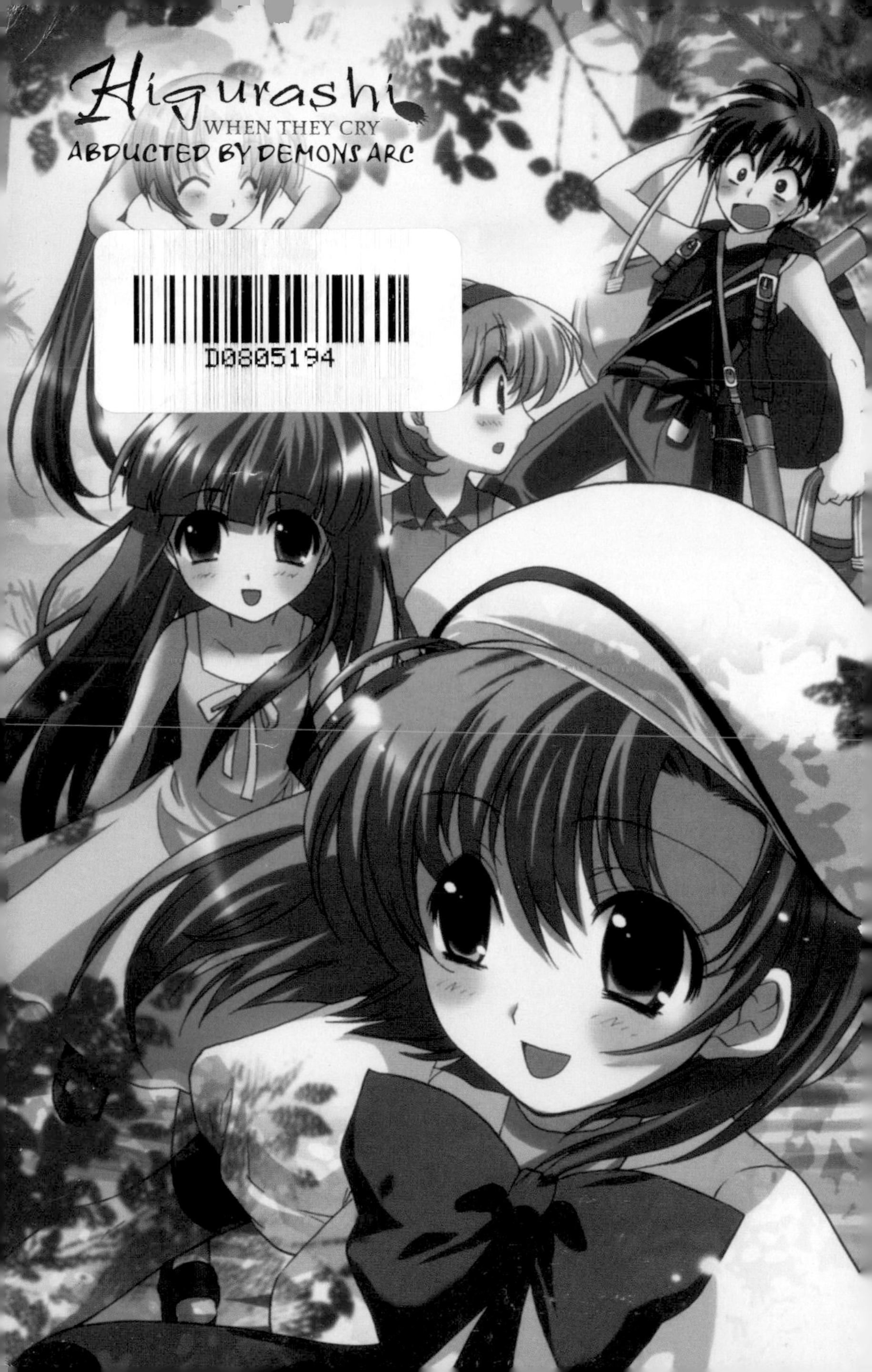
Higurashi
WHEN THEY CRY
ABDUCTED BY DEMONS ARC

Higurashi
WHEN THEY CRY
ABDUCTED BY DEMONS ARC

2

CONTENTS

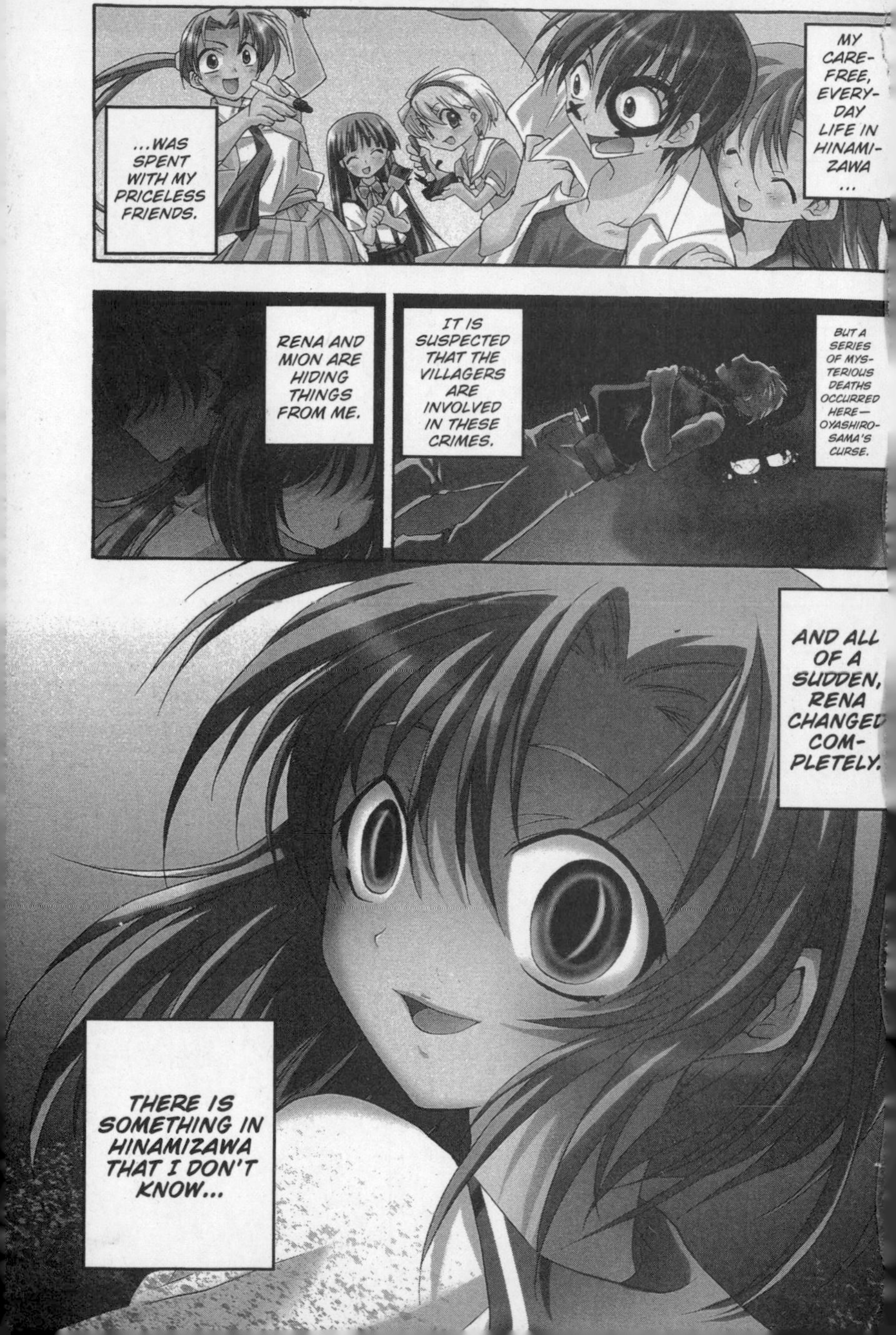
MY CAREFREE, EVERYDAY LIFE IN HINAMIZAWA...
...WAS SPENT WITH MY PRICELESS FRIENDS.
BUT A SERIES OF MYSTERIOUS DEATHS OCCURRED HERE—OYASHIRO-SAMA'S CURSE.
IT IS SUSPECTED THAT THE VILLAGERS ARE INVOLVED IN THESE CRIMES.
RENA AND MION ARE HIDING THINGS FROM ME.
AND ALL OF A SUDDEN, RENA CHANGED COMPLETELY.
THERE IS SOMETHING IN HINAMIZAWA THAT I DON'T KNOW...

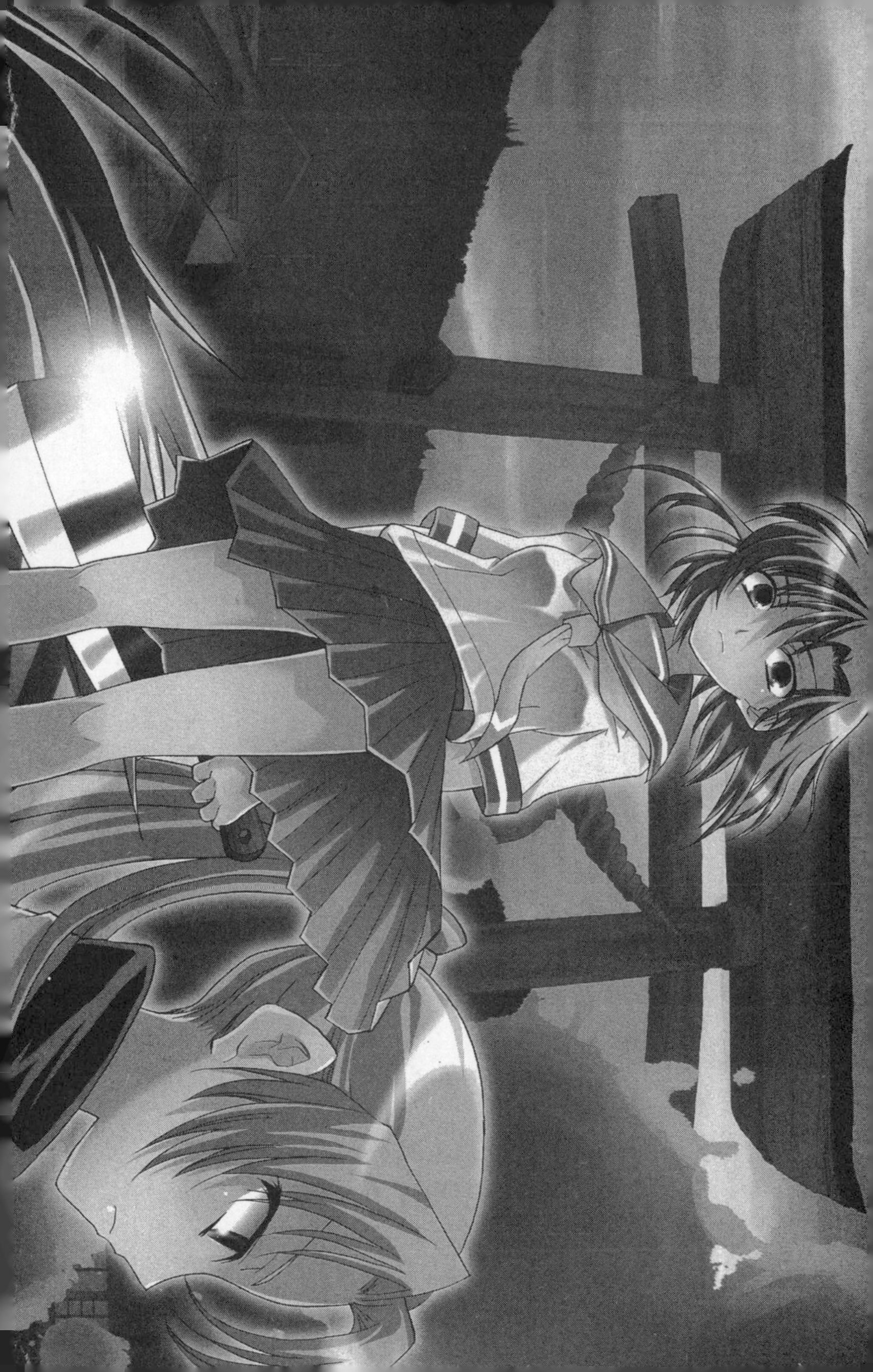

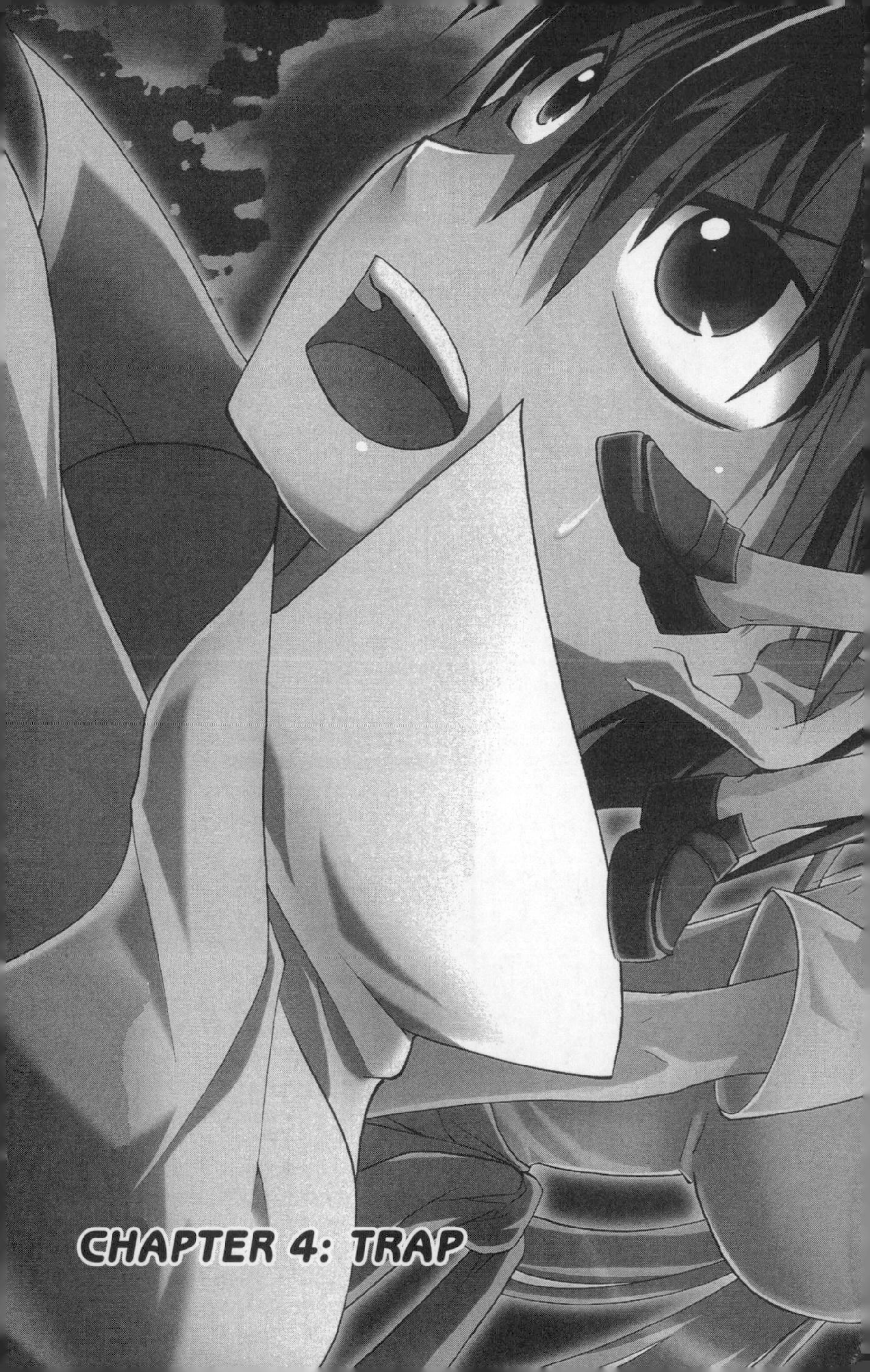
CHAPTER 4: TRAP

Higurashi WHEN THEY CRY
ABDUCTED BY DEMONS ARC

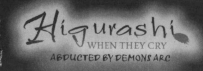

CHARACTER INTRODUCTION

KEIICHI MAEBARA

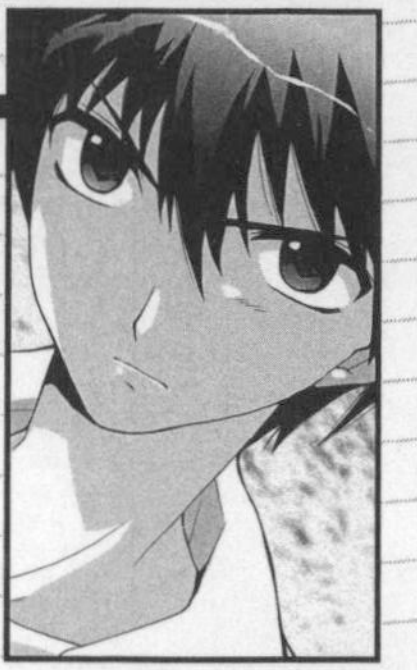

Keiichi recently transferred to Hinamizawa and was enjoying life with newfound friends. A string of mysterious incidents, however, has thrown all he thought he knew about the town and his friends into question.

RENA RYUGU

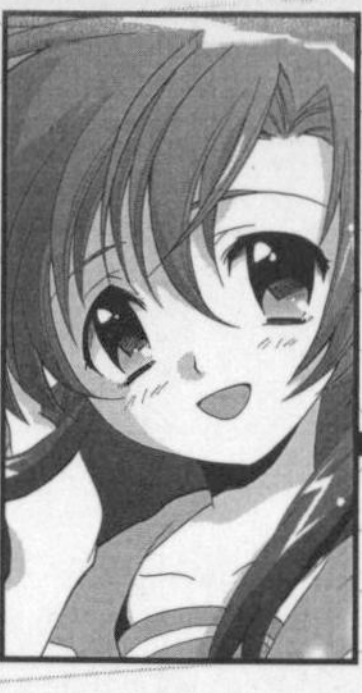

A friend from Keiichi's club who looks out for him, Rena seems to be nothing but a sweet, normal girl. When pressed about the unsettling incidents, though, Rena undergoes a frightening transformation.

SATOKO HOJO

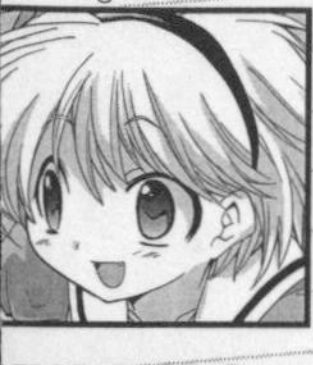

he club's expert at etting traps, Satoko is ery strong-willed, but vhen counter-attacked, he shows she has a nore fragile side...

MION SONOZAKI

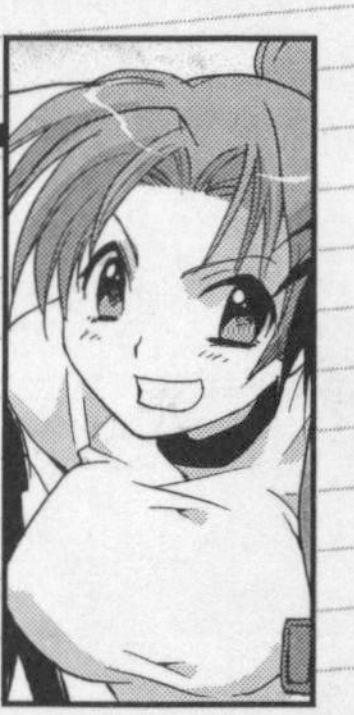

Mion is the ringleader of the club. The Sonozaki family led the anti-dam movement, and it's said the Mion herself had some serious run-ins with the police at the time, but...

RIKA FURUDE

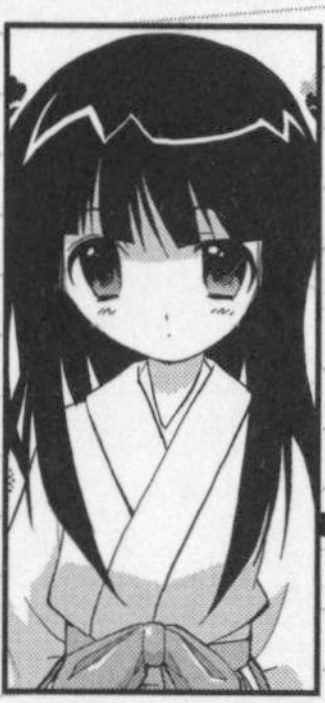

Satoko's best friend and a member of the club. She has a quiet personality. When someone is depressed, she pets their head and comforts them.

KURAUDO OOISHI

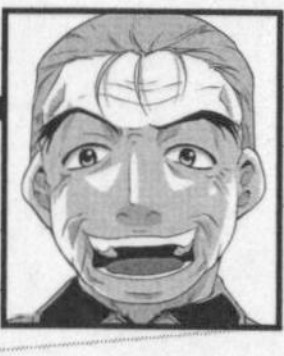

detective from the kinomiya Police. He aims that Oyashiro-ama's Curse is a over for murders ommitted by the ntire village.

JIROU TOMITAKE

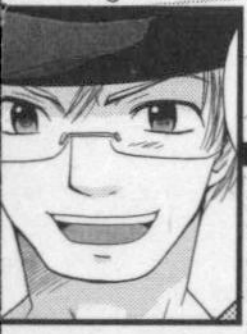

A would-be photographer. On the night of the Cotton Drifting, he tore out his own throat and died.

THE STORY SO FAR...

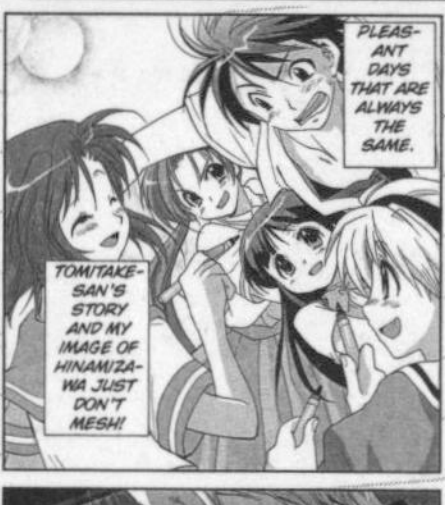
PLEASANT DAYS THAT ARE ALWAYS THE SAME.
TOMITAKE-SAN'S STORY AND MY IMAGE OF HINAMIZAWA JUST DON'T MESH!

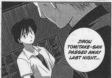

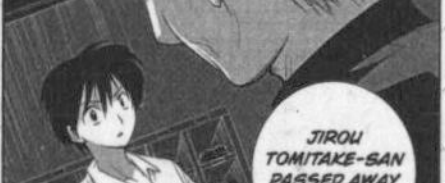
JIROU TOMITAKE-SAN PASSED AWAY LAST NIGHT...

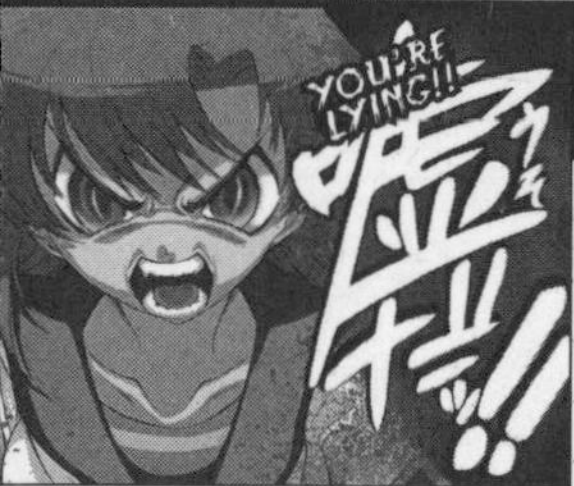
YOU'RE LYING!!

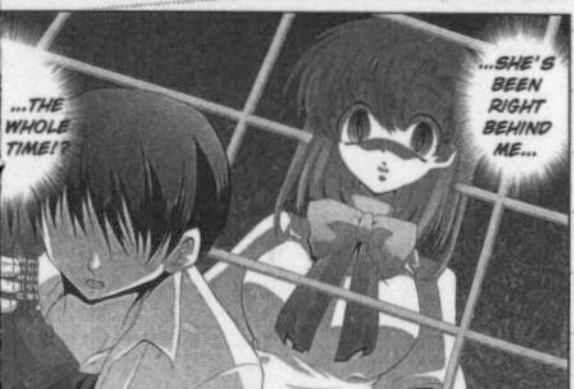
...SHE'S BEEN RIGHT BEHIND ME...
...THE WHOLE TIME!?

Keiichi Maebara just moved to Hinamizawa where he spends his time doing club activities with his friends at school. That is until he learns of a series of mysterious deaths that occur each year on the night of the Cotton Drifting Festival, which have come to be known as Oyashiro-sama's Curse. This year, a man he knew, the photographer Tomitake, died. Keiichi is informed by police detective Ooishi that the deaths were actually murders committed by the village. Ooishi goes on to say that Keiichi's classmate, Mion, could be involved. Wanting to believe in his friends but wavering, Keiichi confronts Rena, prompting a frightening transformation. When he later discovers that Rena has been eavesdropping on his conversation with the detective, Keiichi's suspicions become all the more real...

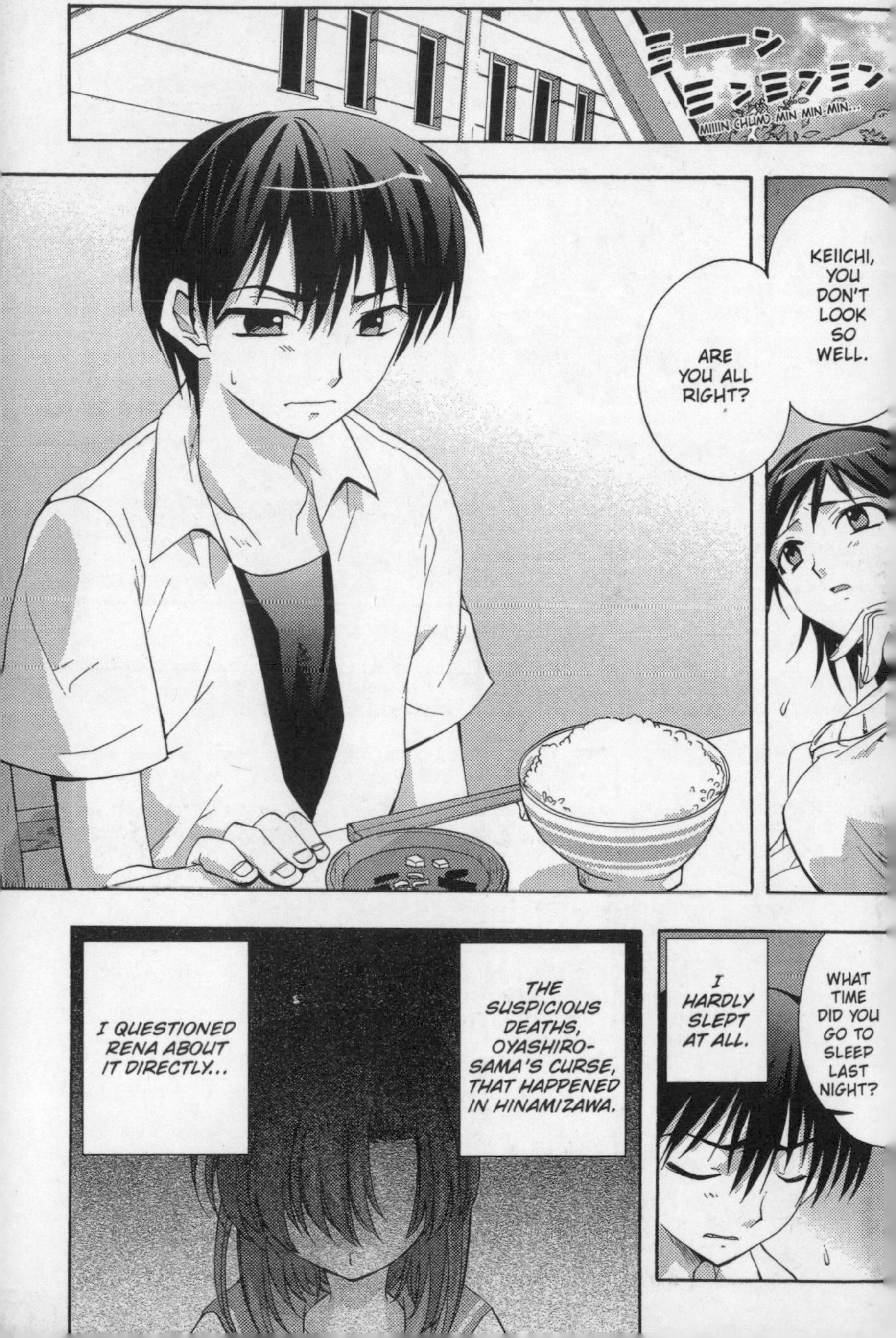
ミーン
ミンミンミン
MIIIIN (HUM) MIN MIN MIN...
KEIICHI, YOU DON'T LOOK SO WELL.
ARE YOU ALL RIGHT?
WHAT TIME DID YOU GO TO SLEEP LAST NIGHT?
I HARDLY SLEPT AT ALL.
THE SUSPICIOUS DEATHS, OYASHIRO-SAMA'S CURSE, THAT HAPPENED IN HINAMIZAWA.
I QUESTIONED RENA ABOUT IT DIRECTLY...

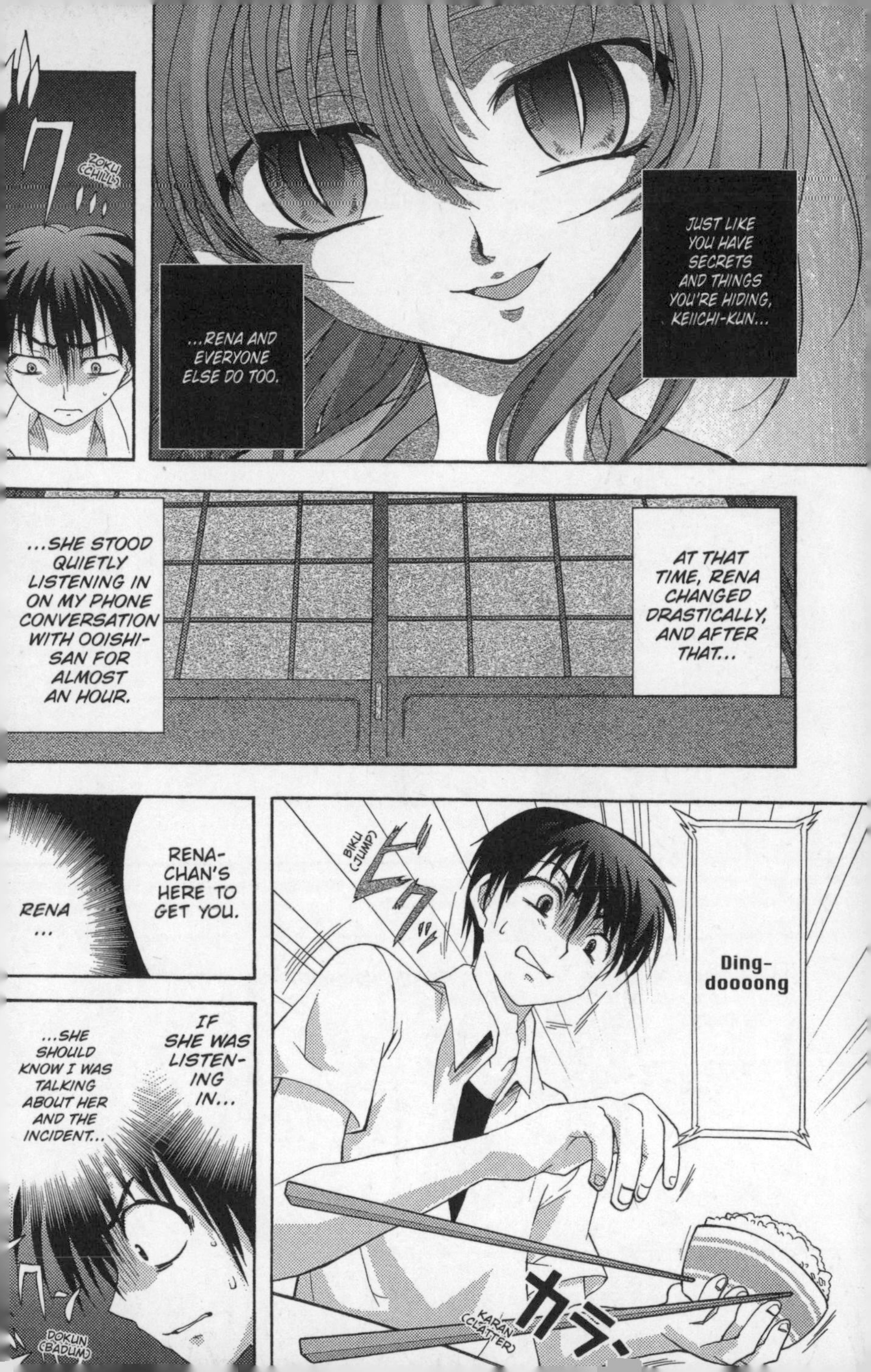
JUST LIKE YOU HAVE SECRETS AND THINGS YOU'RE HIDING, KEIICHI-KUN...
...RENA AND EVERYONE ELSE DO TOO.
ZOKU (CHILL)
AT THAT TIME, RENA CHANGED DRASTICALLY, AND AFTER THAT...
...SHE STOOD QUIETLY LISTENING IN ON MY PHONE CONVERSATION WITH OOISHI-SAN FOR ALMOST AN HOUR.
Ding-dooooong
BIKU (JUMP)
KARAN (CLATTER)
RENA-CHAN'S HERE TO GET YOU.
RENA ...
IF SHE WAS LISTEN-ING IN...
...SHE SHOULD KNOW I WAS TALKING ABOUT HER AND THE INCIDENT...
DOKUN (BADUM)

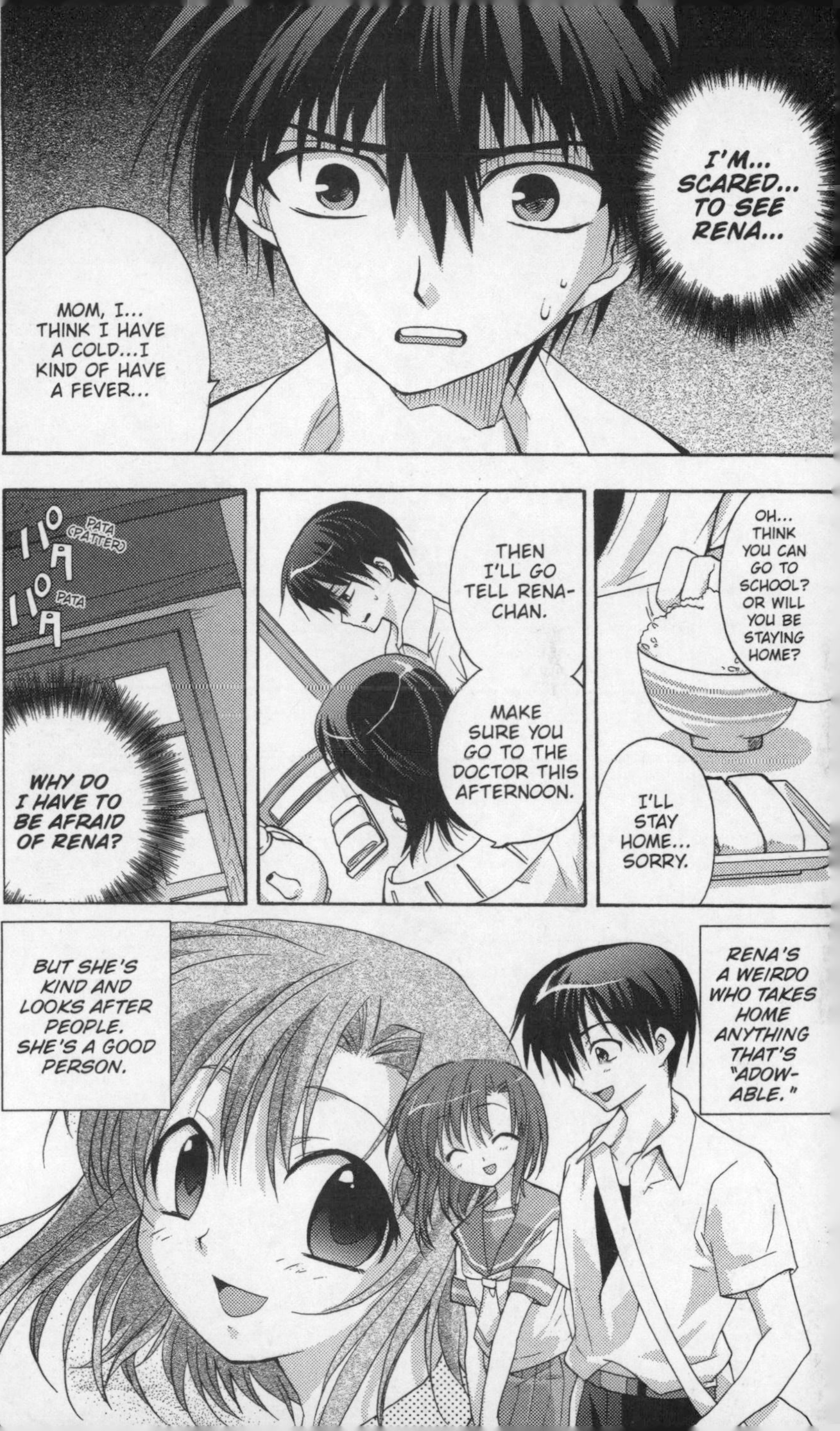
I'M... SCARED... TO SEE RENA...
MOM, I... THINK I HAVE A COLD...I KIND OF HAVE A FEVER...
OH... THINK YOU CAN GO TO SCHOOL? OR WILL YOU BE STAYING HOME?
I'LL STAY HOME... SORRY.
THEN I'LL GO TELL RENA-CHAN.
MAKE SURE YOU GO TO THE DOCTOR THIS AFTERNOON.
PATA (PATTER)
PATA
WHY DO I HAVE TO BE AFRAID OF RENA?
RENA'S A WEIRDO WHO TAKES HOME ANYTHING THAT'S "ADOW-ABLE."
BUT SHE'S KIND AND LOOKS AFTER PEOPLE. SHE'S A GOOD PERSON.

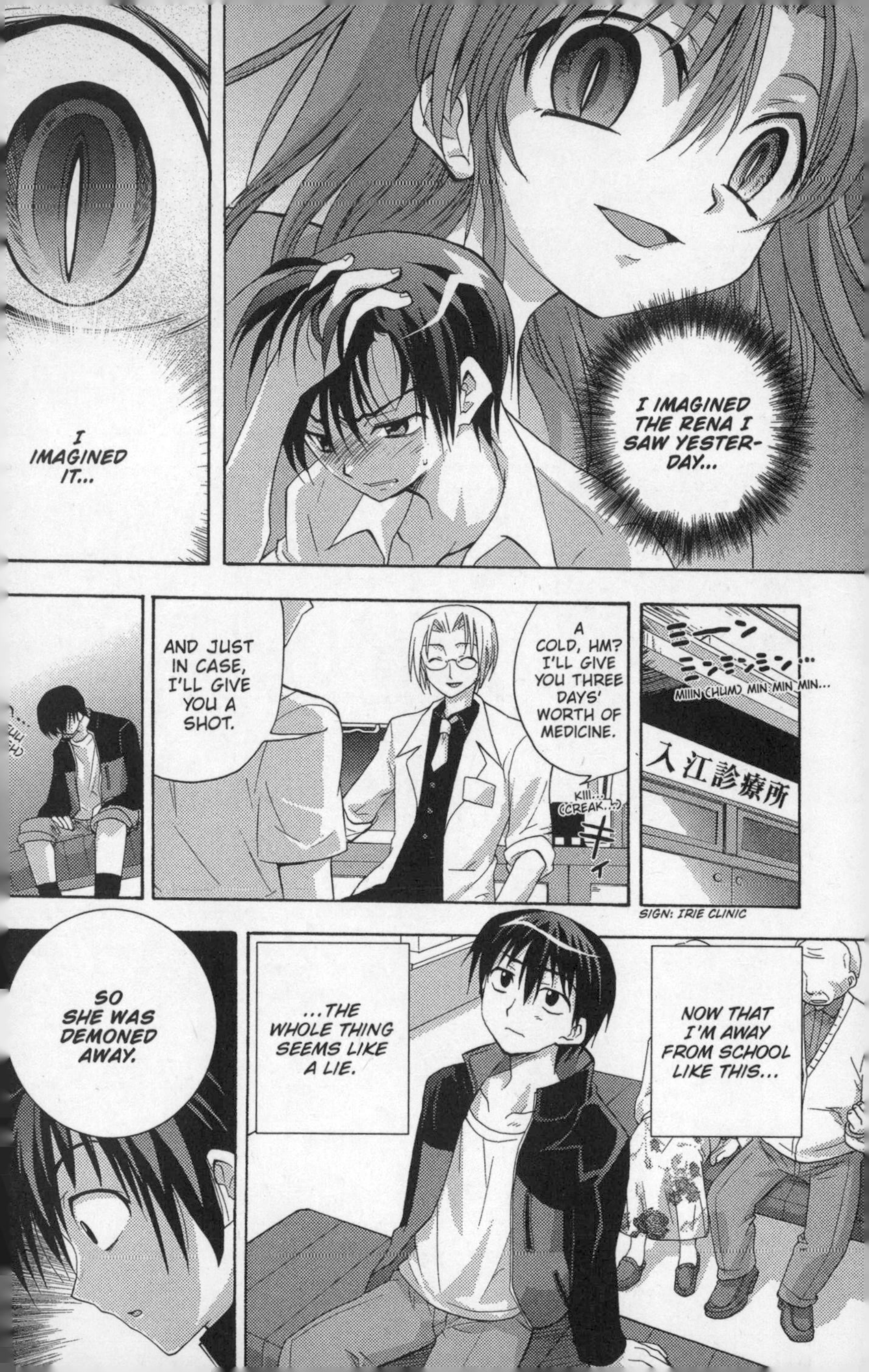

I IMAGINED THE RENA I SAW YESTER-DAY...
I IMAGINED IT...
ミーン ミンミンミン…
MIIN (CHUM) MIN MIN MIN...
入江診療所
SIGN: IRIE CLINIC
A COLD, HM? I'LL GIVE YOU THREE DAYS' WORTH OF MEDICINE.
キィ
KIII... (CREAK...)
AND JUST IN CASE, I'LL GIVE YOU A SHOT.
NOW THAT I'M AWAY FROM SCHOOL LIKE THIS...
...THE WHOLE THING SEEMS LIKE A LIE.
SO SHE WAS DEMONED AWAY.

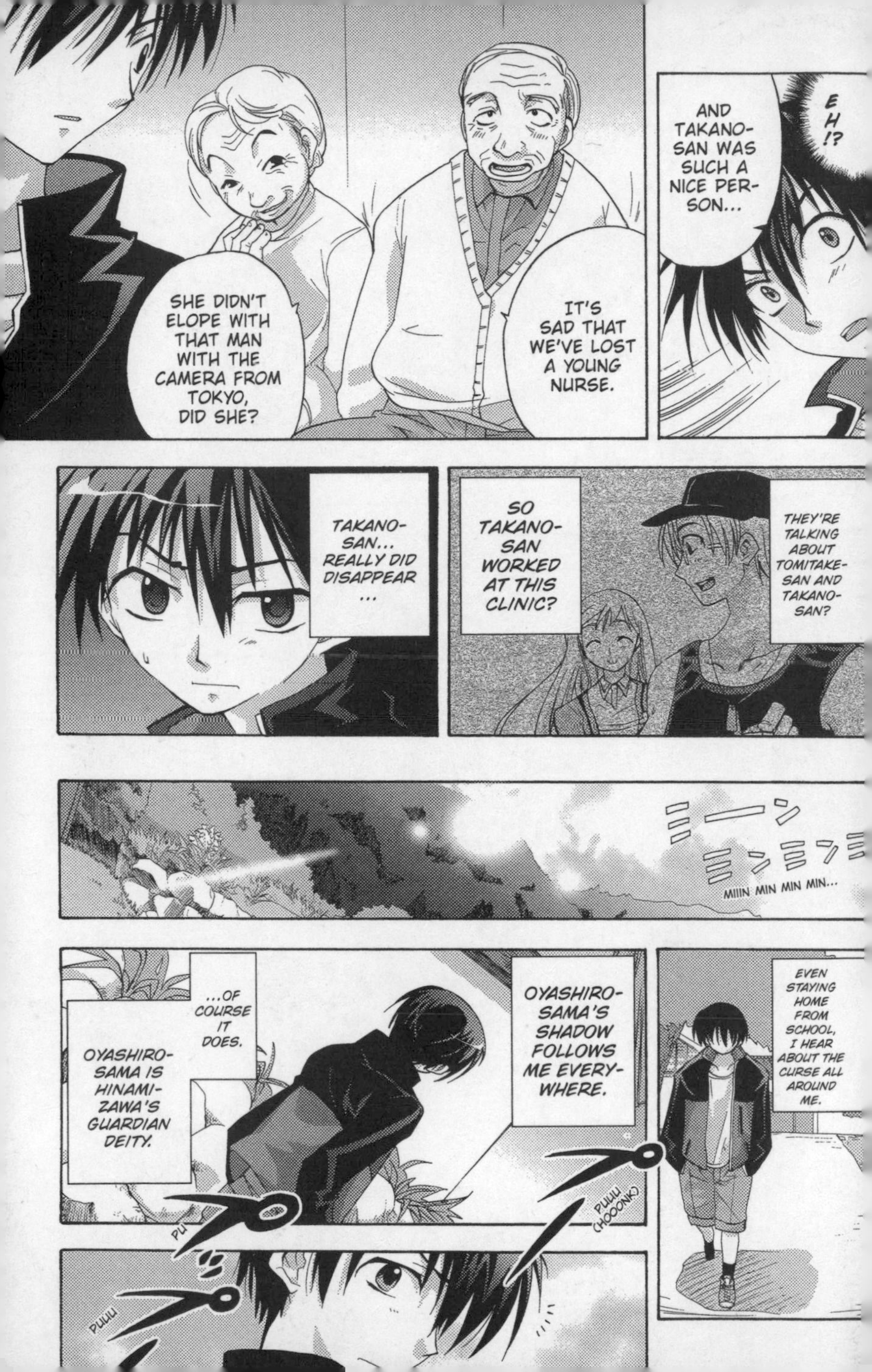
AND TAKANO-SAN WAS SUCH A NICE PERSON...
EH!?
IT'S SAD THAT WE'VE LOST A YOUNG NURSE.
SHE DIDN'T ELOPE WITH THAT MAN WITH THE CAMERA FROM TOKYO, DID SHE?
THEY'RE TALKING ABOUT TOMITAKE-SAN AND TAKANO-SAN?
SO TAKANO-SAN WORKED AT THIS CLINIC?
TAKANO-SAN... REALLY DID DISAPPEAR ...
MIIIN MIN MIN MIN...
EVEN STAYING HOME FROM SCHOOL, I HEAR ABOUT THE CURSE ALL AROUND ME.
OYASHIRO-SAMA'S SHADOW FOLLOWS ME EVERYWHERE.
...OF COURSE IT DOES.
OYASHIRO-SAMA IS HINAMIZAWA'S GUARDIAN DEITY.
PUUU (HOOONK)
PU
PUUU

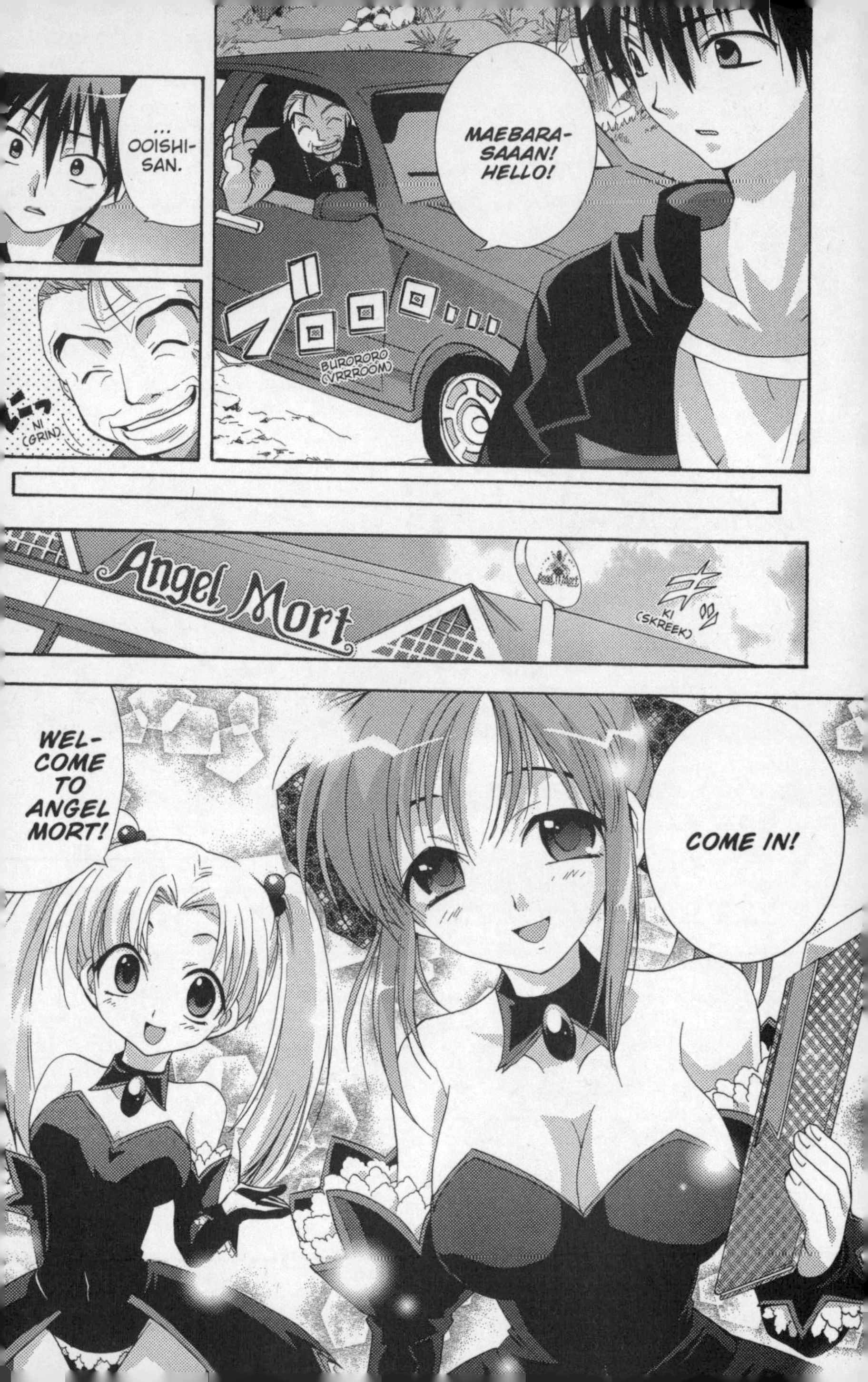
MAEBARA-SAAAN! HELLO!
BURORORO (VRRROOM)
... OOISHI-SAN.
NI (GRIND)
Angel Mort
KI (SKREEK)
COME IN!
WEL-COME TO ANGEL MORT!

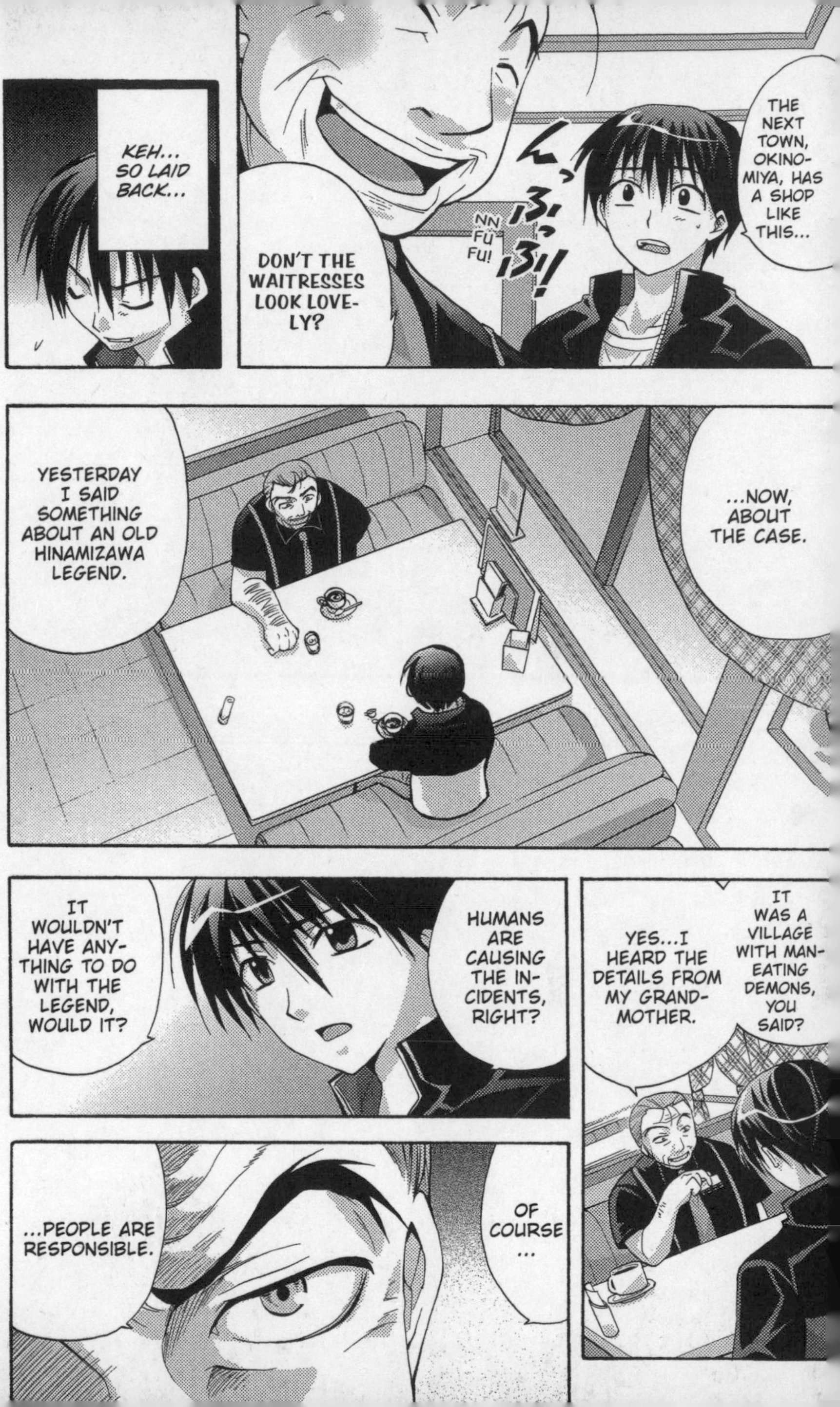
THE NEXT TOWN, OKINO-MIYA, HAS A SHOP LIKE THIS...
NN FU FU!
DON'T THE WAITRESSES LOOK LOVE-LY?
KEH... SO LAID BACK...
...NOW, ABOUT THE CASE.
YESTERDAY I SAID SOMETHING ABOUT AN OLD HINAMIZAWA LEGEND.
IT WAS A VILLAGE WITH MAN-EATING DEMONS, YOU SAID?
YES...I HEARD THE DETAILS FROM MY GRAND-MOTHER.
HUMANS ARE CAUSING THE IN-CIDENTS, RIGHT?
IT WOULDN'T HAVE ANY-THING TO DO WITH THE LEGEND, WOULD IT?
OF COURSE ...
...PEOPLE ARE RESPONSIBLE.

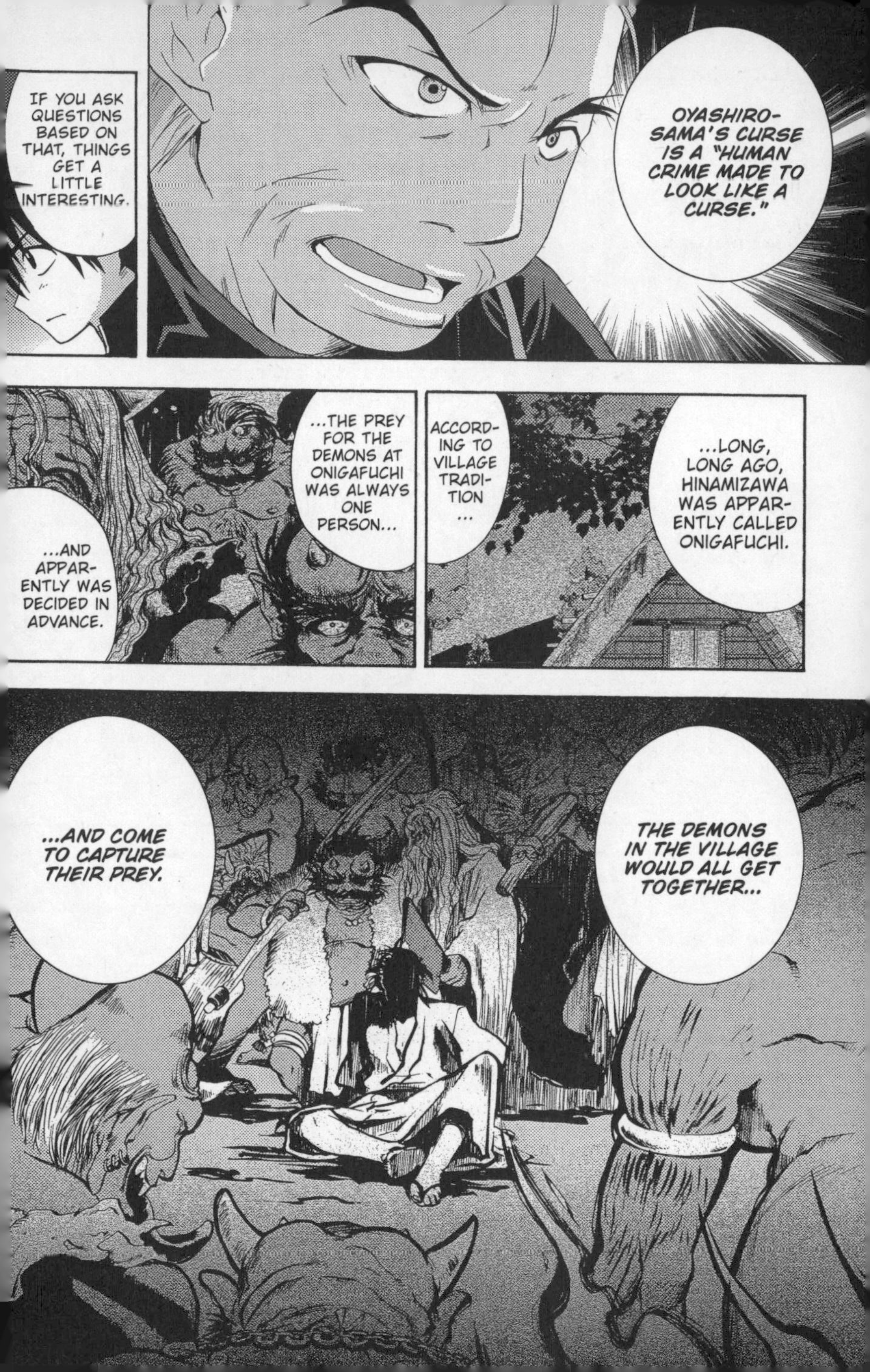
OYASHIRO-SAMA'S CURSE IS A "HUMAN CRIME MADE TO LOOK LIKE A CURSE."
IF YOU ASK QUESTIONS BASED ON THAT, THINGS GET A LITTLE INTERESTING.
...LONG, LONG AGO, HINAMIZAWA WAS APPARENTLY CALLED ONIGAFUCHI.
ACCORDING TO VILLAGE TRADITION...
...THE PREY FOR THE DEMONS AT ONIGAFUCHI WAS ALWAYS ONE PERSON...
...AND APPARENTLY WAS DECIDED IN ADVANCE.
THE DEMONS IN THE VILLAGE WOULD ALL GET TOGETHER...
...AND COME TO CAPTURE THEIR PREY.

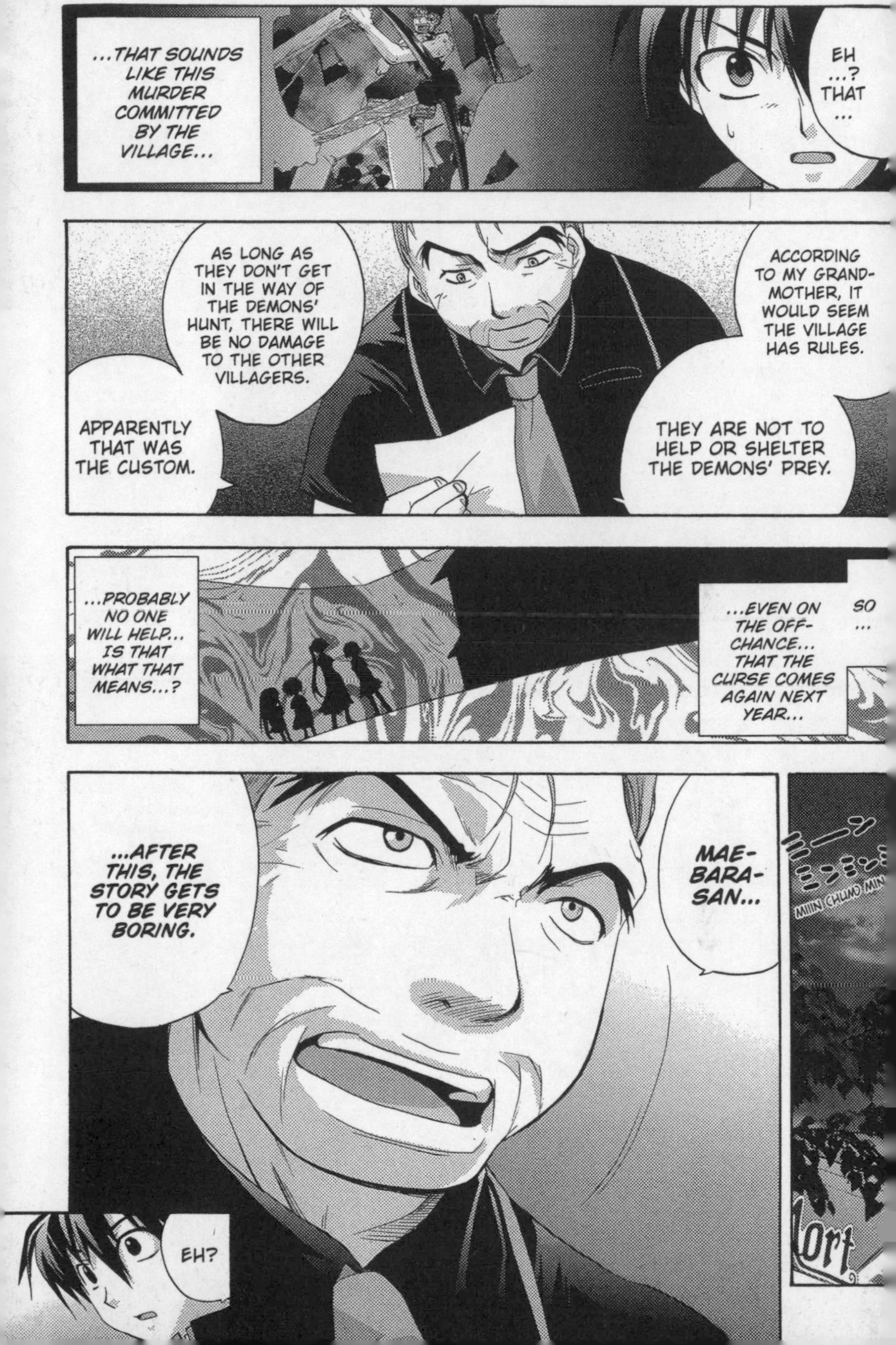
EH ...? THAT ...
...THAT SOUNDS LIKE THIS MURDER COMMITTED BY THE VILLAGE...
ACCORDING TO MY GRAND-MOTHER, IT WOULD SEEM THE VILLAGE HAS RULES.
THEY ARE NOT TO HELP OR SHELTER THE DEMONS' PREY.
AS LONG AS THEY DON'T GET IN THE WAY OF THE DEMONS' HUNT, THERE WILL BE NO DAMAGE TO THE OTHER VILLAGERS.
APPARENTLY THAT WAS THE CUSTOM.
SO ...
...EVEN ON THE OFF-CHANCE... THAT THE CURSE COMES AGAIN NEXT YEAR...
...PROBABLY NO ONE WILL HELP... IS THAT WHAT THAT MEANS...?
MIIN CHUNG MIN
MAE-BARA-SAN...
...AFTER THIS, THE STORY GETS TO BE VERY BORING.
EH?

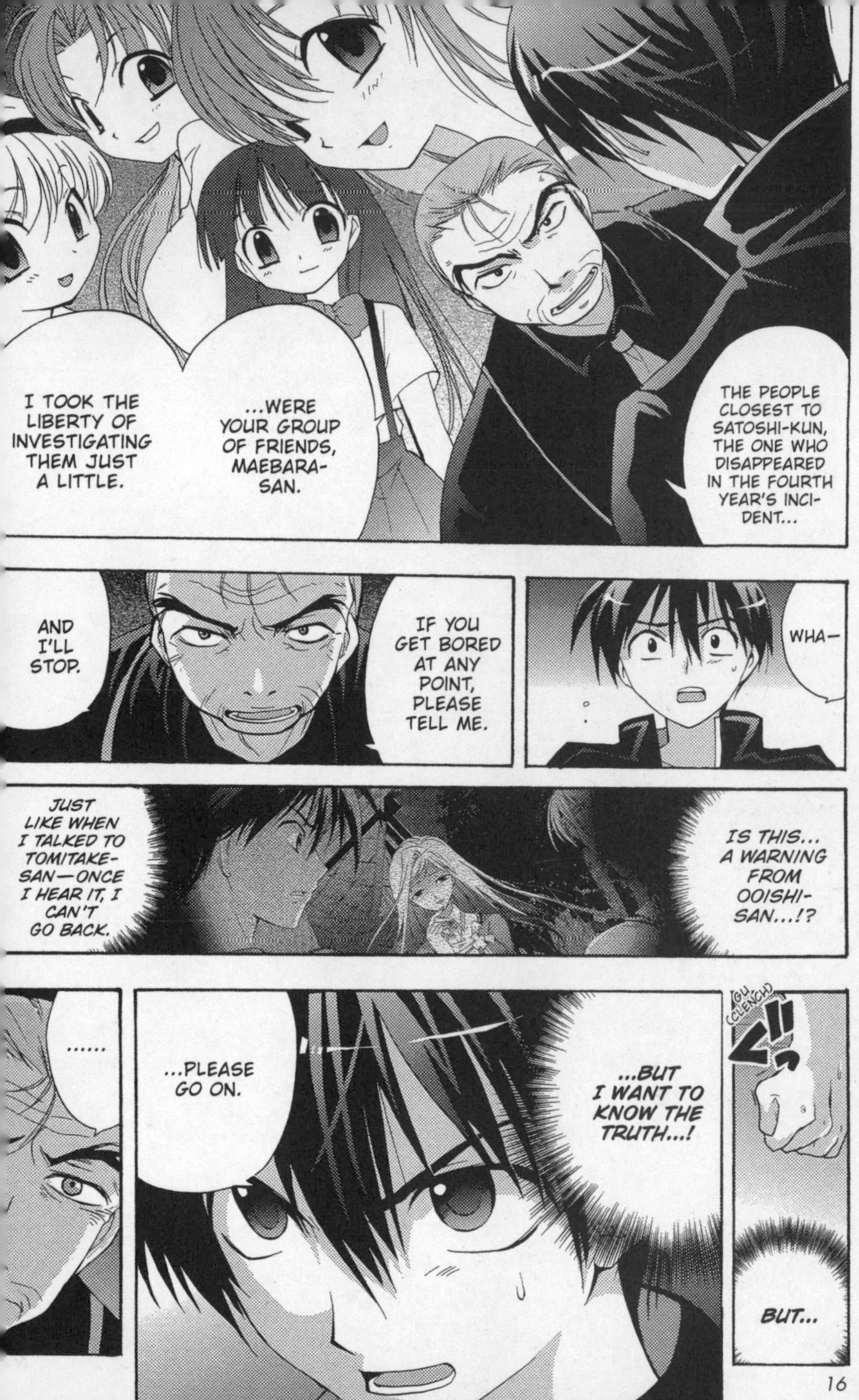
THE PEOPLE CLOSEST TO SATOSHI-KUN, THE ONE WHO DISAPPEARED IN THE FOURTH YEAR'S INCI-DENT...
...WERE YOUR GROUP OF FRIENDS, MAEBARA-SAN.
I TOOK THE LIBERTY OF INVESTIGATING THEM JUST A LITTLE.
WHA—
IF YOU GET BORED AT ANY POINT, PLEASE TELL ME.
AND I'LL STOP.
IS THIS... A WARNING FROM OOISHI-SAN...!?
JUST LIKE WHEN I TALKED TO TOMITAKE-SAN—ONCE I HEAR IT, I CAN'T GO BACK.
GU (CLENCH)
BUT...
...BUT I WANT TO KNOW THE TRUTH...!
...PLEASE GO ON.
......

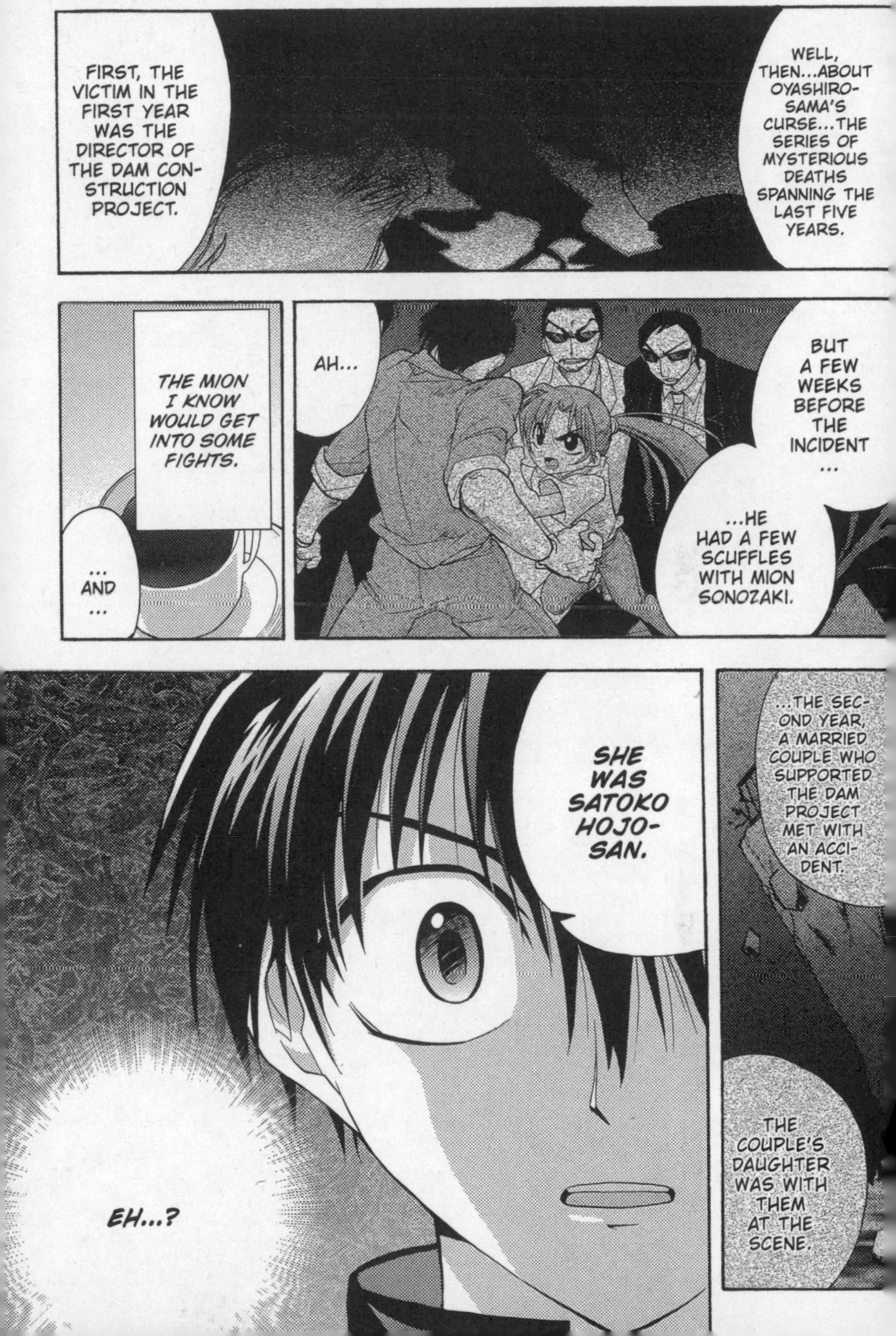
WELL, THEN...ABOUT OYASHIRO-SAMA'S CURSE...THE SERIES OF MYSTERIOUS DEATHS SPANNING THE LAST FIVE YEARS.
FIRST, THE VICTIM IN THE FIRST YEAR WAS THE DIRECTOR OF THE DAM CON-STRUCTION PROJECT.
BUT A FEW WEEKS BEFORE THE INCIDENT ...
...HE HAD A FEW SCUFFLES WITH MION SONOZAKI.
AH...
THE MION I KNOW WOULD GET INTO SOME FIGHTS.
... AND ...
...THE SEC-OND YEAR, A MARRIED COUPLE WHO SUPPORTED THE DAM PROJECT MET WITH AN ACCI-DENT.
THE COUPLE'S DAUGHTER WAS WITH THEM AT THE SCENE.
SHE WAS SATOKO HOJO-SAN.
EH...?

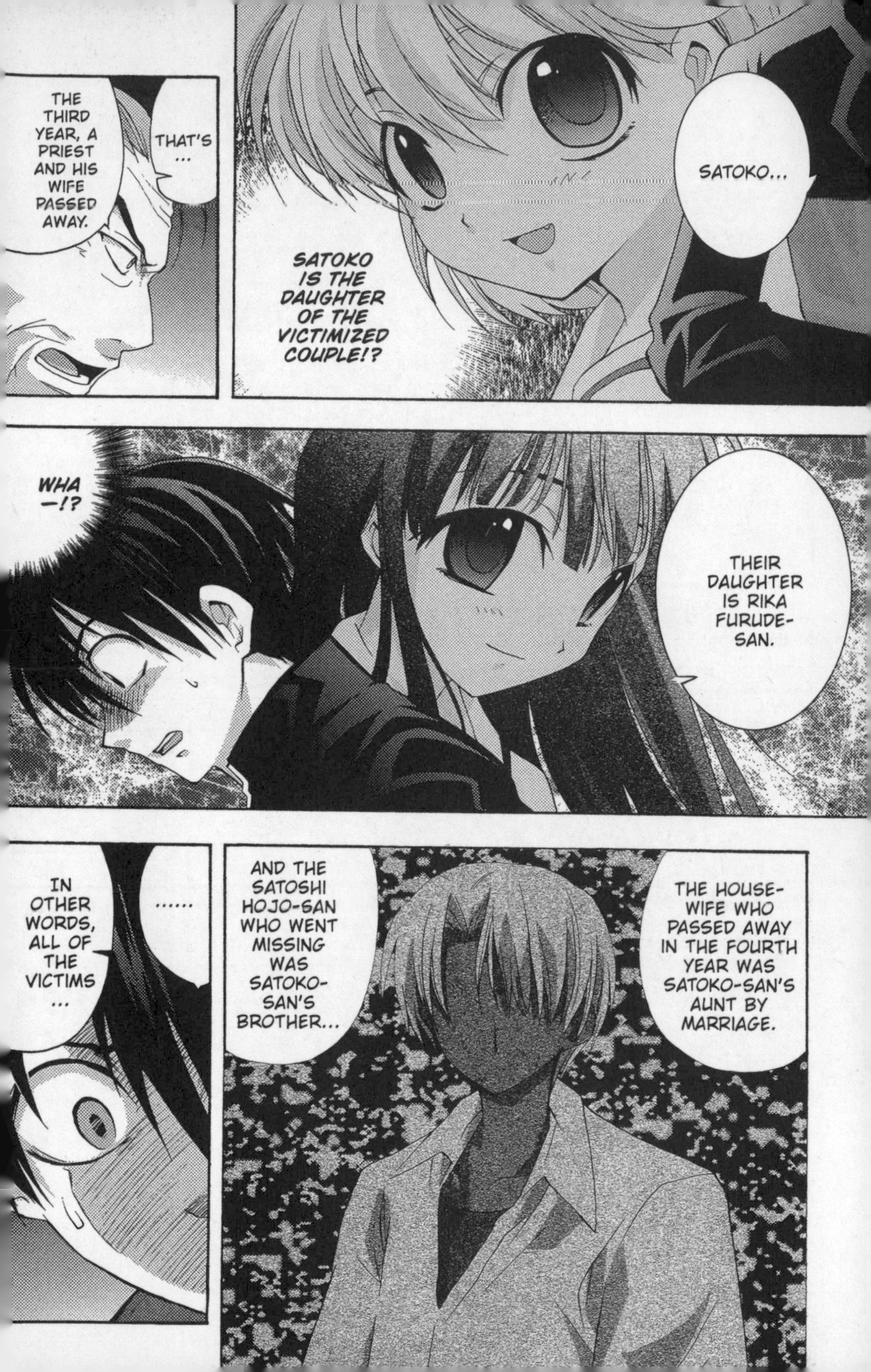
SATOKO...
SATOKO IS THE DAUGHTER OF THE VICTIMIZED COUPLE!?
THAT'S ...
THE THIRD YEAR, A PRIEST AND HIS WIFE PASSED AWAY.
THEIR DAUGHTER IS RIKA FURUDE-SAN.
WHA —!?
THE HOUSE-WIFE WHO PASSED AWAY IN THE FOURTH YEAR WAS SATOKO-SAN'S AUNT BY MARRIAGE.
AND THE SATOSHI HOJO-SAN WHO WENT MISSING WAS SATOKO-SAN'S BROTHER...
......
IN OTHER WORDS, ALL OF THE VICTIMS ...

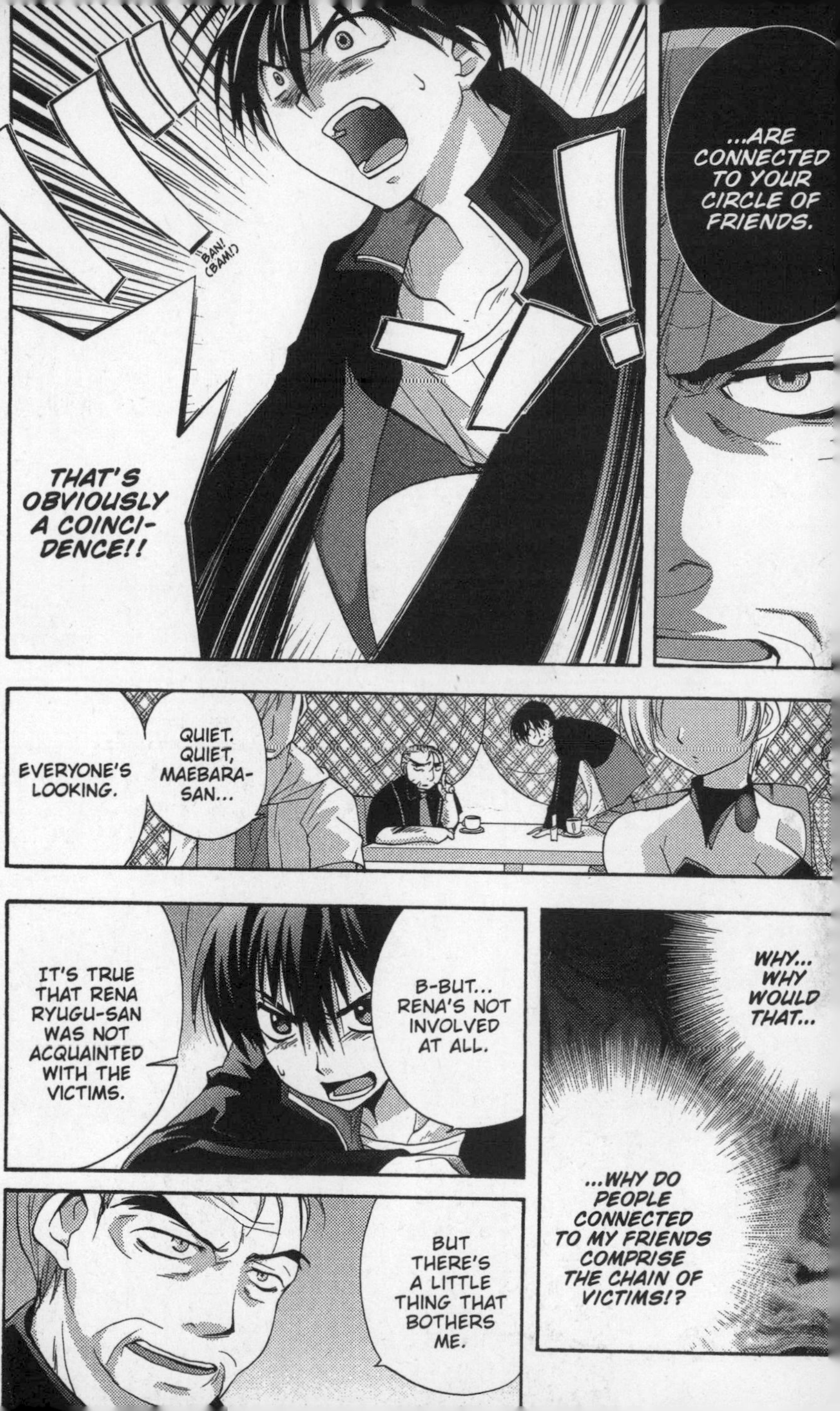
...ARE CONNECTED TO YOUR CIRCLE OF FRIENDS.
BAN! (BAM!)
THAT'S OBVIOUSLY A COINCIDENCE!!
QUIET. QUIET, MAEBARA-SAN...
EVERYONE'S LOOKING.
WHY... WHY WOULD THAT...
...WHY DO PEOPLE CONNECTED TO MY FRIENDS COMPRISE THE CHAIN OF VICTIMS!?
B-BUT... RENA'S NOT INVOLVED AT ALL.
IT'S TRUE THAT RENA RYUGU-SAN WAS NOT ACQUAINTED WITH THE VICTIMS.
BUT THERE'S A LITTLE THING THAT BOTHERS ME.

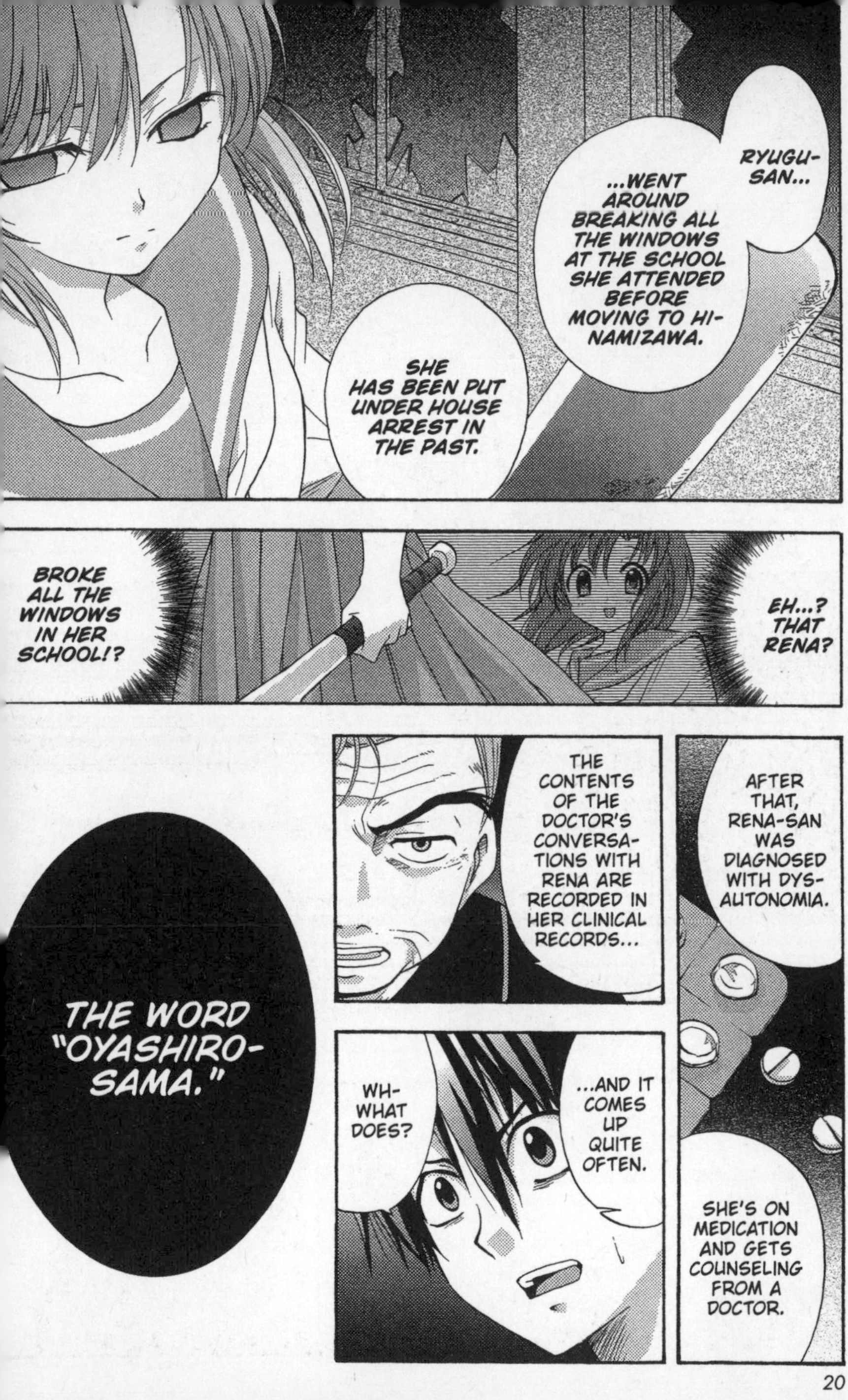

RYUGU-SAN...
...WENT AROUND BREAKING ALL THE WINDOWS AT THE SCHOOL SHE ATTENDED BEFORE MOVING TO HI-NAMIZAWA.
SHE HAS BEEN PUT UNDER HOUSE ARREST IN THE PAST.
EH...? THAT RENA?
BROKE ALL THE WINDOWS IN HER SCHOOL!?
AFTER THAT, RENA-SAN WAS DIAGNOSED WITH DYS-AUTONOMIA.
SHE'S ON MEDICATION AND GETS COUNSELING FROM A DOCTOR.
THE CONTENTS OF THE DOCTOR'S CONVERSA-TIONS WITH RENA ARE RECORDED IN HER CLINICAL RECORDS...
...AND IT COMES UP QUITE OFTEN.
WH-WHAT DOES?
THE WORD "OYASHIRO-SAMA."

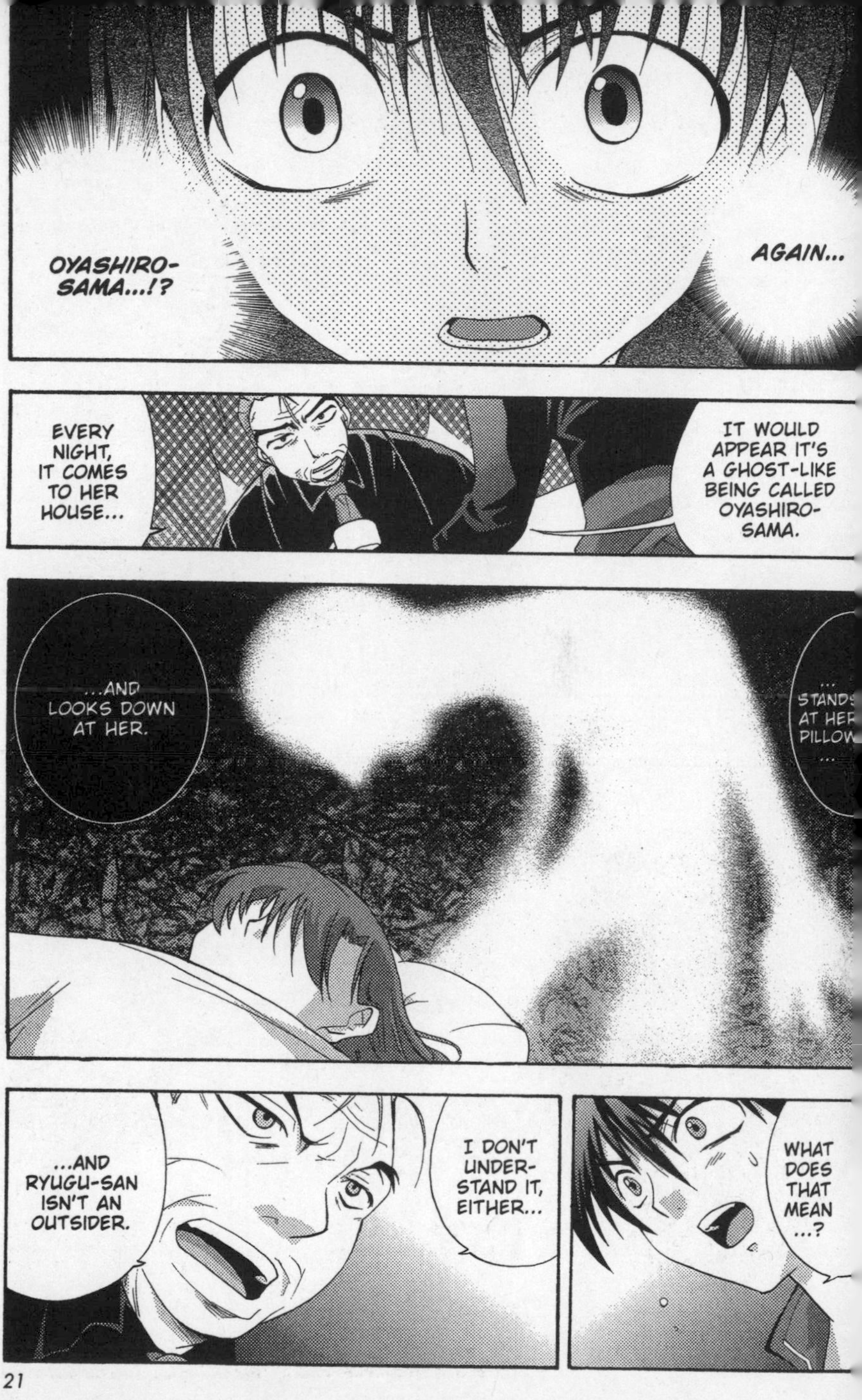
AGAIN...
OYASHIRO-SAMA...!?
IT WOULD APPEAR IT'S A GHOST-LIKE BEING CALLED OYASHIRO-SAMA.
EVERY NIGHT, IT COMES TO HER HOUSE...
...STANDS AT HER PILLOW...
...AND LOOKS DOWN AT HER.
WHAT DOES THAT MEAN...?
I DON'T UNDER-STAND IT, EITHER...
...AND RYUGU-SAN ISN'T AN OUTSIDER.

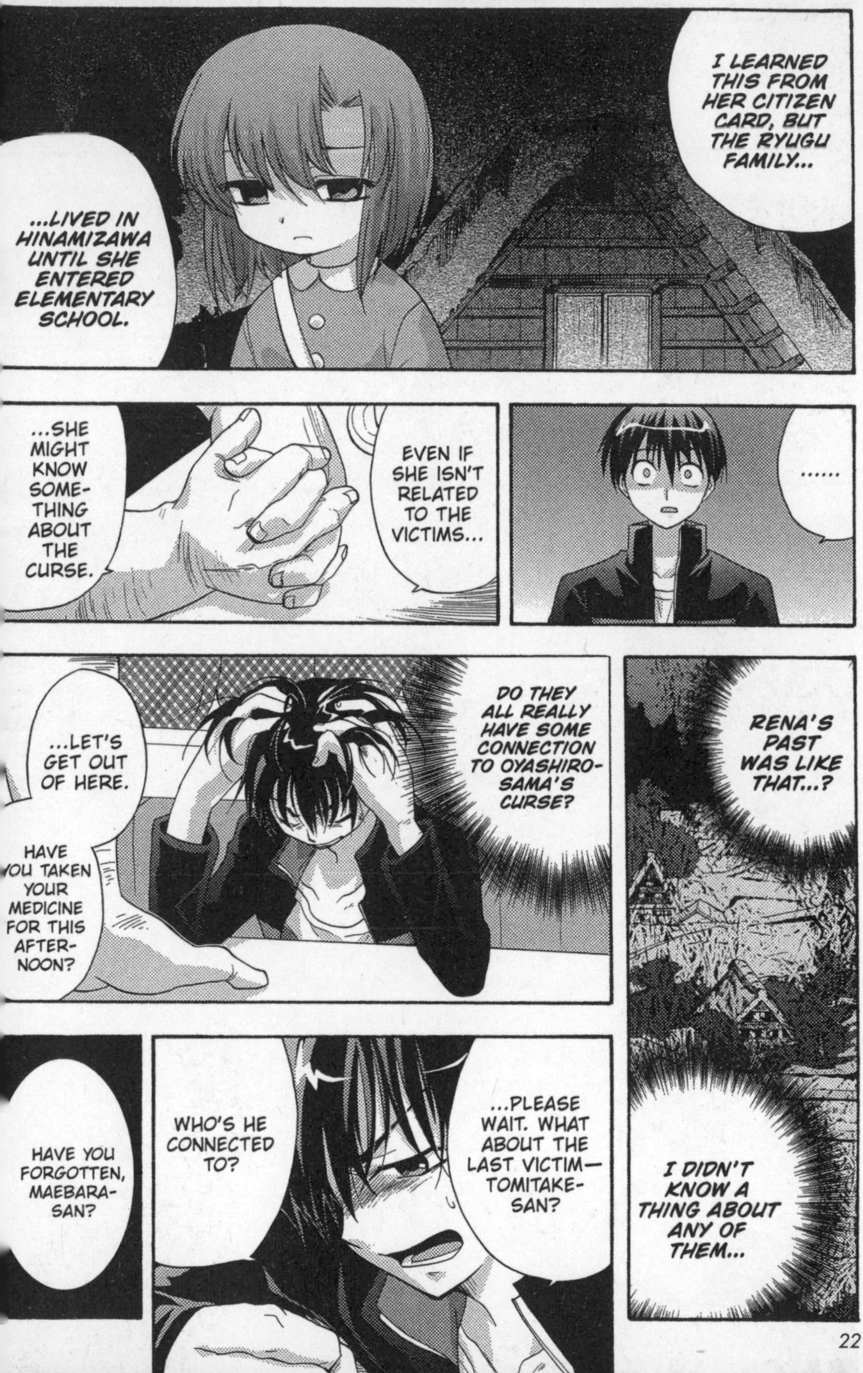
I LEARNED THIS FROM HER CITIZEN CARD, BUT THE RYUGU FAMILY...
...LIVED IN HINAMIZAWA UNTIL SHE ENTERED ELEMENTARY SCHOOL.
......
EVEN IF SHE ISN'T RELATED TO THE VICTIMS...
...SHE MIGHT KNOW SOME-THING ABOUT THE CURSE.
RENA'S PAST WAS LIKE THAT...?
I DIDN'T KNOW A THING ABOUT ANY OF THEM...
DO THEY ALL REALLY HAVE SOME CONNECTION TO OYASHIRO-SAMA'S CURSE?
...LET'S GET OUT OF HERE.
HAVE YOU TAKEN YOUR MEDICINE FOR THIS AFTER-NOON?
...PLEASE WAIT. WHAT ABOUT THE LAST VICTIM—TOMITAKE-SAN?
WHO'S HE CONNECTED TO?
HAVE YOU FORGOTTEN, MAEBARA-SAN?

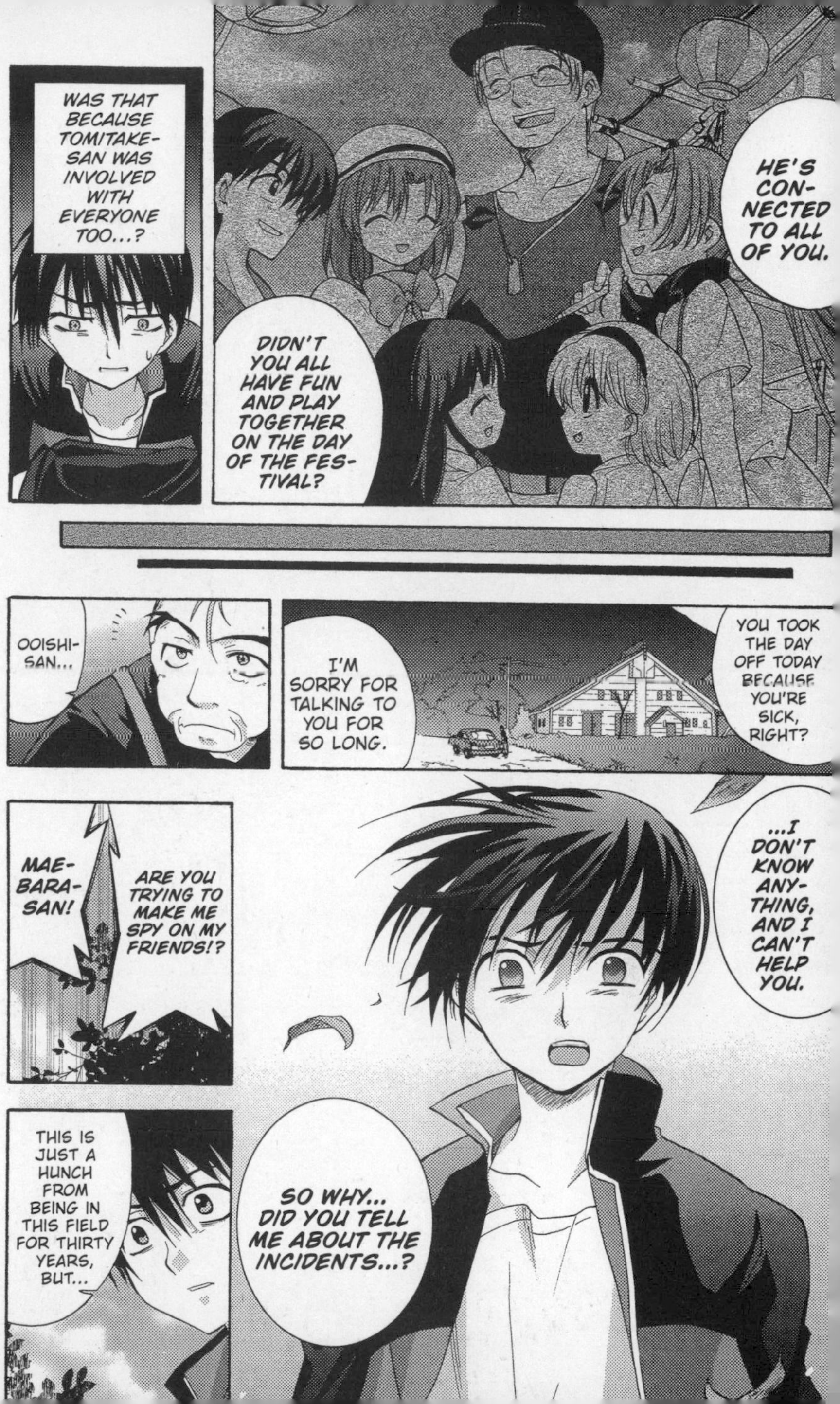
HE'S CONNECTED TO ALL OF YOU.
DIDN'T YOU ALL HAVE FUN AND PLAY TOGETHER ON THE DAY OF THE FESTIVAL?
WAS THAT BECAUSE TOMITAKE-SAN WAS INVOLVED WITH EVERYONE TOO...?
YOU TOOK THE DAY OFF TODAY BECAUSE YOU'RE SICK, RIGHT?
I'M SORRY FOR TALKING TO YOU FOR SO LONG.
OOISHI-SAN...
...I DON'T KNOW ANYTHING, AND I CAN'T HELP YOU.
SO WHY... DID YOU TELL ME ABOUT THE INCIDENTS...?
MAEBARA-SAN!
ARE YOU TRYING TO MAKE ME SPY ON MY FRIENDS!?
THIS IS JUST A HUNCH FROM BEING IN THIS FIELD FOR THIRTY YEARS, BUT...

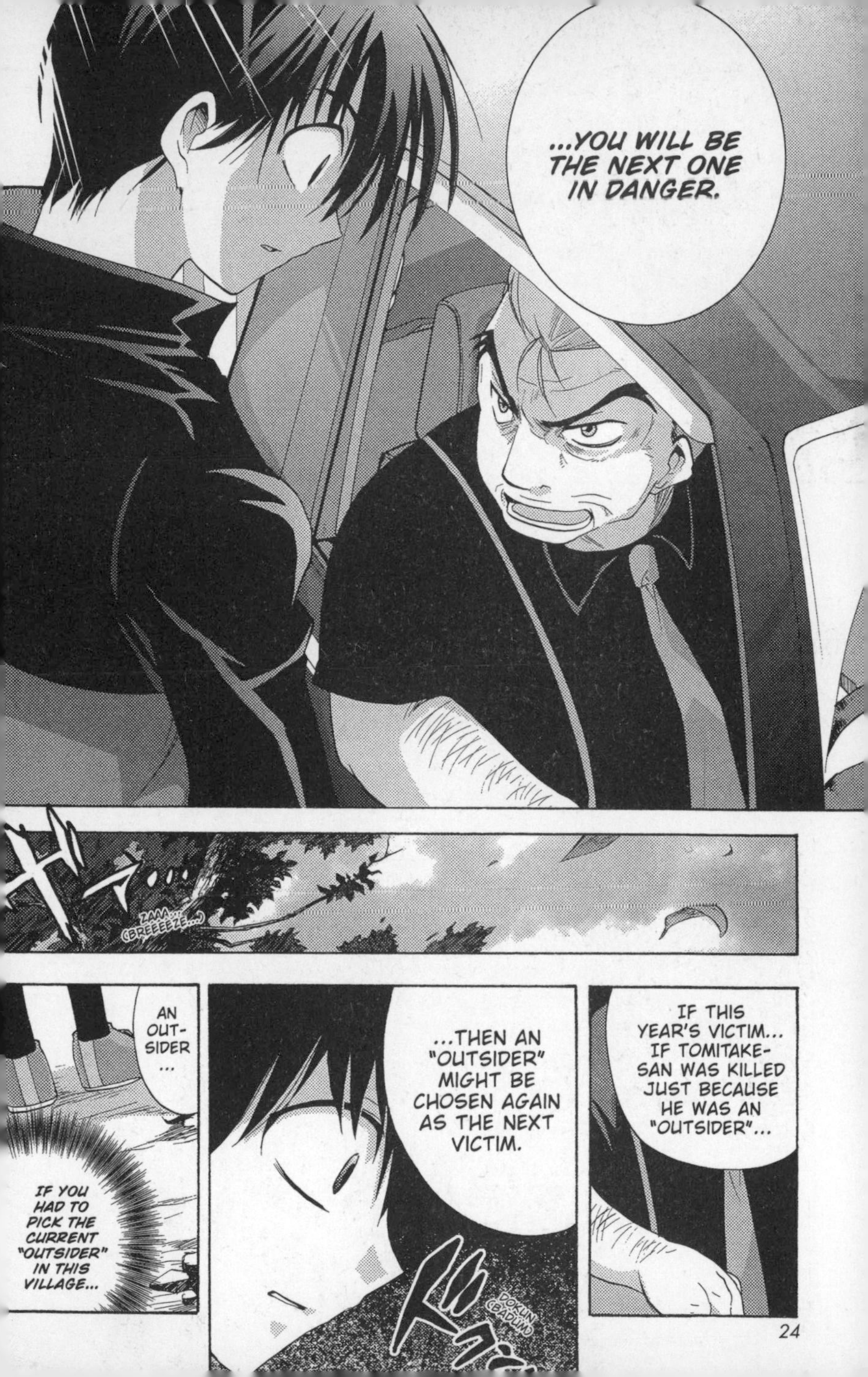
...YOU WILL BE THE NEXT ONE IN DANGER.
ZAAA... (BREEEEZE...)
IF THIS YEAR'S VICTIM... IF TOMITAKE-SAN WAS KILLED JUST BECAUSE HE WAS AN "OUTSIDER"...
...THEN AN "OUTSIDER" MIGHT BE CHOSEN AGAIN AS THE NEXT VICTIM.
DOKUN (BADUM)
AN OUT-SIDER ...
IF YOU HAD TO PICK THE CURRENT "OUTSIDER" IN THIS VILLAGE...

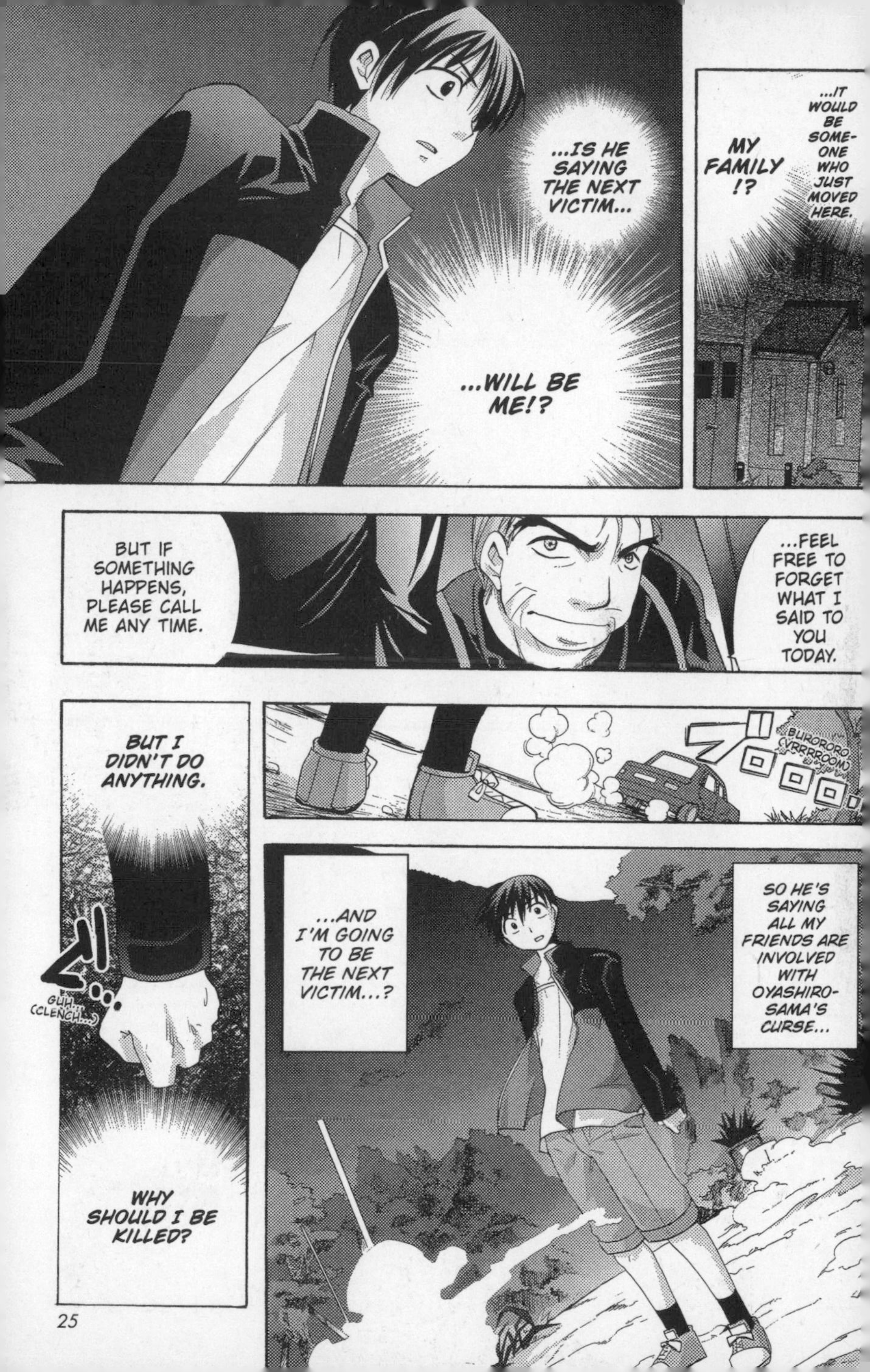
...IT WOULD BE SOME-ONE WHO JUST MOVED HERE.
MY FAMILY!?
...IS HE SAYING THE NEXT VICTIM...
...WILL BE ME!?
...FEEL FREE TO FORGET WHAT I SAID TO YOU TODAY.
BUT IF SOMETHING HAPPENS, PLEASE CALL ME ANY TIME.
BURORORO (VRRRROOM)
SO HE'S SAYING ALL MY FRIENDS ARE INVOLVED WITH OYASHIRO-SAMA'S CURSE...
...AND I'M GOING TO BE THE NEXT VICTIM...?
BUT I DIDN'T DO ANYTHING.
GUH... (CLENCH...)
WHY SHOULD I BE KILLED?

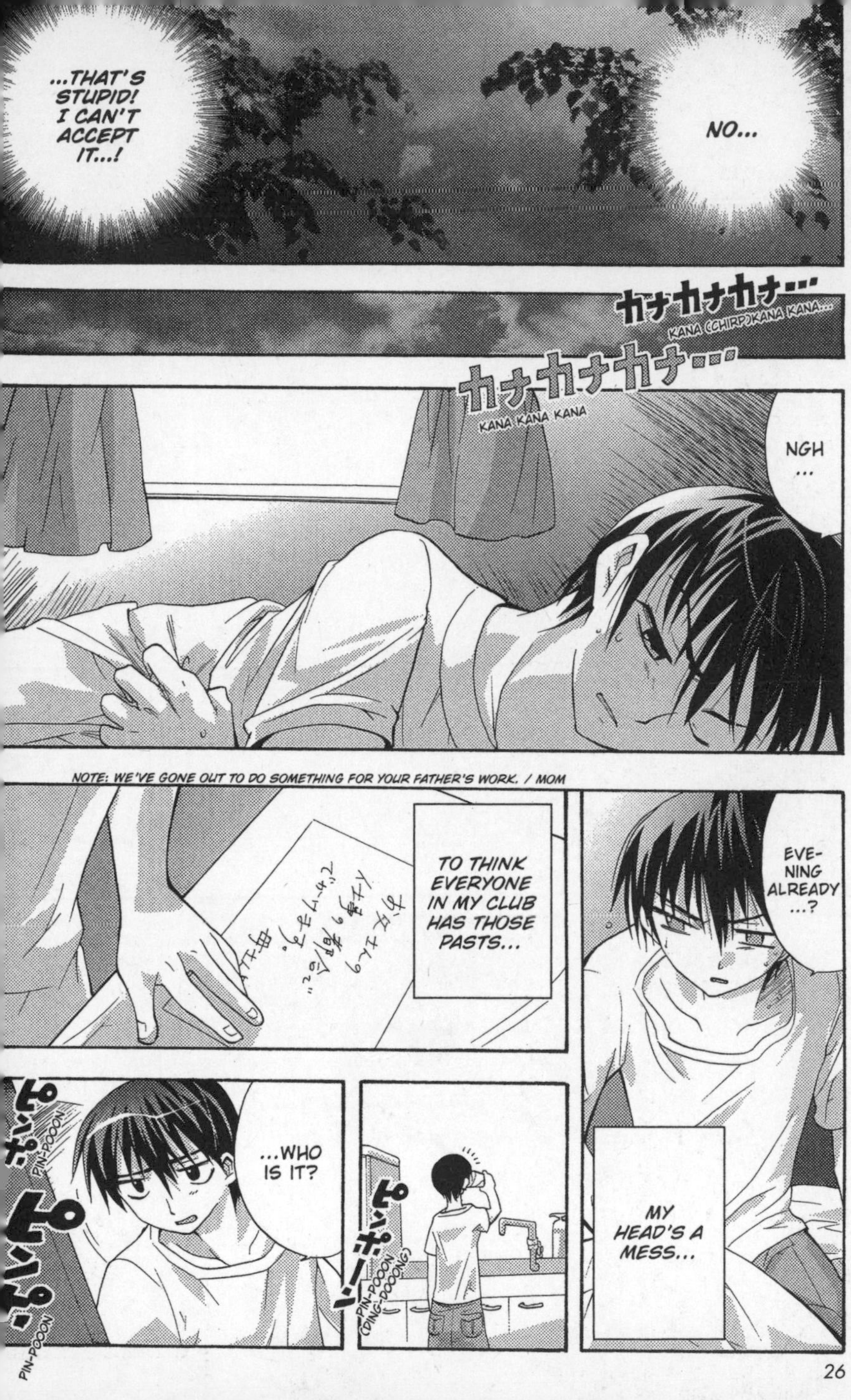
NO...
...THAT'S STUPID! I CAN'T ACCEPT IT...!
カナカナカナ…
KANA (CHIRP) KANA KANA...
カナカナカナ…
KANA KANA KANA
NGH ...
NOTE: WE'VE GONE OUT TO DO SOMETHING FOR YOUR FATHER'S WORK. / MOM
EVE-NING ALREADY ...?
MY HEAD'S A MESS...
TO THINK EVERYONE IN MY CLUB HAS THOSE PASTS...
ピンポーン!
PIN-POOON (DING-DOOONG)
...WHO IS IT?
ピンポーン
PIN-POOON
PIN-POOON

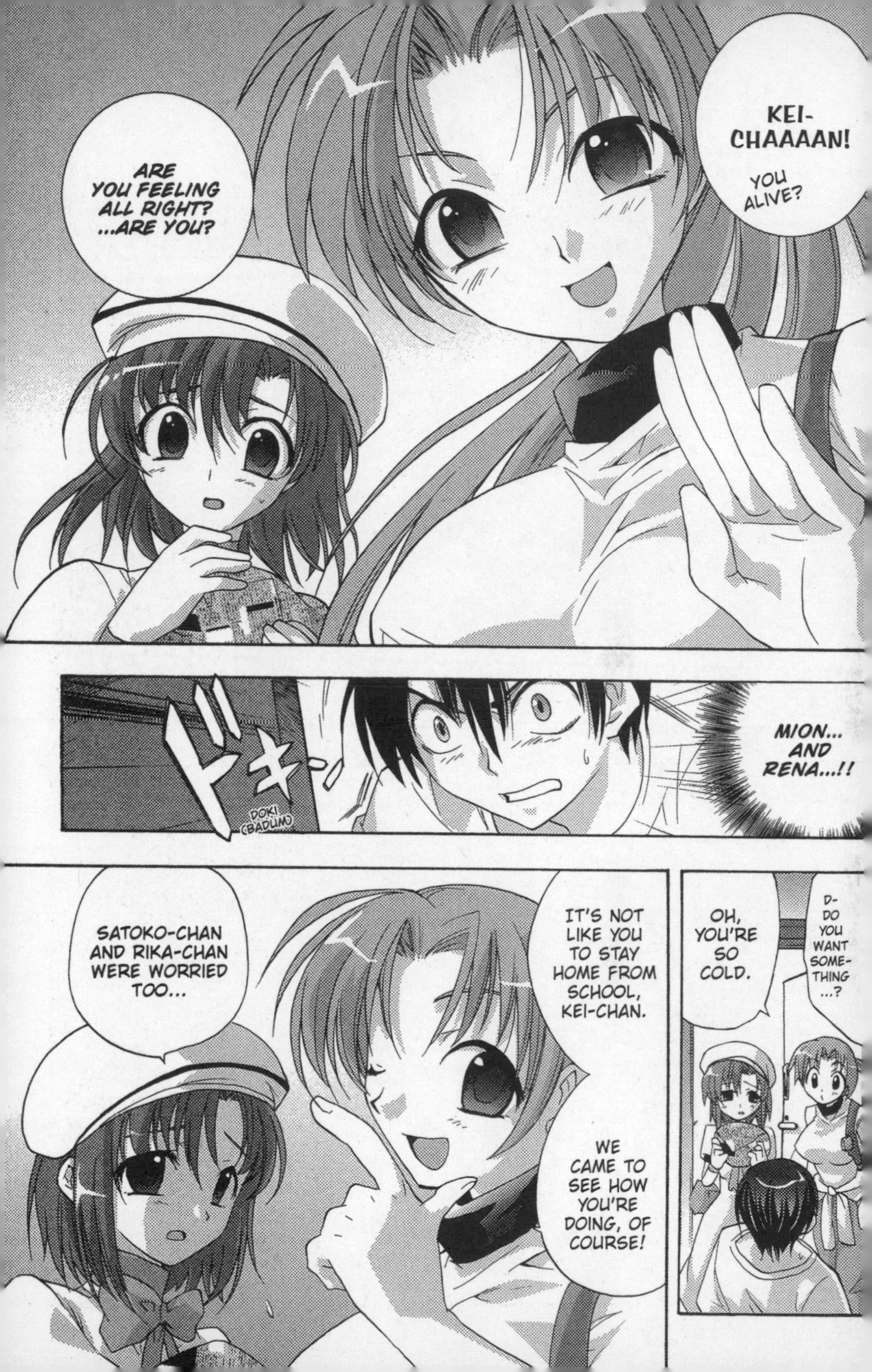
KEI-CHAAAAN! YOU ALIVE?
ARE YOU FEELING ALL RIGHT? ...ARE YOU?
MION... AND RENA...!!
DOKI (BADUM)
D-DO YOU WANT SOME-THING ...?
OH, YOU'RE SO COLD.
IT'S NOT LIKE YOU TO STAY HOME FROM SCHOOL, KEI-CHAN.
WE CAME TO SEE HOW YOU'RE DOING, OF COURSE!
SATOKO-CHAN AND RIKA-CHAN WERE WORRIED TOO...

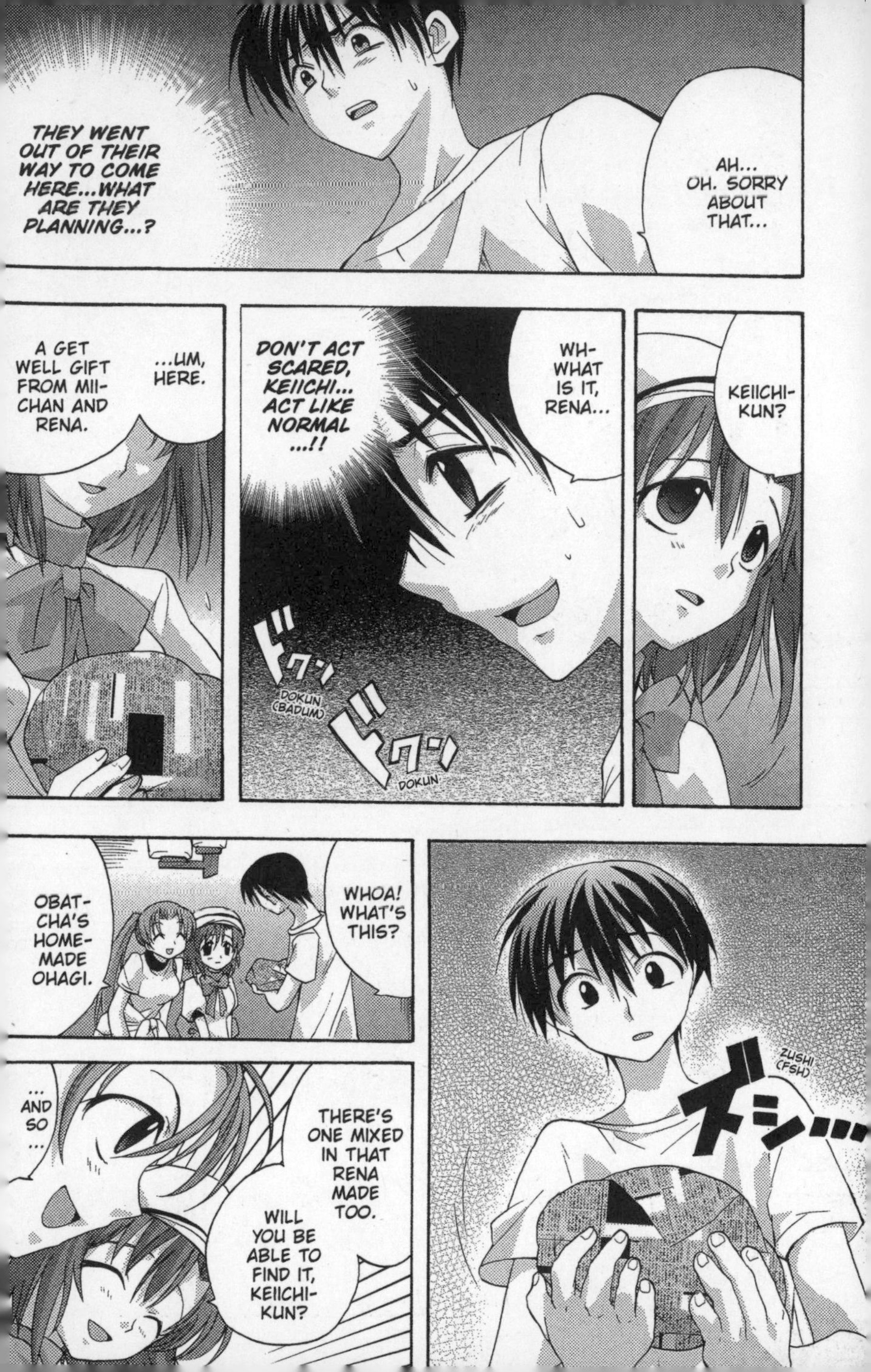
AH... OH. SORRY ABOUT THAT...
THEY WENT OUT OF THEIR WAY TO COME HERE...WHAT ARE THEY PLANNING...?
KEIICHI-KUN?
WH-WHAT IS IT, RENA...
DON'T ACT SCARED, KEIICHI... ACT LIKE NORMAL ...!!
ドクン DOKUN (BADUM)
ドクン DOKUN
...UM, HERE.
A GET WELL GIFT FROM MII-CHAN AND RENA.
ZUSHI (FSH)
WHOA! WHAT'S THIS?
OBAT-CHA'S HOME-MADE OHAGI.
THERE'S ONE MIXED IN THAT RENA MADE TOO.
WILL YOU BE ABLE TO FIND IT, KEIICHI-KUN?
... AND SO ...

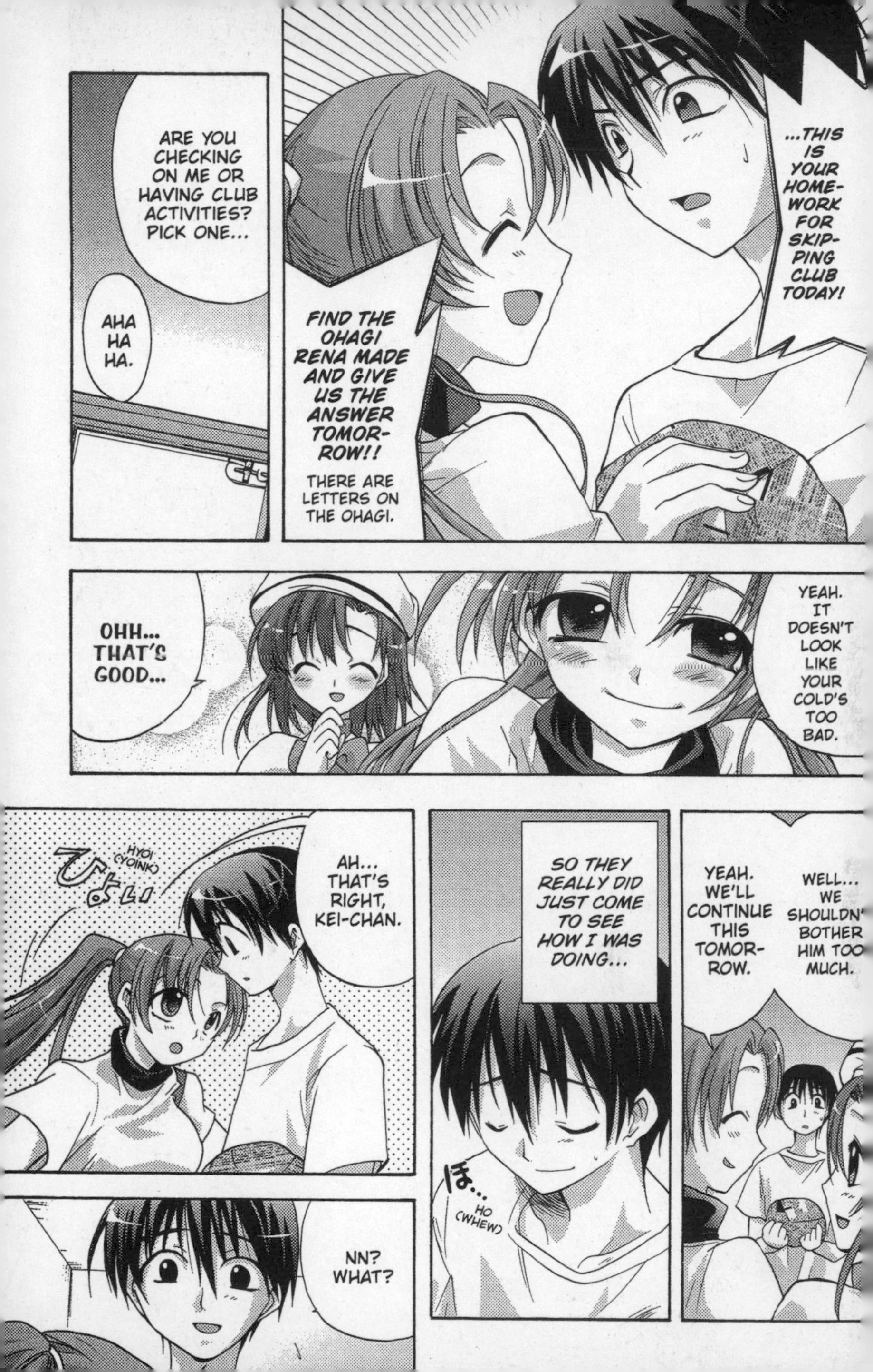
...THIS IS YOUR HOMEWORK FOR SKIPPING CLUB TODAY!
FIND THE OHAGI RENA MADE AND GIVE US THE ANSWER TOMORROW!!
THERE ARE LETTERS ON THE OHAGI.
ARE YOU CHECKING ON ME OR HAVING CLUB ACTIVITIES? PICK ONE...
AHA HA HA.
YEAH. IT DOESN'T LOOK LIKE YOUR COLD'S TOO BAD.
OHH... THAT'S GOOD...
WELL... WE SHOULDN' BOTHER HIM TOO MUCH.
YEAH. WE'LL CONTINUE THIS TOMORROW.
SO THEY REALLY DID JUST COME TO SEE HOW I WAS DOING...
HO (WHEW)
HYOI (YOINK)
AH... THAT'S RIGHT, KEI-CHAN.
NN? WHAT?

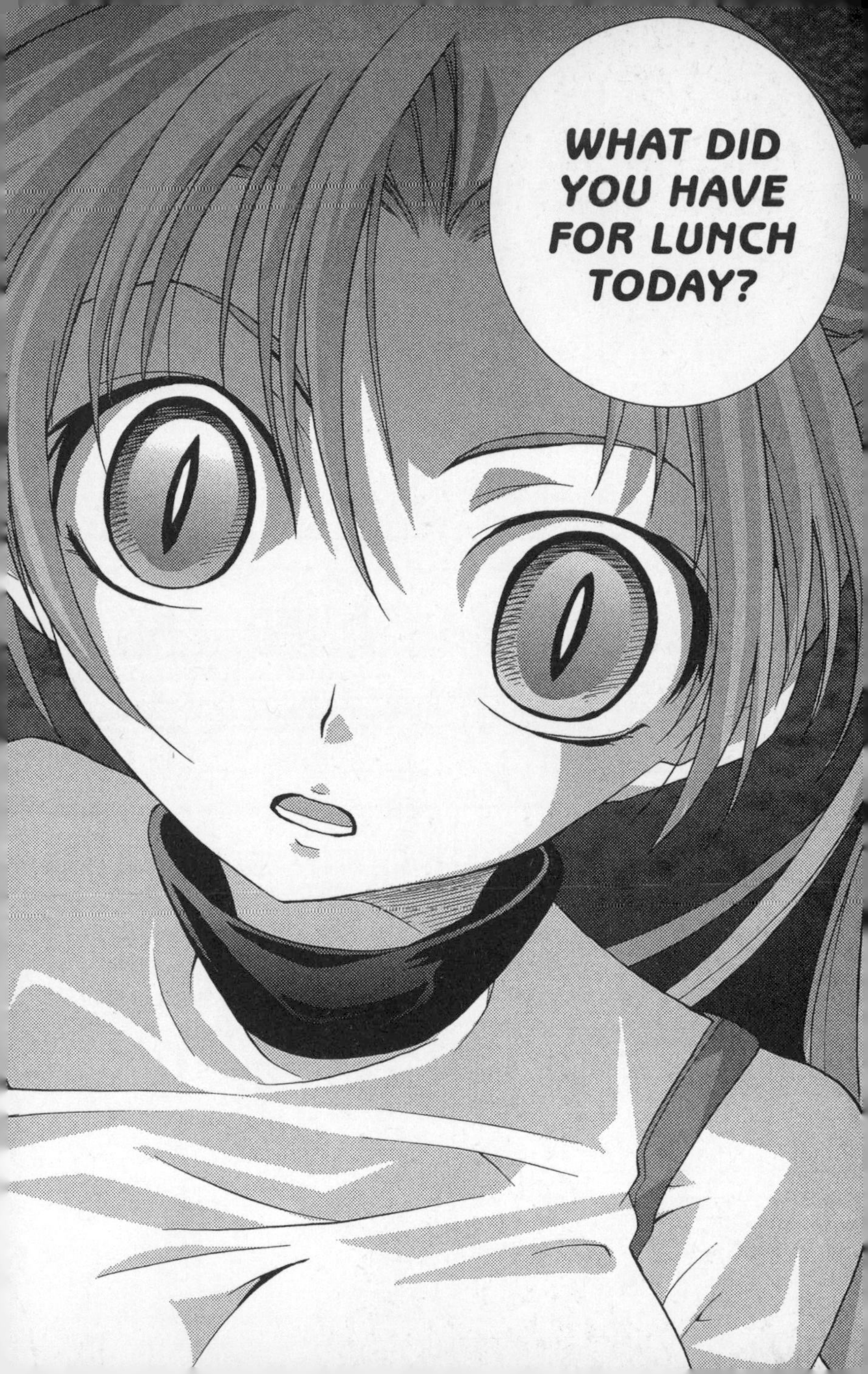
WHAT DID YOU HAVE FOR LUNCH TODAY?

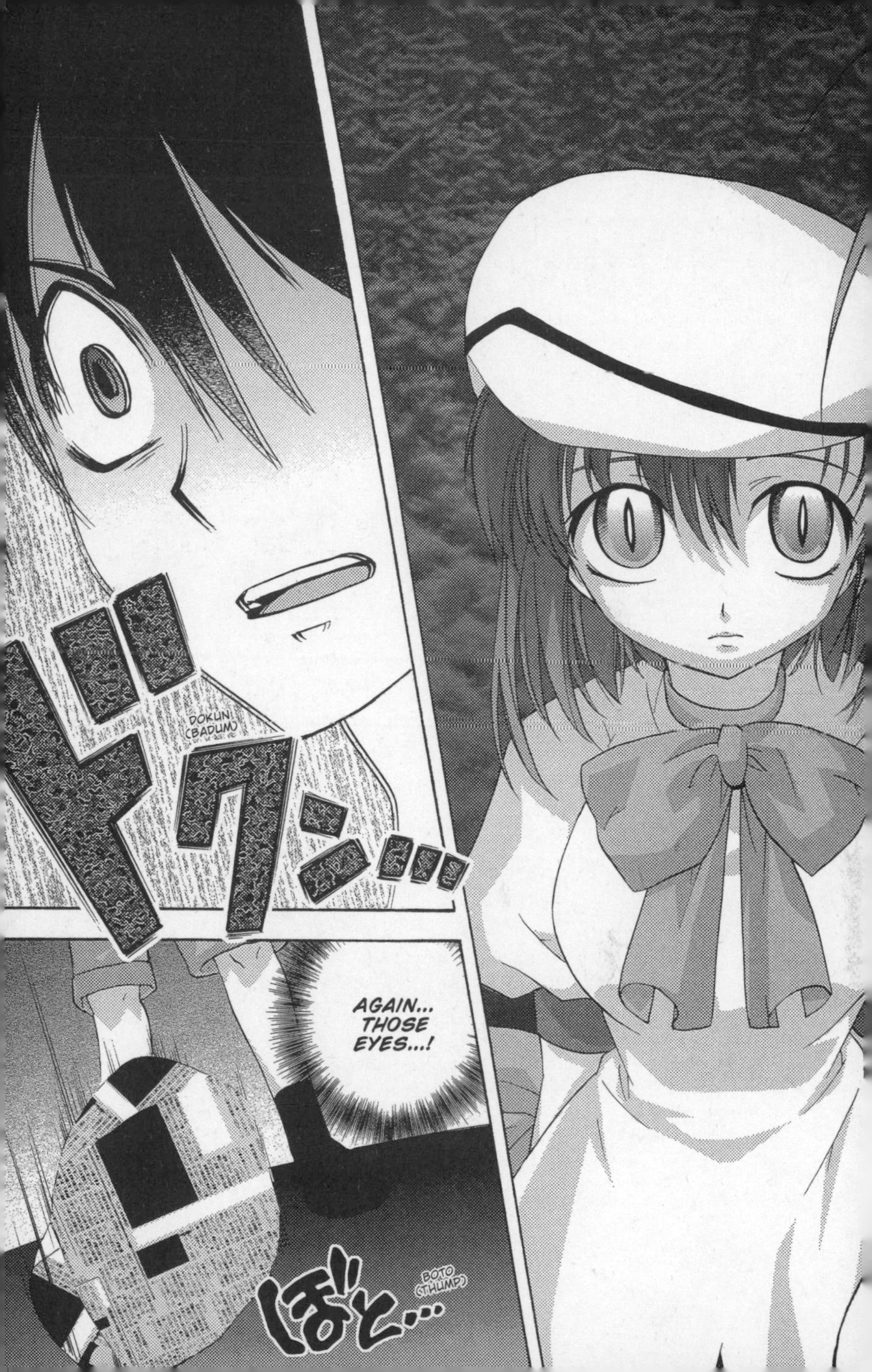
ドクン…
DOKUN! (BADUM)
AGAIN... THOSE EYES...!
ぼとっ…
BOTO (THUMP)

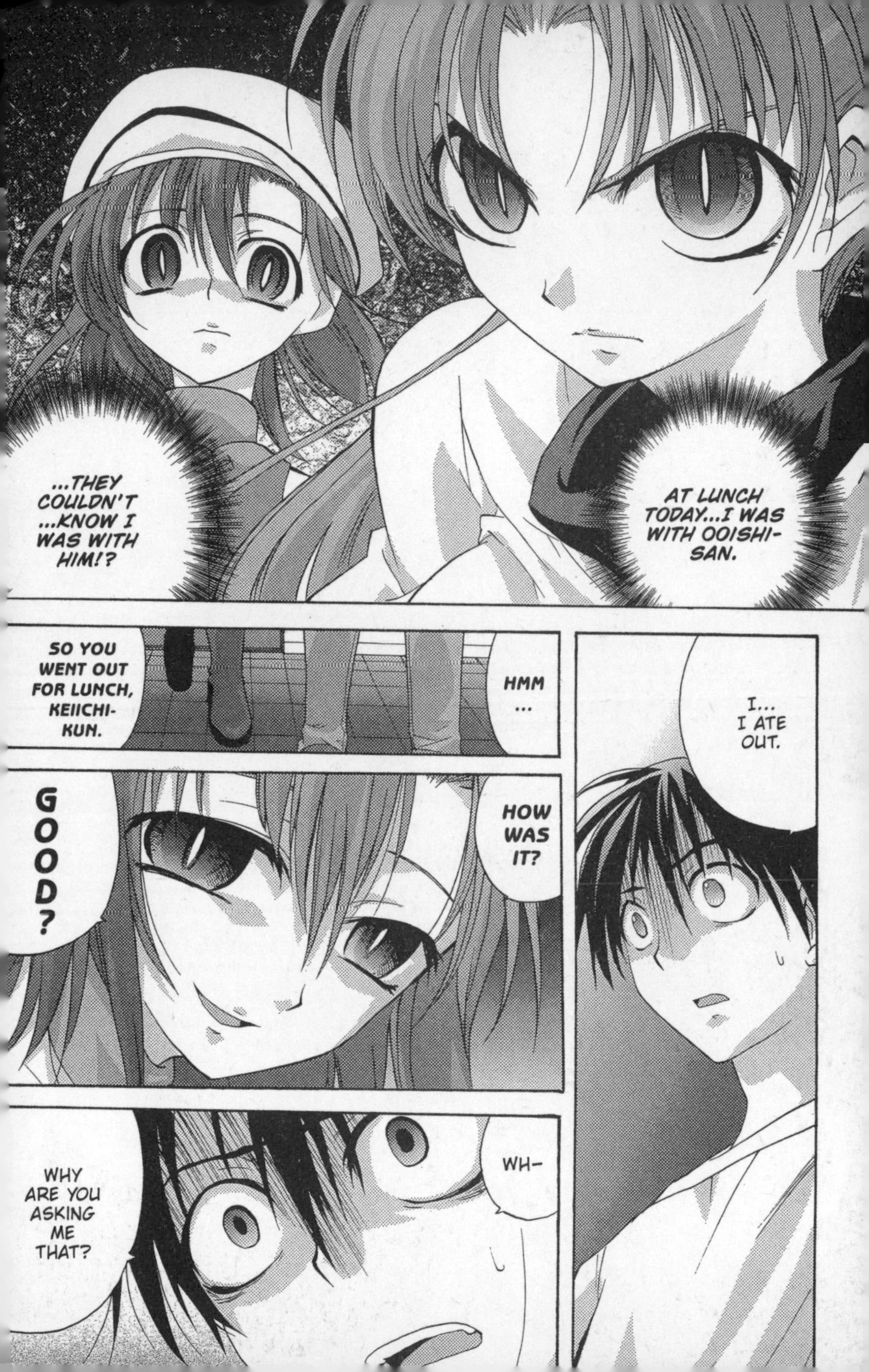
AT LUNCH TODAY...I WAS WITH OOISHI-SAN.
...THEY COULDN'T ...KNOW I WAS WITH HIM!?
I... I ATE OUT.
HMM ...
SO YOU WENT OUT FOR LUNCH, KEIICHI-KUN.
HOW WAS IT?
GOOD?
WH-
WHY ARE YOU ASKING ME THAT?

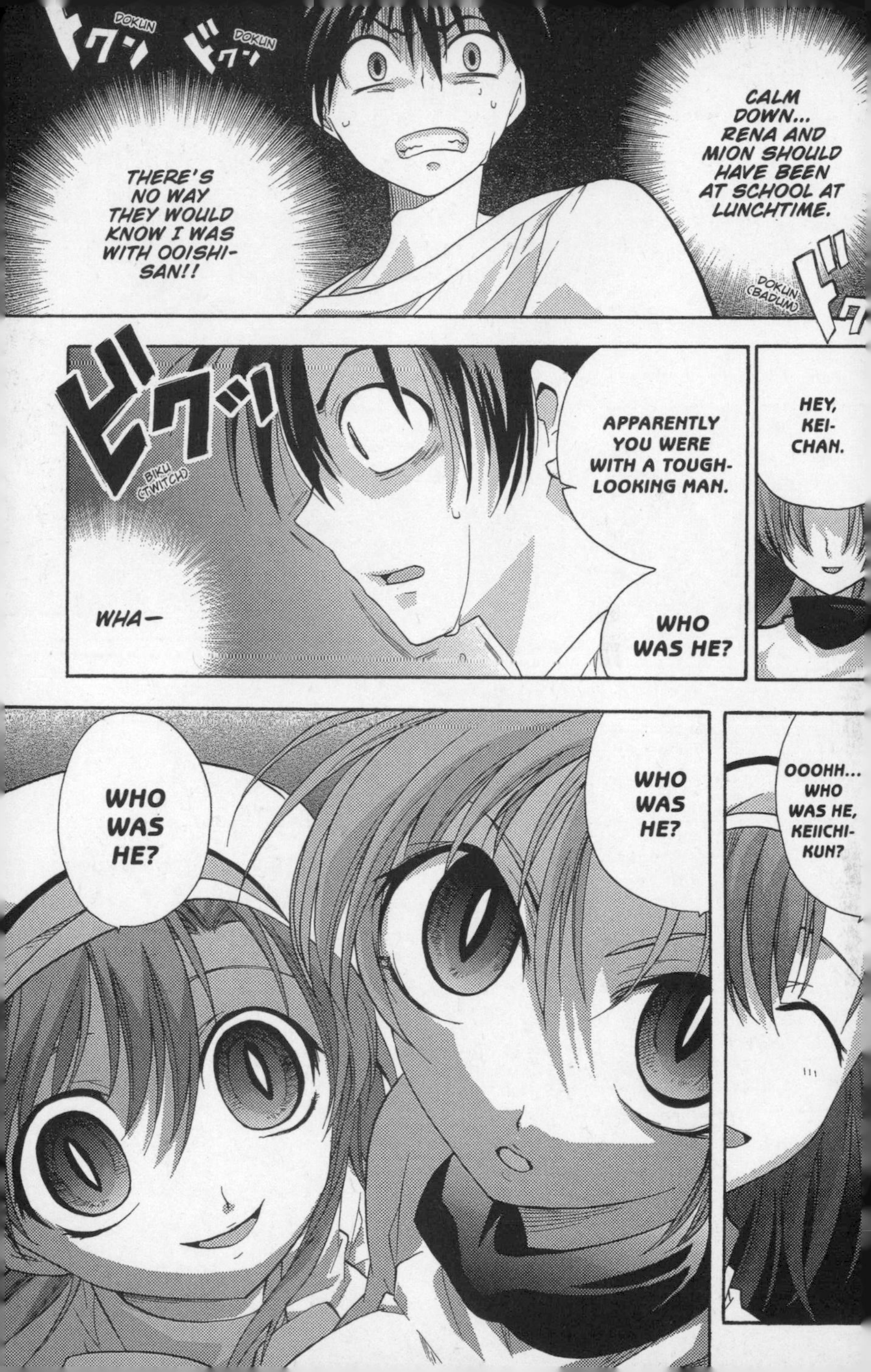
CALM DOWN... RENA AND MION SHOULD HAVE BEEN AT SCHOOL AT LUNCHTIME.
DOKUN (BADUM)
DOKUN
DOKUN
THERE'S NO WAY THEY WOULD KNOW I WAS WITH OOISHI-SAN!!
HEY, KEI-CHAN.
APPARENTLY YOU WERE WITH A TOUGH-LOOKING MAN.
WHO WAS HE?
BIKU (TWITCH)
WHA—
OOOHH... WHO WAS HE, KEIICHI-KUN?
WHO WAS HE?
WHO WAS HE?

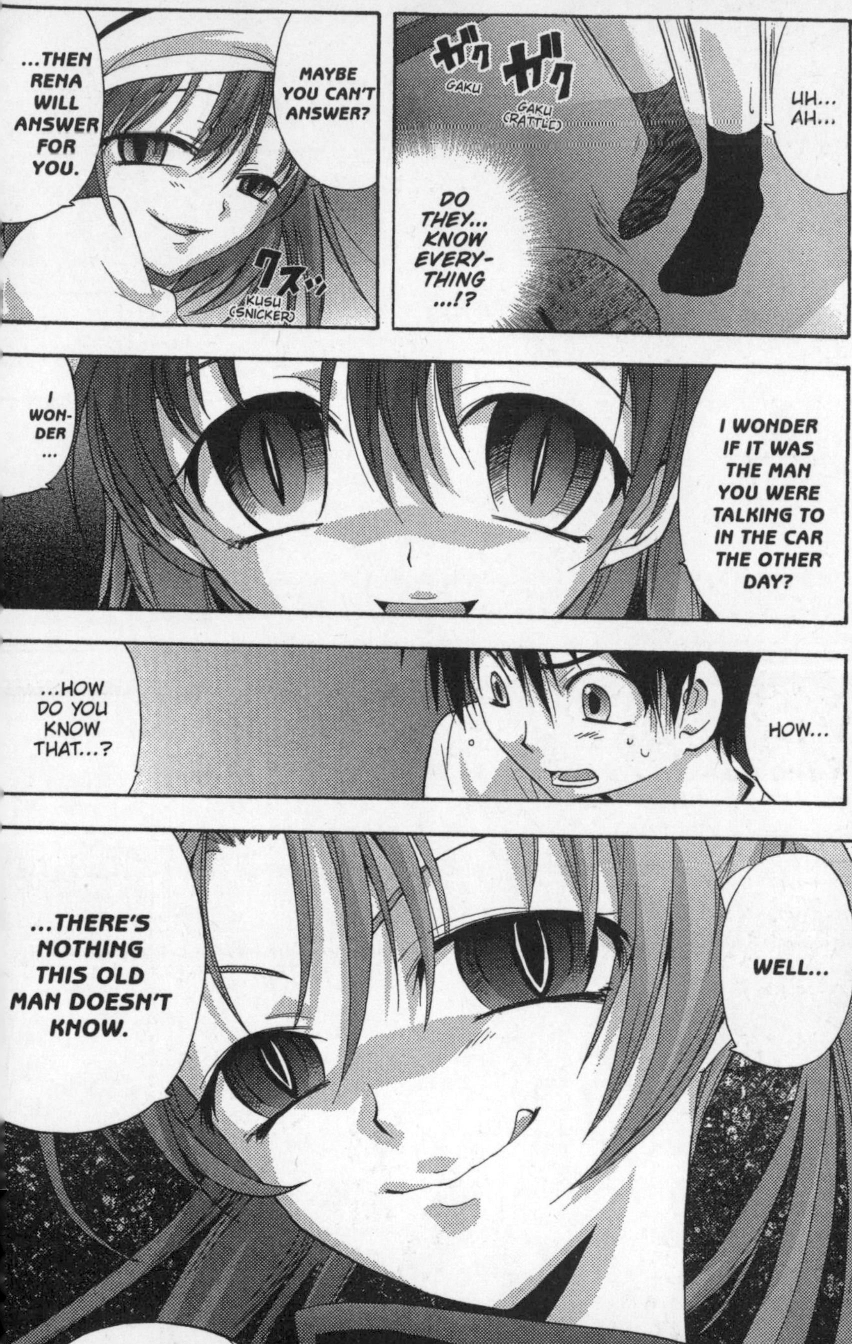
UH... AH...
ガク ガク
GAKU
GAKU (RATTLE)
DO THEY... KNOW EVERY-THING...!?
MAYBE YOU CAN'T ANSWER?
...THEN RENA WILL ANSWER FOR YOU.
クスッ
KUSU (SNICKER)
I WONDER IF IT WAS THE MAN YOU WERE TALKING TO IN THE CAR THE OTHER DAY?
I WON-DER ...
HOW...
...HOW DO YOU KNOW THAT...?
WELL...
...THERE'S NOTHING THIS OLD MAN DOESN'T KNOW.

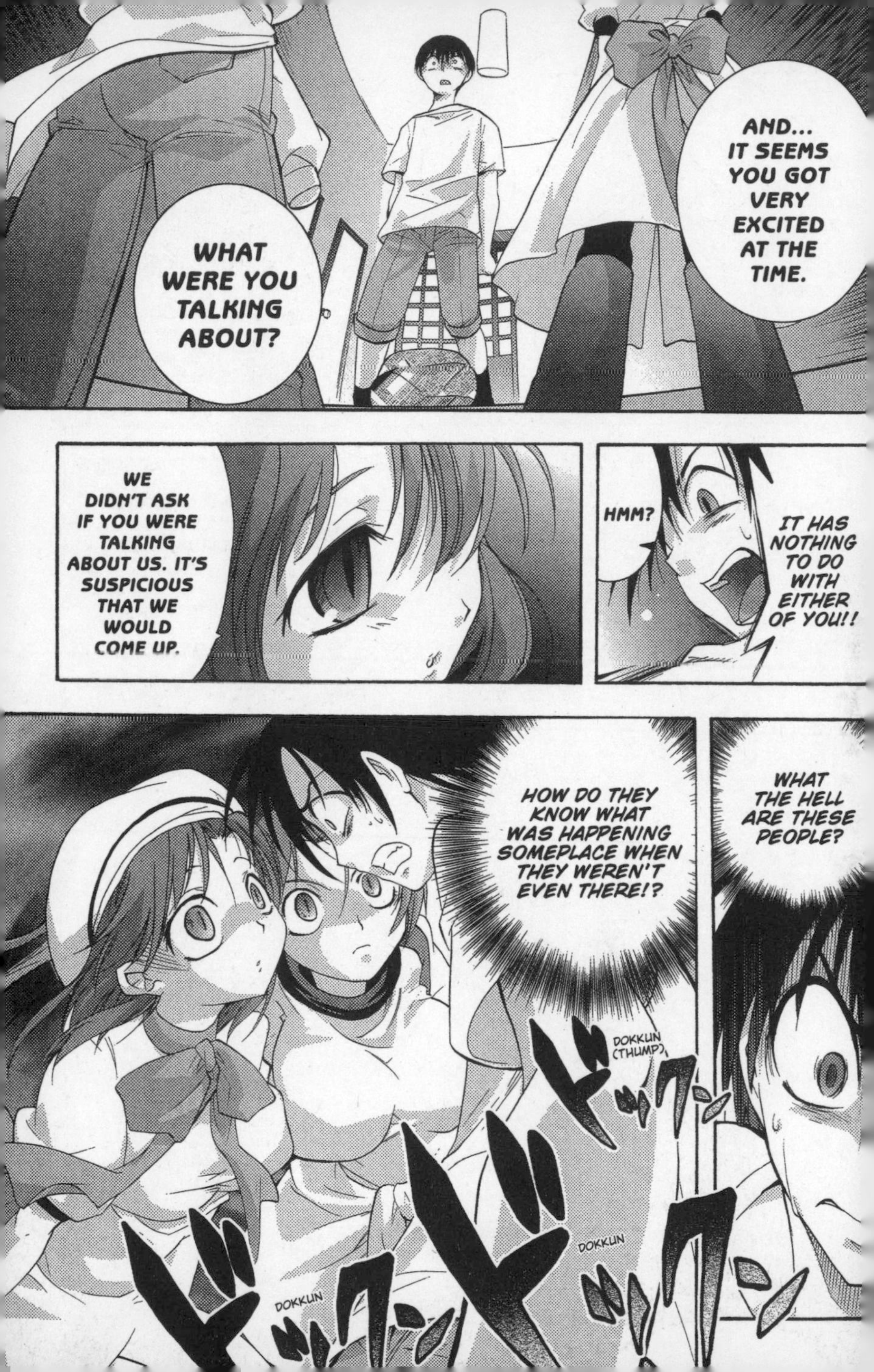
AND... IT SEEMS YOU GOT VERY EXCITED AT THE TIME.
WHAT WERE YOU TALKING ABOUT?
IT HAS NOTHING TO DO WITH EITHER OF YOU!!
HMM?
WE DIDN'T ASK IF YOU WERE TALKING ABOUT US. IT'S SUSPICIOUS THAT WE WOULD COME UP.
WHAT THE HELL ARE THESE PEOPLE?
HOW DO THEY KNOW WHAT WAS HAPPENING SOMEPLACE WHEN THEY WEREN'T EVEN THERE!?
DOKKUN (THUMP)
DOKKUN
DOKKUN

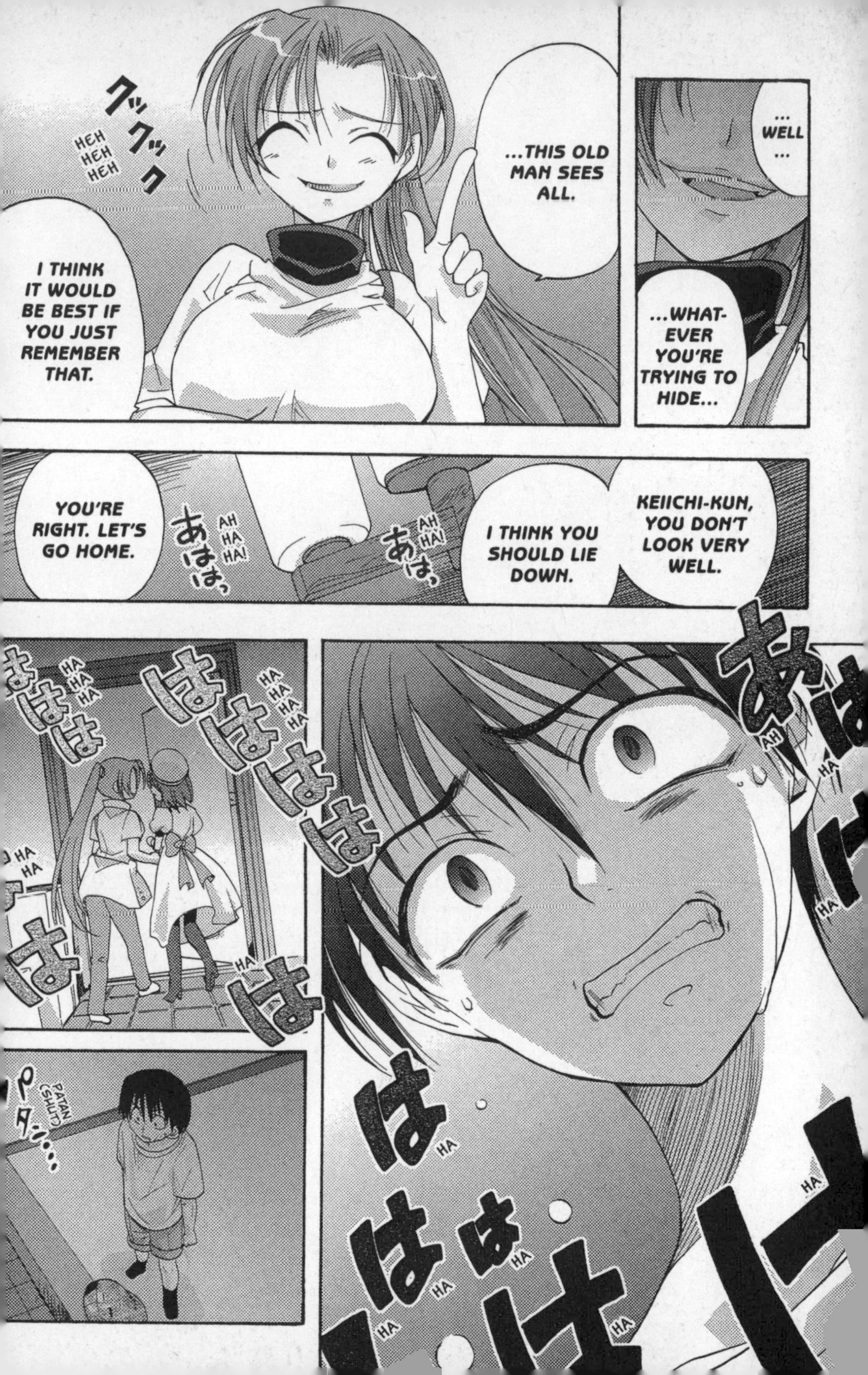

... WELL ...
...WHAT-EVER YOU'RE TRYING TO HIDE...
...THIS OLD MAN SEES ALL.
クックック
HEH HEH HEH
I THINK IT WOULD BE BEST IF YOU JUST REMEMBER THAT.
KEIICHI-KUN, YOU DON'T LOOK VERY WELL.
I THINK YOU SHOULD LIE DOWN.
あは、
AH HA!
あははっ
AH HA HA!
YOU'RE RIGHT. LET'S GO HOME.
あは
AH HA
HA
HA
は
HA
はは
HA HA
HA
HA
ははは
HA HA HA
ははははは
HA HA HA HA HA
HA HA
HA
パタン…
PATAN (SHUT)

OH, THAT'S RIGHT, KEI-CHAN.

BIKU (JUMP)

BAN (BAM)

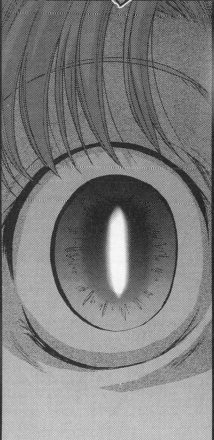

WE DON'T... WANT YOU TO...

...STAY HOME FROM SCHOOL TOMORROW.

BATAN (SHUT)

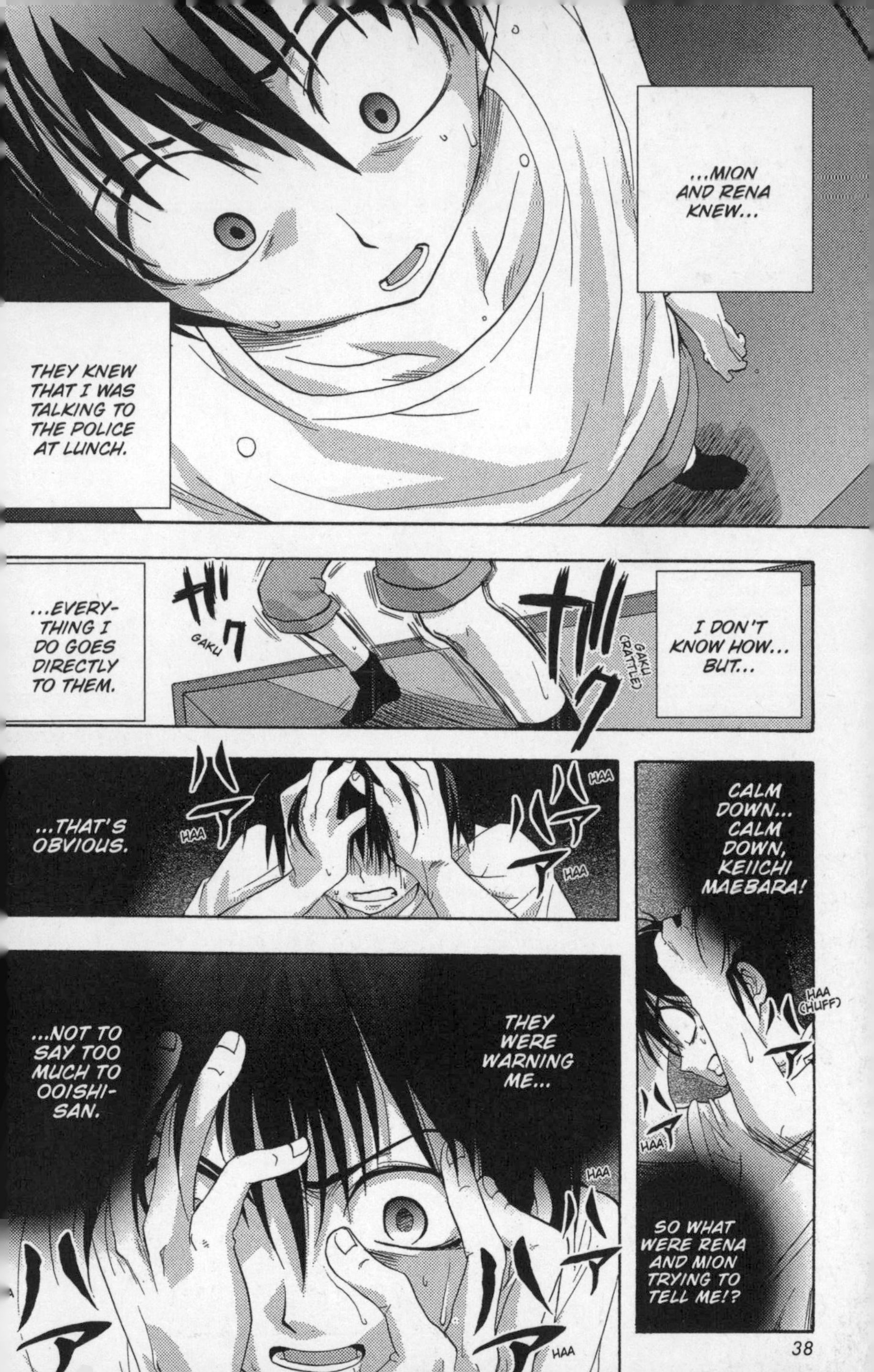
...MION AND RENA KNEW...
THEY KNEW THAT I WAS TALKING TO THE POLICE AT LUNCH.
I DON'T KNOW HOW... BUT...
GAKU (RATTLE)
GAKU
...EVERY-THING I DO GOES DIRECTLY TO THEM.
CALM DOWN... CALM DOWN, KEIICHI MAEBARA!
HAA (HUFF)
HAA
SO WHAT WERE RENA AND MION TRYING TO TELL ME!?
HAA
HAA
...THAT'S OBVIOUS.
HAA
THEY WERE WARNING ME...
...NOT TO SAY TOO MUCH TO OOISHI-SAN.
HAA
HAA

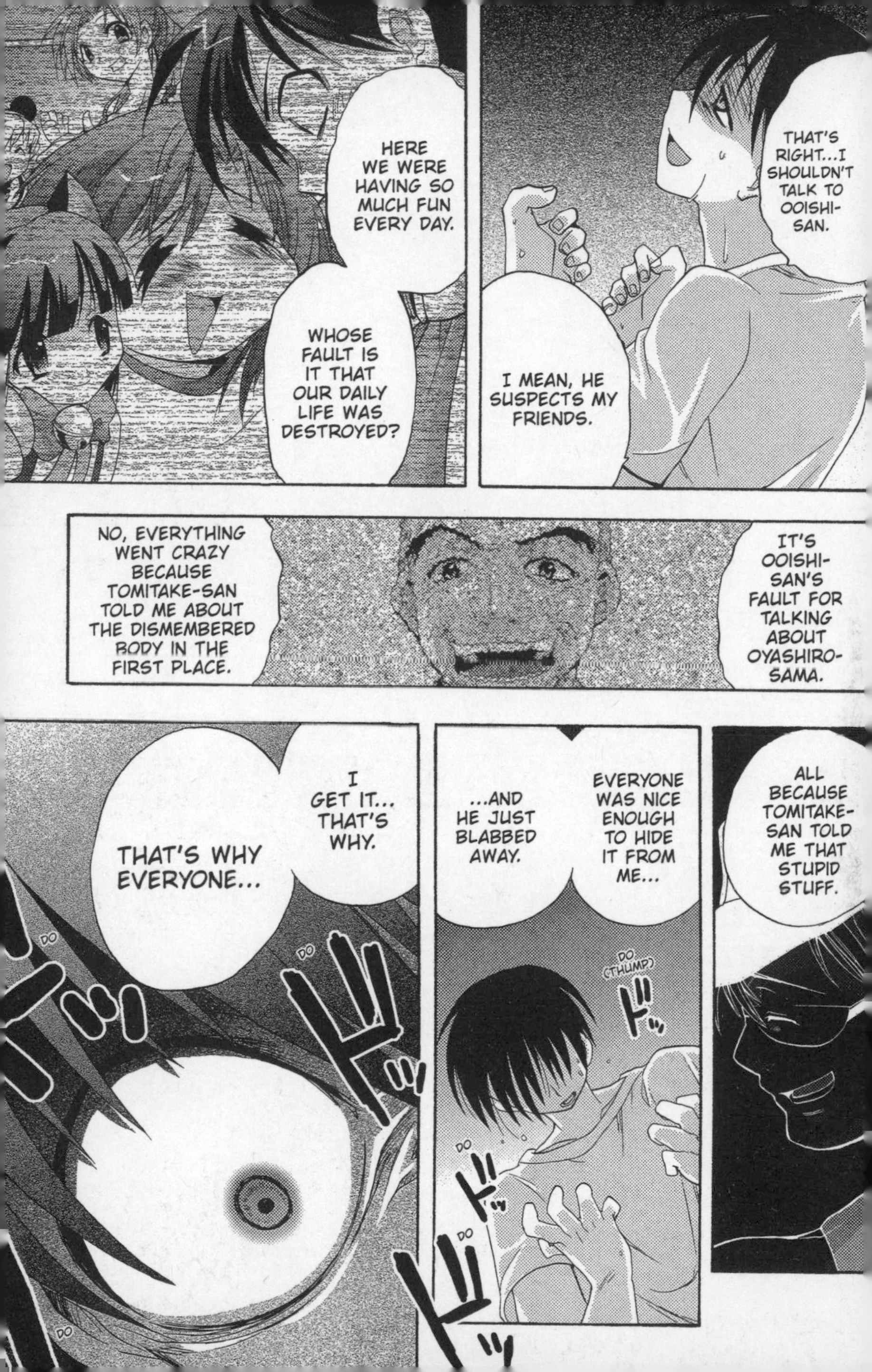
THAT'S RIGHT...I SHOULDN'T TALK TO OOISHI-SAN.
I MEAN, HE SUSPECTS MY FRIENDS.
HERE WE WERE HAVING SO MUCH FUN EVERY DAY.
WHOSE FAULT IS IT THAT OUR DAILY LIFE WAS DESTROYED?
IT'S OOISHI-SAN'S FAULT FOR TALKING ABOUT OYASHIRO-SAMA.
NO, EVERYTHING WENT CRAZY BECAUSE TOMITAKE-SAN TOLD ME ABOUT THE DISMEMBERED BODY IN THE FIRST PLACE.
ALL BECAUSE TOMITAKE-SAN TOLD ME THAT STUPID STUFF.
EVERYONE WAS NICE ENOUGH TO HIDE IT FROM ME...
...AND HE JUST BLABBED AWAY.
DO (THUMP)
DO
DO
I GET IT... THAT'S WHY.
THAT'S WHY EVERYONE...
DO
DO
DO

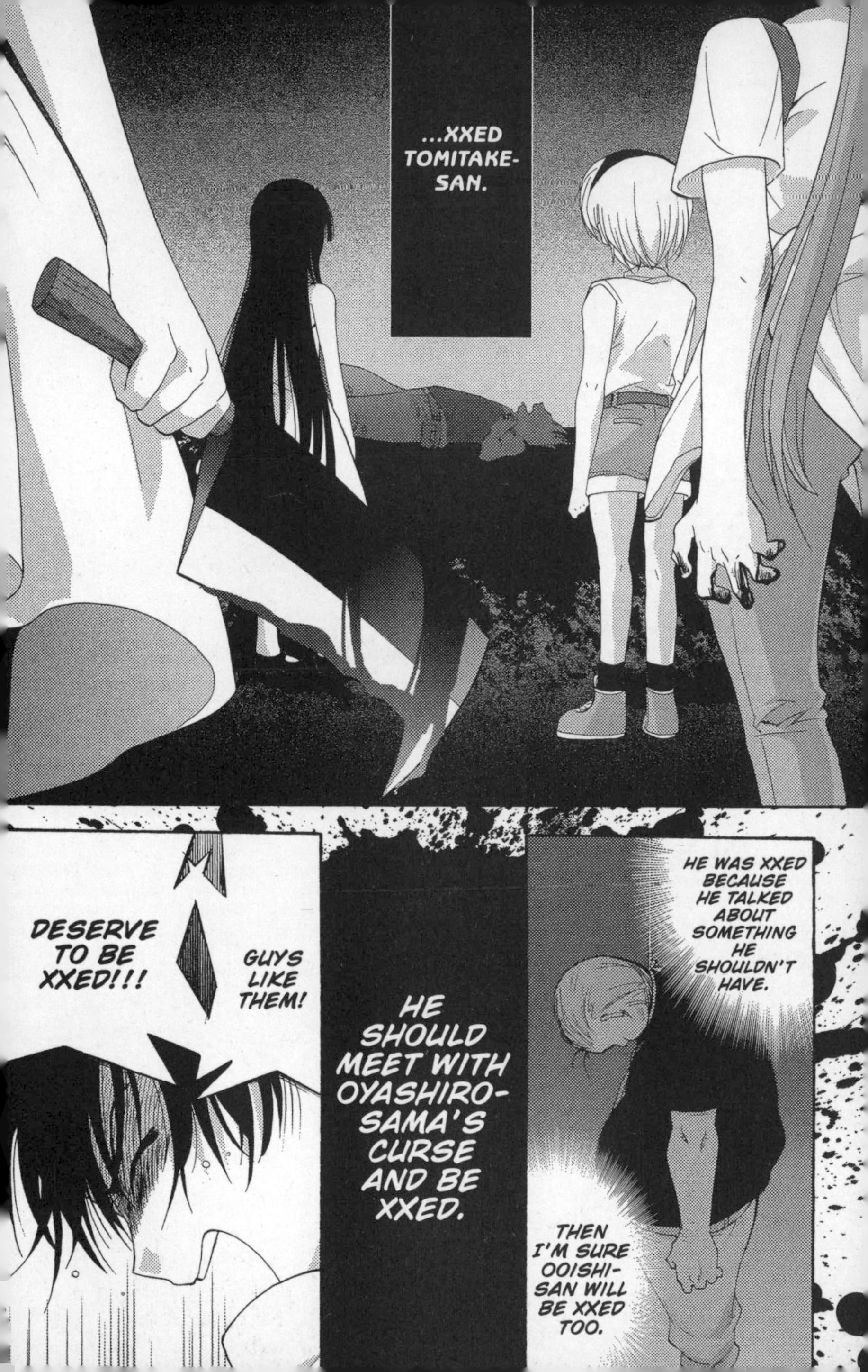
...XXED TOMITAKE-SAN.
HE WAS XXED BECAUSE HE TALKED ABOUT SOMETHING HE SHOULDN'T HAVE.
THEN I'M SURE OOISHI-SAN WILL BE XXED TOO.
HE SHOULD MEET WITH OYASHIRO-SAMA'S CURSE AND BE XXED.
GUYS LIKE THEM!
DESERVE TO BE XXED!!!

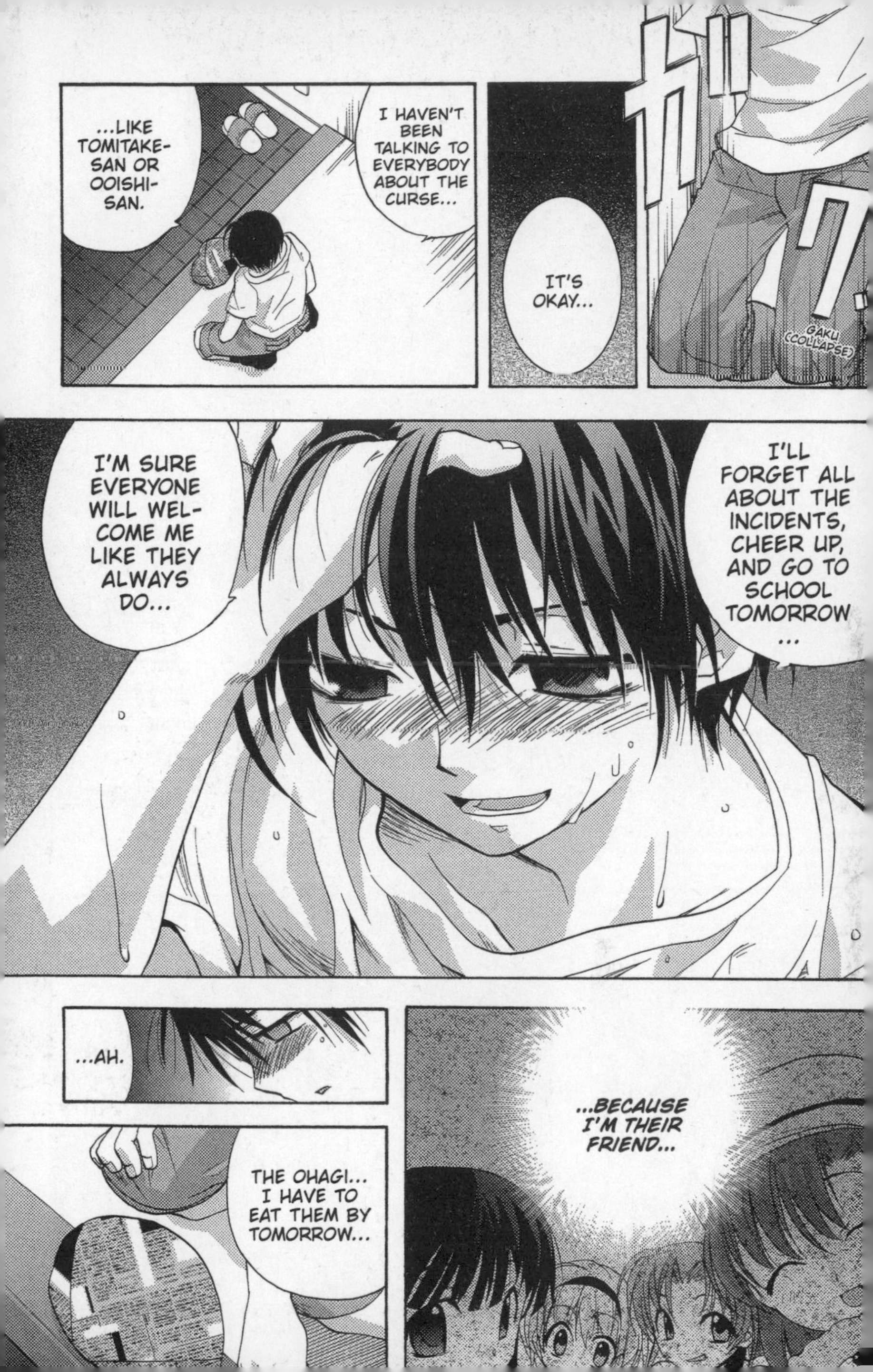
ガク
GAKU (COLLAPSE)
IT'S OKAY...
I HAVEN'T BEEN TALKING TO EVERYBODY ABOUT THE CURSE...
...LIKE TOMITAKE-SAN OR OOISHI-SAN.
I'LL FORGET ALL ABOUT THE INCIDENTS, CHEER UP, AND GO TO SCHOOL TOMORROW ...
I'M SURE EVERYONE WILL WEL-COME ME LIKE THEY ALWAYS DO...
...BECAUSE I'M THEIR FRIEND...
...AH.
THE OHAGI... I HAVE TO EAT THEM BY TOMORROW...

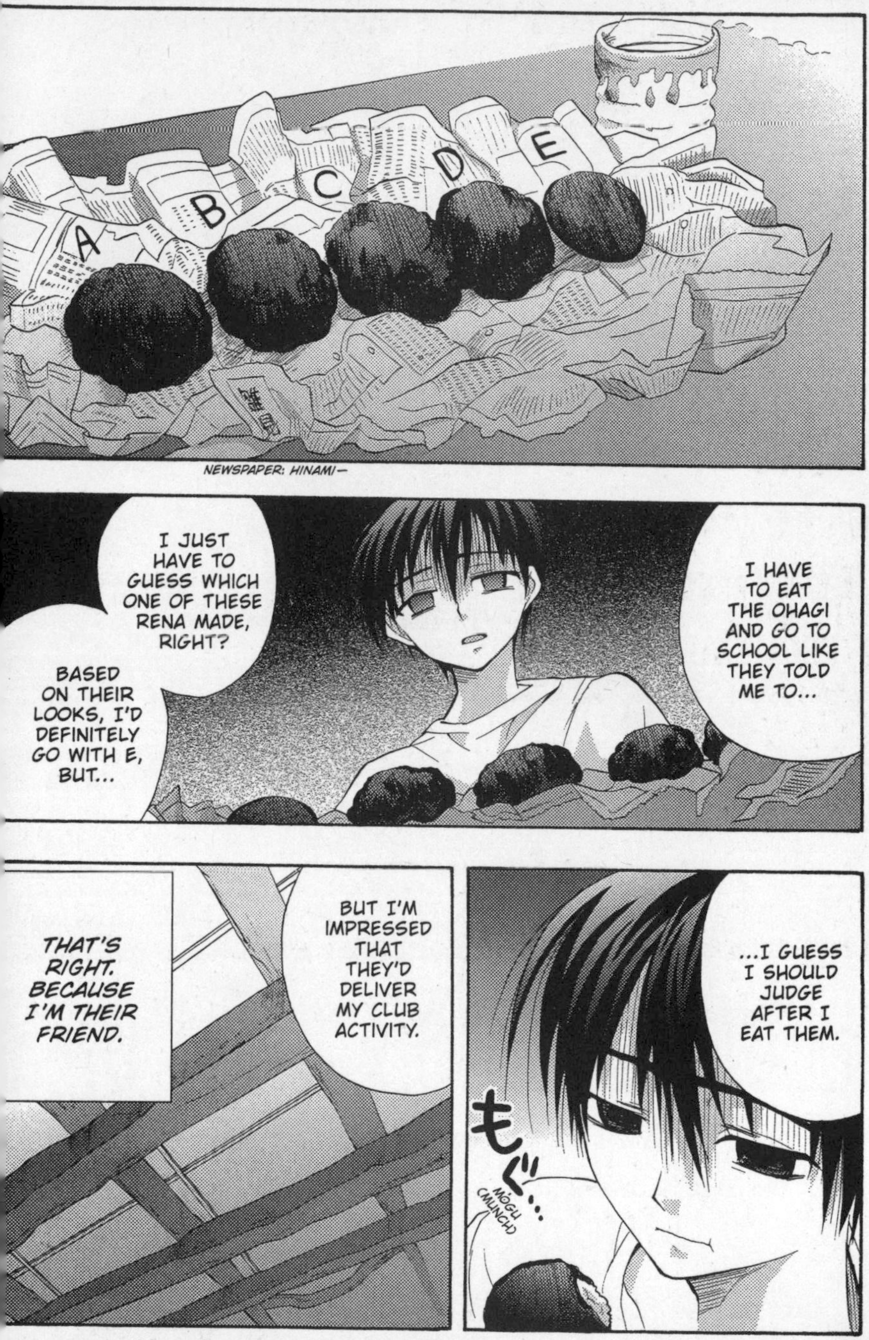
A
B
C
D
E
NEWSPAPER: HINAMI—
I HAVE TO EAT THE OHAGI AND GO TO SCHOOL LIKE THEY TOLD ME TO...
I JUST HAVE TO GUESS WHICH ONE OF THESE RENA MADE, RIGHT?
BASED ON THEIR LOOKS, I'D DEFINITELY GO WITH E, BUT...
...I GUESS I SHOULD JUDGE AFTER I EAT THEM.
もぐ…
MOGU (MUNCH)
BUT I'M IMPRESSED THAT THEY'D DELIVER MY CLUB ACTIVITY.
THAT'S RIGHT. BECAUSE I'M THEIR FRIEND.

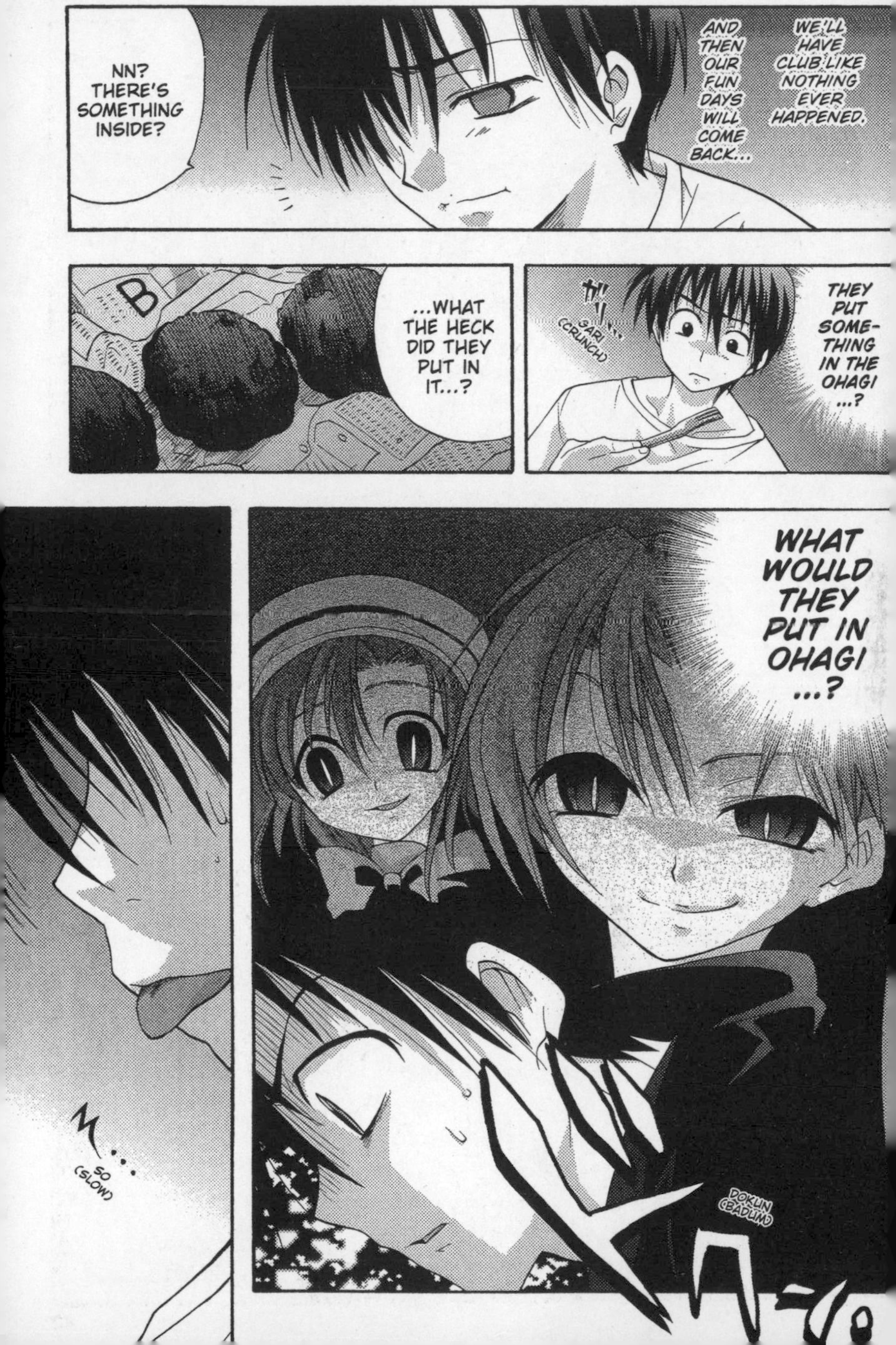
WE'LL HAVE CLUB LIKE NOTHING EVER HAPPENED.
AND THEN OUR FUN DAYS WILL COME BACK...
NN? THERE'S SOMETHING INSIDE?
SARI (CRUNCH)
THEY PUT SOMETHING IN THE OHAGI ...?
...WHAT THE HECK DID THEY PUT IN IT...?
WHAT WOULD THEY PUT IN OHAGI ...?
DOKUN (BADUM)
SO (SLOW)

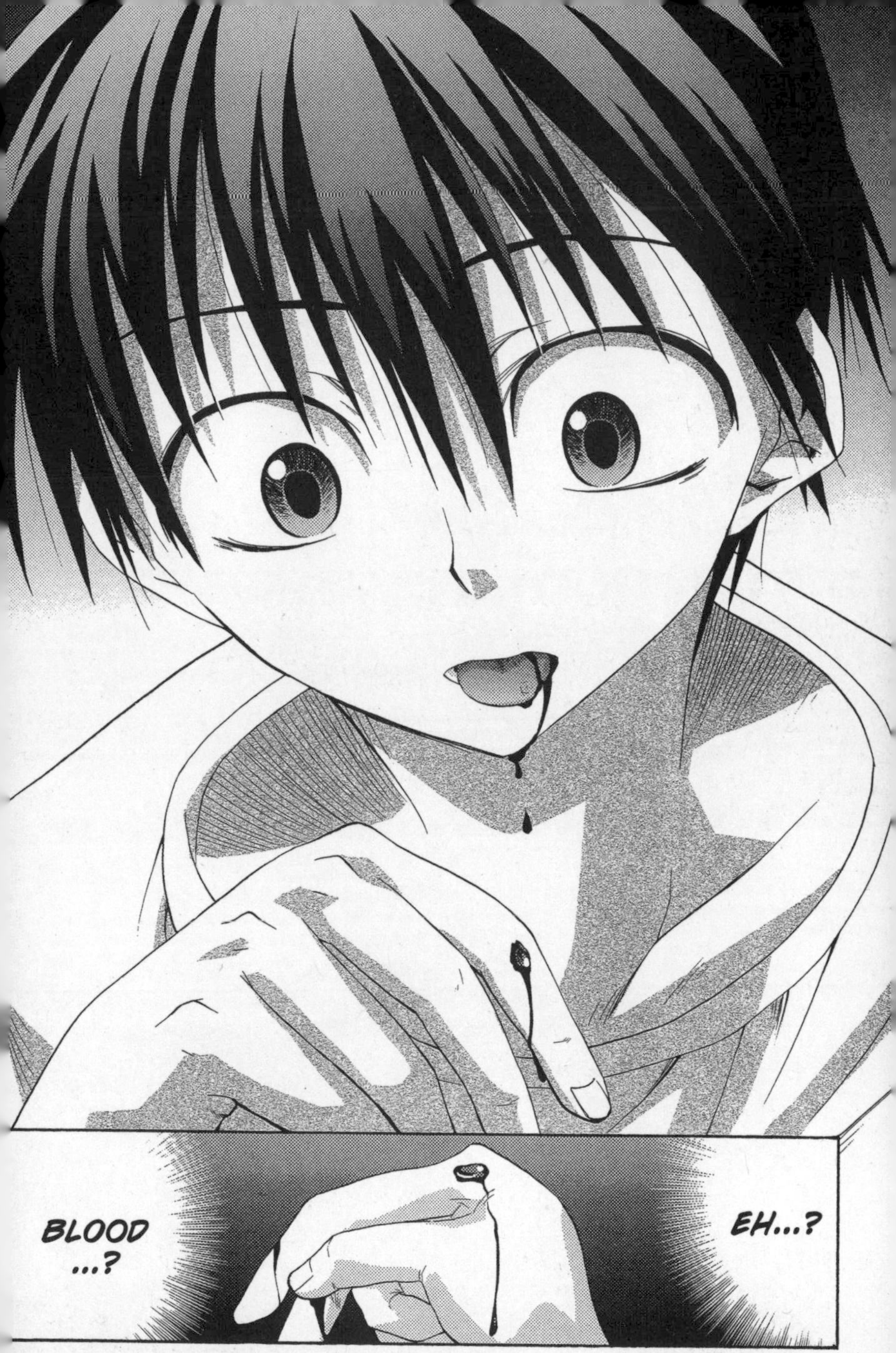
EH...?
BLOOD ...?

WHA!?

WHY ....?

A SEWING NEEDLE?

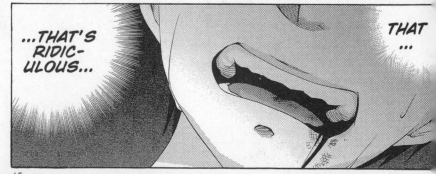

...THAT'S RIDIC- ULOUS...

THAT ...

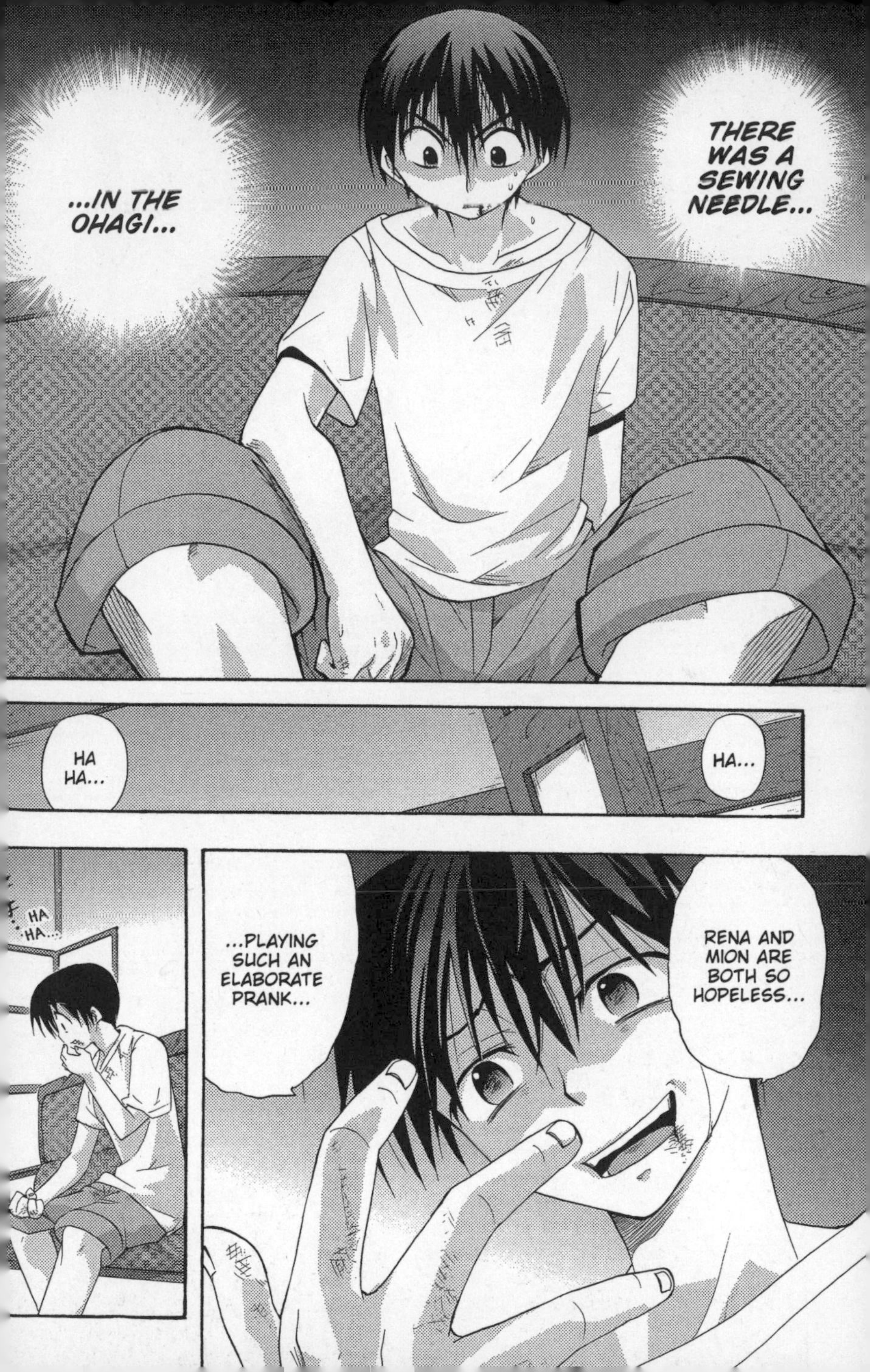
THERE WAS A SEWING NEEDLE...
...IN THE OHAGI...
HA...
HA HA...
RENA AND MION ARE BOTH SO HOPELESS...
...PLAYING SUCH AN ELABORATE PRANK...
HA HA...

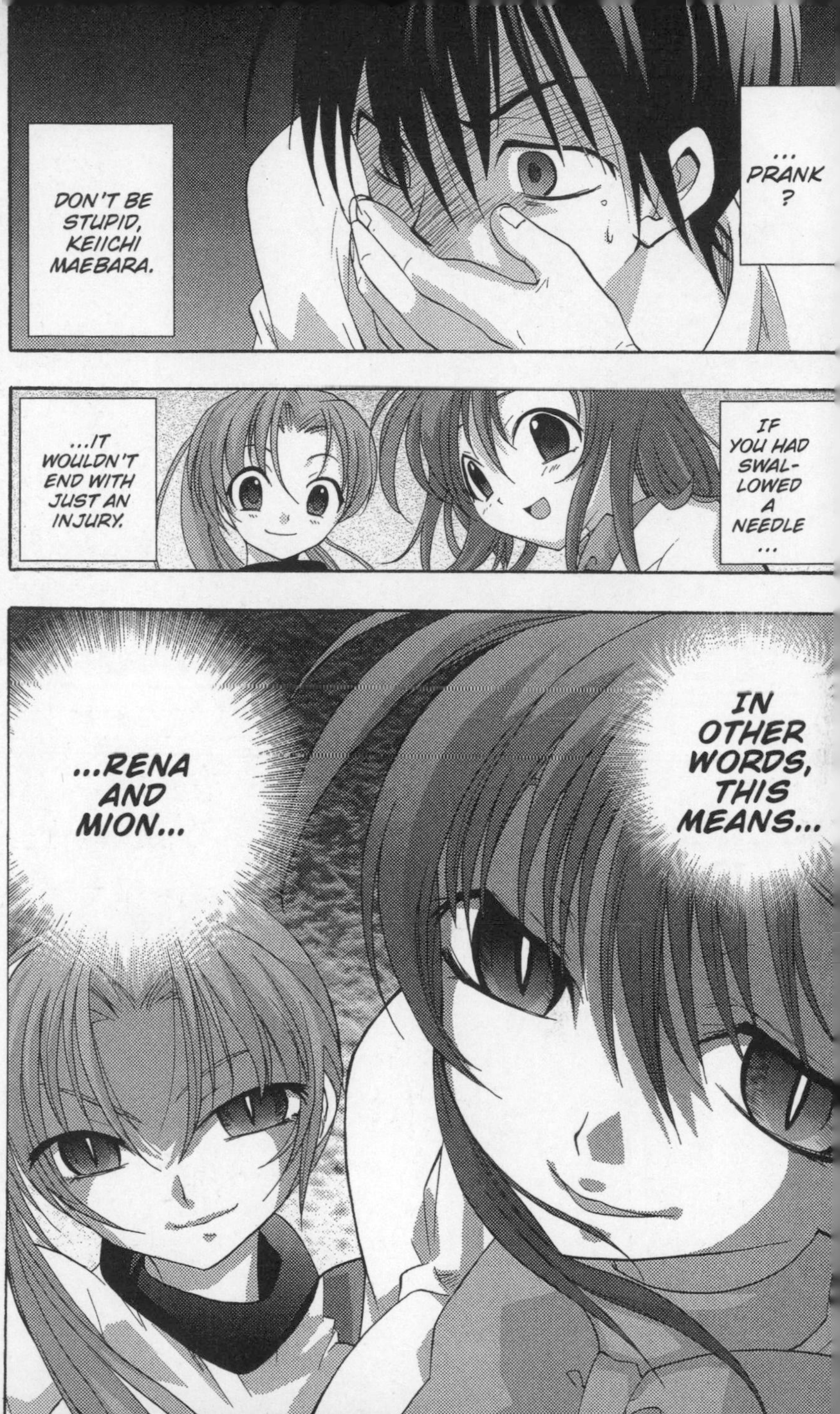
...PRANK?
DON'T BE STUPID, KEIICHI MAEBARA.
IF YOU HAD SWAL-LOWED A NEEDLE...
...IT WOULDN'T END WITH JUST AN INJURY.
IN OTHER WORDS, THIS MEANS...
...RENA AND MION...

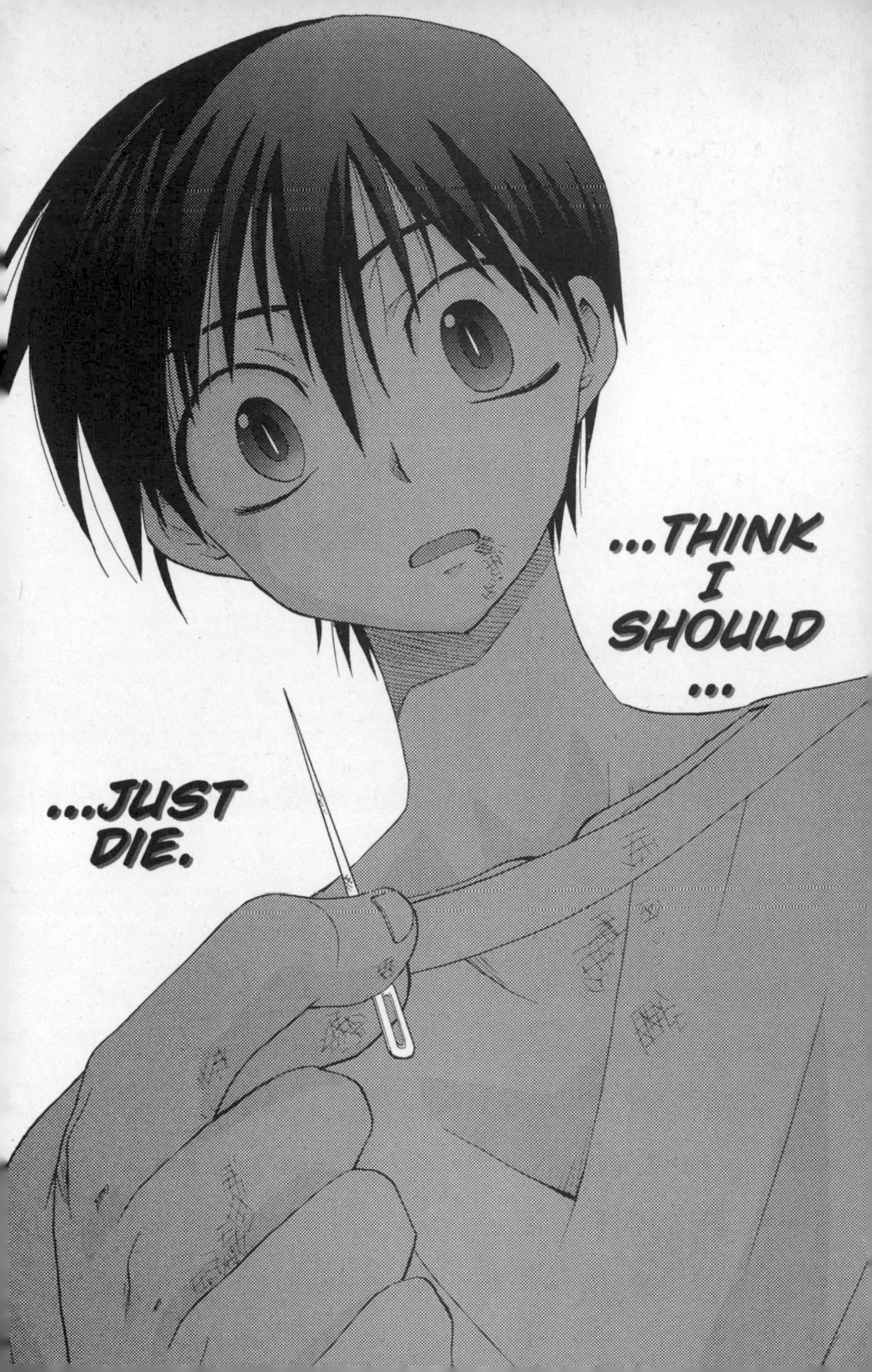
...THINK I SHOULD ...
...JUST DIE.

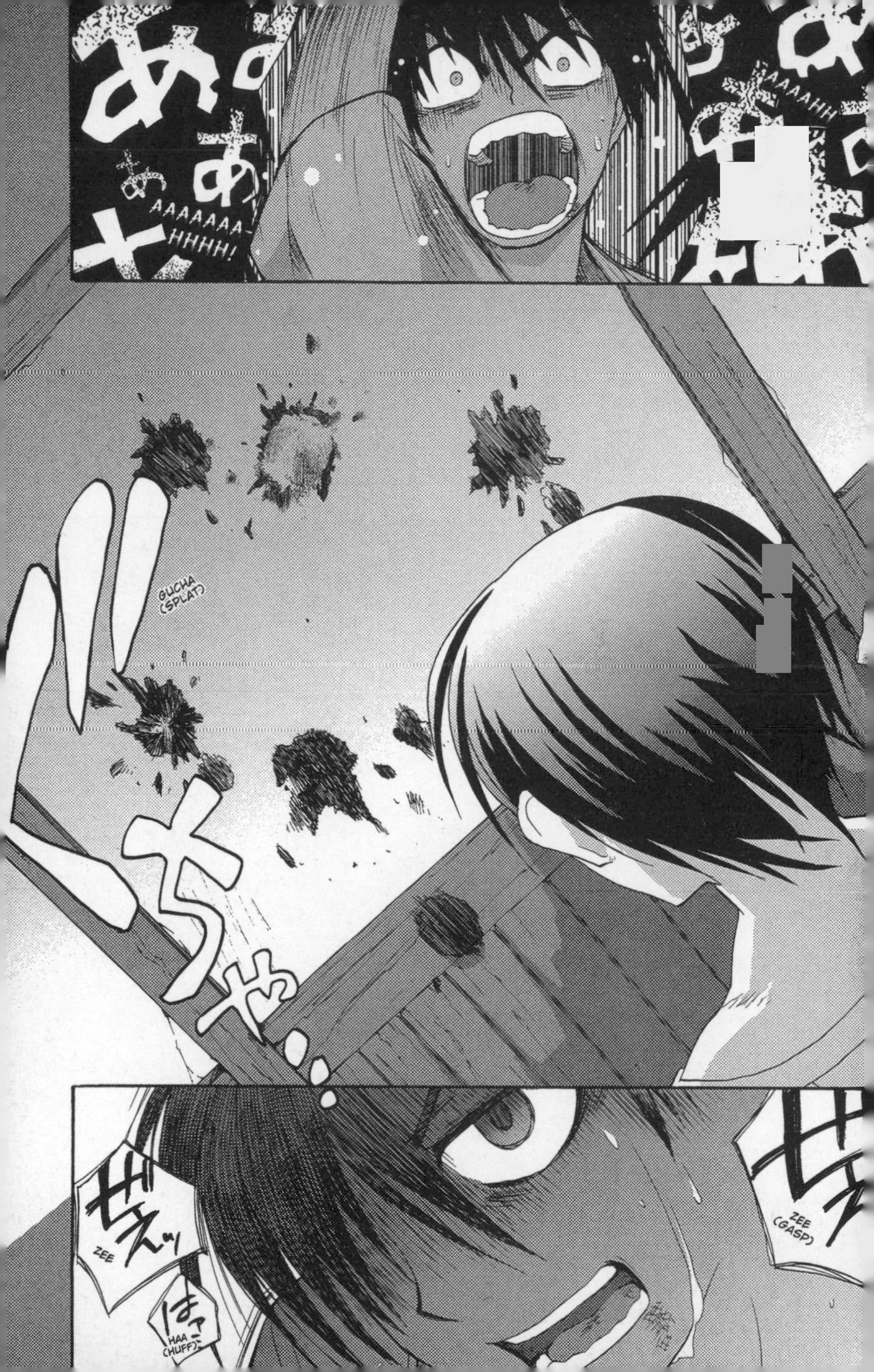
AAAAAHH
AAAAAAA-HHHH!
GUCHA (SPLAT)
ZEE (GASP)
ZEE
HAA (HUFF)

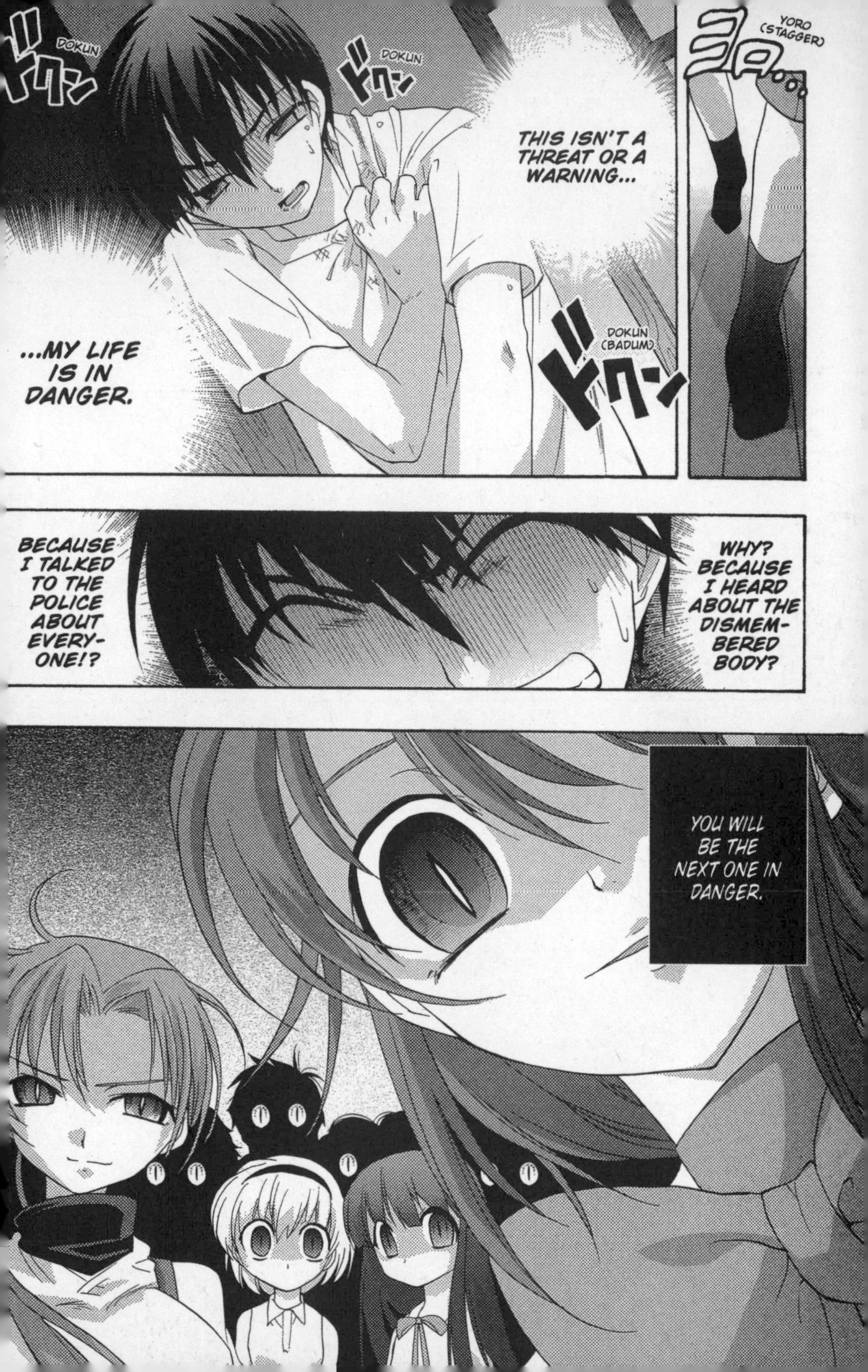
ヨロ…
YORO (STAGGER)
ドクン
DOKUN
THIS ISN'T A THREAT OR A WARNING...
ドクン
DOKUN
ドクン
DOKUN (BADUM)
...MY LIFE IS IN DANGER.
WHY? BECAUSE I HEARD ABOUT THE DISMEM-BERED BODY?
BECAUSE I TALKED TO THE POLICE ABOUT EVERY-ONE!?
YOU WILL BE THE NEXT ONE IN DANGER.

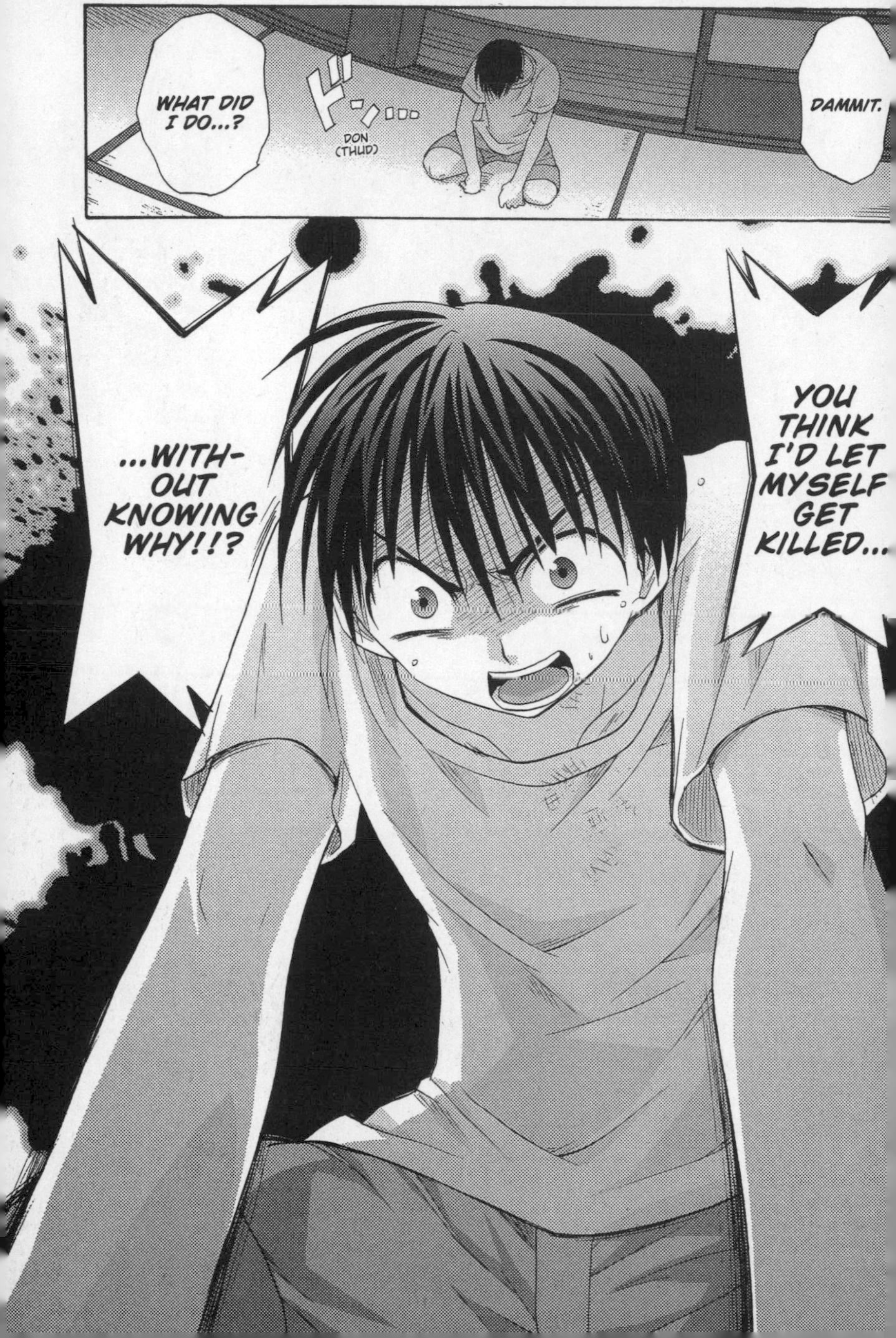
DAMMIT.
ドーン
DON (THUD)
WHAT DID I DO...?
YOU THINK I'D LET MYSELF GET KILLED...
...WITH-OUT KNOWING WHY!!?

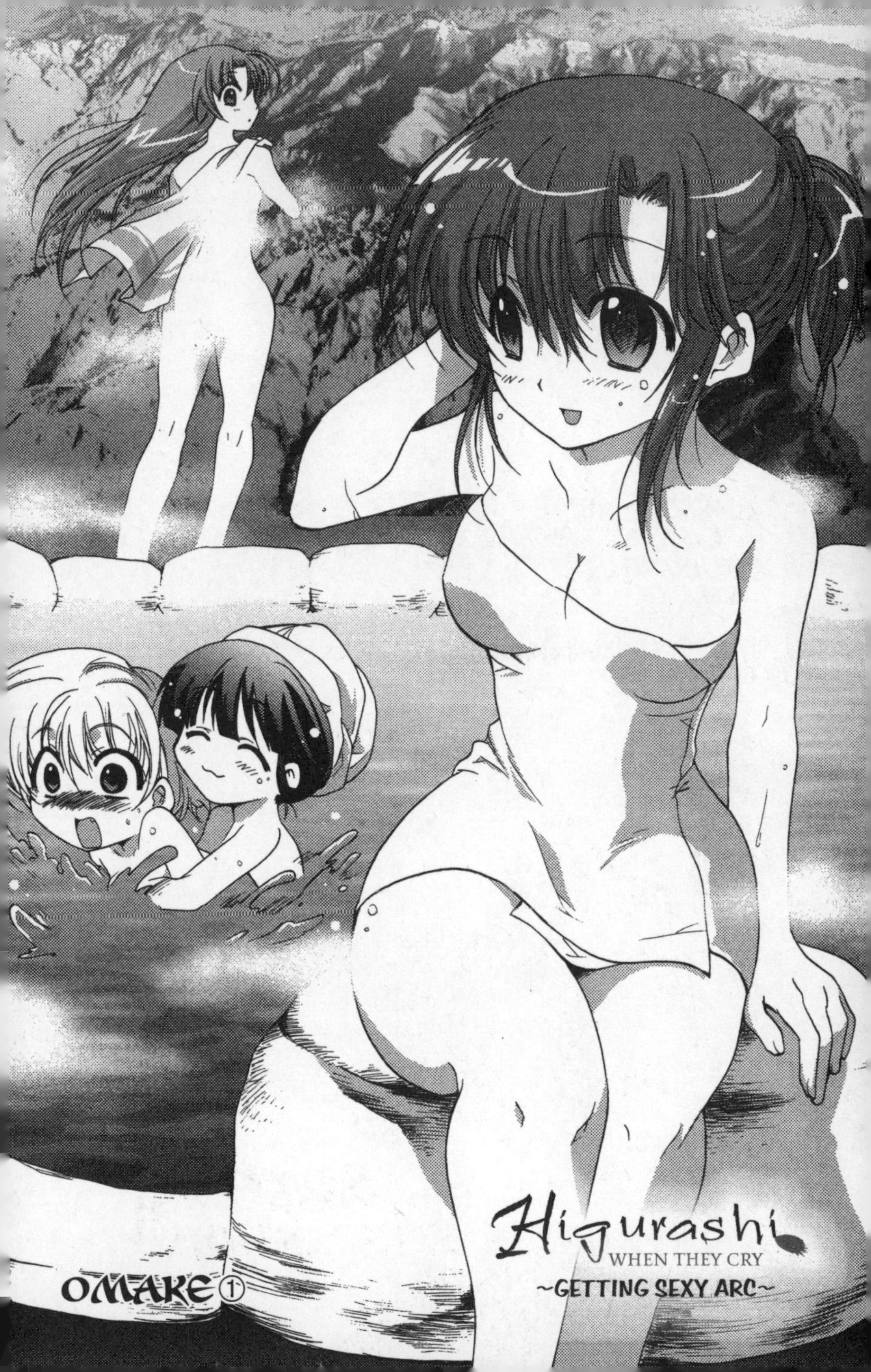
Higurashi
WHEN THEY CRY
~GETTING SEXY ARC~
OMAKE 1

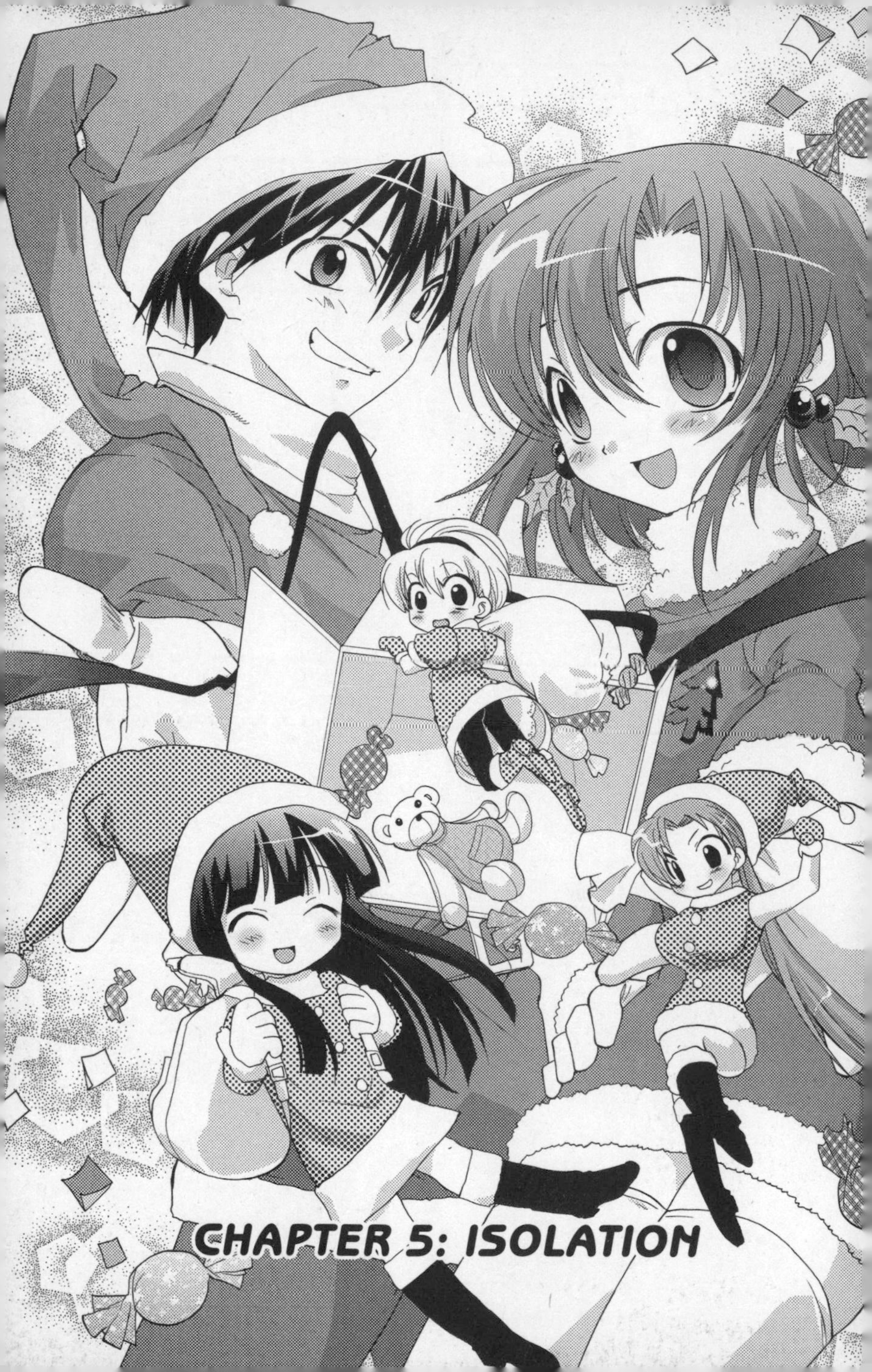
CHAPTER 5: ISOLATION

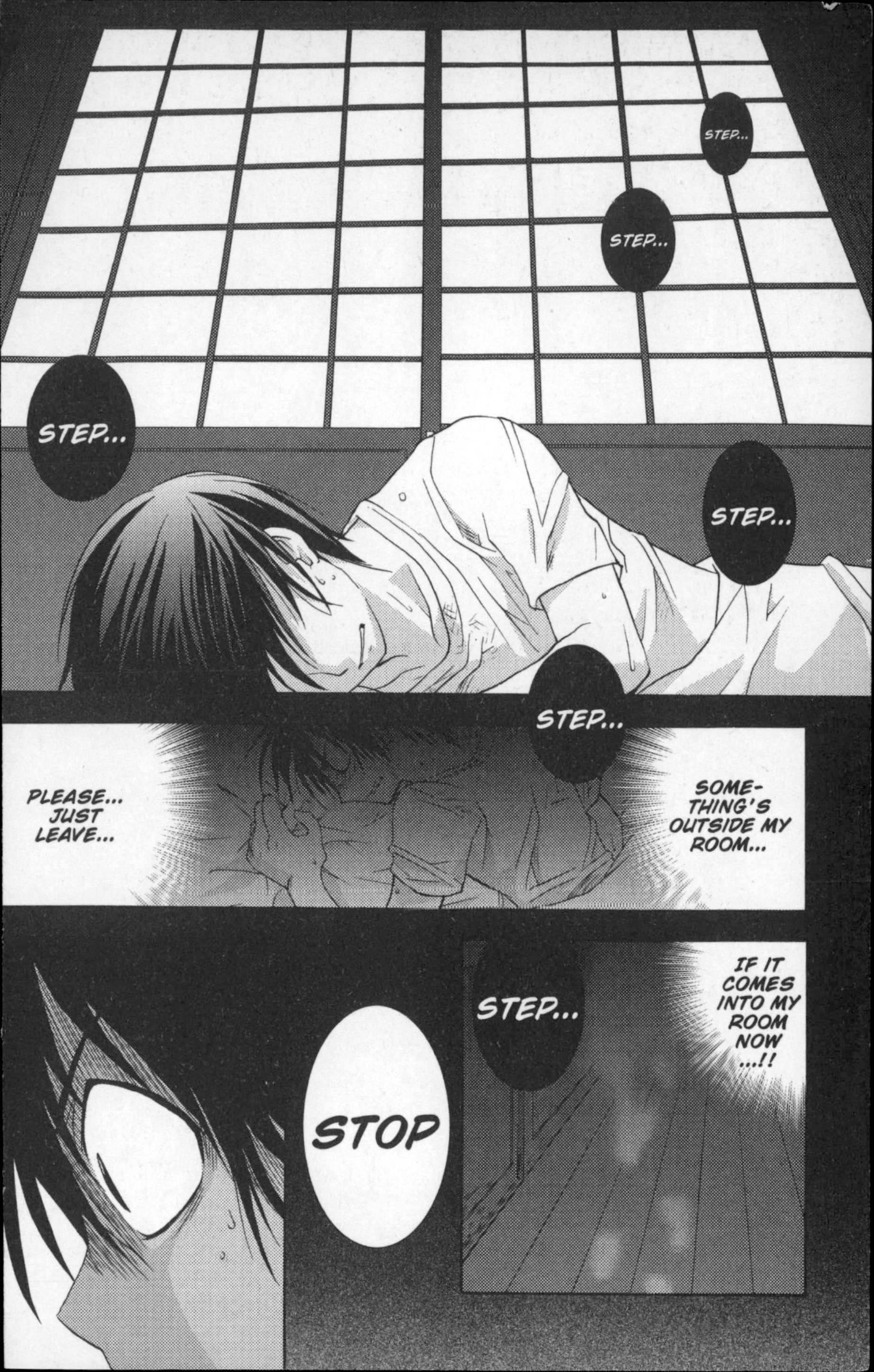
STEP...
STEP...
STEP...
STEP...
STEP...
SOMETHING'S OUTSIDE MY ROOM...
PLEASE... JUST LEAVE...
IF IT COMES INTO MY ROOM NOW ...!!
STEP...
STOP

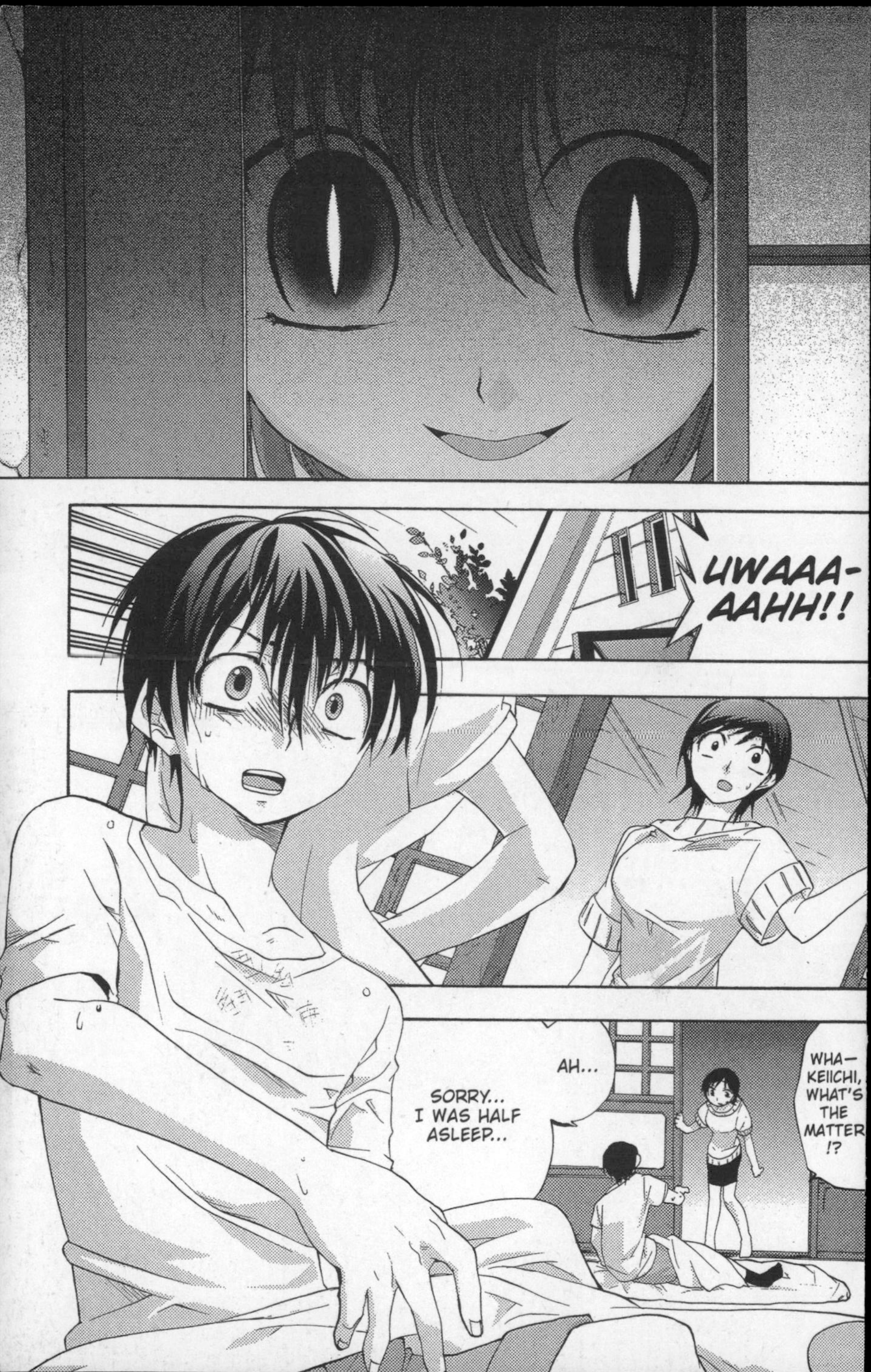
UWAAA-AAHH!!
WHA— KEIICHI, WHAT'S THE MATTER!?
AH...
SORRY... I WAS HALF ASLEEP...

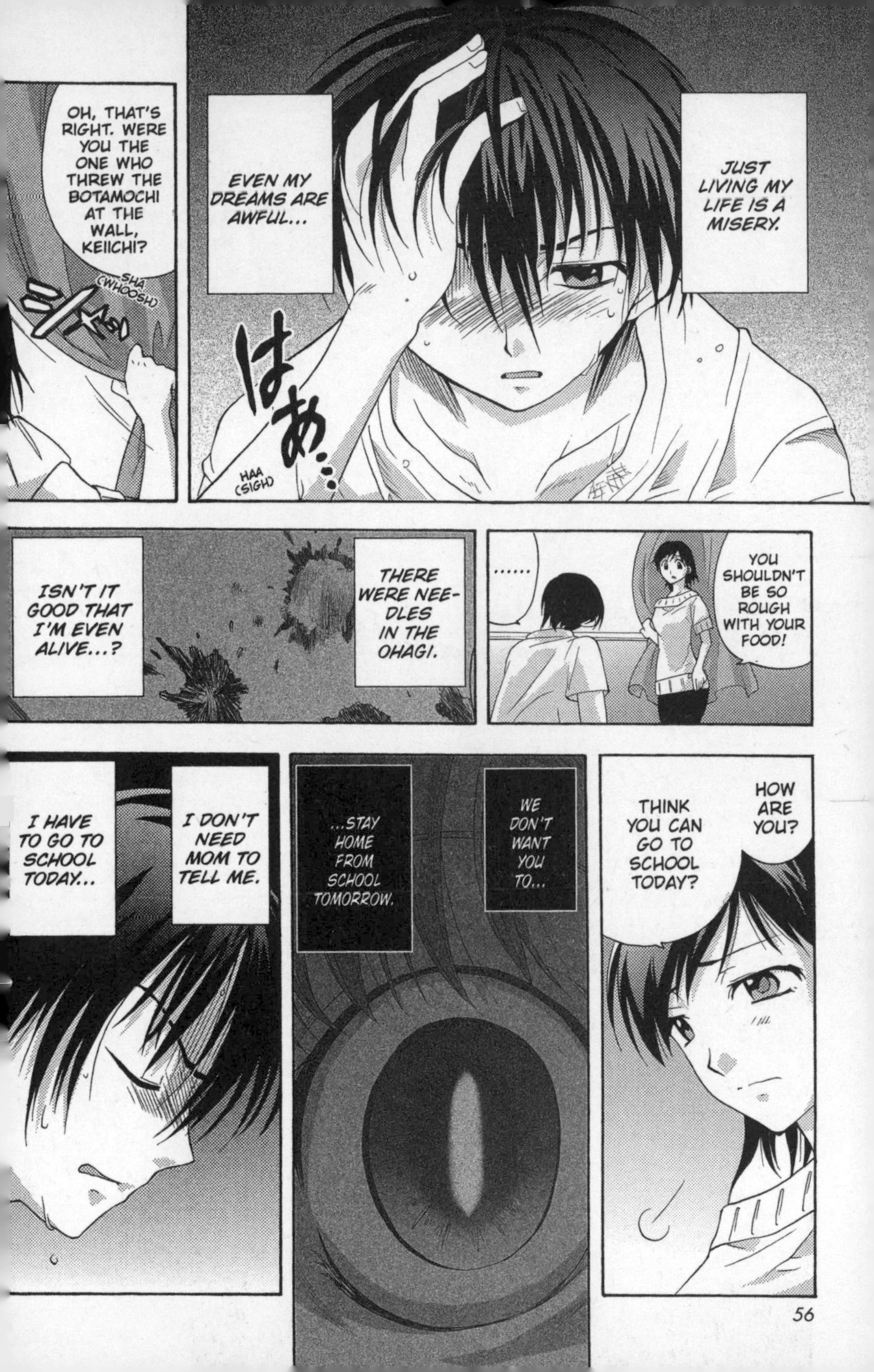

JUST LIVING MY LIFE IS A MISERY.
EVEN MY DREAMS ARE AWFUL...
はあ…
HAA (SIGH)
OH, THAT'S RIGHT. WERE YOU THE ONE WHO THREW THE BOTAMOCHI AT THE WALL, KEIICHI?
SHA (WHOOSH)
YOU SHOULDN'T BE SO ROUGH WITH YOUR FOOD!
......
THERE WERE NEE-DLES IN THE OHAGI.
ISN'T IT GOOD THAT I'M EVEN ALIVE...?
HOW ARE YOU?
THINK YOU CAN GO TO SCHOOL TODAY?
WE DON'T WANT YOU TO...
...STAY HOME FROM SCHOOL TOMORROW.
I DON'T NEED MOM TO TELL ME.
I HAVE TO GO TO SCHOOL TODAY...

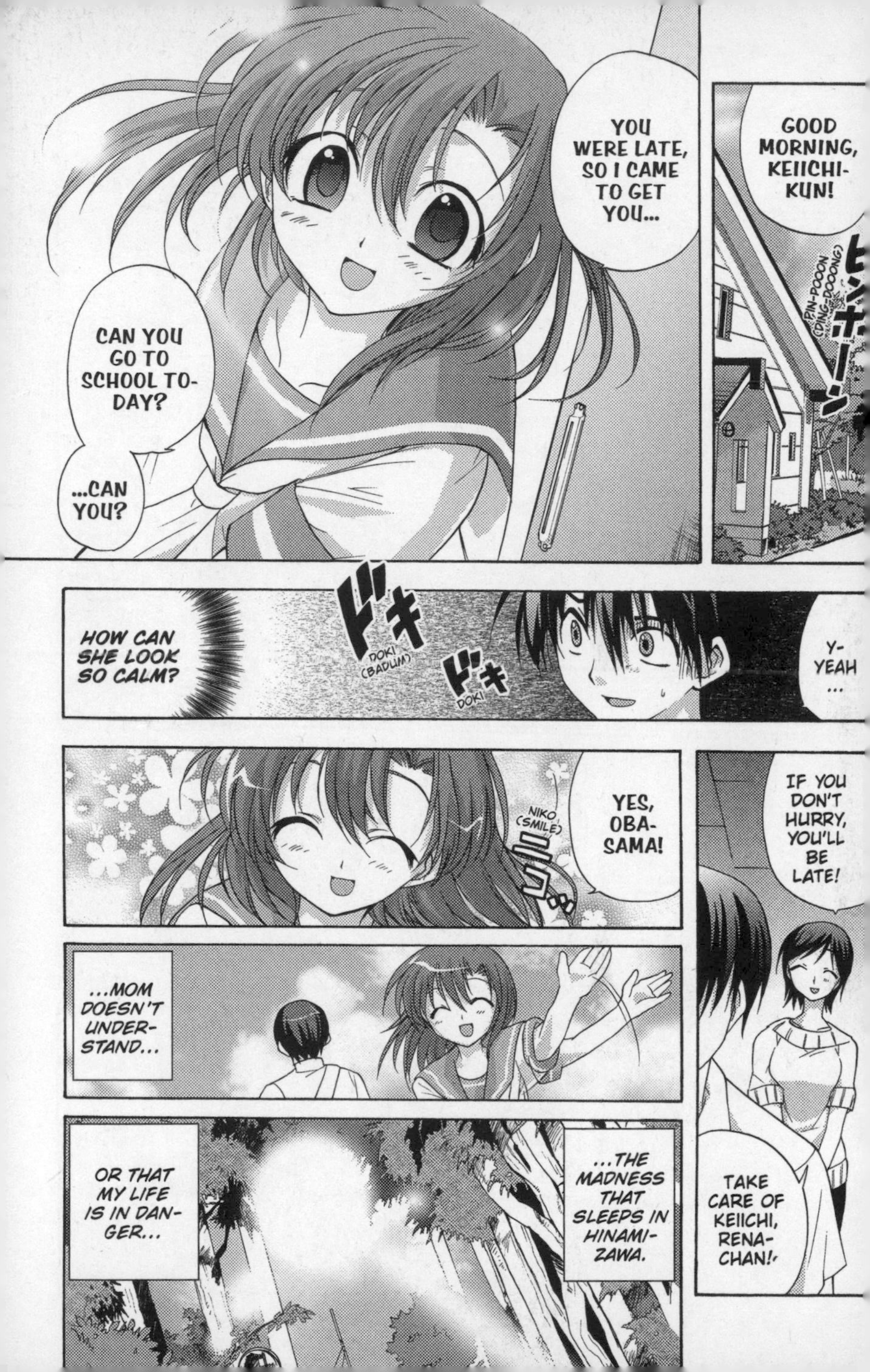
GOOD MORNING, KEIICHI-KUN!
PIN-POOON (DING-DOOONG)
YOU WERE LATE, SO I CAME TO GET YOU...
CAN YOU GO TO SCHOOL TO-DAY?
...CAN YOU?
Y-YEAH ...
DOKI (BADUM)
DOKI
HOW CAN SHE LOOK SO CALM?
IF YOU DON'T HURRY, YOU'LL BE LATE!
TAKE CARE OF KEIICHI, RENA-CHAN!
YES, OBA-SAMA!
NIKO (SMILE)
...MOM DOESN'T UNDER-STAND...
...THE MADNESS THAT SLEEPS IN HINAMI-ZAWA.
OR THAT MY LIFE IS IN DAN-GER...

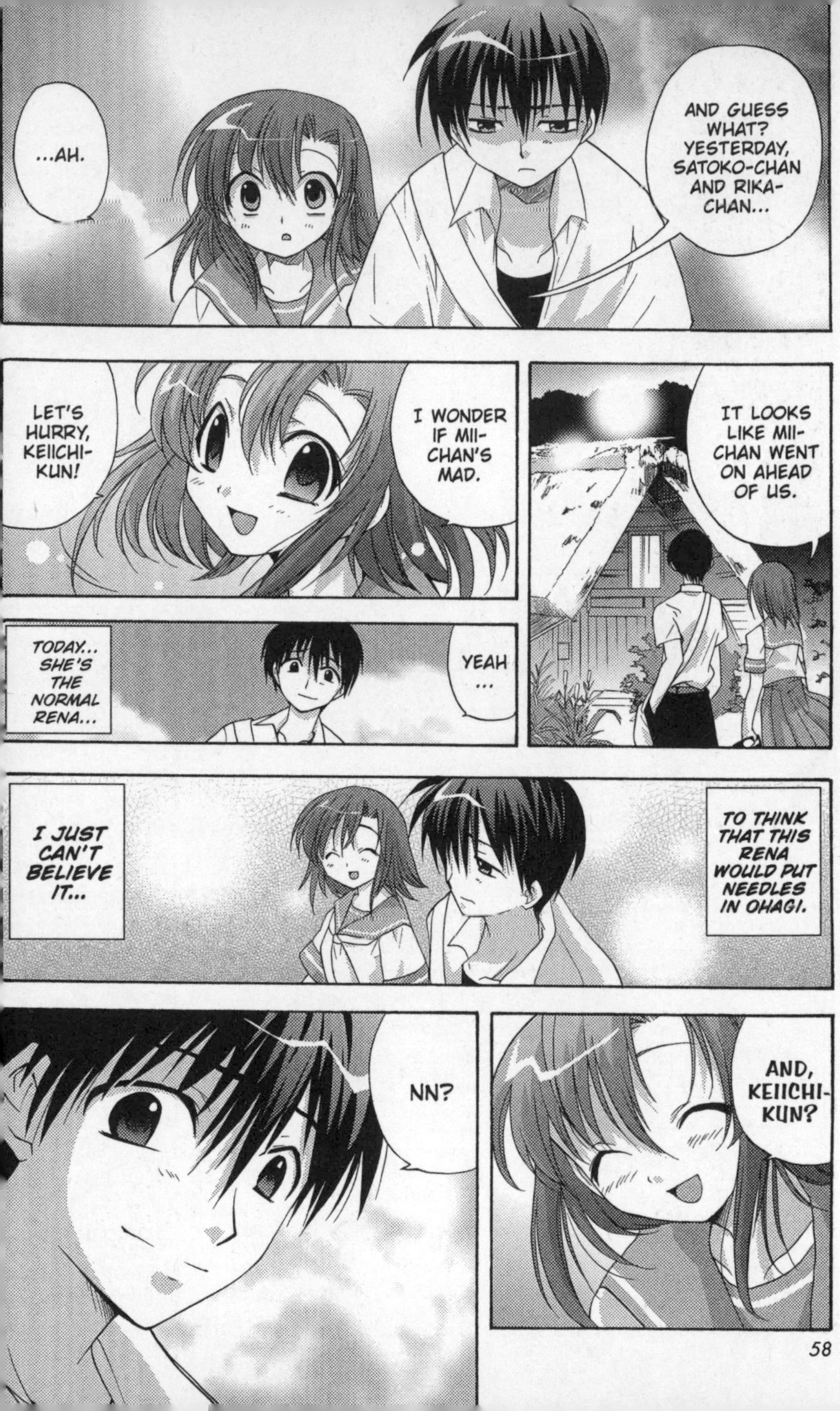
AND GUESS WHAT? YESTERDAY, SATOKO-CHAN AND RIKA-CHAN...
...AH.
IT LOOKS LIKE MII-CHAN WENT ON AHEAD OF US.
I WONDER IF MII-CHAN'S MAD.
LET'S HURRY, KEIICHI-KUN!
YEAH ...
TODAY... SHE'S THE NORMAL RENA...
TO THINK THAT THIS RENA WOULD PUT NEEDLES IN OHAGI.
I JUST CAN'T BELIEVE IT...
AND, KEIICHI-KUN?
NN?

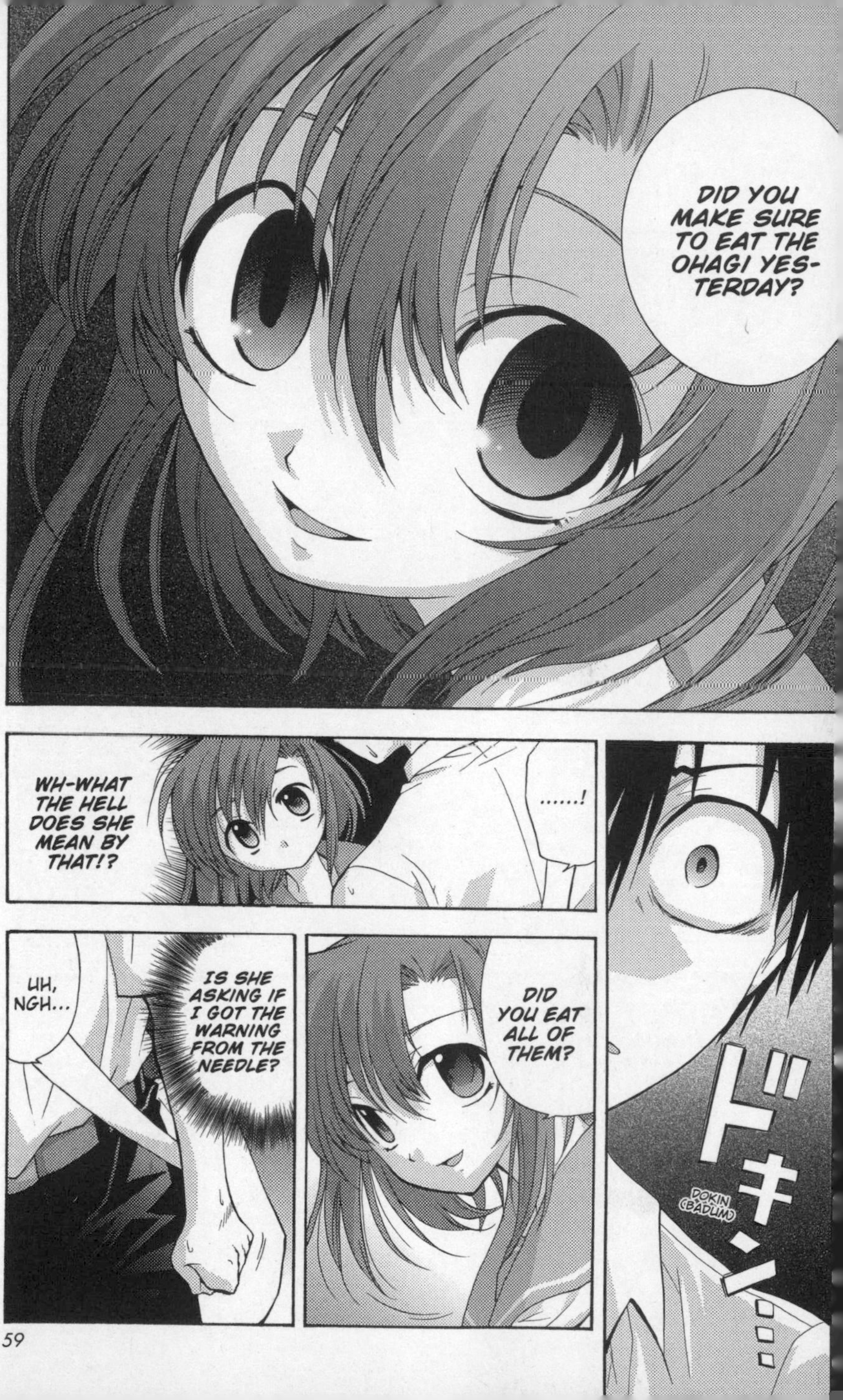
DID YOU MAKE SURE TO EAT THE OHAGI YES-TERDAY?
DOKIN (BADUM)
......!
WH-WHAT THE HELL DOES SHE MEAN BY THAT!?
DID YOU EAT ALL OF THEM?
IS SHE ASKING IF I GOT THE WARNING FROM THE NEEDLE?
UH, NGH...

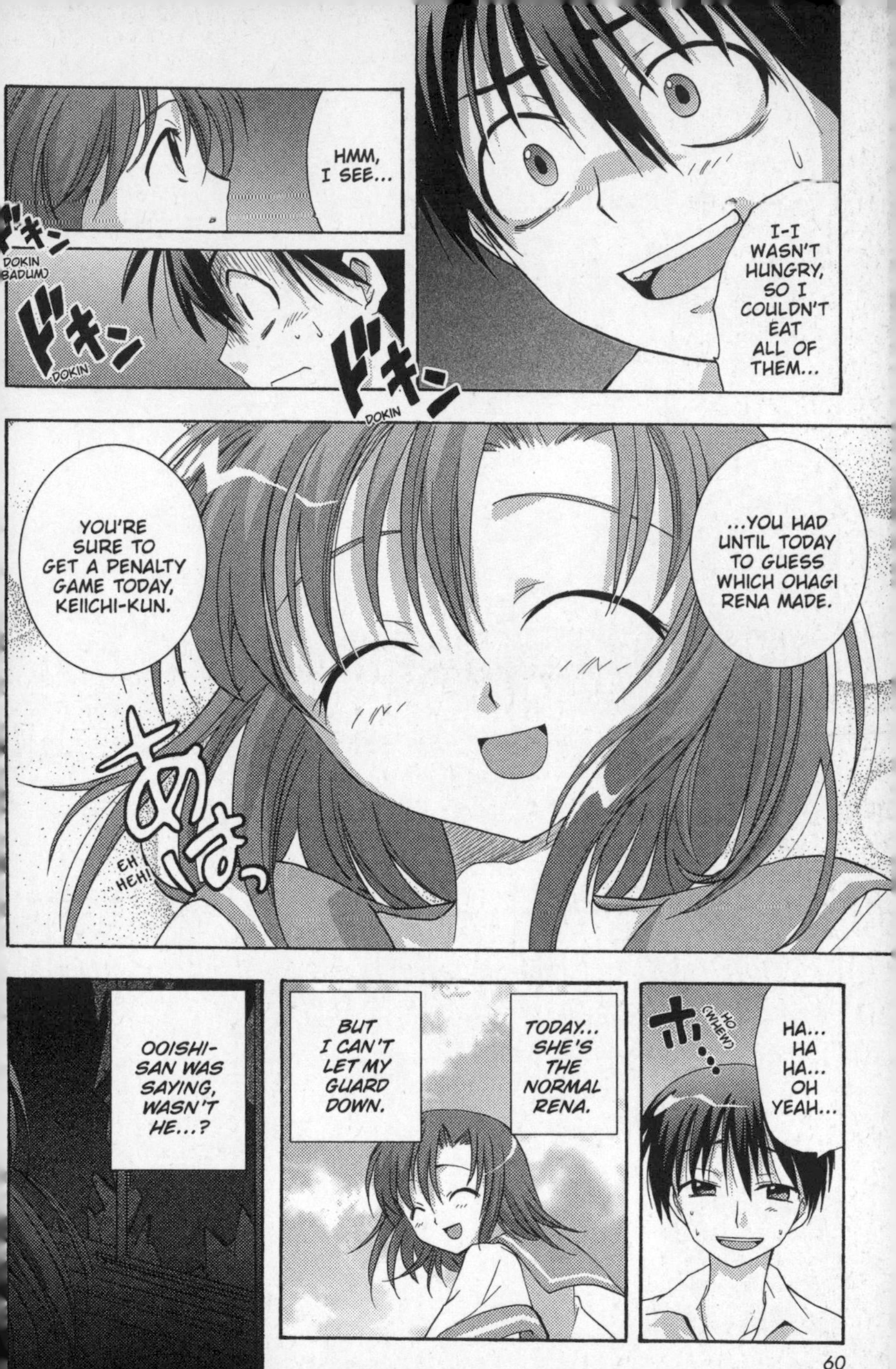
I-I WASN'T HUNGRY, SO I COULDN'T EAT ALL OF THEM...
HMM, I SEE...
ドキン
DOKIN BADUMP
ドキン
DOKIN
ドキン
DOKIN
...YOU HAD UNTIL TODAY TO GUESS WHICH OHAGI RENA MADE.
YOU'RE SURE TO GET A PENALTY GAME TODAY, KEIICHI-KUN.
あはっ
EH HEH!
ホ…
HO (WHEW)
HA... HA HA... OH YEAH...
TODAY... SHE'S THE NORMAL RENA.
BUT I CAN'T LET MY GUARD DOWN.
OOISHI-SAN WAS SAYING, WASN'T HE...?

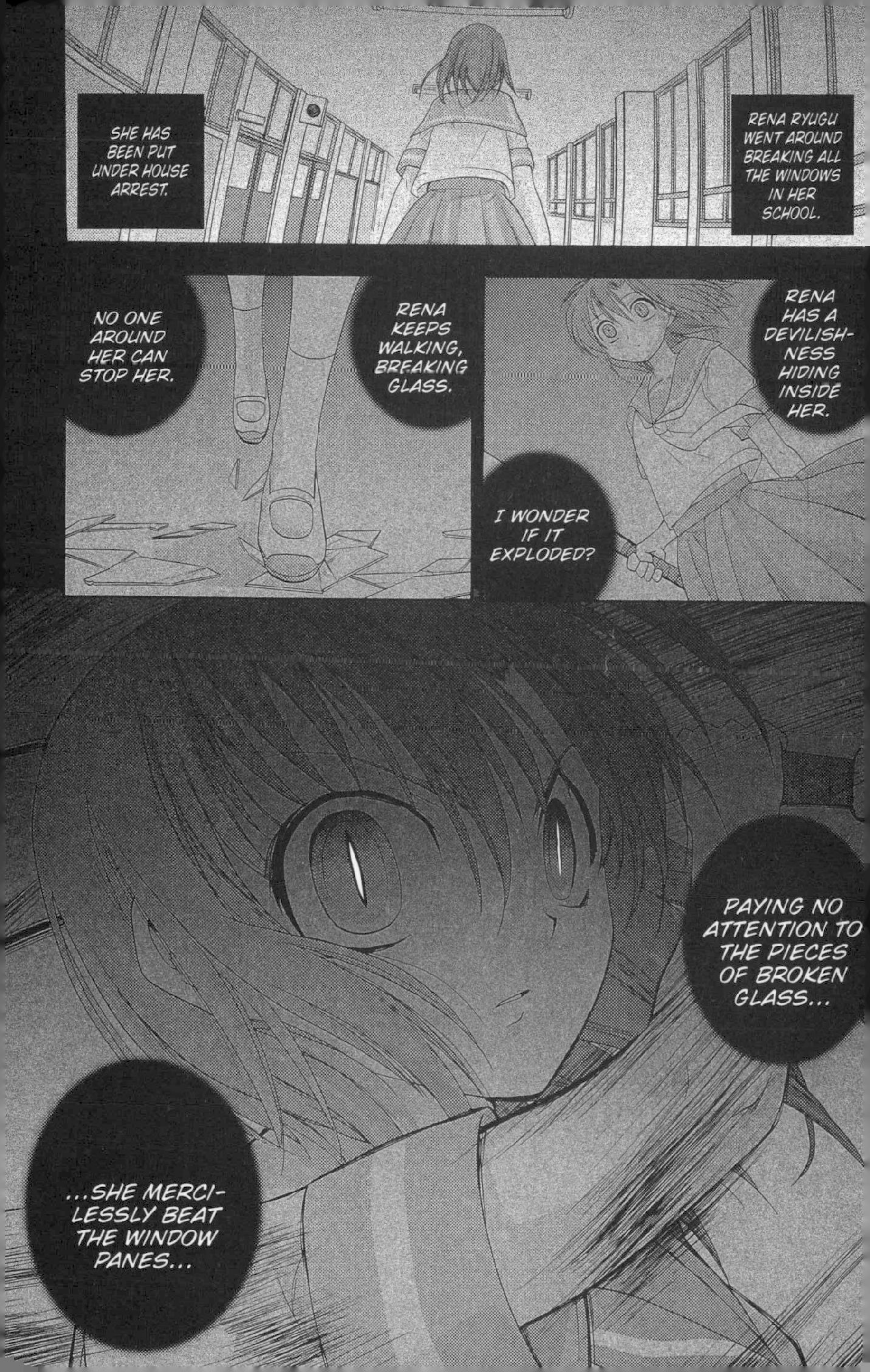
RENA RYUGU WENT AROUND BREAKING ALL THE WINDOWS IN HER SCHOOL.
SHE HAS BEEN PUT UNDER HOUSE ARREST.
RENA HAS A DEVILISH-NESS HIDING INSIDE HER.
I WONDER IF IT EXPLODED?
RENA KEEPS WALKING, BREAKING GLASS.
NO ONE AROUND HER CAN STOP HER.
PAYING NO ATTENTION TO THE PIECES OF BROKEN GLASS...
...SHE MERCI-LESSLY BEAT THE WINDOW PANES...

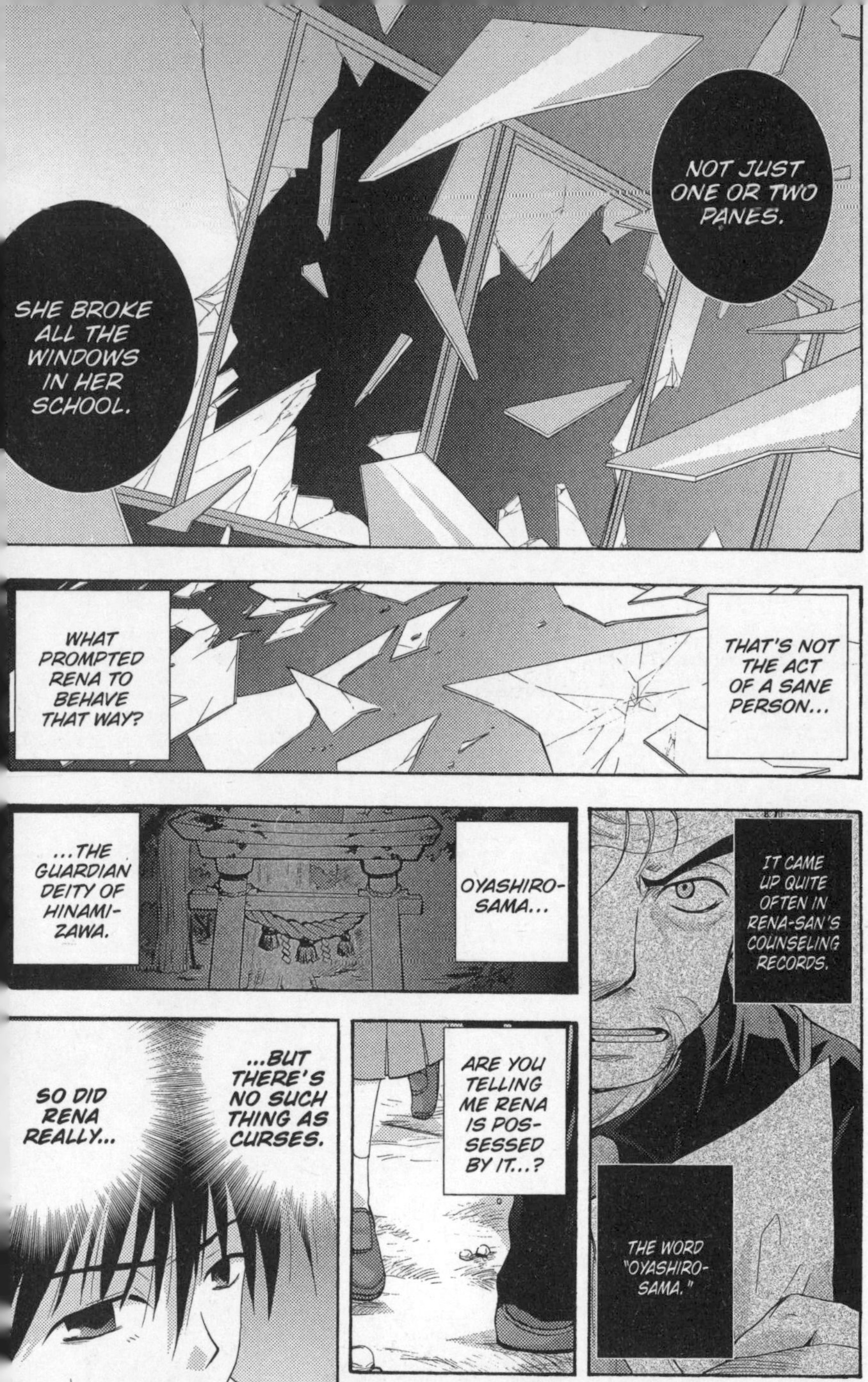
NOT JUST ONE OR TWO PANES.
SHE BROKE ALL THE WINDOWS IN HER SCHOOL.
THAT'S NOT THE ACT OF A SANE PERSON...
WHAT PROMPTED RENA TO BEHAVE THAT WAY?
IT CAME UP QUITE OFTEN IN RENA-SAN'S COUNSELING RECORDS.
THE WORD "OYASHIRO-SAMA."
OYASHIRO-SAMA...
...THE GUARDIAN DEITY OF HINAMI-ZAWA.
ARE YOU TELLING ME RENA IS POS-SESSED BY IT...?
...BUT THERE'S NO SUCH THING AS CURSES.
SO DID RENA REALLY...

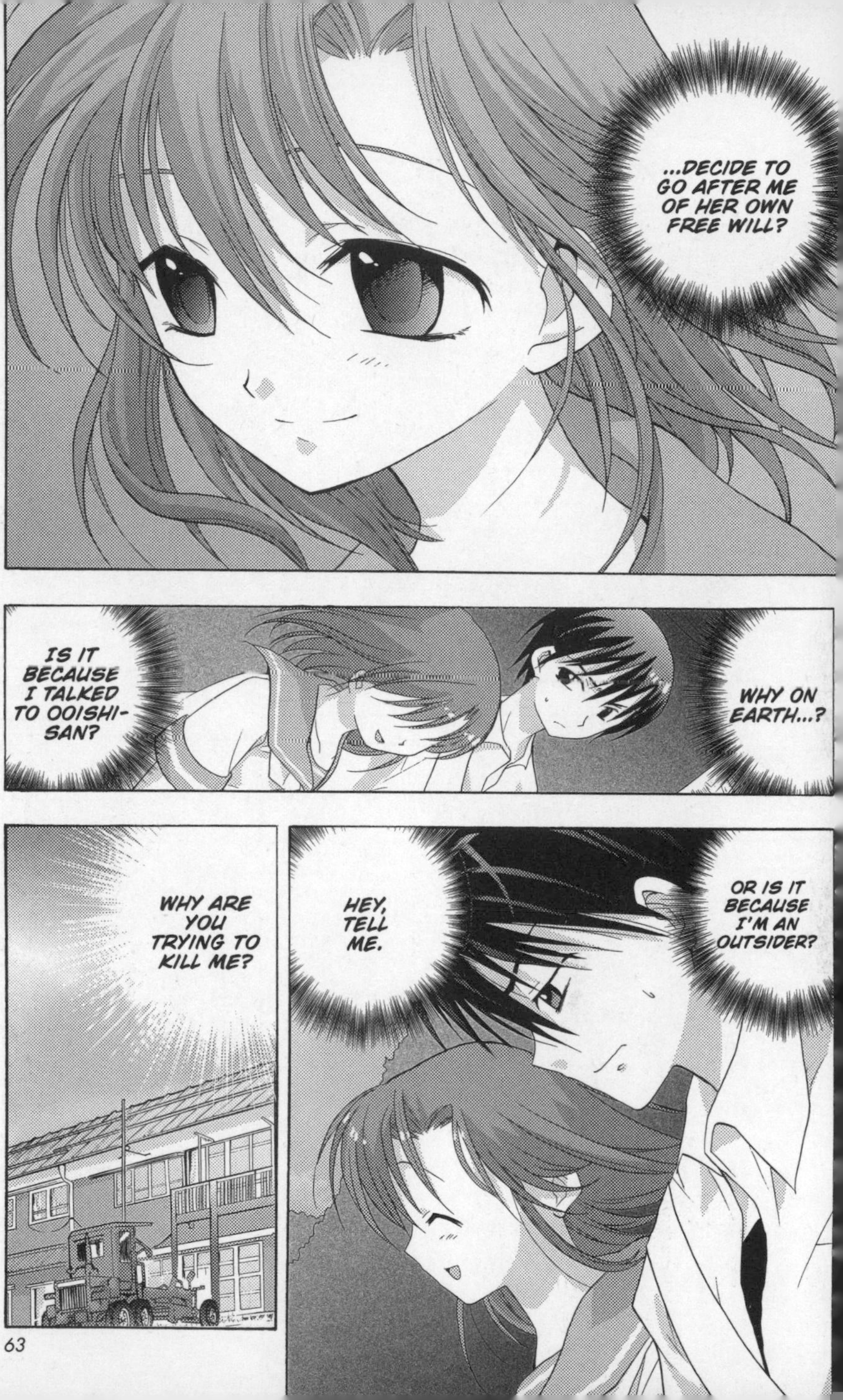
...DECIDE TO GO AFTER ME OF HER OWN FREE WILL?
WHY ON EARTH...?
IS IT BECAUSE I TALKED TO OOISHI-SAN?
OR IS IT BECAUSE I'M AN OUTSIDER?
HEY, TELL ME.
WHY ARE YOU TRYING TO KILL ME?

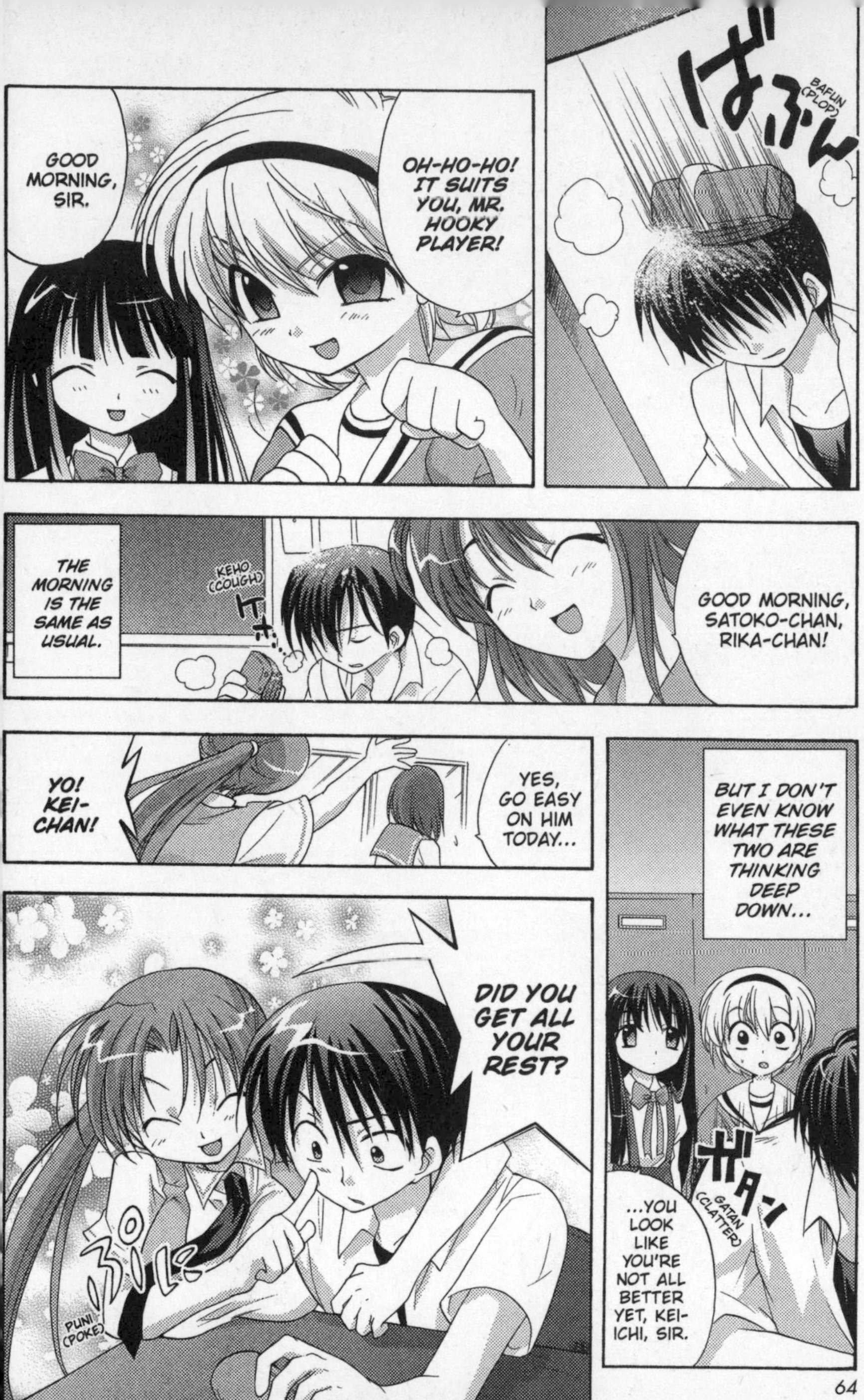

ばふん
BAFUN (PLOP)
OH-HO-HO! IT SUITS YOU, MR. HOOKY PLAYER!
GOOD MORNING, SIR.
GOOD MORNING, SATOKO-CHAN, RIKA-CHAN!
KEHO (COUGH)
THE MORNING IS THE SAME AS USUAL.
BUT I DON'T EVEN KNOW WHAT THESE TWO ARE THINKING DEEP DOWN...
GATAN (CLATTER)
...YOU LOOK LIKE YOU'RE NOT ALL BETTER YET, KEI-ICHI, SIR.
YES, GO EASY ON HIM TODAY...
YO! KEI-CHAN!
DID YOU GET ALL YOUR REST?
PUNI (POKE)

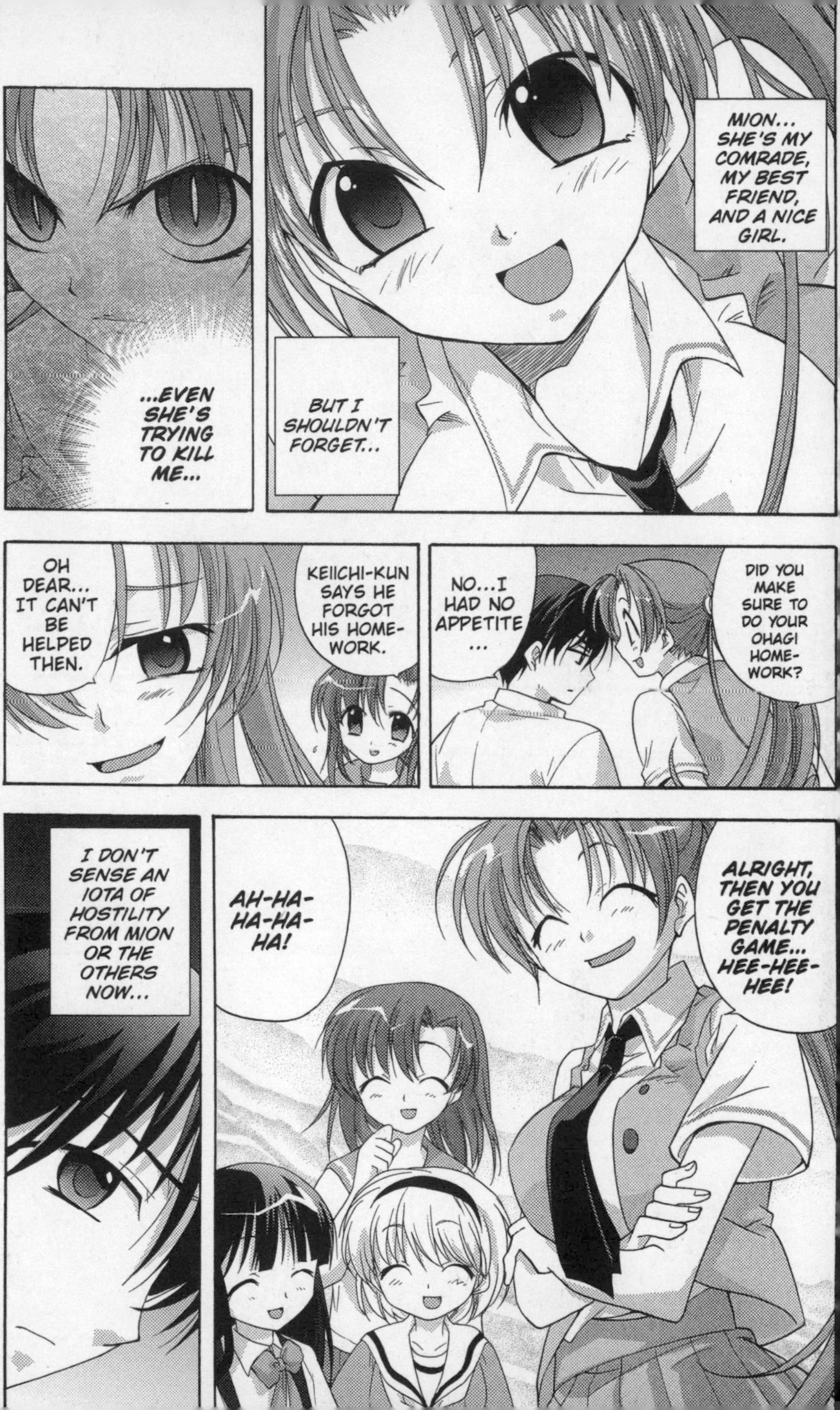
MION... SHE'S MY COMRADE, MY BEST FRIEND, AND A NICE GIRL.
BUT I SHOULDN'T FORGET...
...EVEN SHE'S TRYING TO KILL ME...
DID YOU MAKE SURE TO DO YOUR OHAGI HOME-WORK?
NO...I HAD NO APPETITE...
KEIICHI-KUN SAYS HE FORGOT HIS HOME-WORK.
OH DEAR... IT CAN'T BE HELPED THEN.
ALRIGHT, THEN YOU GET THE PENALTY GAME... HEE-HEE-HEE!
AH-HA-HA-HA-HA!
I DON'T SENSE AN IOTA OF HOSTILITY FROM MION OR THE OTHERS NOW...

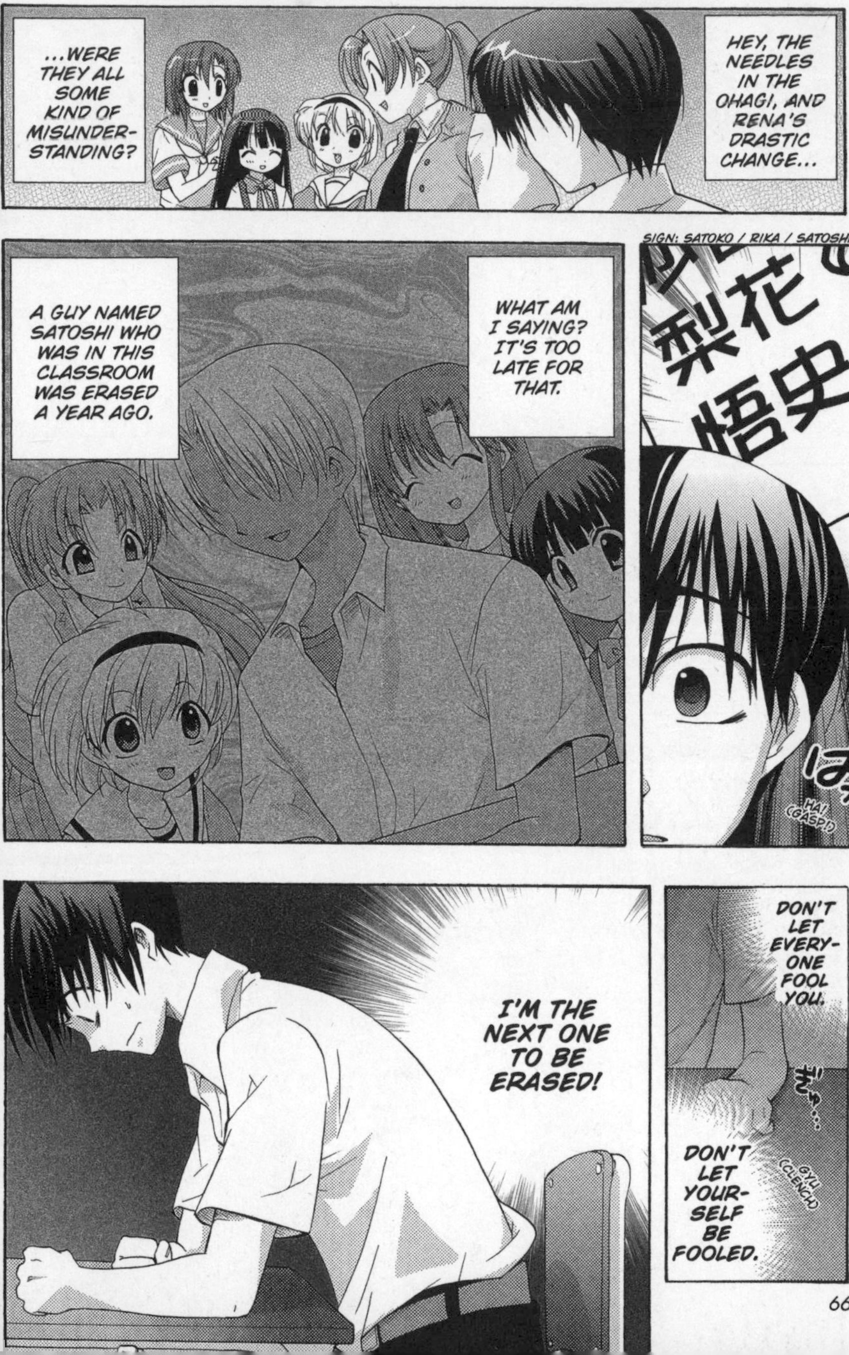
HEY, THE NEEDLES IN THE OHAGI, AND RENA'S DRASTIC CHANGE...
...WERE THEY ALL SOME KIND OF MISUNDER-STANDING?
SIGN: SATOKO / RIKA / SATOSHI
梨花
悟史
はっ
HA! (GASP!)
WHAT AM I SAYING? IT'S TOO LATE FOR THAT.
A GUY NAMED SATOSHI WHO WAS IN THIS CLASSROOM WAS ERASED A YEAR AGO.
DON'T LET EVERY-ONE FOOL YOU.
ぎゅ...
GYU (CLENCH)
DON'T LET YOUR-SELF BE FOOLED.
I'M THE NEXT ONE TO BE ERASED!

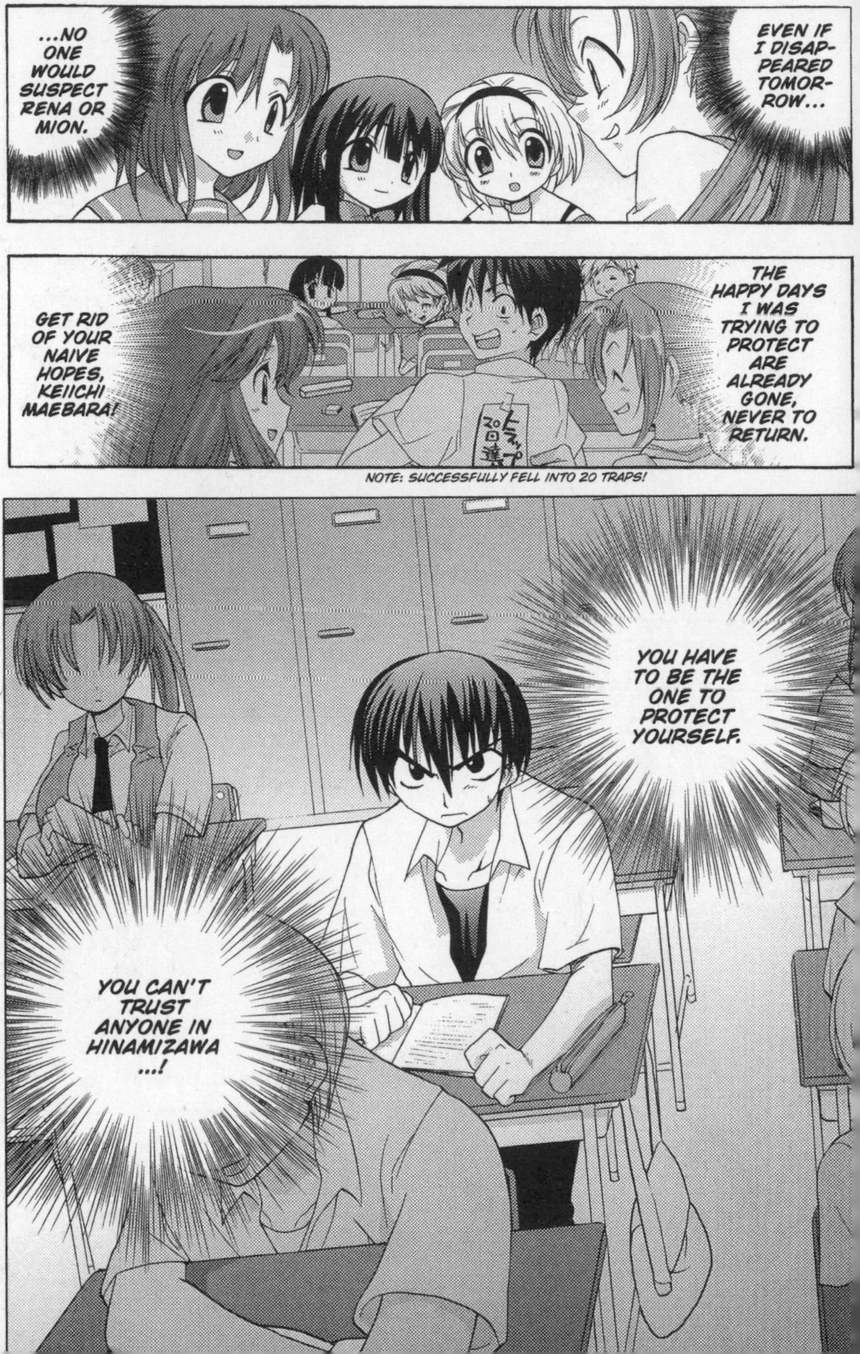
EVEN IF I DISAPPEARED TOMORROW...
...NO ONE WOULD SUSPECT RENA OR MION.
THE HAPPY DAYS I WAS TRYING TO PROTECT ARE ALREADY GONE, NEVER TO RETURN.
GET RID OF YOUR NAIVE HOPES, KEIICHI MAEBARA!
NOTE: SUCCESSFULLY FELL INTO 20 TRAPS!
YOU HAVE TO BE THE ONE TO PROTECT YOURSELF.
YOU CAN'T TRUST ANYONE IN HINAMIZAWA ...!

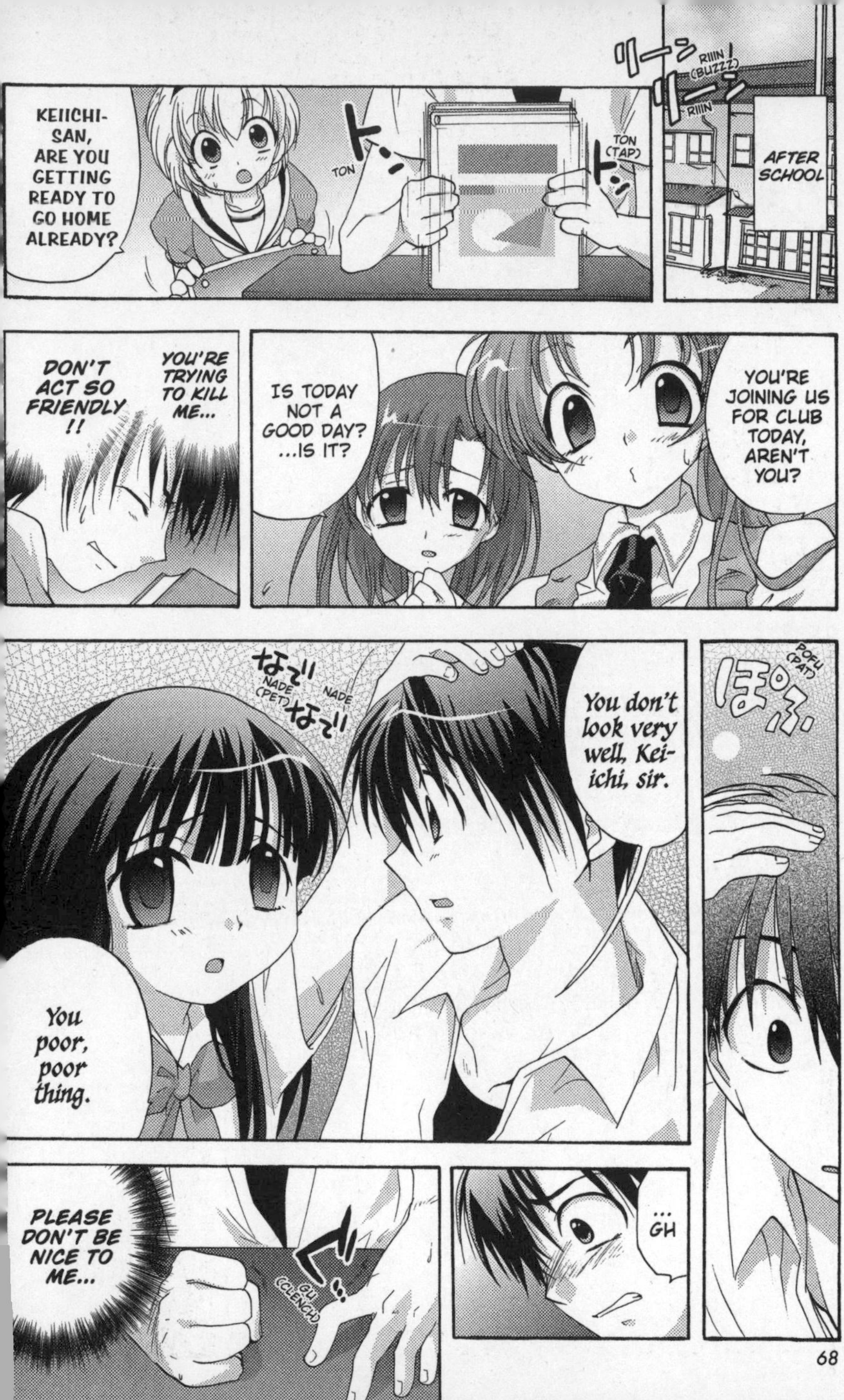
RIIIN (BUZZZ)
RIIIN
AFTER SCHOOL
TON (TAP)
TON
KEIICHI-SAN, ARE YOU GETTING READY TO GO HOME ALREADY?
YOU'RE JOINING US FOR CLUB TODAY, AREN'T YOU?
IS TODAY NOT A GOOD DAY? ...IS IT?
YOU'RE TRYING TO KILL ME...
DON'T ACT SO FRIENDLY!!
POFU (PAT)
NADE (PET)
NADE
You don't look very well, Kei-ichi, sir.
You poor, poor thing.
...GH
PLEASE DON'T BE NICE TO ME...
GU (CLENCH)

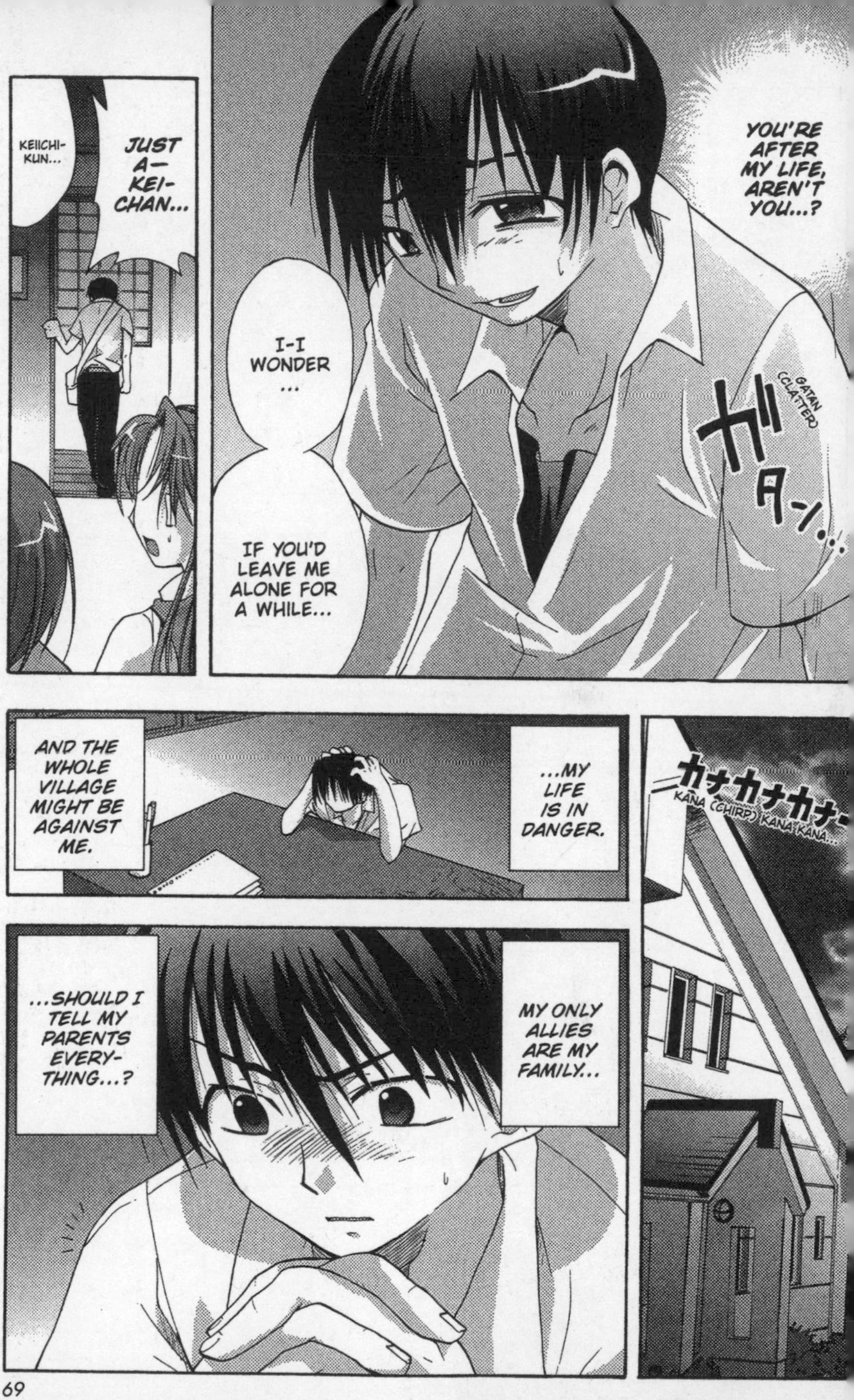
YOU'RE AFTER MY LIFE, AREN'T YOU...?
I-I WONDER ...
IF YOU'D LEAVE ME ALONE FOR A WHILE...
GATAN (CLATTER)
JUST A— KEI-CHAN...
KEIICHI-KUN...
KANA (CHIRP) KANA KANA...
...MY LIFE IS IN DANGER.
AND THE WHOLE VILLAGE MIGHT BE AGAINST ME.
MY ONLY ALLIES ARE MY FAMILY...
...SHOULD I TELL MY PARENTS EVERY-THING...?

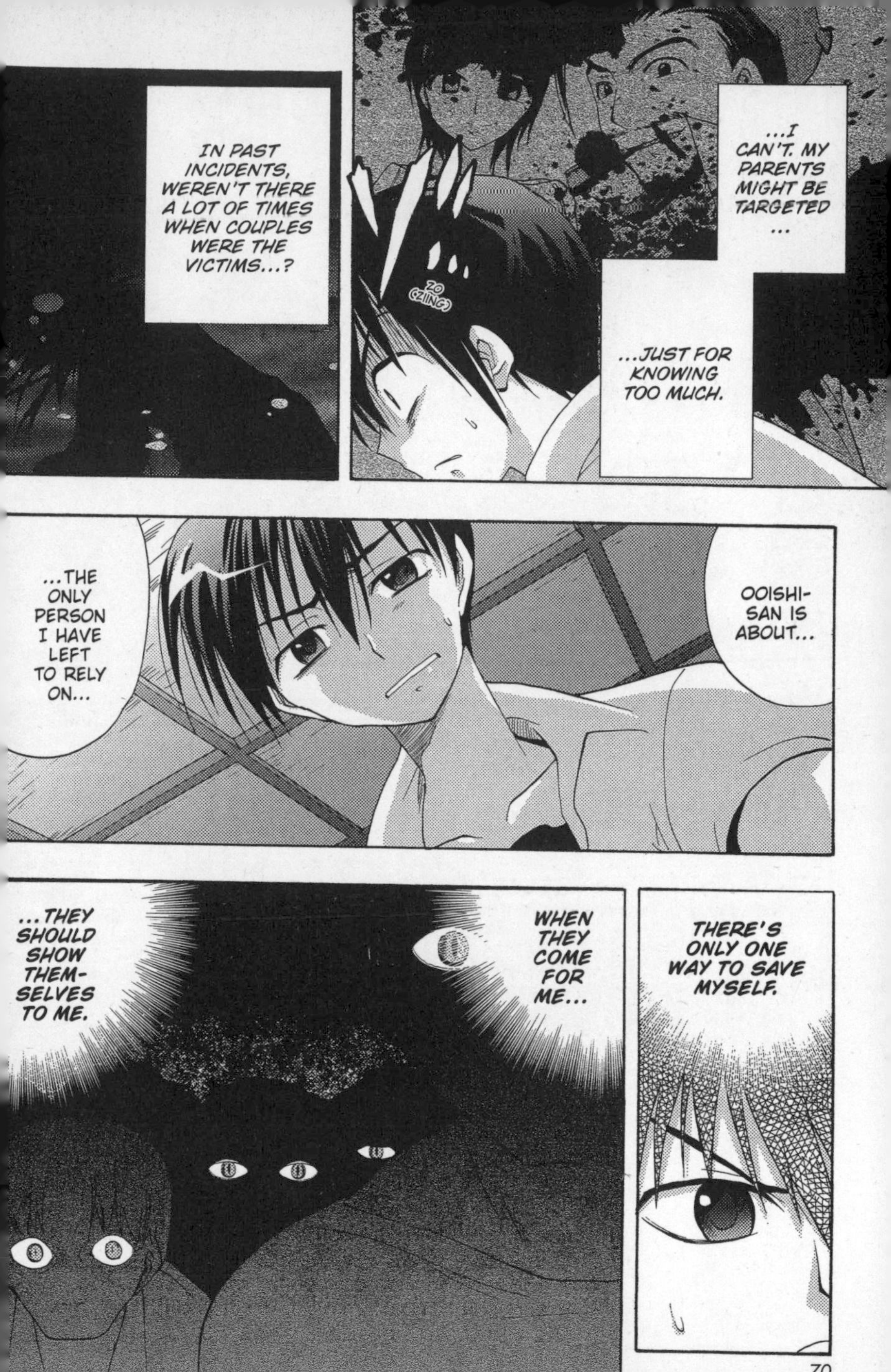
...I CAN'T. MY PARENTS MIGHT BE TARGETED...
ZO (ZING)
...JUST FOR KNOWING TOO MUCH.
IN PAST INCIDENTS, WEREN'T THERE A LOT OF TIMES WHEN COUPLES WERE THE VICTIMS...?
OOISHI-SAN IS ABOUT...
...THE ONLY PERSON I HAVE LEFT TO RELY ON...
THERE'S ONLY ONE WAY TO SAVE MYSELF.
WHEN THEY COME FOR ME...
...THEY SHOULD SHOW THEMSELVES TO ME.

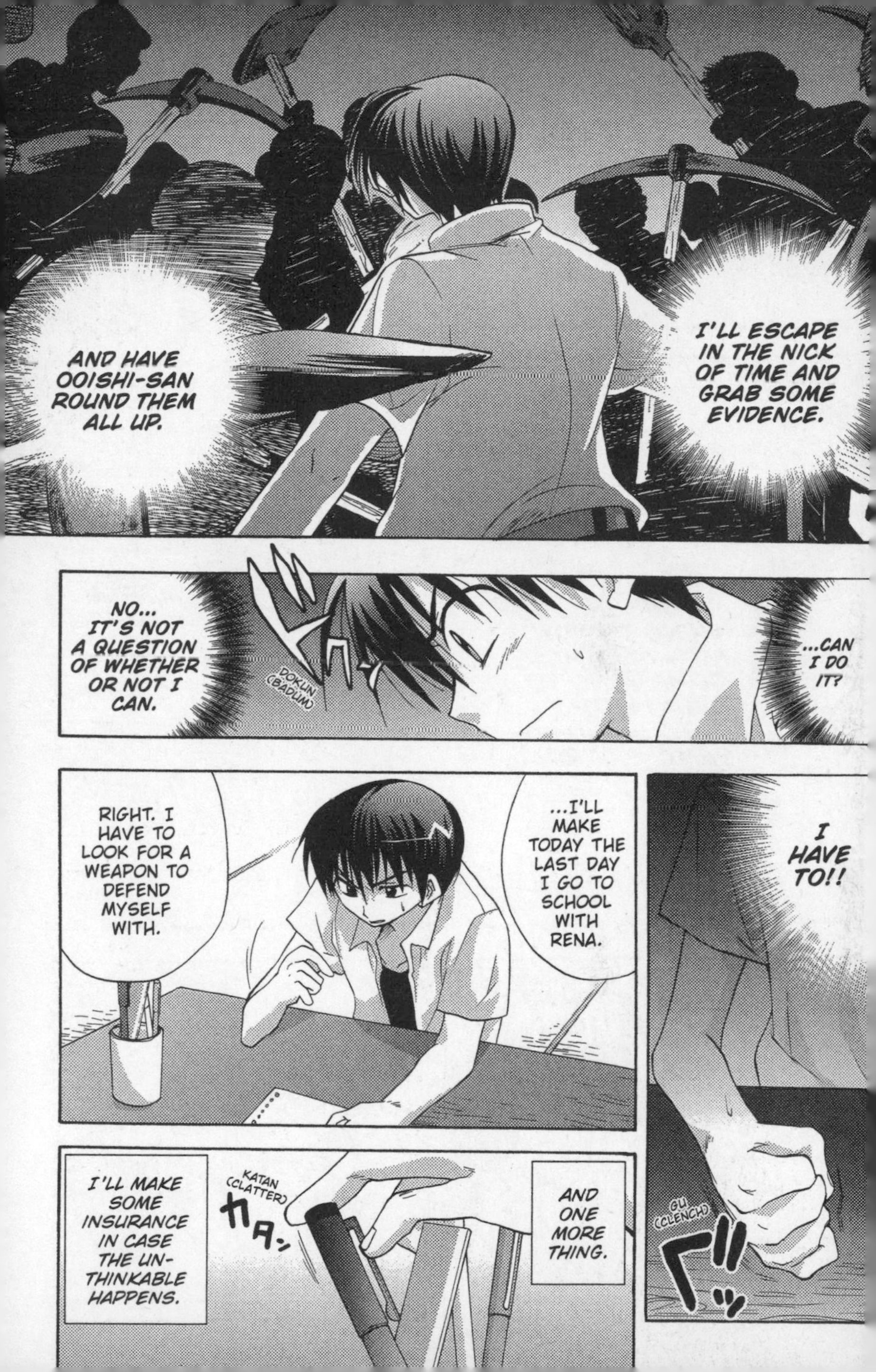
I'LL ESCAPE IN THE NICK OF TIME AND GRAB SOME EVIDENCE.
AND HAVE OOISHI-SAN ROUND THEM ALL UP.
...CAN I DO IT?
DOKUN (BADUM)
NO... IT'S NOT A QUESTION OF WHETHER OR NOT I CAN.
I HAVE TO!!
GU (CLENCH)
...I'LL MAKE TODAY THE LAST DAY I GO TO SCHOOL WITH RENA.
RIGHT. I HAVE TO LOOK FOR A WEAPON TO DEFEND MYSELF WITH.
AND ONE MORE THING.
KATAN (CLATTER)
I'LL MAKE SOME INSURANCE IN CASE THE UN-THINKABLE HAPPENS.

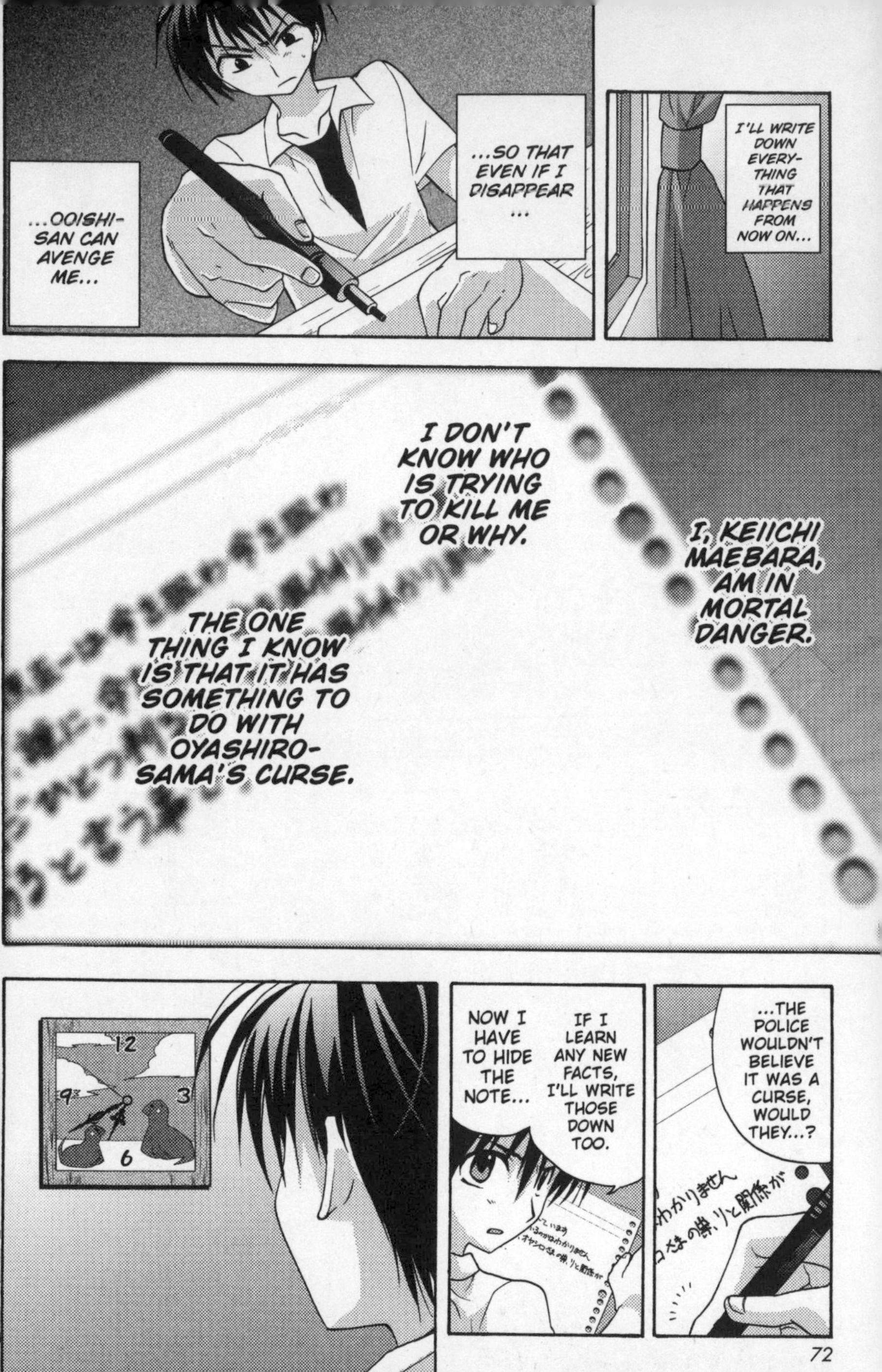
I'LL WRITE DOWN EVERY-THING THAT HAPPENS FROM NOW ON...
...SO THAT EVEN IF I DISAPPEAR ...
...OOISHI-SAN CAN AVENGE ME...
I, KEIICHI MAEBARA, AM IN MORTAL DANGER.
I DON'T KNOW WHO IS TRYING TO KILL ME OR WHY.
THE ONE THING I KNOW IS THAT IT HAS SOMETHING TO DO WITH OYASHIRO-SAMA'S CURSE.
...THE POLICE WOULDN'T BELIEVE IT WAS A CURSE, WOULD THEY...?
わかりません
ロさまの祟りと関係が
IF I LEARN ANY NEW FACTS, I'LL WRITE THOSE DOWN TOO.
NOW I HAVE TO HIDE THE NOTE...
12
3
6
9

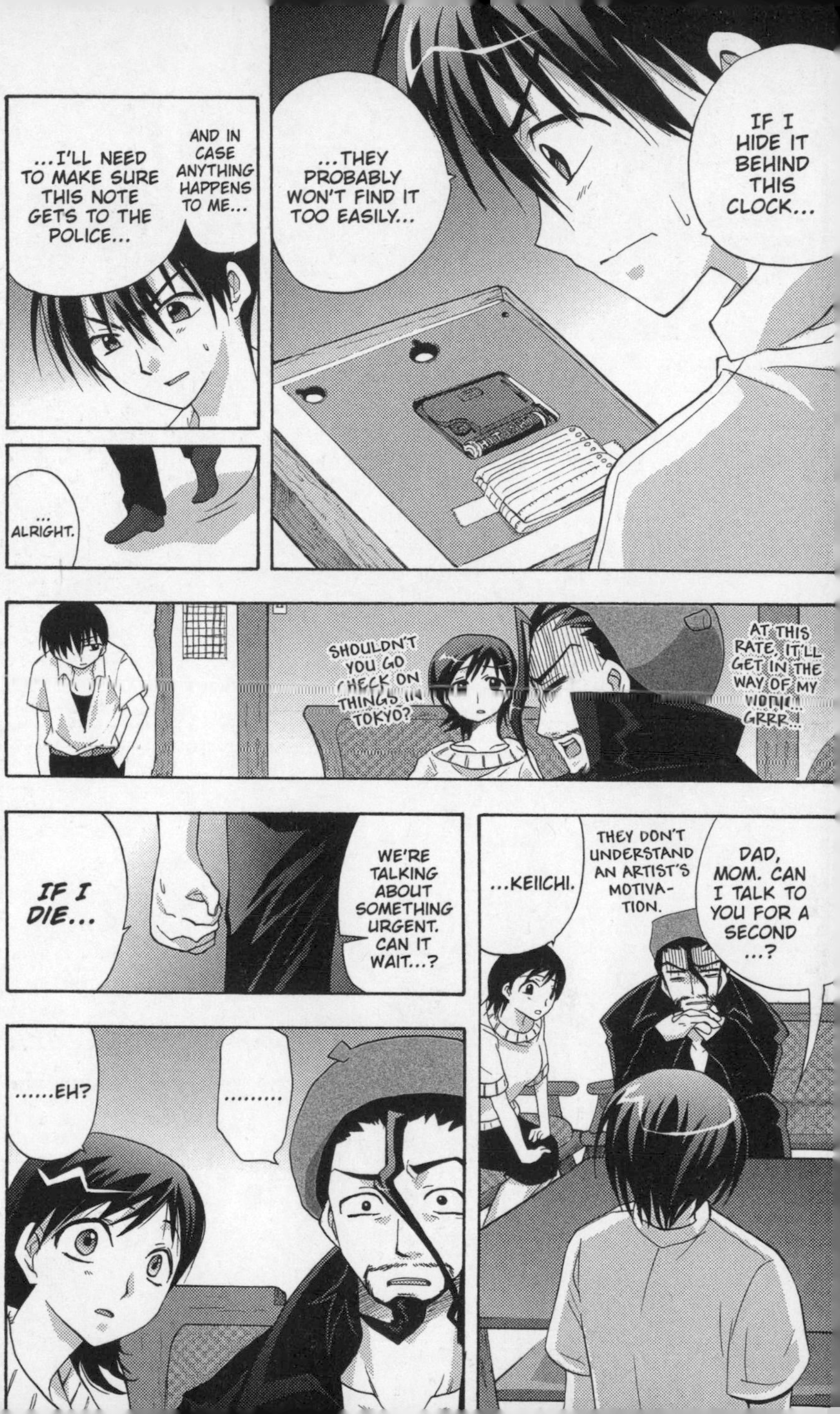

IF I HIDE IT BEHIND THIS CLOCK...
...THEY PROBABLY WON'T FIND IT TOO EASILY...
AND IN CASE ANYTHING HAPPENS TO ME...
...I'LL NEED TO MAKE SURE THIS NOTE GETS TO THE POLICE...
... ALRIGHT.
AT THIS RATE, IT'LL GET IN THE WAY OF MY
GRRR...
SHOULDN'T YOU GO CHECK ON THINGS IN TOKYO?
DAD, MOM. CAN I TALK TO YOU FOR A SECOND ...?
THEY DON'T UNDERSTAND AN ARTIST'S MOTIVATION.
...KEIICHI.
WE'RE TALKING ABOUT SOMETHING URGENT. CAN IT WAIT...?
IF I DIE...
....
......EH?

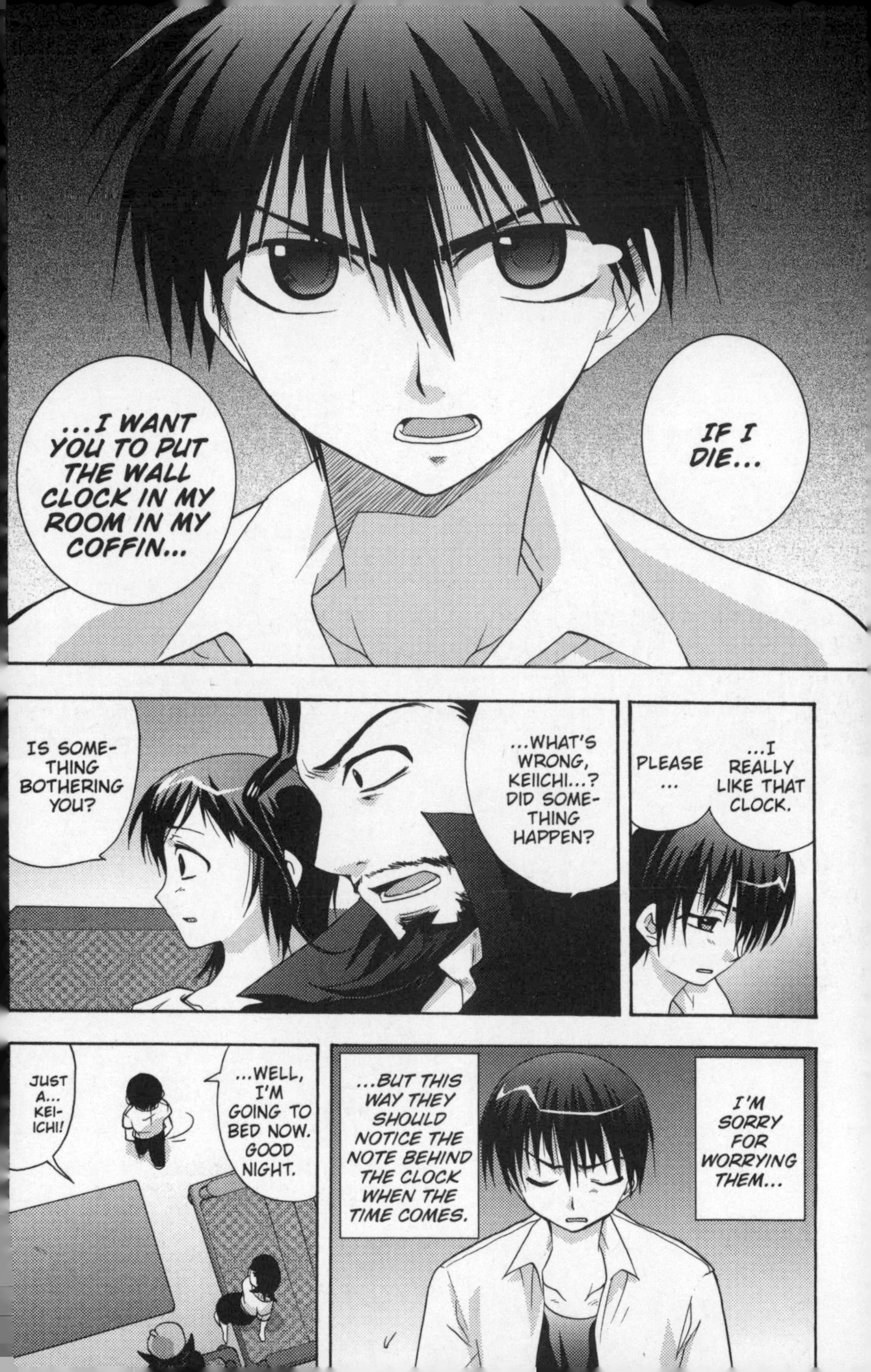
IF I DIE...
...I WANT YOU TO PUT THE WALL CLOCK IN MY ROOM IN MY COFFIN...
...I REALLY LIKE THAT CLOCK.
PLEASE ...
...WHAT'S WRONG, KEIICHI...? DID SOME-THING HAPPEN?
IS SOME-THING BOTHERING YOU?
I'M SORRY FOR WORRYING THEM...
...BUT THIS WAY THEY SHOULD NOTICE THE NOTE BEHIND THE CLOCK WHEN THE TIME COMES.
...WELL, I'M GOING TO BED NOW. GOOD NIGHT.
JUST A... KEI-ICHI!

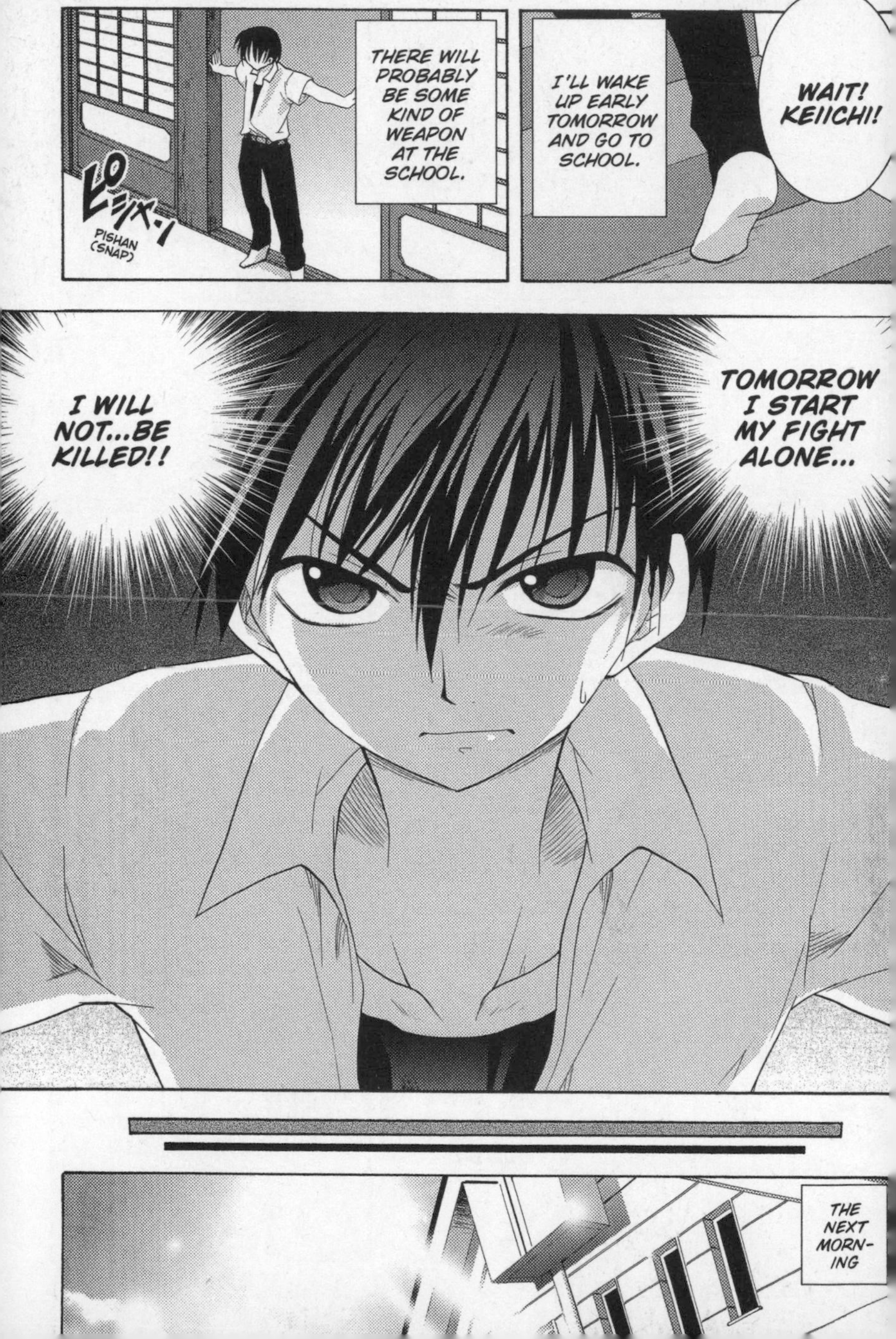
WAIT! KEIICHI!
I'LL WAKE UP EARLY TOMORROW AND GO TO SCHOOL.
THERE WILL PROBABLY BE SOME KIND OF WEAPON AT THE SCHOOL.
PISHAN (SNAP)
TOMORROW I START MY FIGHT ALONE...
I WILL NOT...BE KILLED!!
THE NEXT MORN-ING

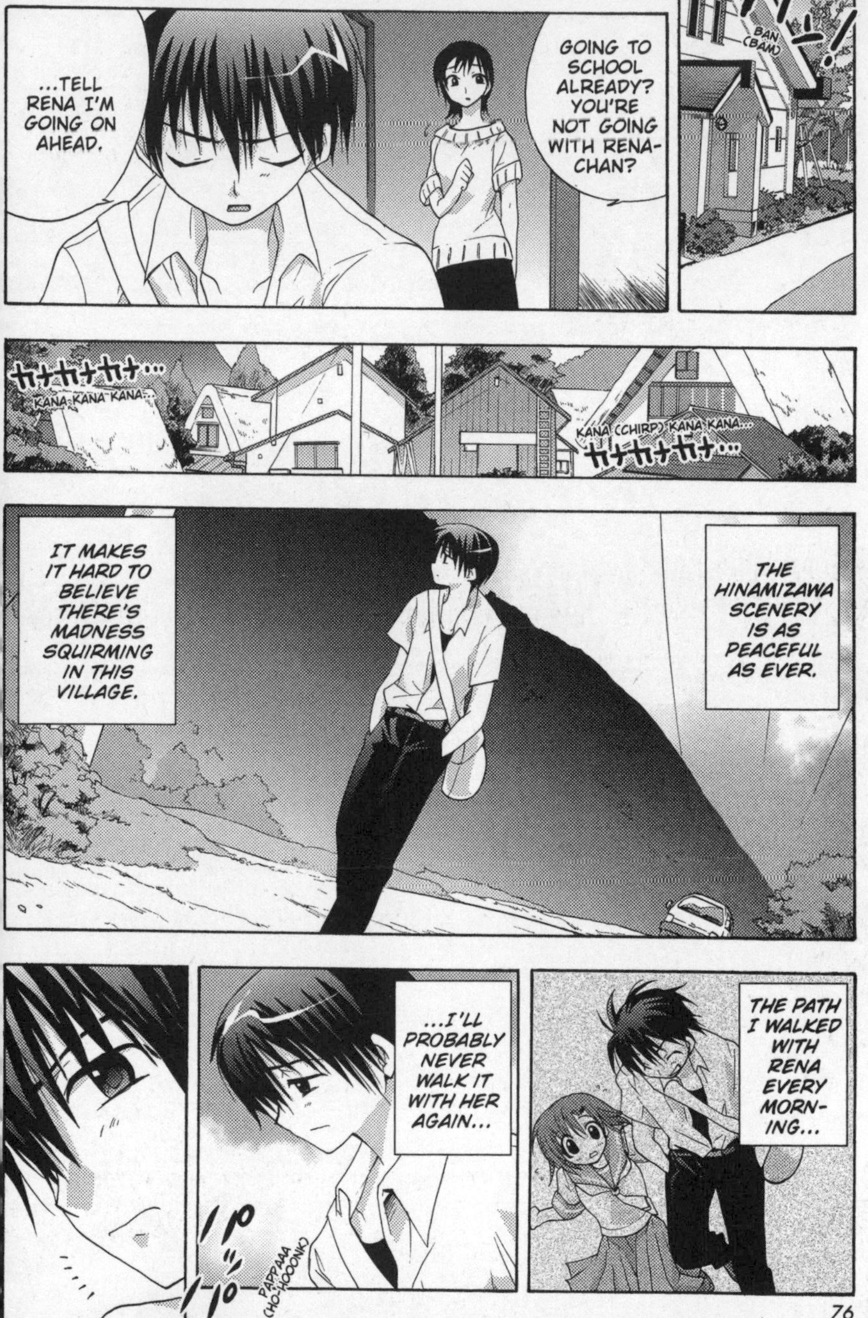
BAN (BAM)
GOING TO SCHOOL ALREADY? YOU'RE NOT GOING WITH RENA-CHAN?
...TELL RENA I'M GOING ON AHEAD.
カナカナカナ…
KANA (CHIRP) KANA KANA...
カナカナカナ…
KANA KANA KANA...
THE HINAMIZAWA SCENERY IS AS PEACEFUL AS EVER.
IT MAKES IT HARD TO BELIEVE THERE'S MADNESS SQUIRMING IN THIS VILLAGE.
THE PATH I WALKED WITH RENA EVERY MORNING...
...I'LL PROBABLY NEVER WALK IT WITH HER AGAIN...
PAPPAAA (HO-HOOONK)

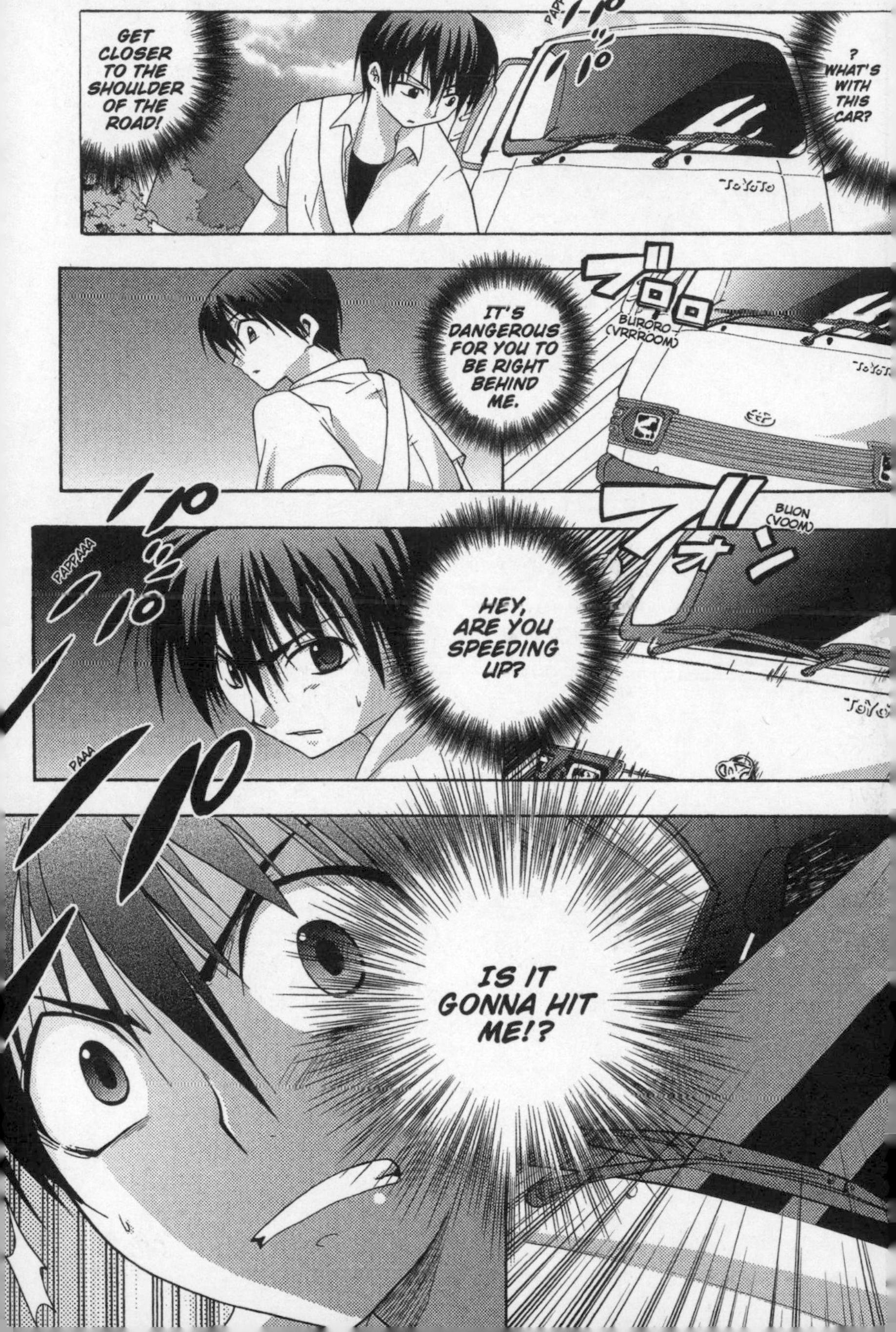
PAPPA
? WHAT'S WITH THIS CAR?
GET CLOSER TO THE SHOULDER OF THE ROAD!
BURORO (VRRROOM)
IT'S DANGEROUS FOR YOU TO BE RIGHT BEHIND ME.
BUON (VOOM)
HEY, ARE YOU SPEEDING UP?
PAPPAA
PAAA
IS IT GONNA HIT ME!?

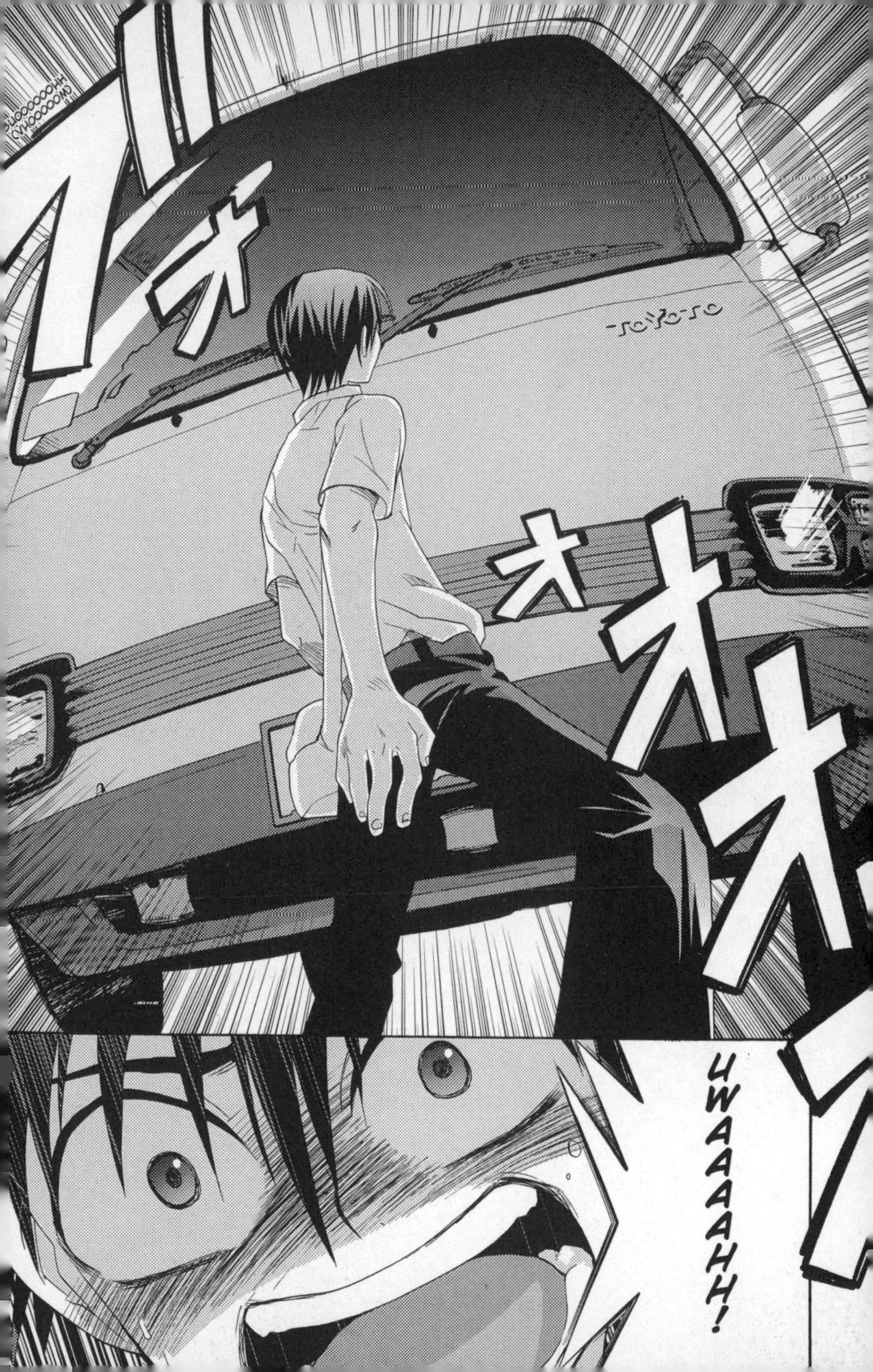
UWAAAAAAH!

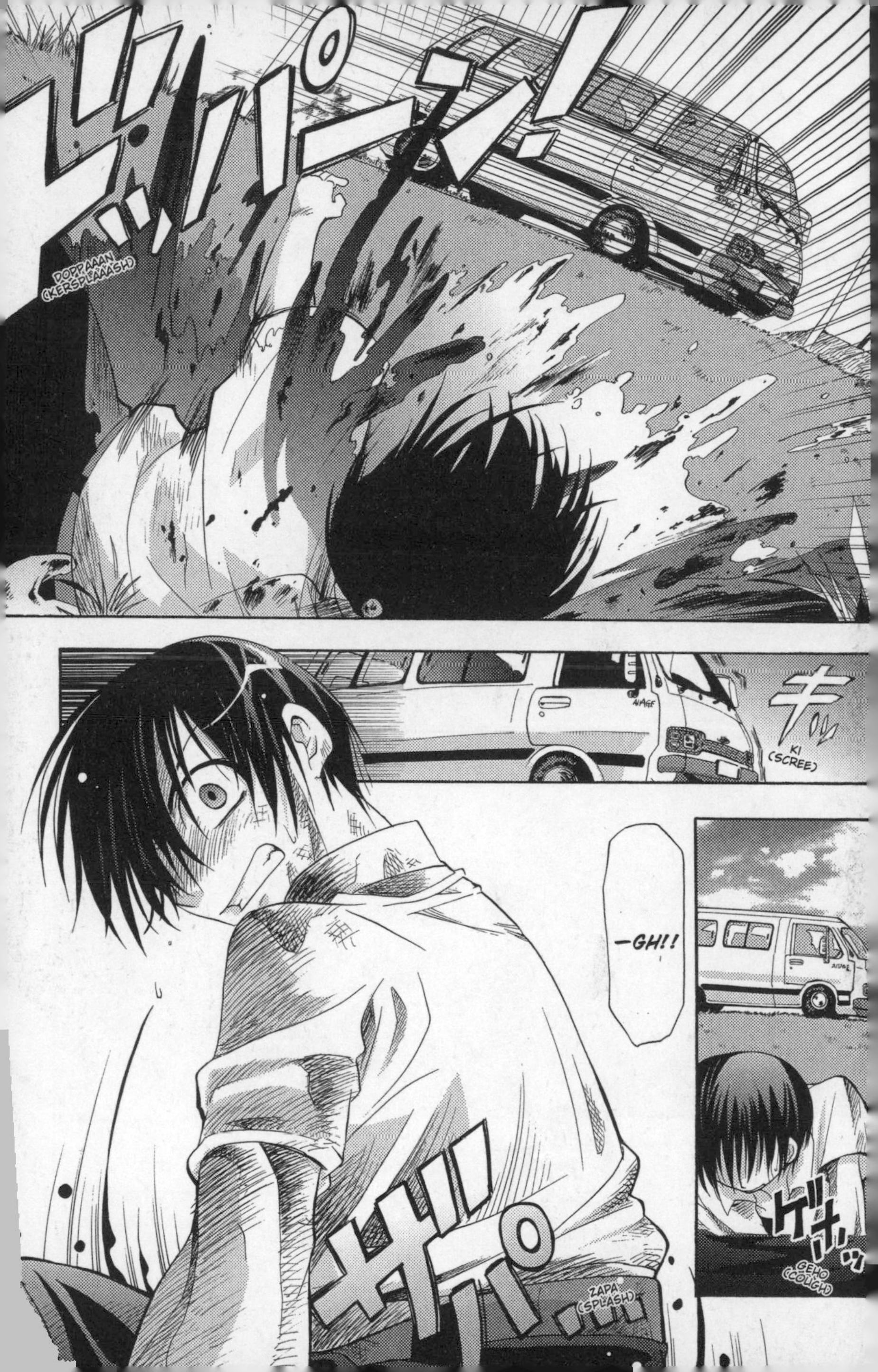
DOPPAAAN (KERSPLAAASH)
KI (SCREE)
GEHO (COUGH)
—GH!!
ZAPA (SPLASH)

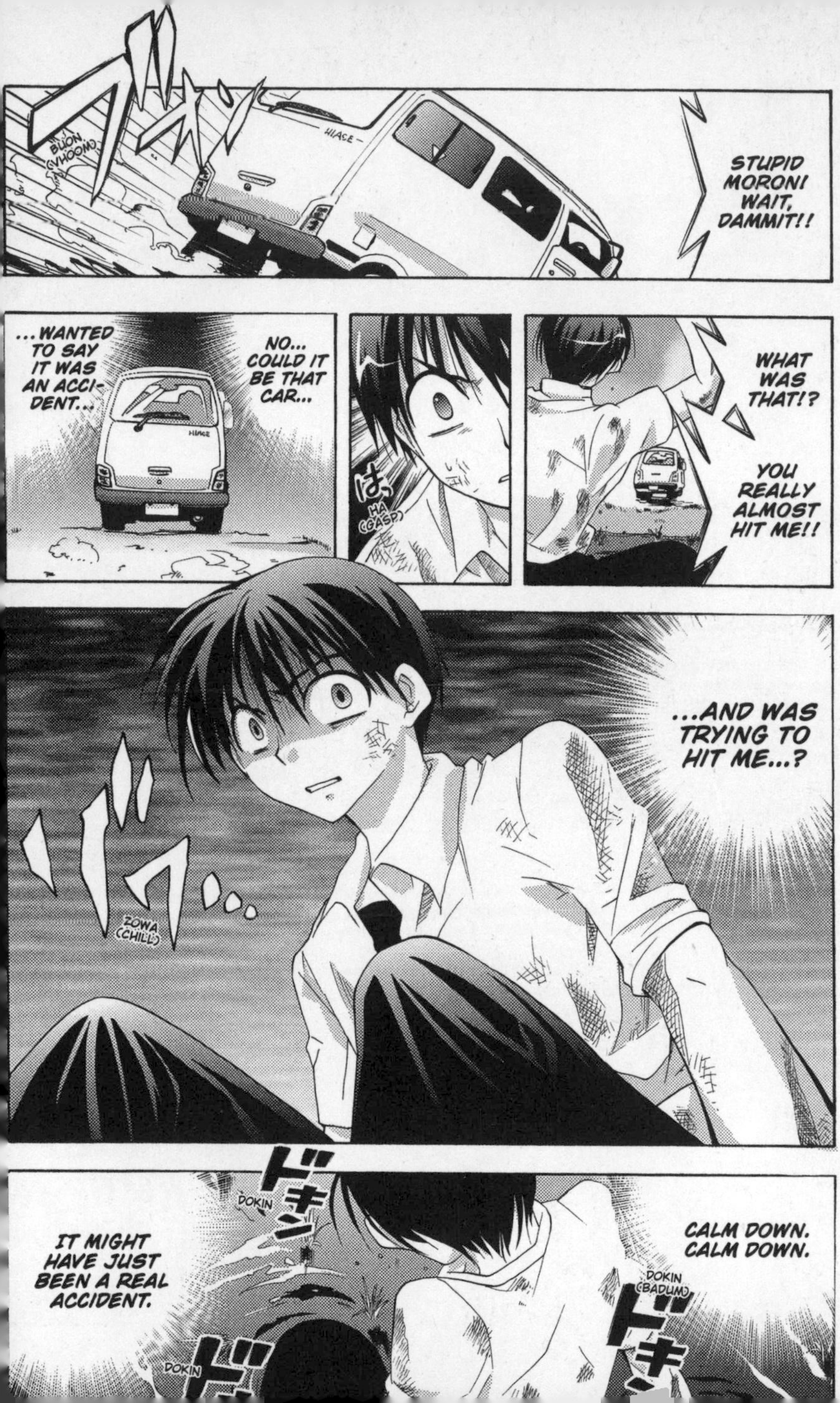
STUPID MORON! WAIT, DAMMIT!!
HIACE
BUON (VHOOM)
WHAT WAS THAT!?
YOU REALLY ALMOST HIT ME!!
HA (GASP)
NO... COULD IT BE THAT CAR...
...WANTED TO SAY IT WAS AN ACCI-DENT...
HIACE
...AND WAS TRYING TO HIT ME...?
ZOWA (CHILL)
CALM DOWN. CALM DOWN.
DOKIN (BADUM)
DOKIN
IT MIGHT HAVE JUST BEEN A REAL ACCIDENT.
DOKIN

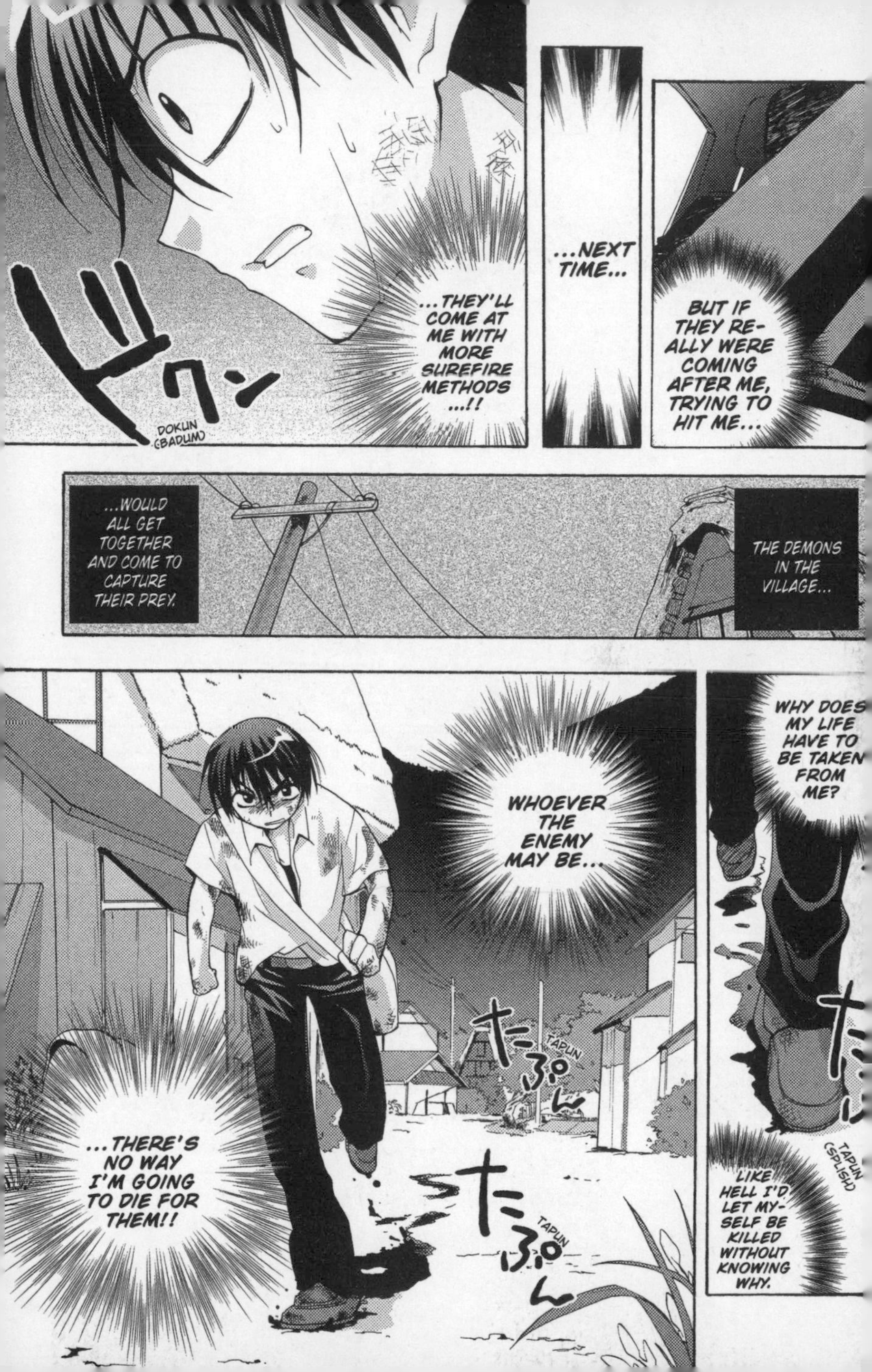
BUT IF THEY REALLY WERE COMING AFTER ME, TRYING TO HIT ME...
...NEXT TIME...
...THEY'LL COME AT ME WITH MORE SUREFIRE METHODS...!!
ドクン
DOKUN (BADUM)
THE DEMONS IN THE VILLAGE...
...WOULD ALL GET TOGETHER AND COME TO CAPTURE THEIR PREY.
WHY DOES MY LIFE HAVE TO BE TAKEN FROM ME?
TAPUN (SPLISH)
LIKE HELL I'D LET MYSELF BE KILLED WITHOUT KNOWING WHY.
WHOEVER THE ENEMY MAY BE...
たーぷん
TAPUN
...THERE'S NO WAY I'M GOING TO DIE FOR THEM!!
たぷん
TAPUN

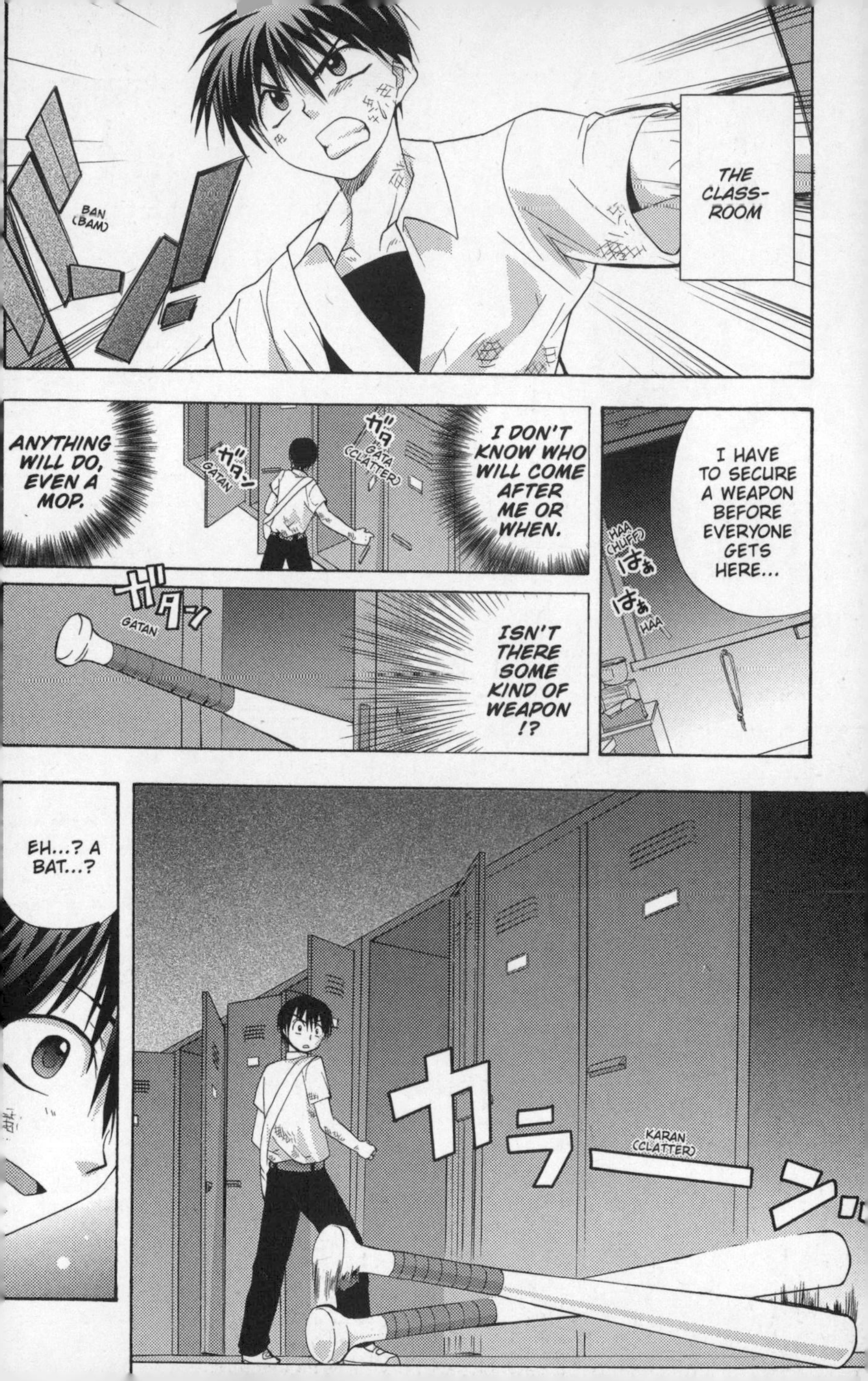
THE CLASS-ROOM
BAN (BAM)
I HAVE TO SECURE A WEAPON BEFORE EVERYONE GETS HERE...
HAA (CHUFF)
HAA
I DON'T KNOW WHO WILL COME AFTER ME OR WHEN.
GATA (CLATTER)
GATAN
ANYTHING WILL DO, EVEN A MOP.
ISN'T THERE SOME KIND OF WEAPON!?
GATAN
KARAN (CLATTER)
EH...? A BAT...?

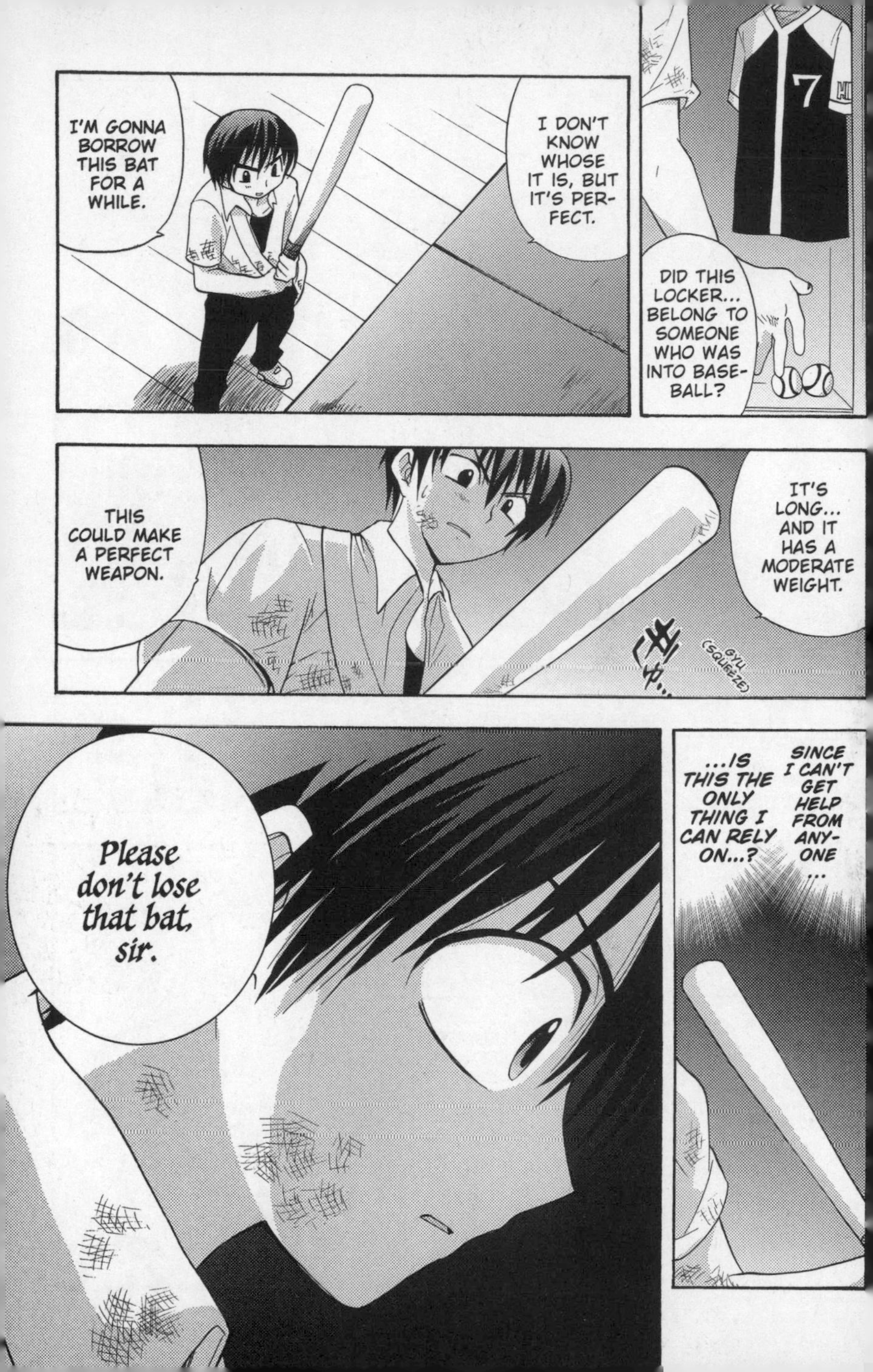
DID THIS LOCKER... BELONG TO SOMEONE WHO WAS INTO BASEBALL?
I DON'T KNOW WHOSE IT IS, BUT IT'S PERFECT.
I'M GONNA BORROW THIS BAT FOR A WHILE.
IT'S LONG... AND IT HAS A MODERATE WEIGHT.
GYU (SQUEEZE)
THIS COULD MAKE A PERFECT WEAPON.
SINCE I CAN'T GET HELP FROM ANYONE...
...IS THIS THE ONLY THING I CAN RELY ON...?
Please don't lose that bat, sir.

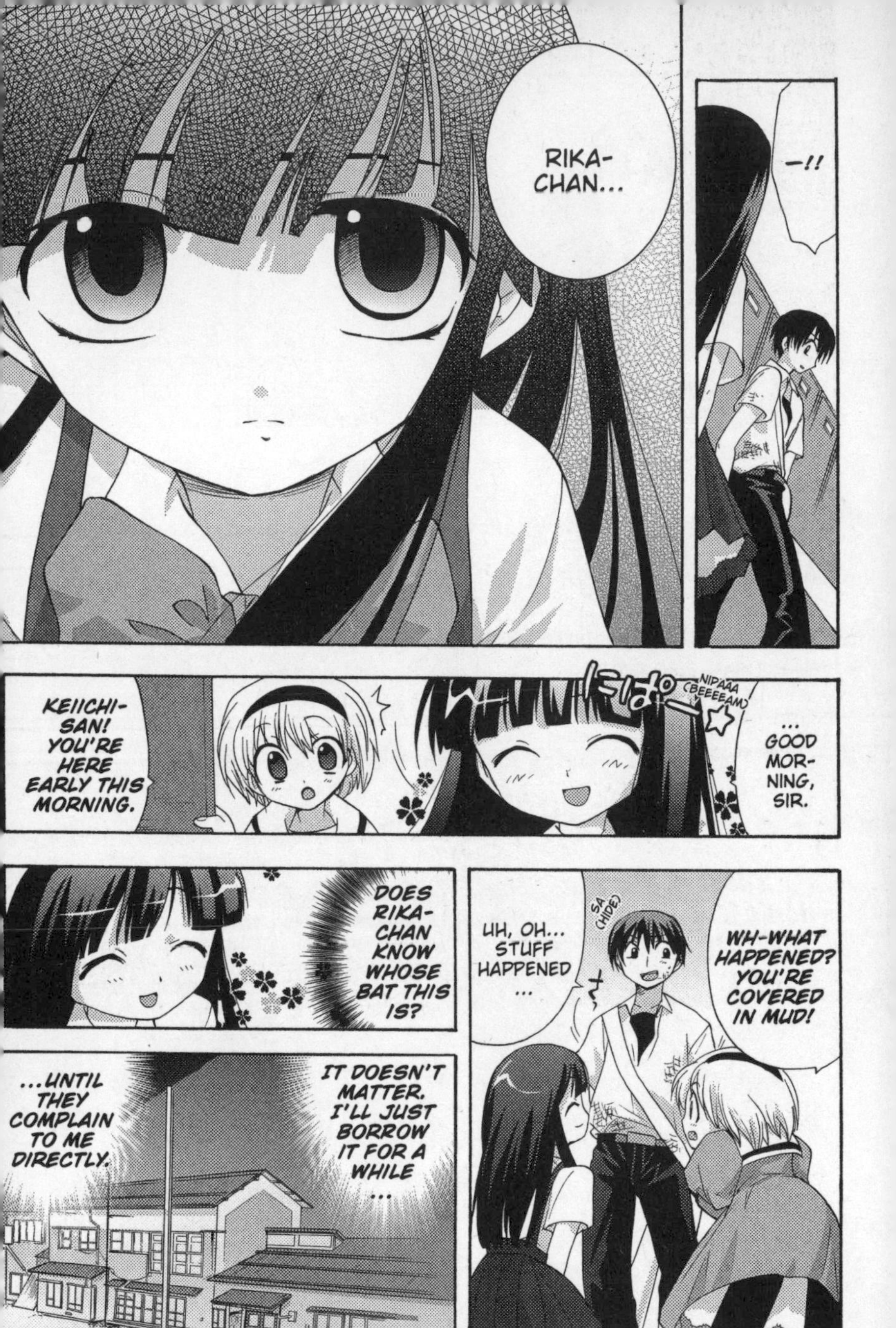
—!!
RIKA-CHAN...
... GOOD MORNING, SIR.
にぱー
NIPAAA (BEEEEAM)
KEIICHI-SAN! YOU'RE HERE EARLY THIS MORNING.
WH-WHAT HAPPENED? YOU'RE COVERED IN MUD!
SA (HIDE)
UH, OH... STUFF HAPPENED ...
DOES RIKA-CHAN KNOW WHOSE BAT THIS IS?
IT DOESN'T MATTER. I'LL JUST BORROW IT FOR A WHILE ...
...UNTIL THEY COMPLAIN TO ME DIRECTLY.

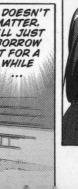

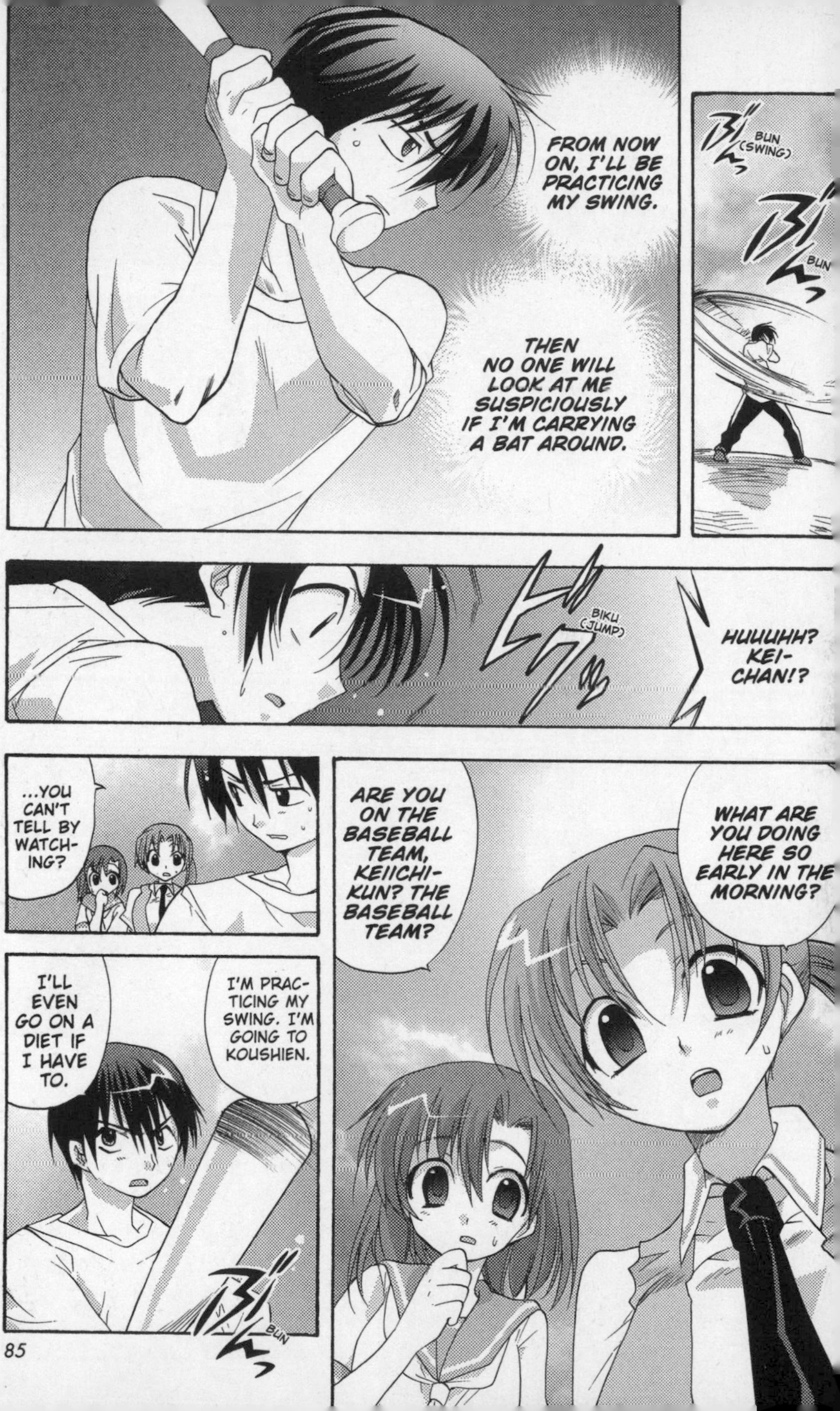
BUN (SWING)
BUN
FROM NOW ON, I'LL BE PRACTICING MY SWING.
THEN NO ONE WILL LOOK AT ME SUSPICIOUSLY IF I'M CARRYING A BAT AROUND.
HUUUHH? KEI-CHAN!?
BIKU (JUMP)
WHAT ARE YOU DOING HERE SO EARLY IN THE MORNING?
ARE YOU ON THE BASEBALL TEAM, KEIICHI-KUN? THE BASEBALL TEAM?
...YOU CAN'T TELL BY WATCHING?
I'M PRAC-TICING MY SWING. I'M GOING TO KOUSHIEN.
I'LL EVEN GO ON A DIET IF I HAVE TO.
BUN

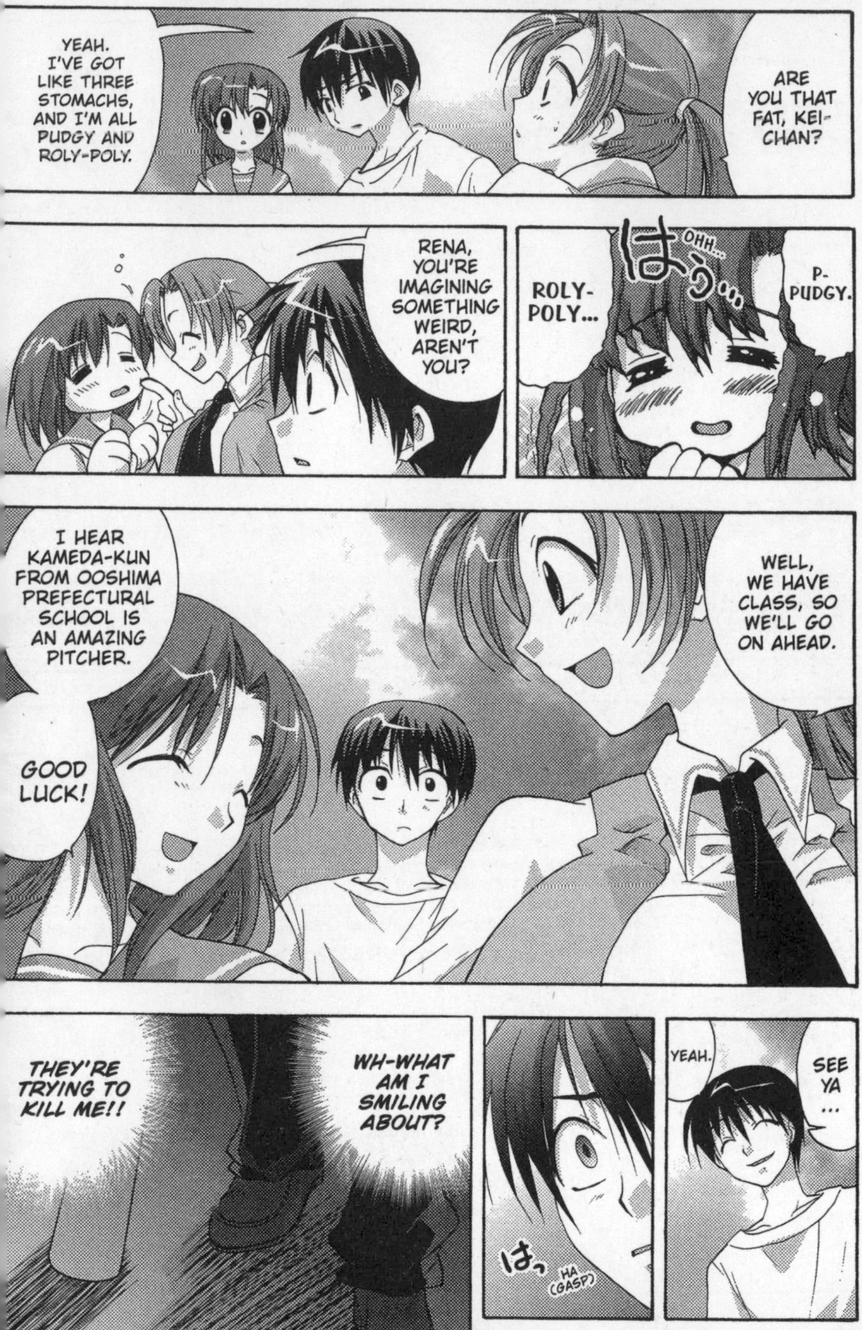
ARE YOU THAT FAT, KEI-CHAN?
YEAH. I'VE GOT LIKE THREE STOMACHS, AND I'M ALL PUDGY AND ROLY-POLY.
はぅ…
OHH...
P-PUDGY.
ROLY-POLY...
RENA, YOU'RE IMAGINING SOMETHING WEIRD, AREN'T YOU?
WELL, WE HAVE CLASS, SO WE'LL GO ON AHEAD.
I HEAR KAMEDA-KUN FROM OOSHIMA PREFECTURAL SCHOOL IS AN AMAZING PITCHER.
GOOD LUCK!
SEE YA ...
YEAH.
はっ
HA (GASP)
WH-WHAT AM I SMILING ABOUT?
THEY'RE TRYING TO KILL ME!!

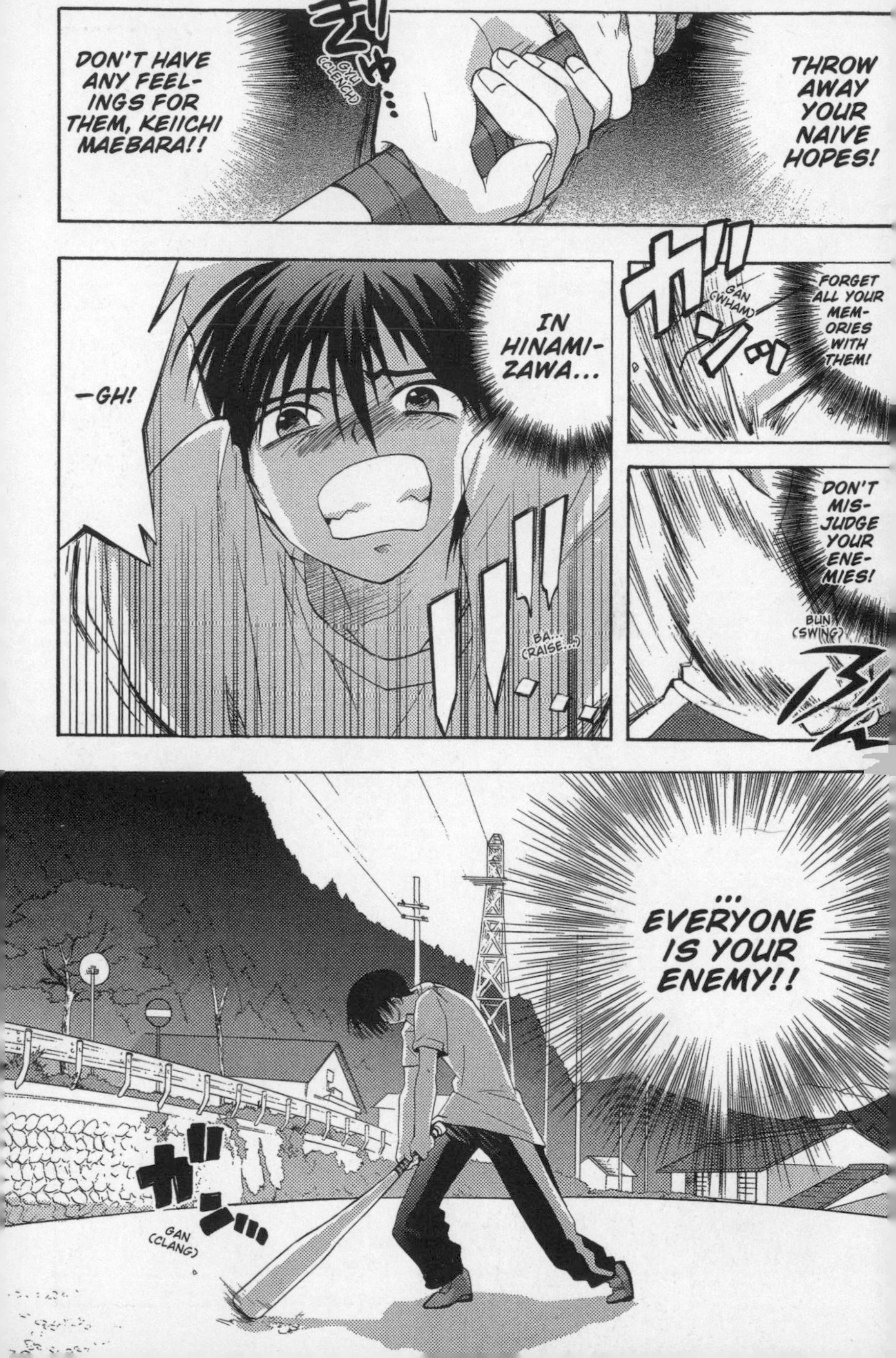
GYU (CLENCH)
THROW AWAY YOUR NAIVE HOPES!
DON'T HAVE ANY FEEL-INGS FOR THEM, KEIICHI MAEBARA!!
GAN (WHAM)
FORGET ALL YOUR MEM-ORIES WITH THEM!
DON'T MIS-JUDGE YOUR ENE-MIES!
BUN (SWING)
IN HINAMI-ZAWA...
-GH!
BA... (RAISE...)
...EVERYONE IS YOUR ENEMY!!
GAN (CLANG)

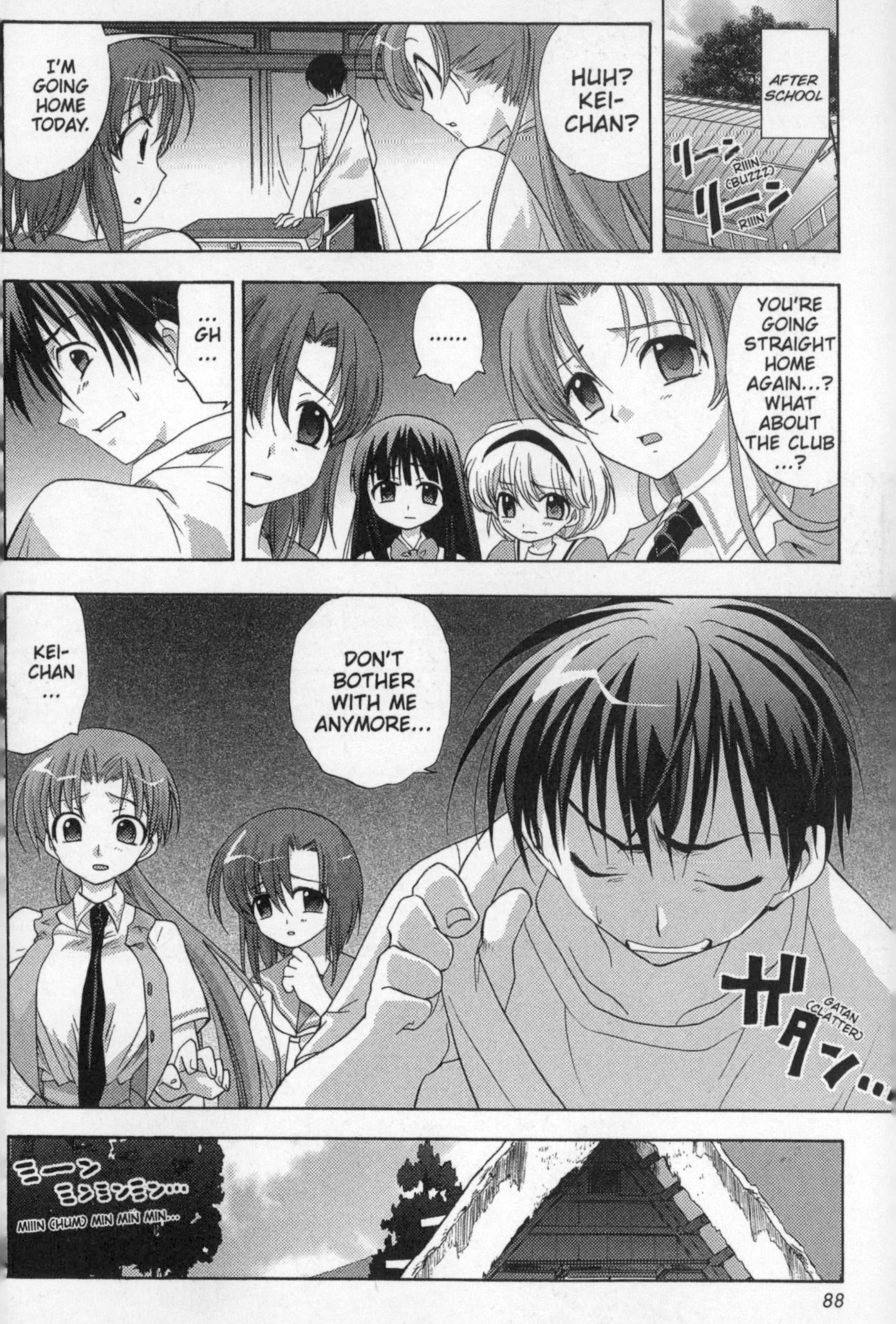
AFTER SCHOOL
リーン リーン
RIIIN (BUZZZ) RIIIN
HUH? KEI-CHAN?
I'M GOING HOME TODAY.
YOU'RE GOING STRAIGHT HOME AGAIN...? WHAT ABOUT THE CLUB ...?
......
... GH ...
DON'T BOTHER WITH ME ANYMORE...
KEI-CHAN ...
ガタン...
GATAN (CLATTER)
ミーン ミンミンミン...
MIIIN (HUM) MIN MIN MIN...

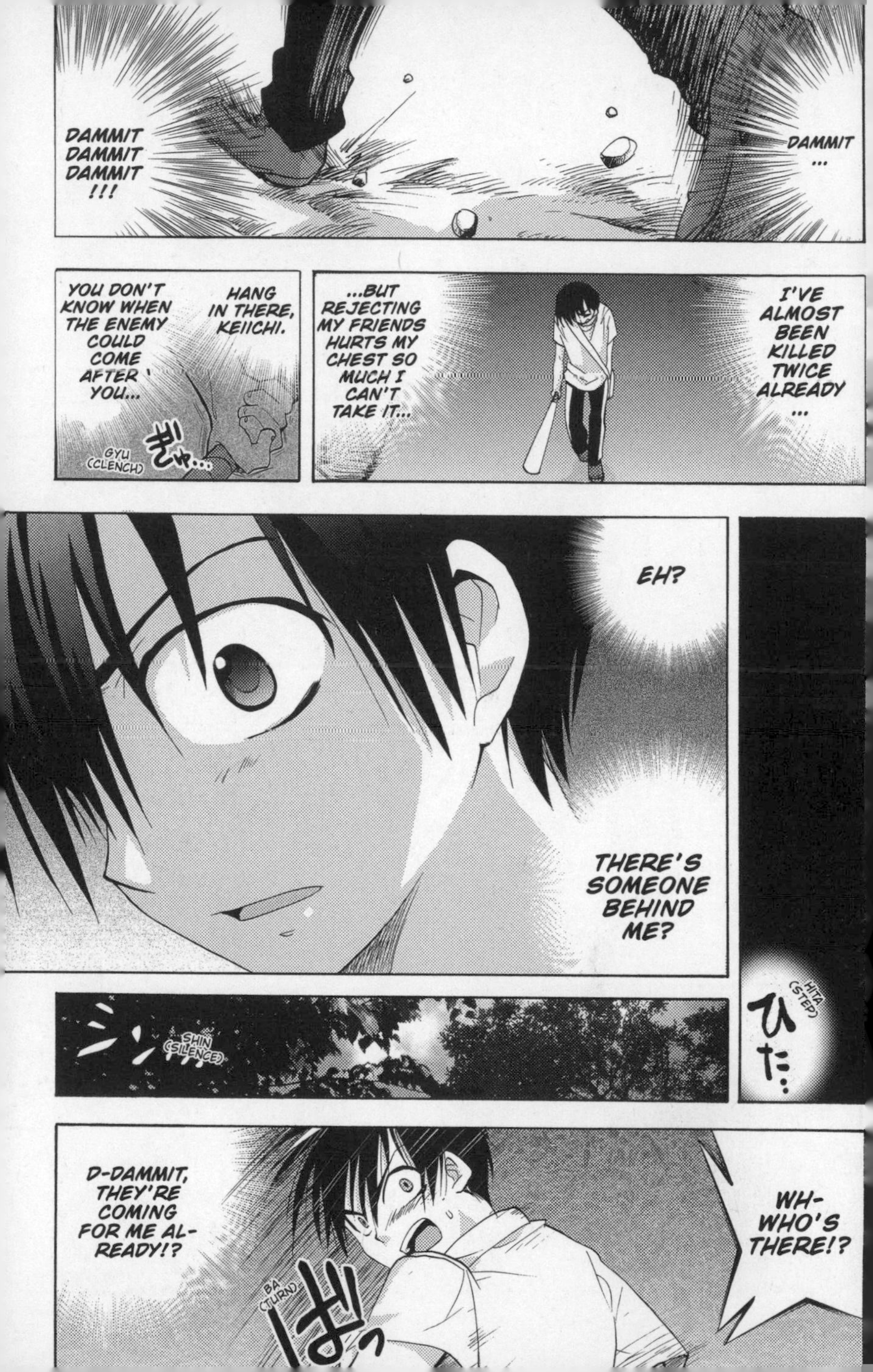
DAMMIT ...
DAMMIT DAMMIT DAMMIT !!!
I'VE ALMOST BEEN KILLED TWICE ALREADY ...
...BUT REJECTING MY FRIENDS HURTS MY CHEST SO MUCH I CAN'T TAKE IT...
HANG IN THERE, KEIICHI.
YOU DON'T KNOW WHEN THE ENEMY COULD COME AFTER YOU...
ぎゅ…
GYU (CLENCH)
ひた…
HITA (STEP)
EH?
THERE'S SOMEONE BEHIND ME?
SHIN (SILENCE)
WH-WHO'S THERE!?
D-DAMMIT, THEY'RE COMING FOR ME AL-READY!?
ばっ
BA (TURN)

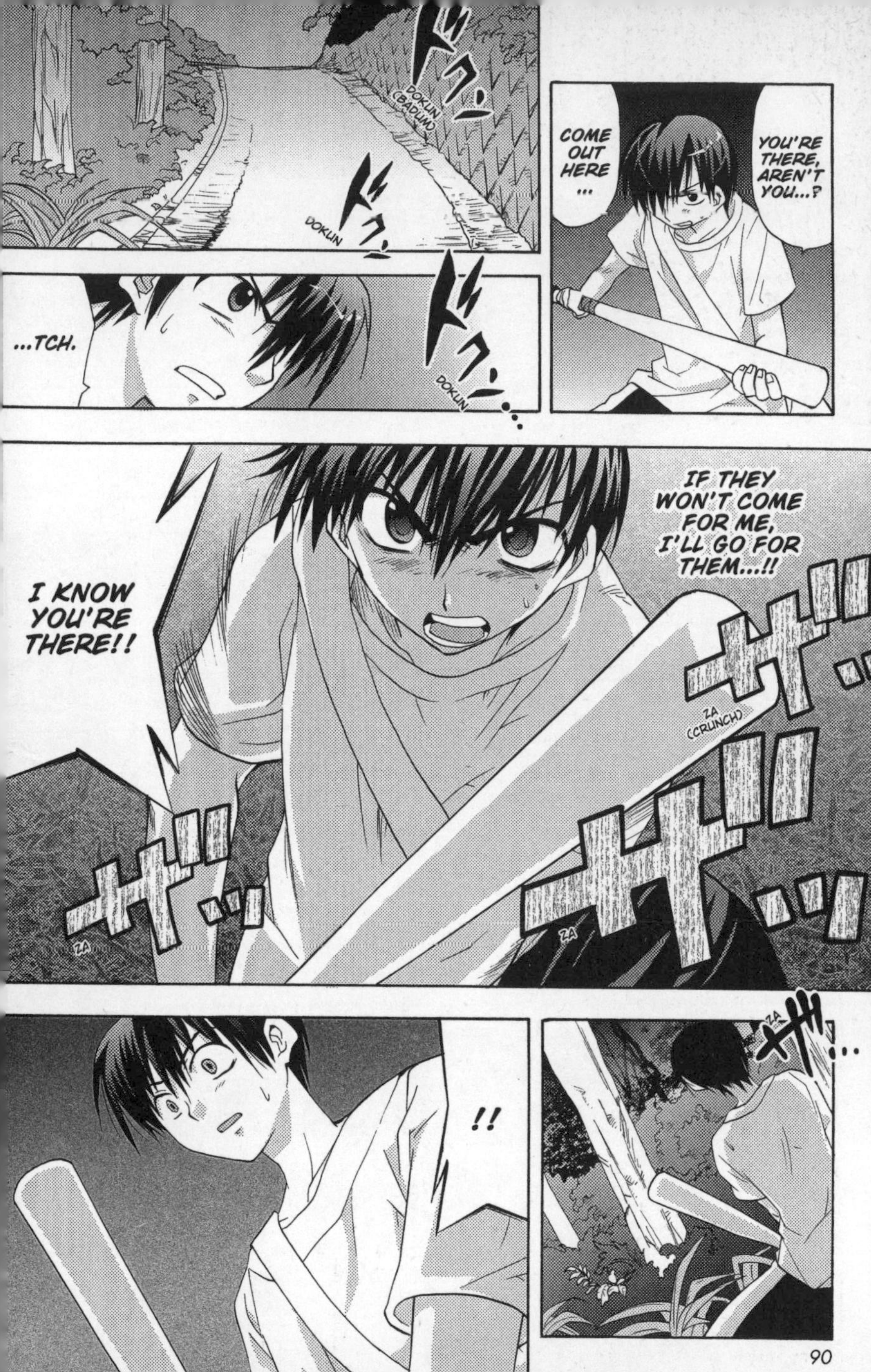
YOU'RE THERE, AREN'T YOU...?
COME OUT HERE ...
DOKUN (BADUM)
DOKUN
DOKUN
...TCH.
IF THEY WON'T COME FOR ME, I'LL GO FOR THEM...!!
I KNOW YOU'RE THERE!!
ZA (CRUNCH)
ZA
ZA
ZA
!!

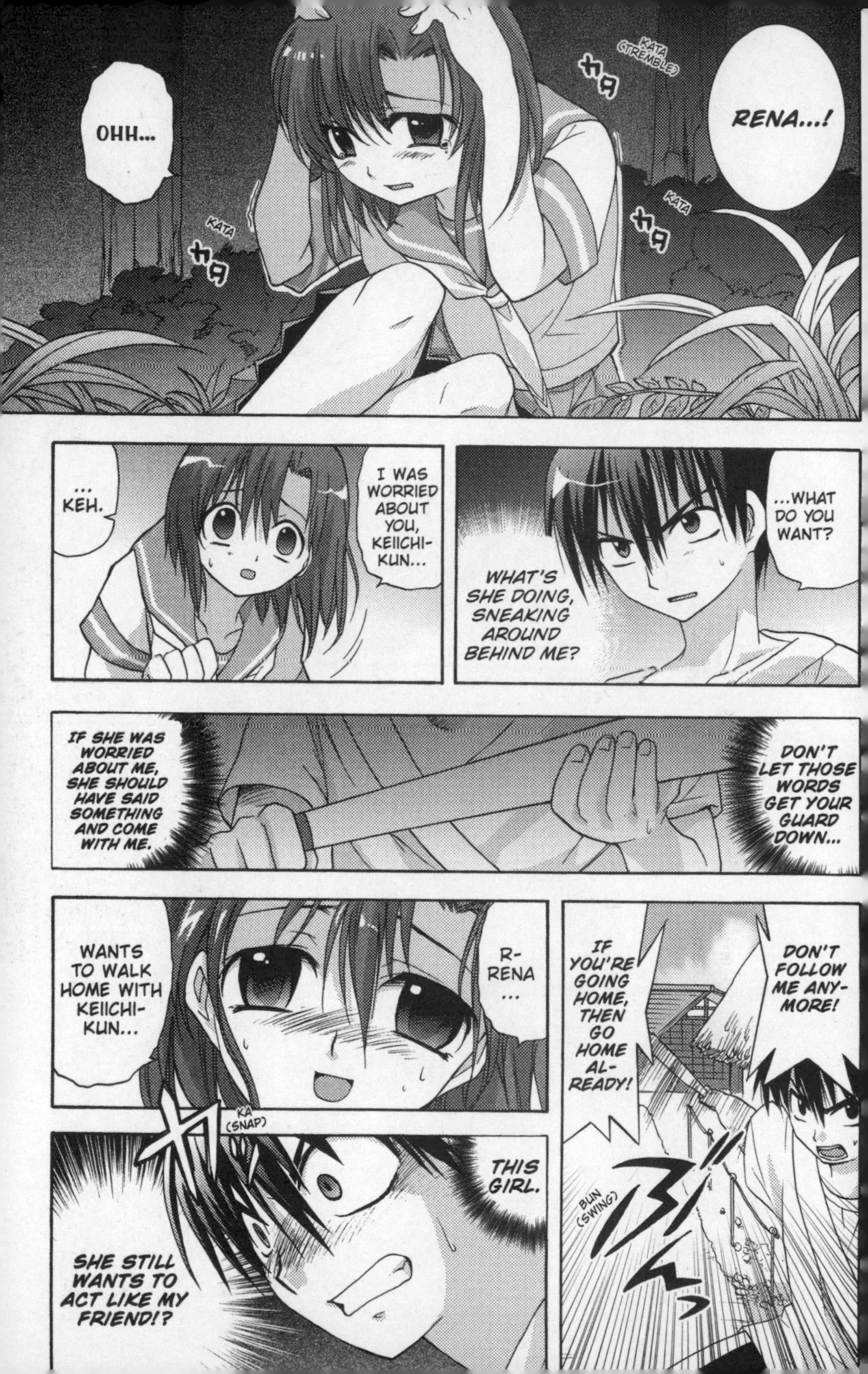
KATA (TREMBLE)
RENA...!
KATA
OHH...
KATA
...WHAT DO YOU WANT?
WHAT'S SHE DOING, SNEAKING AROUND BEHIND ME?
I WAS WORRIED ABOUT YOU, KEIICHI-KUN...
... KEH.
DON'T LET THOSE WORDS GET YOUR GUARD DOWN...
IF SHE WAS WORRIED ABOUT ME, SHE SHOULD HAVE SAID SOMETHING AND COME WITH ME.
DON'T FOLLOW ME ANYMORE!
IF YOU'RE GOING HOME, THEN GO HOME ALREADY!
BUN (SWING)
R-RENA ...
WANTS TO WALK HOME WITH KEIICHI-KUN...
KA (SNAP)
THIS GIRL.
SHE STILL WANTS TO ACT LIKE MY FRIEND!?

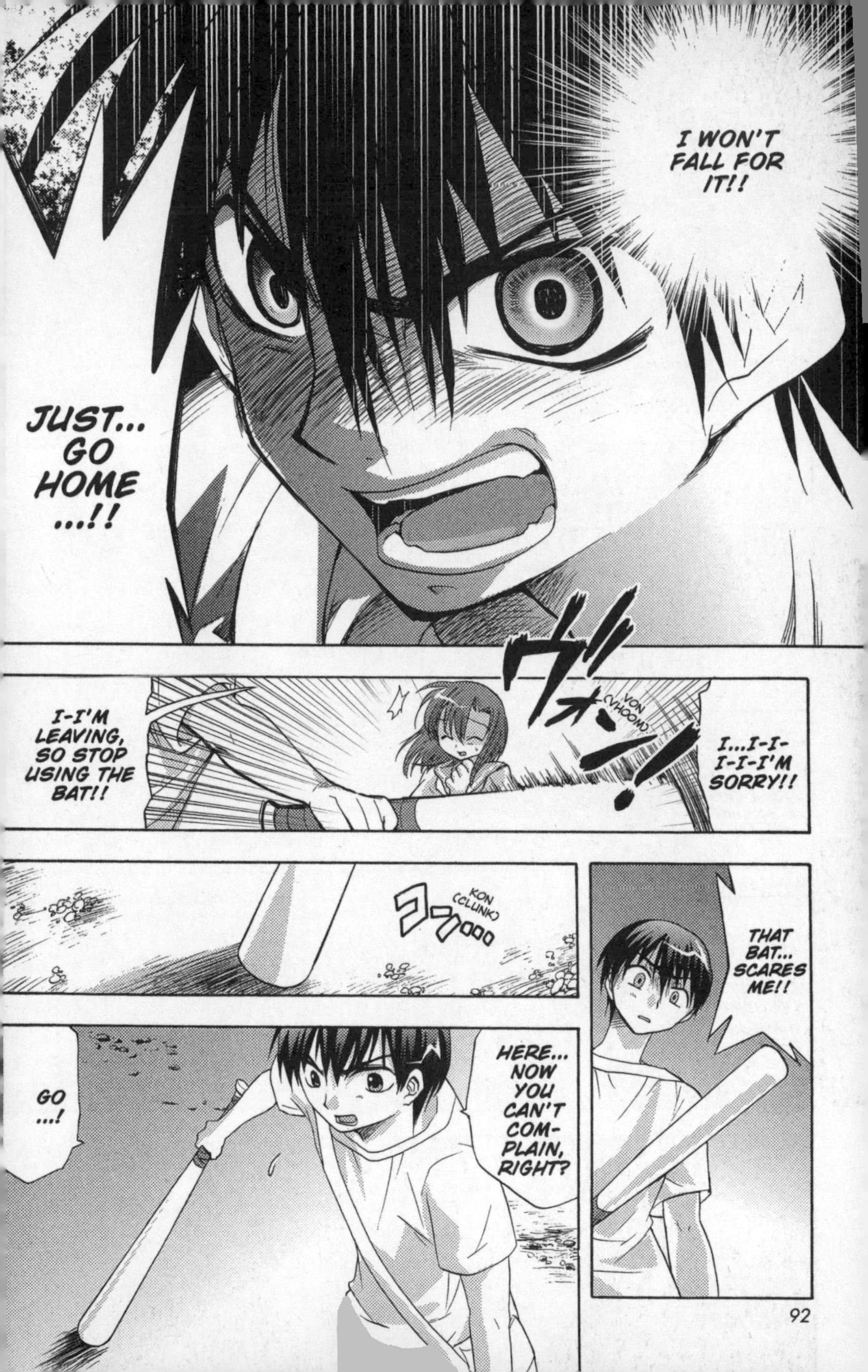
I WON'T FALL FOR IT!!
JUST... GO HOME ...!!
I...I-I-I-I-I'M SORRY!!
VON (VHOOM)
I-I'M LEAVING, SO STOP USING THE BAT!!
THAT BAT... SCARES ME!!
KON (CLUNK)
HERE... NOW YOU CAN'T COM-PLAIN, RIGHT?
GO ...!

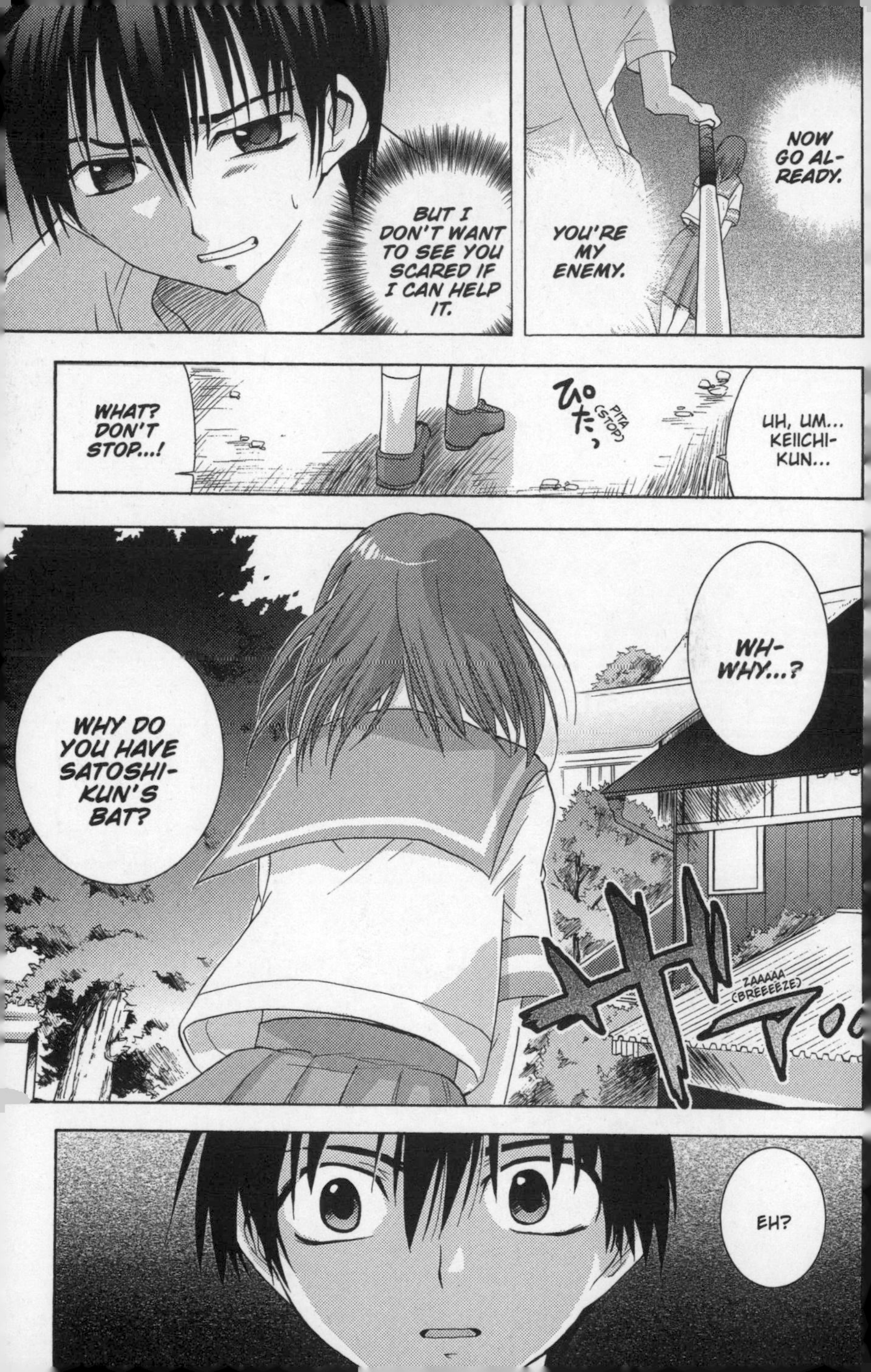
NOW GO AL-READY.
YOU'RE MY ENEMY.
BUT I DON'T WANT TO SEE YOU SCARED IF I CAN HELP IT.
UH, UM... KEIICHI-KUN...
ぴた、
PITA (STOP)
WHAT? DON'T STOP...!
WH-WHY...?
WHY DO YOU HAVE SATOSHI-KUN'S BAT?
ZAAAAA (BREEEEZE)
EH?

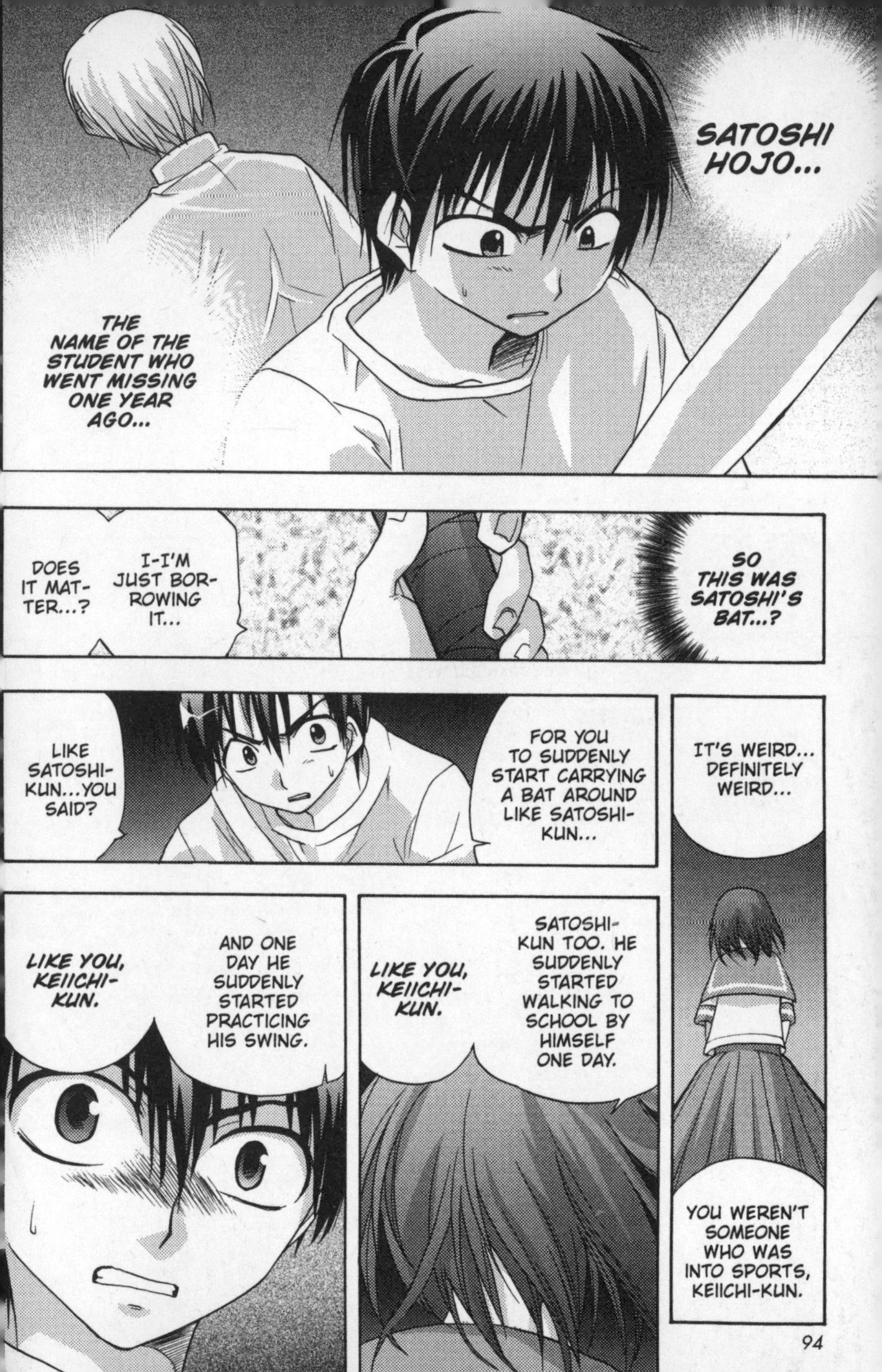
SATOSHI HOJO...
THE NAME OF THE STUDENT WHO WENT MISSING ONE YEAR AGO...
SO THIS WAS SATOSHI'S BAT...?
I-I'M JUST BOR-ROWING IT...
DOES IT MAT-TER...?
IT'S WEIRD... DEFINITELY WEIRD...
YOU WEREN'T SOMEONE WHO WAS INTO SPORTS, KEIICHI-KUN.
FOR YOU TO SUDDENLY START CARRYING A BAT AROUND LIKE SATOSHI-KUN...
LIKE SATOSHI-KUN...YOU SAID?
SATOSHI-KUN TOO. HE SUDDENLY STARTED WALKING TO SCHOOL BY HIMSELF ONE DAY.
LIKE YOU, KEIICHI-KUN.
AND ONE DAY HE SUDDENLY STARTED PRACTICING HIS SWING.
LIKE YOU, KEIICHI-KUN.

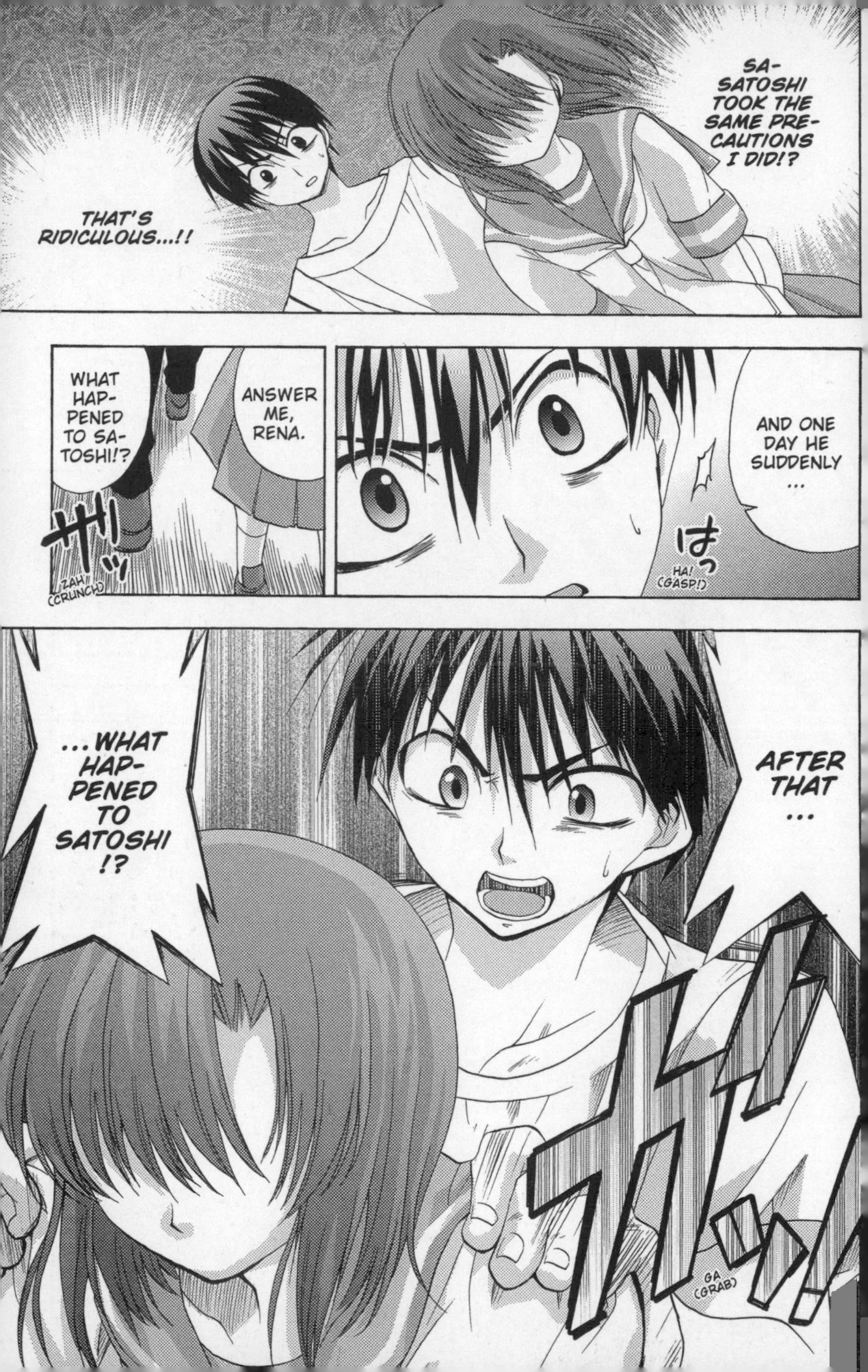
SA-SATOSHI TOOK THE SAME PRE-CAUTIONS I DID!?
THAT'S RIDICULOUS...!!
AND ONE DAY HE SUDDENLY ...
はっ
HA! (GASP!)
ANSWER ME, RENA.
WHAT HAP-PENED TO SA-TOSHI!?
ザッ
ZAH (CRUNCH)
AFTER THAT ...
...WHAT HAP-PENED TO SATOSHI !?
GA (GRAB)

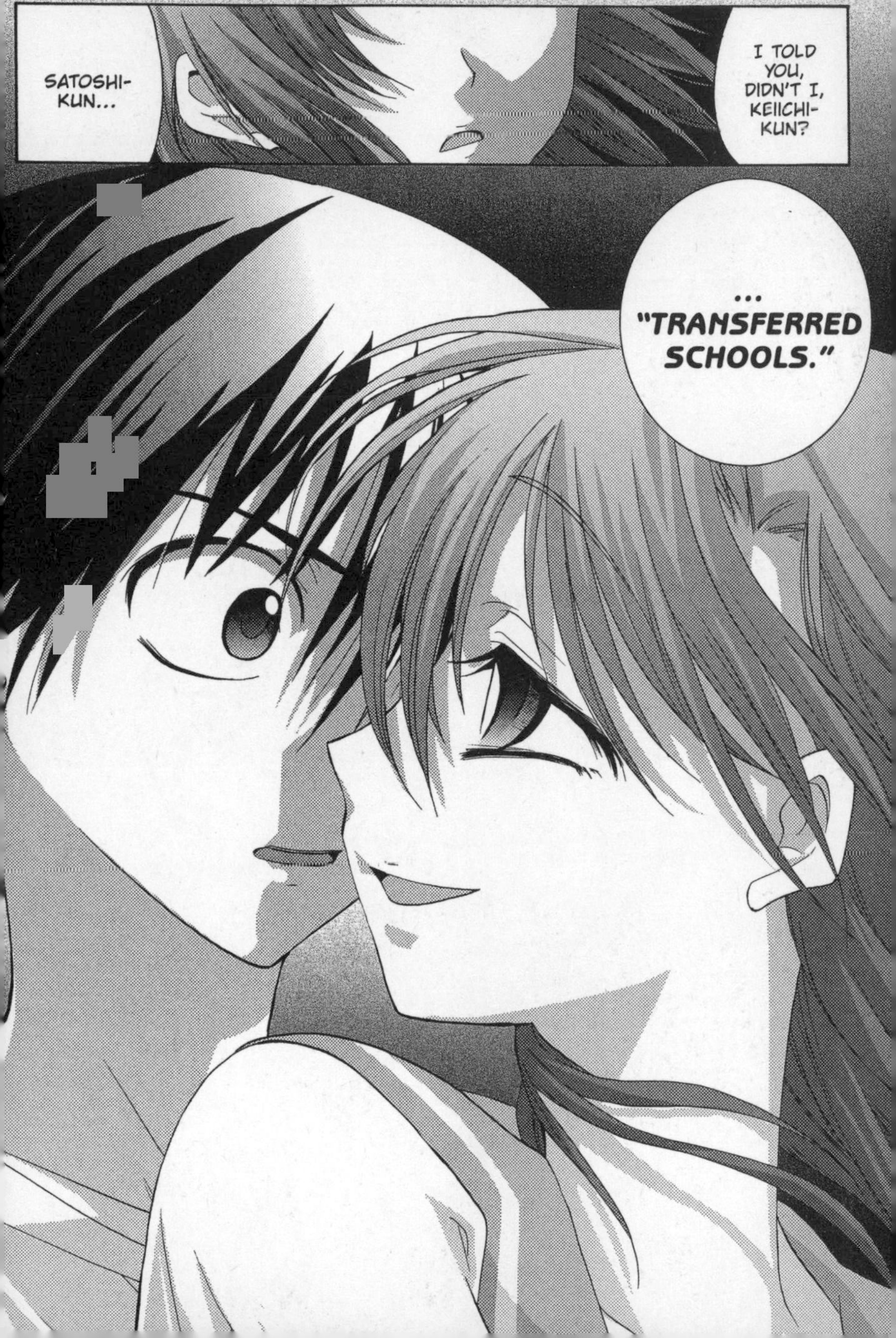
I TOLD YOU, DIDN'T I, KEIICHI-KUN?
SATOSHI-KUN...
... "TRANSFERRED SCHOOLS."

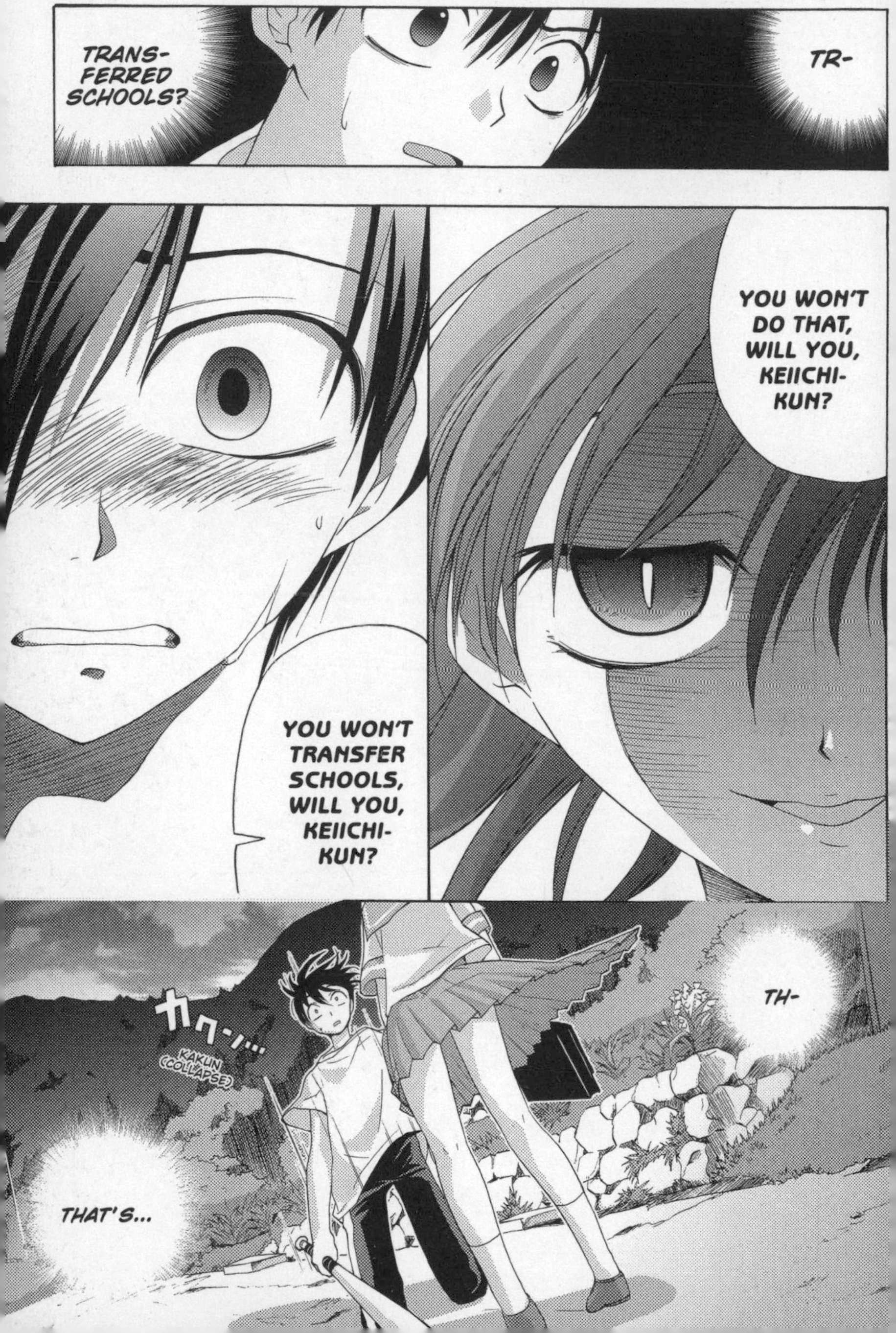
TR-
TRANS-FERRED SCHOOLS?
YOU WON'T DO THAT, WILL YOU, KEIICHI-KUN?
YOU WON'T TRANSFER SCHOOLS, WILL YOU, KEIICHI-KUN?
TH-
カクーン…
KAKUN (COLLAPSE)
THAT'S...

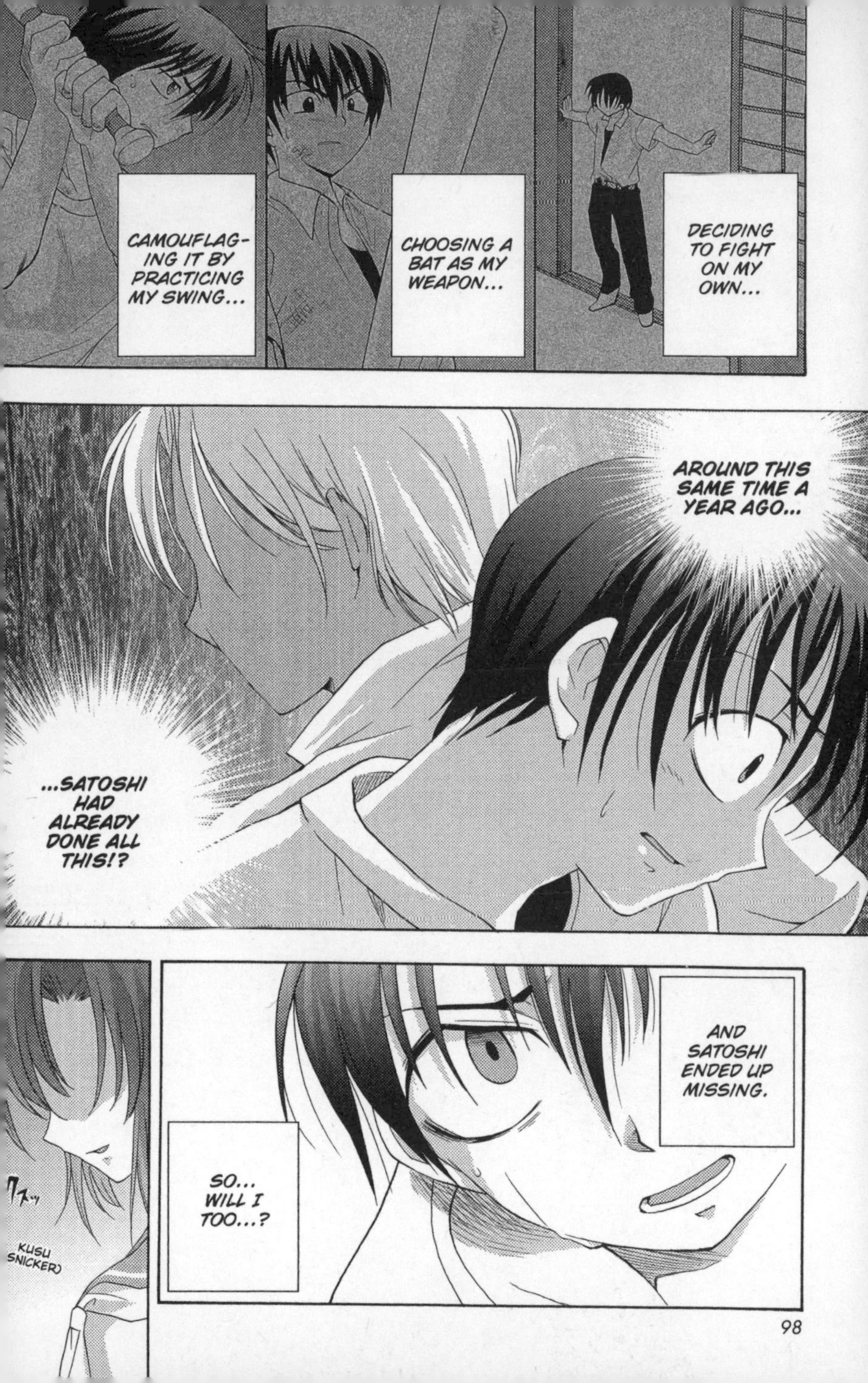
DECIDING TO FIGHT ON MY OWN...
CHOOSING A BAT AS MY WEAPON...
CAMOUFLAGING IT BY PRACTICING MY SWING...
AROUND THIS SAME TIME A YEAR AGO...
...SATOSHI HAD ALREADY DONE ALL THIS!?
AND SATOSHI ENDED UP MISSING.
SO... WILL I TOO...?
KUSU (SNICKER)

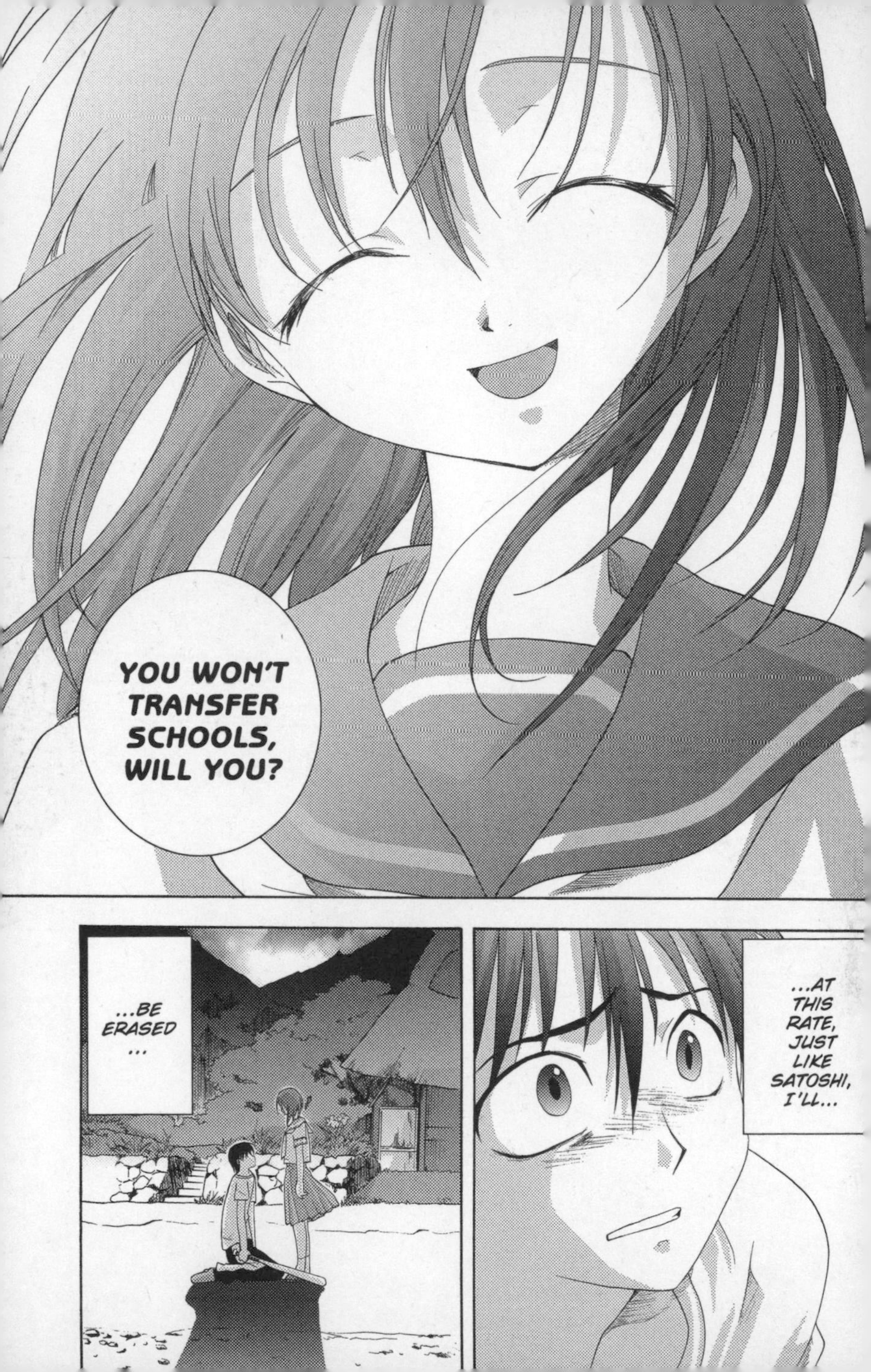
YOU WON'T TRANSFER SCHOOLS, WILL YOU?
...AT THIS RATE, JUST LIKE SATOSHI, I'LL...
...BE ERASED ...

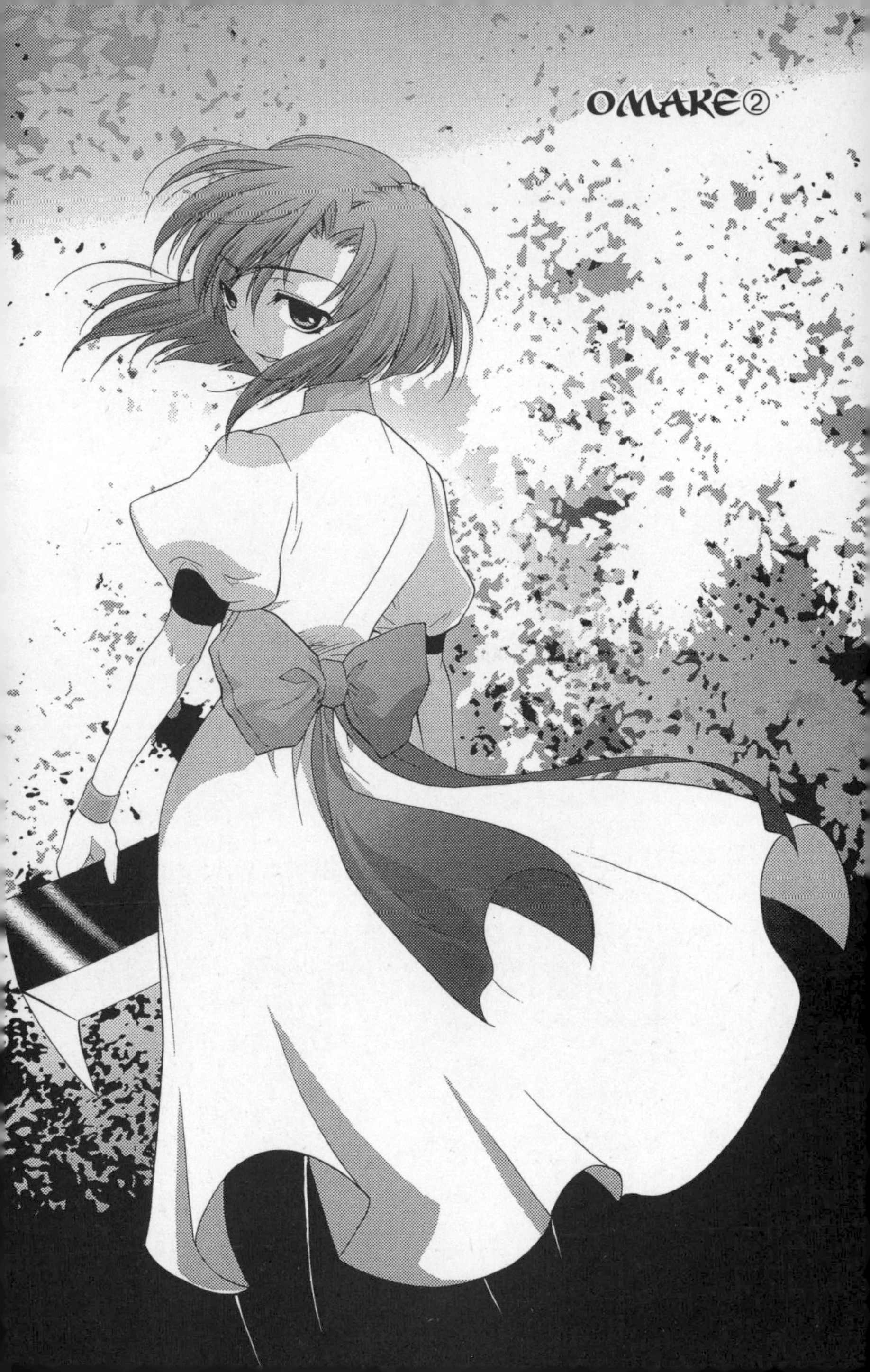
OMAKE②

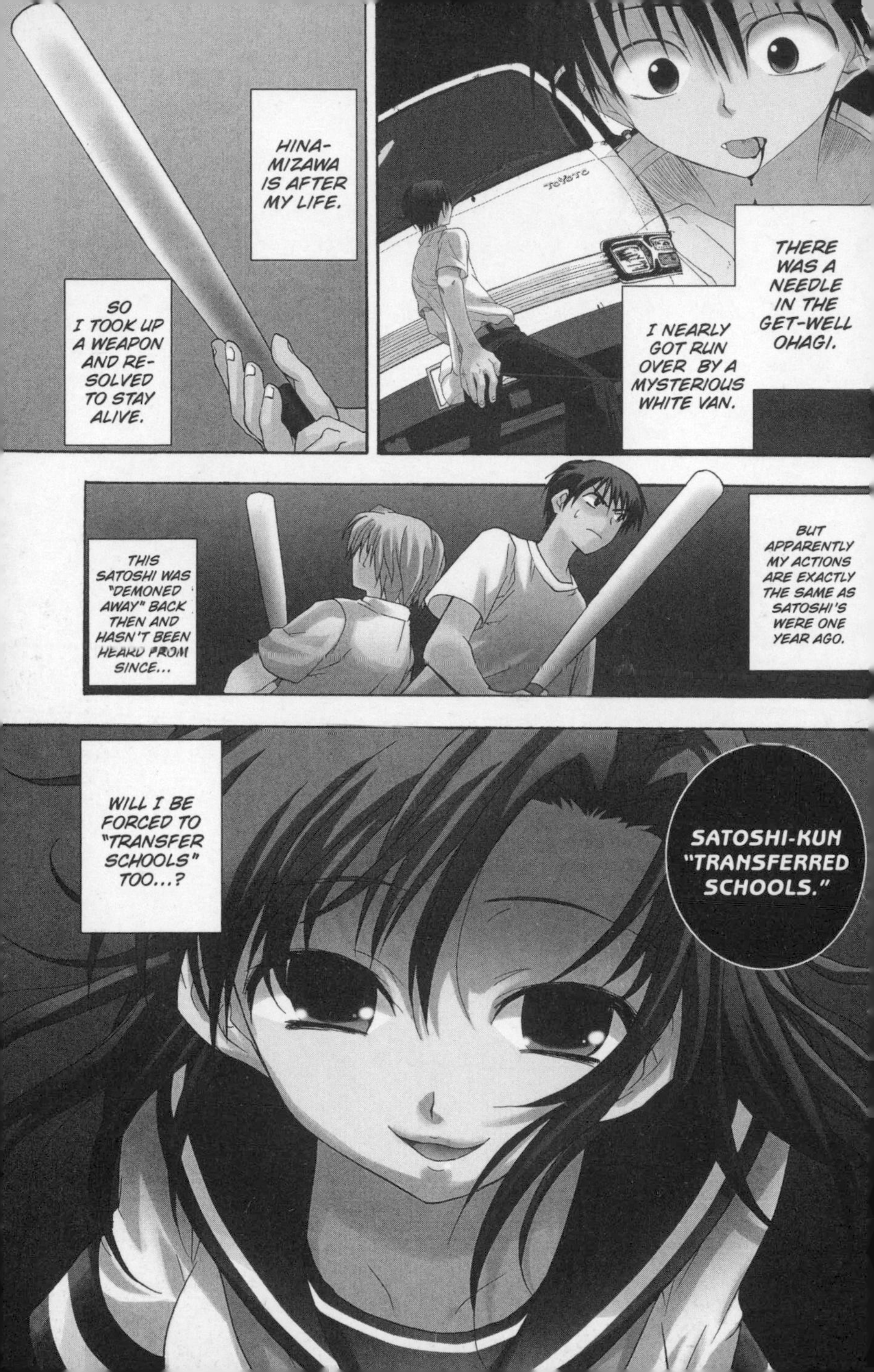
THERE WAS A NEEDLE IN THE GET-WELL OHAGI.
I NEARLY GOT RUN OVER BY A MYSTERIOUS WHITE VAN.
HINA-MIZAWA IS AFTER MY LIFE.
SO I TOOK UP A WEAPON AND RE-SOLVED TO STAY ALIVE.
BUT APPARENTLY MY ACTIONS ARE EXACTLY THE SAME AS SATOSHI'S WERE ONE YEAR AGO.
THIS SATOSHI WAS "DEMONED AWAY" BACK THEN AND HASN'T BEEN HEARD FROM SINCE...
SATOSHI-KUN "TRANSFERRED SCHOOLS."
WILL I BE FORCED TO "TRANSFER SCHOOLS" TOO...?

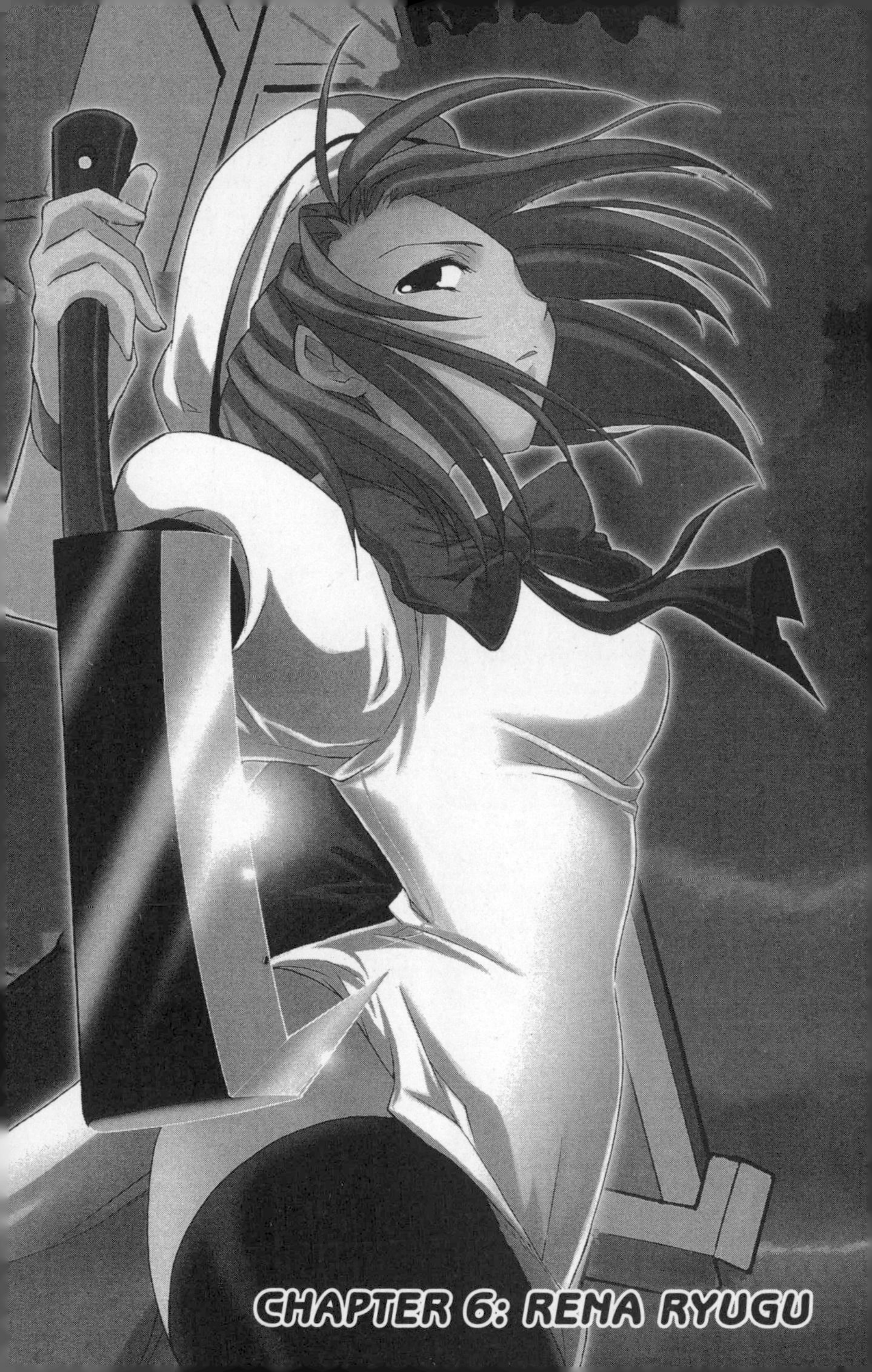
CHAPTER 6: RENA RYUGU

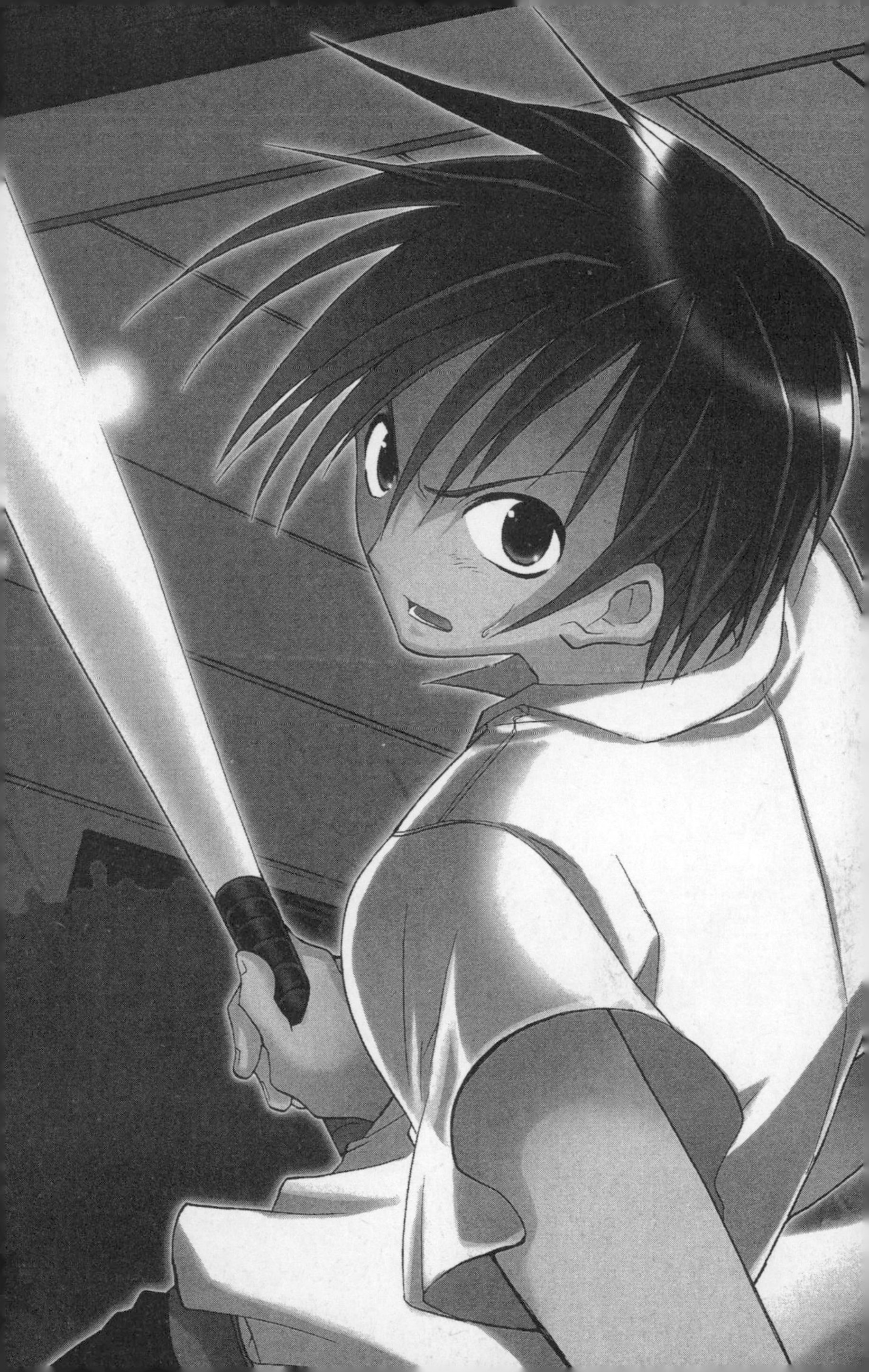

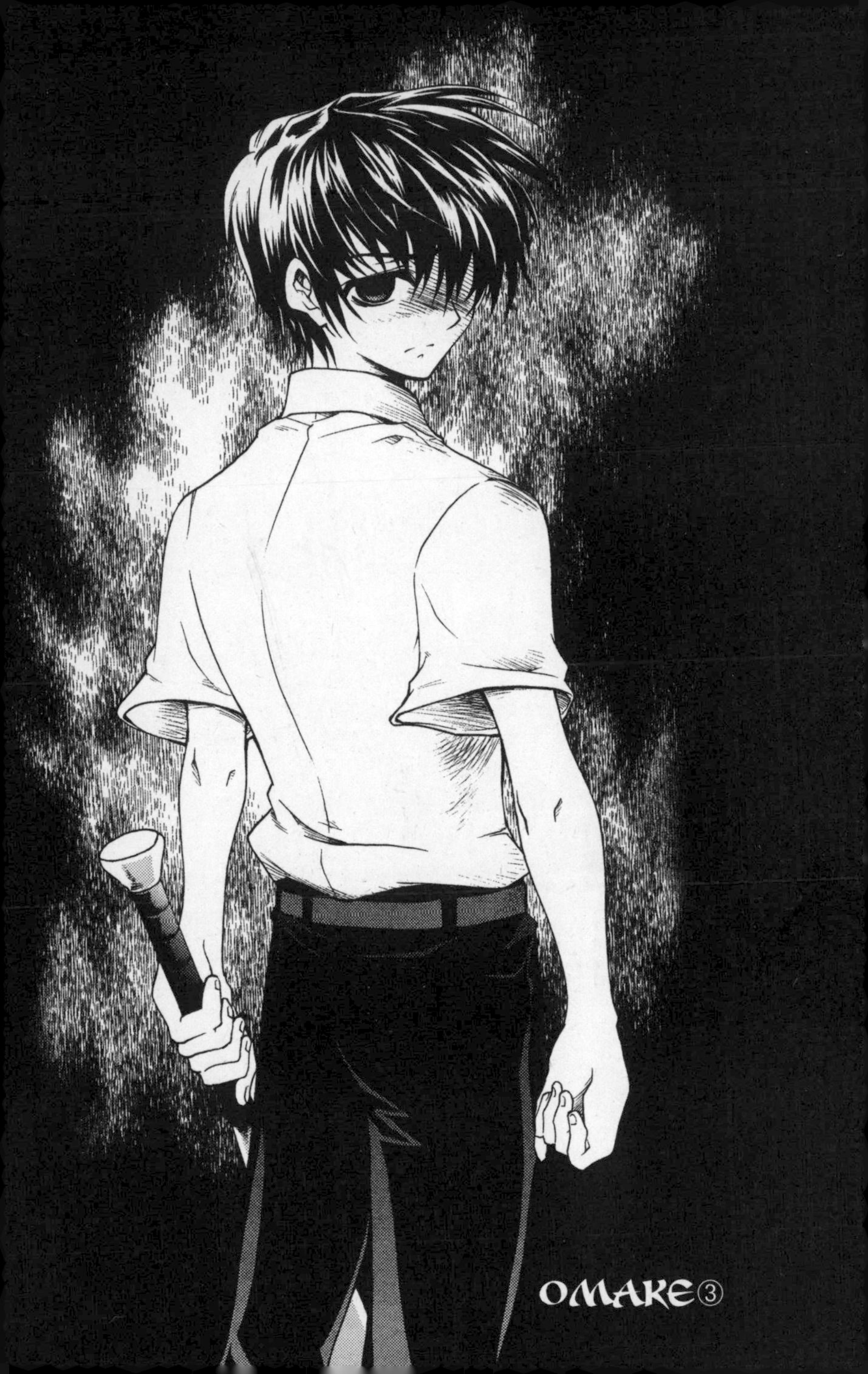
OMAKE③

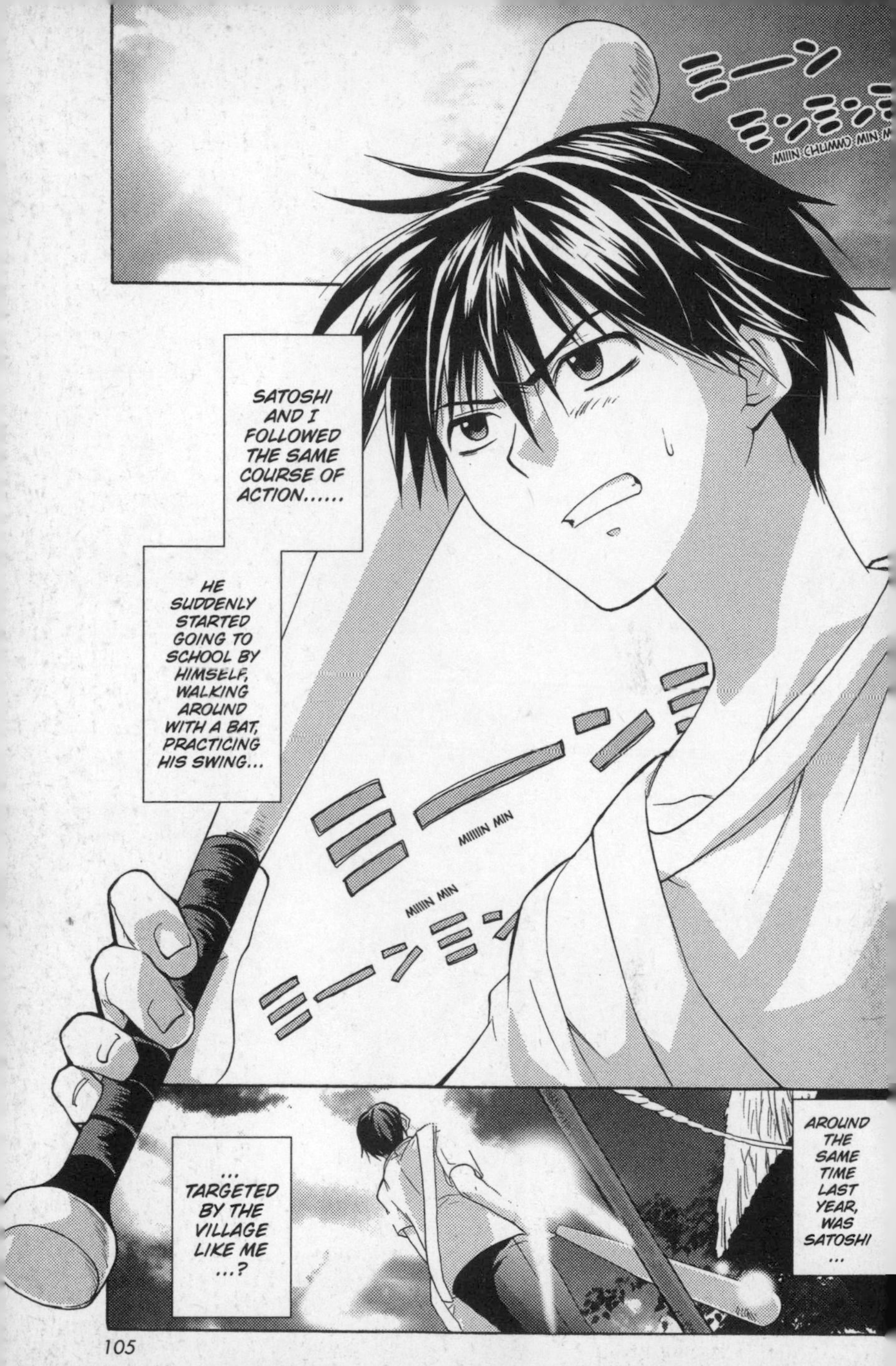
ミーン ミンミンミ
MIIIN (HUMM) MIN M
SATOSHI AND I FOLLOWED THE SAME COURSE OF ACTION......
HE SUDDENLY STARTED GOING TO SCHOOL BY HIMSELF, WALKING AROUND WITH A BAT, PRACTICING HIS SWING...
ミーン
MIIIIN MIN
MIIIIN MIN
ミーンミン
AROUND THE SAME TIME LAST YEAR, WAS SATOSHI ...
... TARGETED BY THE VILLAGE LIKE ME ...?

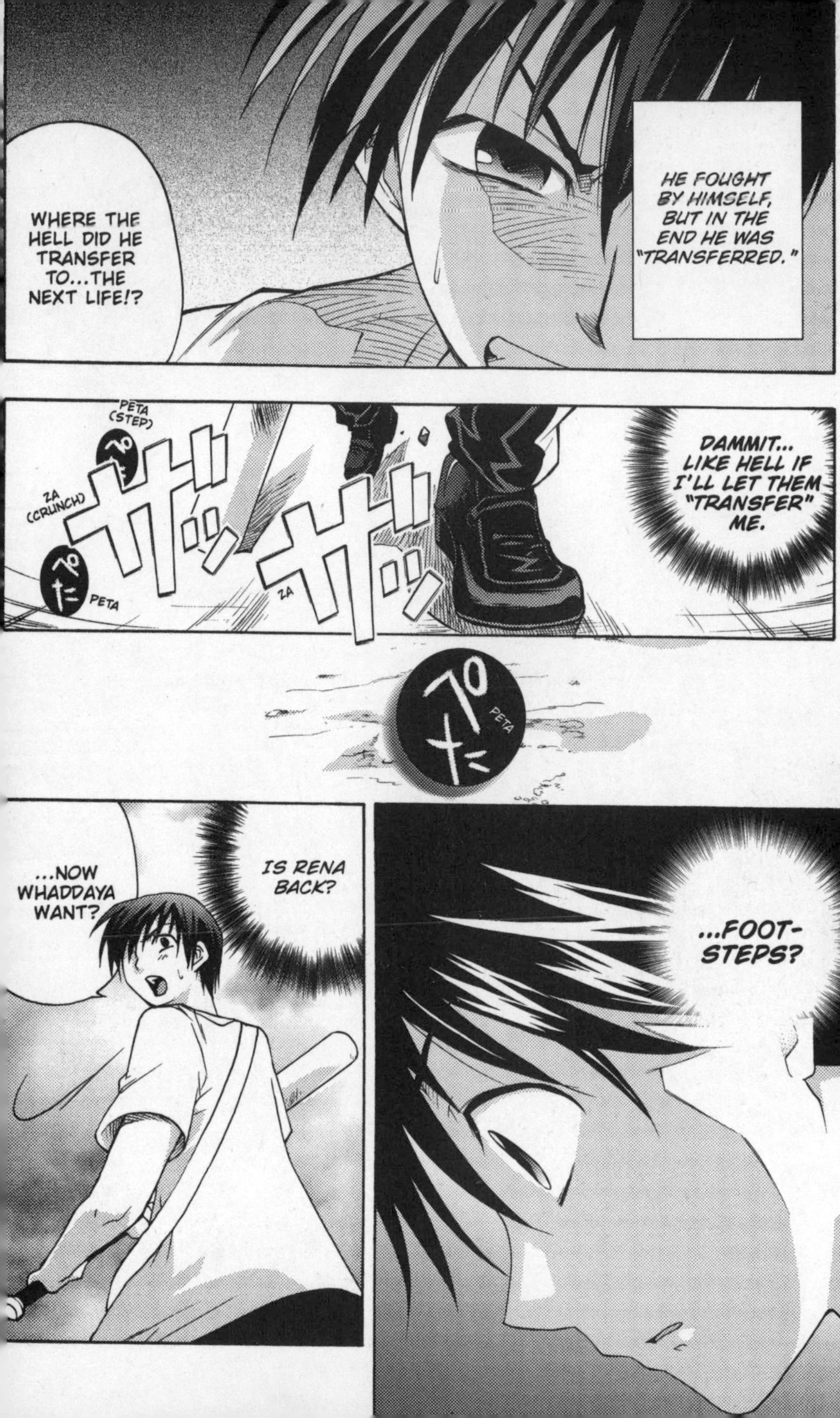

HE FOUGHT BY HIMSELF, BUT IN THE END HE WAS "TRANSFERRED."
WHERE THE HELL DID HE TRANSFER TO...THE NEXT LIFE!?
DAMMIT... LIKE HELL IF I'LL LET THEM "TRANSFER" ME.
ZA
PETA (STEP)
ZA (CRUNCH)
PETA
PETA
...FOOT-STEPS?
IS RENA BACK?
...NOW WHADDAYA WANT?

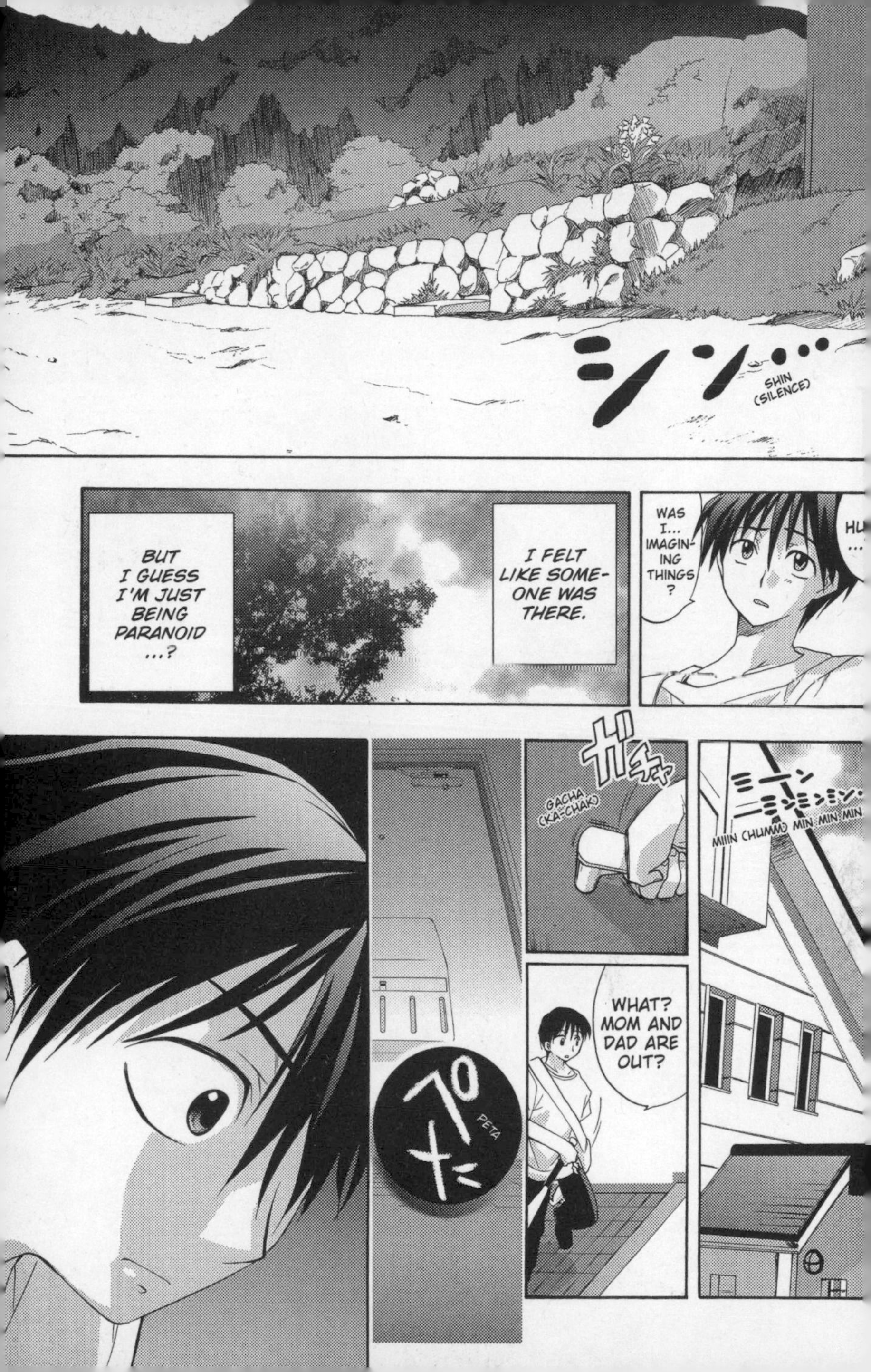
シン…
SHIN (SILENCE)
HU...
WAS I... IMAGINING THINGS?
I FELT LIKE SOME-ONE WAS THERE.
BUT I GUESS I'M JUST BEING PARANOID ...?
ミーン ミンミンミン
MIIN (CHUMM) MIN MIN MIN
ガチャ
GACHA (KA-CHAK)
WHAT? MOM AND DAD ARE OUT?
ペタ
PETA

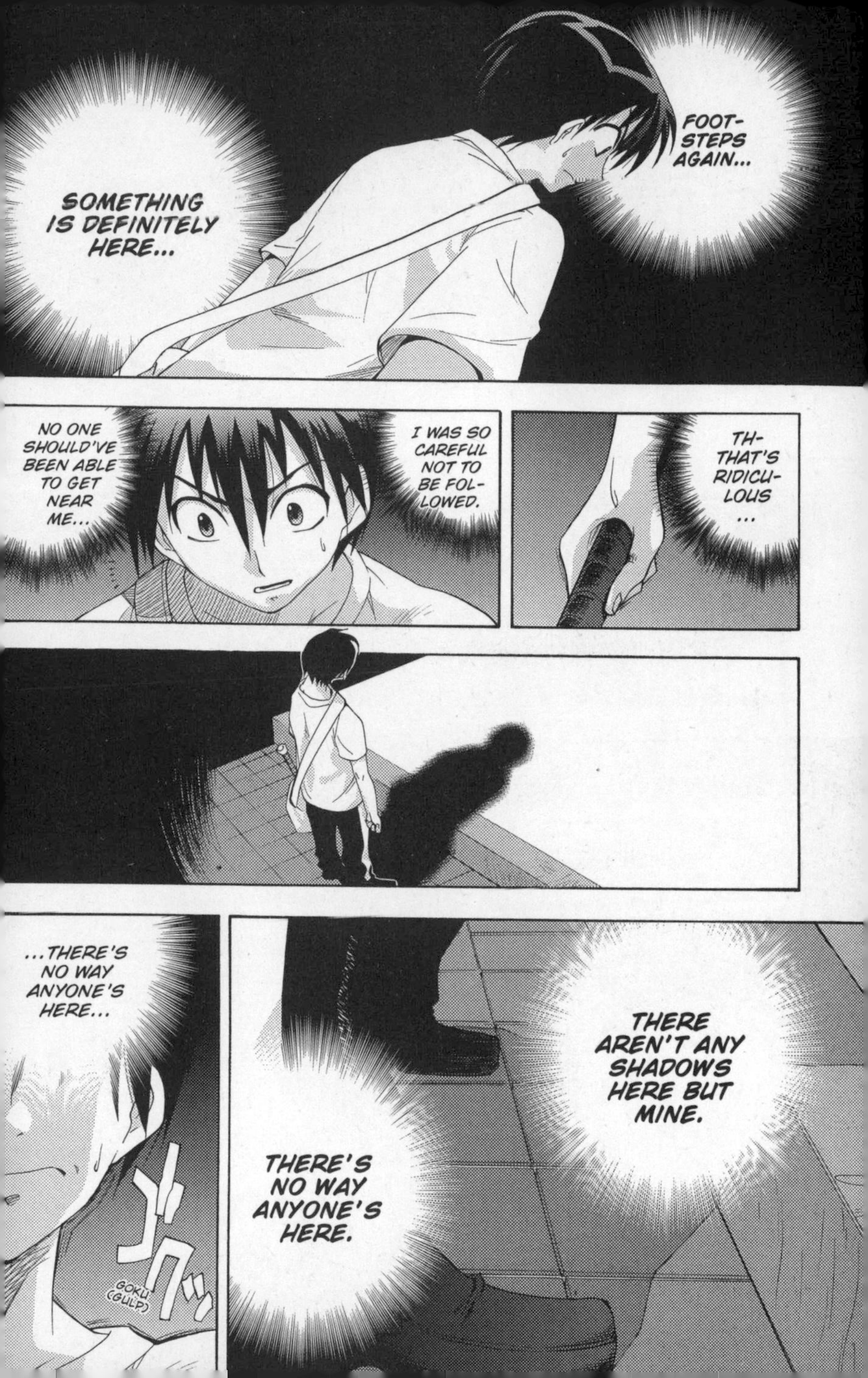
FOOTSTEPS AGAIN...
SOMETHING IS DEFINITELY HERE...
TH-THAT'S RIDICULOUS...
I WAS SO CAREFUL NOT TO BE FOLLOWED.
NO ONE SHOULD'VE BEEN ABLE TO GET NEAR ME...
THERE AREN'T ANY SHADOWS HERE BUT MINE.
THERE'S NO WAY ANYONE'S HERE.
...THERE'S NO WAY ANYONE'S HERE...
GOKU (GULP)

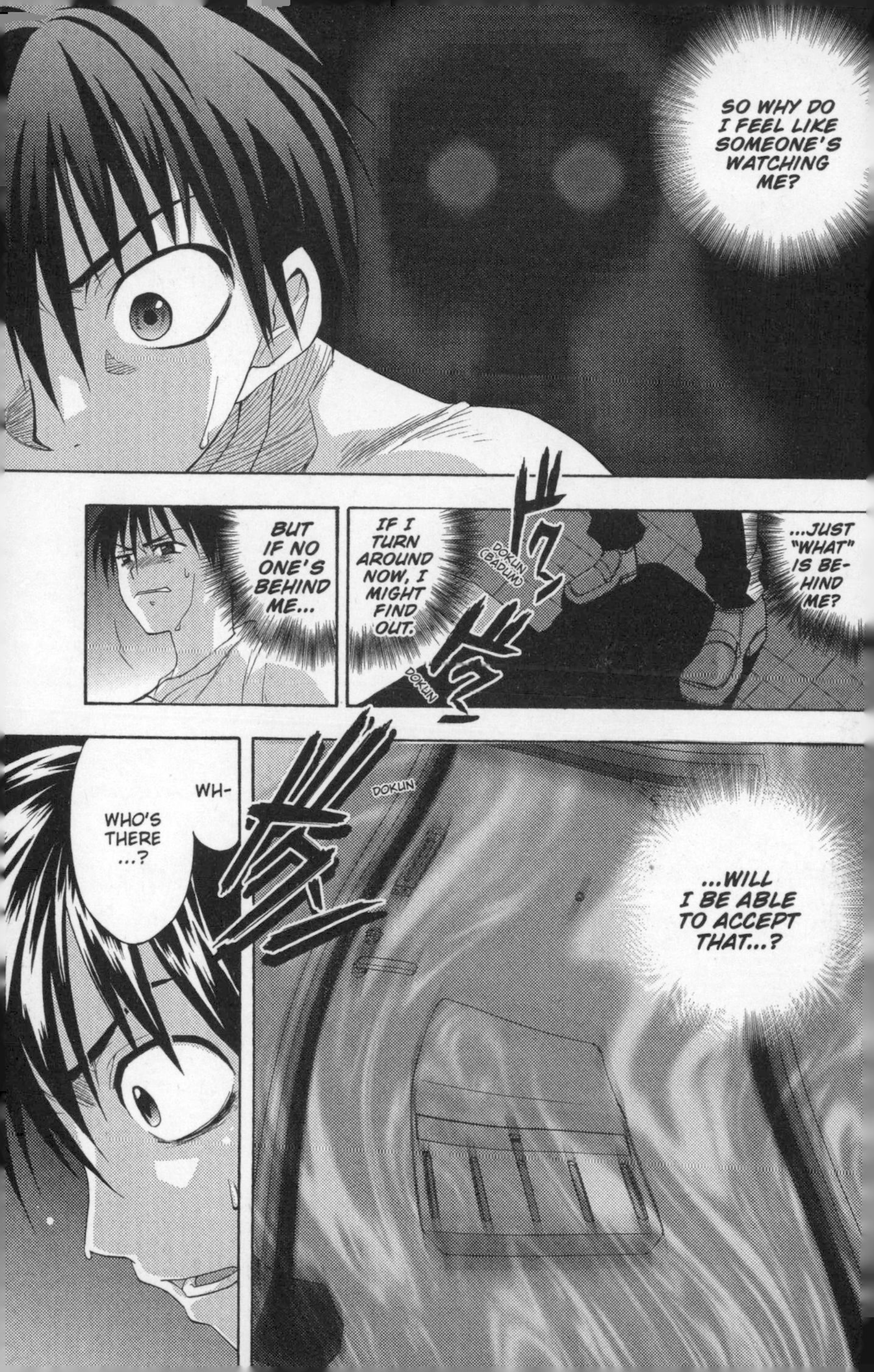
SO WHY DO I FEEL LIKE SOMEONE'S WATCHING ME?
...JUST "WHAT" IS BEHIND ME?
DOKUN (BADUM)
IF I TURN AROUND NOW, I MIGHT FIND OUT.
DOKUN
BUT IF NO ONE'S BEHIND ME...
...WILL I BE ABLE TO ACCEPT THAT...?
DOKUN
WH-
WHO'S THERE ...?

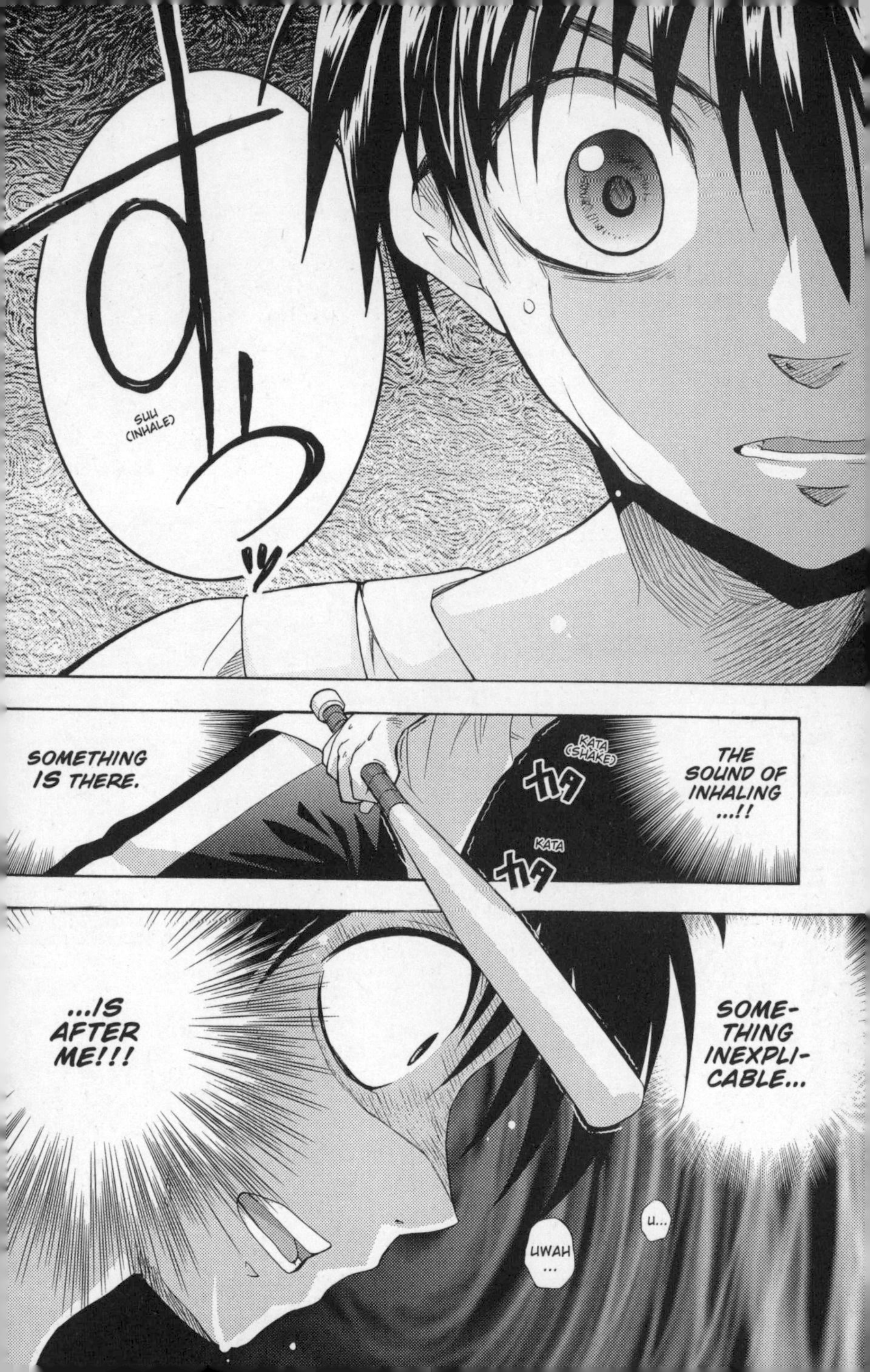
SUU (INHALE)
THE SOUND OF INHALING ...!!
KATA (SHAKE)
KATA
SOMETHING IS THERE.
SOME-THING INEXPLI-CABLE...
...IS AFTER ME!!!
U...
UWAH ...

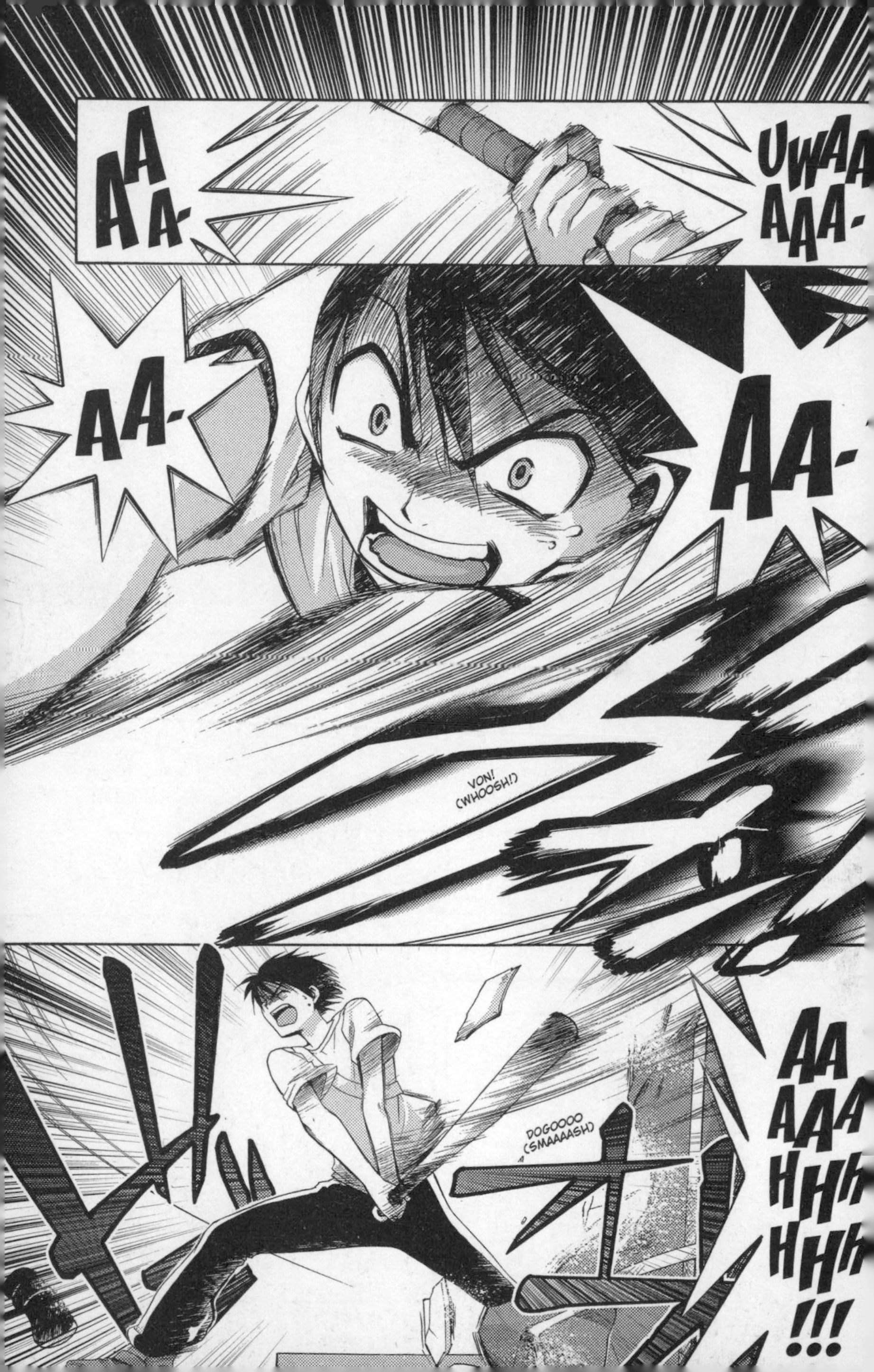
UWAAAAA-
AAA-
AA-
AA-
VON! (WHOOSH!)
AAAAAHHHHHH!!!
DOGOOOO (SMAAAASH)

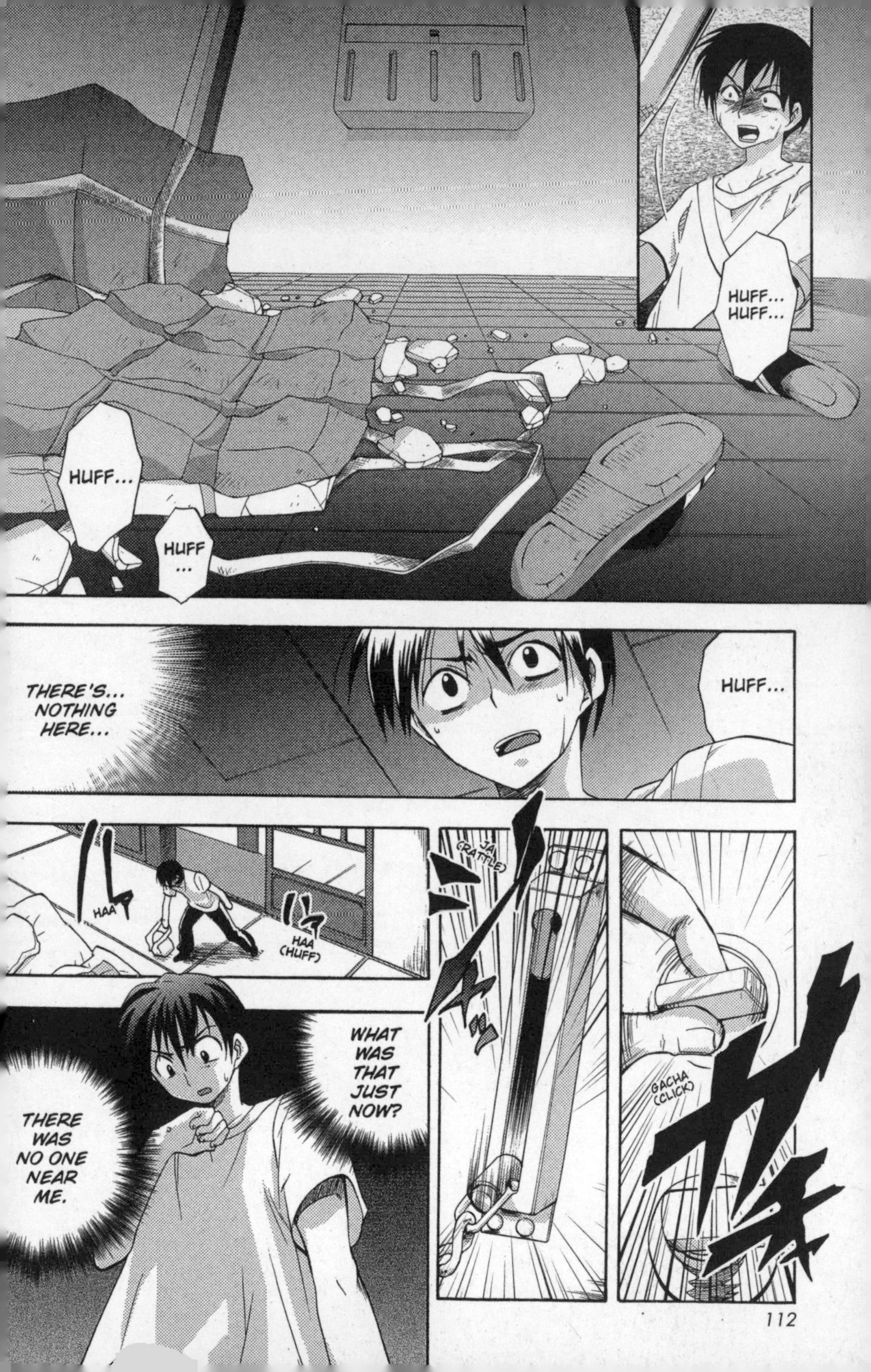
HUFF... HUFF...
HUFF...
HUFF ...
HUFF...
THERE'S... NOTHING HERE...
GACHA (CLICK)
JA (RATTLE)
HAA (HUFF)
HAA
WHAT WAS THAT JUST NOW?
THERE WAS NO ONE NEAR ME.

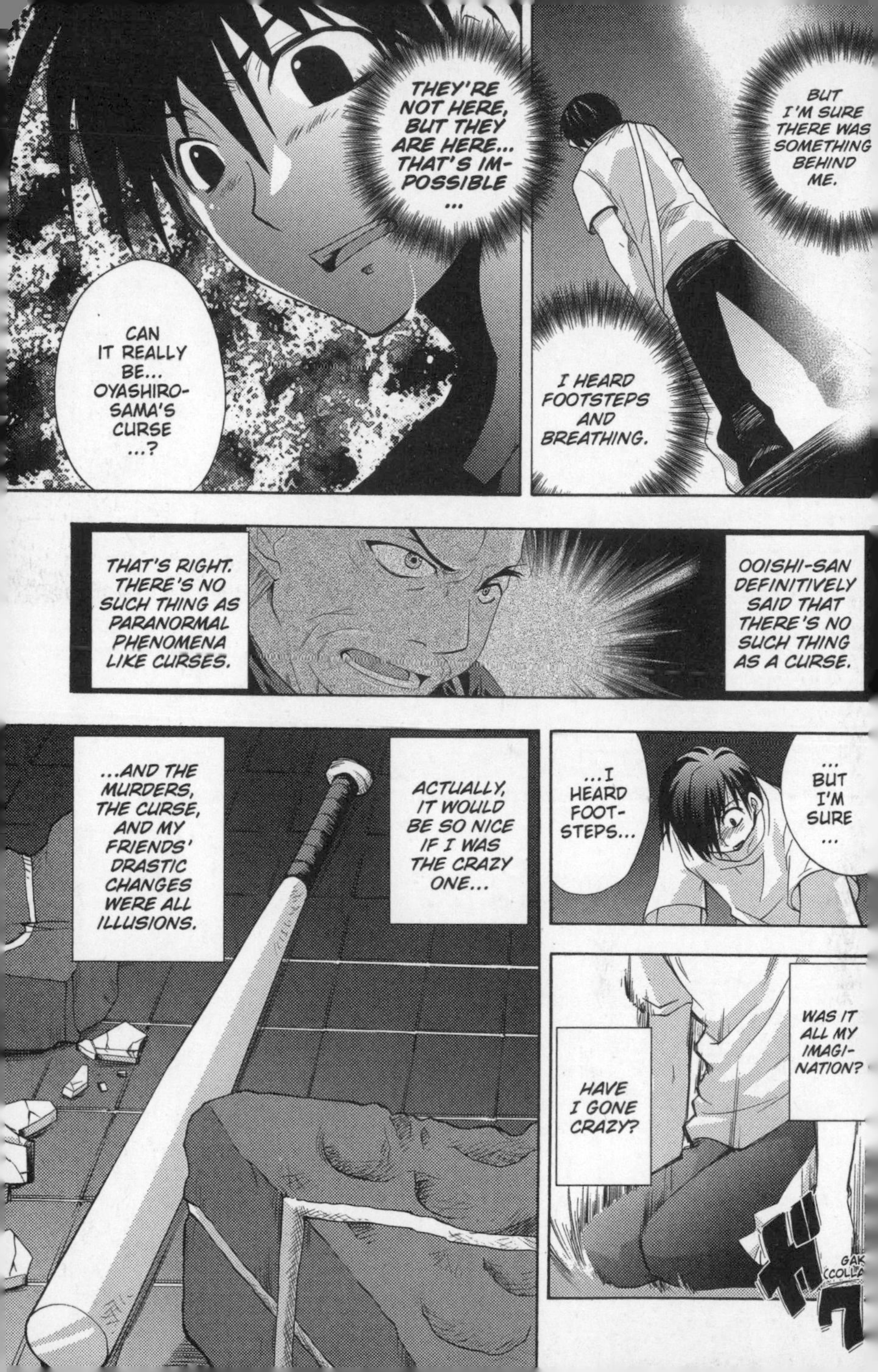
BUT I'M SURE THERE WAS SOMETHING BEHIND ME.
I HEARD FOOTSTEPS AND BREATHING.
THEY'RE NOT HERE, BUT THEY ARE HERE... THAT'S IMPOSSIBLE ...
CAN IT REALLY BE... OYASHIRO-SAMA'S CURSE ...?
OOISHI-SAN DEFINITIVELY SAID THAT THERE'S NO SUCH THING AS A CURSE.
THAT'S RIGHT. THERE'S NO SUCH THING AS PARANORMAL PHENOMENA LIKE CURSES.
... BUT I'M SURE ...
...I HEARD FOOTSTEPS...
WAS IT ALL MY IMAGINATION?
HAVE I GONE CRAZY?
GAK
ACTUALLY, IT WOULD BE SO NICE IF I WAS THE CRAZY ONE...
...AND THE MURDERS, THE CURSE, AND MY FRIENDS' DRASTIC CHANGES WERE ALL ILLUSIONS.

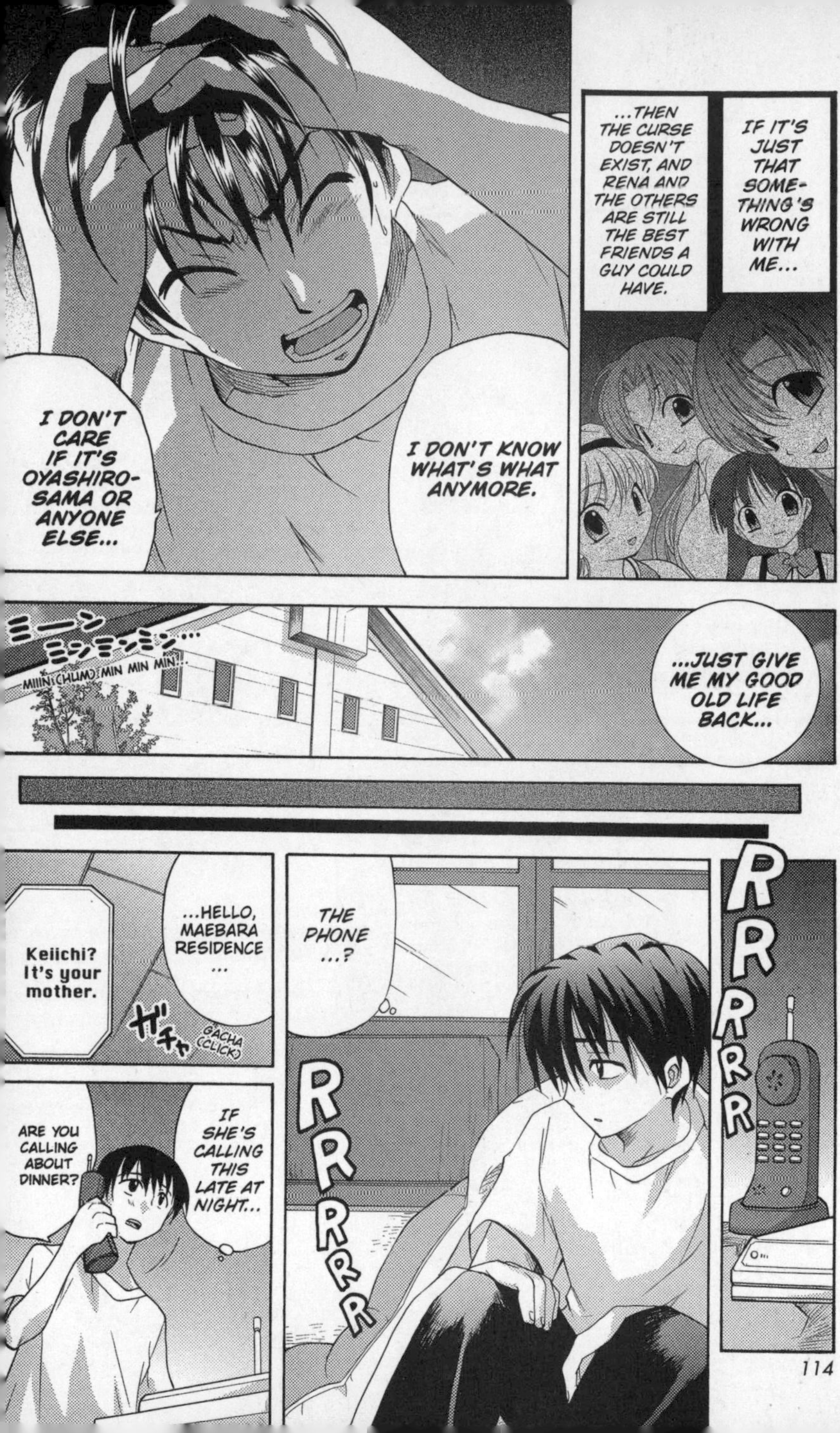
IF IT'S JUST THAT SOME-THING'S WRONG WITH ME...
...THEN THE CURSE DOESN'T EXIST, AND RENA AND THE OTHERS ARE STILL THE BEST FRIENDS A GUY COULD HAVE.
I DON'T KNOW WHAT'S WHAT ANYMORE.
I DON'T CARE IF IT'S OYASHIRO-SAMA OR ANYONE ELSE...
...JUST GIVE ME MY GOOD OLD LIFE BACK...
ミーン ミンミンミン…
MIIIN (HUM) MIN MIN MIN...
RRRRR
THE PHONE ...?
RRRRR
...HELLO, MAEBARA RESIDENCE ...
ガチャ
GACHA (CLICK)
Keiichi? It's your mother.
IF SHE'S CALLING THIS LATE AT NIGHT...
ARE YOU CALLING ABOUT DINNER?

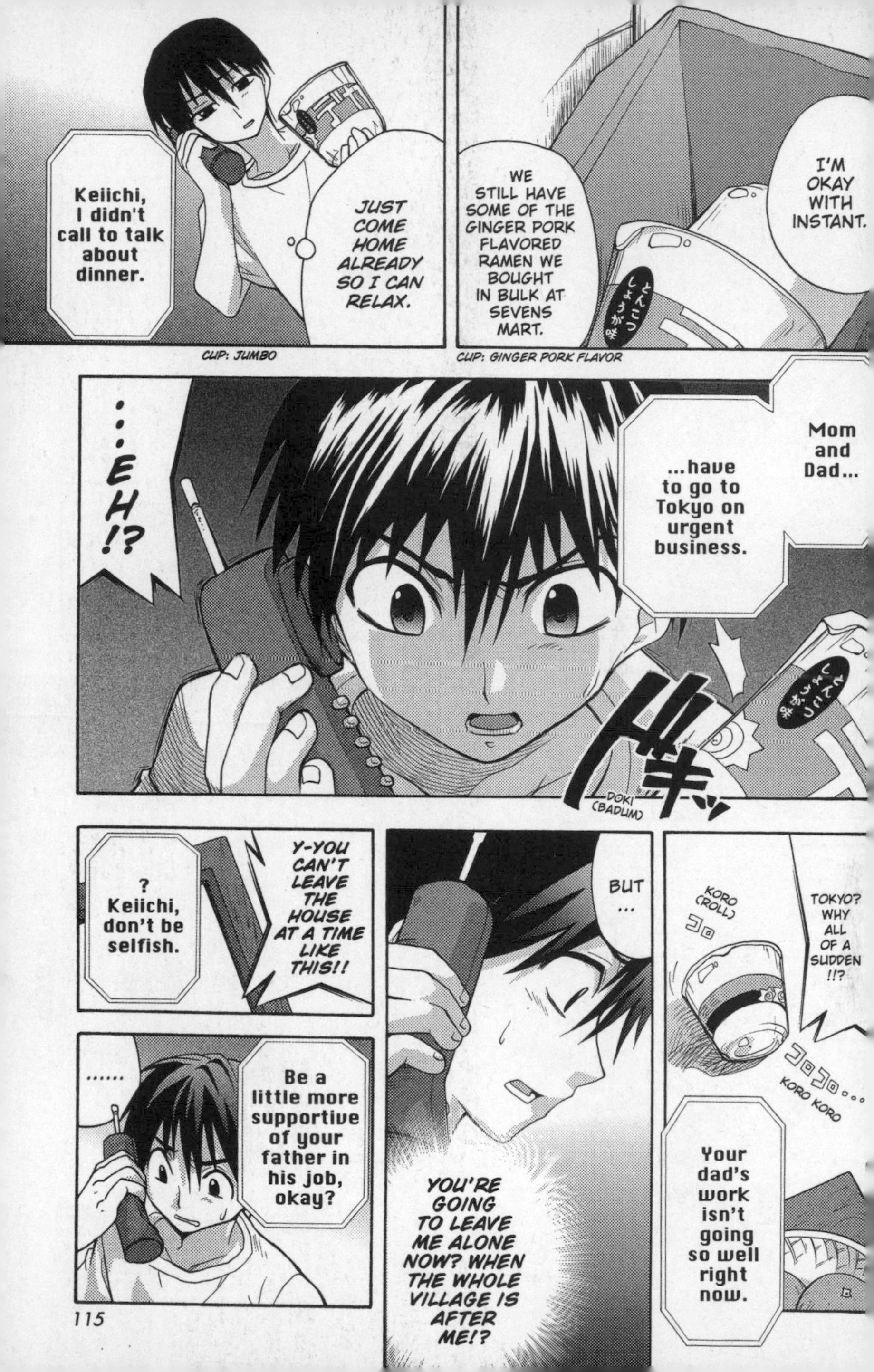
I'M OKAY WITH INSTANT.
WE STILL HAVE SOME OF THE GINGER PORK FLAVORED RAMEN WE BOUGHT IN BULK AT SEVENS MART.
CUP: GINGER PORK FLAVOR
JUST COME HOME ALREADY SO I CAN RELAX.
Keiichi, I didn't call to talk about dinner.
CUP: JUMBO
Mom and Dad...
...have to go to Tokyo on urgent business.
DOKI (BADUM)
...EH!?
TOKYO? WHY ALL OF A SUDDEN!?
KORO (ROLL)
KORO KORO
Your dad's work isn't going so well right now.
BUT...
YOU'RE GOING TO LEAVE ME ALONE NOW? WHEN THE WHOLE VILLAGE IS AFTER ME!?
Y-YOU CAN'T LEAVE THE HOUSE AT A TIME LIKE THIS!!
? Keiichi, don't be selfish.
Be a little more supportive of your father in his job, okay?
......

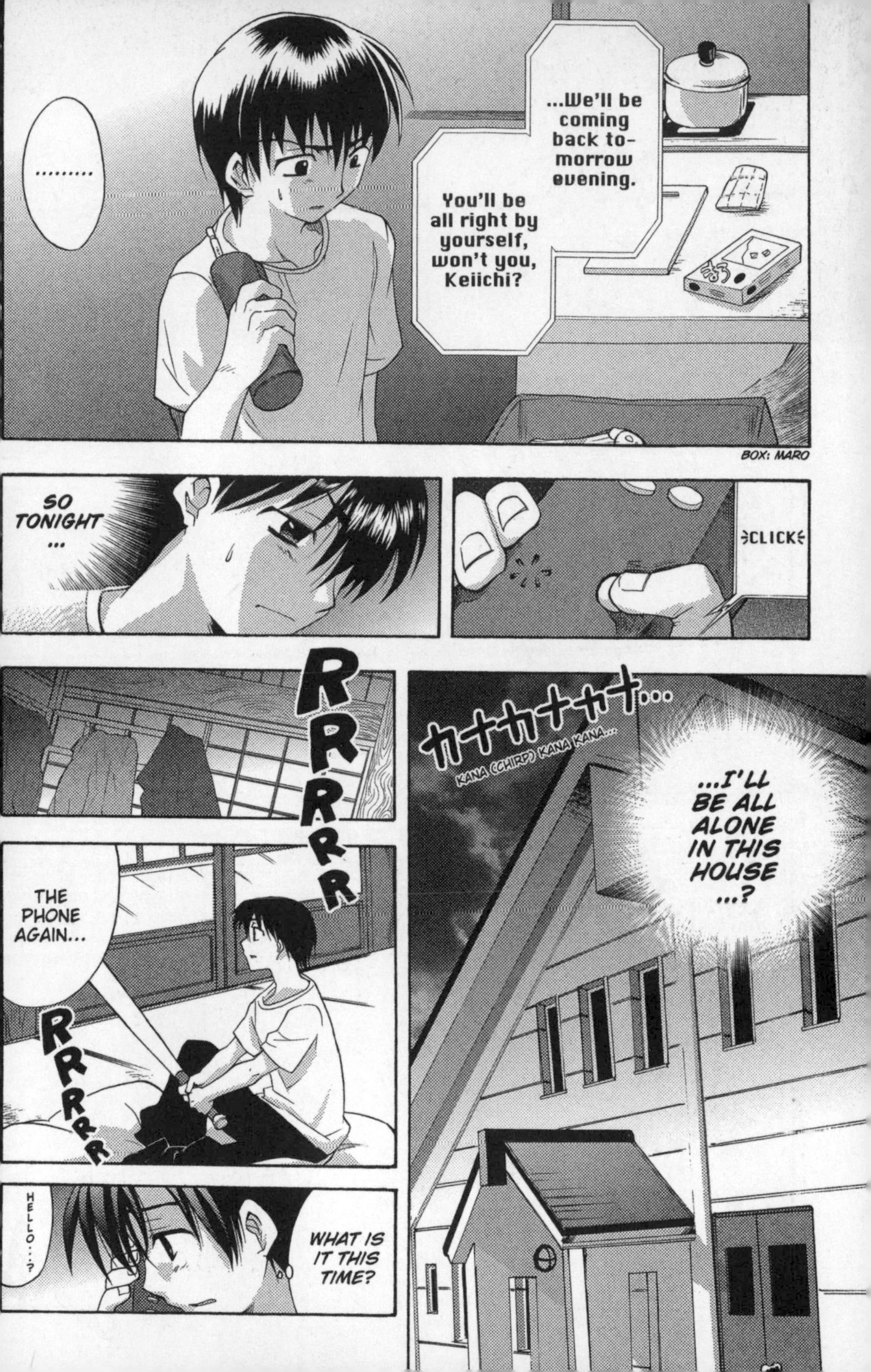
...We'll be coming back to-morrow evening.
You'll be all right by yourself, won't you, Keiichi?
....
BOX: MARO
CLICK
SO TONIGHT ...
カナカナカナ...
KANA (CHIRP) KANA KANA...
...I'LL BE ALL ALONE IN THIS HOUSE ...?
RRRRR
THE PHONE AGAIN...
RRRRR
WHAT IS IT THIS TIME?
HELLO...?

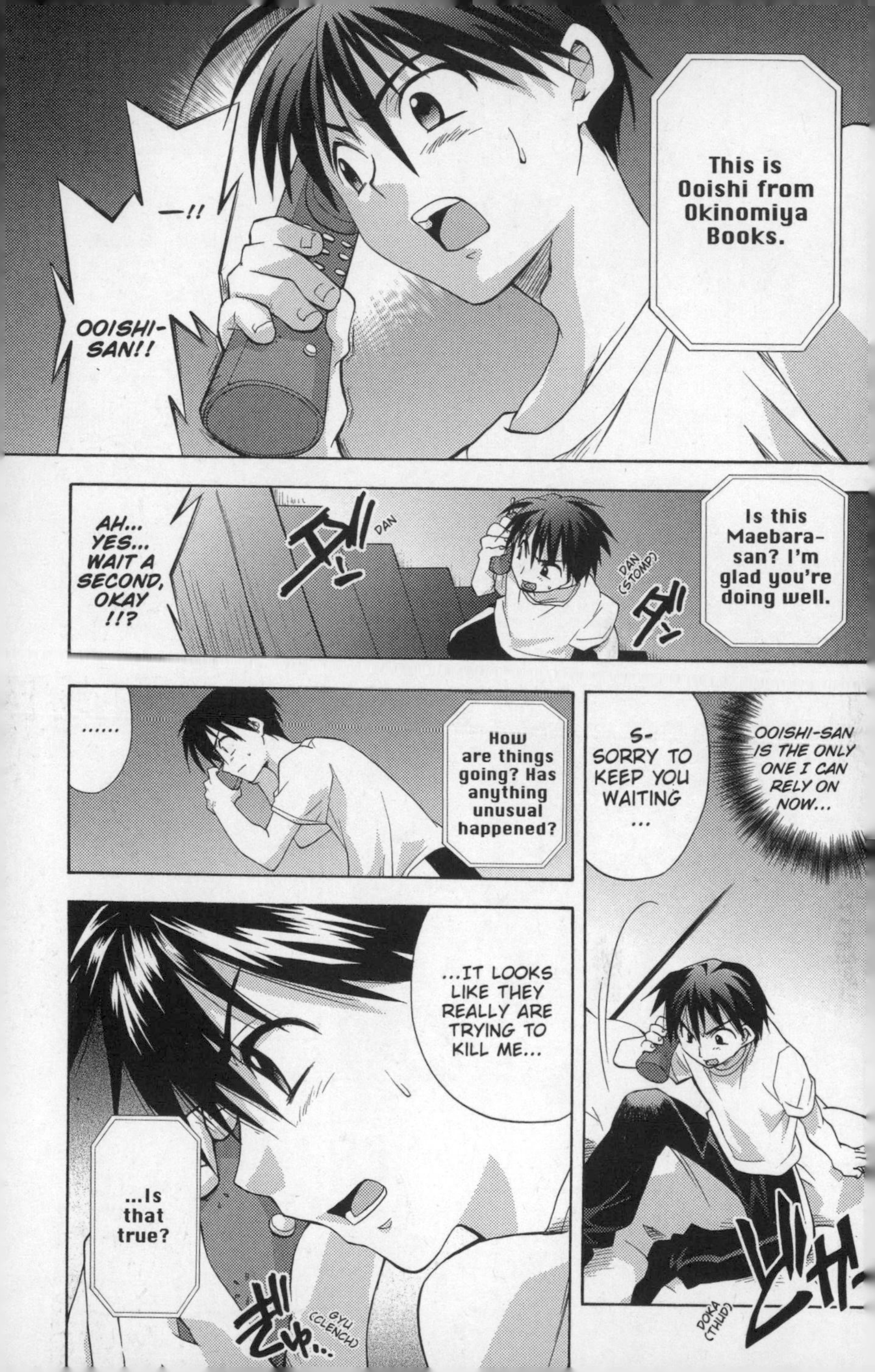
This is Ooishi from Okinomiya Books.
—!!
OOISHI-SAN!!
Is this Maebara-san? I'm glad you're doing well.
DAN (STOMP)
DAN
AH... YES... WAIT A SECOND, OKAY!!?
OOISHI-SAN IS THE ONLY ONE I CAN RELY ON NOW...
S- SORRY TO KEEP YOU WAITING ...
DOKA (THUD)
How are things going? Has anything unusual happened?
......
...IT LOOKS LIKE THEY REALLY ARE TRYING TO KILL ME...
...Is that true?
GYU (CLENCH)

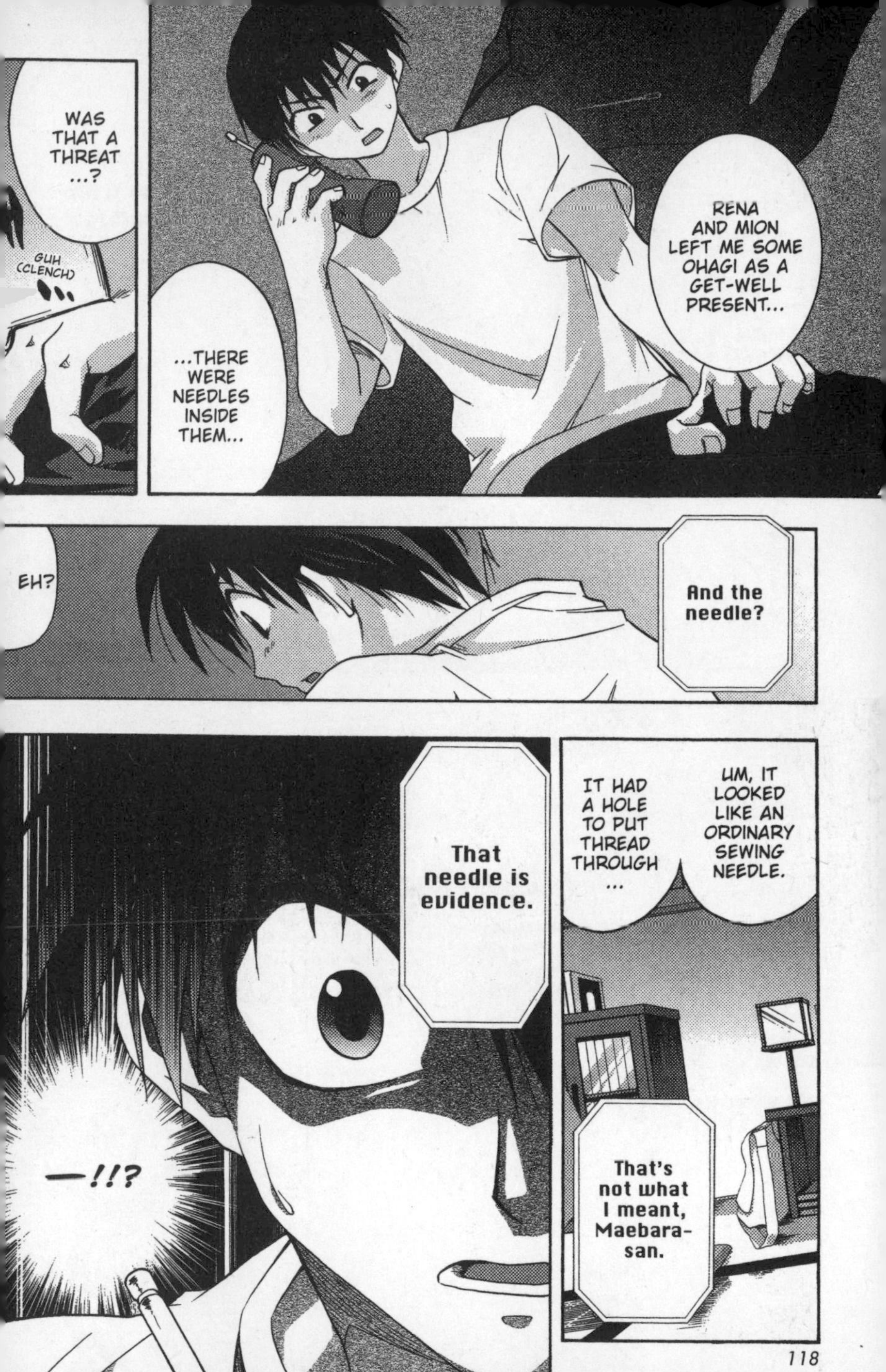
RENA AND MION LEFT ME SOME OHAGI AS A GET-WELL PRESENT...
...THERE WERE NEEDLES INSIDE THEM...
WAS THAT A THREAT ...?
GUH (CLENCH)
And the needle?
EH?
UM, IT LOOKED LIKE AN ORDINARY SEWING NEEDLE.
IT HAD A HOLE TO PUT THREAD THROUGH ...
That's not what I meant, Maebara-san.
That needle is evidence.
—!!?

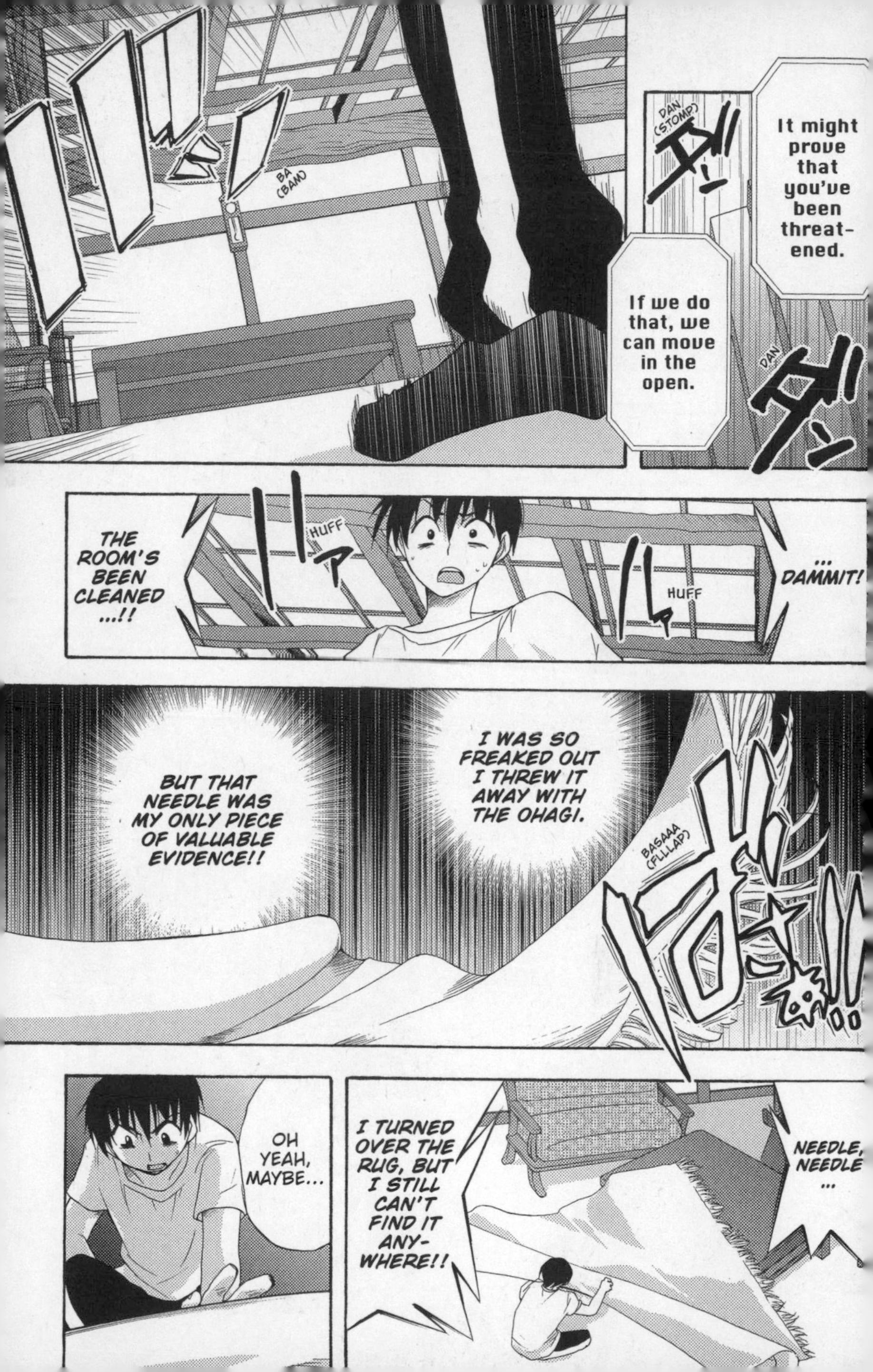

It might prove that you've been threatened.
DAN (STOMP)
DAN
If we do that, we can move in the open.
BA (BAM)
... DAMMIT!
HUFF
HUFF
THE ROOM'S BEEN CLEANED ...!!
BASAAA (FLLLAP)
I WAS SO FREAKED OUT I THREW IT AWAY WITH THE OHAGI.
BUT THAT NEEDLE WAS MY ONLY PIECE OF VALUABLE EVIDENCE!!
NEEDLE, NEEDLE ...
I TURNED OVER THE RUG, BUT I STILL CAN'T FIND IT ANYWHERE!!
OH YEAH, MAYBE...

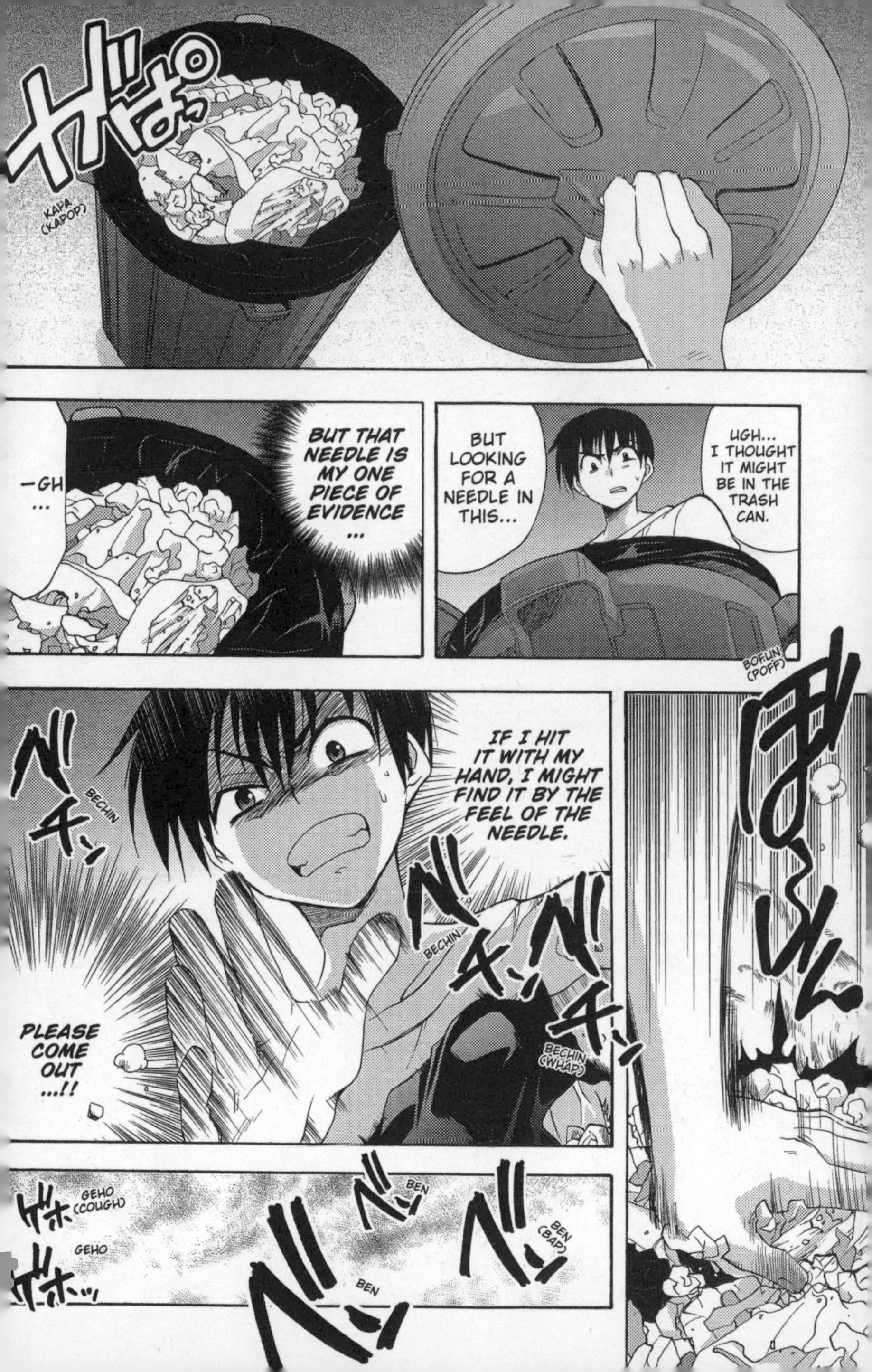
KAPA (KAPOP)
UGH... I THOUGHT IT MIGHT BE IN THE TRASH CAN.
BUT LOOKING FOR A NEEDLE IN THIS...
BUT THAT NEEDLE IS MY ONE PIECE OF EVIDENCE ...
-GH ...
BOFUN (POFF)
IF I HIT IT WITH MY HAND, I MIGHT FIND IT BY THE FEEL OF THE NEEDLE.
BECHIN
BECHIN
BECHIN (WHAP)
PLEASE COME OUT ...!!
BEN
BEN (BAP)
BEN
GEHO (COUGH)
GEHO

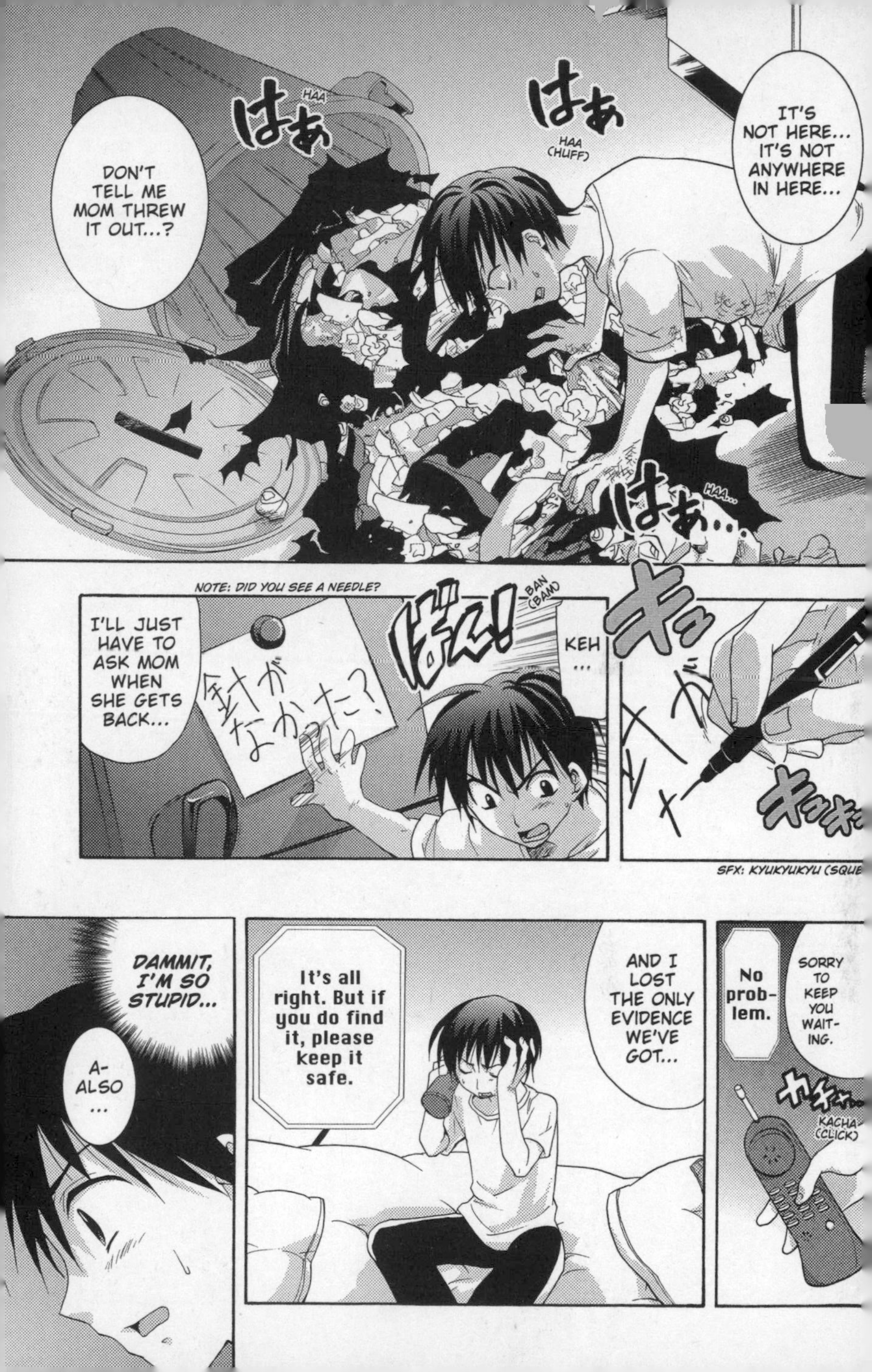
IT'S NOT HERE... IT'S NOT ANYWHERE IN HERE...
はぁ
HAA (HUFF)
はぁ
HAA
DON'T TELL ME MOM THREW IT OUT...?
はぁ...
HAA...
SFX: KYUKYUKYU (SQUE
ばん!
BAN (BAM)
KEH...
針がなかった?
NOTE: DID YOU SEE A NEEDLE?
I'LL JUST HAVE TO ASK MOM WHEN SHE GETS BACK...
SORRY TO KEEP YOU WAITING.
No problem.
KACHA (CLICK)
AND I LOST THE ONLY EVIDENCE WE'VE GOT...
It's all right. But if you do find it, please keep it safe.
DAMMIT, I'M SO STUPID...
A- ALSO...

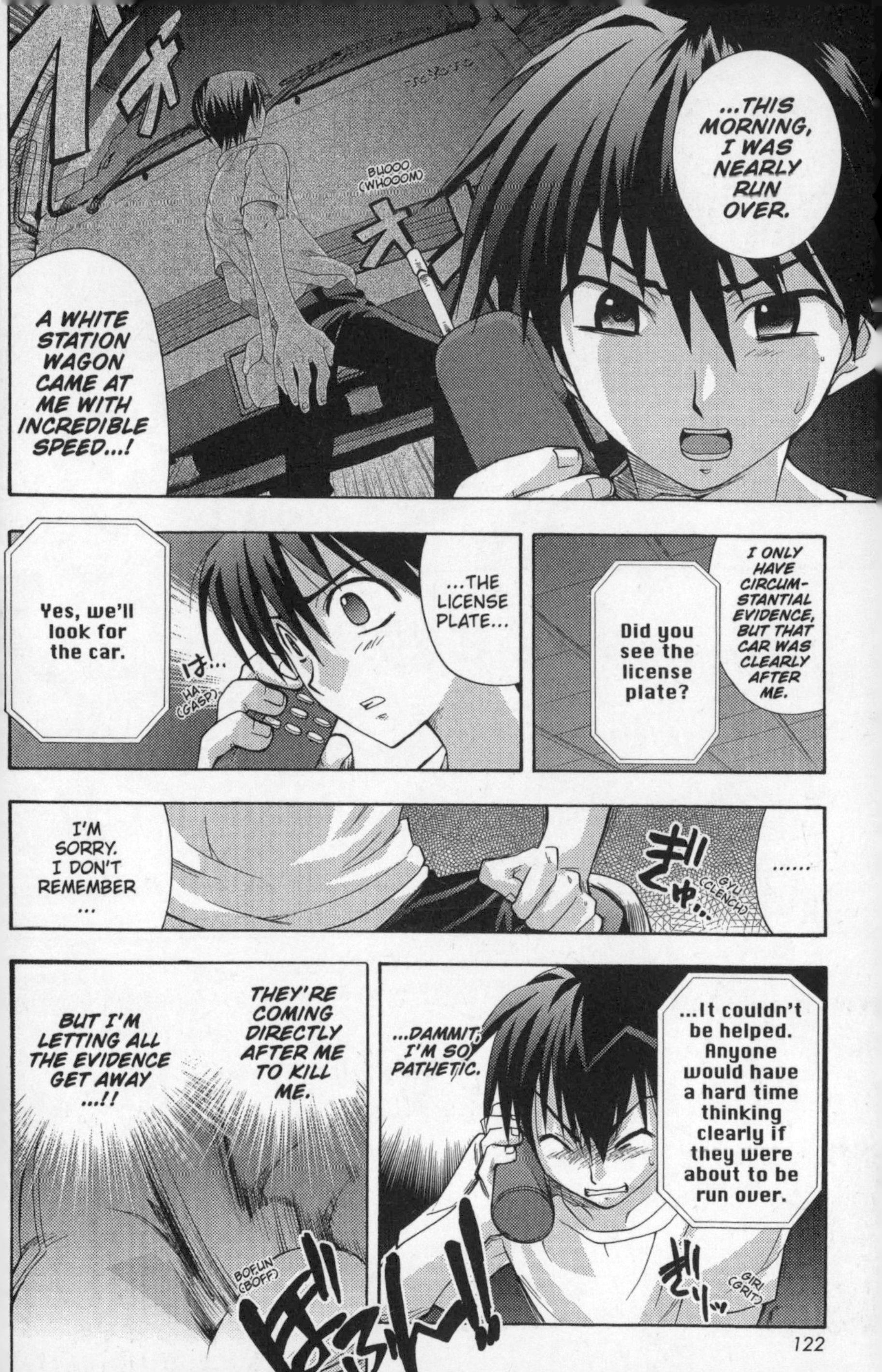
...THIS MORNING, I WAS NEARLY RUN OVER.
BUOOO (WHOOOM)
A WHITE STATION WAGON CAME AT ME WITH INCREDIBLE SPEED...!
I ONLY HAVE CIRCUM-STANTIAL EVIDENCE, BUT THAT CAR WAS CLEARLY AFTER ME.
Did you see the license plate?
...THE LICENSE PLATE...
は... HA (GASP)
Yes, we'll look for the car.
......
ぎゅ... GYU (CLENCH)
I'M SORRY. I DON'T REMEMBER ...
...It couldn't be helped. Anyone would have a hard time thinking clearly if they were about to be run over.
...DAMMIT, I'M SO PATHETIC.
ぎり GIRI (GRIT)
THEY'RE COMING DIRECTLY AFTER ME TO KILL ME.
BUT I'M LETTING ALL THE EVIDENCE GET AWAY ...!!
ぼふん BOFUN (BOFF)

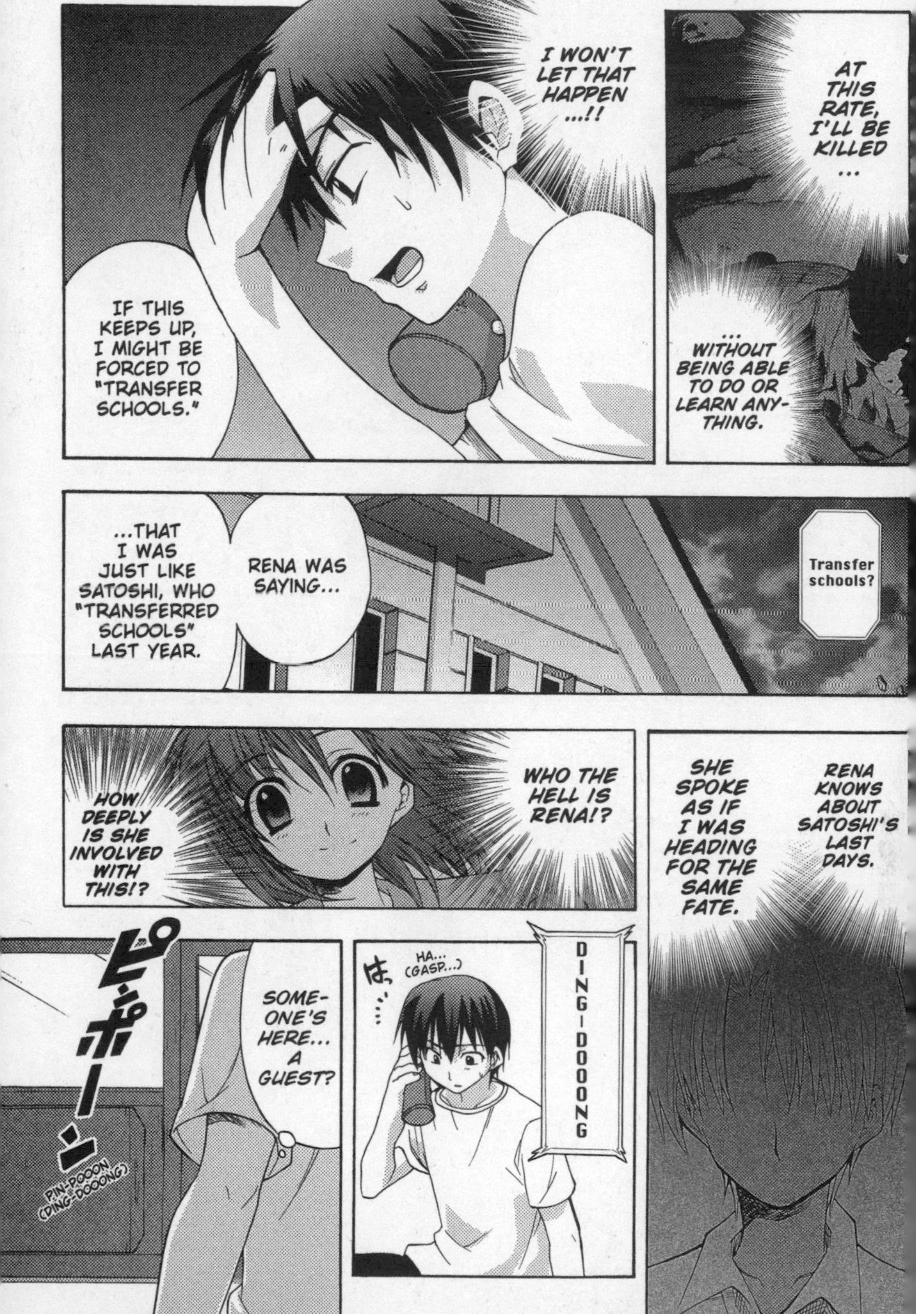
AT THIS RATE, I'LL BE KILLED...
...WITHOUT BEING ABLE TO DO OR LEARN ANY-THING.
I WON'T LET THAT HAPPEN...!!
IF THIS KEEPS UP, I MIGHT BE FORCED TO "TRANSFER SCHOOLS."
Transfer schools?
RENA WAS SAYING...
...THAT I WAS JUST LIKE SATOSHI, WHO "TRANSFERRED SCHOOLS" LAST YEAR.
RENA KNOWS ABOUT SATOSHI'S LAST DAYS.
SHE SPOKE AS IF I WAS HEADING FOR THE SAME FATE.
WHO THE HELL IS RENA!?
HOW DEEPLY IS SHE INVOLVED WITH THIS!?
DING-DOOONG
HA... (GASP...)
SOME-ONE'S HERE... A GUEST?
PIN-POOON (DING-DOOONG)

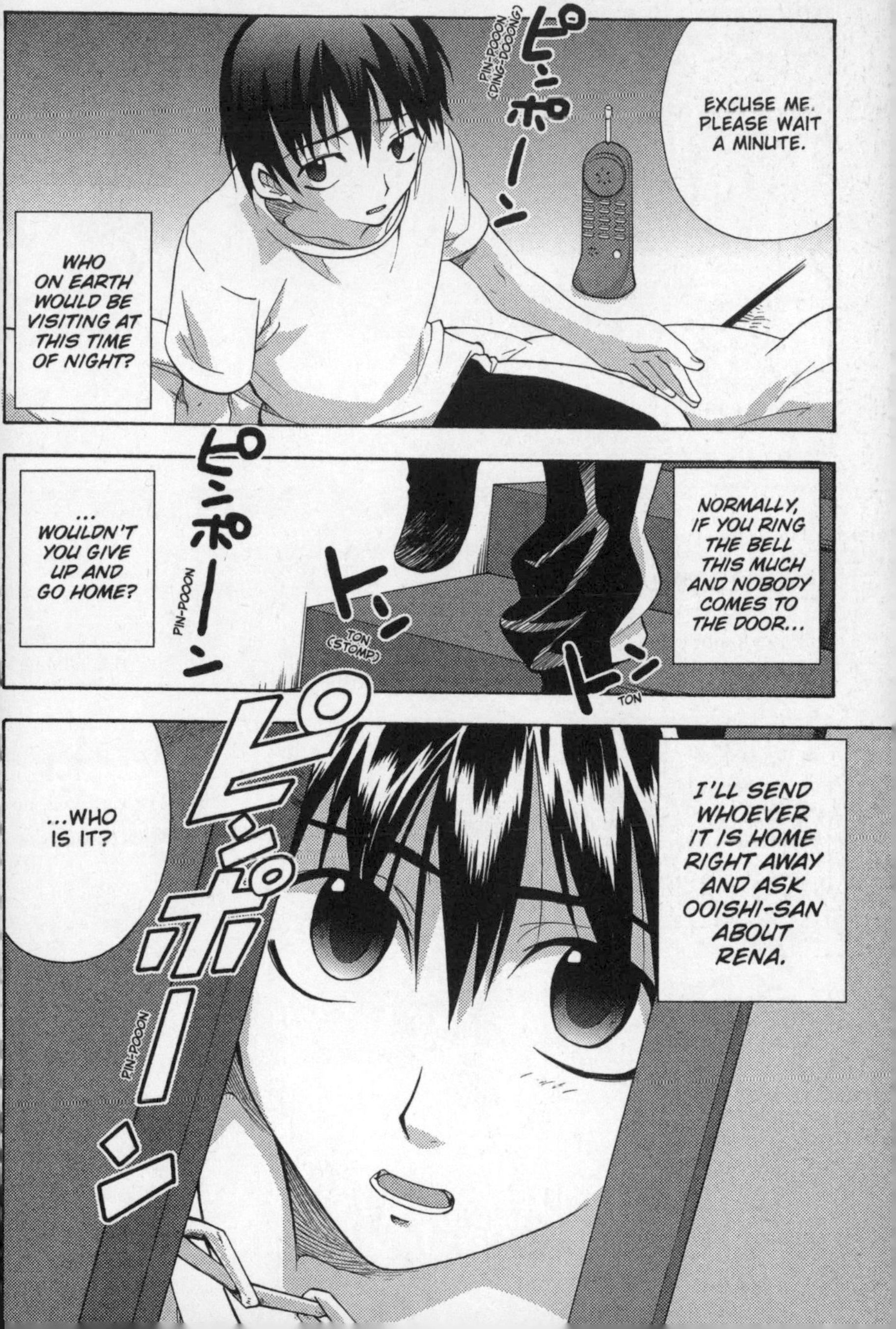
EXCUSE ME. PLEASE WAIT A MINUTE.
PIN-POOON (DING-DOOONG)
WHO ON EARTH WOULD BE VISITING AT THIS TIME OF NIGHT?
NORMALLY, IF YOU RING THE BELL THIS MUCH AND NOBODY COMES TO THE DOOR...
TON
TON (STOMP)
PIN-POOON
...WOULDN'T YOU GIVE UP AND GO HOME?
I'LL SEND WHOEVER IT IS HOME RIGHT AWAY AND ASK OOISHI-SAN ABOUT RENA.
PIN-POOON
...WHO IS IT?

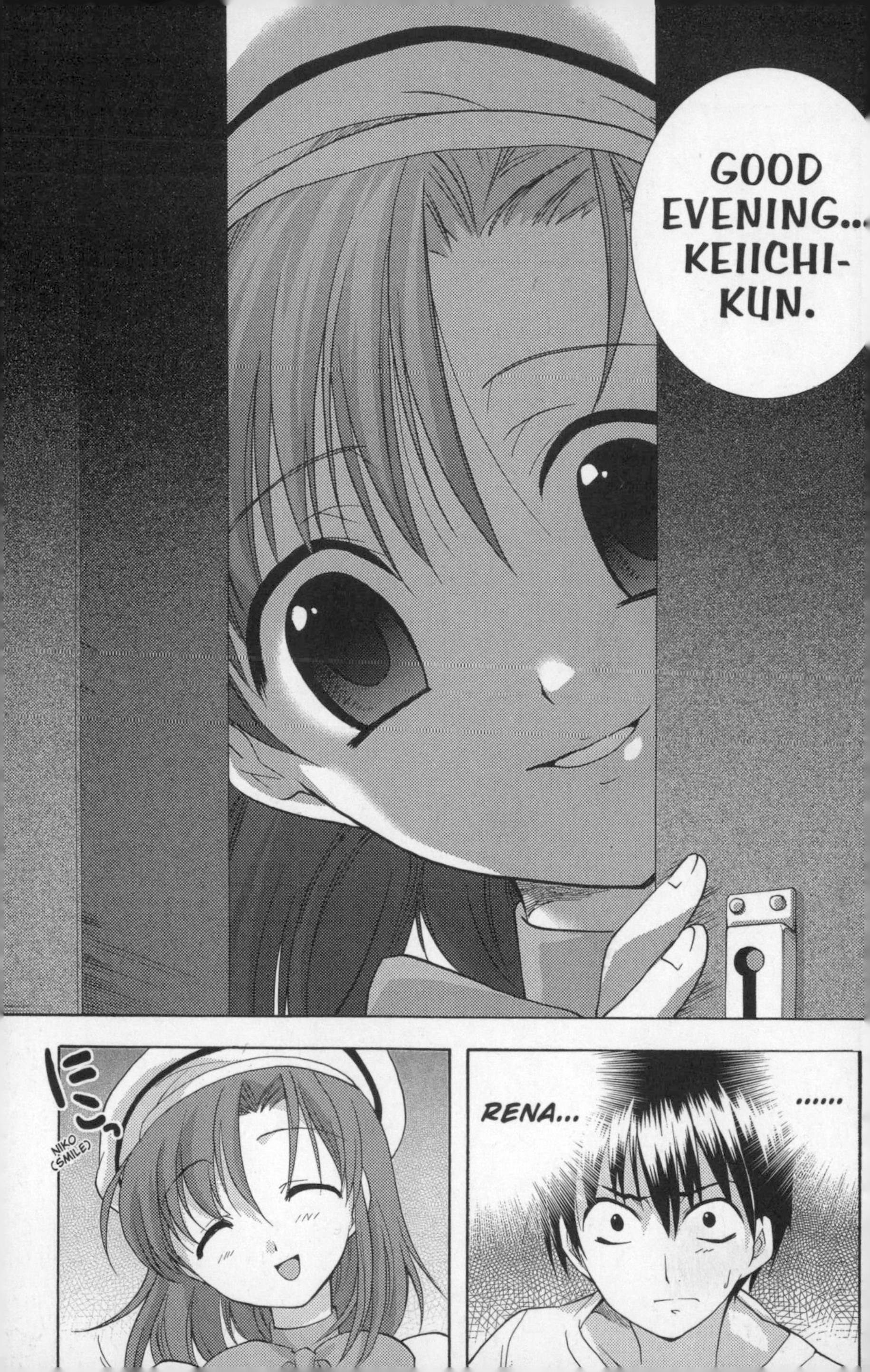
GOOD EVENING... KEIICHI-KUN.
......
RENA...
NIKO (SMILE)

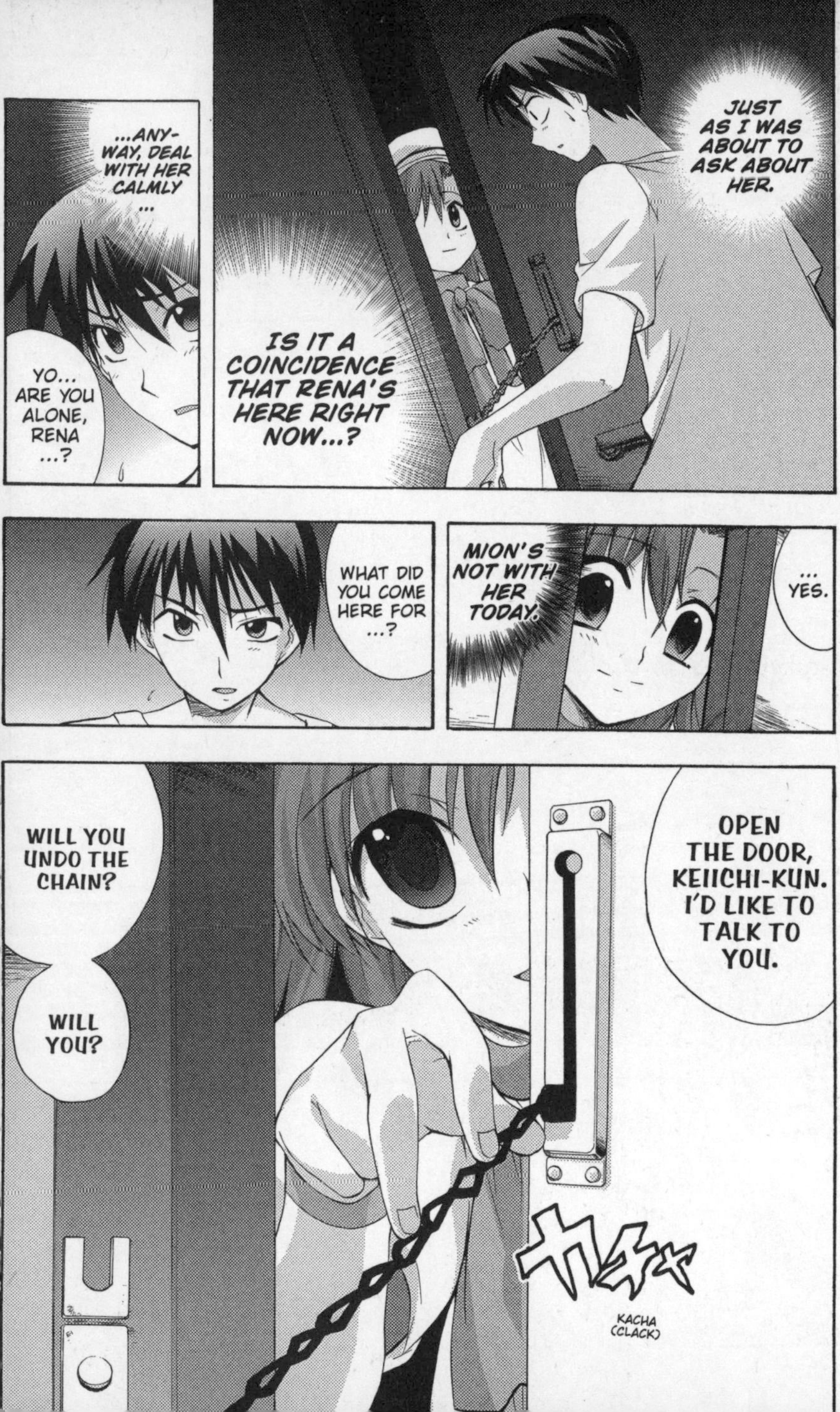
JUST AS I WAS ABOUT TO ASK ABOUT HER.
IS IT A COINCIDENCE THAT RENA'S HERE RIGHT NOW...?
...ANYWAY, DEAL WITH HER CALMLY...
YO... ARE YOU ALONE, RENA...?
...YES.
MION'S NOT WITH HER TODAY.
WHAT DID YOU COME HERE FOR...?
OPEN THE DOOR, KEIICHI-KUN. I'D LIKE TO TALK TO YOU.
WILL YOU UNDO THE CHAIN?
WILL YOU?
KACHA (CLACK)

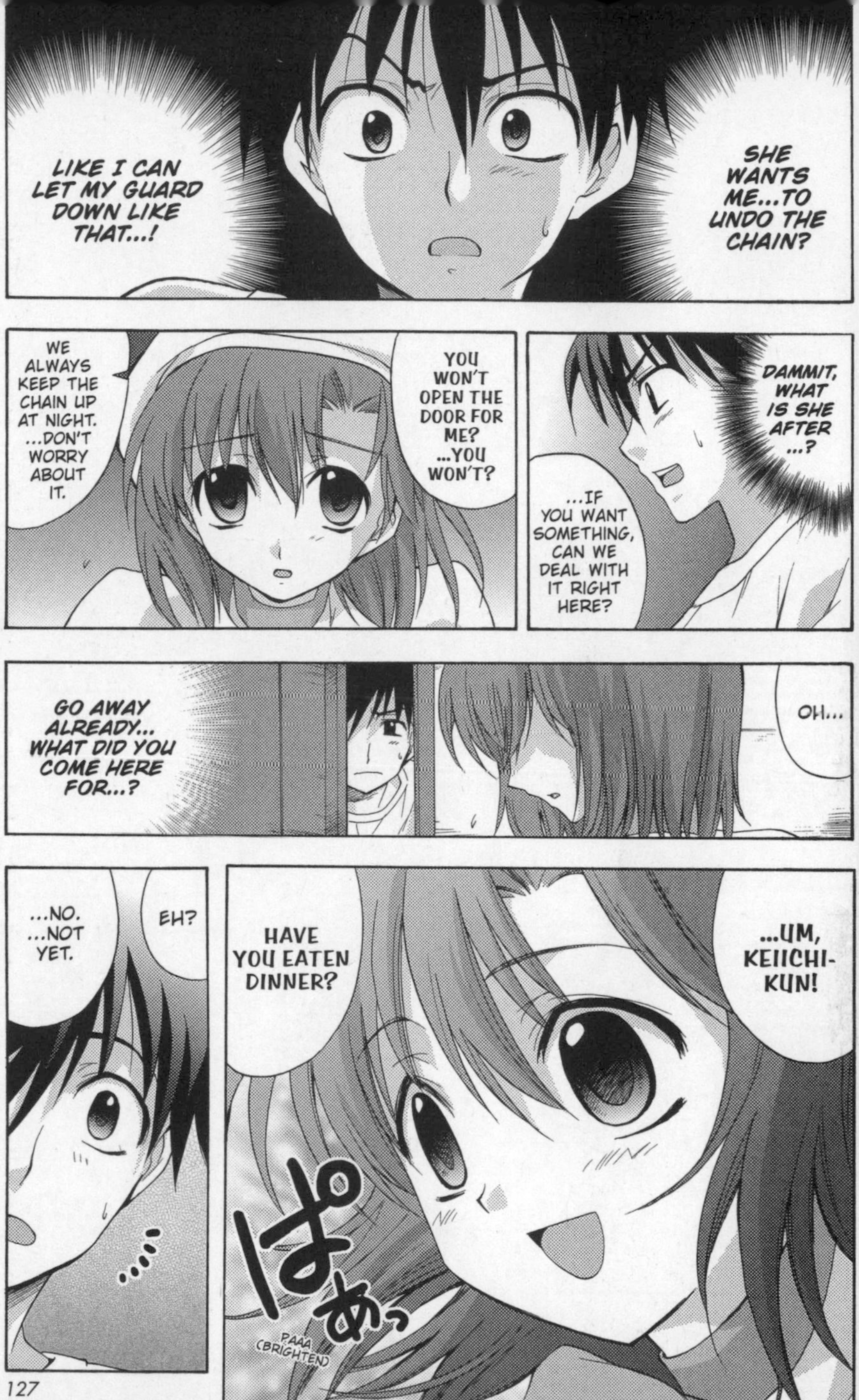
SHE WANTS ME...TO UNDO THE CHAIN?
LIKE I CAN LET MY GUARD DOWN LIKE THAT...!
DAMMIT, WHAT IS SHE AFTER ...?
...IF YOU WANT SOMETHING, CAN WE DEAL WITH IT RIGHT HERE?
YOU WON'T OPEN THE DOOR FOR ME? ...YOU WON'T?
WE ALWAYS KEEP THE CHAIN UP AT NIGHT. ...DON'T WORRY ABOUT IT.
OH...
GO AWAY ALREADY... WHAT DID YOU COME HERE FOR...?
...UM, KEIICHI-KUN!
HAVE YOU EATEN DINNER?
ぱあっ
PAAA (BRIGHTEN)
EH?
...NO. ...NOT YET.

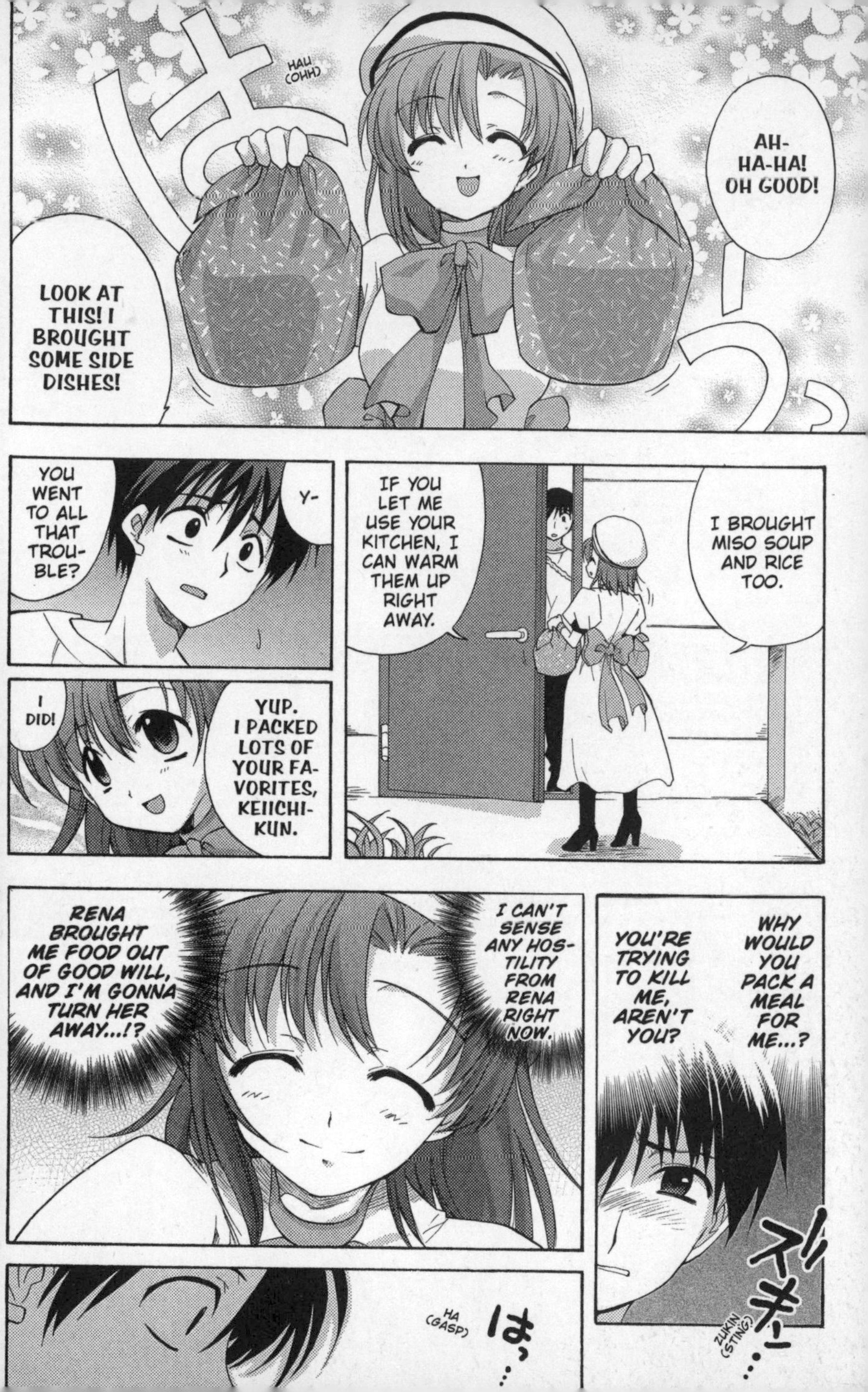
AH-HA-HA! OH GOOD!
HAU (OHH)
LOOK AT THIS! I BROUGHT SOME SIDE DISHES!
I BROUGHT MISO SOUP AND RICE TOO.
IF YOU LET ME USE YOUR KITCHEN, I CAN WARM THEM UP RIGHT AWAY.
Y-
YOU WENT TO ALL THAT TROUBLE?
YUP. I PACKED LOTS OF YOUR FAVORITES, KEIICHI-KUN.
I DID!
WHY WOULD YOU PACK A MEAL FOR ME...?
YOU'RE TRYING TO KILL ME, AREN'T YOU?
ZUKIN (STING)
I CAN'T SENSE ANY HOSTILITY FROM RENA RIGHT NOW.
RENA BROUGHT ME FOOD OUT OF GOOD WILL, AND I'M GONNA TURN HER AWAY...!?
HA (GASP)

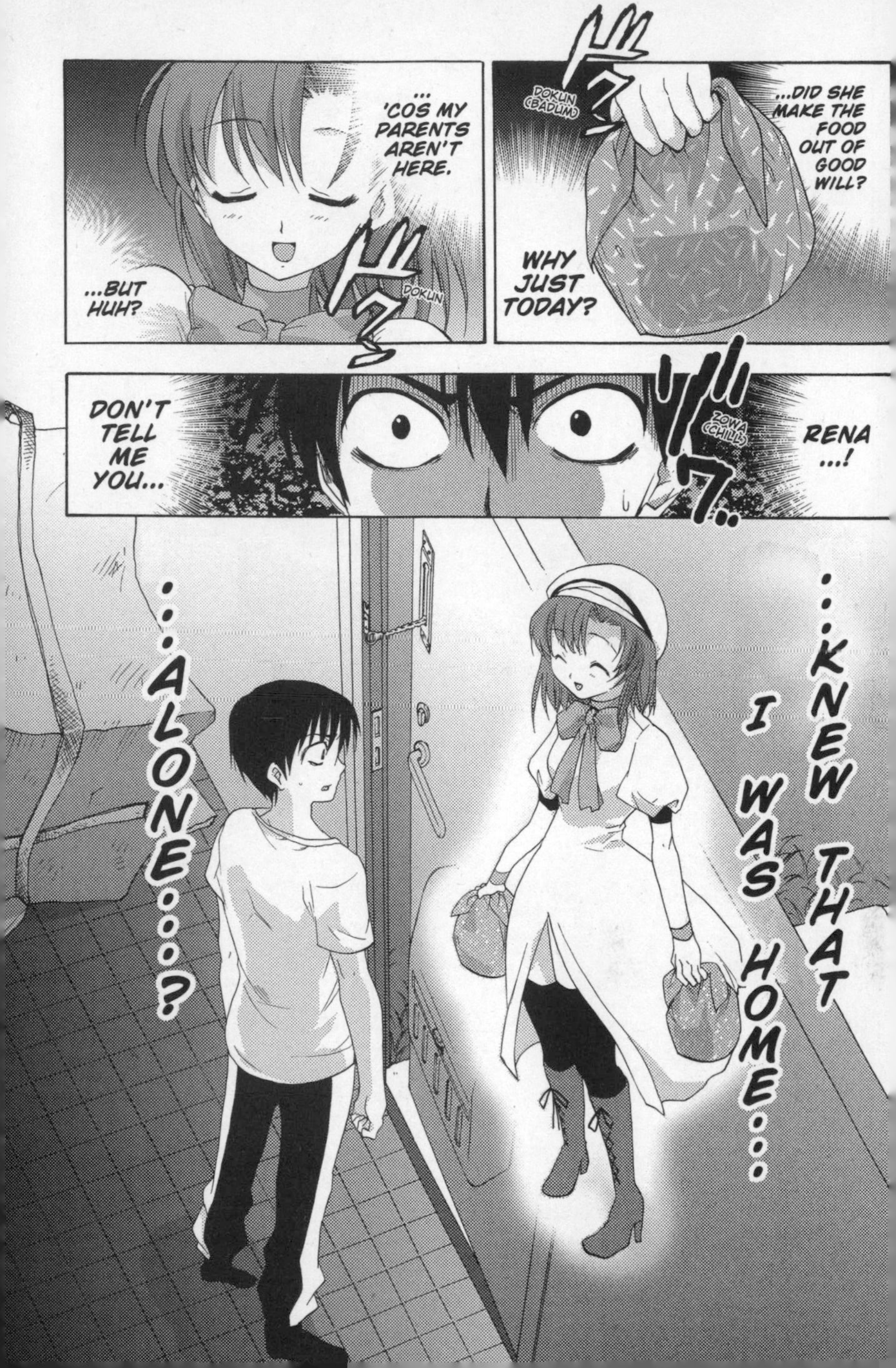
DOKUN (BADUM)
...DID SHE MAKE THE FOOD OUT OF GOOD WILL?
WHY JUST TODAY?
...'COS MY PARENTS AREN'T HERE.
DOKUN
...BUT HUH?
RENA ...!
ZOWA (CHILL)
DON'T TELL ME YOU...
...KNEW THAT I WAS HOME...
...ALONE...?

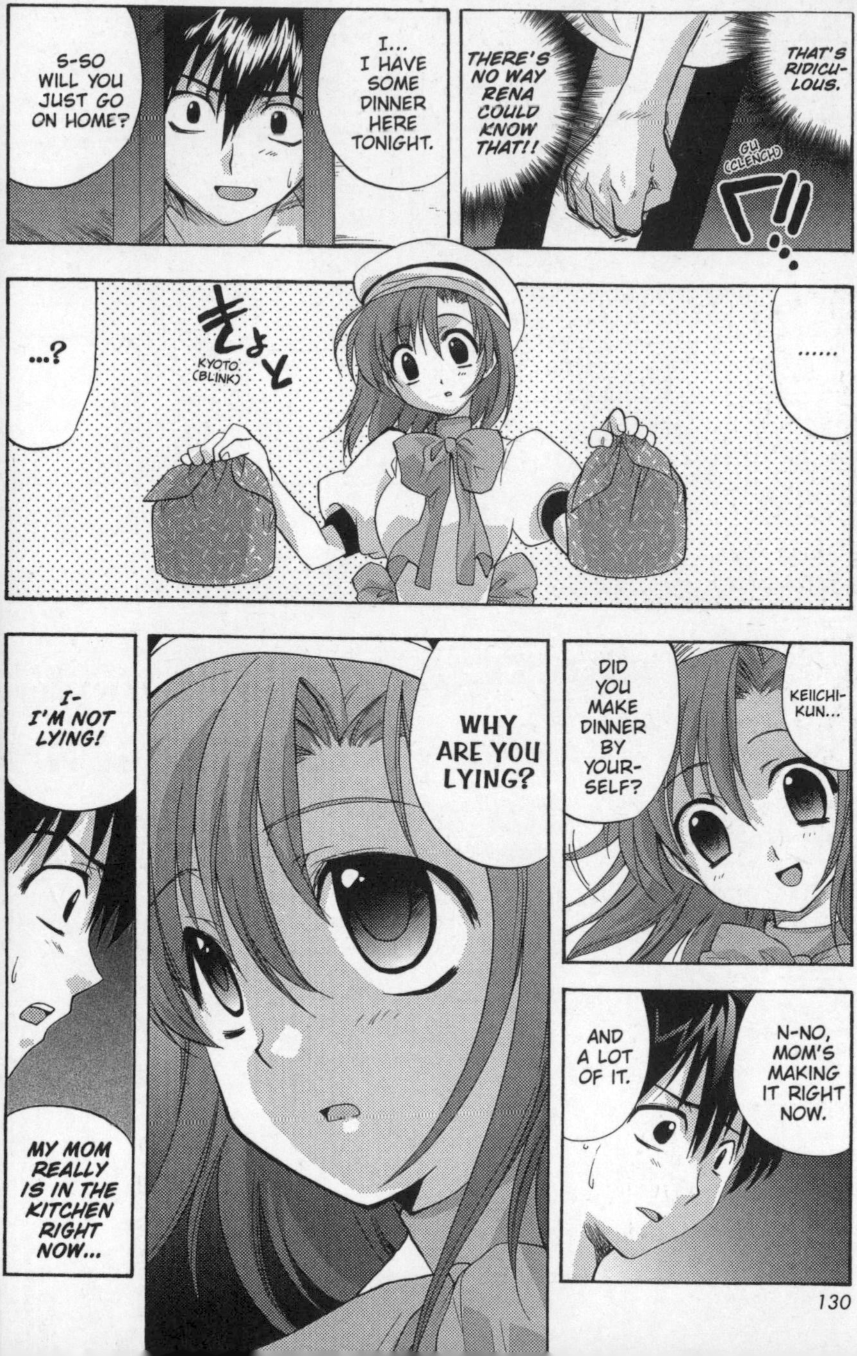
THAT'S RIDICU-LOUS.
THERE'S NO WAY RENA COULD KNOW THAT!!
GU (CLENCH)
I... I HAVE SOME DINNER HERE TONIGHT.
S-SO WILL YOU JUST GO ON HOME?
......
KYOTO (BLINK)
...?
KEIICHI-KUN...
DID YOU MAKE DINNER BY YOUR-SELF?
N-NO, MOM'S MAKING IT RIGHT NOW.
AND A LOT OF IT.
WHY ARE YOU LYING?
I- I'M NOT LYING!
MY MOM REALLY IS IN THE KITCHEN RIGHT NOW...

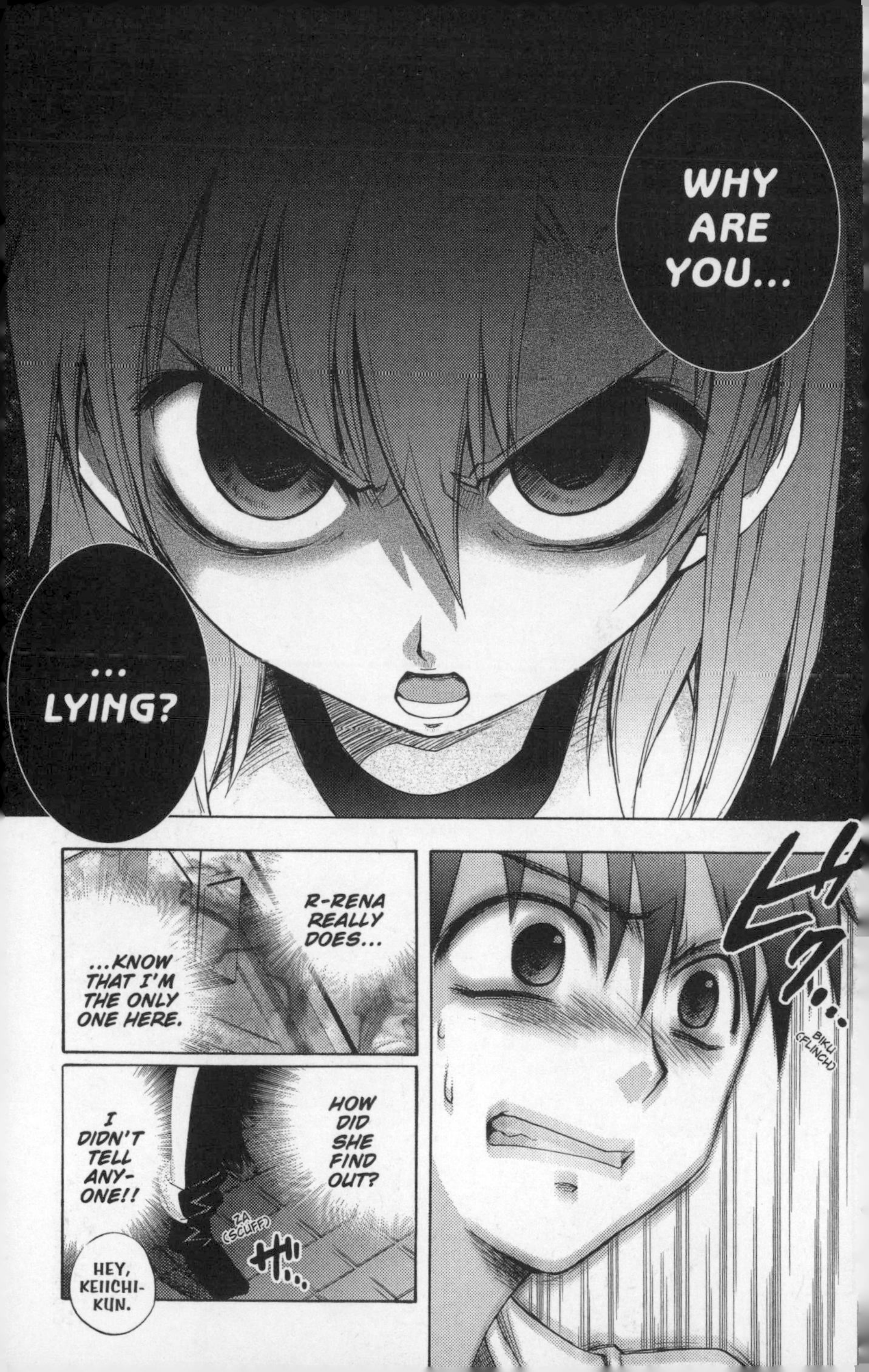
WHY ARE YOU...
...LYING?
BIKU (FLINCH)
R-RENA REALLY DOES...
...KNOW THAT I'M THE ONLY ONE HERE.
HOW DID SHE FIND OUT?
I DIDN'T TELL ANY-ONE!!
ZA (SCUFF)
HEY, KEIICHI-KUN.

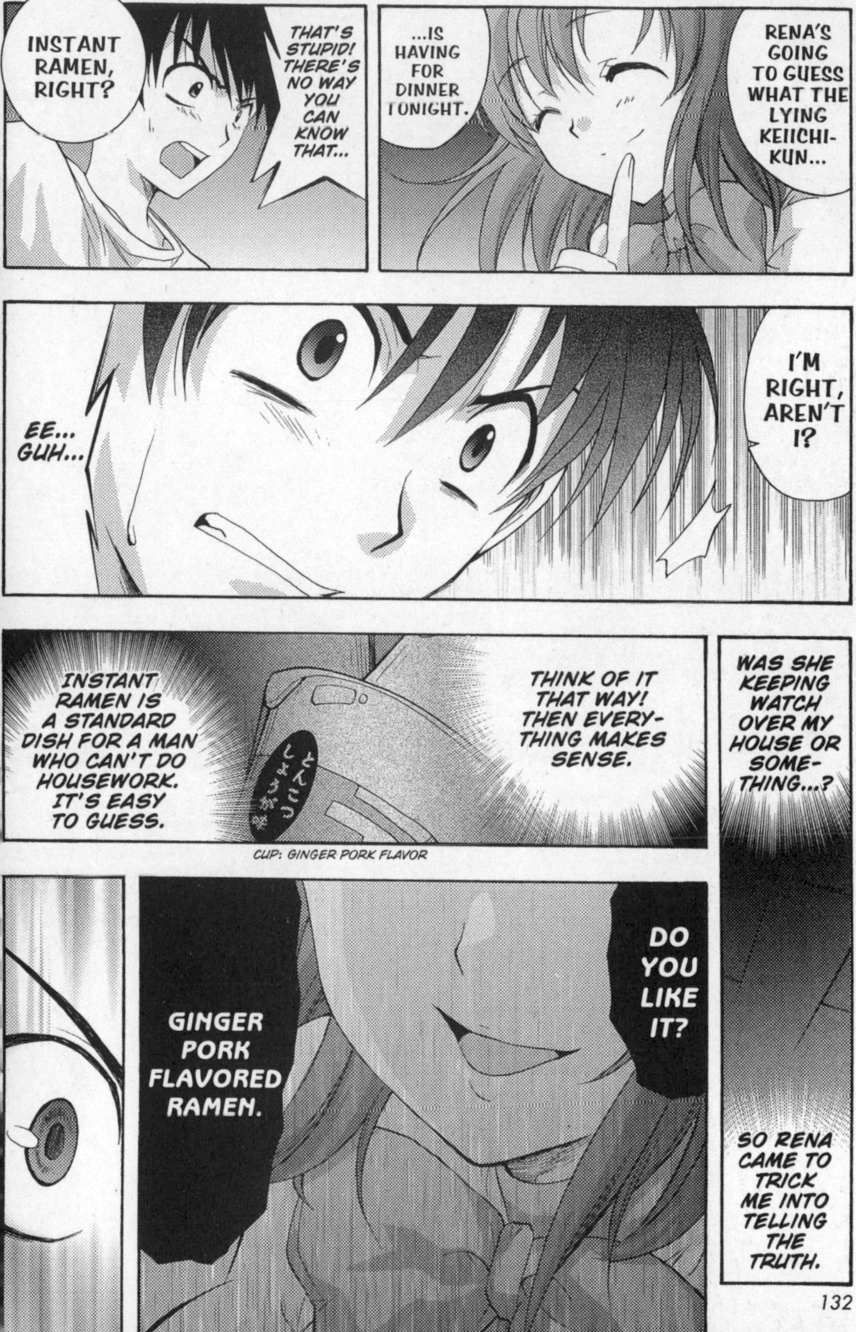
RENA'S GOING TO GUESS WHAT THE LYING KEIICHI-KUN...
...IS HAVING FOR DINNER TONIGHT.
THAT'S STUPID! THERE'S NO WAY YOU CAN KNOW THAT...
INSTANT RAMEN, RIGHT?
I'M RIGHT, AREN'T I?
EE... GUH...
WAS SHE KEEPING WATCH OVER MY HOUSE OR SOMETHING...?
SO RENA CAME TO TRICK ME INTO TELLING THE TRUTH.
THINK OF IT THAT WAY! THEN EVERYTHING MAKES SENSE.
INSTANT RAMEN IS A STANDARD DISH FOR A MAN WHO CAN'T DO HOUSEWORK. IT'S EASY TO GUESS.
とんこつしょうが味
CUP: GINGER PORK FLAVOR
DO YOU LIKE IT?
GINGER PORK FLAVORED RAMEN.

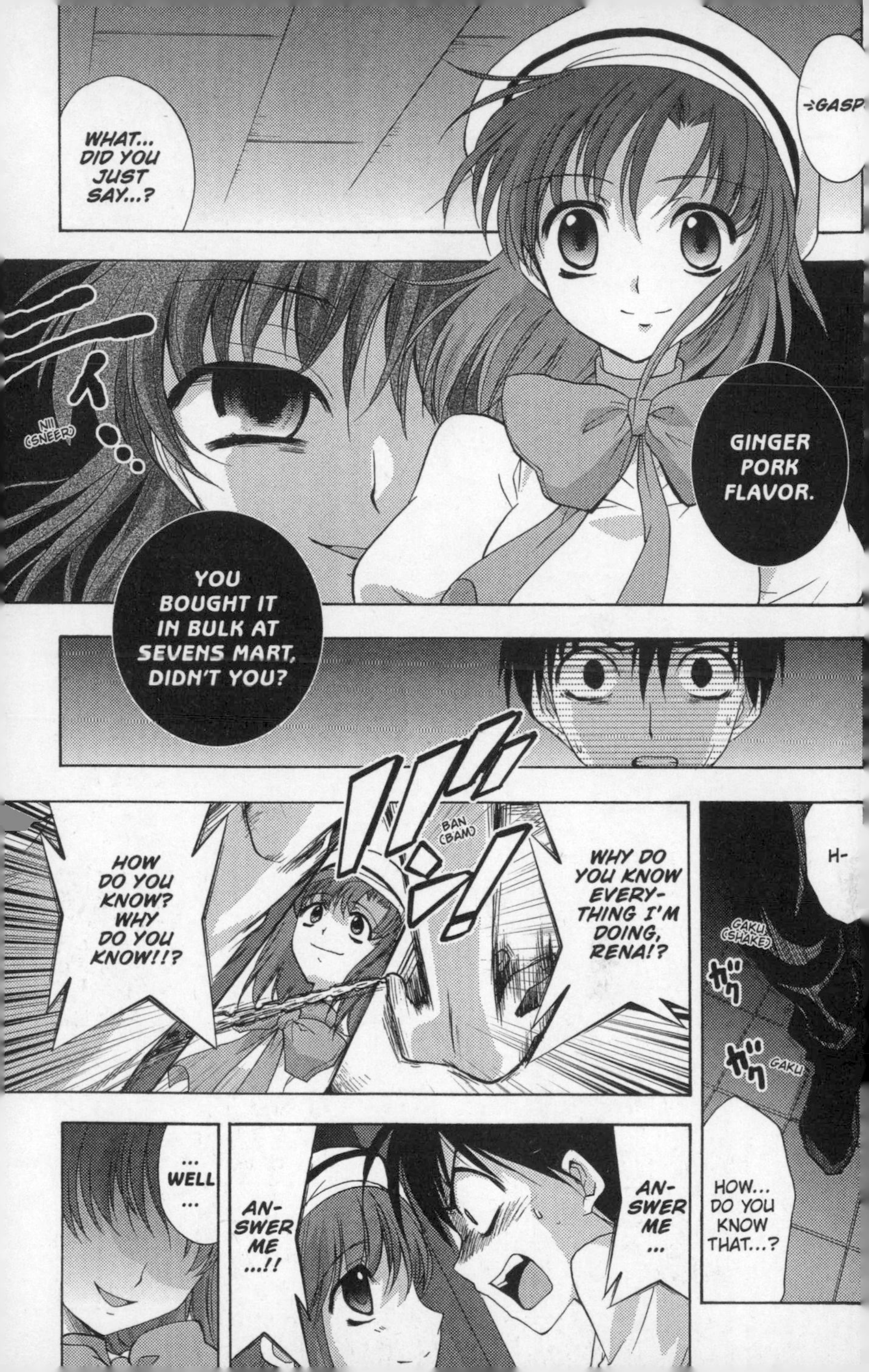
⇒GASP
WHAT... DID YOU JUST SAY...?
GINGER PORK FLAVOR.
NII (SNEER)
YOU BOUGHT IT IN BULK AT SEVENS MART, DIDN'T YOU?
H-
GAKU (SHAKE)
GAKU
HOW... DO YOU KNOW THAT...?
WHY DO YOU KNOW EVERY-THING I'M DOING, RENA!?
BAN (BAM)
HOW DO YOU KNOW? WHY DO YOU KNOW!!?
AN-SWER ME ...
AN-SWER ME ...!!
... WELL ...

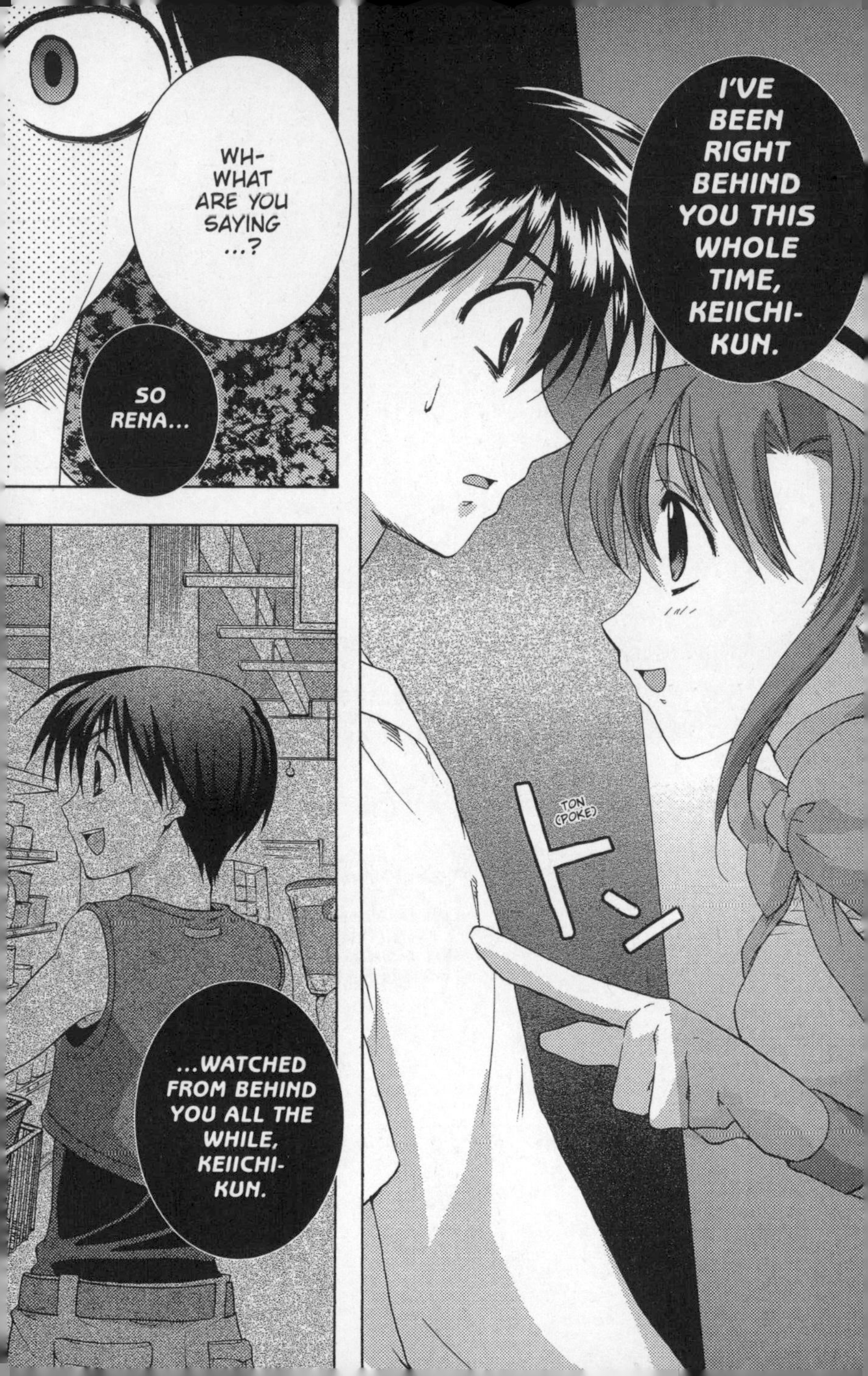
I'VE BEEN RIGHT BEHIND YOU THIS WHOLE TIME, KEIICHI-KUN.
TON (POKE)
WH-WHAT ARE YOU SAYING ...?
SO RENA...
...WATCHED FROM BEHIND YOU ALL THE WHILE, KEIICHI-KUN.

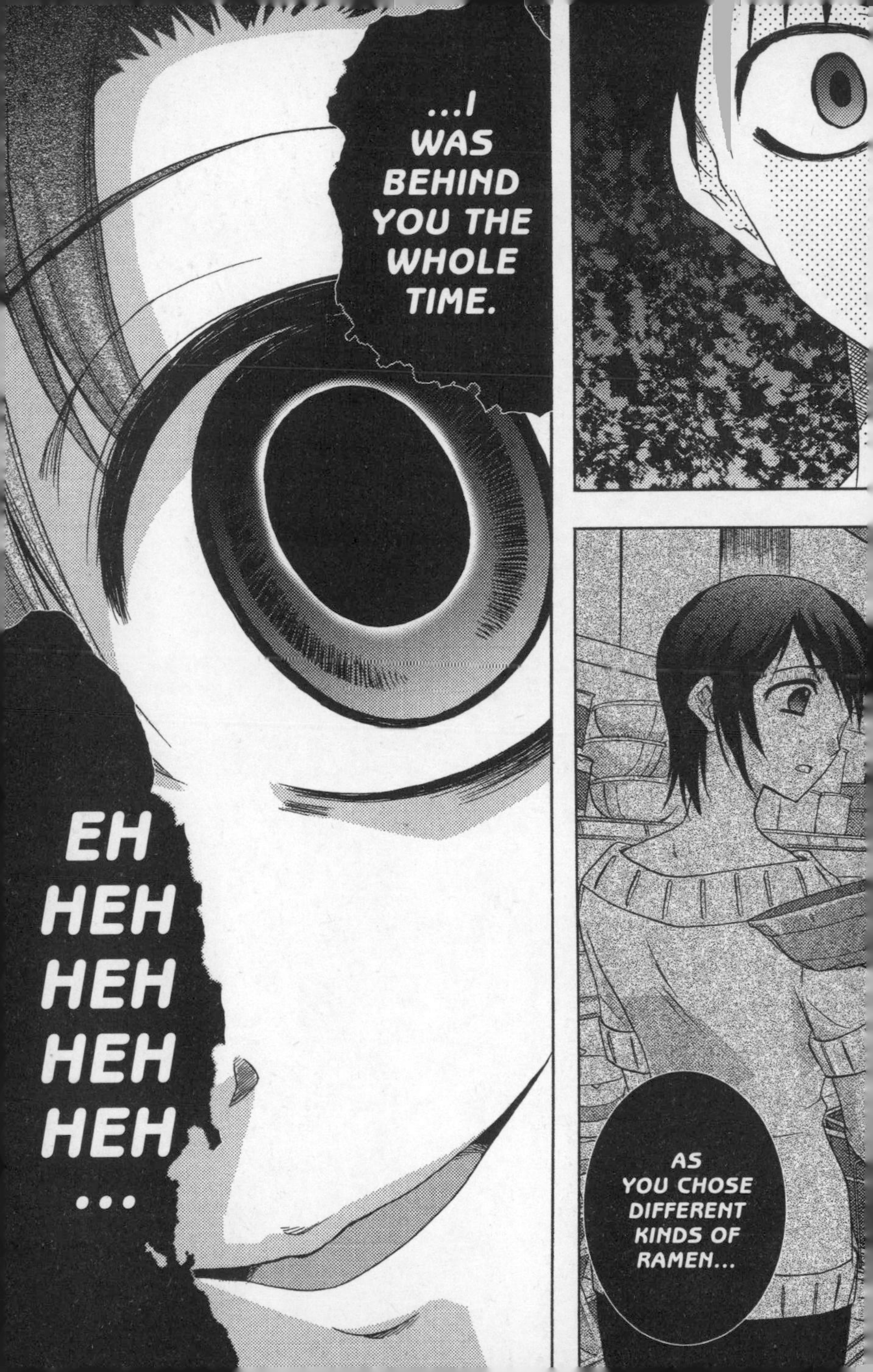
AS YOU CHOSE DIFFERENT KINDS OF RAMEN...
...I WAS BEHIND YOU THE WHOLE TIME.
EH HEH HEH HEH HEH...

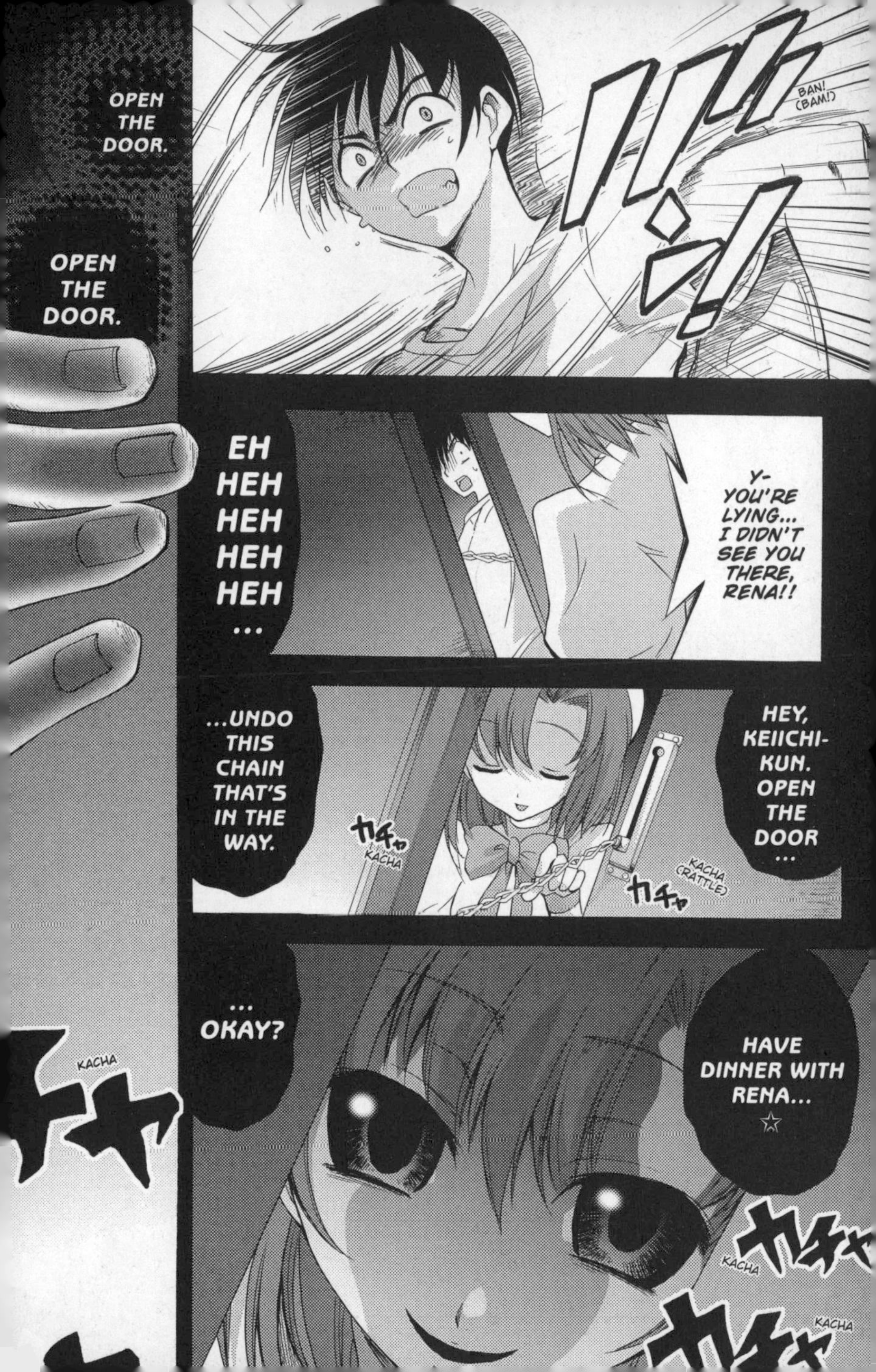
BAN! (BAM!)
Y-YOU'RE LYING... I DIDN'T SEE YOU THERE, RENA!!
EH HEH HEH HEH HEH...
HEY, KEIICHI-KUN. OPEN THE DOOR...
カチャ
KACHA (RATTLE)
カチャ
KACHA
...UNDO THIS CHAIN THAT'S IN THE WAY.
HAVE DINNER WITH RENA... ☆
KACHA
KACHA
...OKAY?
OPEN THE DOOR.
OPEN THE DOOR.
KACHA

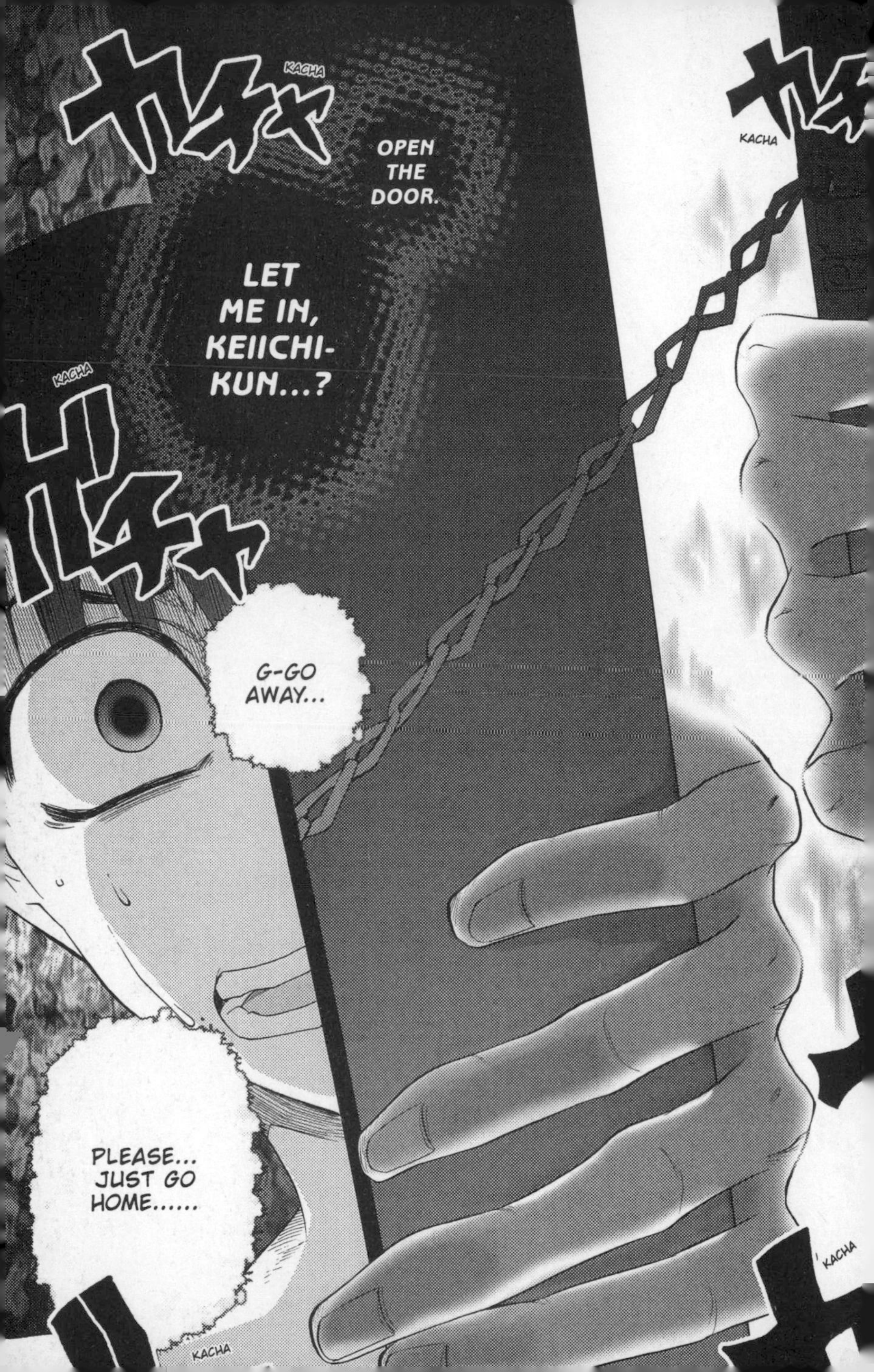
KACHA
KACHA
OPEN THE DOOR.
LET ME IN, KEIICHI-KUN...?
KACHA
G-GO AWAY...
KACHA
PLEASE... JUST GO HOME......
KACHA

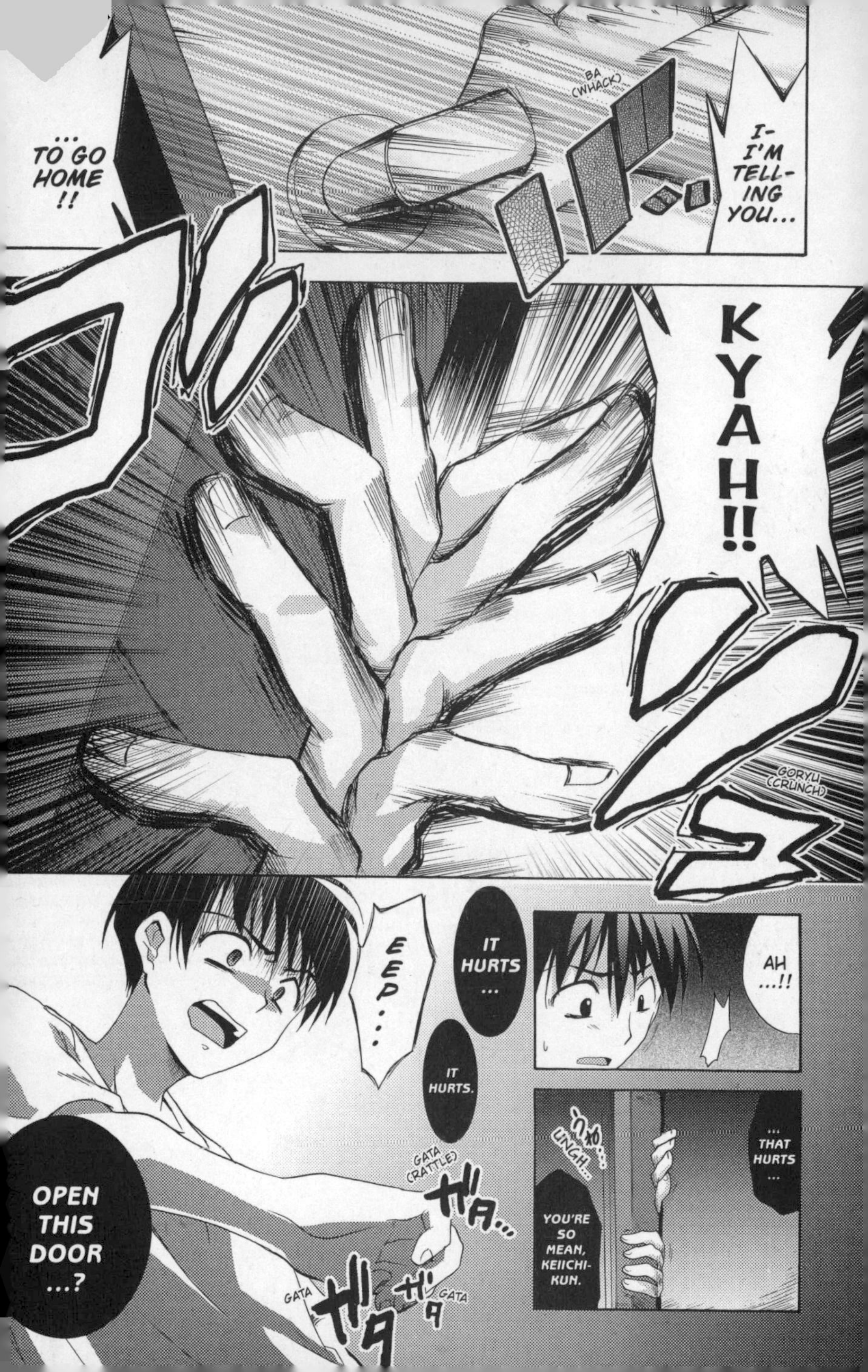
I-I'M TELLING YOU...
BA (WHACK)
...TO GO HOME!!
KYAH!!
GORYU (CRUNCH)
AH ...!!
IT HURTS...
EEP...
IT HURTS.
...THAT HURTS...
UNGH...
YOU'RE SO MEAN, KEIICHI-KUN.
GATA (RATTLE)
GATA
GATA
OPEN THIS DOOR ...?

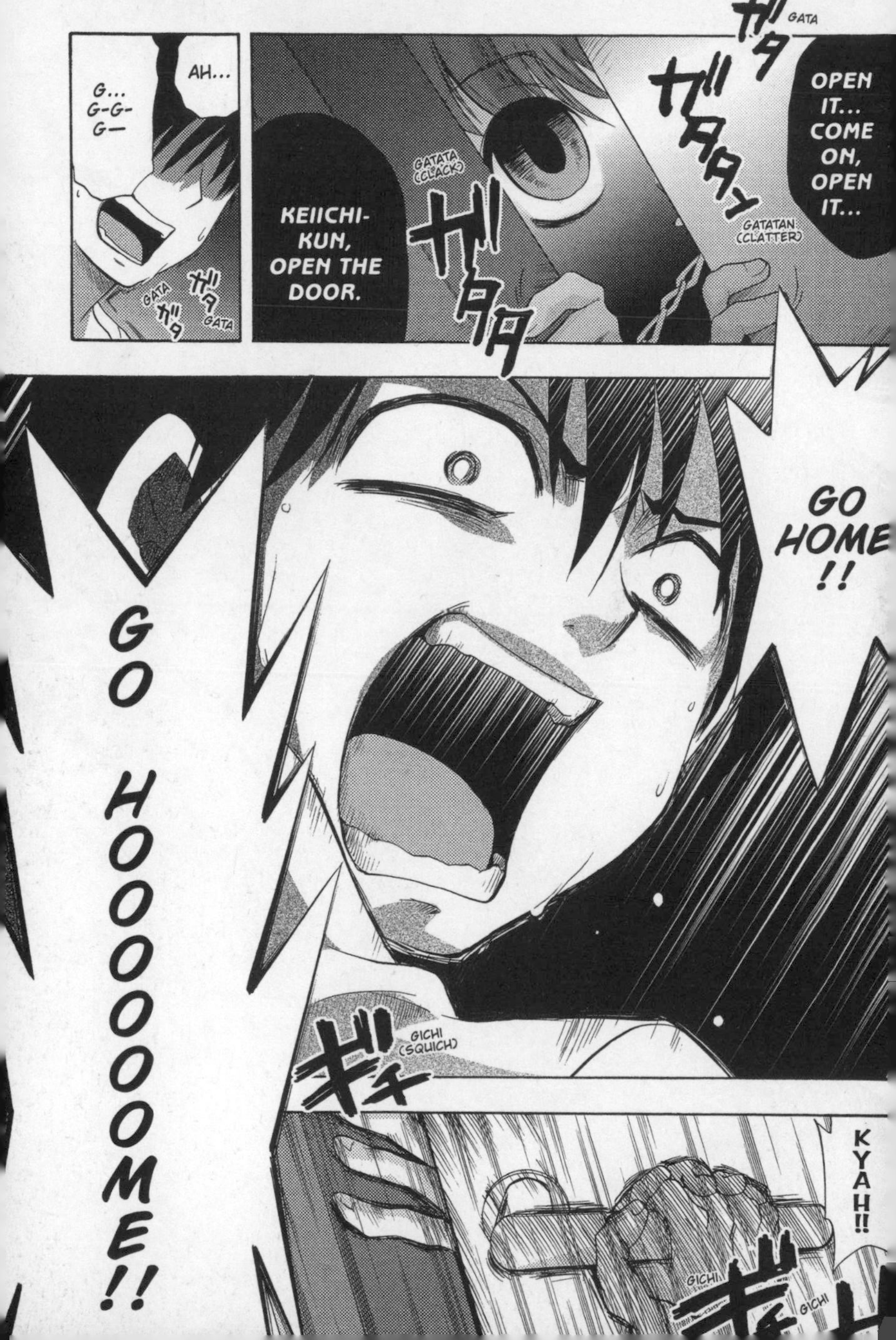
GATA
OPEN IT... COME ON, OPEN IT...
GATATAN (CLATTER)
GATATA (CLACK)
KEIICHI-KUN, OPEN THE DOOR.
AH...
G... G-G-G—
GATA GATA
GO HOME!!
GO HOOOOOOOME!!
GICHI (SQUICH)
KYAH!!
GICHI GICHI

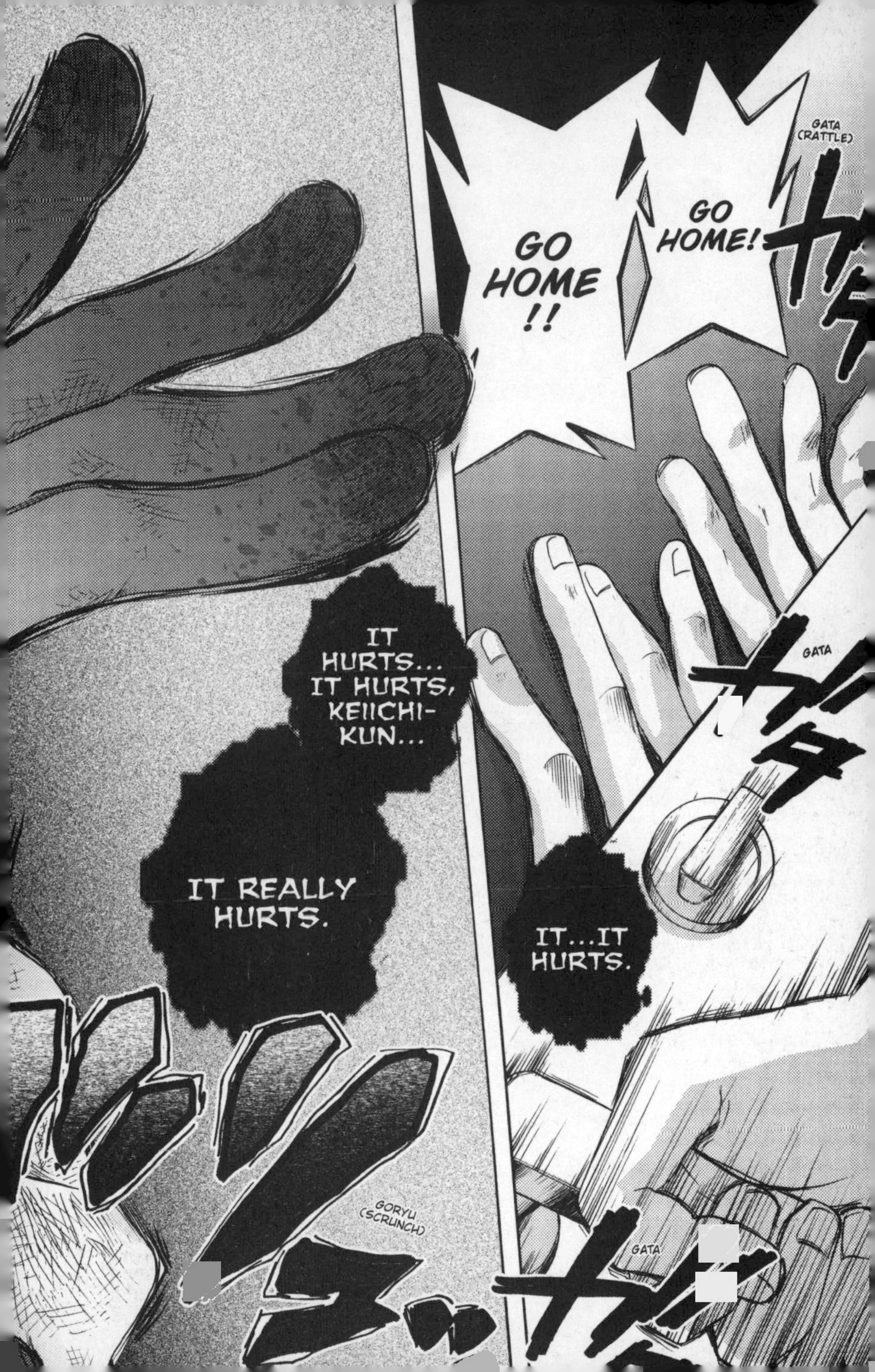
GATA (RATTLE)
GO HOME!
GO HOME !!
GATA
IT...IT HURTS.
GATA
IT HURTS... IT HURTS, KEIICHI-KUN...
IT REALLY HURTS.
GORYU (SCRUNCH)

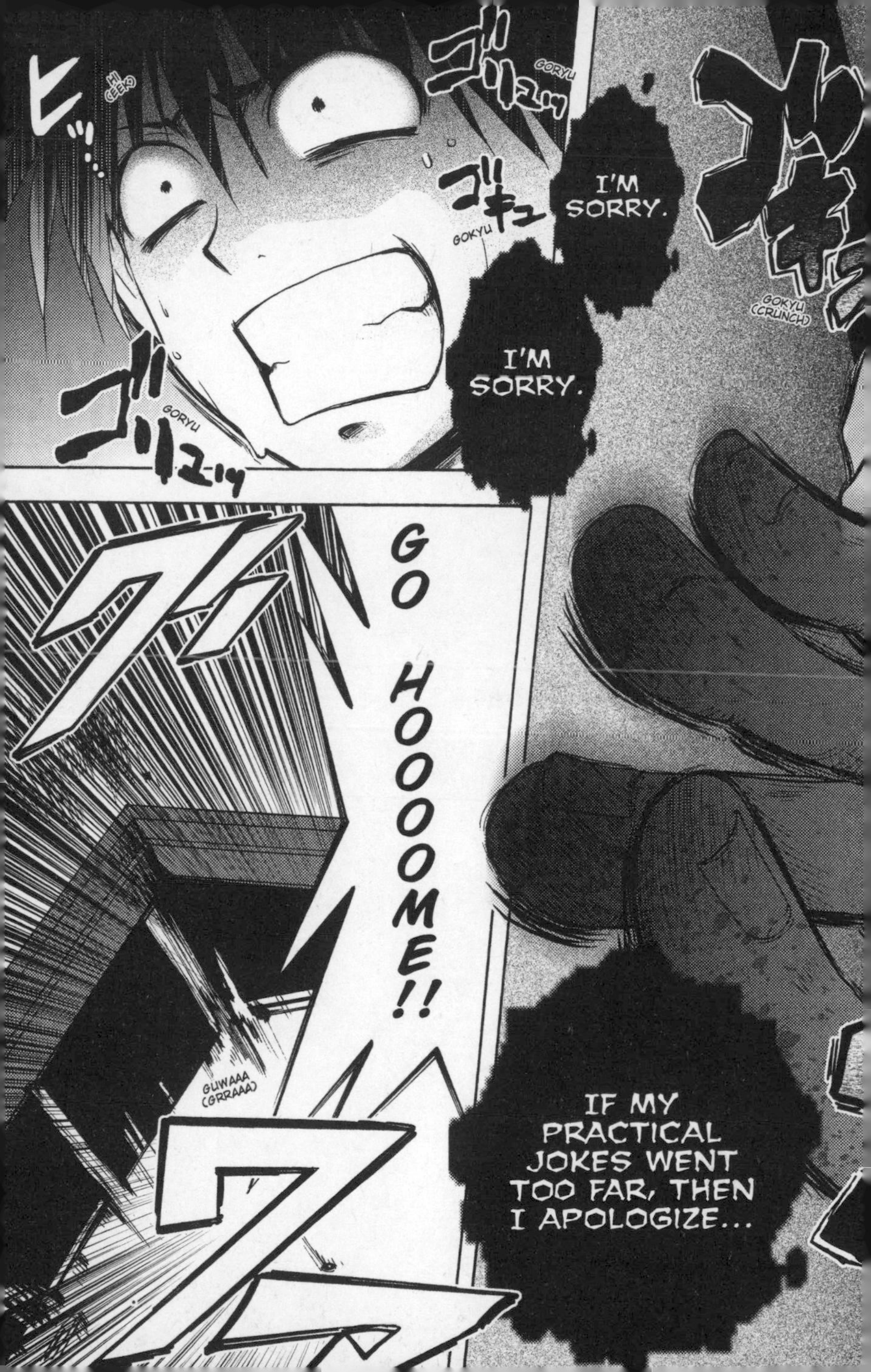

GOKYU (CRUNCH)
I'M SORRY.
I'M SORRY.
IF MY PRACTICAL JOKES WENT TOO FAR, THEN I APOLOGIZE...
HI (EEK)
GORYU
GOKYU
GORYU
GO HOOOOOME!!
GUWAAA (GRRAAA)

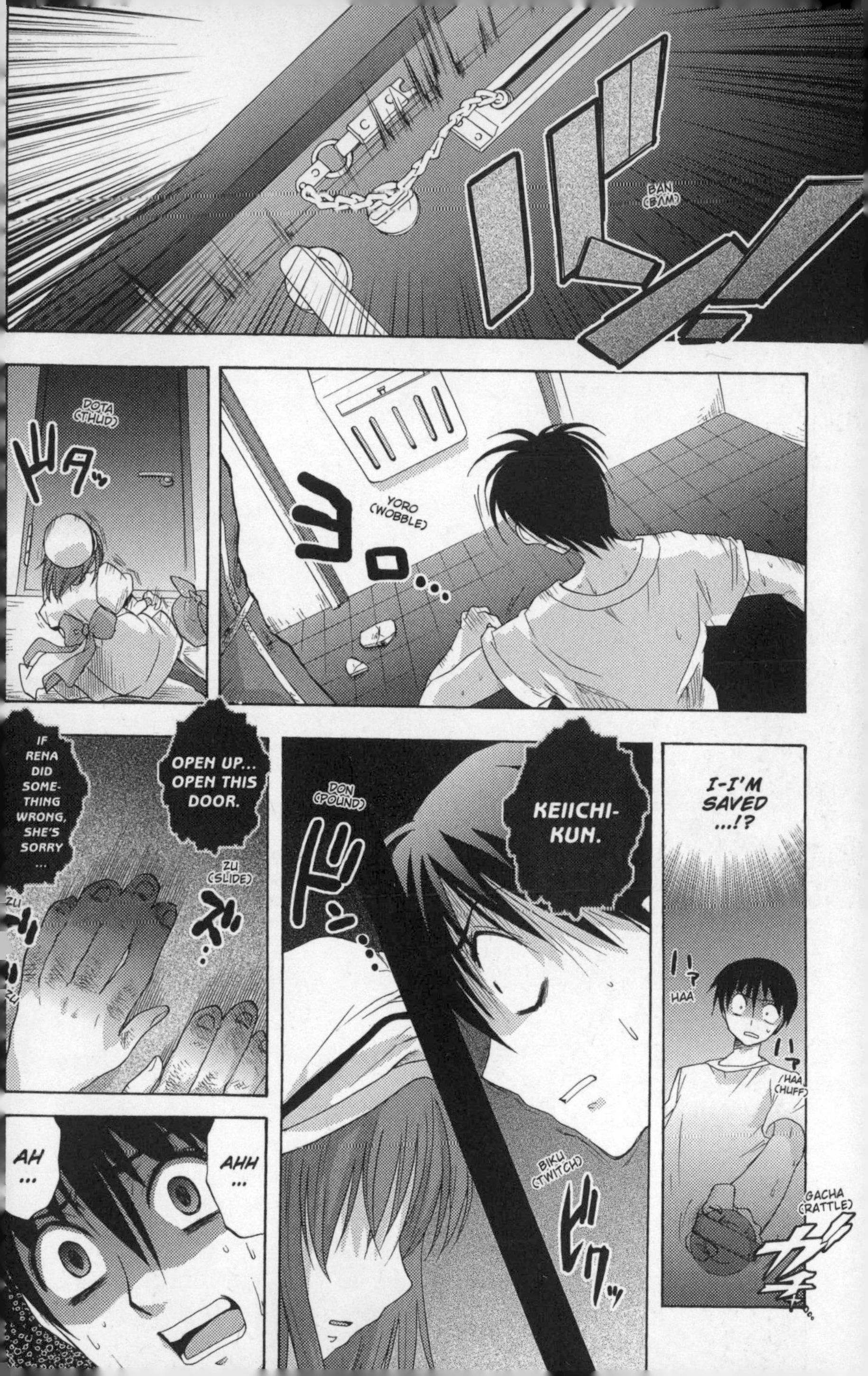
BAN (BAM)
YORO (WOBBLE)
DOTA (THUD)
I-I'M SAVED ...!?
HAA
HAA (CHUFF)
GACHA (RATTLE)
KEIICHI-KUN.
DON (POUND)
BIKU (TWITCH)
OPEN UP... OPEN THIS DOOR.
IF RENA DID SOME-THING WRONG, SHE'S SORRY ...
ZU (SLIDE)
ZU
AHH ...
AH ...

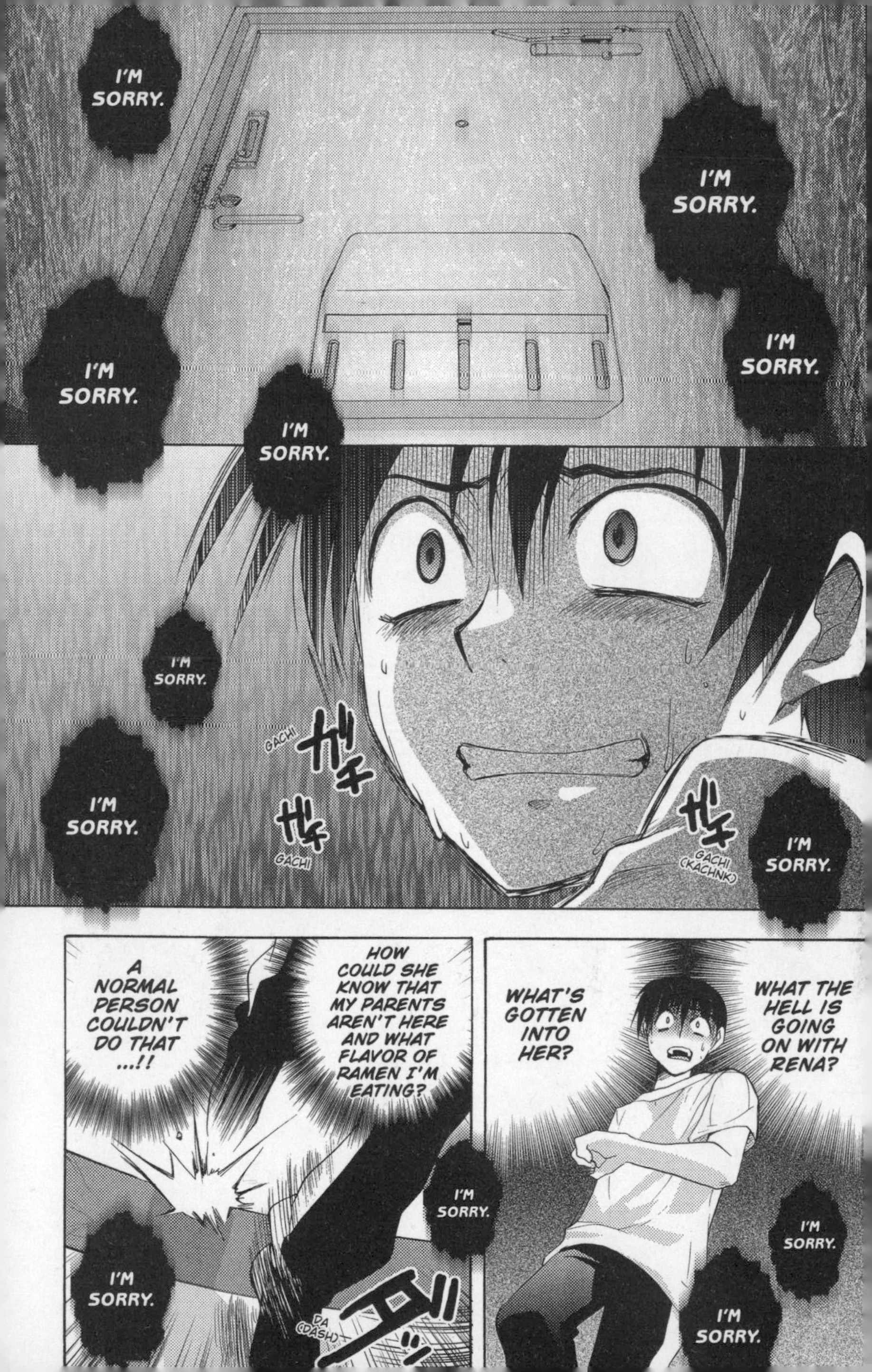
I'M SORRY.
I'M SORRY.
I'M SORRY.
I'M SORRY.
I'M SORRY.
GACHI (KACHNK)
I'M SORRY.
GACHI
GACHI
I'M SORRY.
I'M SORRY.
WHAT THE HELL IS GOING ON WITH RENA?
WHAT'S GOTTEN INTO HER?
I'M SORRY.
I'M SORRY.
HOW COULD SHE KNOW THAT MY PARENTS AREN'T HERE AND WHAT FLAVOR OF RAMEN I'M EATING?
A NORMAL PERSON COULDN'T DO THAT ...!!
I'M SORRY.
DA (DASH)
I'M SORRY.

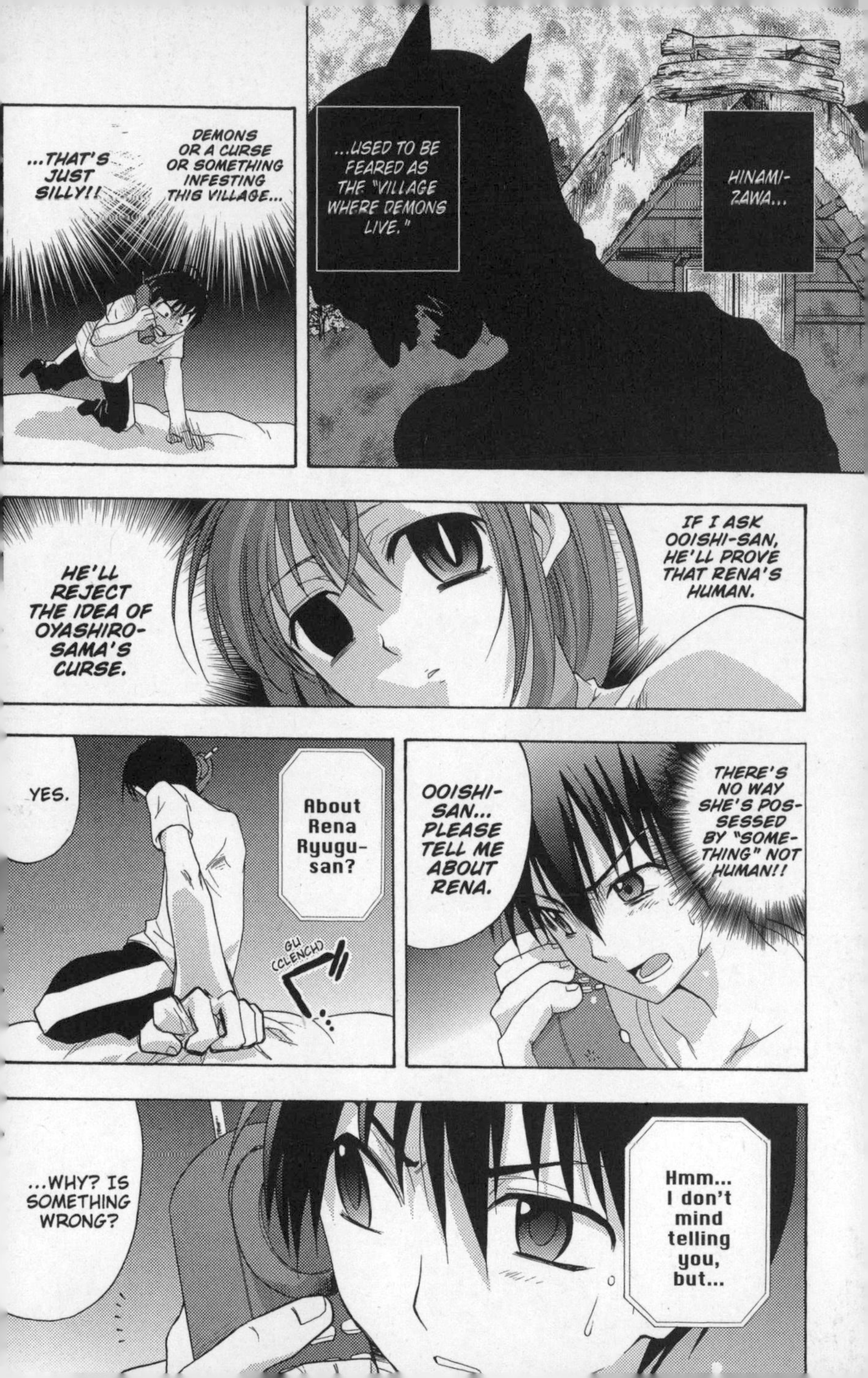

HINAMI-ZAWA...
...USED TO BE FEARED AS THE "VILLAGE WHERE DEMONS LIVE."
DEMONS OR A CURSE OR SOMETHING INFESTING THIS VILLAGE...
...THAT'S JUST SILLY!!
IF I ASK OOISHI-SAN, HE'LL PROVE THAT RENA'S HUMAN.
HE'LL REJECT THE IDEA OF OYASHIRO-SAMA'S CURSE.
THERE'S NO WAY SHE'S POSSESSED BY "SOMETHING" NOT HUMAN!!
OOISHI-SAN... PLEASE TELL ME ABOUT RENA.
About Rena Ryugu-san?
GU (CLENCH)
YES.
Hmm... I don't mind telling you, but...
...WHY? IS SOMETHING WRONG?

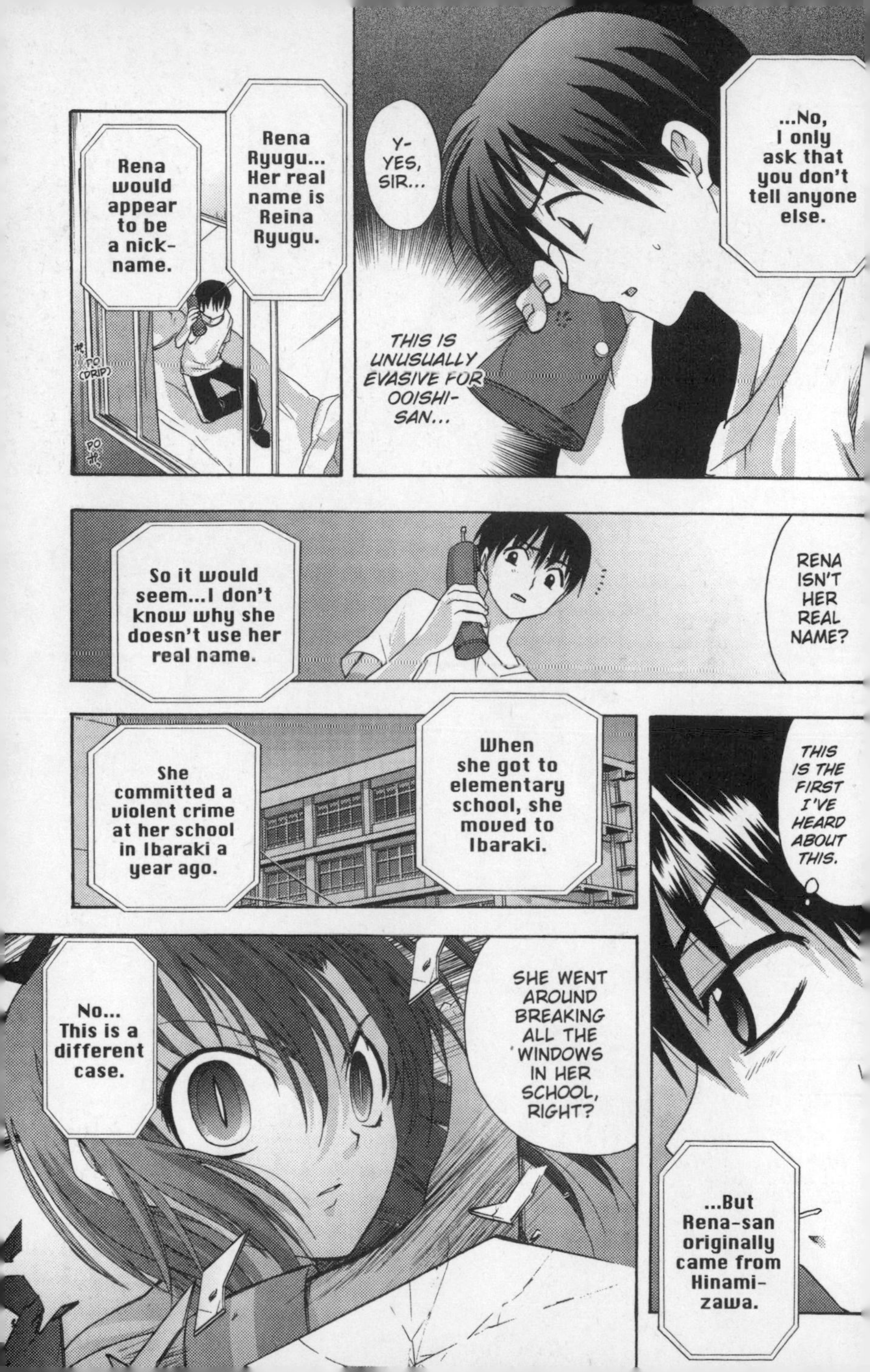
...No, I only ask that you don't tell anyone else.
Y-YES, SIR...
THIS IS UNUSUALLY EVASIVE FOR OOISHI-SAN...
Rena Ryugu... Her real name is Reina Ryugu.
Rena would appear to be a nick-name.
PO (DRIP)
PO
RENA ISN'T HER REAL NAME?
So it would seem...I don't know why she doesn't use her real name.
THIS IS THE FIRST I'VE HEARD ABOUT THIS.
...But Rena-san originally came from Hinami-zawa.
When she got to elementary school, she moved to Ibaraki.
She committed a violent crime at her school in Ibaraki a year ago.
SHE WENT AROUND BREAKING ALL THE WINDOWS IN HER SCHOOL, RIGHT?
No... This is a different case.

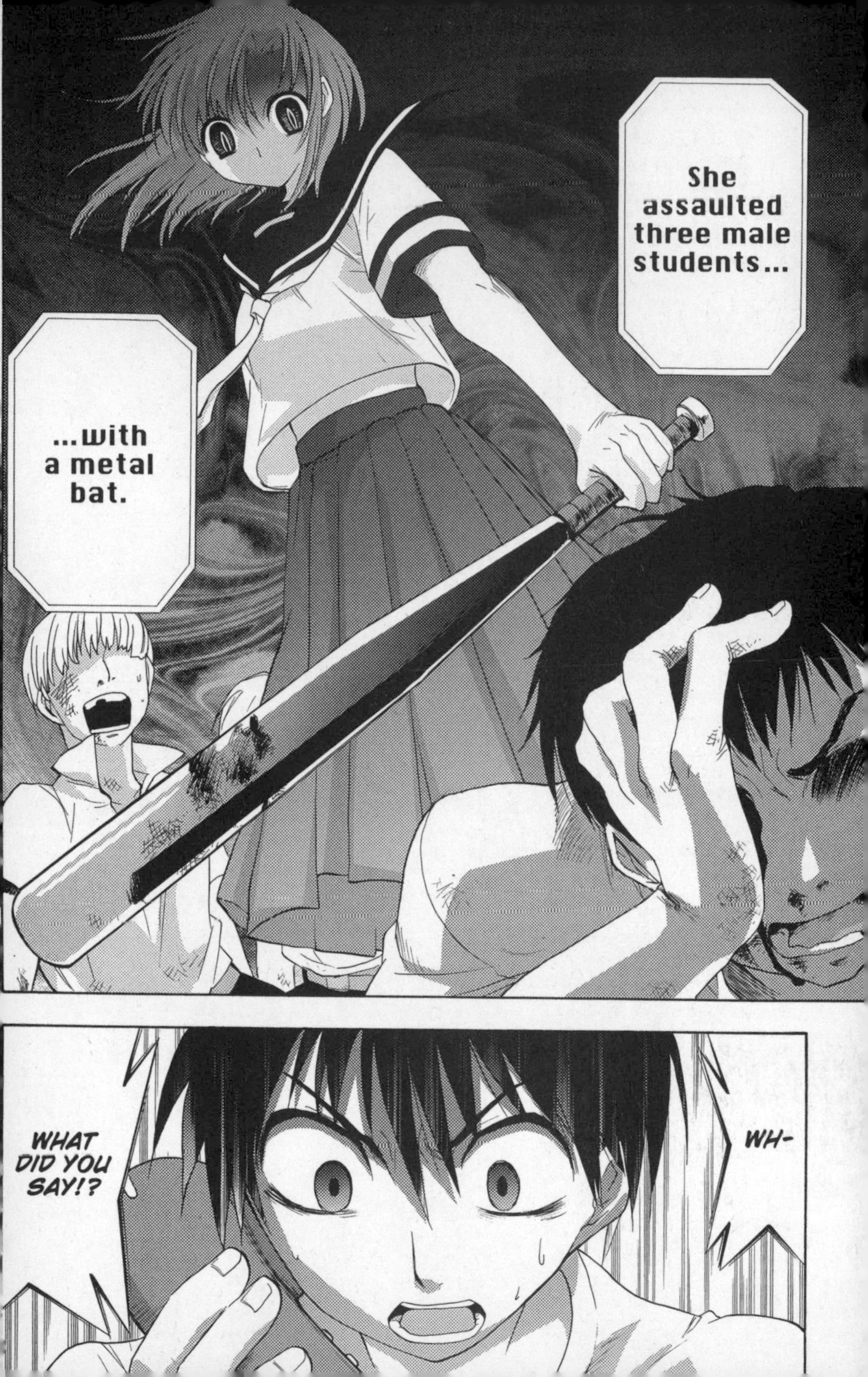
She assaulted three male students...
...with a metal bat.
WH-
WHAT DID YOU SAY!?

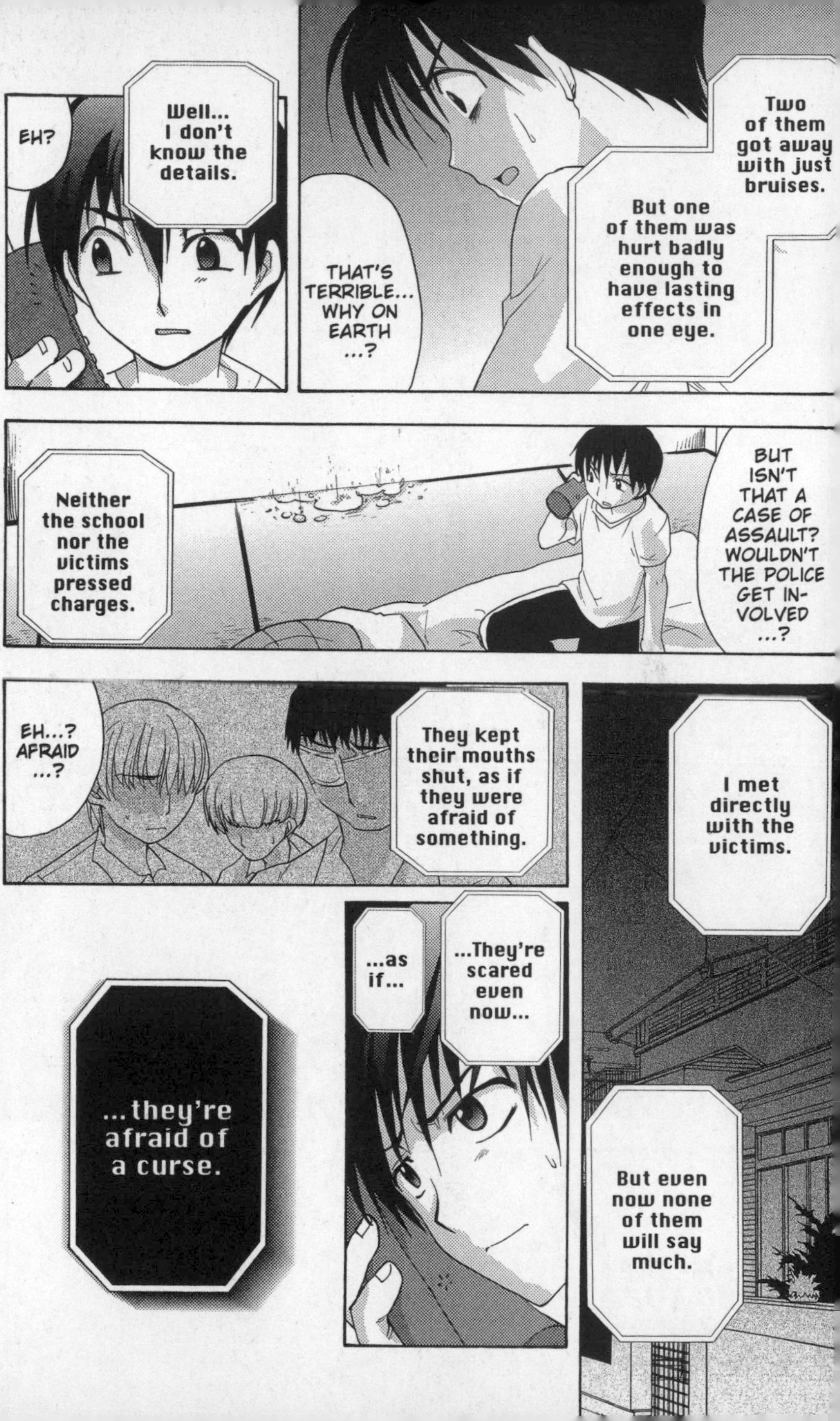
Two of them got away with just bruises.
But one of them was hurt badly enough to have lasting effects in one eye.
THAT'S TERRIBLE... WHY ON EARTH ...?
Well... I don't know the details.
EH?
BUT ISN'T THAT A CASE OF ASSAULT? WOULDN'T THE POLICE GET IN-VOLVED ...?
Neither the school nor the victims pressed charges.
I met directly with the victims.
But even now none of them will say much.
They kept their mouths shut, as if they were afraid of something.
EH...? AFRAID ...?
...They're scared even now...
...as if...
...they're afraid of a curse.

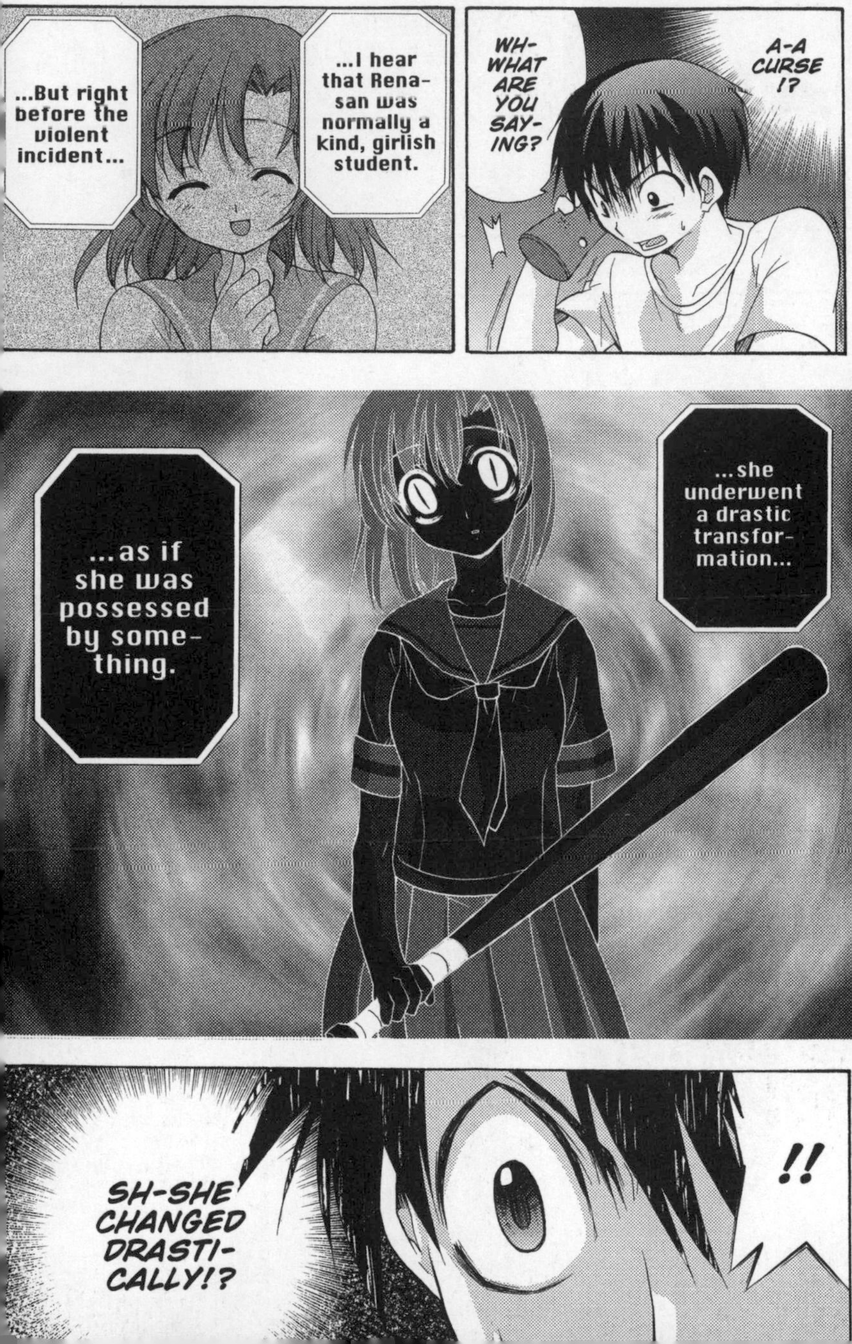
A-A CURSE !?
WH-WHAT ARE YOU SAY-ING?
...I hear that Rena-san was normally a kind, girlish student.
...But right before the violent incident...
...she underwent a drastic transfor-mation...
...as if she was possessed by some-thing.
!!
SH-SHE CHANGED DRASTI-CALLY!?

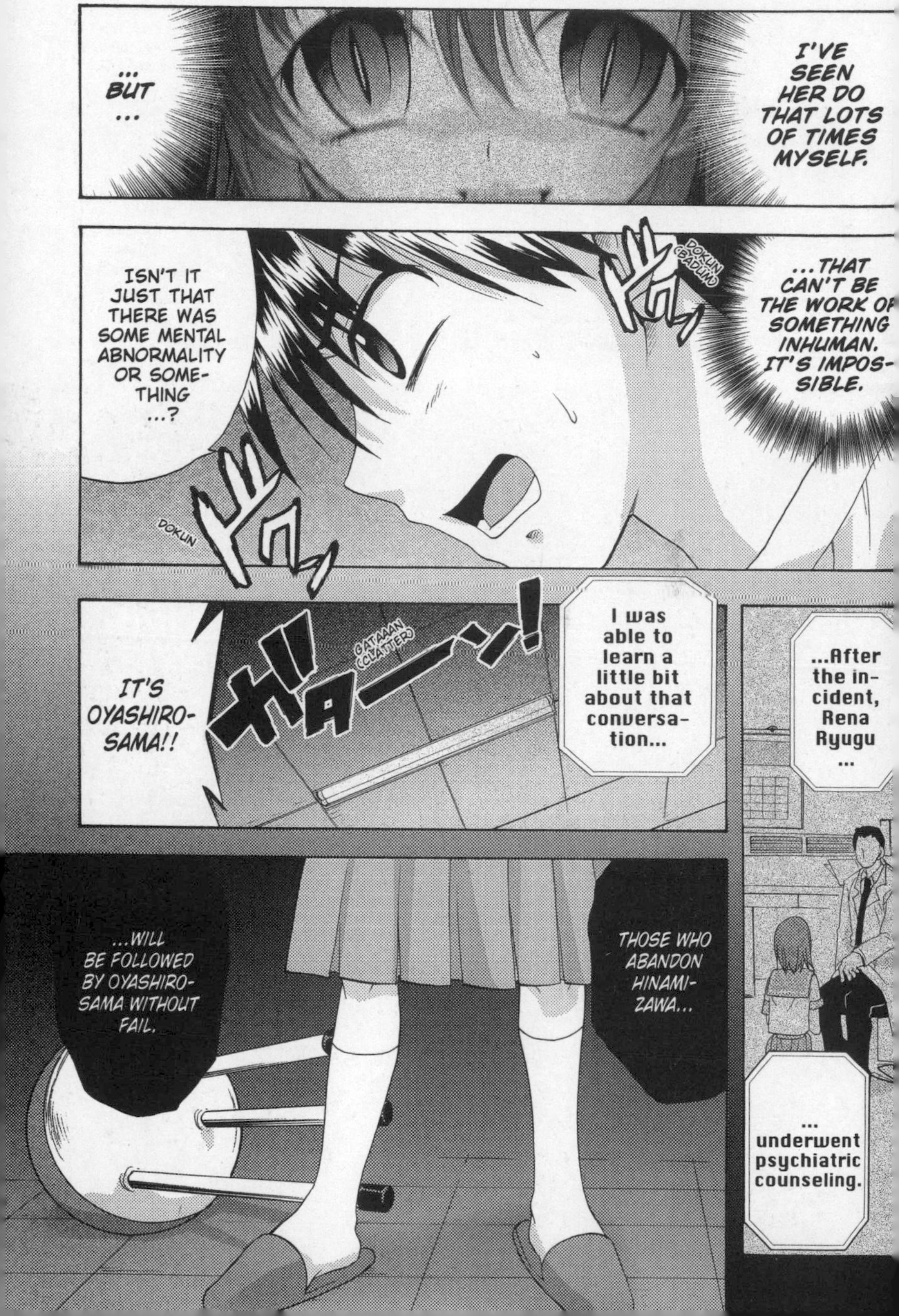
I'VE SEEN HER DO THAT LOTS OF TIMES MYSELF.
...BUT...
...THAT CAN'T BE THE WORK OF SOMETHING INHUMAN. IT'S IMPOSSIBLE.
DOKUN (BADUM)
ISN'T IT JUST THAT THERE WAS SOME MENTAL ABNORMALITY OR SOMETHING...?
DOKUN
...After the incident, Rena Ryugu ...
... underwent psychiatric counseling.
I was able to learn a little bit about that conversation...
GATAAAN (CLATTER)
IT'S OYASHIRO-SAMA!!
THOSE WHO ABANDON HINAMIZAWA...
...WILL BE FOLLOWED BY OYASHIRO-SAMA WITHOUT FAIL.

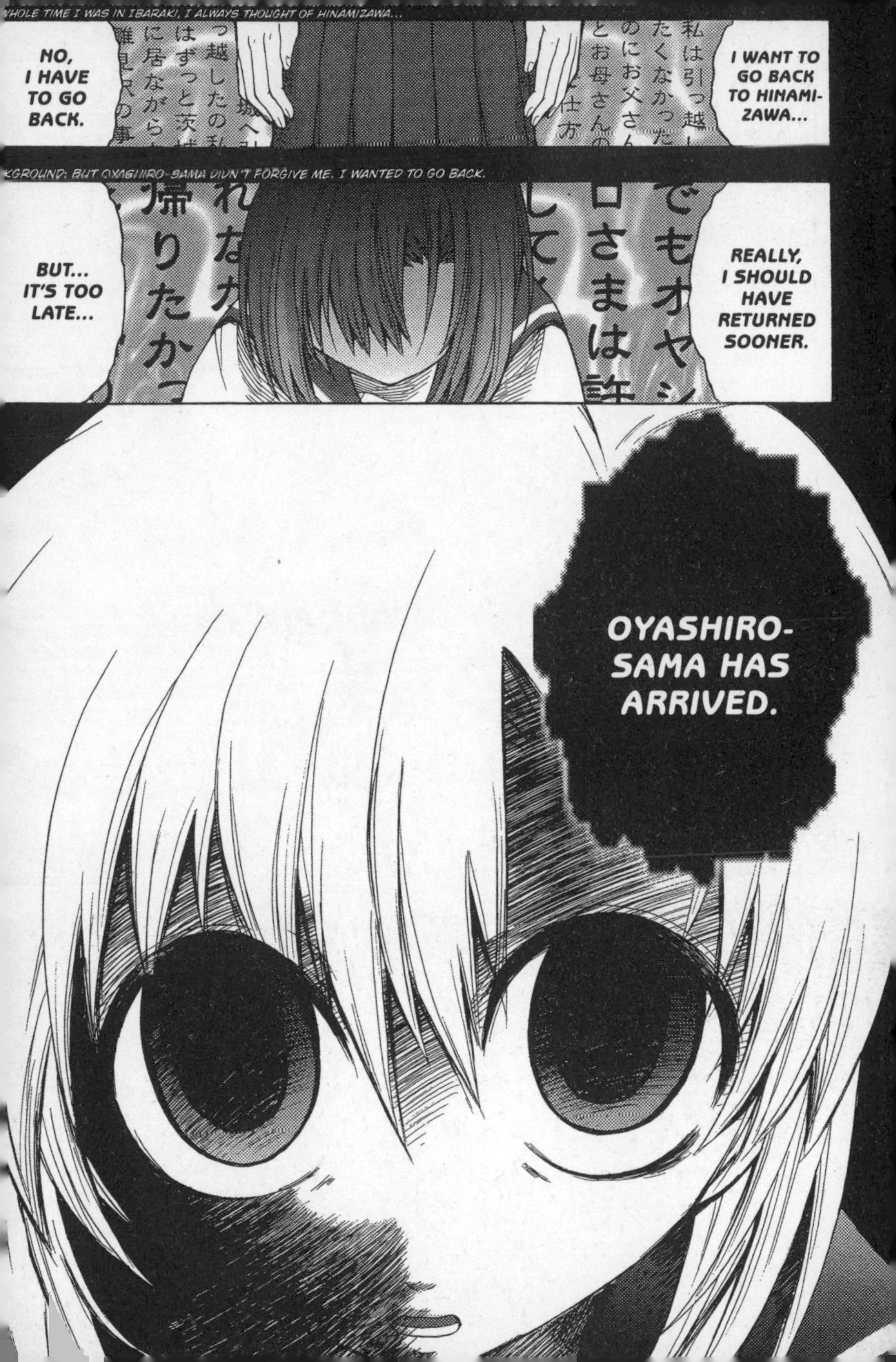
WHOLE TIME I WAS IN IBARAKI, I ALWAYS THOUGHT OF HINAMIZAWA...
I WANT TO GO BACK TO HINAMI-ZAWA...
NO, I HAVE TO GO BACK.
KGROUND: BUT OYASHIRO-SAMA DIDN'T FORGIVE ME. I WANTED TO GO BACK.
REALLY, I SHOULD HAVE RETURNED SOONER.
BUT... IT'S TOO LATE...
OYASHIRO-SAMA HAS ARRIVED.

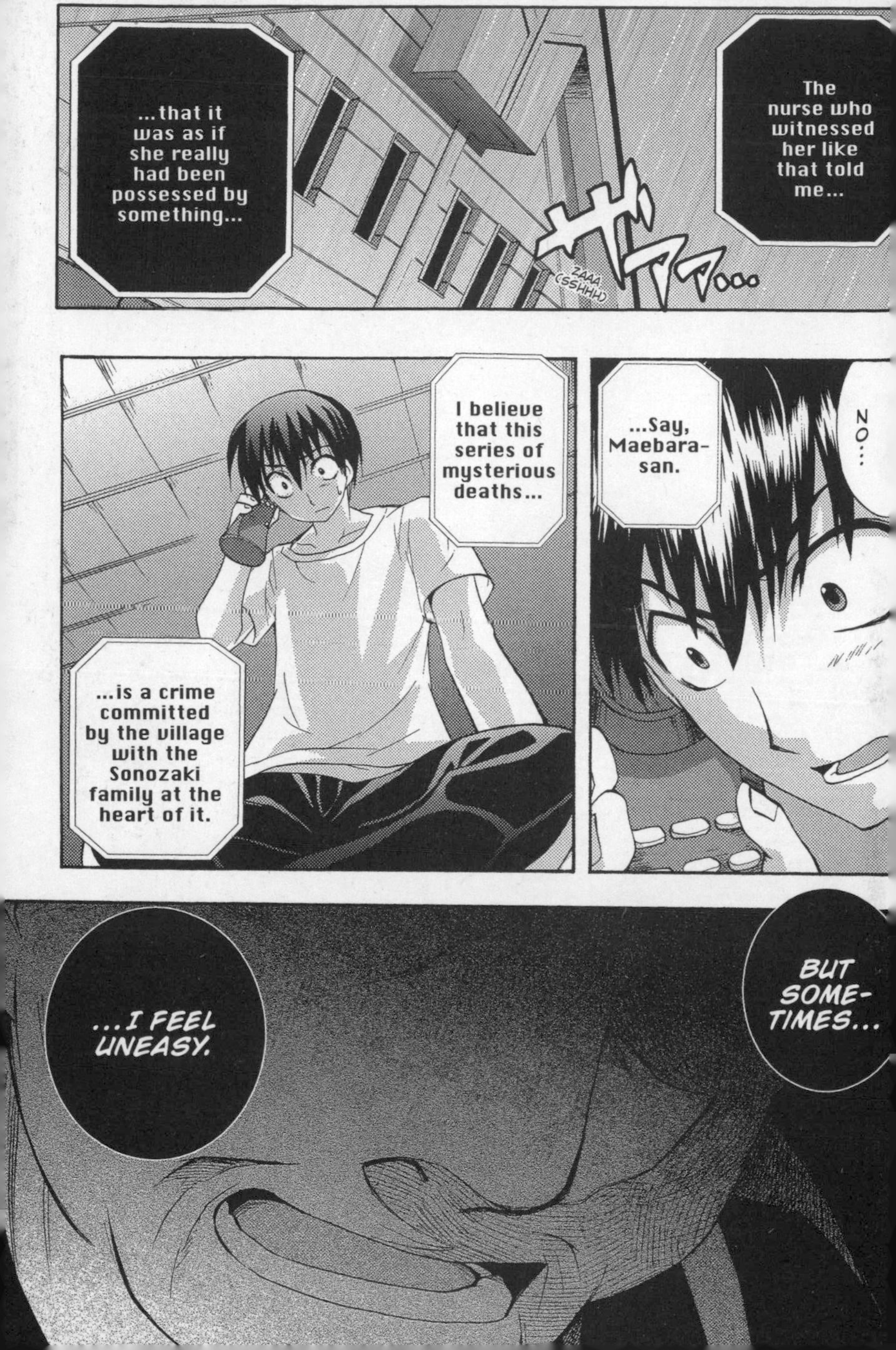
The nurse who witnessed her like that told me...
...that it was as if she really had been possessed by something...
ZAAA (SSHHH)
NO...
...Say, Maebara-san.
I believe that this series of mysterious deaths...
...is a crime committed by the village with the Sonozaki family at the heart of it.
BUT SOMETIMES...
...I FEEL UNEASY.

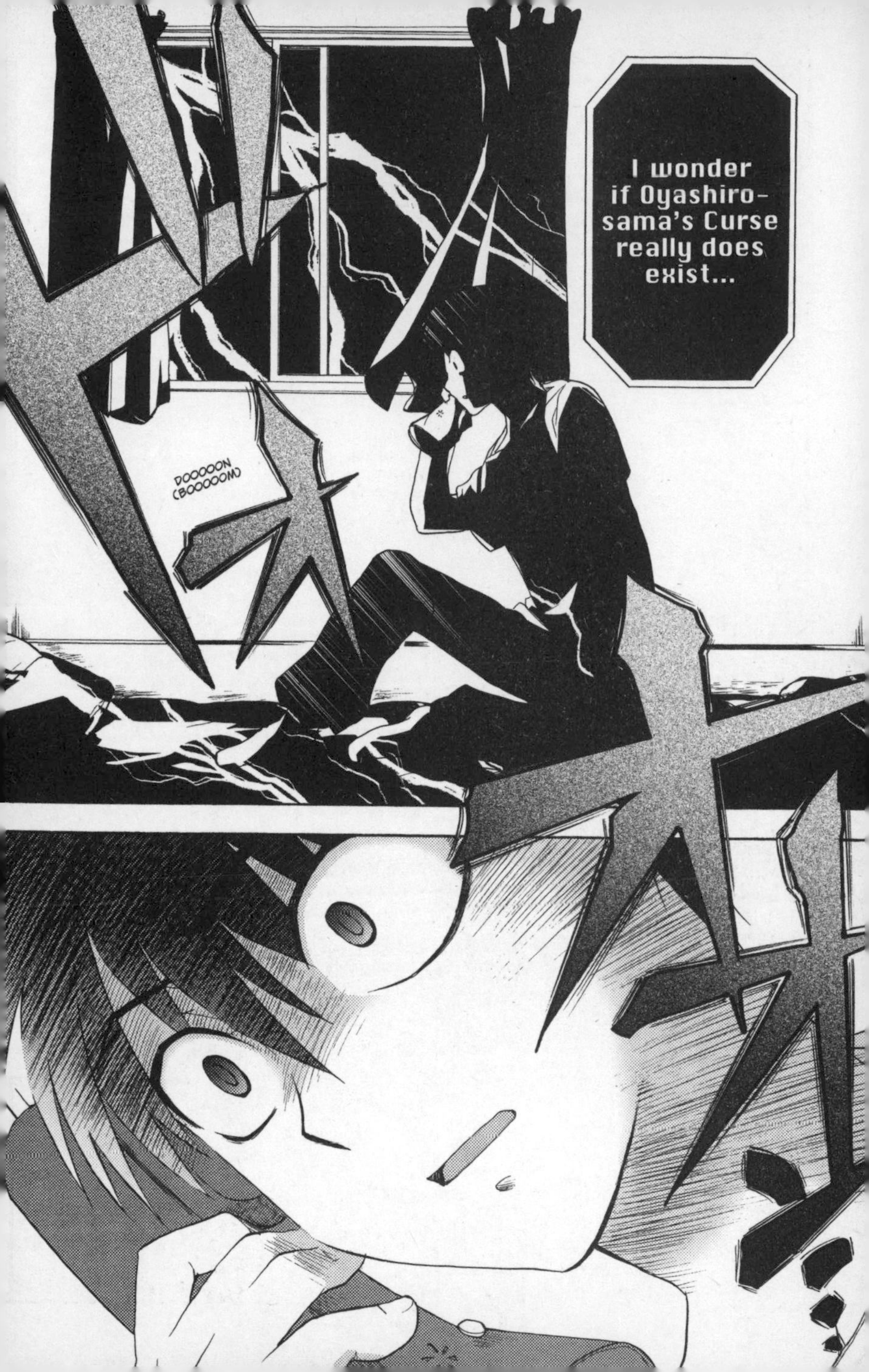
I wonder if Oyashiro-sama's Curse really does exist...
DOOOOON (BOOOOOM)

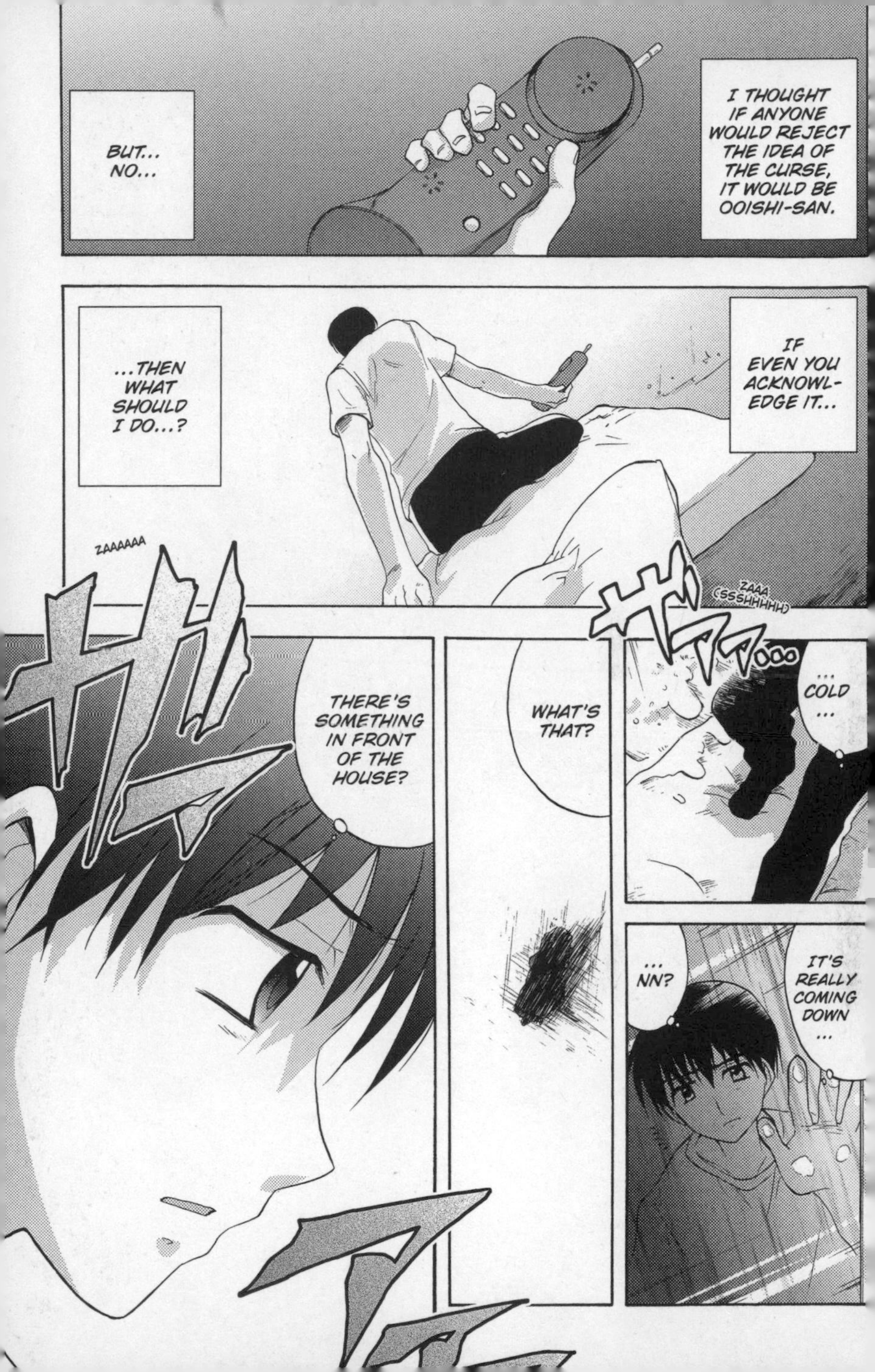
I THOUGHT IF ANYONE WOULD REJECT THE IDEA OF THE CURSE, IT WOULD BE OOISHI-SAN.
BUT... NO...
IF EVEN YOU ACKNOWL-EDGE IT...
...THEN WHAT SHOULD I DO...?
ZAAAAAA
ZAAA (SSSHHHHHH)
...COLD...
IT'S REALLY COMING DOWN...
...NN?
WHAT'S THAT?
THERE'S SOMETHING IN FRONT OF THE HOUSE?

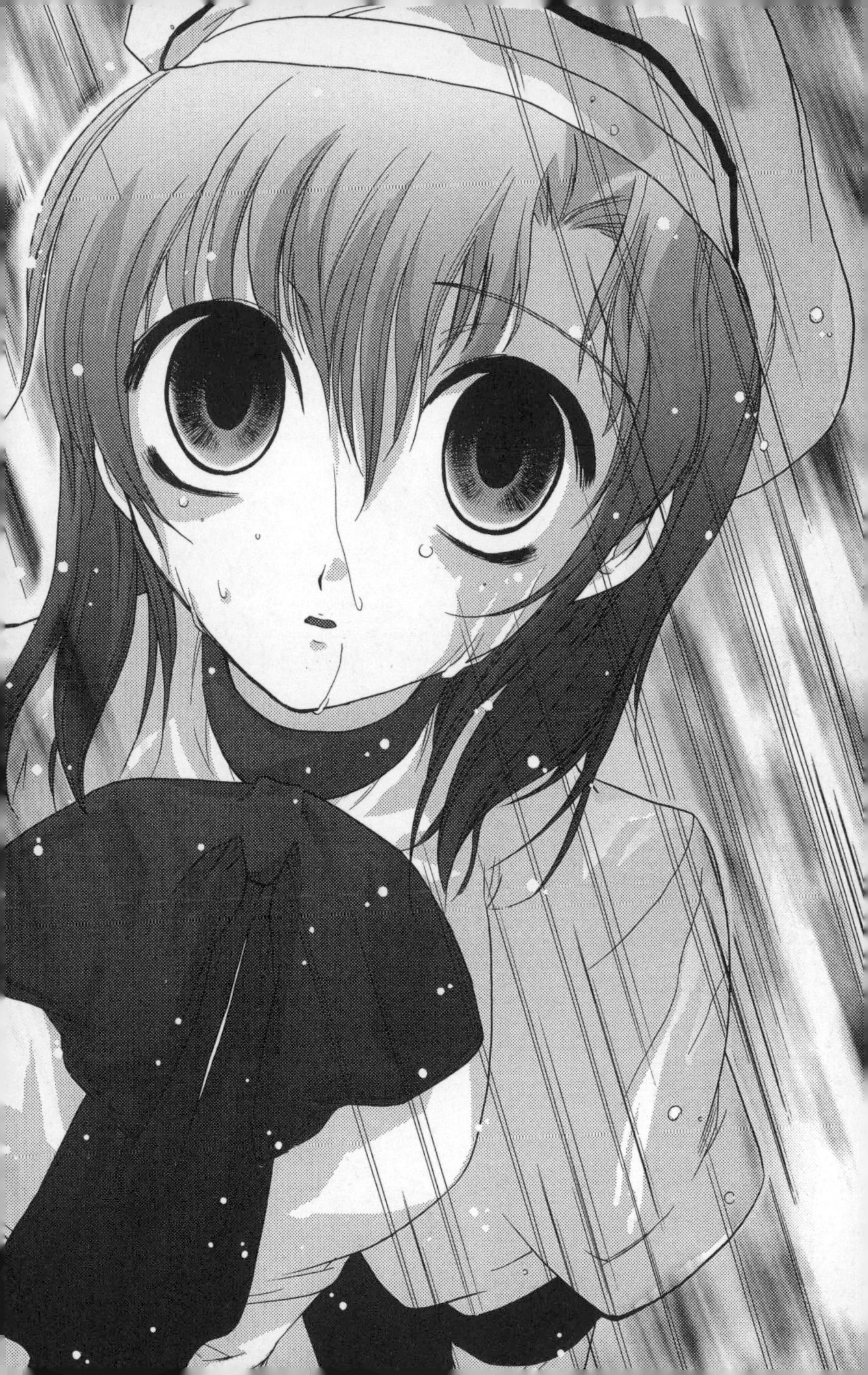

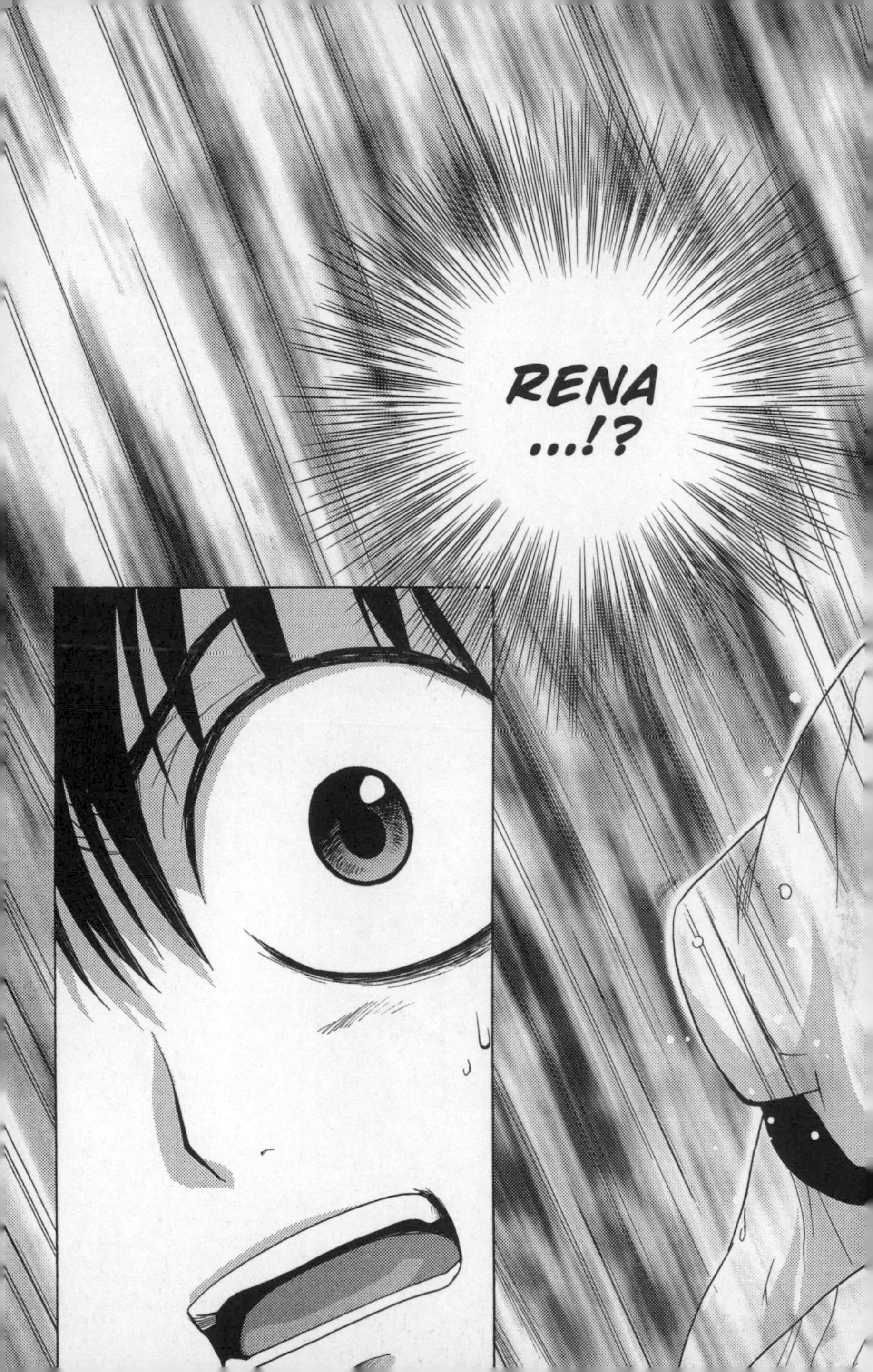
RENA ...!?

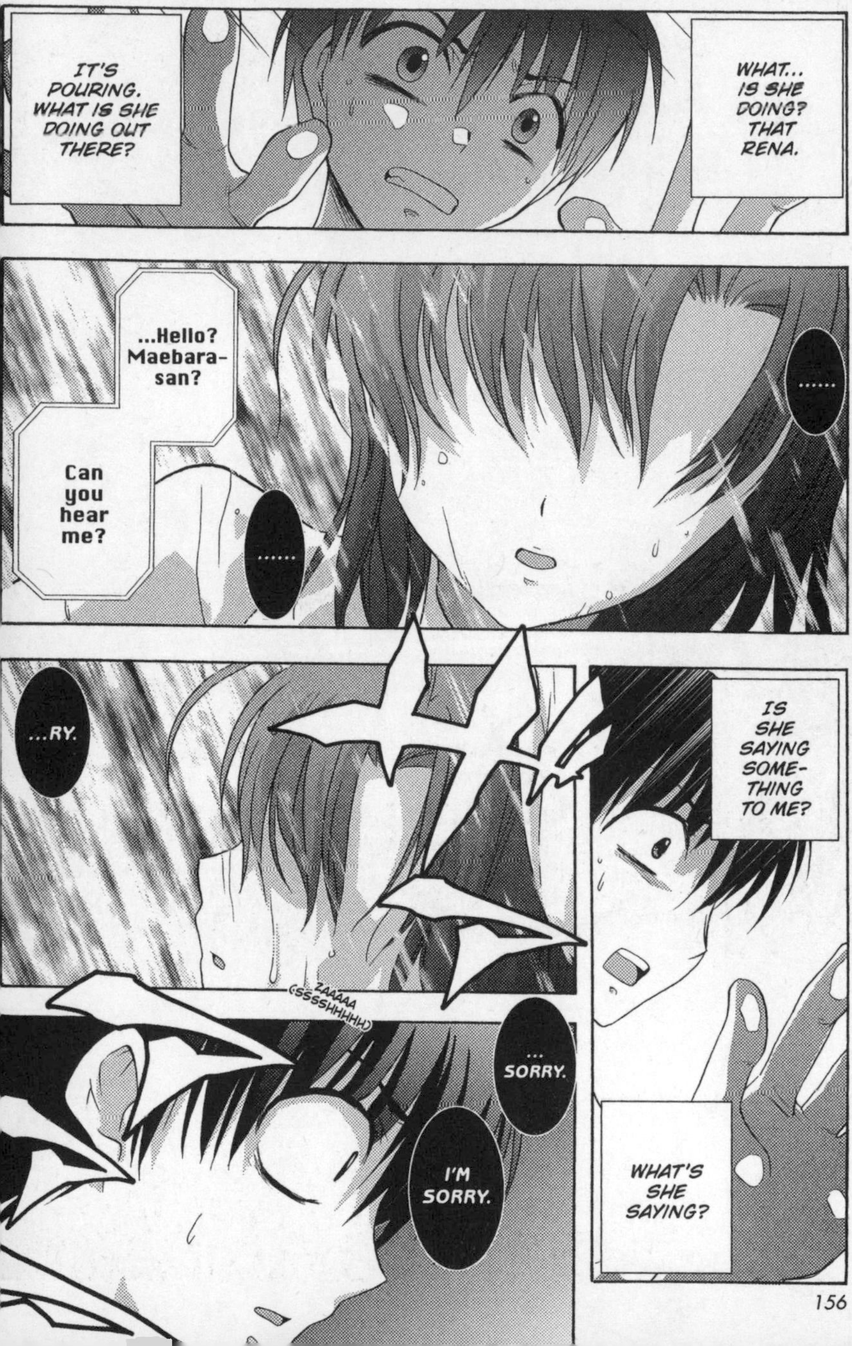
WHAT... IS SHE DOING? THAT RENA.
IT'S POURING. WHAT IS SHE DOING OUT THERE?
......
...Hello? Maebara-san?
Can you hear me?
......
IS SHE SAYING SOME-THING TO ME?
WHAT'S SHE SAYING?
...RY.
ZAAAAA (SSSSHHHHHH)
... SORRY.
I'M SORRY.

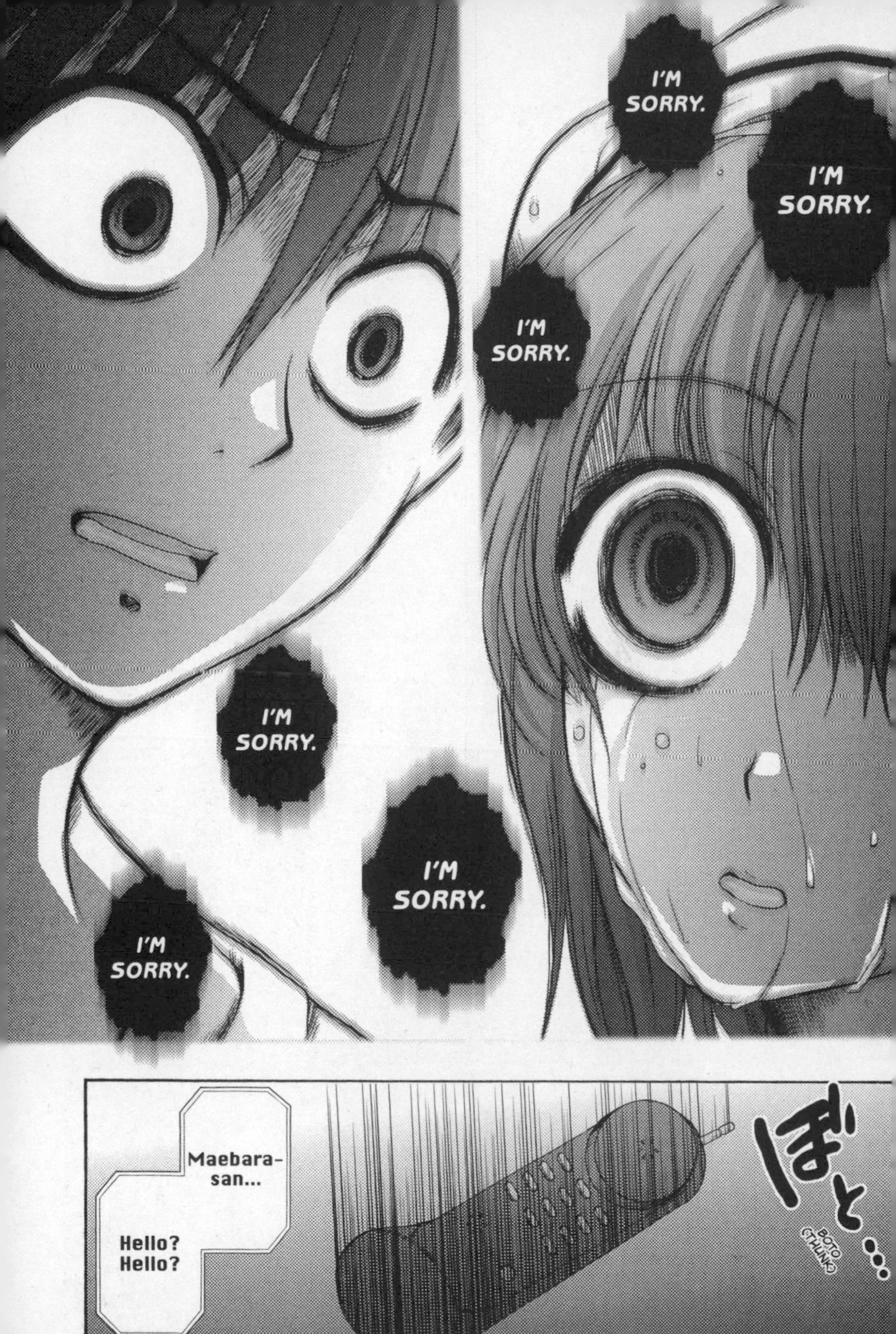
I'M SORRY.
I'M SORRY.
I'M SORRY.
I'M SORRY.
I'M SORRY.
I'M SORRY.
ぼと…
BOTO (THUNK)
Maebara-san...
Hello? Hello?

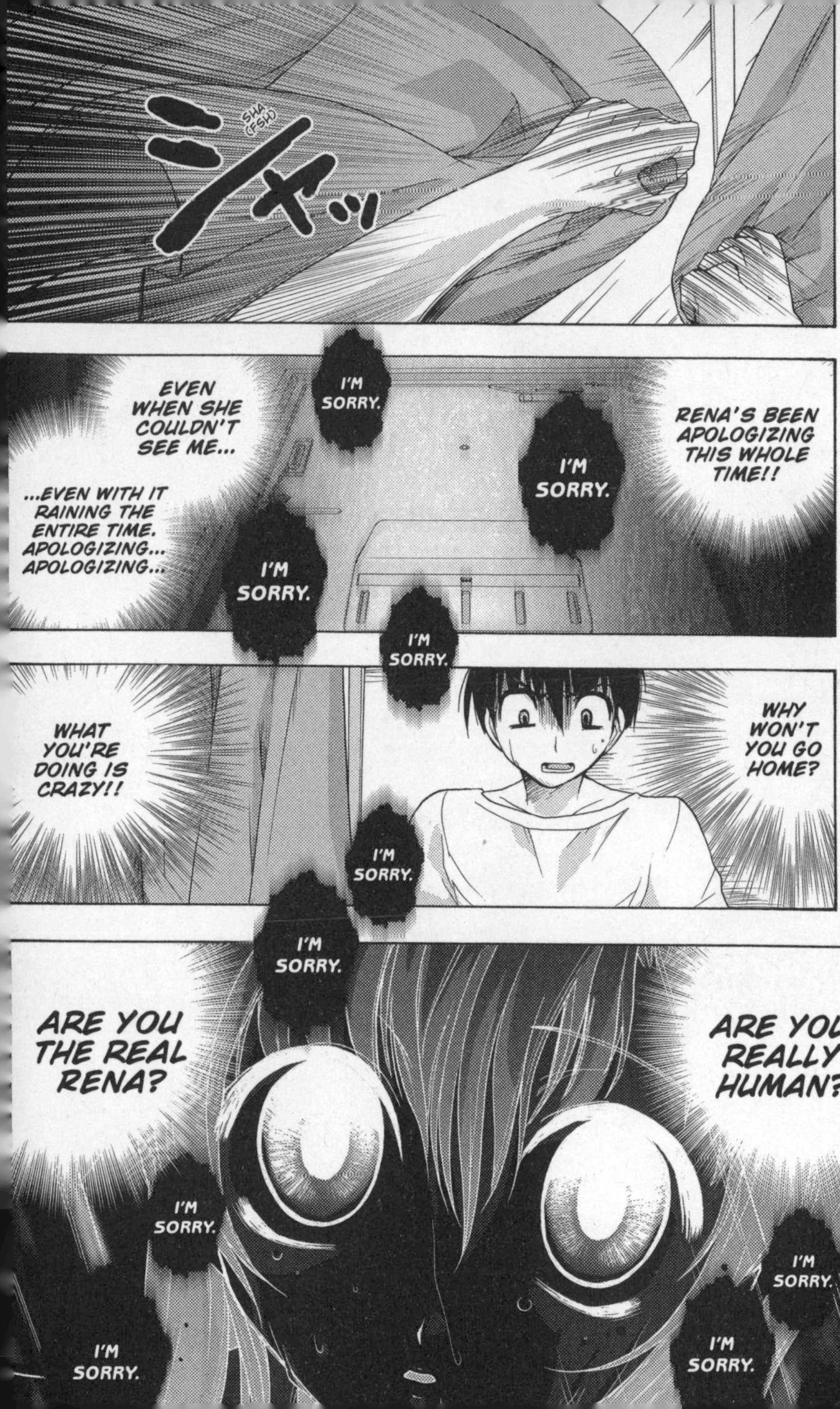

SHA (FSH)
RENA'S BEEN APOLOGIZING THIS WHOLE TIME!!
I'M SORRY.
I'M SORRY.
EVEN WHEN SHE COULDN'T SEE ME...
...EVEN WITH IT RAINING THE ENTIRE TIME. APOLOGIZING... APOLOGIZING...
I'M SORRY.
I'M SORRY.
WHY WON'T YOU GO HOME?
WHAT YOU'RE DOING IS CRAZY!!
I'M SORRY.
I'M SORRY.
ARE YOU REALLY HUMAN?
ARE YOU THE REAL RENA?
I'M SORRY.
I'M SORRY.
I'M SORRY.
I'M SORRY.

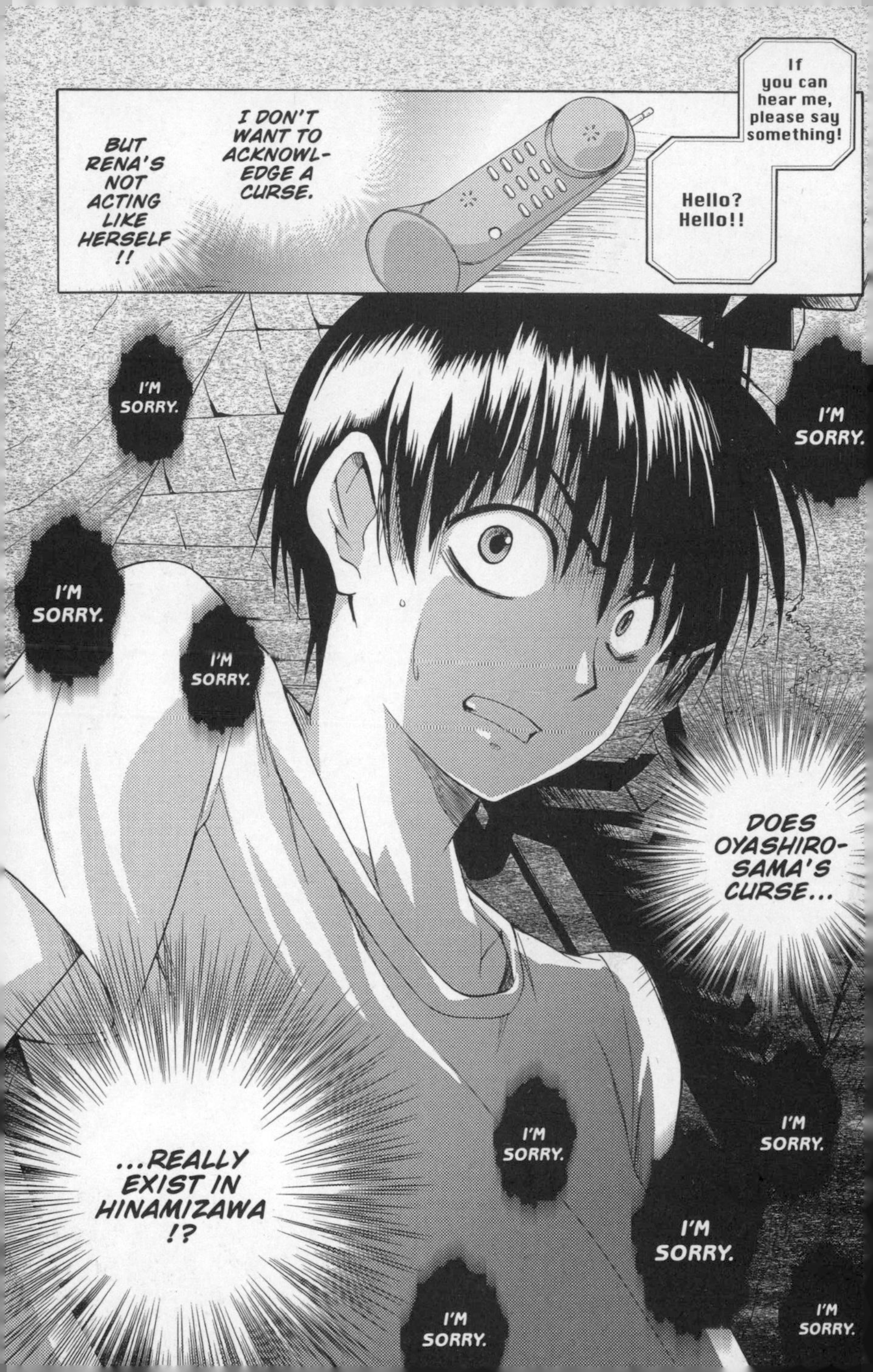
If you can hear me, please say something!
Hello? Hello!!
I DON'T WANT TO ACKNOWL-EDGE A CURSE.
BUT RENA'S NOT ACTING LIKE HERSELF!!
I'M SORRY.
I'M SORRY.
DOES OYASHIRO-SAMA'S CURSE...
I'M SORRY.
I'M SORRY.
I'M SORRY.
I'M SORRY.
...REALLY EXIST IN HINAMIZAWA!?
I'M SORRY.
I'M SORRY.
I'M SORRY.

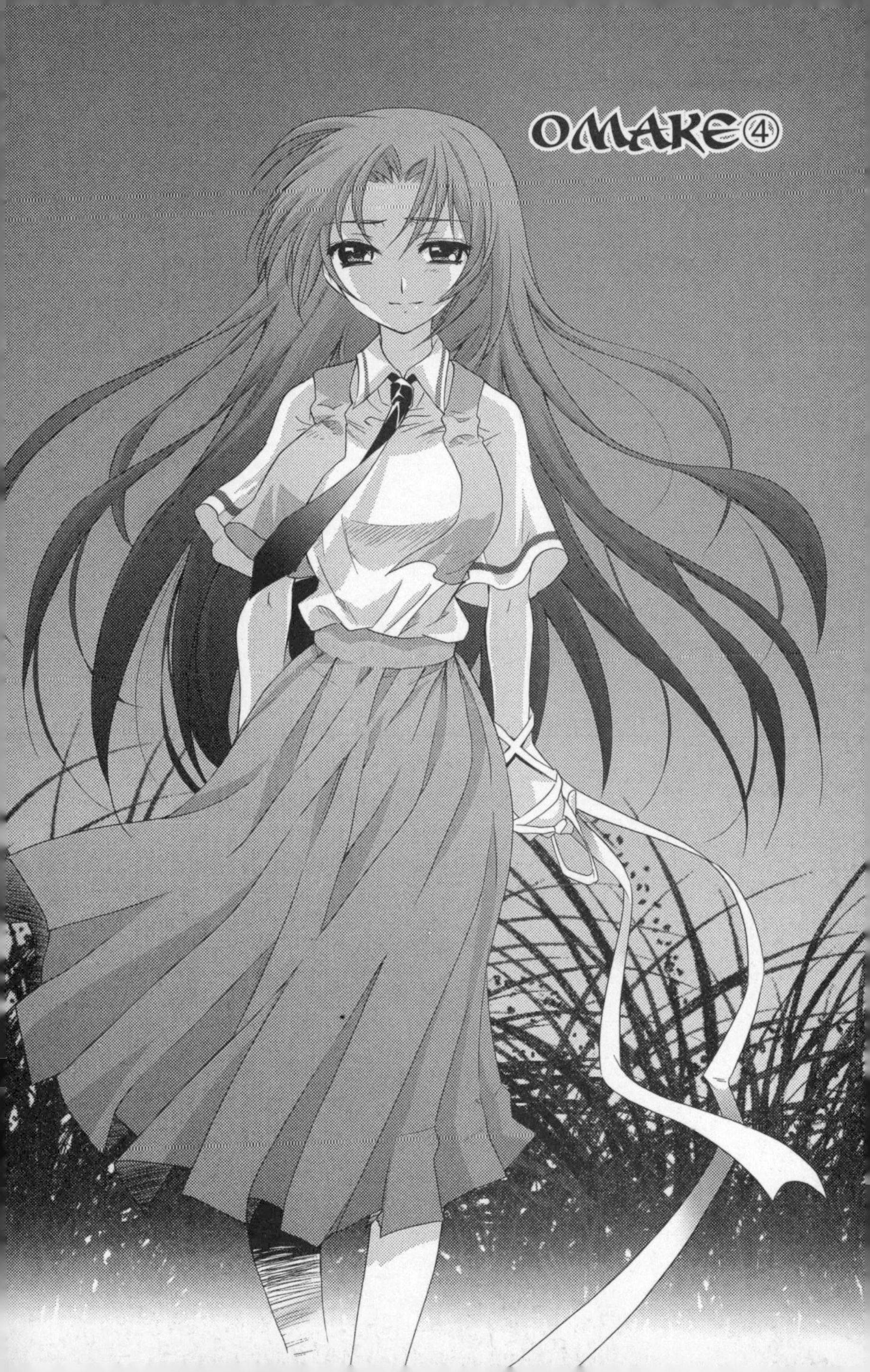
OMAKE④

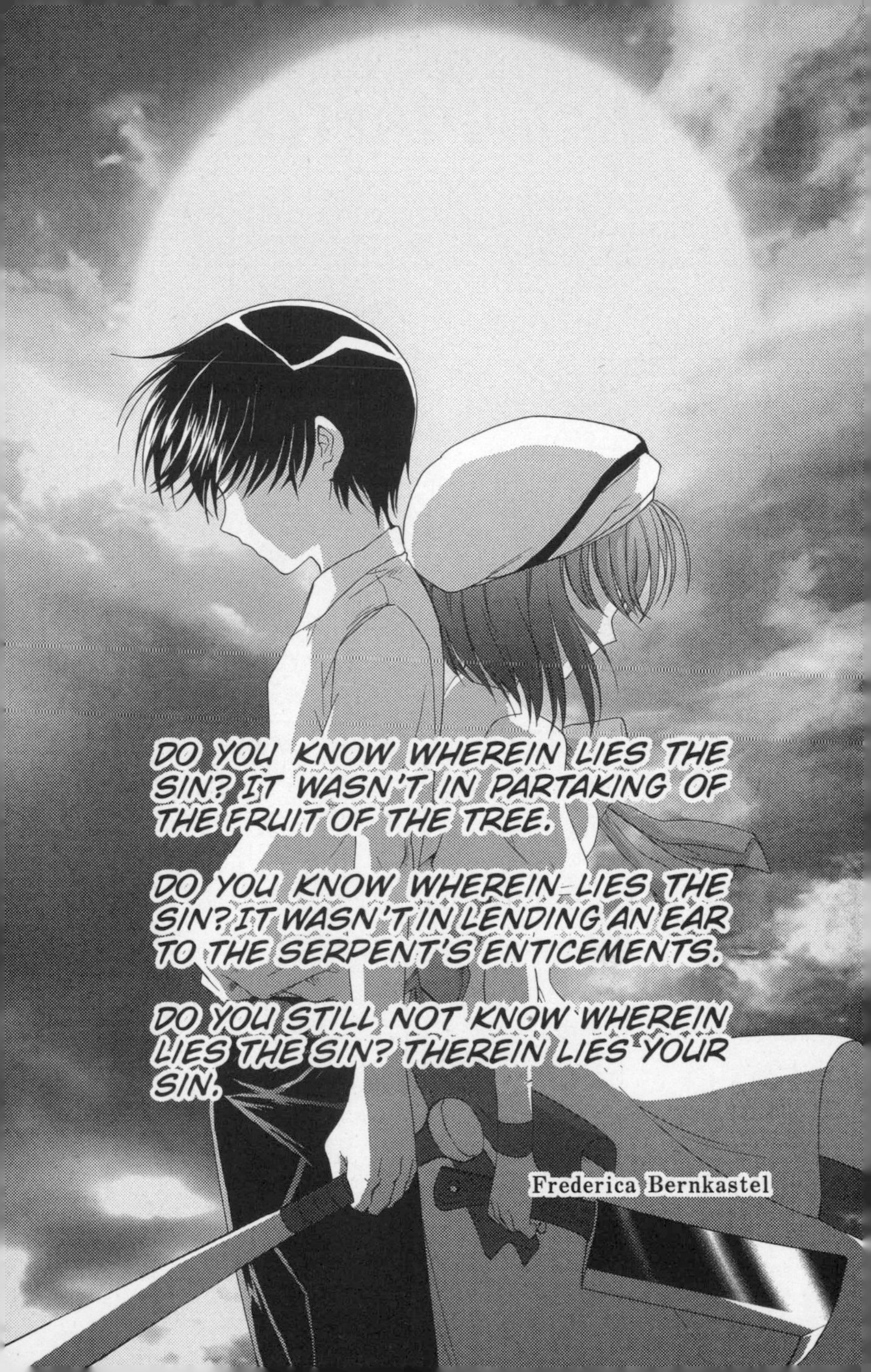
DO YOU KNOW WHEREIN LIES THE SIN? IT WASN'T IN PARTAKING OF THE FRUIT OF THE TREE.
DO YOU KNOW WHEREIN LIES THE SIN? IT WASN'T IN LENDING AN EAR TO THE SERPENT'S ENTICEMENTS.
DO YOU STILL NOT KNOW WHEREIN LIES THE SIN? THEREIN LIES YOUR SIN.
Frederica Bernkastel

FINAL CHAPTER: WISH

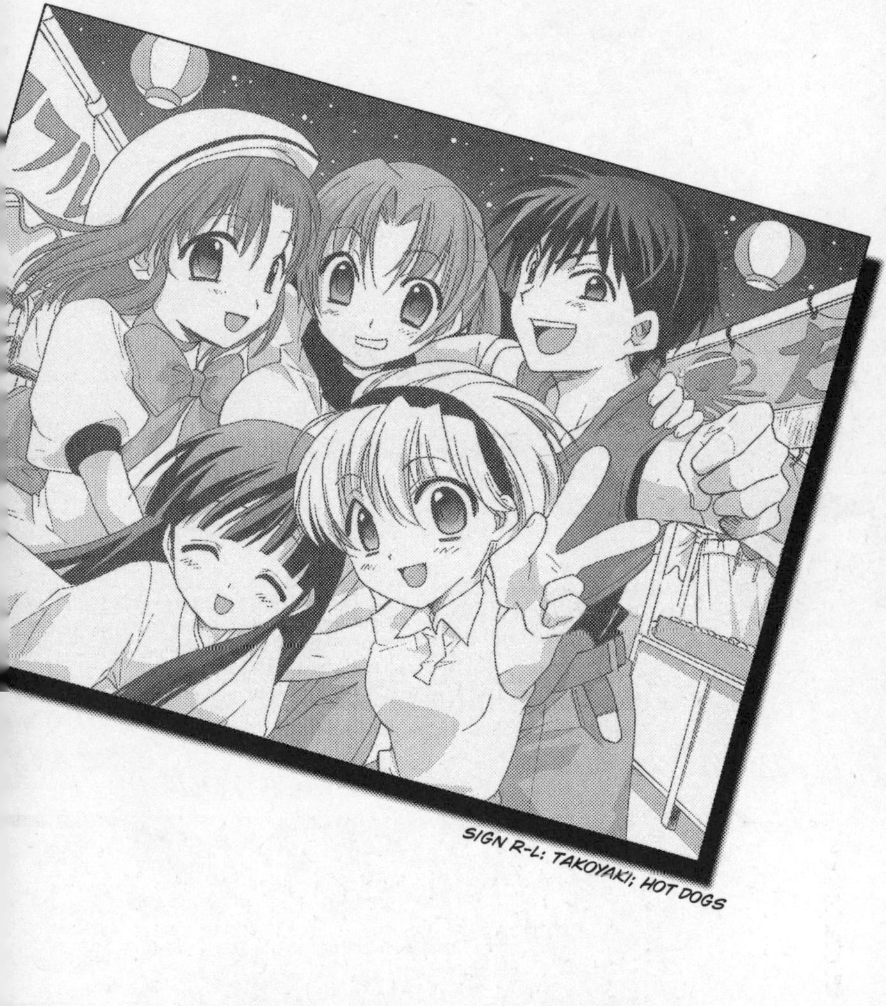

SIGN R-L: TAKOYAKI; HOT DOGS

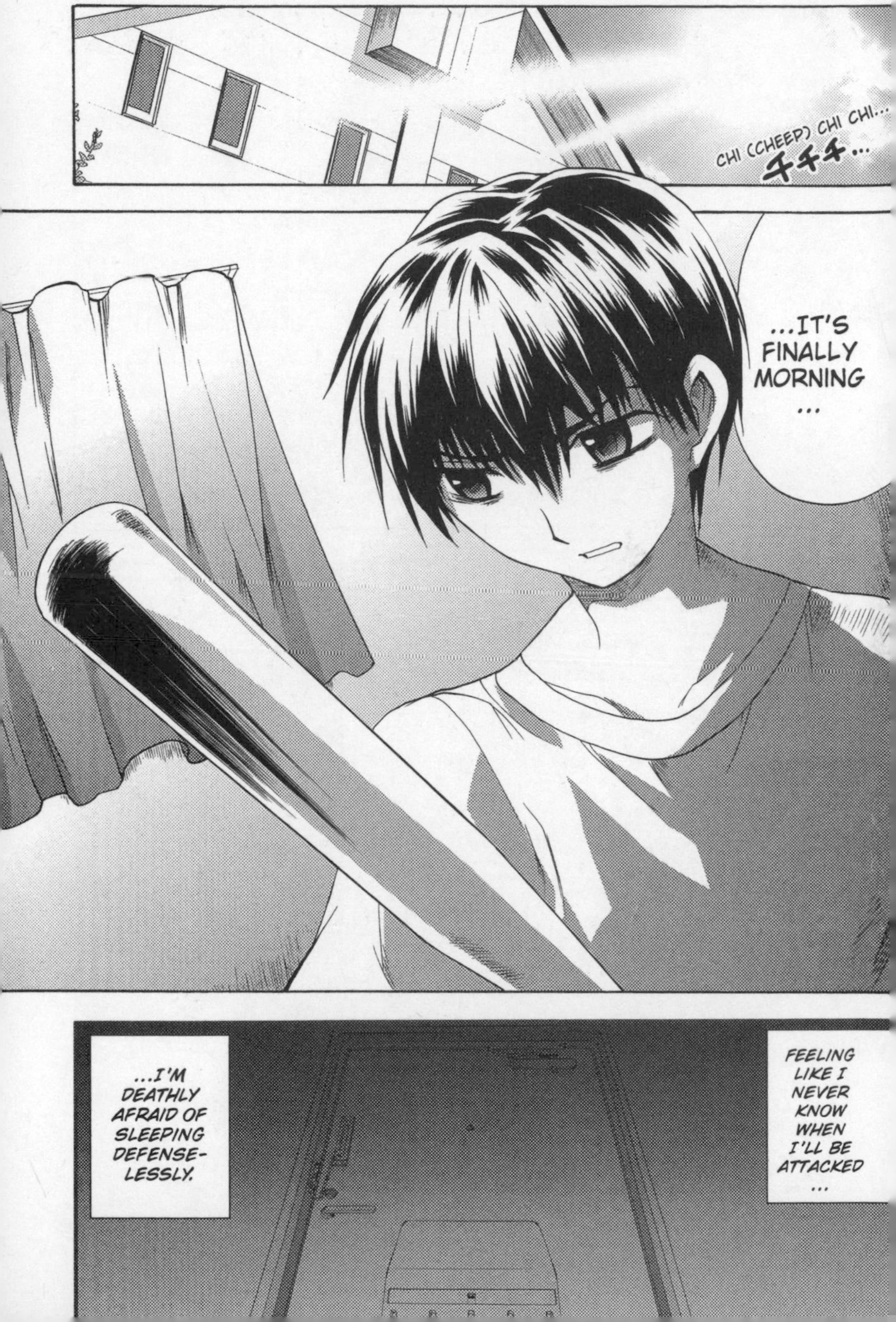
CHI (CHEEP) CHI CHI...
チチチ...
...IT'S FINALLY MORNING ...
FEELING LIKE I NEVER KNOW WHEN I'LL BE ATTACKED ...
...I'M DEATHLY AFRAID OF SLEEPING DEFENSELESSLY.

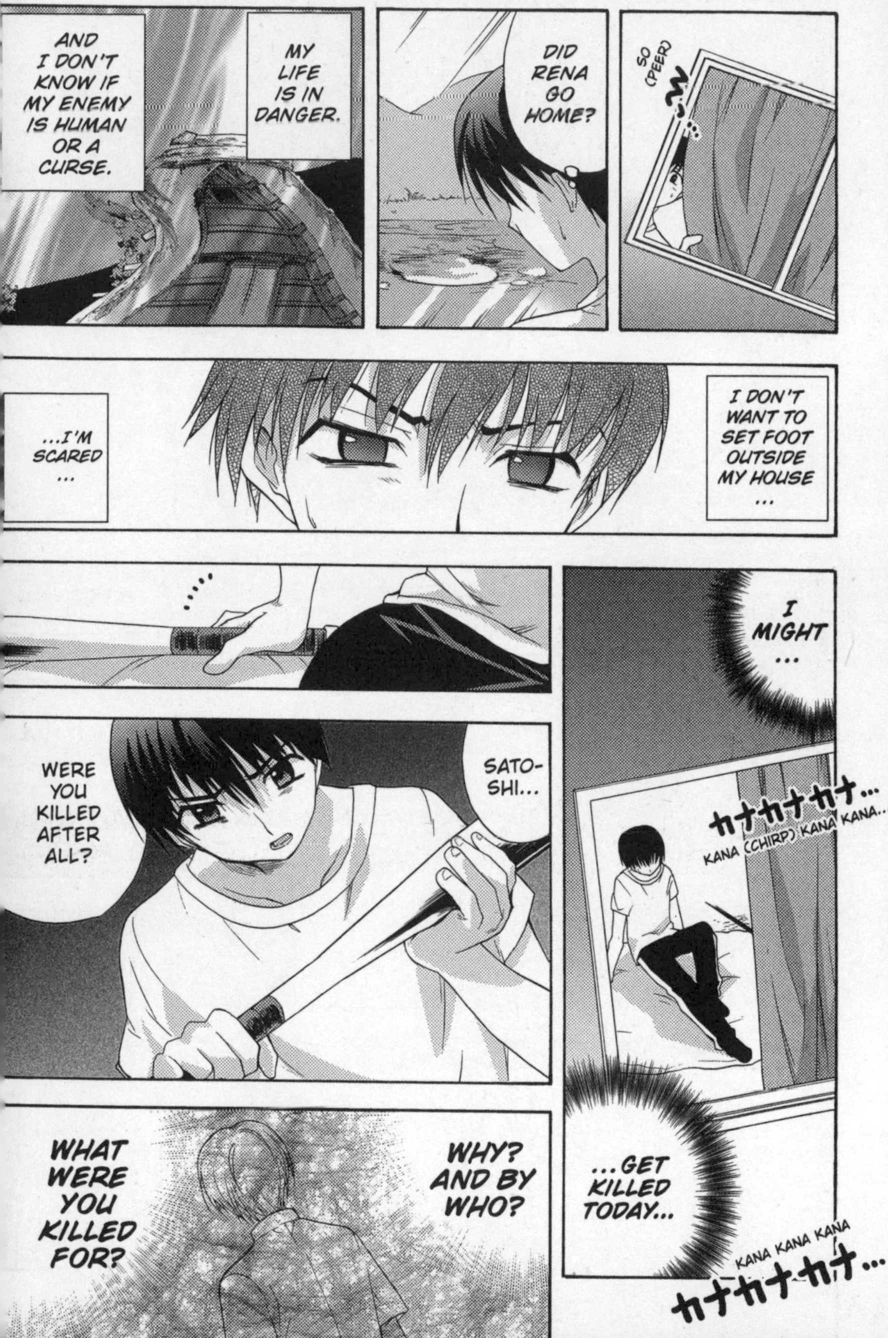
SO (PEER)
DID RENA GO HOME?
MY LIFE IS IN DANGER.
AND I DON'T KNOW IF MY ENEMY IS HUMAN OR A CURSE.
I DON'T WANT TO SET FOOT OUTSIDE MY HOUSE...
...I'M SCARED...
I MIGHT...
カナカナカナ... KANA (CHIRP) KANA KANA...
...GET KILLED TODAY...
KANA KANA KANA カナカナカナ...
....
SATO-SHI...
WERE YOU KILLED AFTER ALL?
WHY? AND BY WHO?
WHAT WERE YOU KILLED FOR?

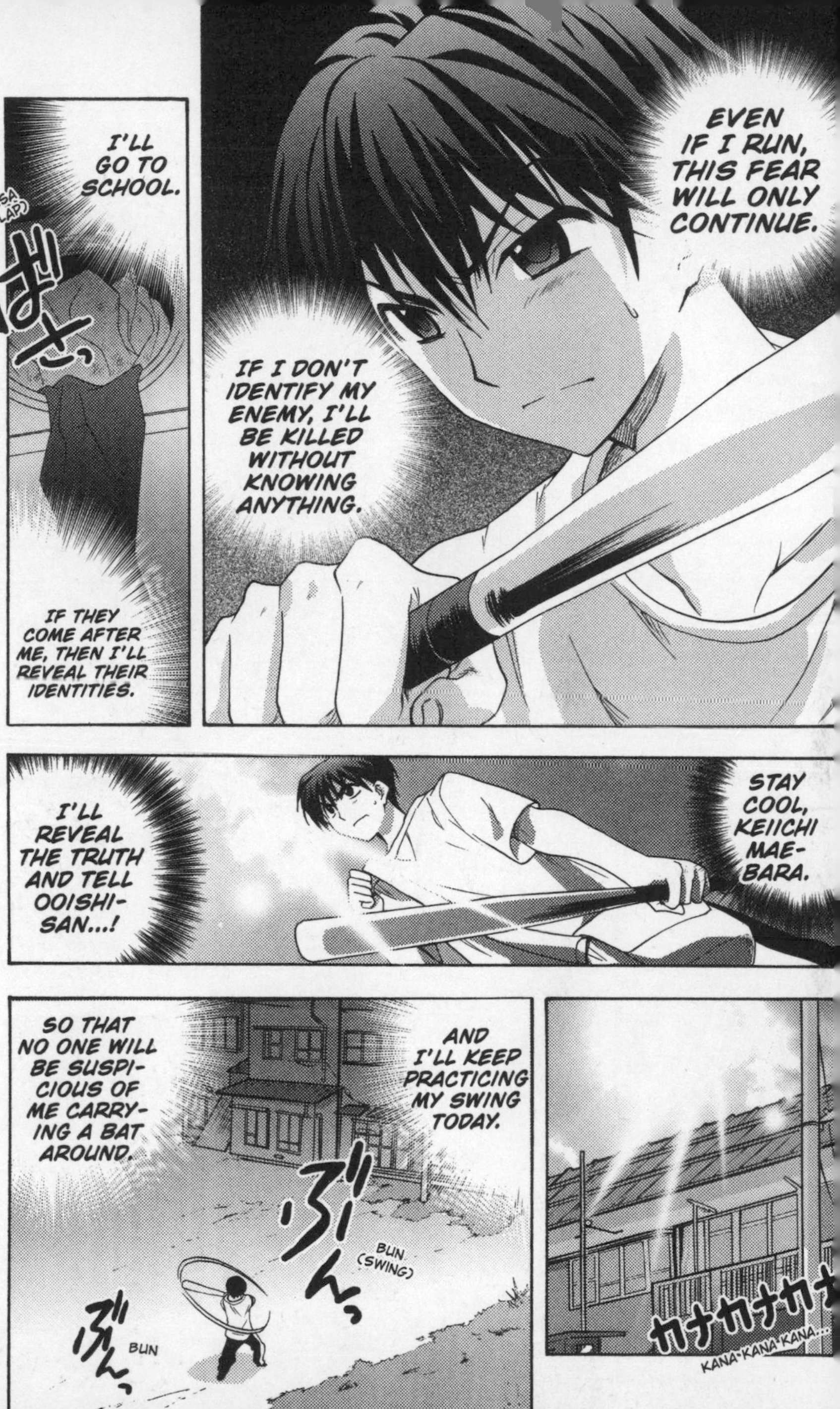
EVEN IF I RUN, THIS FEAR WILL ONLY CONTINUE.
IF I DON'T IDENTIFY MY ENEMY, I'LL BE KILLED WITHOUT KNOWING ANYTHING.
I'LL GO TO SCHOOL.
ばさっ
BASA (FLAP)
IF THEY COME AFTER ME, THEN I'LL REVEAL THEIR IDENTITIES.
STAY COOL, KEIICHI MAE-BARA.
I'LL REVEAL THE TRUTH AND TELL OOISHI-SAN...!
カナカナカナ
KANA KANA KANA...
AND I'LL KEEP PRACTICING MY SWING TODAY.
SO THAT NO ONE WILL BE SUSPI-CIOUS OF ME CARRY-ING A BAT AROUND.
ぶーん
BUN (SWING)
ぶん
BUN

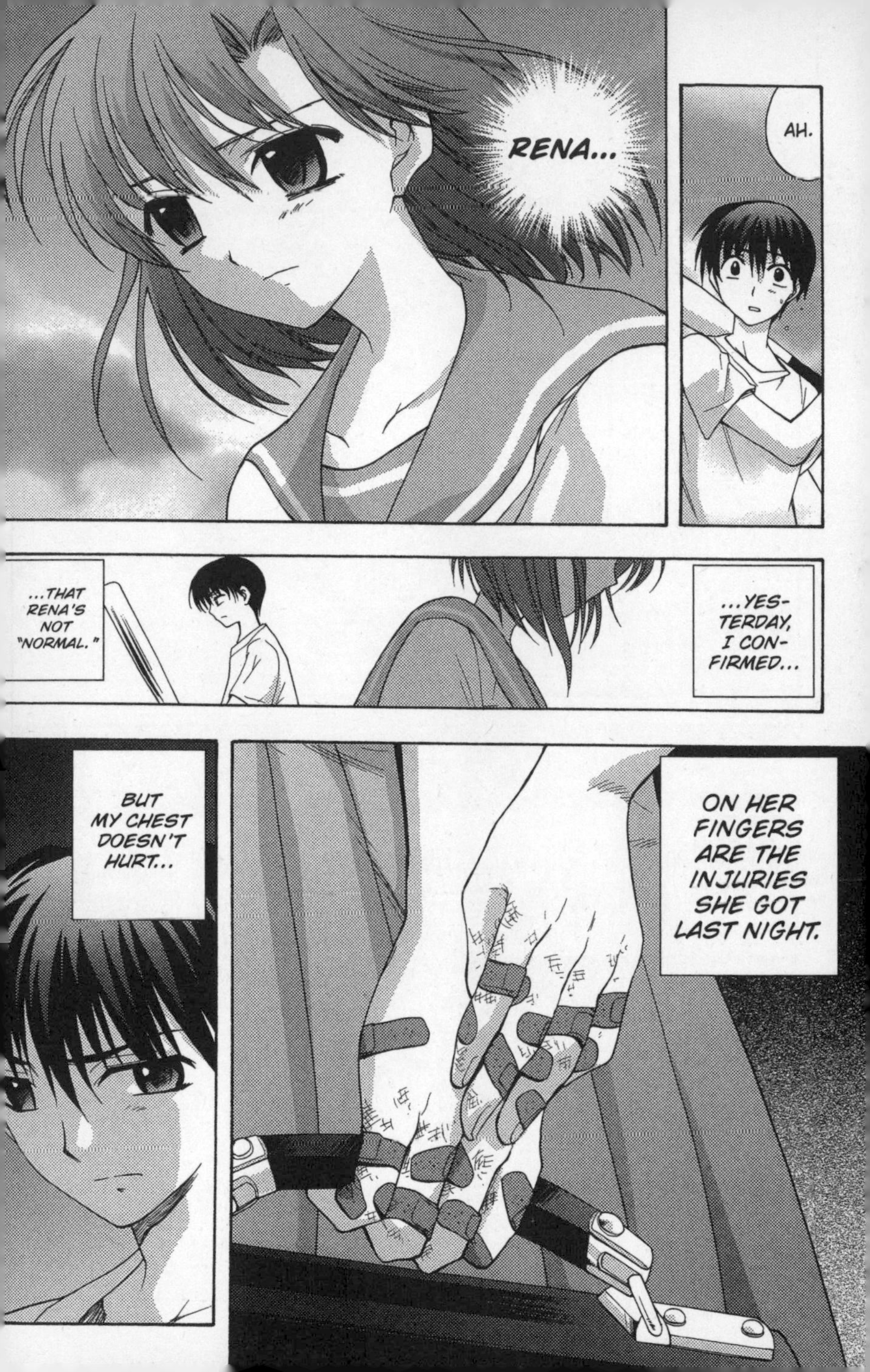
AH.
RENA...
...YES-TERDAY, I CON-FIRMED...
...THAT RENA'S NOT "NORMAL."
ON HER FINGERS ARE THE INJURIES SHE GOT LAST NIGHT.
BUT MY CHEST DOESN'T HURT...

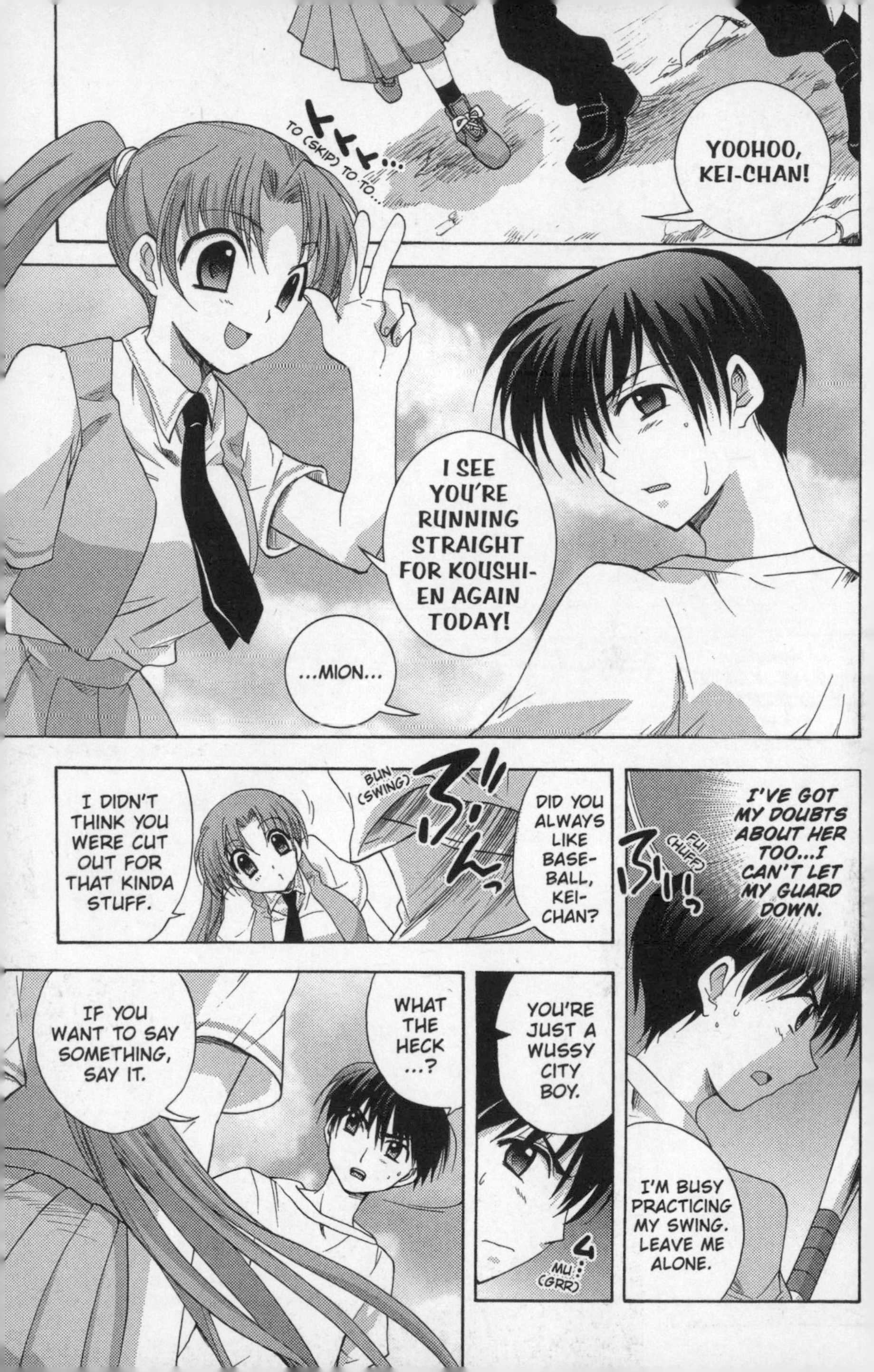
YOOHOO, KEI-CHAN!
TO (SKIP) TO TO...
I SEE YOU'RE RUNNING STRAIGHT FOR KOUSHI-EN AGAIN TODAY!
...MION...
I'VE GOT MY DOUBTS ABOUT HER TOO...I CAN'T LET MY GUARD DOWN.
FU! (HUFF)
I'M BUSY PRACTICING MY SWING. LEAVE ME ALONE.
BUN (SWING)
DID YOU ALWAYS LIKE BASE-BALL, KEI-CHAN?
I DIDN'T THINK YOU WERE CUT OUT FOR THAT KINDA STUFF.
YOU'RE JUST A WUSSY CITY BOY.
MU (GRR)
WHAT THE HECK ...?
IF YOU WANT TO SAY SOMETHING, SAY IT.

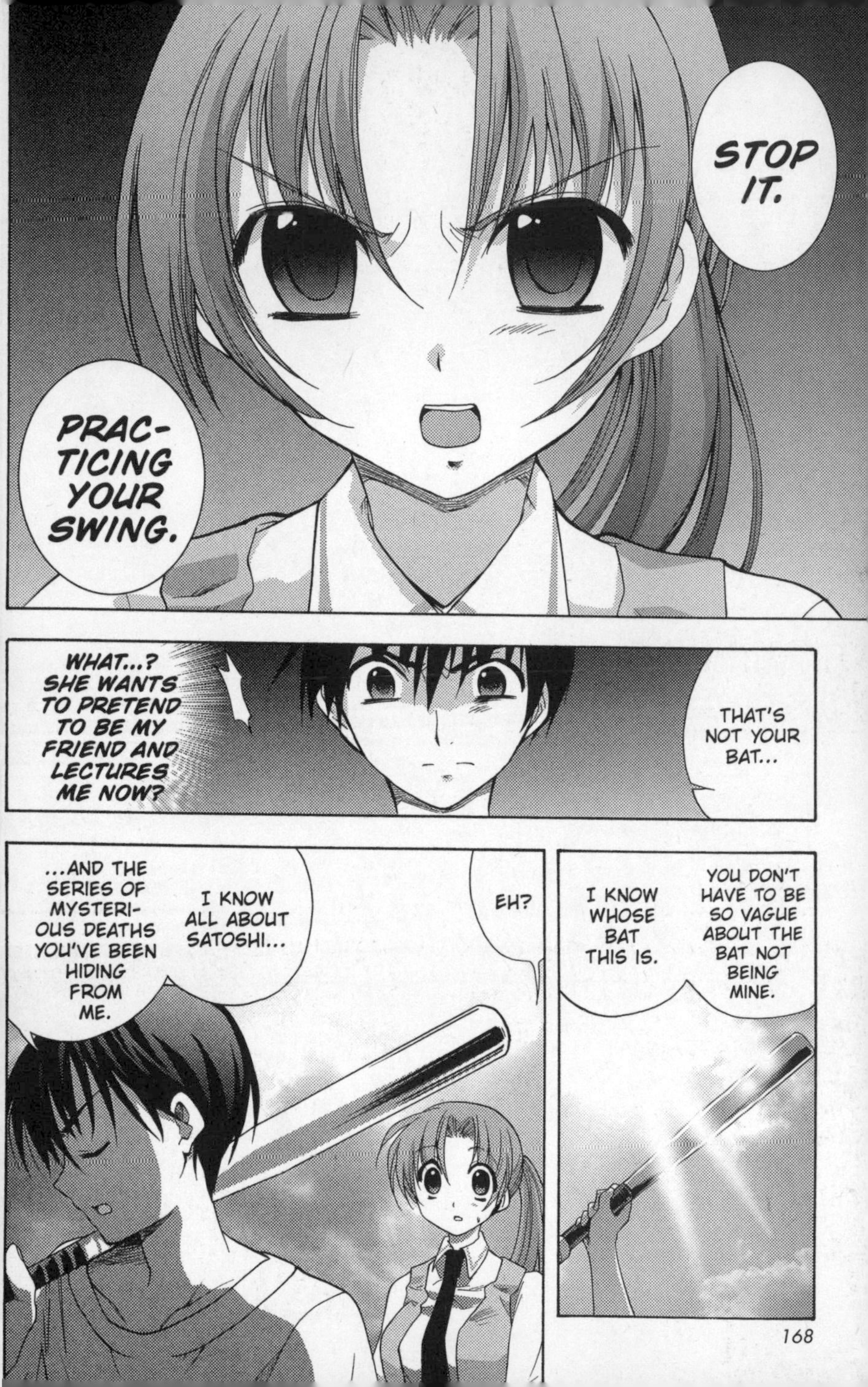
STOP IT.
PRAC-TICING YOUR SWING.
THAT'S NOT YOUR BAT...
WHAT...? SHE WANTS TO PRETEND TO BE MY FRIEND AND LECTURES ME NOW?
YOU DON'T HAVE TO BE SO VAGUE ABOUT THE BAT NOT BEING MINE.
I KNOW WHOSE BAT THIS IS.
EH?
I KNOW ALL ABOUT SATOSHI...
...AND THE SERIES OF MYSTERI-OUS DEATHS YOU'VE BEEN HIDING FROM ME.

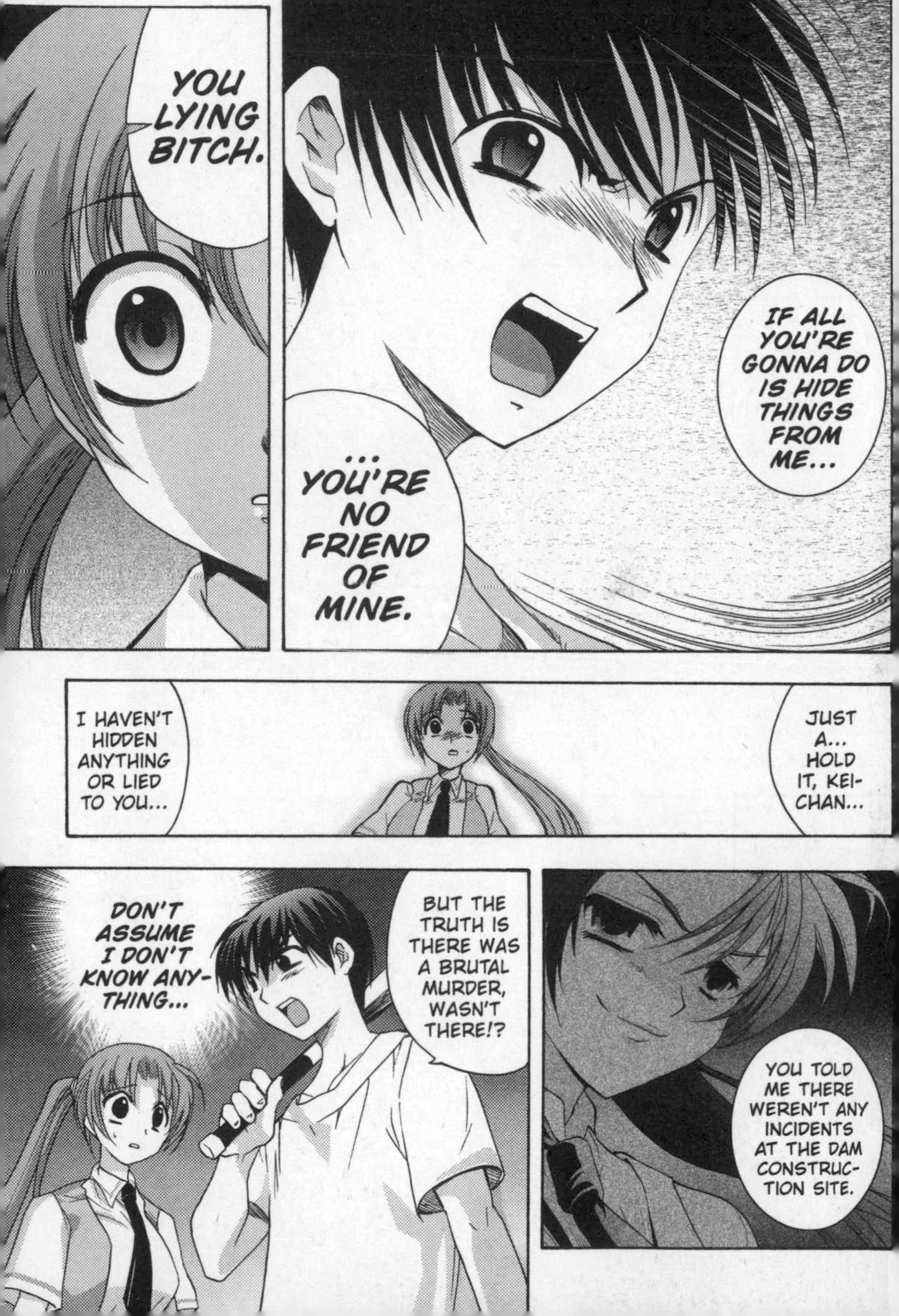
IF ALL YOU'RE GONNA DO IS HIDE THINGS FROM ME...
...YOU'RE NO FRIEND OF MINE.
YOU LYING BITCH.
JUST A... HOLD IT, KEI-CHAN...
I HAVEN'T HIDDEN ANYTHING OR LIED TO YOU...
YOU TOLD ME THERE WEREN'T ANY INCIDENTS AT THE DAM CONSTRUCTION SITE.
BUT THE TRUTH IS THERE WAS A BRUTAL MURDER, WASN'T THERE!?
DON'T ASSUME I DON'T KNOW ANYTHING...

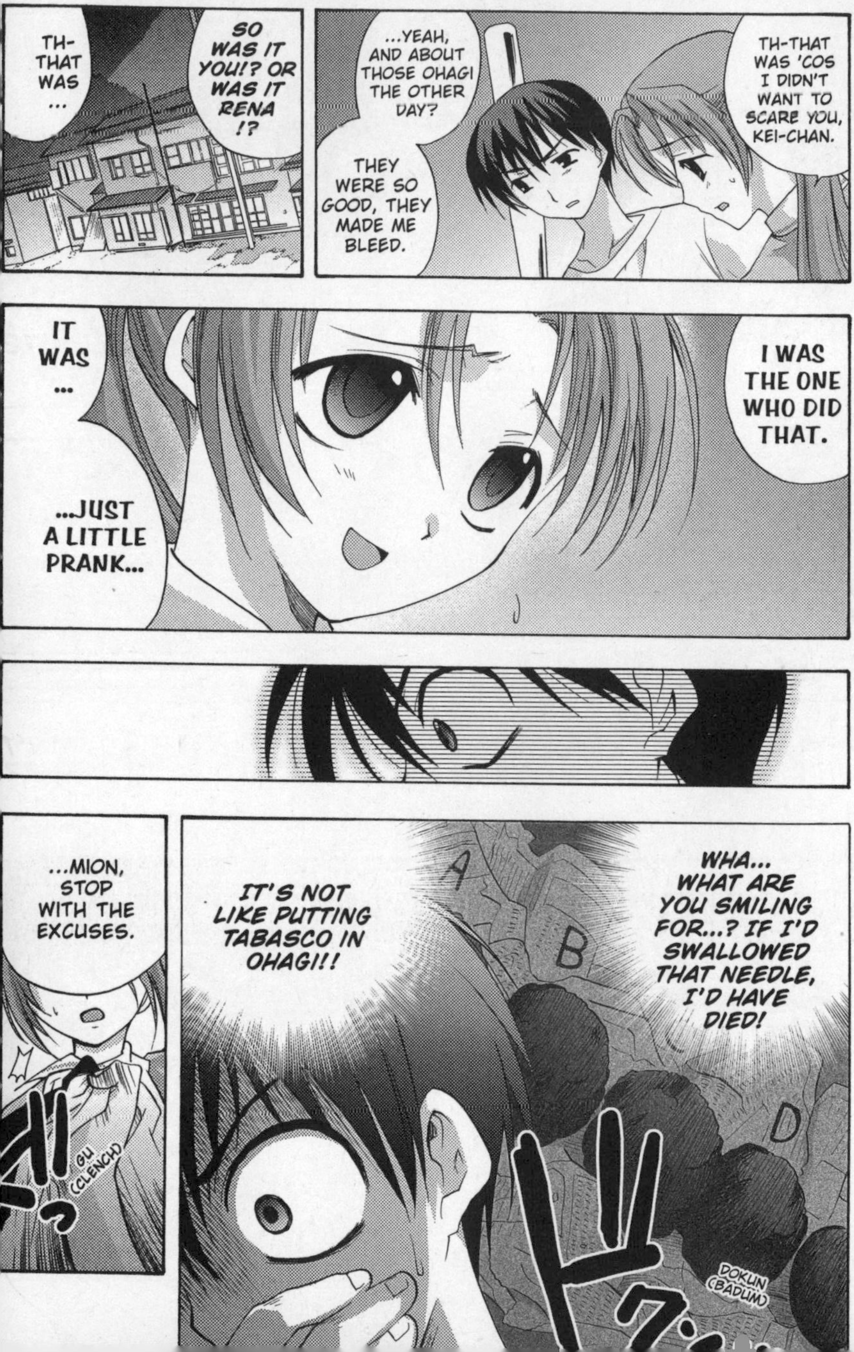
TH-THAT WAS 'COS I DIDN'T WANT TO SCARE YOU, KEI-CHAN.
...YEAH, AND ABOUT THOSE OHAGI THE OTHER DAY?
THEY WERE SO GOOD, THEY MADE ME BLEED.
SO WAS IT YOU!? OR WAS IT RENA !?
TH-THAT WAS ...
I WAS THE ONE WHO DID THAT.
IT WAS ...
...JUST A LITTLE PRANK...
WHA... WHAT ARE YOU SMILING FOR...? IF I'D SWALLOWED THAT NEEDLE, I'D HAVE DIED!
IT'S NOT LIKE PUTTING TABASCO IN OHAGI!!
DOKUN (BADUM)
...MION, STOP WITH THE EXCUSES.
GU (CLENCH)

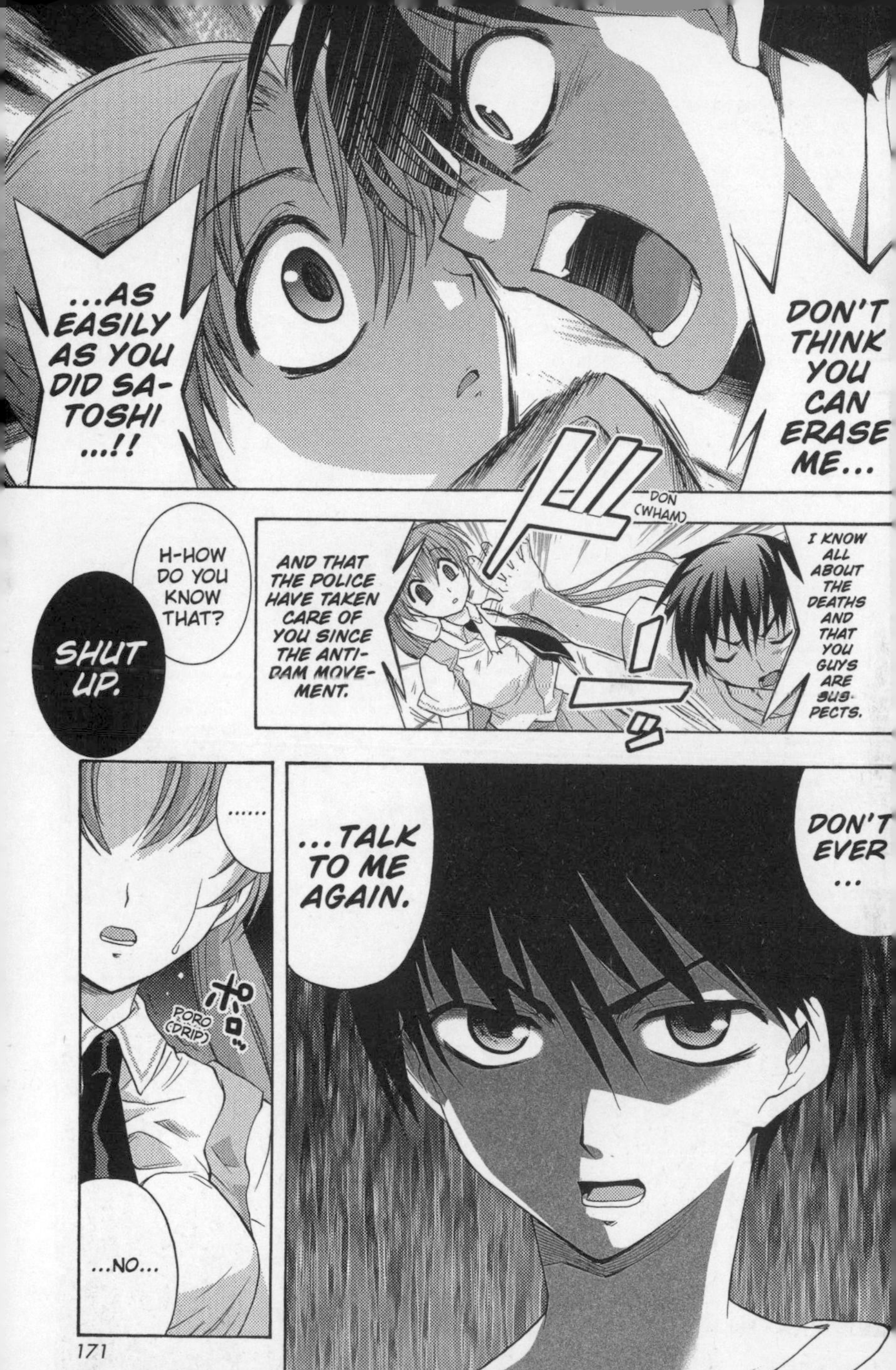
DON'T THINK YOU CAN ERASE ME...
...AS EASILY AS YOU DID SA-TOSHI...!!
I KNOW ALL ABOUT THE DEATHS AND THAT YOU GUYS ARE SUS-PECTS.
DON (WHAM)
AND THAT THE POLICE HAVE TAKEN CARE OF YOU SINCE THE ANTI-DAM MOVE-MENT.
H-HOW DO YOU KNOW THAT?
SHUT UP.
DON'T EVER...
...TALK TO ME AGAIN.
......
PORO (DRIP)
...NO...

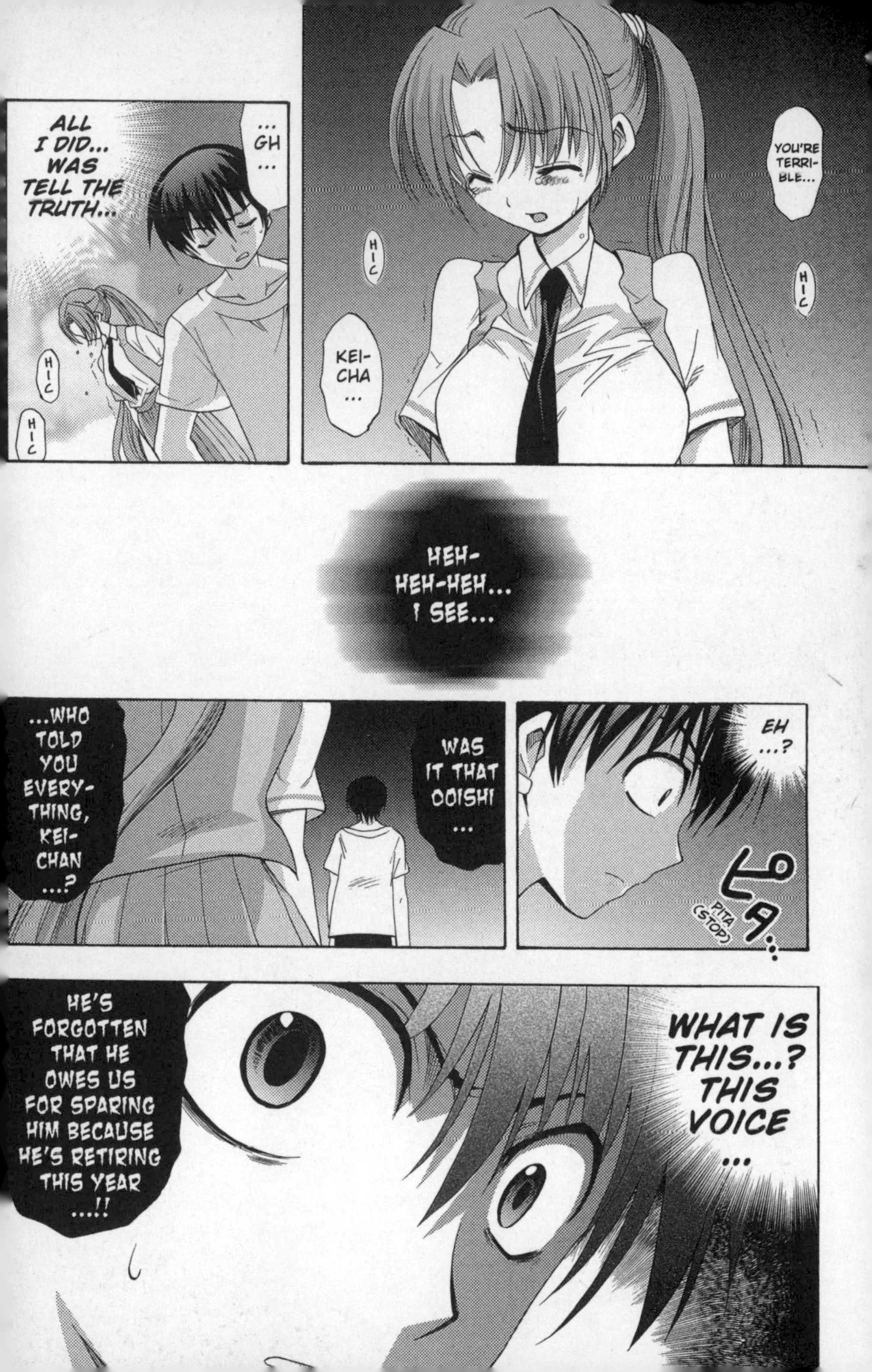
YOU'RE TERRIBLE...
HIC
HIC
KEI-CHA...
...GH...
ALL I DID... WAS TELL THE TRUTH...
HIC
HIC
HEH-HEH-HEH... I SEE...
EH...?
ピタ
PITA (STOP)
WAS IT THAT OOISHI...
...WHO TOLD YOU EVERYTHING, KEI-CHAN...?
WHAT IS THIS...? THIS VOICE...
HE'S FORGOTTEN THAT HE OWES US FOR SPARING HIM BECAUSE HE'S RETIRING THIS YEAR...!!

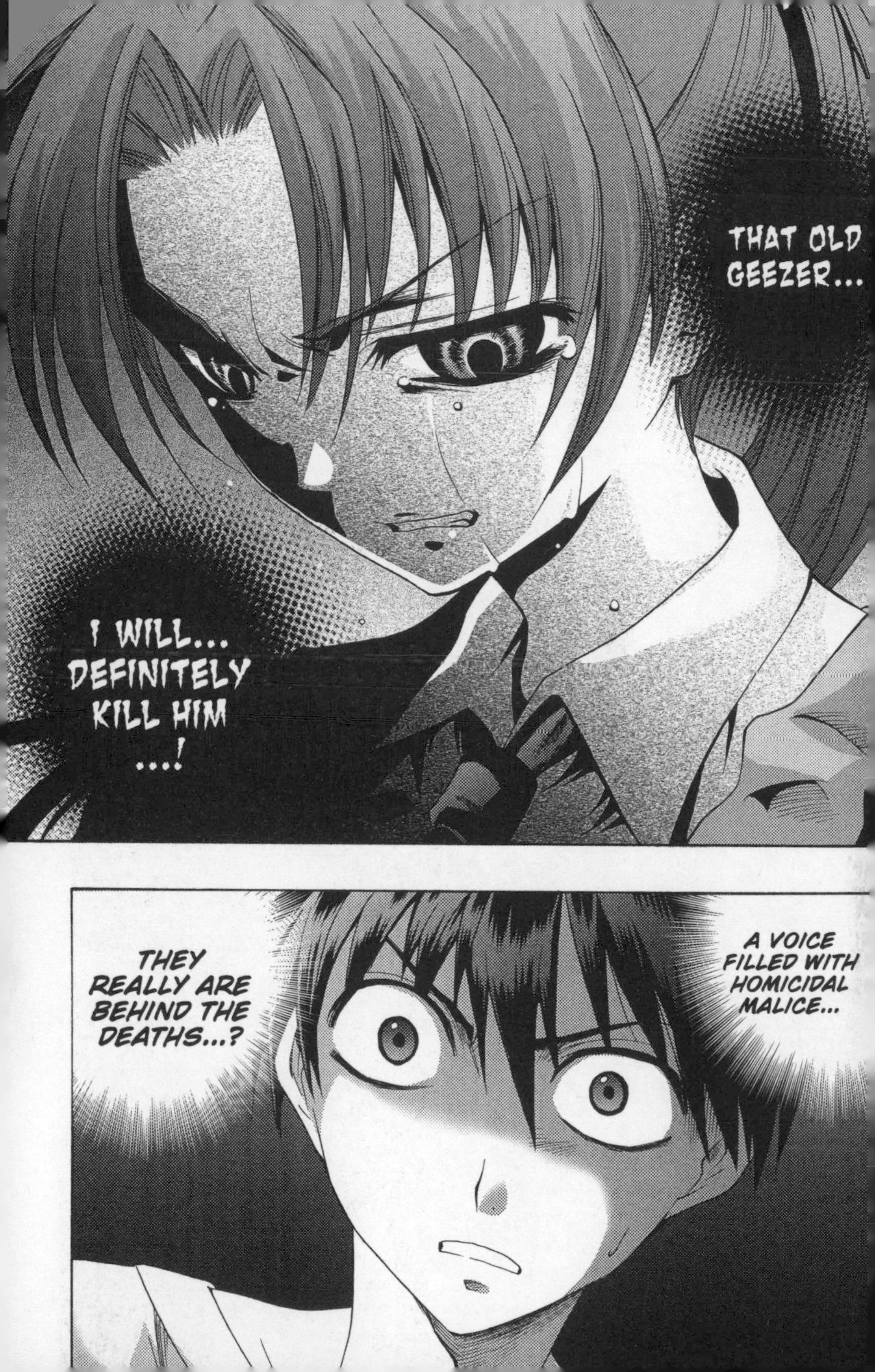
THAT OLD GEEZER...
I WILL... DEFINITELY KILL HIM ...!
A VOICE FILLED WITH HOMICIDAL MALICE...
THEY REALLY ARE BEHIND THE DEATHS...?

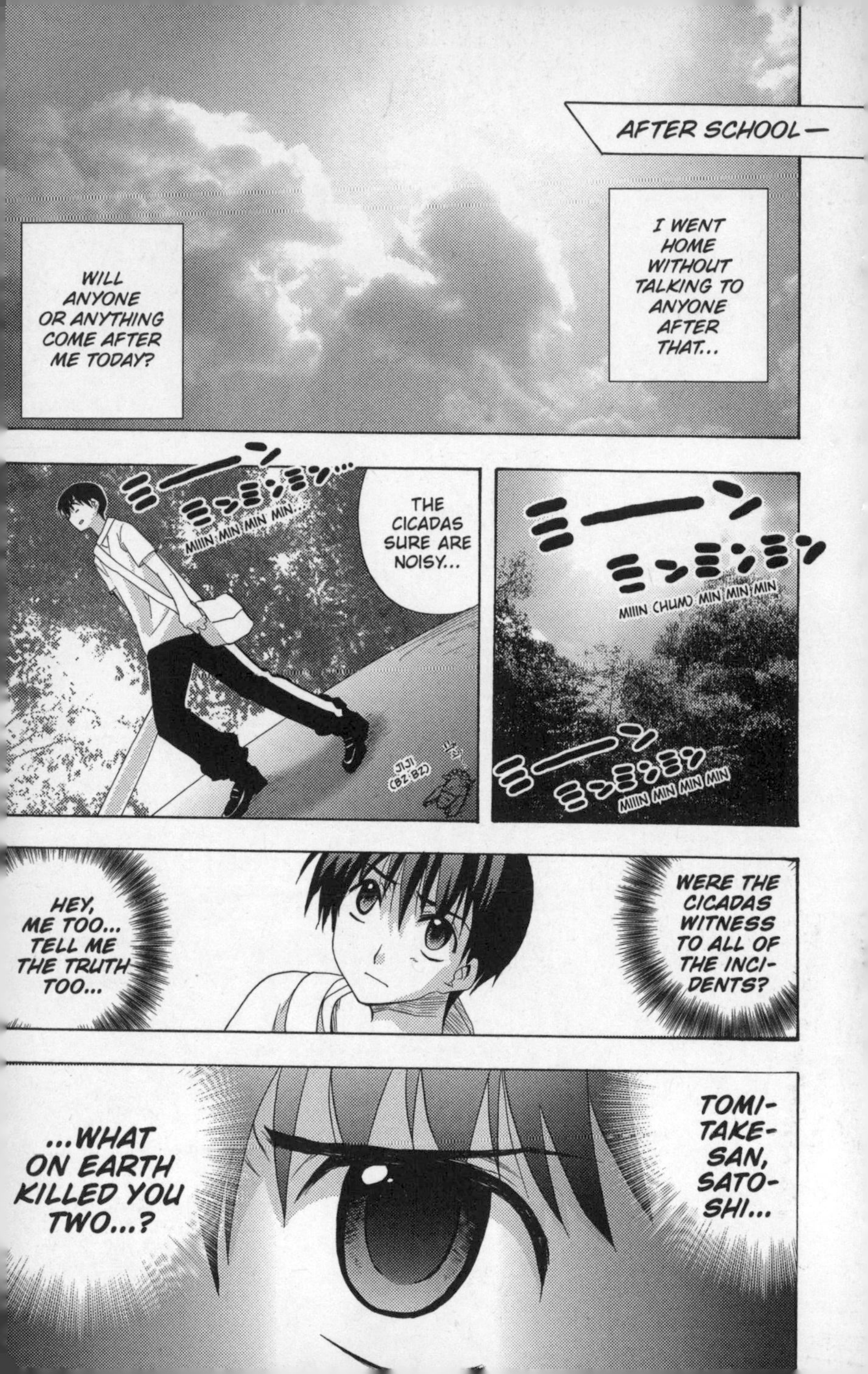
AFTER SCHOOL—
I WENT HOME WITHOUT TALKING TO ANYONE AFTER THAT...
WILL ANYONE OR ANYTHING COME AFTER ME TODAY?
ミーーン ミンミンミン
MIIIN (CHUM) MIN MIN MIN
ミーーン ミンミンミン
MIIIN MIN MIN MIN
ミーーン ミンミンミン...
MIIIN MIN MIN MIN...
THE CICADAS SURE ARE NOISY...
JIJI (BZ BZ)
WERE THE CICADAS WITNESS TO ALL OF THE INCIDENTS?
HEY, ME TOO... TELL ME THE TRUTH TOO...
TOMITAKE-SAN, SATOSHI...
...WHAT ON EARTH KILLED YOU TWO...?

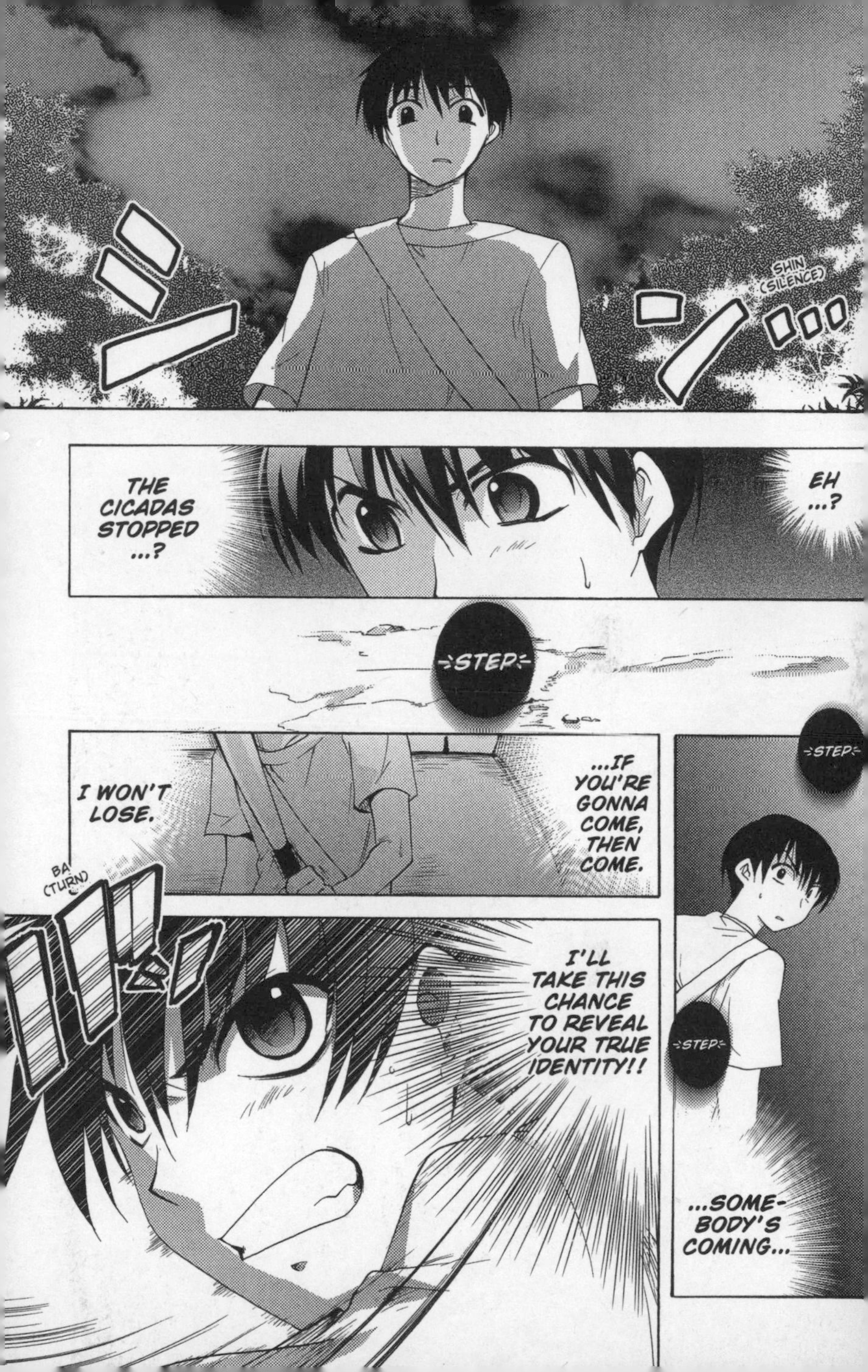
SHIN (SILENCE)
EH ...?
THE CICADAS STOPPED ...?
STEP
STEP
STEP
...SOME-BODY'S COMING...
...IF YOU'RE GONNA COME, THEN COME.
I WON'T LOSE.
I'LL TAKE THIS CHANCE TO REVEAL YOUR TRUE IDENTITY!!
BA (TURN)

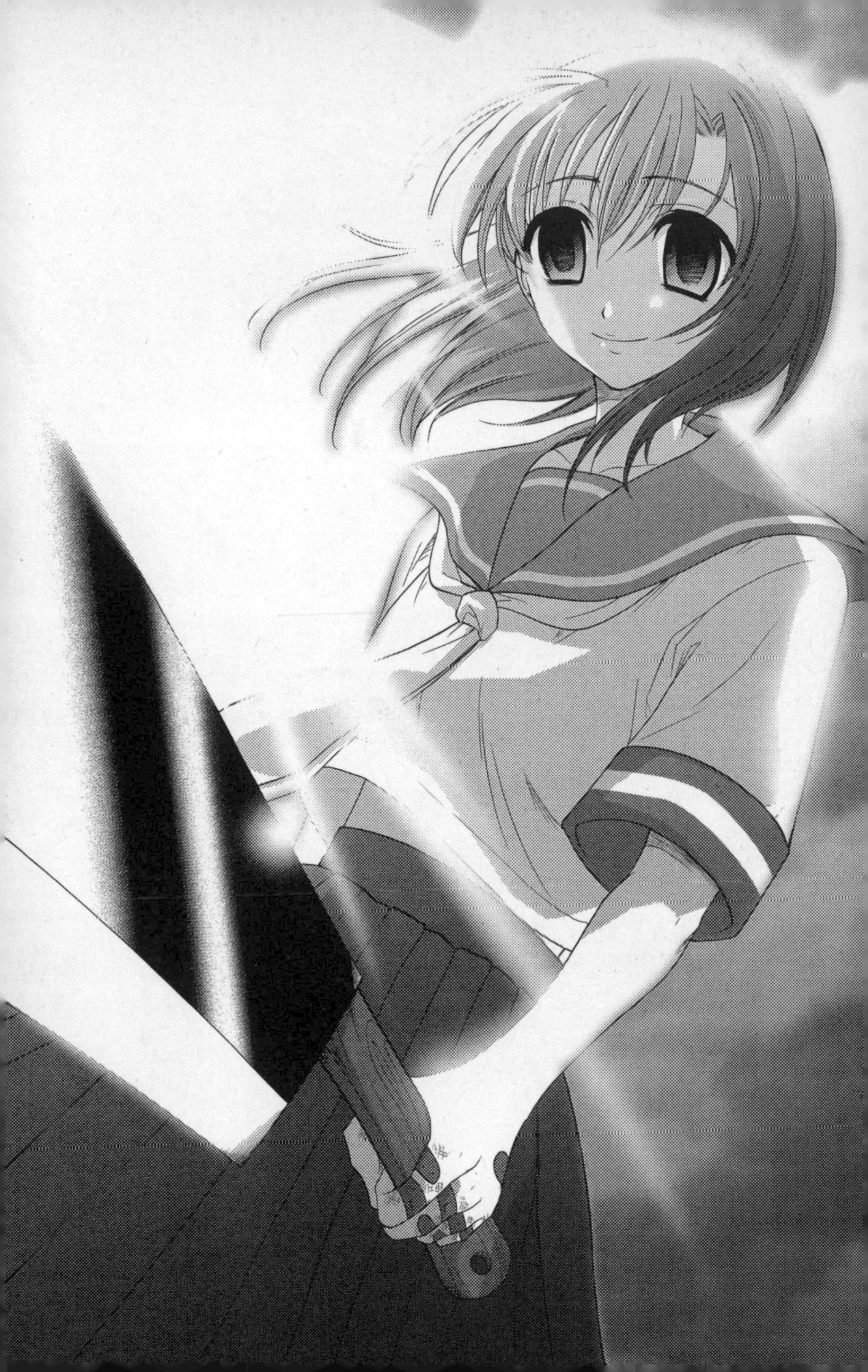

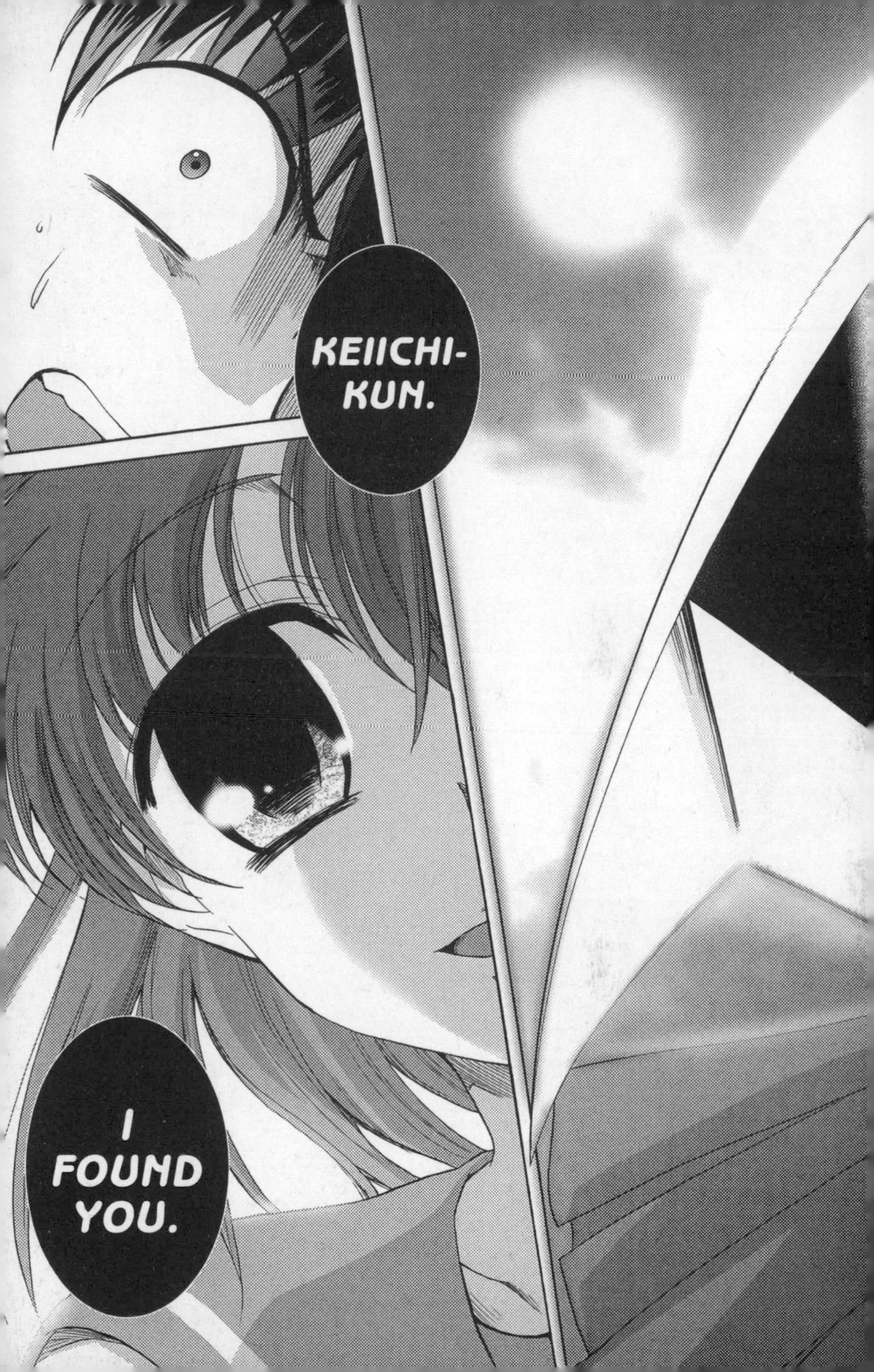
KEIICHI-KUN.
I FOUND YOU.

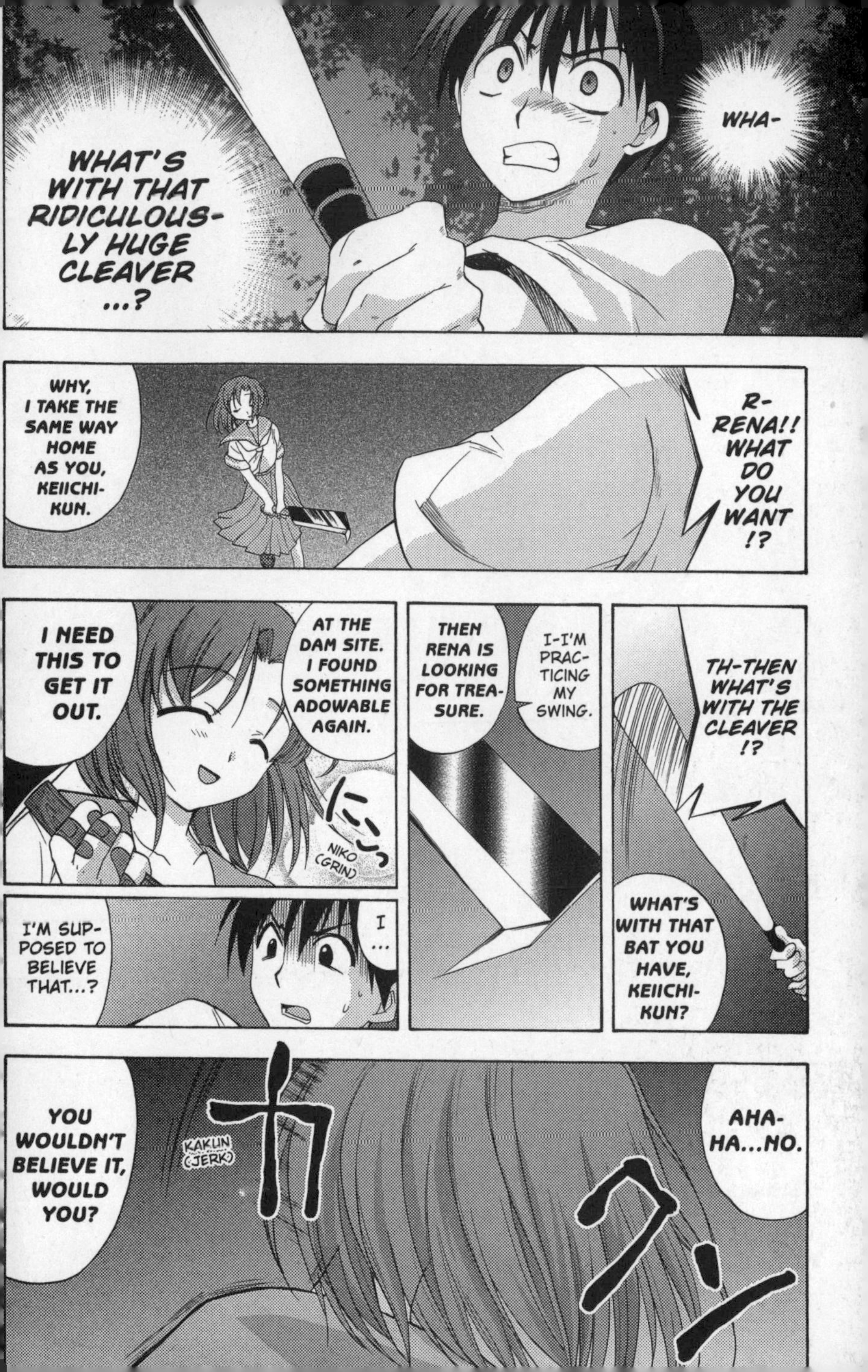
WHA-
WHAT'S WITH THAT RIDICULOUSLY HUGE CLEAVER ...?
R-RENA!! WHAT DO YOU WANT!?
WHY, I TAKE THE SAME WAY HOME AS YOU, KEIICHI-KUN.
TH-THEN WHAT'S WITH THE CLEAVER!?
WHAT'S WITH THAT BAT YOU HAVE, KEIICHI-KUN?
I-I'M PRACTICING MY SWING.
THEN RENA IS LOOKING FOR TREASURE.
AT THE DAM SITE. I FOUND SOMETHING ADOWABLE AGAIN.
I NEED THIS TO GET IT OUT.
にこっ
NIKO (GRIN)
I ...
I'M SUPPOSED TO BELIEVE THAT...?
AHAHA...NO.
YOU WOULDN'T BELIEVE IT, WOULD YOU?
カクン
KAKUN (JERK)

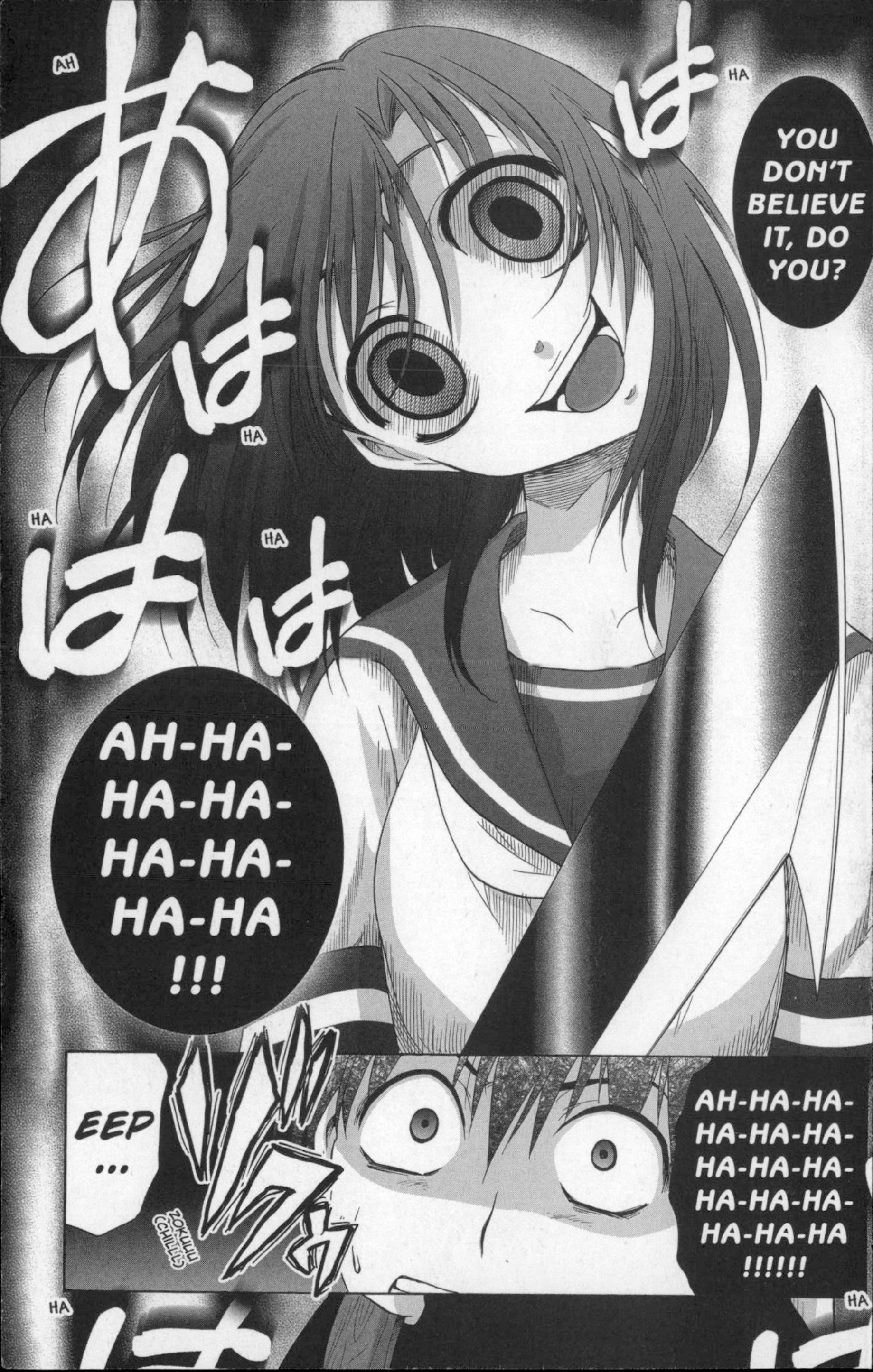

YOU DON'T BELIEVE IT, DO YOU?
HA
は
AH
あ
HA
は
HA
は
HA
は
AH-HA-HA-HA-HA-HA-HA-HA-HA !!!
AH-HA-HA-HA-HA-HA-HA-HA-HA-HA-HA-HA-HA-HA-HA !!!!!!
ZOKUUU (CHILL!)
EEP ...
HA
HA

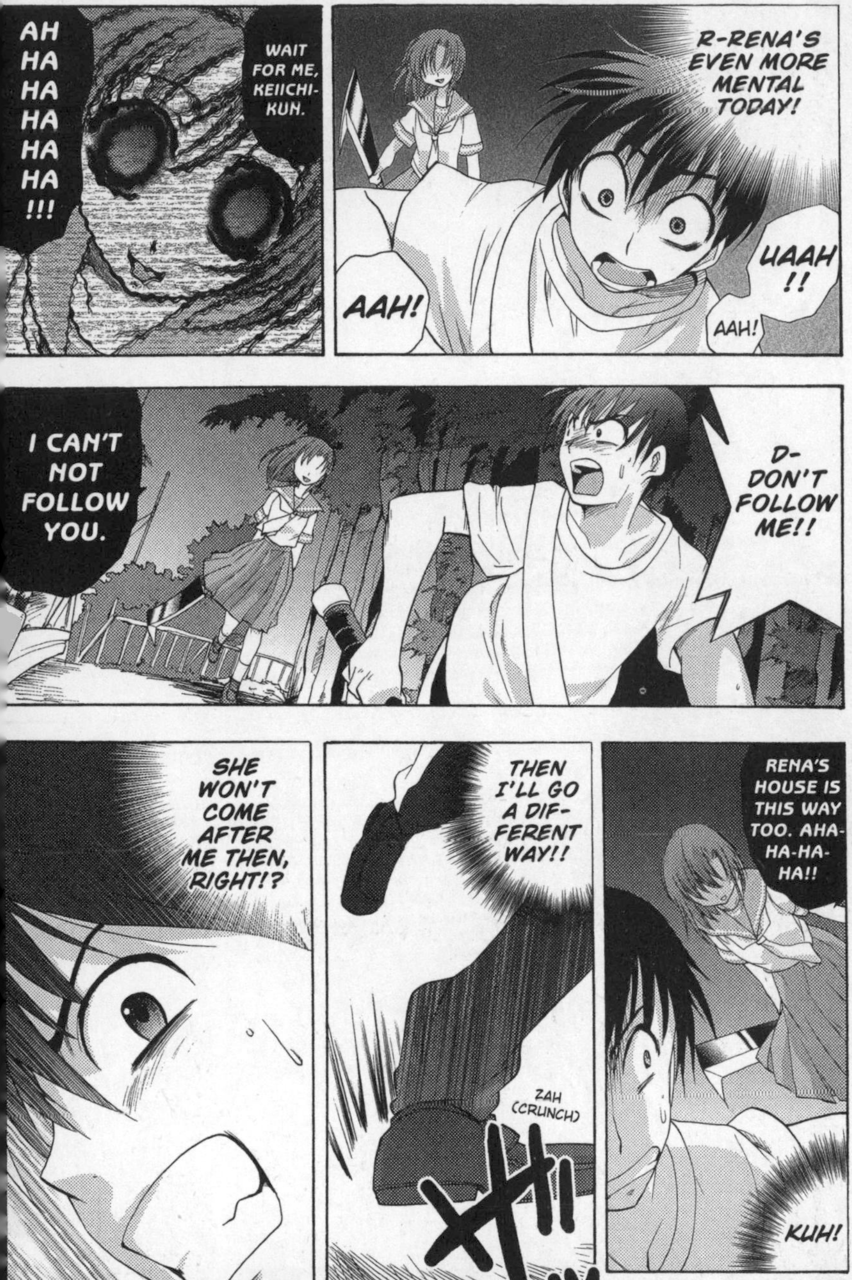

R-RENA'S EVEN MORE MENTAL TODAY!
UAAH!!
AAH!
AAH!
WAIT FOR ME, KEIICHI-KUN.
AH HA HA HA HA HA!!!
D-DON'T FOLLOW ME!!
I CAN'T NOT FOLLOW YOU.
RENA'S HOUSE IS THIS WAY TOO. AHA-HA-HA-HA!!
KUH!
THEN I'LL GO A DIF-FERENT WAY!!
ZAH (CRUNCH)
SHE WON'T COME AFTER ME THEN, RIGHT!?

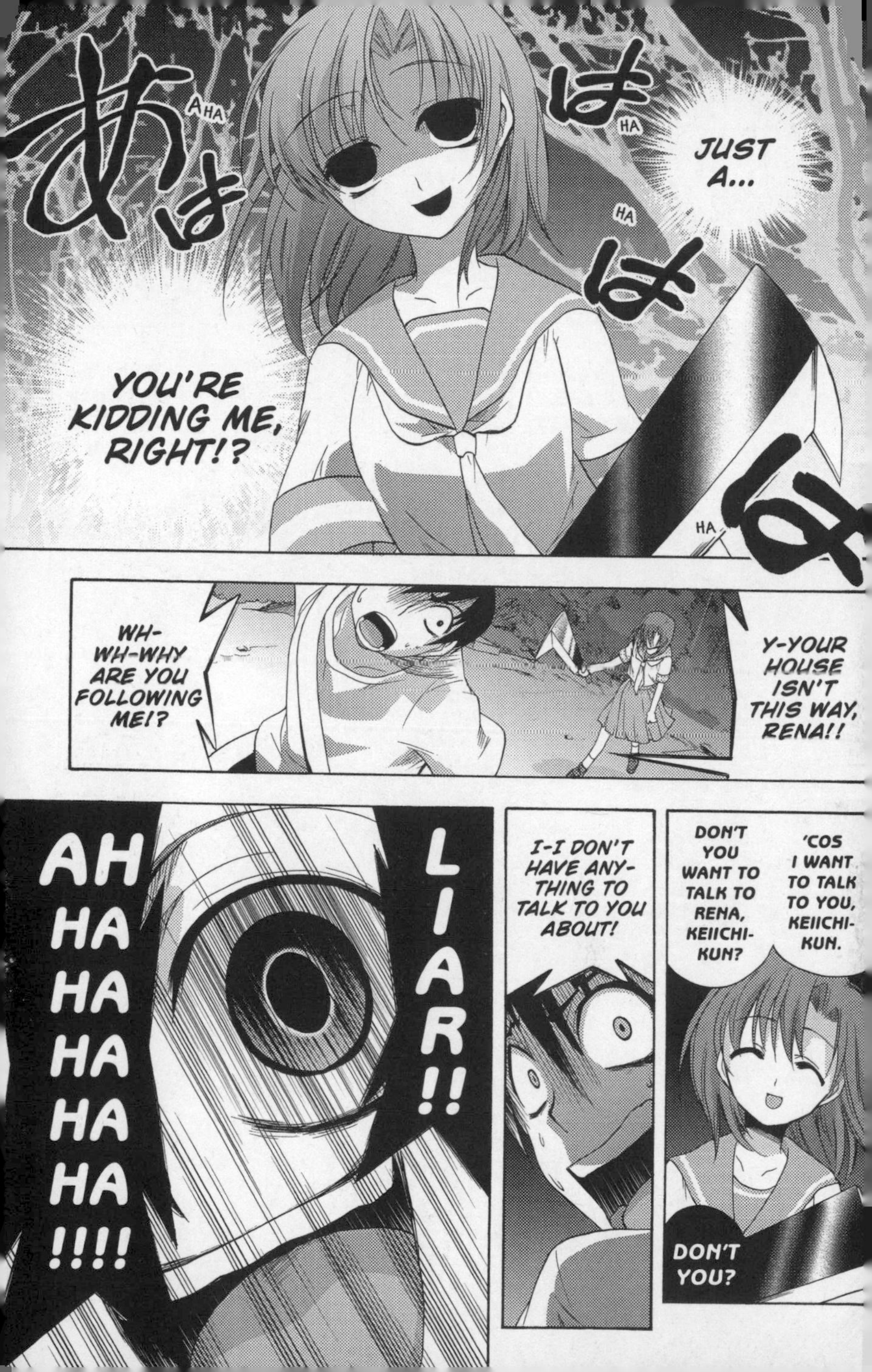
は
HA
JUST A...
HA
は
HA
は
あは
AHA
YOU'RE KIDDING ME, RIGHT!?
Y-YOUR HOUSE ISN'T THIS WAY, RENA!!
WH-WH-WHY ARE YOU FOLLOWING ME!?
'COS I WANT TO TALK TO YOU, KEIICHI-KUN.
DON'T YOU WANT TO TALK TO RENA, KEIICHI-KUN?
DON'T YOU?
I-I DON'T HAVE ANYTHING TO TALK TO YOU ABOUT!
LIAR!!
AH HA HA HA HA HA HA HA!!!!

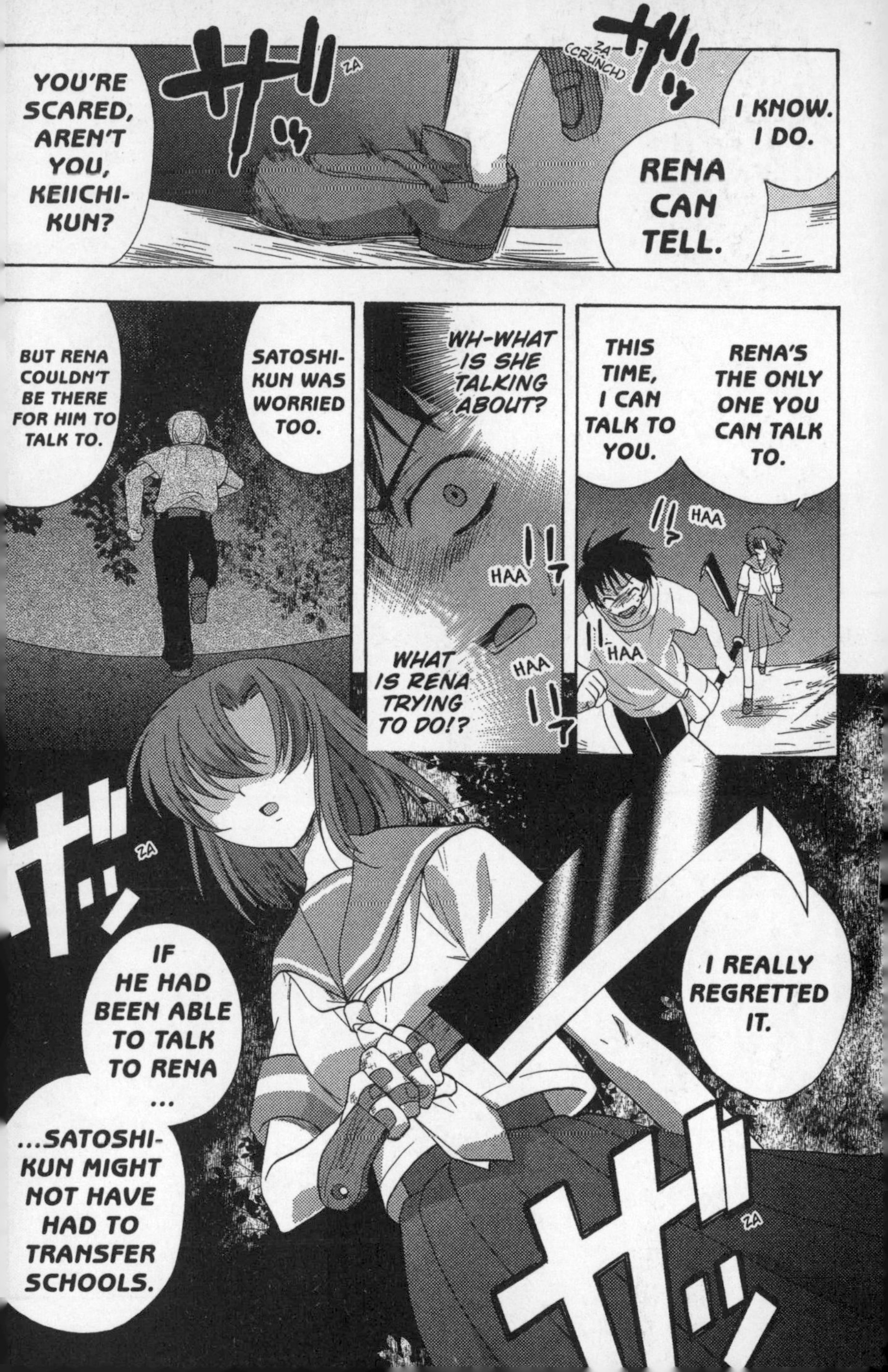
ZA (CRUNCH)
I KNOW. I DO.
RENA CAN TELL.
ZA
YOU'RE SCARED, AREN'T YOU, KEIICHI-KUN?
RENA'S THE ONLY ONE YOU CAN TALK TO.
THIS TIME, I CAN TALK TO YOU.
HAA
HAA
WH-WHAT IS SHE TALKING ABOUT?
HAA
HAA
WHAT IS RENA TRYING TO DO!?
SATOSHI-KUN WAS WORRIED TOO.
BUT RENA COULDN'T BE THERE FOR HIM TO TALK TO.
I REALLY REGRETTED IT.
ZA
IF HE HAD BEEN ABLE TO TALK TO RENA ...
...SATOSHI-KUN MIGHT NOT HAVE HAD TO TRANSFER SCHOOLS.
ZA

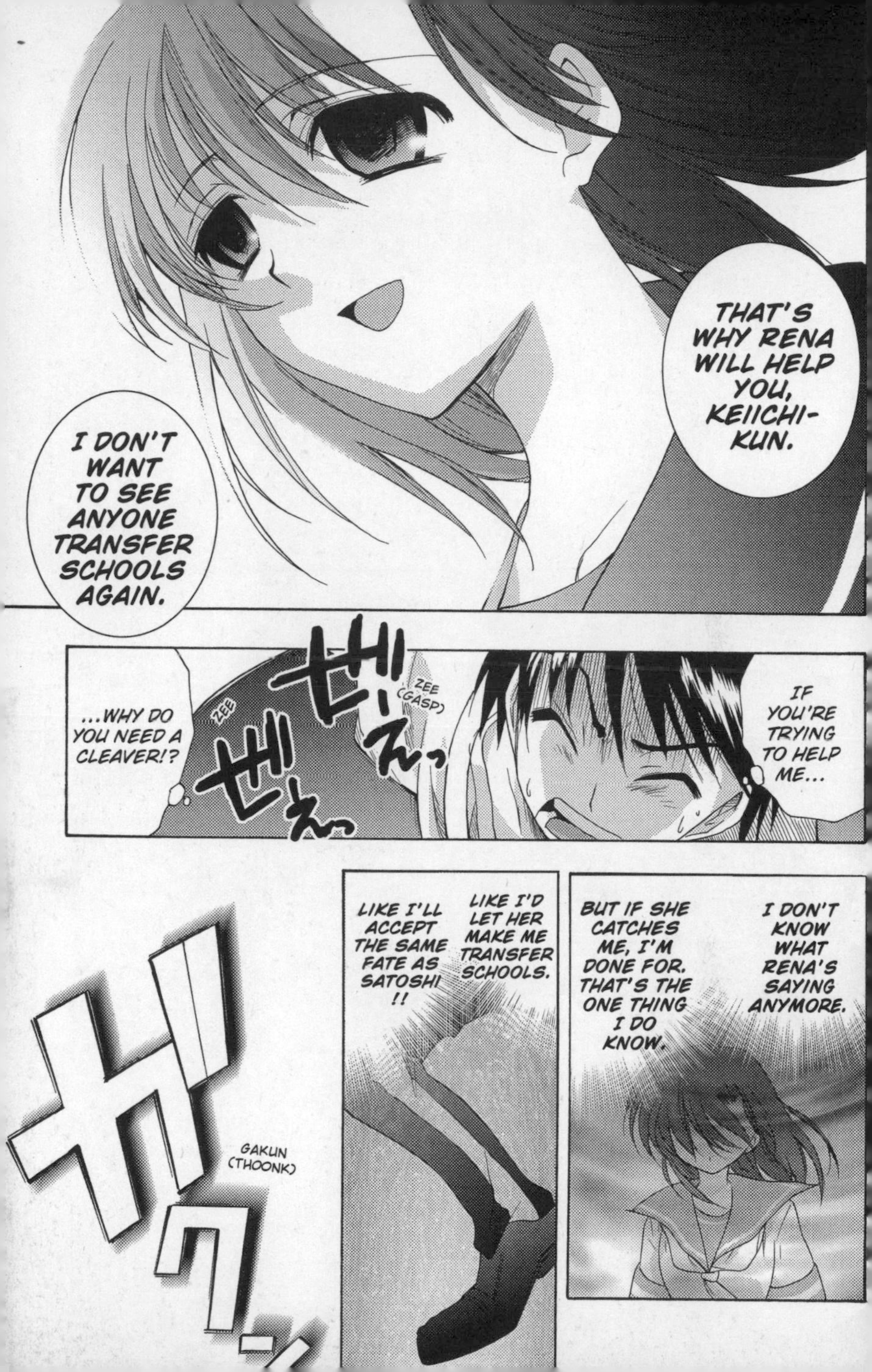
THAT'S WHY RENA WILL HELP YOU, KEIICHI-KUN.
I DON'T WANT TO SEE ANYONE TRANSFER SCHOOLS AGAIN.
IF YOU'RE TRYING TO HELP ME...
ZEE (GASP)
ZEE
...WHY DO YOU NEED A CLEAVER!?
I DON'T KNOW WHAT RENA'S SAYING ANYMORE.
BUT IF SHE CATCHES ME, I'M DONE FOR. THAT'S THE ONE THING I DO KNOW.
LIKE I'D LET HER MAKE ME TRANSFER SCHOOLS.
LIKE I'LL ACCEPT THE SAME FATE AS SATOSHI!!
GAKUN (THOONK)

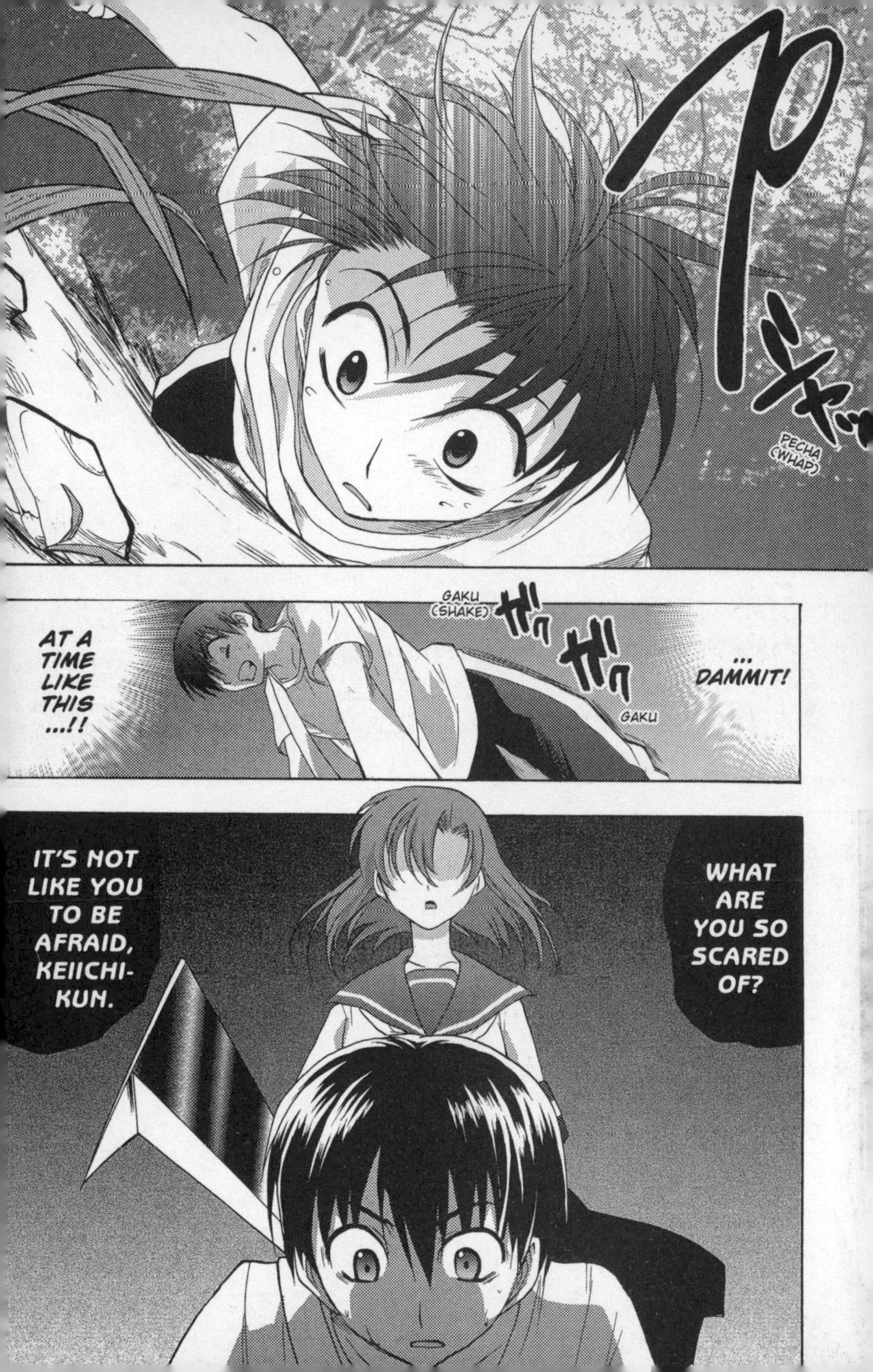
PECHA (WHAP)
... DAMMIT!
GAKU (SHAKE)
GAKU
AT A TIME LIKE THIS ...!!
WHAT ARE YOU SO SCARED OF?
IT'S NOT LIKE YOU TO BE AFRAID, KEIICHI-KUN.

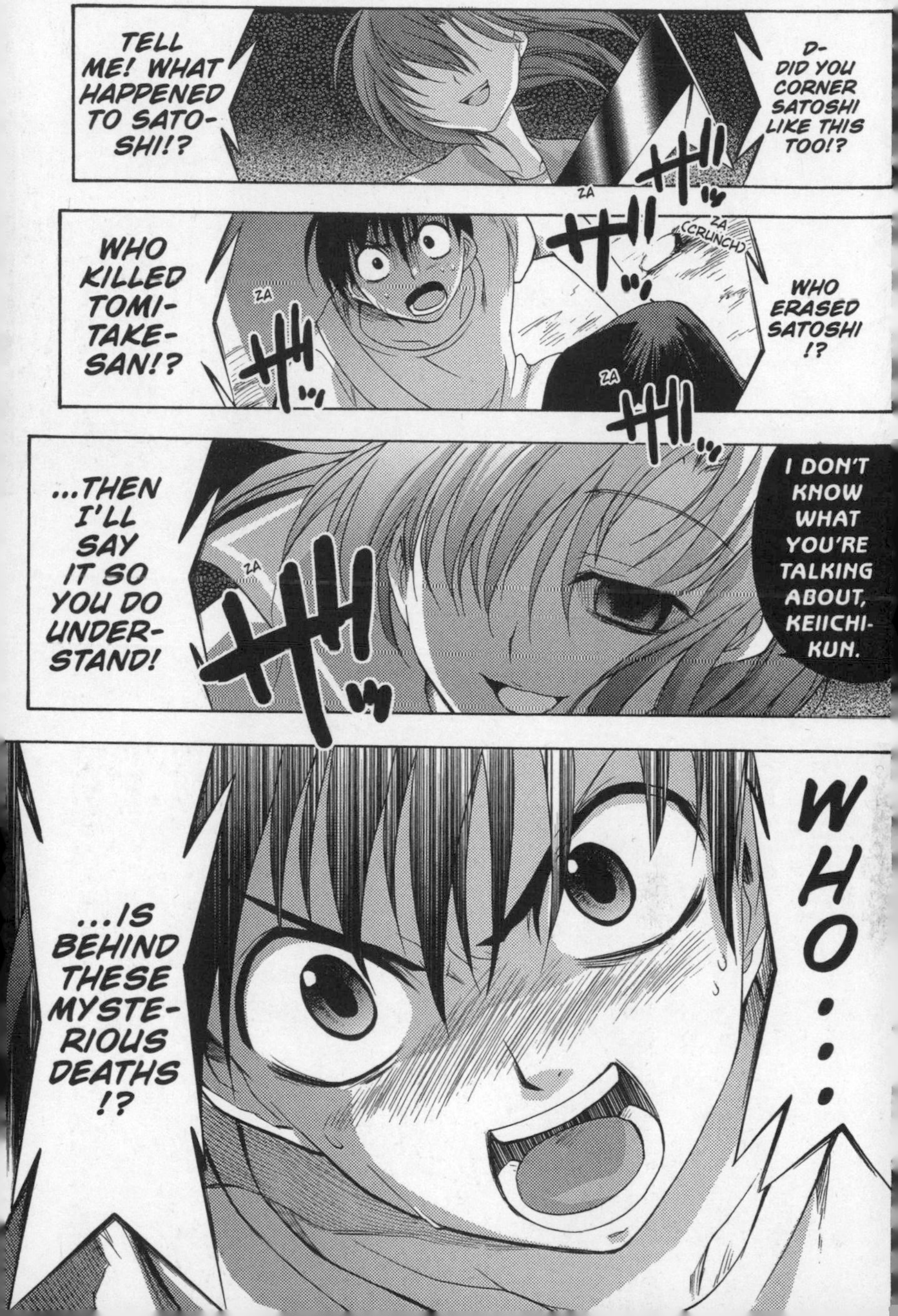
D- DID YOU CORNER SATOSHI LIKE THIS TOO!?
TELL ME! WHAT HAPPENED TO SATO-SHI!?
ZA
ZA (CRUNCH)
WHO ERASED SATOSHI !?
ZA
WHO KILLED TOMI-TAKE-SAN!?
ZA
I DON'T KNOW WHAT YOU'RE TALKING ABOUT, KEIICHI-KUN.
ZA
...THEN I'LL SAY IT SO YOU DO UNDER-STAND!
WHO...
...IS BEHIND THESE MYSTE-RIOUS DEATHS!?

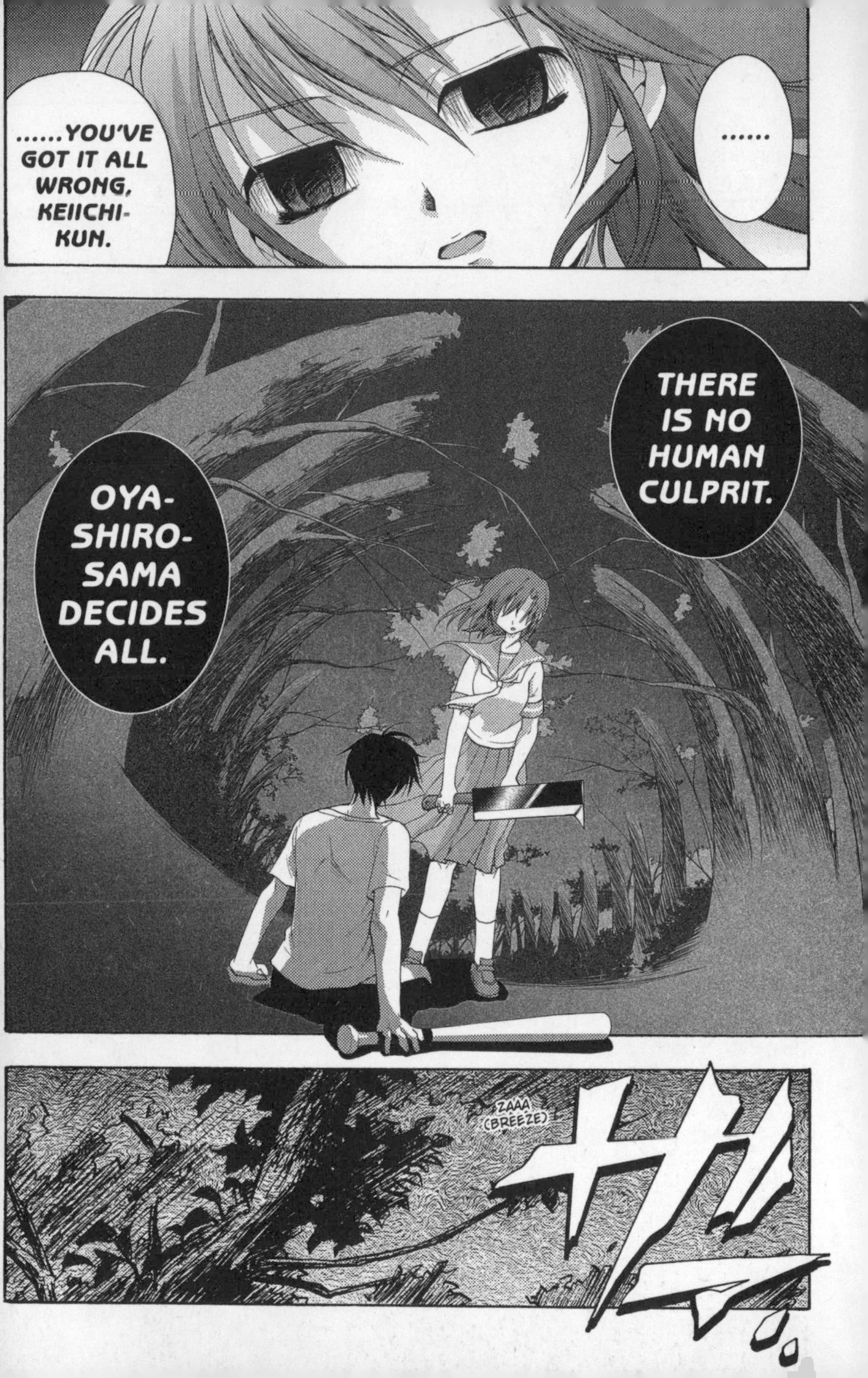
......
......YOU'VE GOT IT ALL WRONG, KEIICHI-KUN.
THERE IS NO HUMAN CULPRIT.
OYA-SHIRO-SAMA DECIDES ALL.
ZAAA (BREEZE)

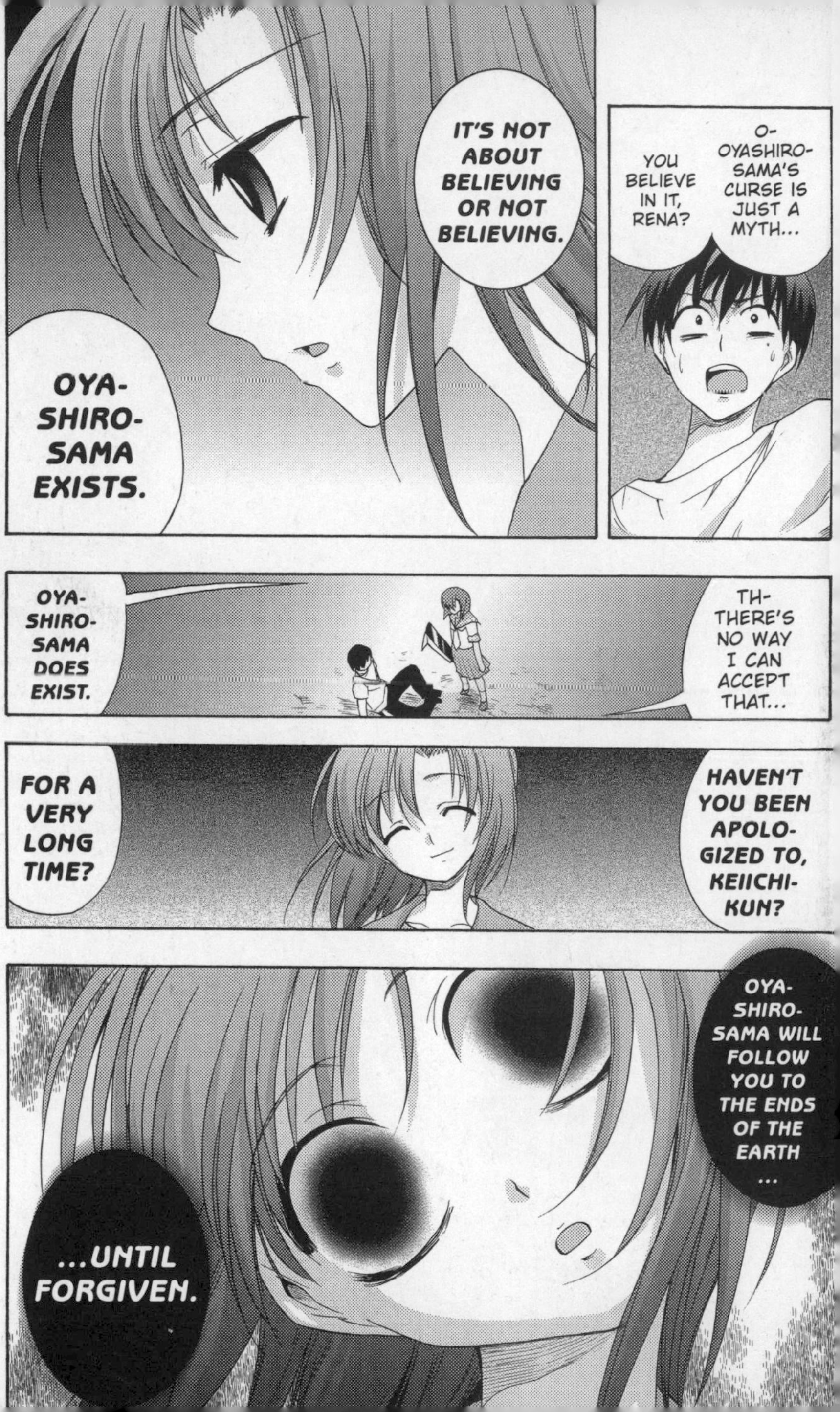
O-OYASHIRO-SAMA'S CURSE IS JUST A MYTH...
YOU BELIEVE IN IT, RENA?
IT'S NOT ABOUT BELIEVING OR NOT BELIEVING.
OYA-SHIRO-SAMA EXISTS.
TH-THERE'S NO WAY I CAN ACCEPT THAT...
OYA-SHIRO-SAMA DOES EXIST.
HAVEN'T YOU BEEN APOLO-GIZED TO, KEIICHI-KUN?
FOR A VERY LONG TIME?
OYA-SHIRO-SAMA WILL FOLLOW YOU TO THE ENDS OF THE EARTH ...
...UNTIL FORGIVEN.

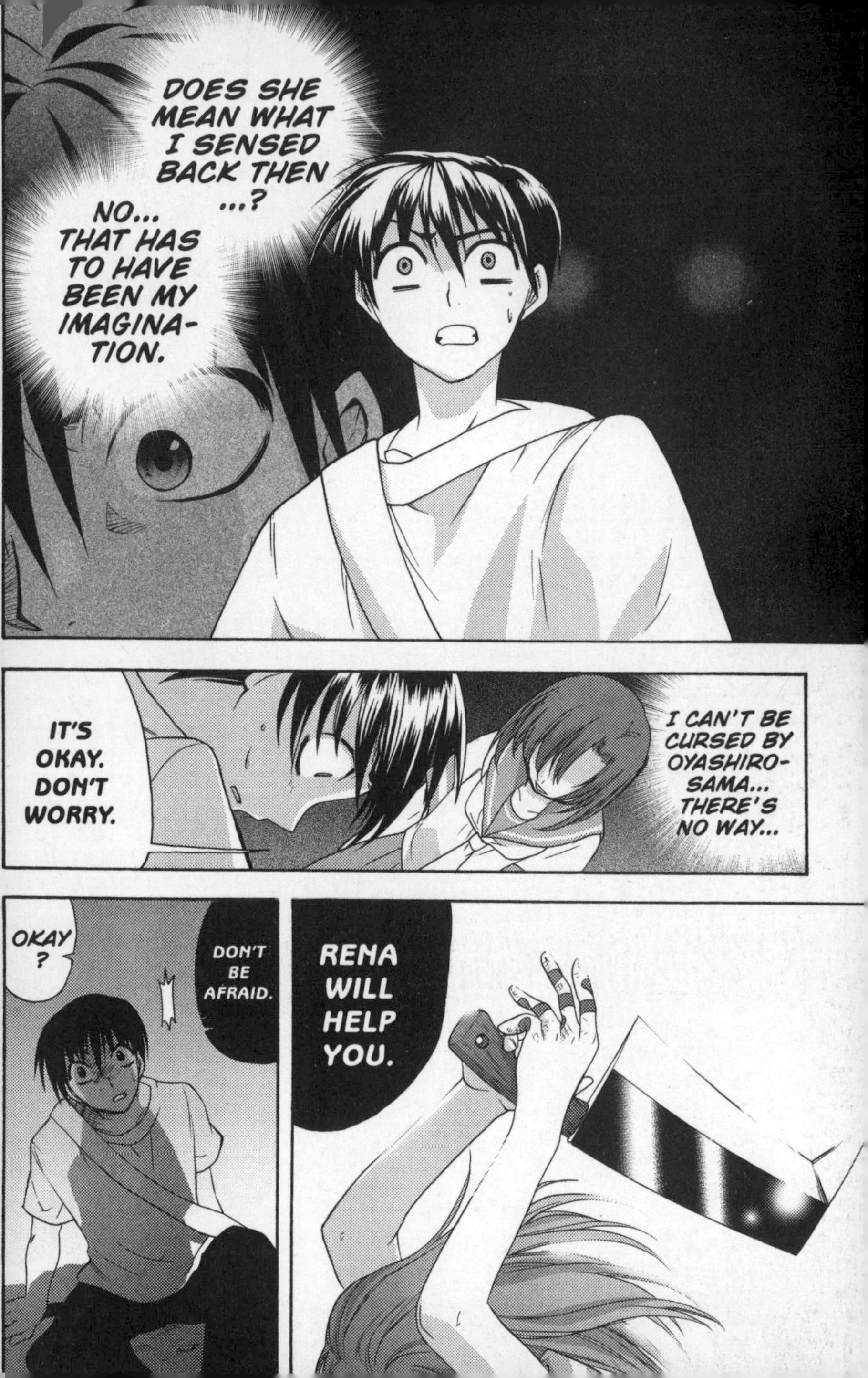
DOES SHE MEAN WHAT I SENSED BACK THEN ...?
NO... THAT HAS TO HAVE BEEN MY IMAGINATION.
I CAN'T BE CURSED BY OYASHIRO-SAMA... THERE'S NO WAY...
IT'S OKAY. DON'T WORRY.
RENA WILL HELP YOU.
DON'T BE AFRAID.
!
OKAY?

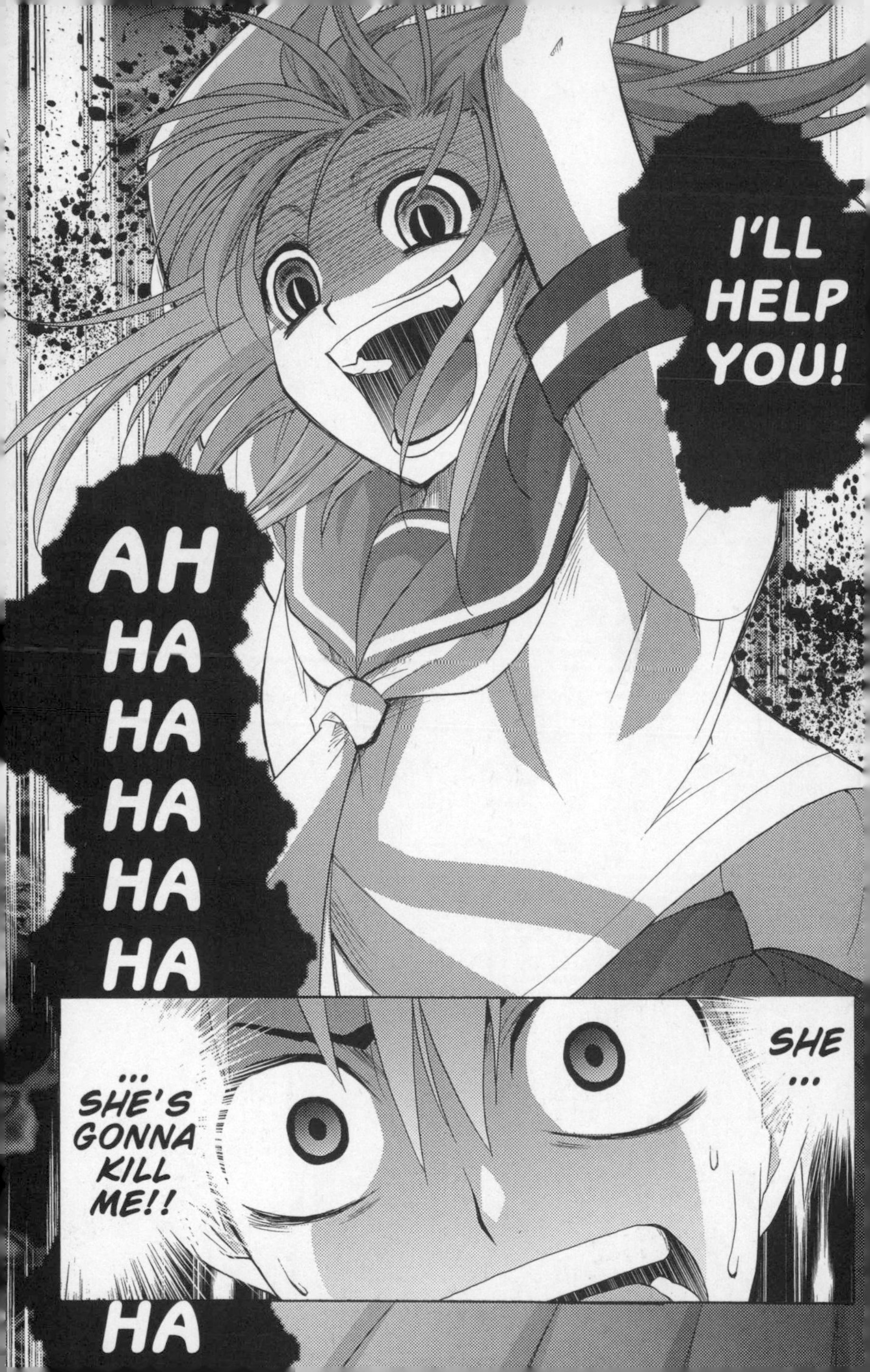
I'LL HELP YOU!
AH HA HA HA HA HA HA
SHE ...
... SHE'S GONNA KILL ME!!
HA

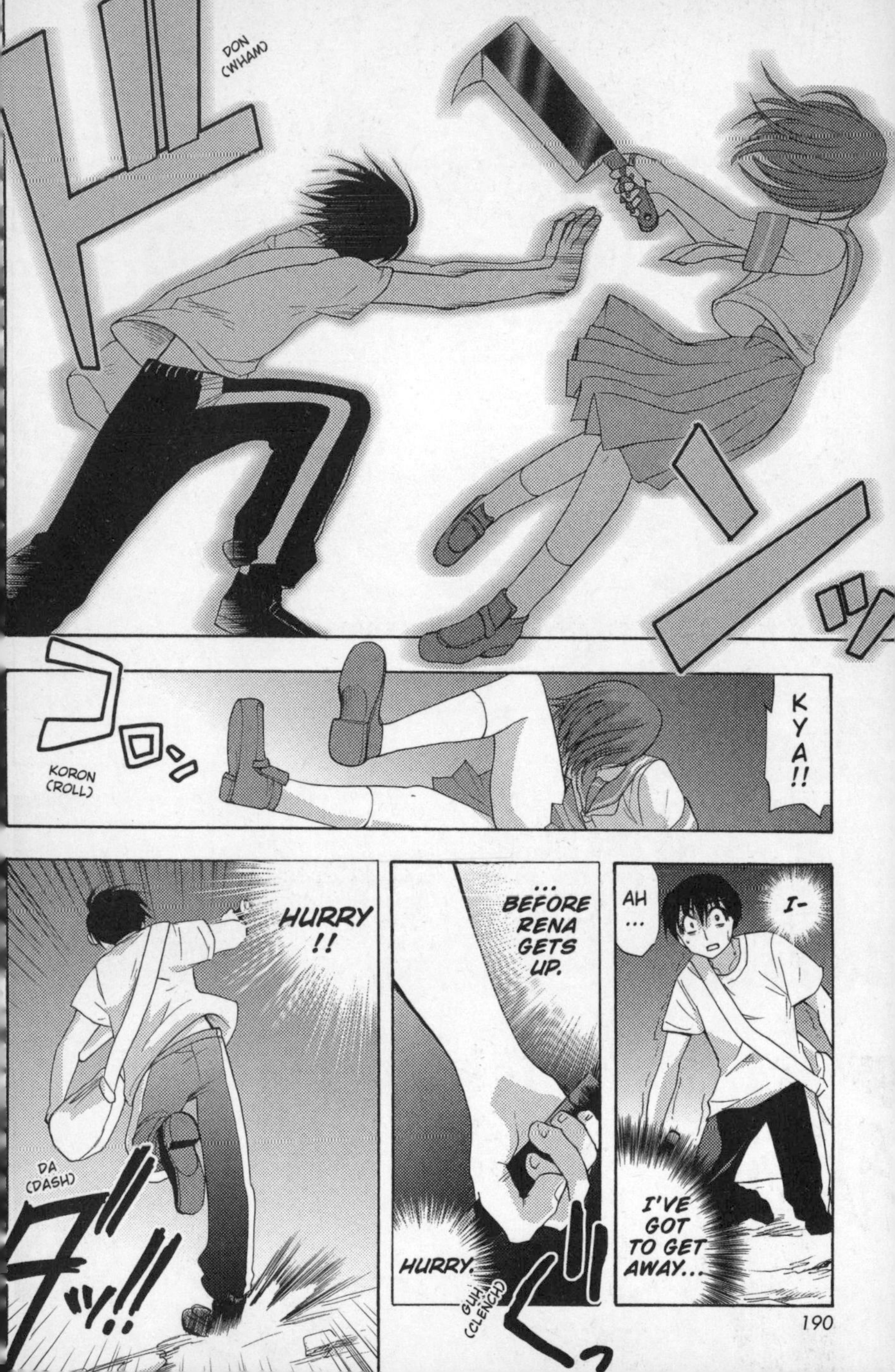
DON (WHAM)
KYA!!
KORON (ROLL)
AH ...
I-
I'VE GOT TO GET AWAY...
... BEFORE RENA GETS UP.
HURRY.
GUH (CLENCH)
HURRY !!
DA (DASH)

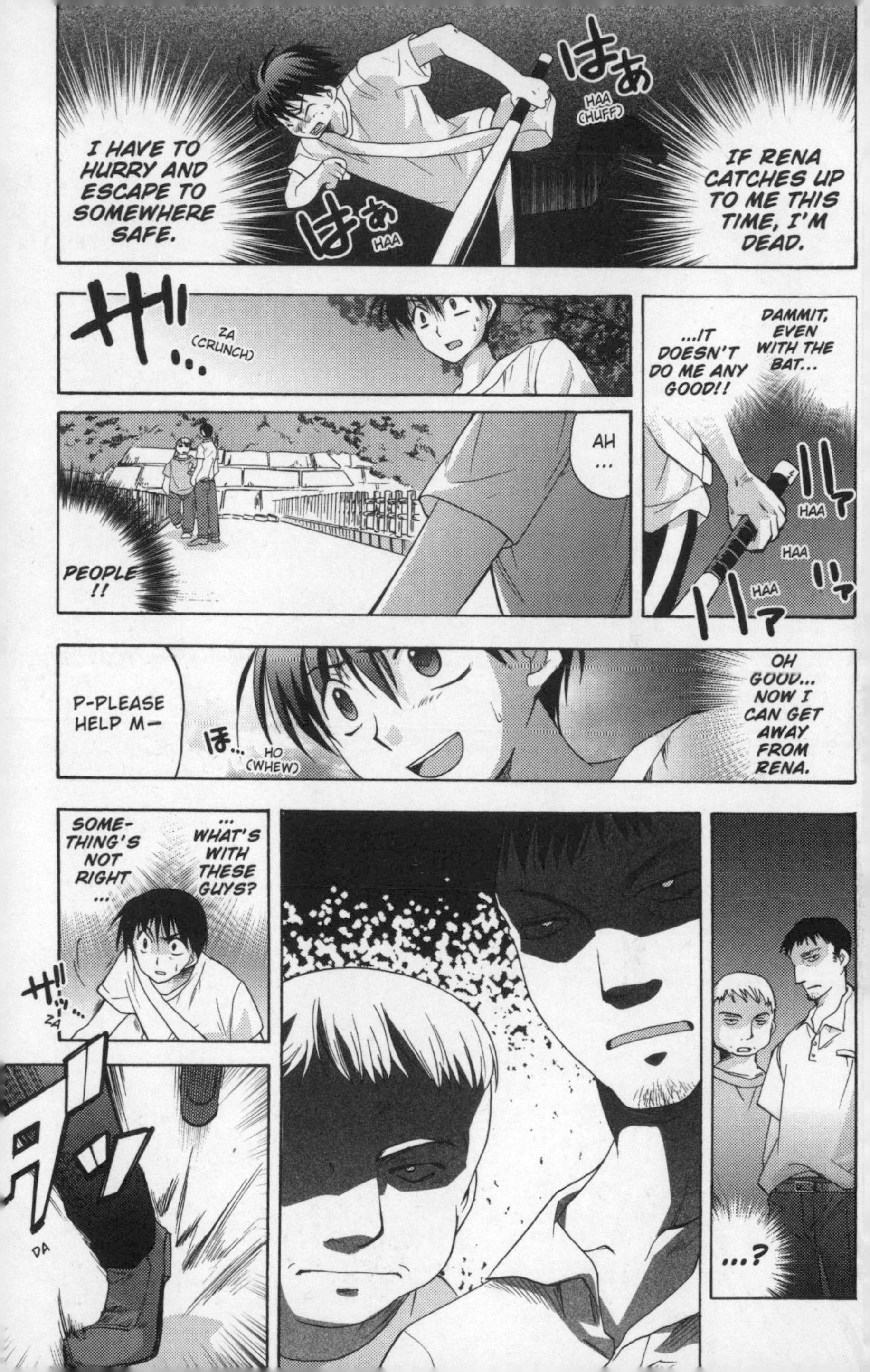
IF RENA CATCHES UP TO ME THIS TIME, I'M DEAD.
はぁ
HAA (HUFF)
I HAVE TO HURRY AND ESCAPE TO SOMEWHERE SAFE.
はぁ
HAA
DAMMIT, EVEN WITH THE BAT...
...IT DOESN'T DO ME ANY GOOD!!
ハァ
HAA
HAA
ハァ
HAA
ハァ
ザ...
ZA (CRUNCH)
AH ...
PEOPLE !!
OH GOOD... NOW I CAN GET AWAY FROM RENA.
ほ...
HO (WHEW)
P-PLEASE HELP M—
...?
...WHAT'S WITH THESE GUYS?
SOME-THING'S NOT RIGHT ...
ザッ...
ZA
ダッ
DA

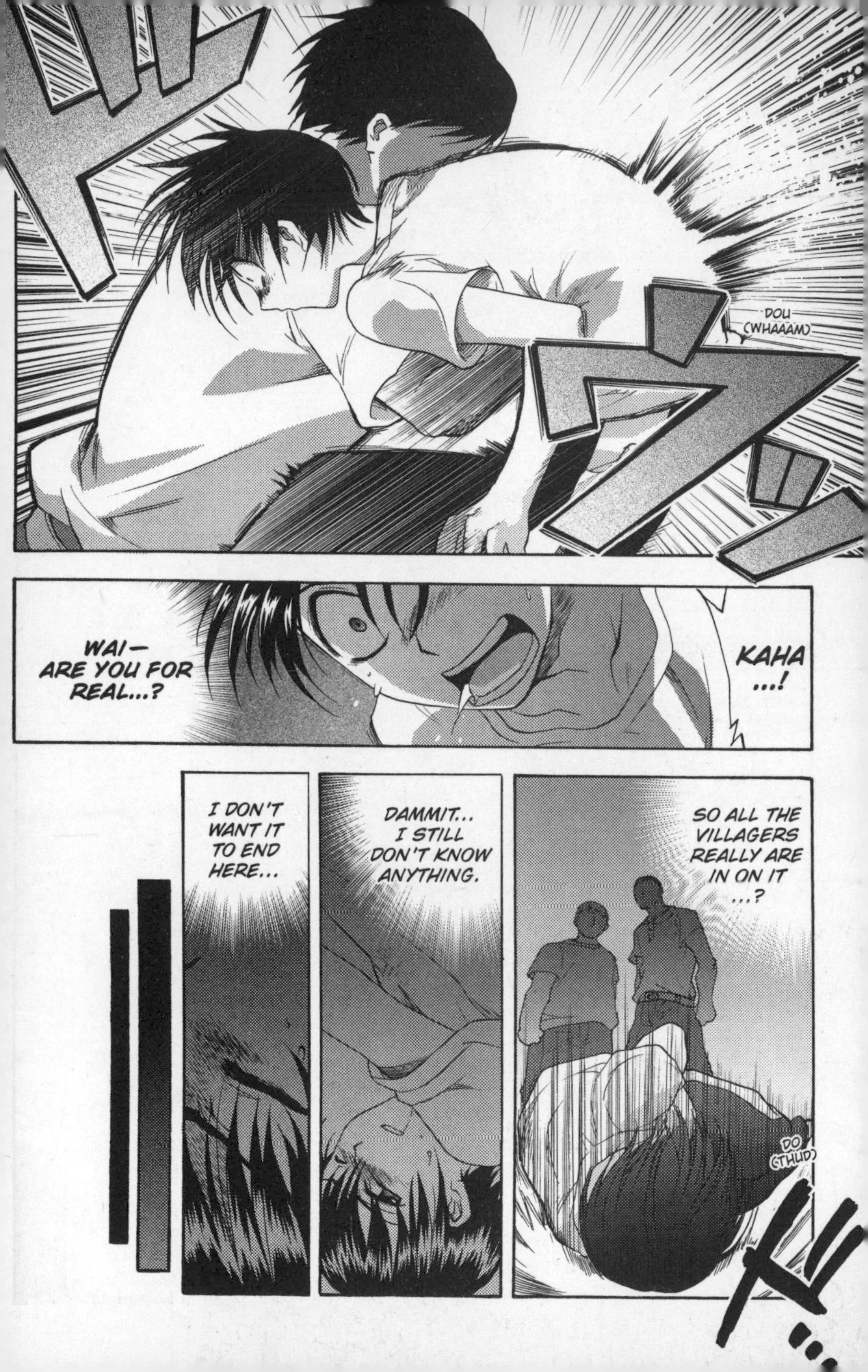
DOU (WHAAAM)
KAHA ...!
WAI— ARE YOU FOR REAL...?
SO ALL THE VILLAGERS REALLY ARE IN ON IT ...?
DO (THUD)
DAMMIT... I STILL DON'T KNOW ANYTHING.
I DON'T WANT IT TO END HERE...

カナカナカナ…
KANA (CHIRP) KANA KANA…

カナカナカナ…
KANA KANA KANA…

...UNGH...

...KEIICHI-KUN...

...I'M SURE RENA WAS CHASING ME...

I'M...

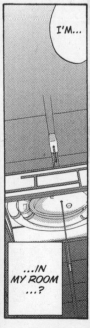

...KEIICHI-KUN, ARE YOU AWAKE...?

...IN MY ROOM...?

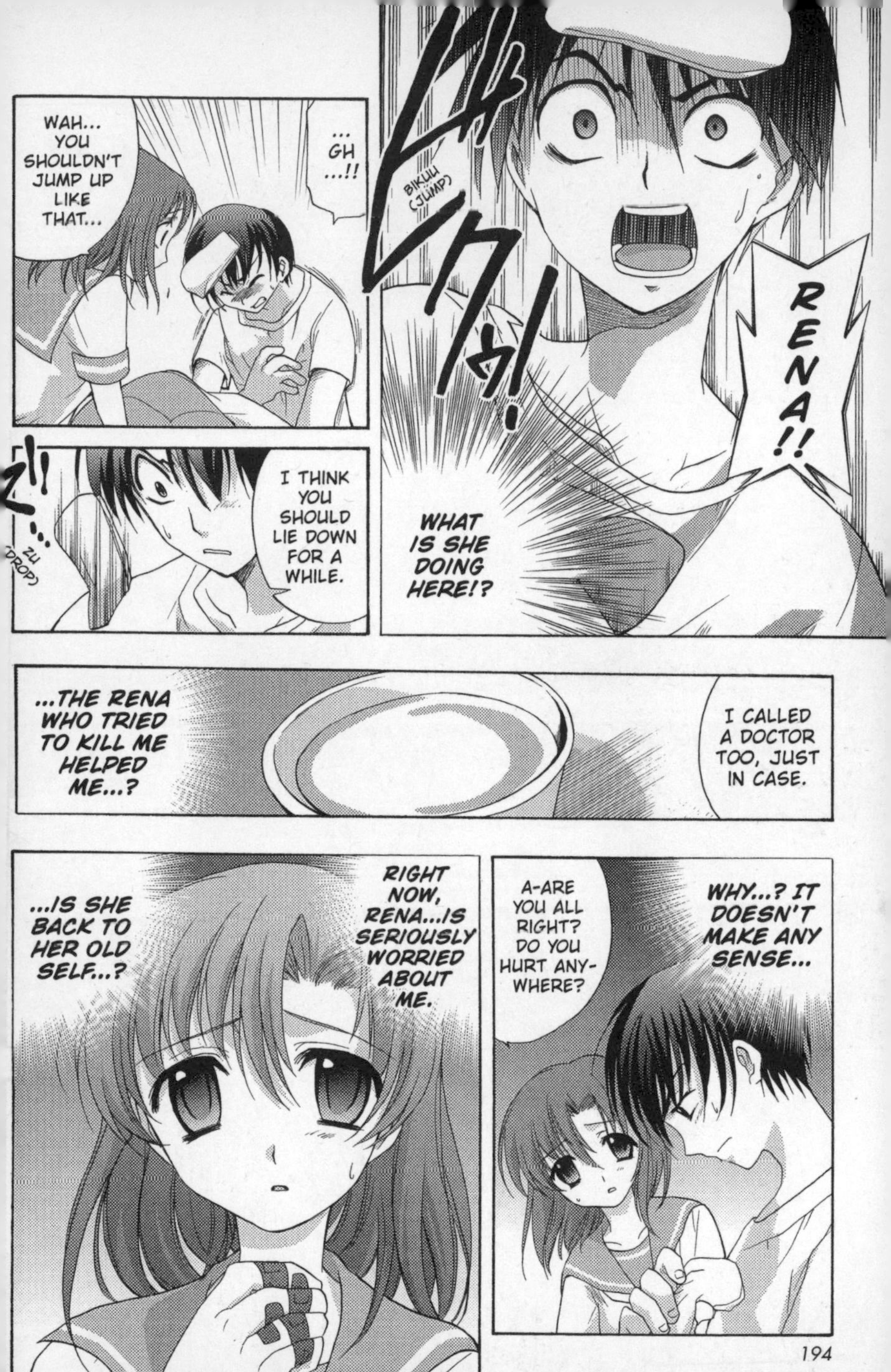
BIKUU (JUMP)
RENA!!
WHAT IS SHE DOING HERE!?
...GH...!!
WAH... YOU SHOULDN'T JUMP UP LIKE THAT...
I THINK YOU SHOULD LIE DOWN FOR A WHILE.
ZU (DROP)
I CALLED A DOCTOR TOO, JUST IN CASE.
...THE RENA WHO TRIED TO KILL ME HELPED ME...?
WHY...? IT DOESN'T MAKE ANY SENSE...
A-ARE YOU ALL RIGHT? DO YOU HURT ANY-WHERE?
RIGHT NOW, RENA...IS SERIOUSLY WORRIED ABOUT ME.
...IS SHE BACK TO HER OLD SELF...?

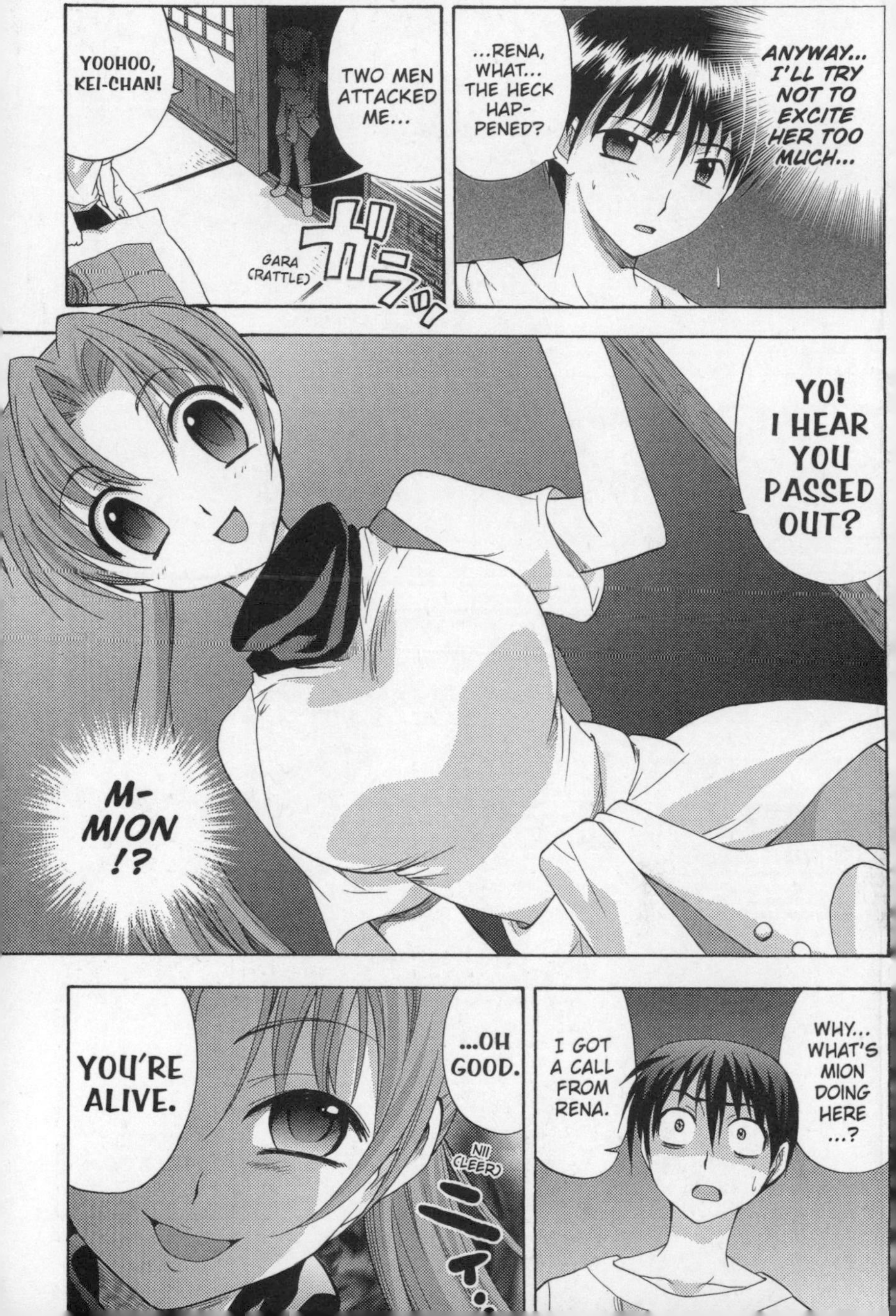
ANYWAY... I'LL TRY NOT TO EXCITE HER TOO MUCH...
...RENA, WHAT... THE HECK HAP-PENED?
TWO MEN ATTACKED ME...
YOOHOO, KEI-CHAN!
GARA (RATTLE)
YO! I HEAR YOU PASSED OUT?
M-MION!?
WHY... WHAT'S MION DOING HERE ...?
I GOT A CALL FROM RENA.
...OH GOOD.
YOU'RE ALIVE.
NII (LEER)

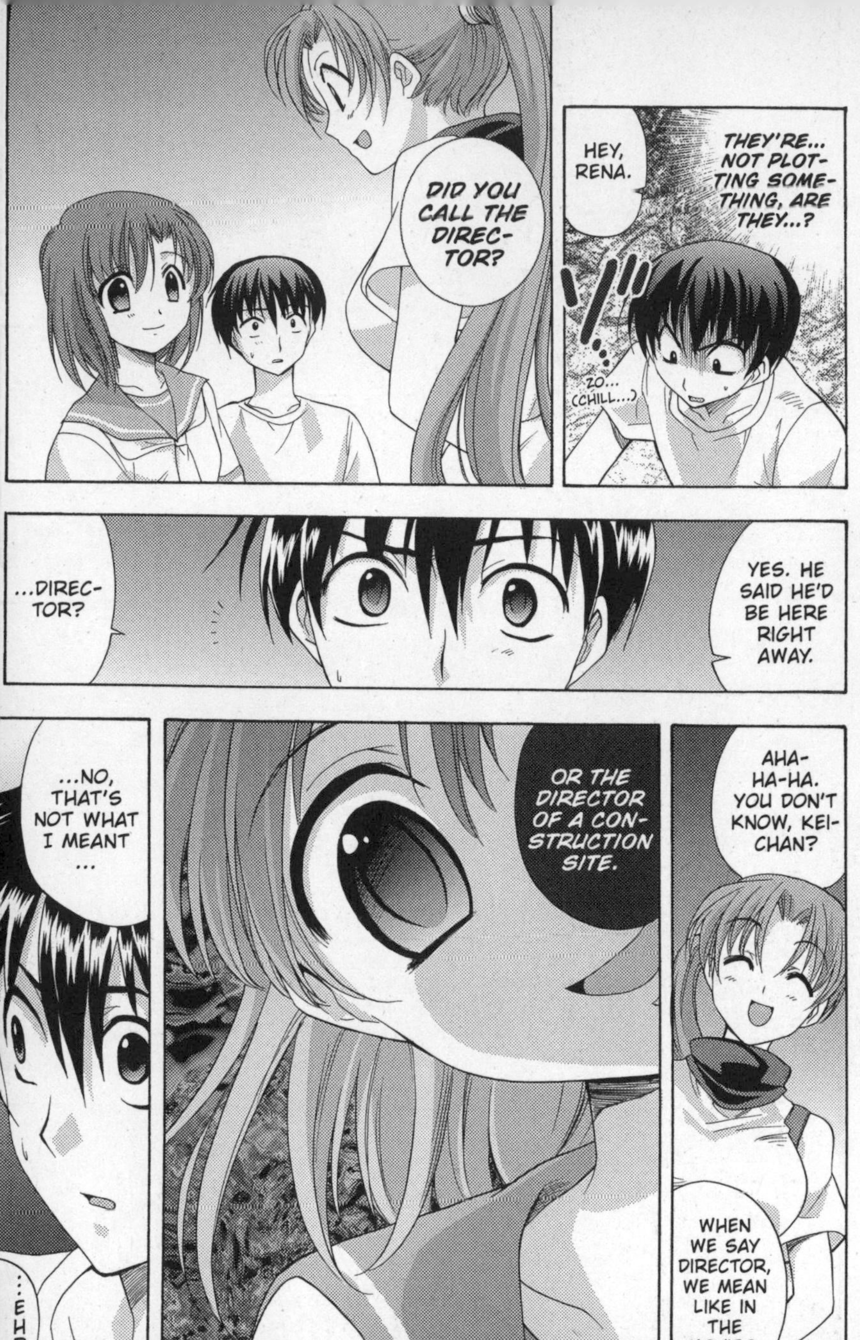
THEY'RE... NOT PLOTTING SOMETHING, ARE THEY...?
HEY, RENA.
ZO... (CHILL...)
DID YOU CALL THE DIRECTOR?
YES. HE SAID HE'D BE HERE RIGHT AWAY.
...DIRECTOR?
AHA-HA-HA. YOU DON'T KNOW, KEI-CHAN?
WHEN WE SAY DIRECTOR, WE MEAN LIKE IN THE MOVIES.
OR THE DIRECTOR OF A CONSTRUCTION SITE.
...NO, THAT'S NOT WHAT I MEANT...
...EH?

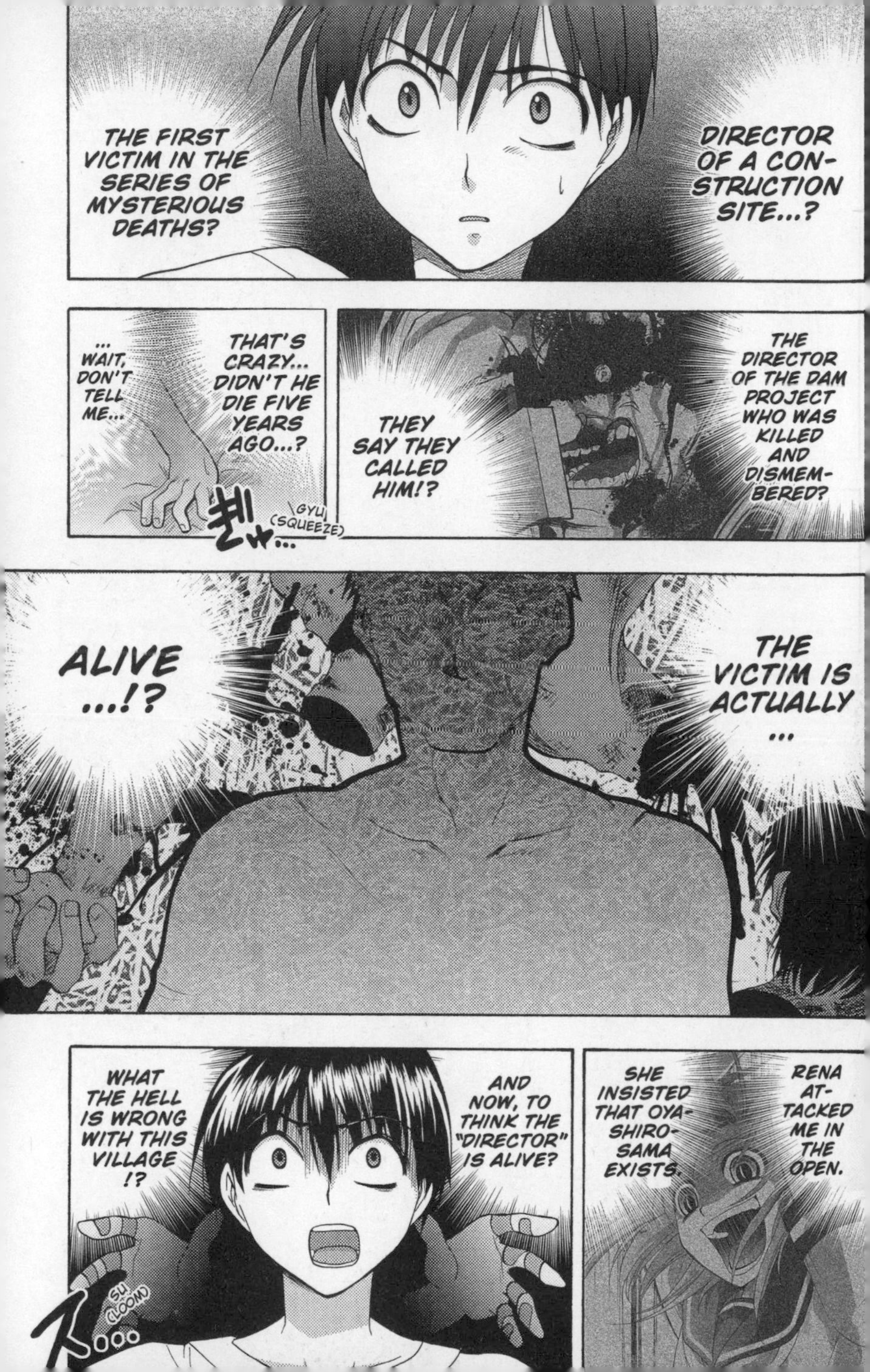
DIRECTOR OF A CONSTRUCTION SITE...?
THE FIRST VICTIM IN THE SERIES OF MYSTERIOUS DEATHS?
THE DIRECTOR OF THE DAM PROJECT WHO WAS KILLED AND DISMEMBERED?
THEY SAY THEY CALLED HIM!?
THAT'S CRAZY... DIDN'T HE DIE FIVE YEARS AGO...?
... WAIT, DON'T TELL ME...
GYU (SQUEEZE)
THE VICTIM IS ACTUALLY ...
ALIVE ...!?
RENA ATTACKED ME IN THE OPEN.
SHE INSISTED THAT OYASHIRO-SAMA EXISTS.
AND NOW, TO THINK THE "DIRECTOR" IS ALIVE?
WHAT THE HELL IS WRONG WITH THIS VILLAGE !?
SU (LOOM)

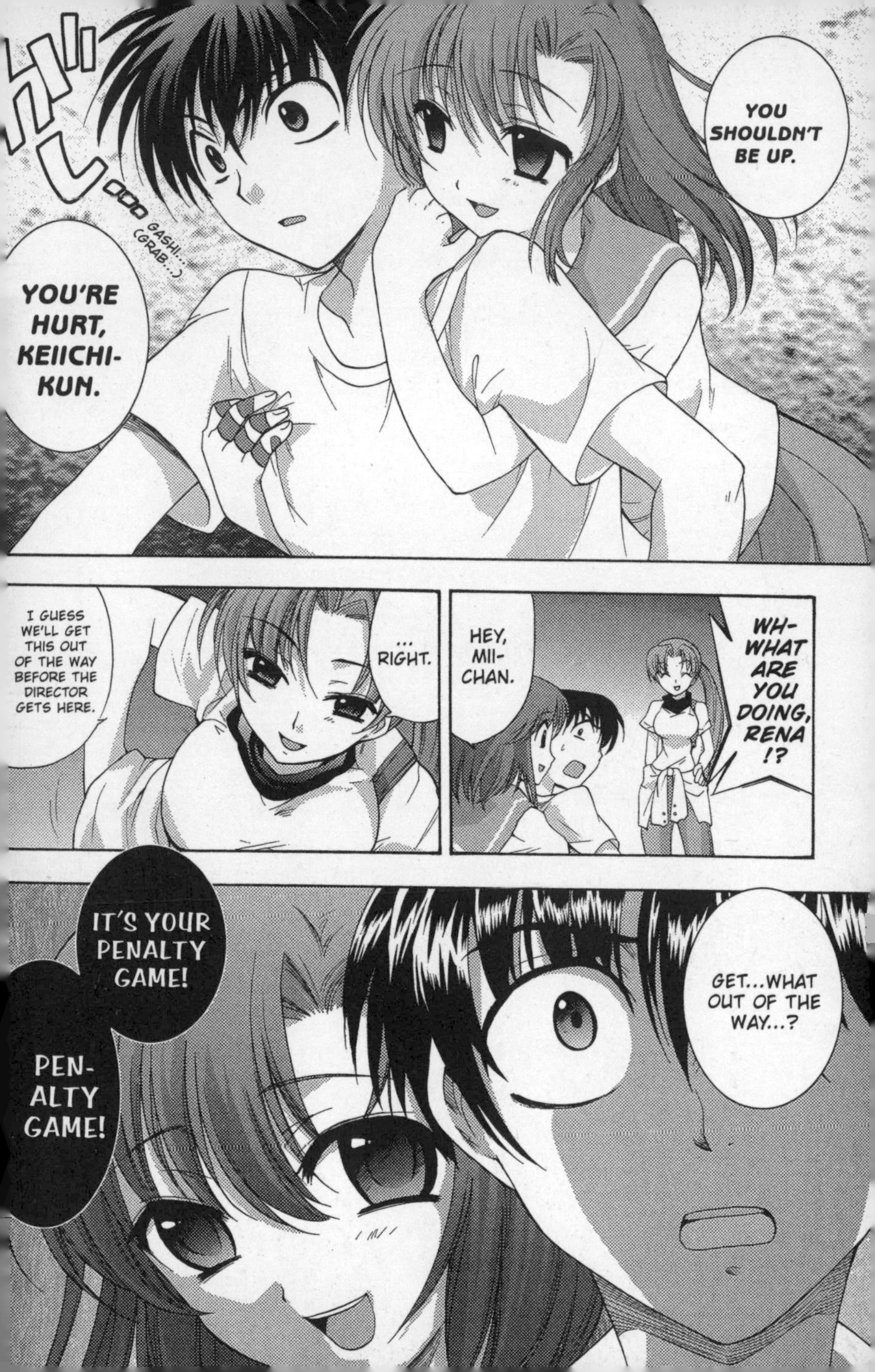
YOU SHOULDN'T BE UP.
GASHI... (GRAB...)
YOU'RE HURT, KEIICHI-KUN.
WH-WHAT ARE YOU DOING, RENA!?
HEY, MII-CHAN.
...RIGHT.
I GUESS WE'LL GET THIS OUT OF THE WAY BEFORE THE DIRECTOR GETS HERE.
GET...WHAT OUT OF THE WAY...?
IT'S YOUR PENALTY GAME!
PEN-ALTY GAME!

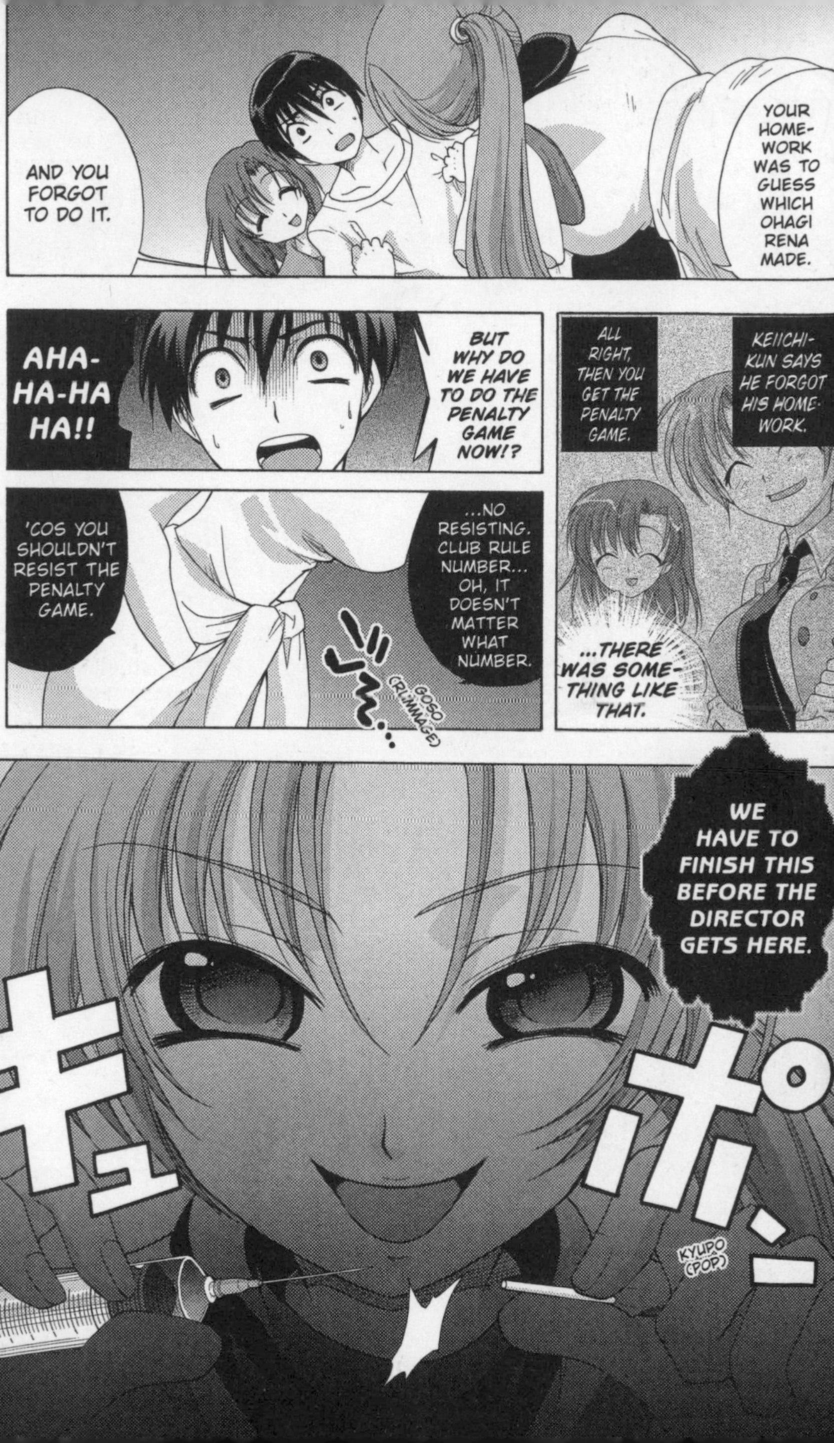
YOUR HOMEWORK WAS TO GUESS WHICH OHAGI RENA MADE.
AND YOU FORGOT TO DO IT.
KEIICHI-KUN SAYS HE FORGOT HIS HOMEWORK.
ALL RIGHT, THEN YOU GET THE PENALTY GAME.
...THERE WAS SOMETHING LIKE THAT.
BUT WHY DO WE HAVE TO DO THE PENALTY GAME NOW!?
AHA-HA-HA HA!!
...NO RESISTING. CLUB RULE NUMBER... OH, IT DOESN'T MATTER WHAT NUMBER.
'COS YOU SHOULDN'T RESIST THE PENALTY GAME.
GOSO (RUMMAGE)
WE HAVE TO FINISH THIS BEFORE THE DIRECTOR GETS HERE.
キュポッ
KYUPO (POP)

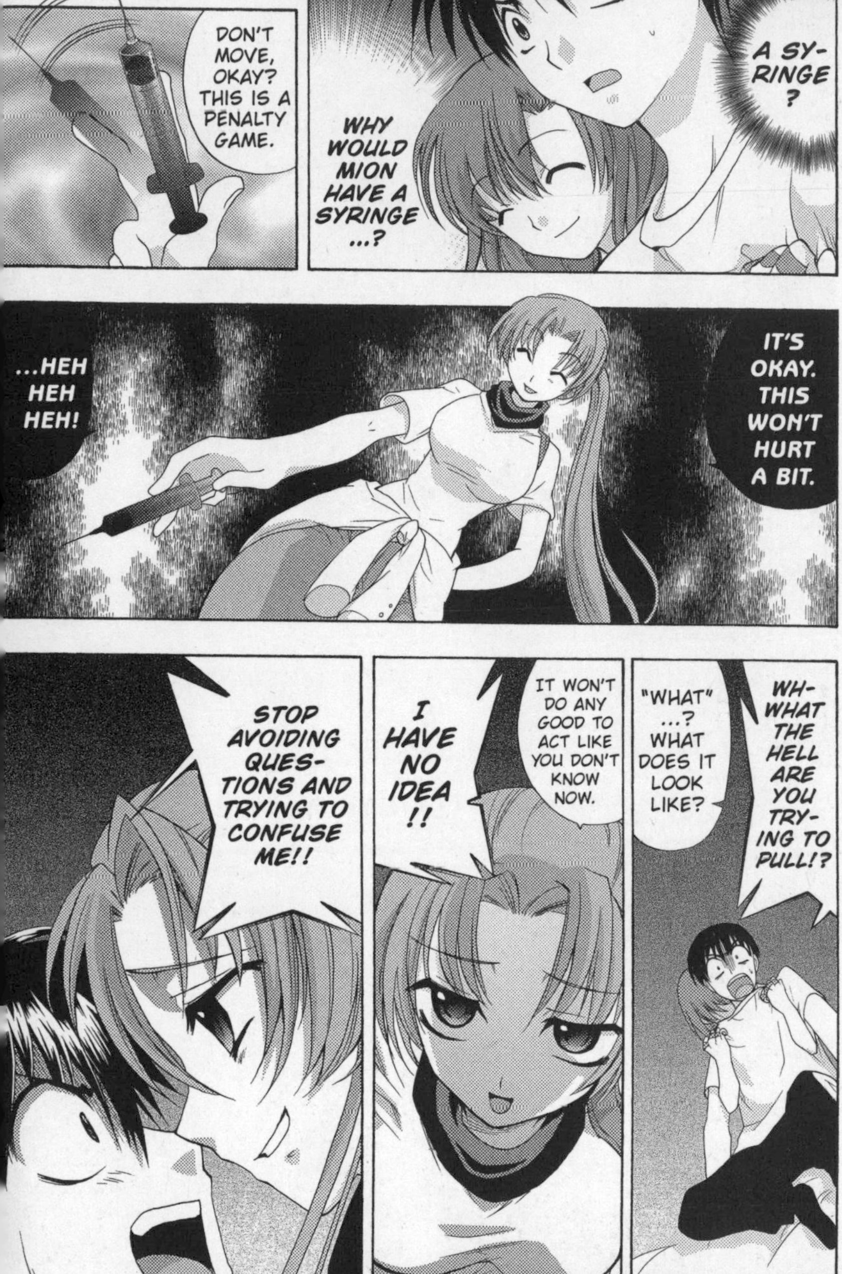
A SY-RINGE?
WHY WOULD MION HAVE A SYRINGE ...?
DON'T MOVE, OKAY? THIS IS A PENALTY GAME.
IT'S OKAY. THIS WON'T HURT A BIT.
...HEH HEH HEH!
WH-WHAT THE HELL ARE YOU TRY-ING TO PULL!?
"WHAT" ...? WHAT DOES IT LOOK LIKE?
IT WON'T DO ANY GOOD TO ACT LIKE YOU DON'T KNOW NOW.
I HAVE NO IDEA!!
STOP AVOIDING QUES-TIONS AND TRYING TO CONFUSE ME!!

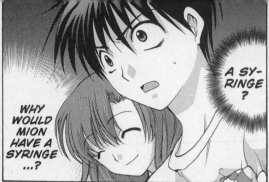

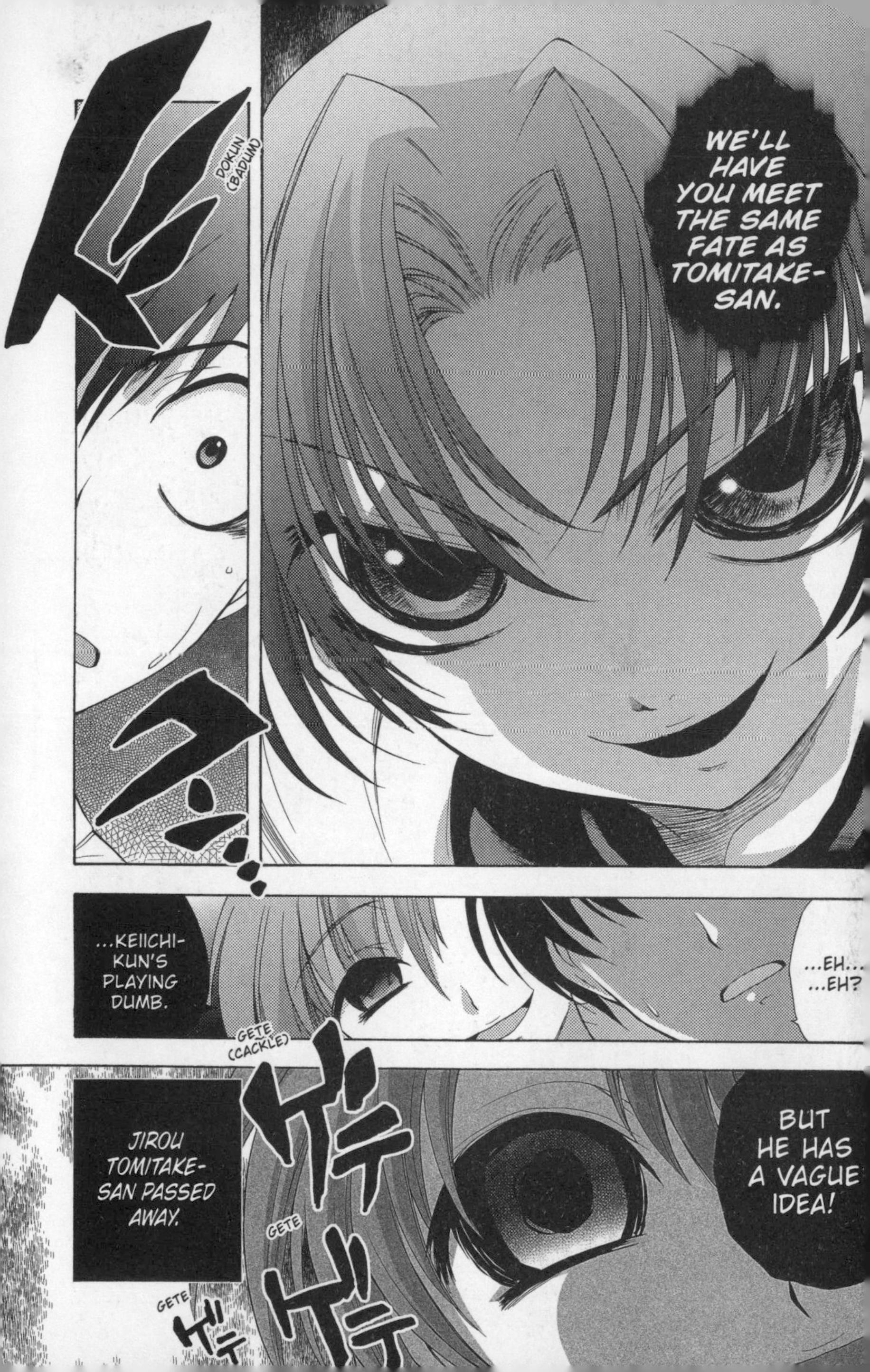
WE'LL HAVE YOU MEET THE SAME FATE AS TOMITAKE-SAN.
DOKUN (BADUM)
...EH... ...EH?
...KEIICHI-KUN'S PLAYING DUMB.
BUT HE HAS A VAGUE IDEA!
GETE (CACKLE)
GETE
GETE
JIROU TOMITAKE-SAN PASSED AWAY.

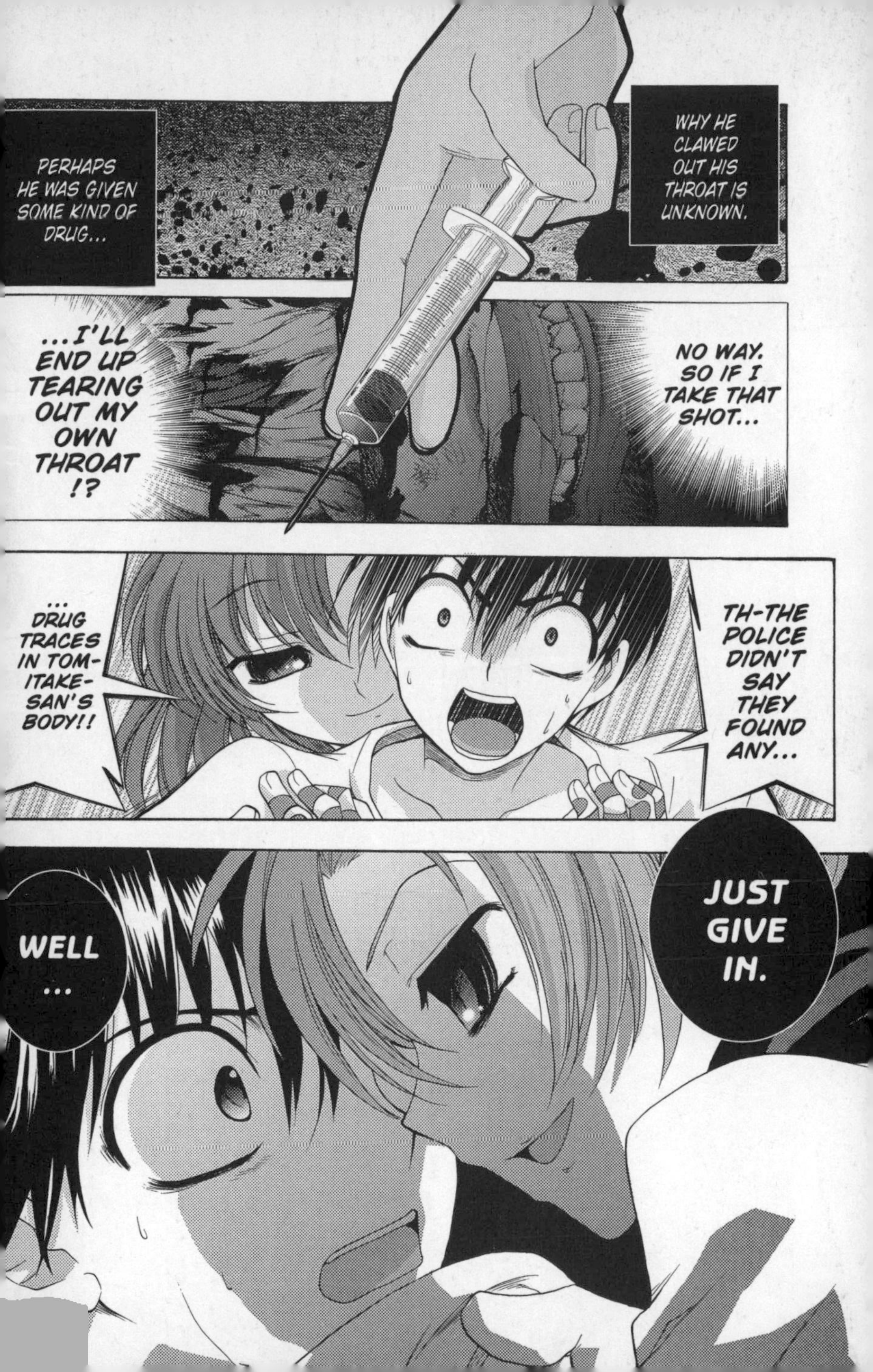
WHY HE CLAWED OUT HIS THROAT IS UNKNOWN.
PERHAPS HE WAS GIVEN SOME KIND OF DRUG...
NO WAY. SO IF I TAKE THAT SHOT...
...I'LL END UP TEARING OUT MY OWN THROAT !?
TH-THE POLICE DIDN'T SAY THEY FOUND ANY...
... DRUG TRACES IN TOM-ITAKE-SAN'S BODY!!
JUST GIVE IN.
WELL ...

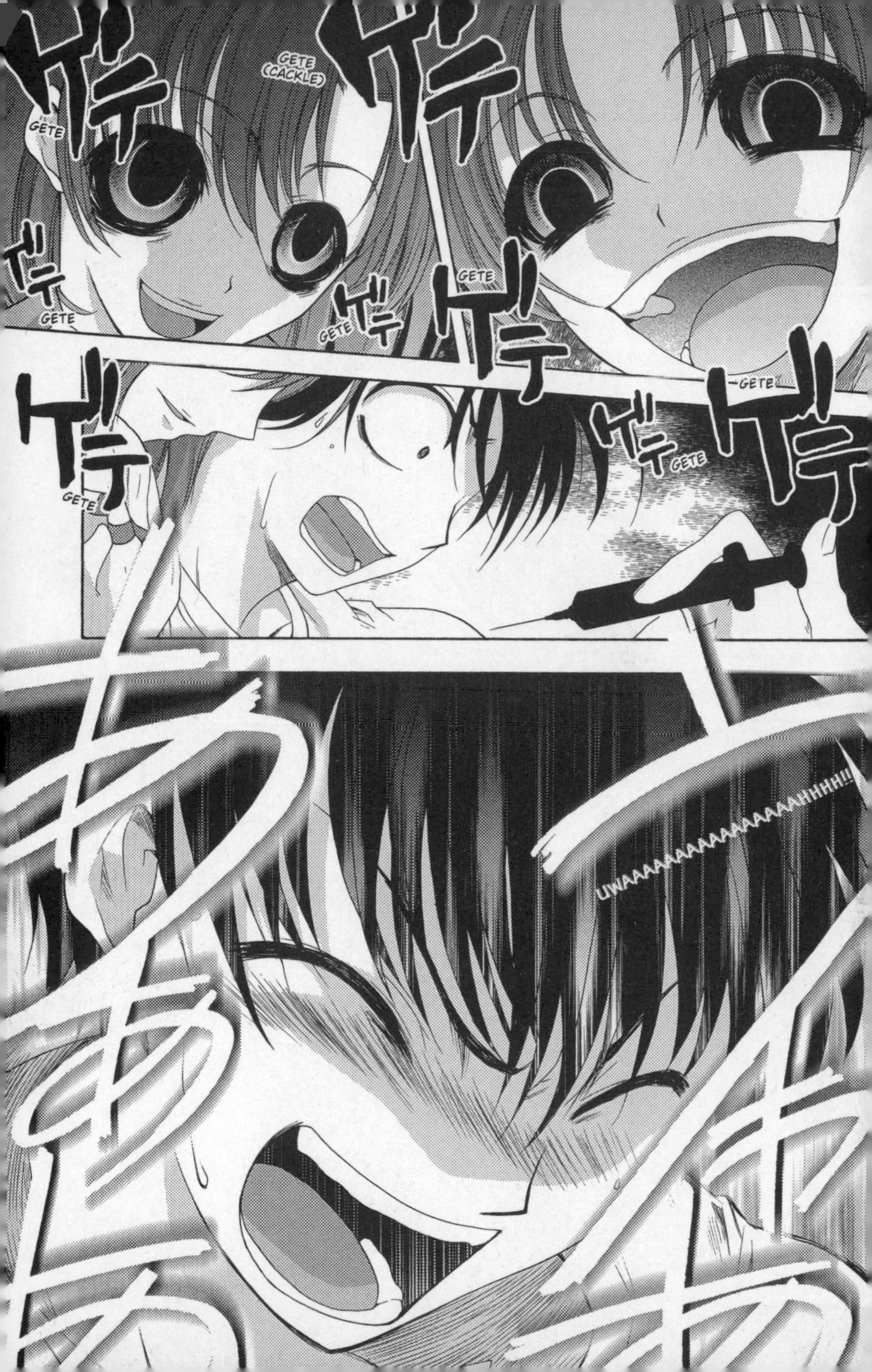
ゲテ
GETE
(CACKLE)
ゲテ
GETE
ゲテ
GETE
ゲテ
GETE
ゲテ
GETE
ゲテ
GETE
ゲテ
GETE
ゲテ
GETE
UWAAAAAAAAAAAAAAAAAHHHH!!

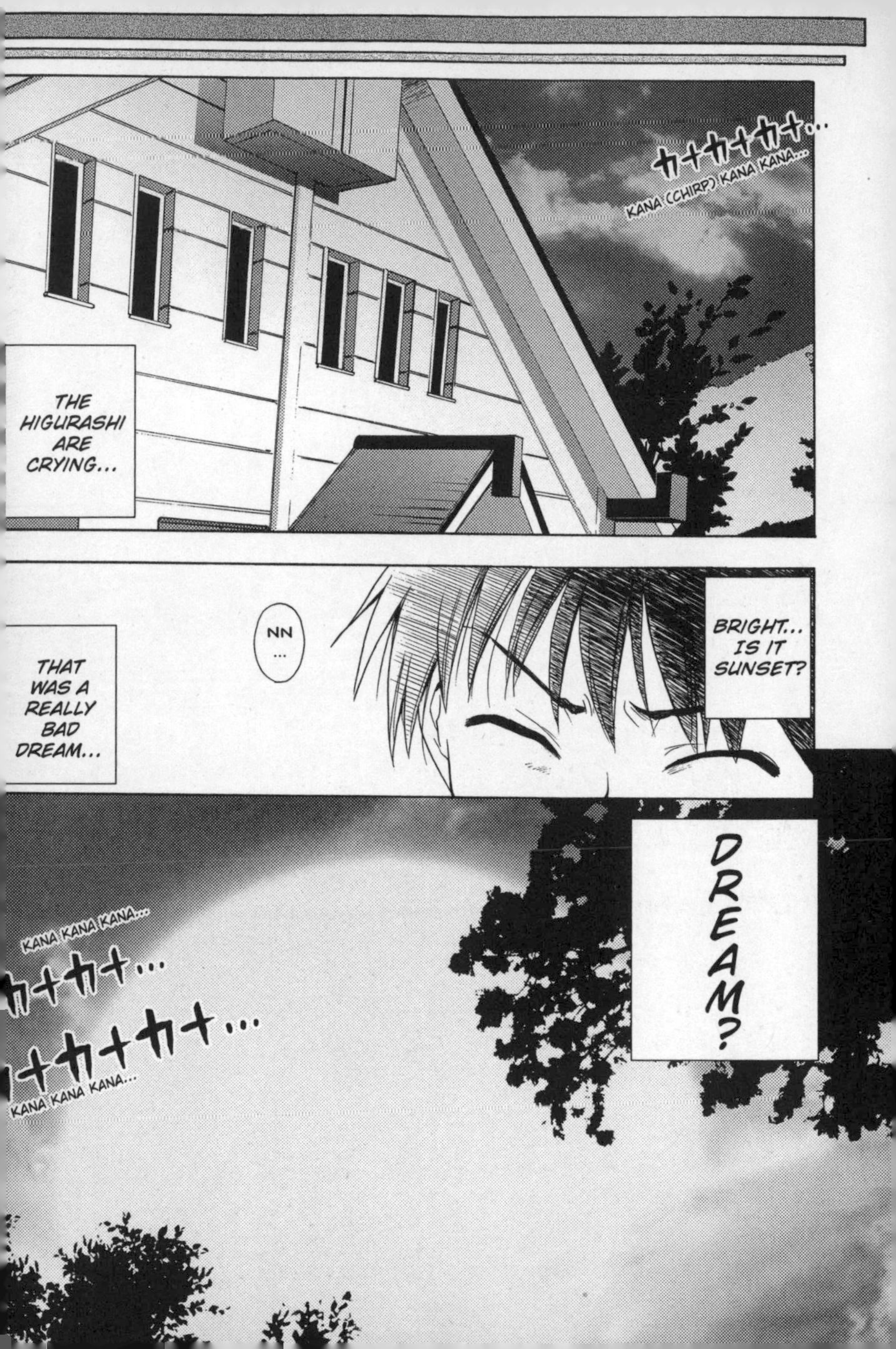
カナカナカナ…
KANA (CHIRP) KANA KANA...
THE HIGURASHI ARE CRYING...
BRIGHT... IS IT SUNSET?
NN ...
THAT WAS A REALLY BAD DREAM...
DREAM?
KANA KANA KANA...
カナカナ…
ナカナカナ…
KANA KANA KANA...

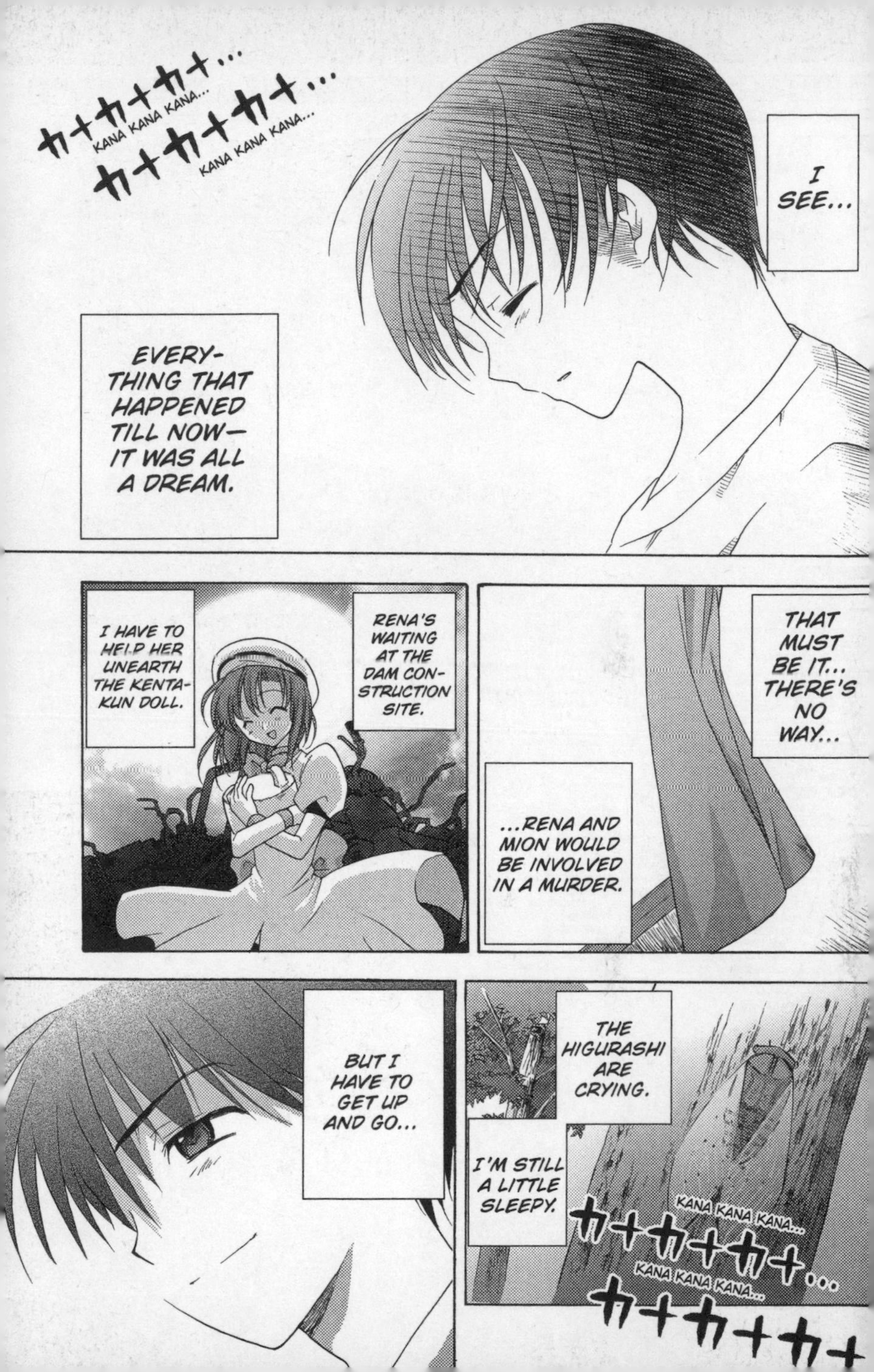
I SEE...
カナカナカナ…
KANA KANA KANA...
カナカナカナ…
KANA KANA KANA...
EVERY-THING THAT HAPPENED TILL NOW—IT WAS ALL A DREAM.
THAT MUST BE IT... THERE'S NO WAY...
...RENA AND MION WOULD BE INVOLVED IN A MURDER.
RENA'S WAITING AT THE DAM CON-STRUCTION SITE.
I HAVE TO HELP HER UNEARTH THE KENTA-KUN DOLL.
THE HIGURASHI ARE CRYING.
I'M STILL A LITTLE SLEEPY.
KANA KANA KANA...
カナカナカナ…
KANA KANA KANA...
カナカナカナ
BUT I HAVE TO GET UP AND GO...

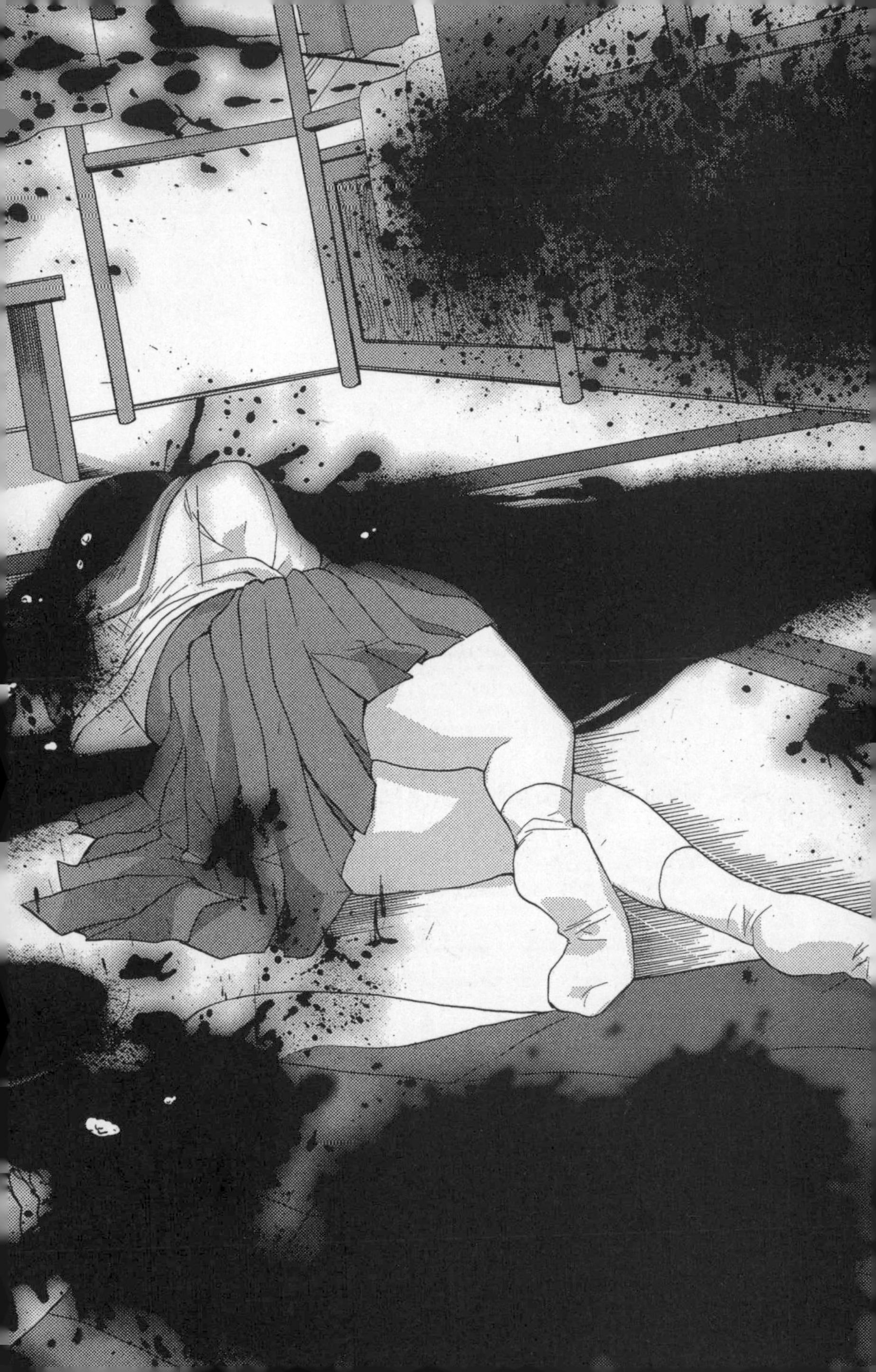

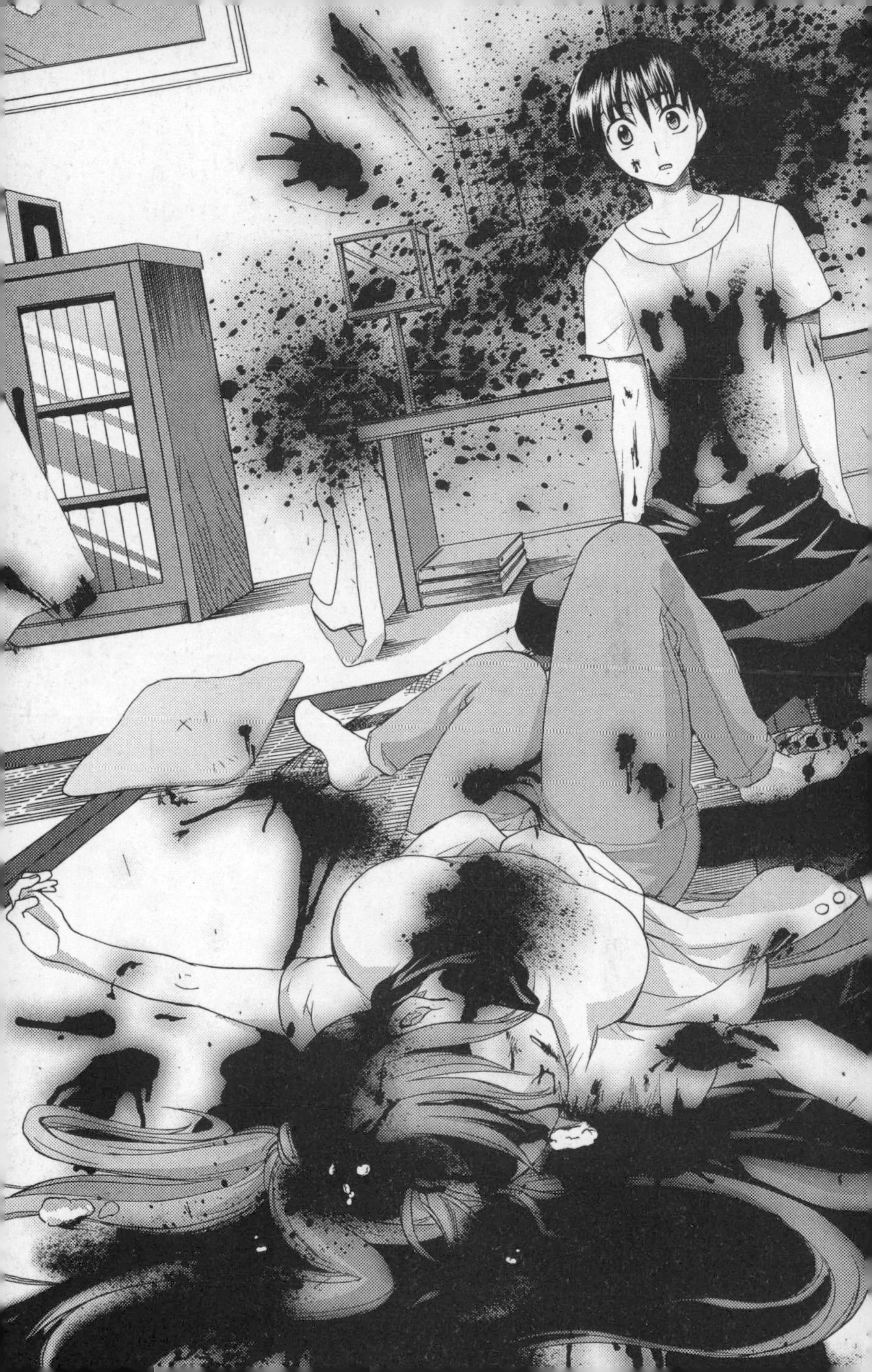

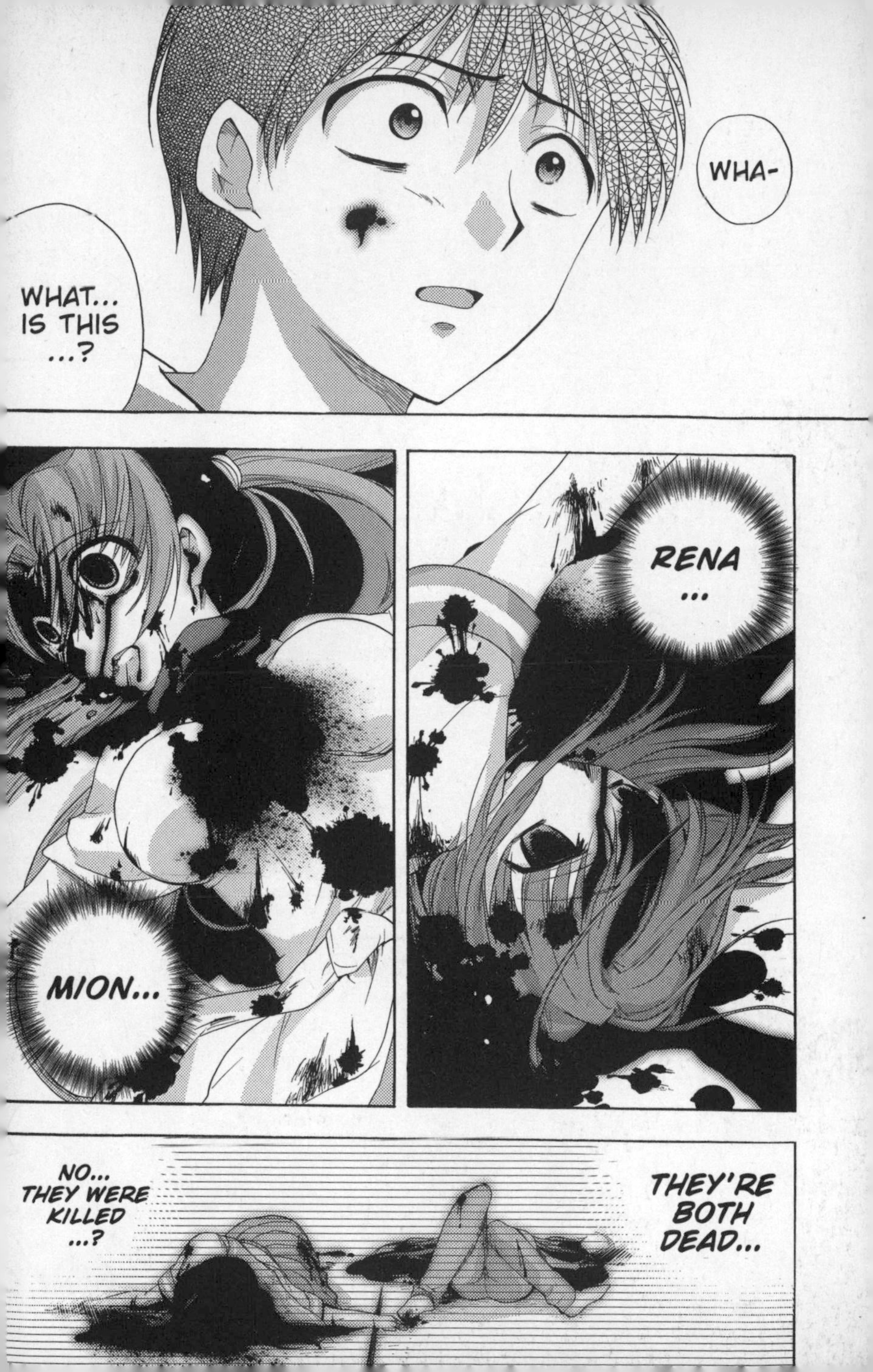
WHA-
WHAT... IS THIS ...?
RENA ...
MION...
THEY'RE BOTH DEAD...
NO... THEY WERE KILLED ...?

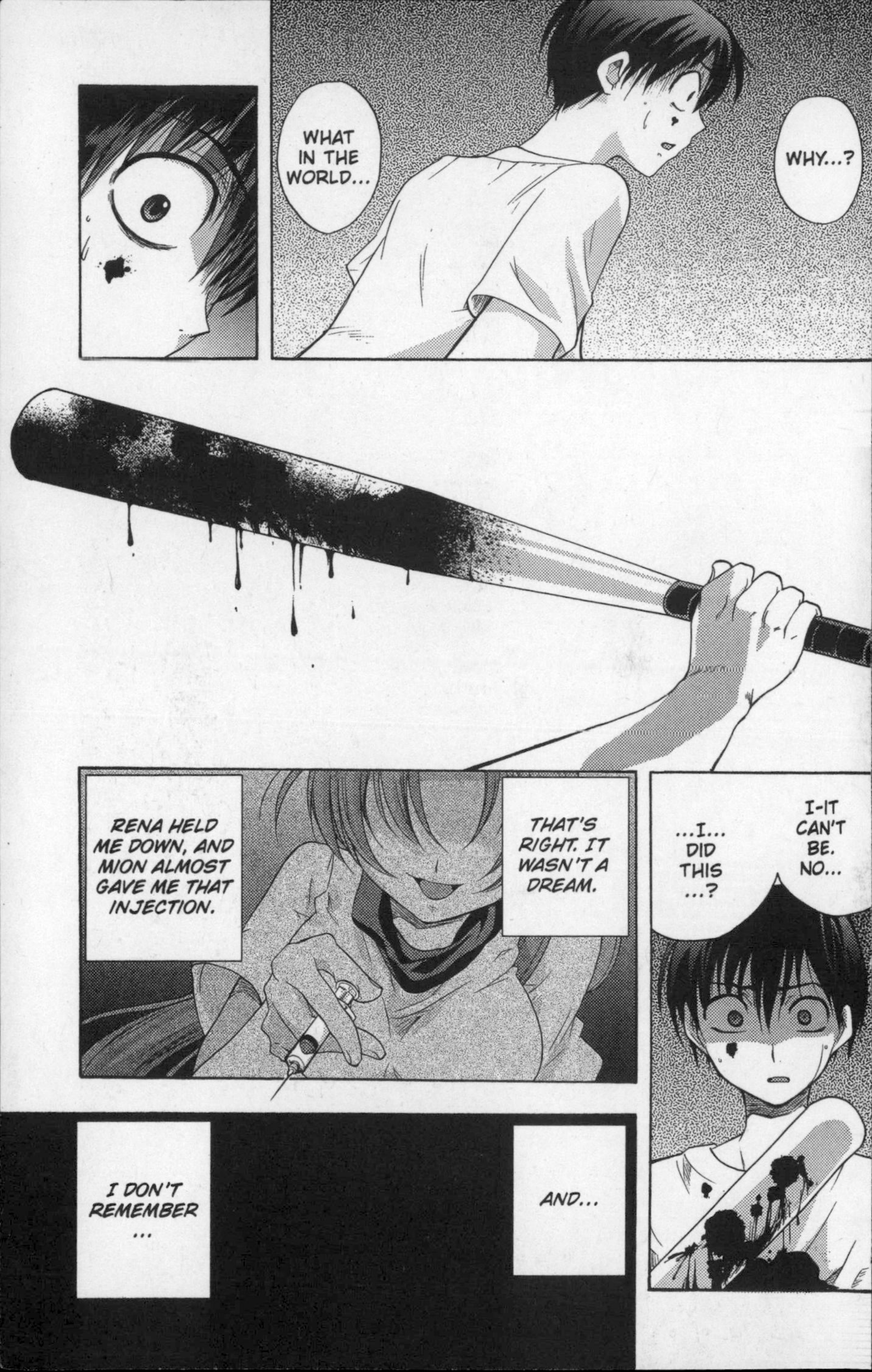
WHY...?
WHAT IN THE WORLD...
I-IT CAN'T BE. NO...
...I... DID THIS ...?
THAT'S RIGHT. IT WASN'T A DREAM.
RENA HELD ME DOWN, AND MION ALMOST GAVE ME THAT INJECTION.
AND...
I DON'T REMEMBER ...

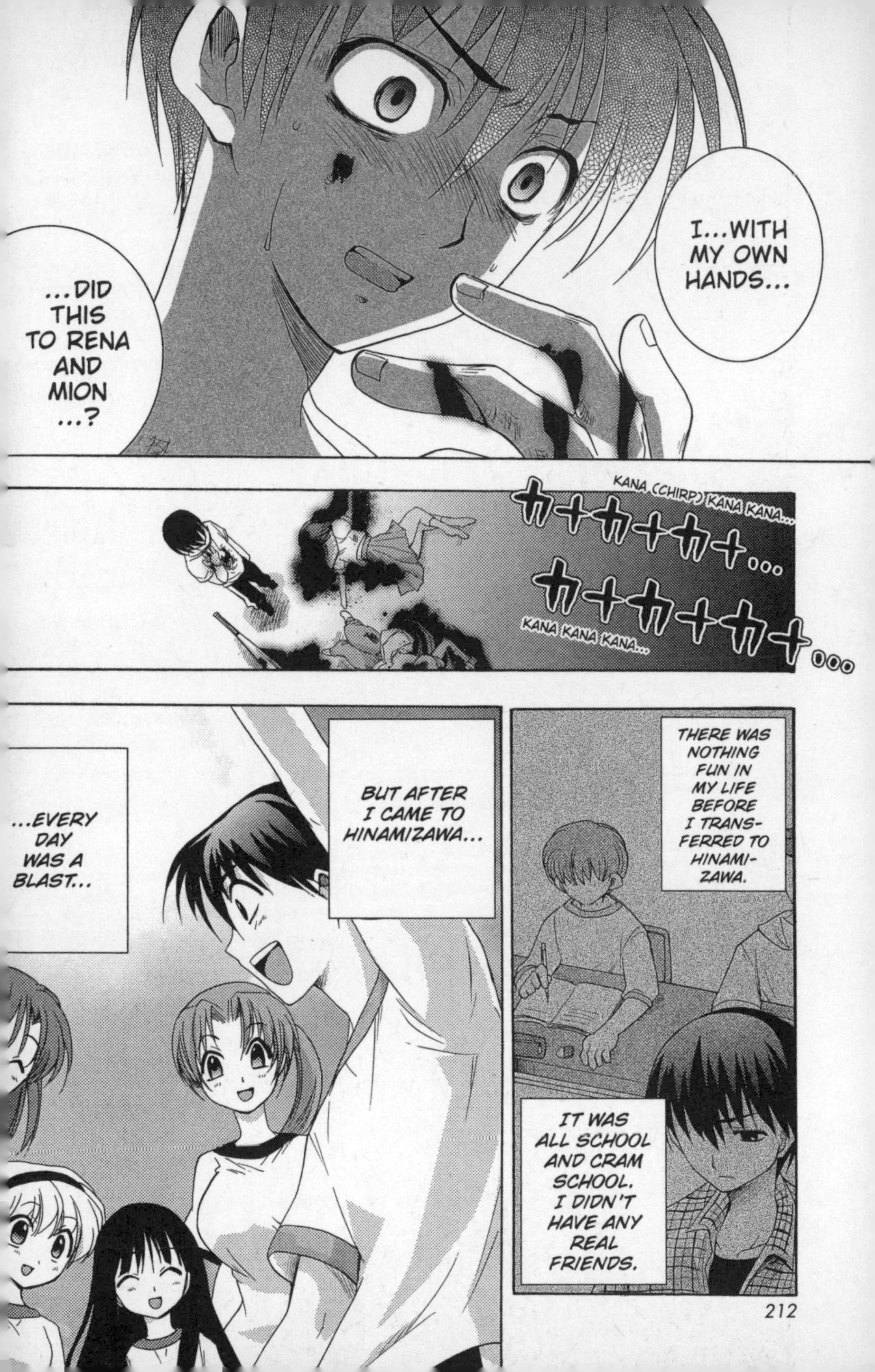
I...WITH MY OWN HANDS...
...DID THIS TO RENA AND MION ...?
KANA (CHIRP) KANA KANA...
カナカナカナ…
カナカナカナ…
KANA KANA KANA...
THERE WAS NOTHING FUN IN MY LIFE BEFORE I TRANS-FERRED TO HINAMI-ZAWA.
IT WAS ALL SCHOOL AND CRAM SCHOOL. I DIDN'T HAVE ANY REAL FRIENDS.
BUT AFTER I CAME TO HINAMIZAWA...
...EVERY DAY WAS A BLAST...

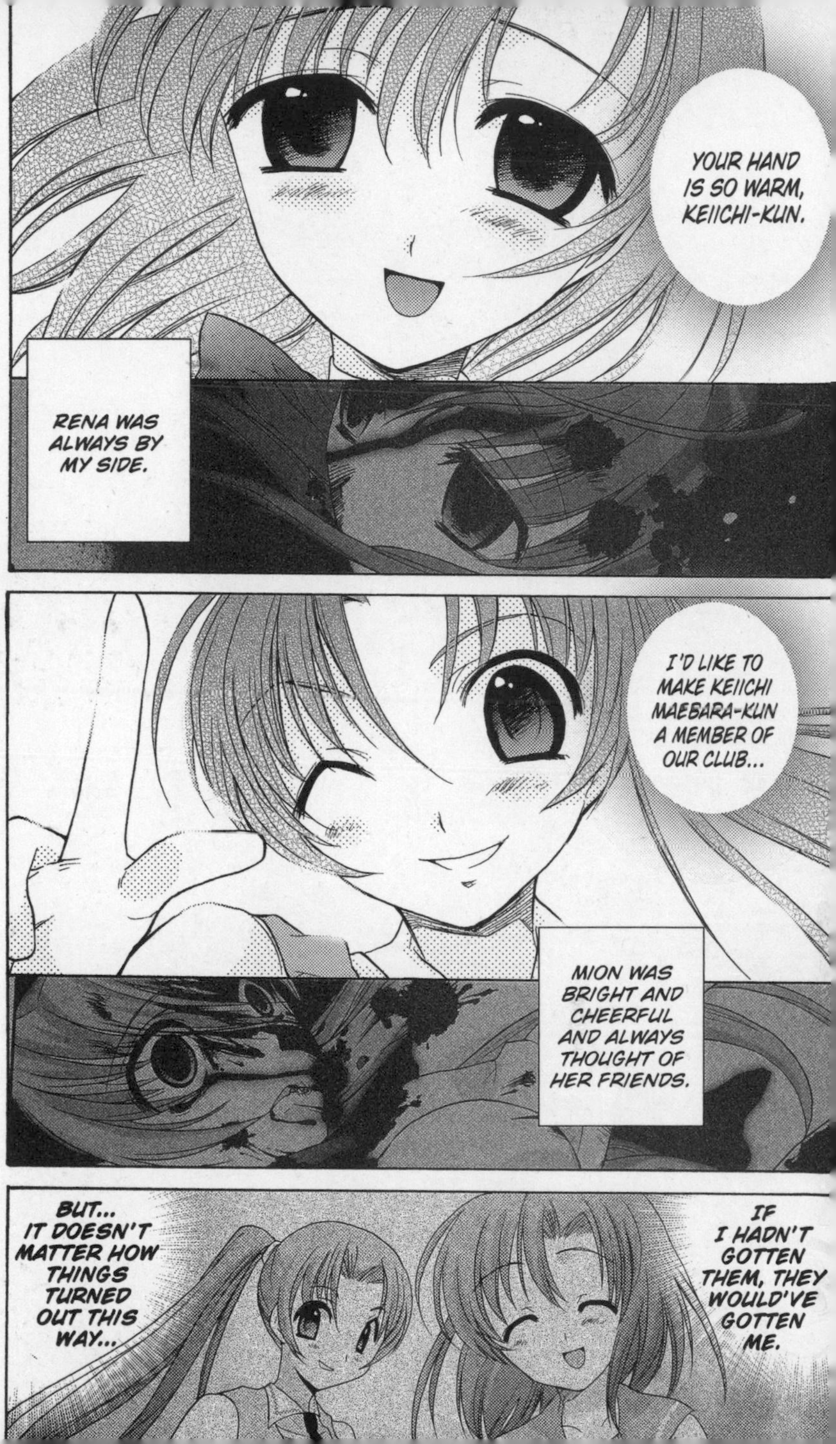
YOUR HAND IS SO WARM, KEIICHI-KUN.
RENA WAS ALWAYS BY MY SIDE.
I'D LIKE TO MAKE KEIICHI MAEBARA-KUN A MEMBER OF OUR CLUB...
MION WAS BRIGHT AND CHEERFUL AND ALWAYS THOUGHT OF HER FRIENDS.
IF I HADN'T GOTTEN THEM, THEY WOULD'VE GOTTEN ME.
BUT... IT DOESN'T MATTER HOW THINGS TURNED OUT THIS WAY...

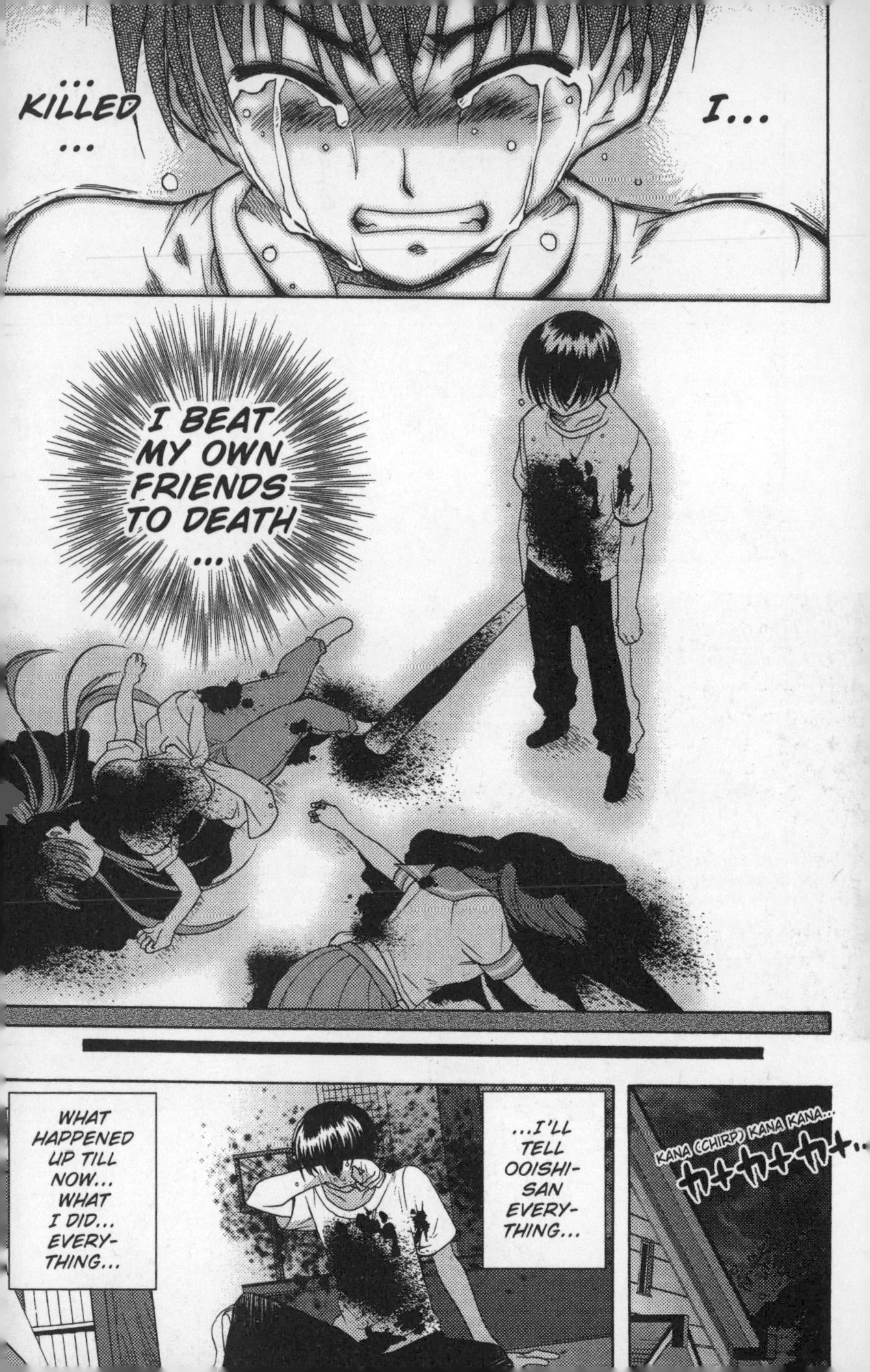
I...
...KILLED...
I BEAT MY OWN FRIENDS TO DEATH ...
KANA (CHIRP) KANA KANA...
カナカナカナ...
...I'LL TELL OOISHI-SAN EVERYTHING...
WHAT HAPPENED UP TILL NOW... WHAT I DID... EVERYTHING...

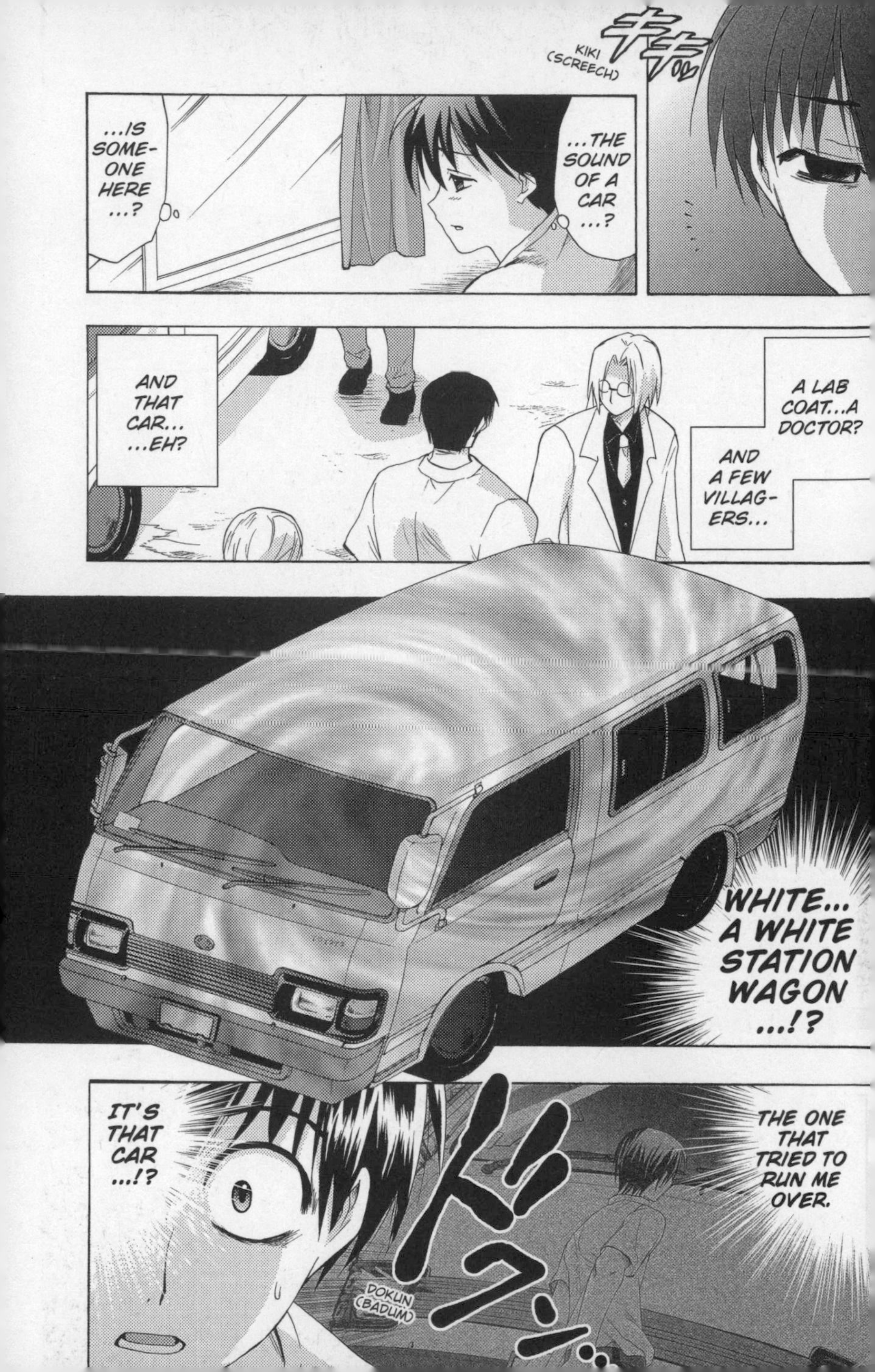
KIKI (SCREECH)
...THE SOUND OF A CAR ...?
...IS SOME-ONE HERE ...?
A LAB COAT...A DOCTOR?
AND A FEW VILLAG-ERS...
AND THAT CAR... ...EH?
WHITE... A WHITE STATION WAGON ...!?
THE ONE THAT TRIED TO RUN ME OVER.
IT'S THAT CAR ...!?
DOKUN (BADUM)

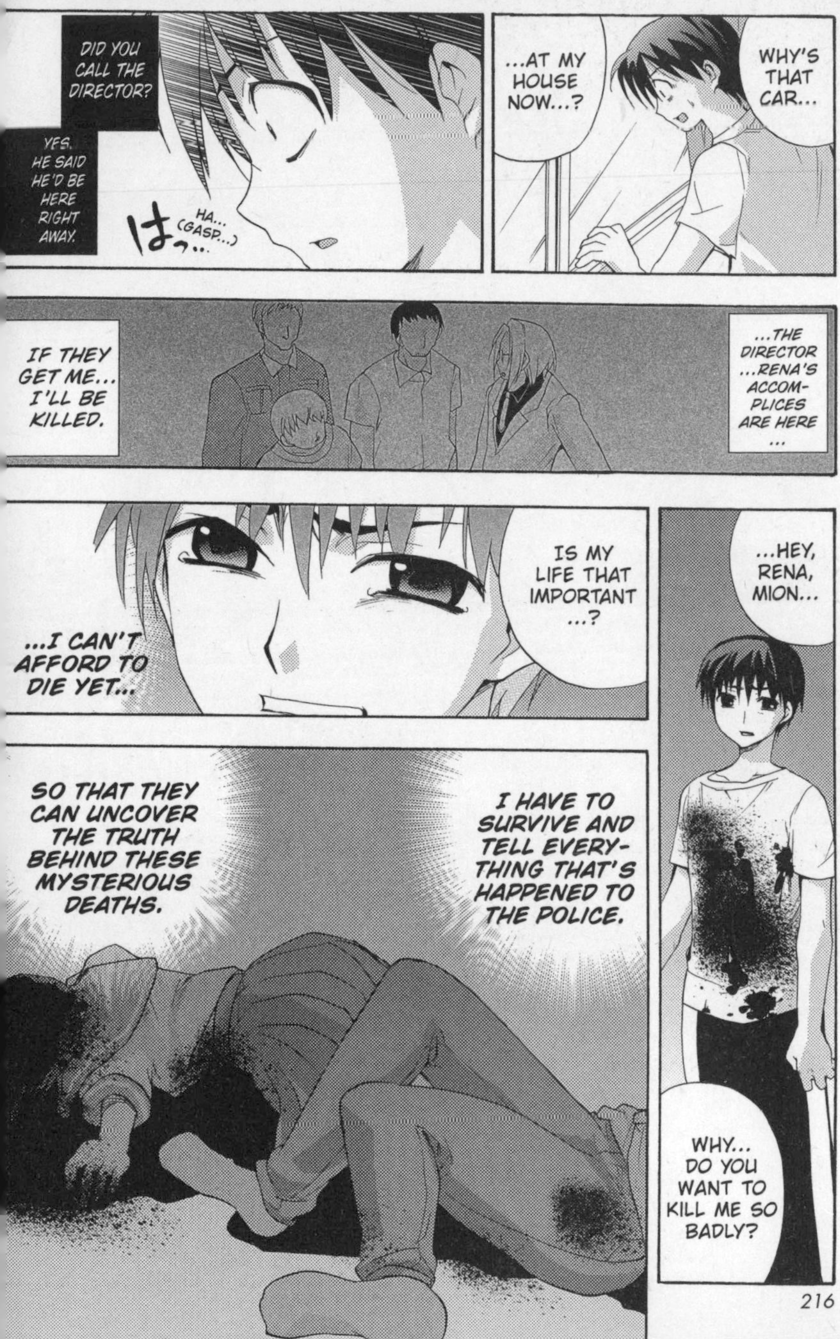
WHY'S THAT CAR...
...AT MY HOUSE NOW...?
DID YOU CALL THE DIRECTOR?
YES. HE SAID HE'D BE HERE RIGHT AWAY.
はっ...
HA... (GASP...)
...THE DIRECTOR ...RENA'S ACCOMPLICES ARE HERE ...
IF THEY GET ME... I'LL BE KILLED.
...HEY, RENA, MION...
WHY... DO YOU WANT TO KILL ME SO BADLY?
IS MY LIFE THAT IMPORTANT ...?
...I CAN'T AFFORD TO DIE YET...
I HAVE TO SURVIVE AND TELL EVERYTHING THAT'S HAPPENED TO THE POLICE.
SO THAT THEY CAN UNCOVER THE TRUTH BEHIND THESE MYSTERIOUS DEATHS.

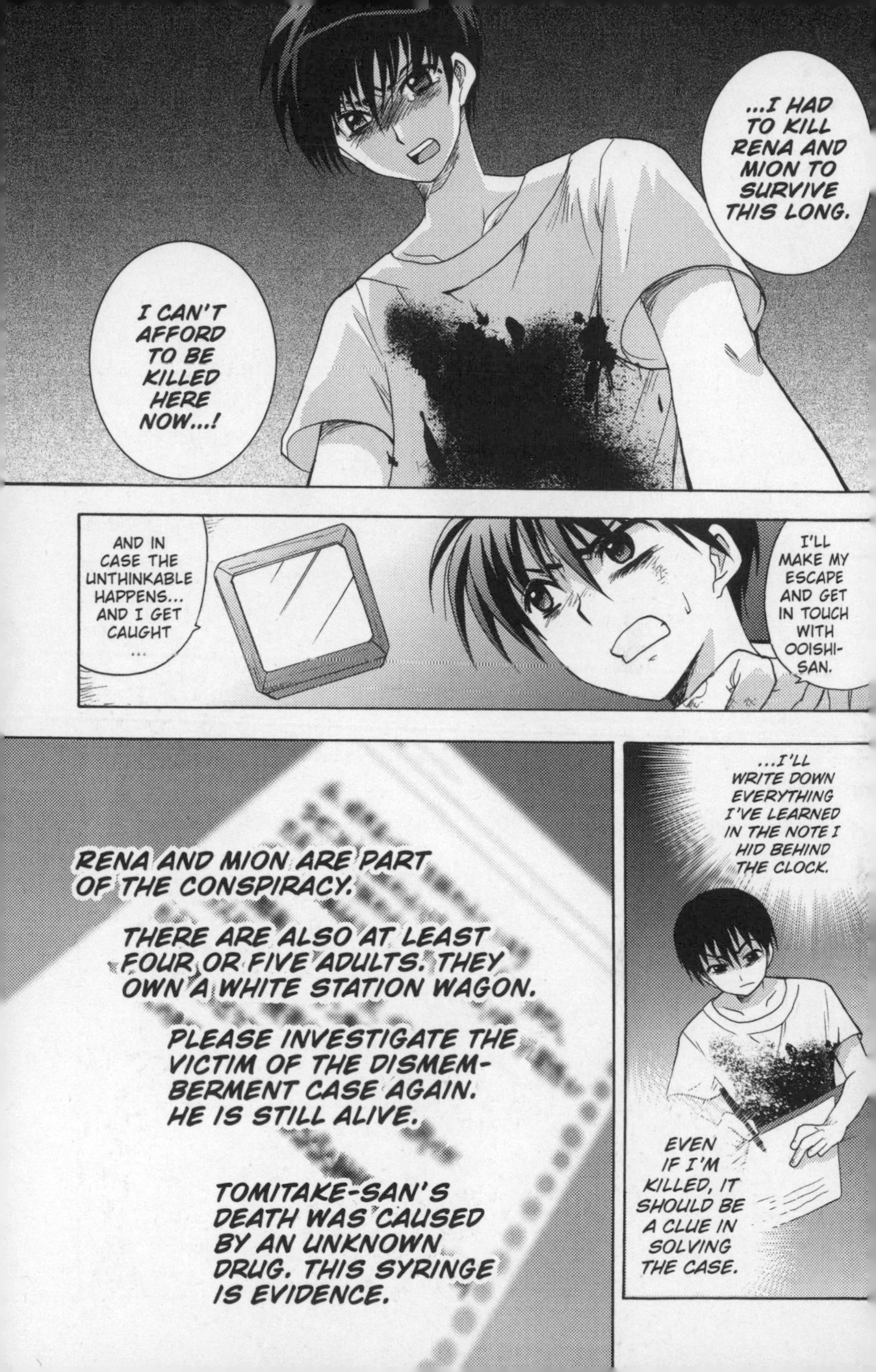
...I HAD TO KILL RENA AND MION TO SURVIVE THIS LONG.
I CAN'T AFFORD TO BE KILLED HERE NOW...!
I'LL MAKE MY ESCAPE AND GET IN TOUCH WITH OOISHI-SAN.
AND IN CASE THE UNTHINKABLE HAPPENS... AND I GET CAUGHT ...
...I'LL WRITE DOWN EVERYTHING I'VE LEARNED IN THE NOTE I HID BEHIND THE CLOCK.
EVEN IF I'M KILLED, IT SHOULD BE A CLUE IN SOLVING THE CASE.
RENA AND MION ARE PART OF THE CONSPIRACY.
THERE ARE ALSO AT LEAST FOUR OR FIVE ADULTS. THEY OWN A WHITE STATION WAGON.
PLEASE INVESTIGATE THE VICTIM OF THE DISMEMBERMENT CASE AGAIN. HE IS STILL ALIVE.
TOMITAKE-SAN'S DEATH WAS CAUSED BY AN UNKNOWN DRUG. THIS SYRINGE IS EVIDENCE.

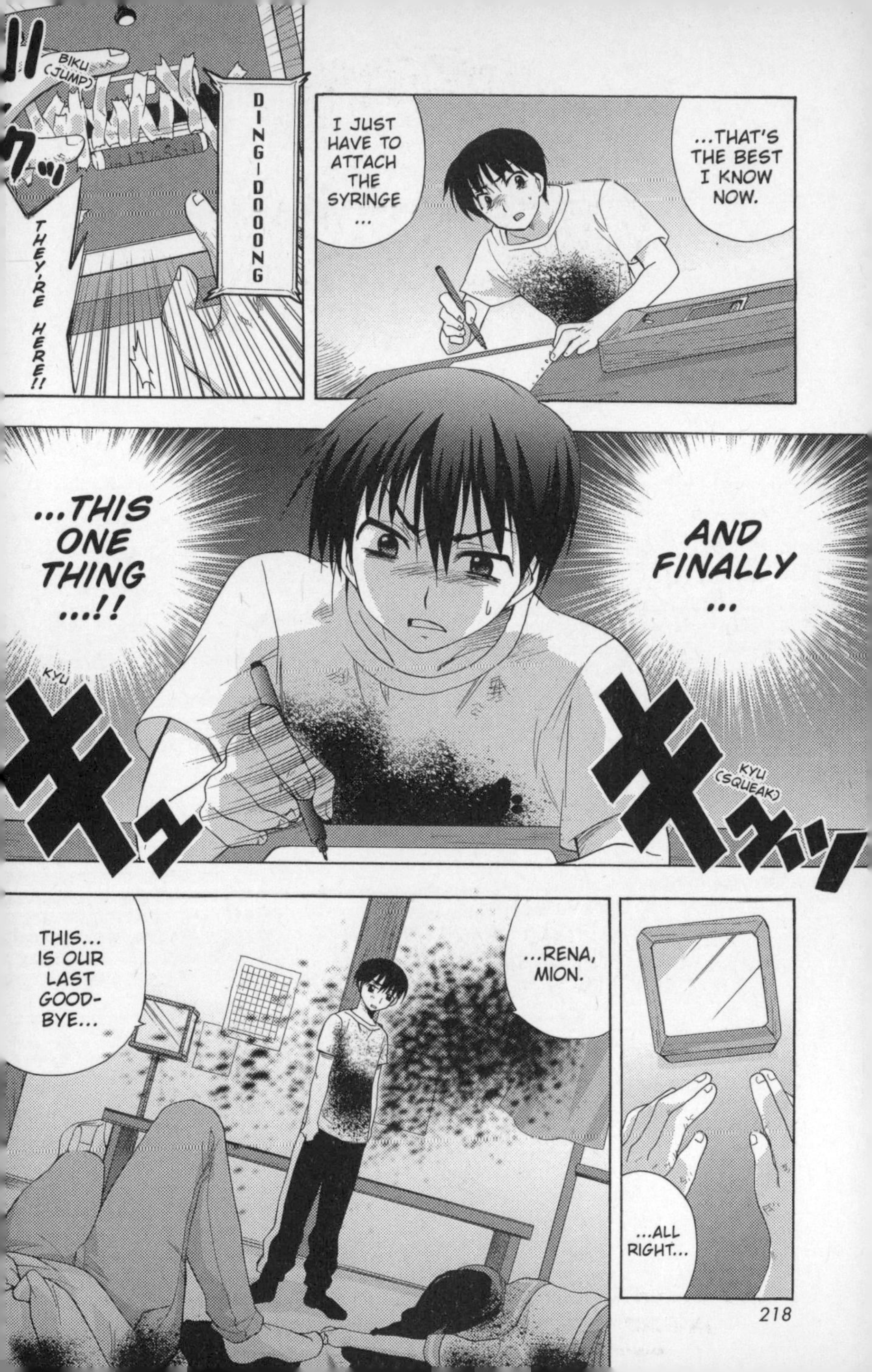
...THAT'S THE BEST I KNOW NOW.
I JUST HAVE TO ATTACH THE SYRINGE ...
DING-DOOONG
BIKU (JUMP)
THEY'RE HERE!!
AND FINALLY ...
...THIS ONE THING ...!!
KYU (SQUEAK)
KYU
...ALL RIGHT...
...RENA, MION.
THIS... IS OUR LAST GOOD-BYE...

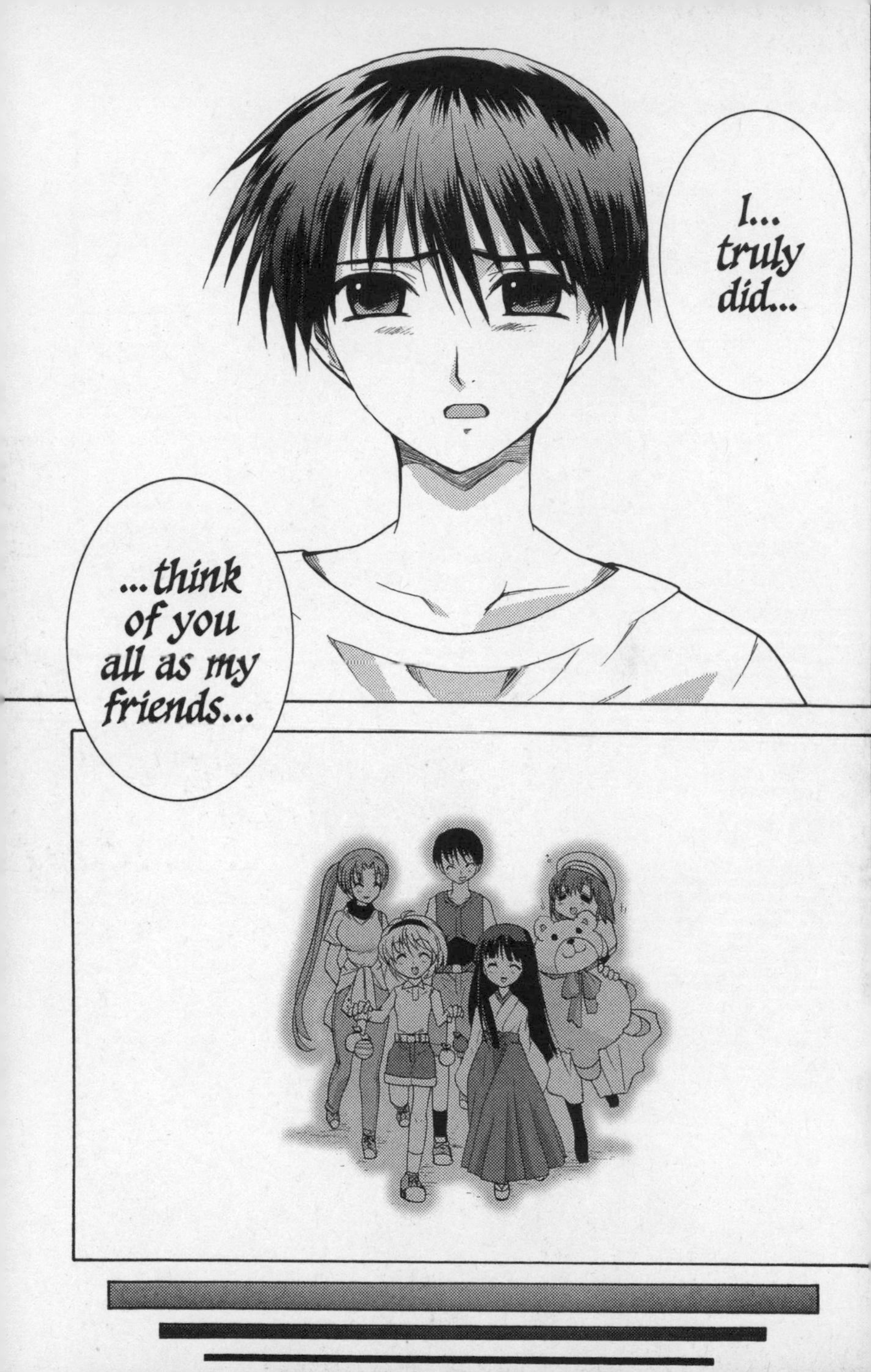
I... truly did...
...think of you all as my friends...

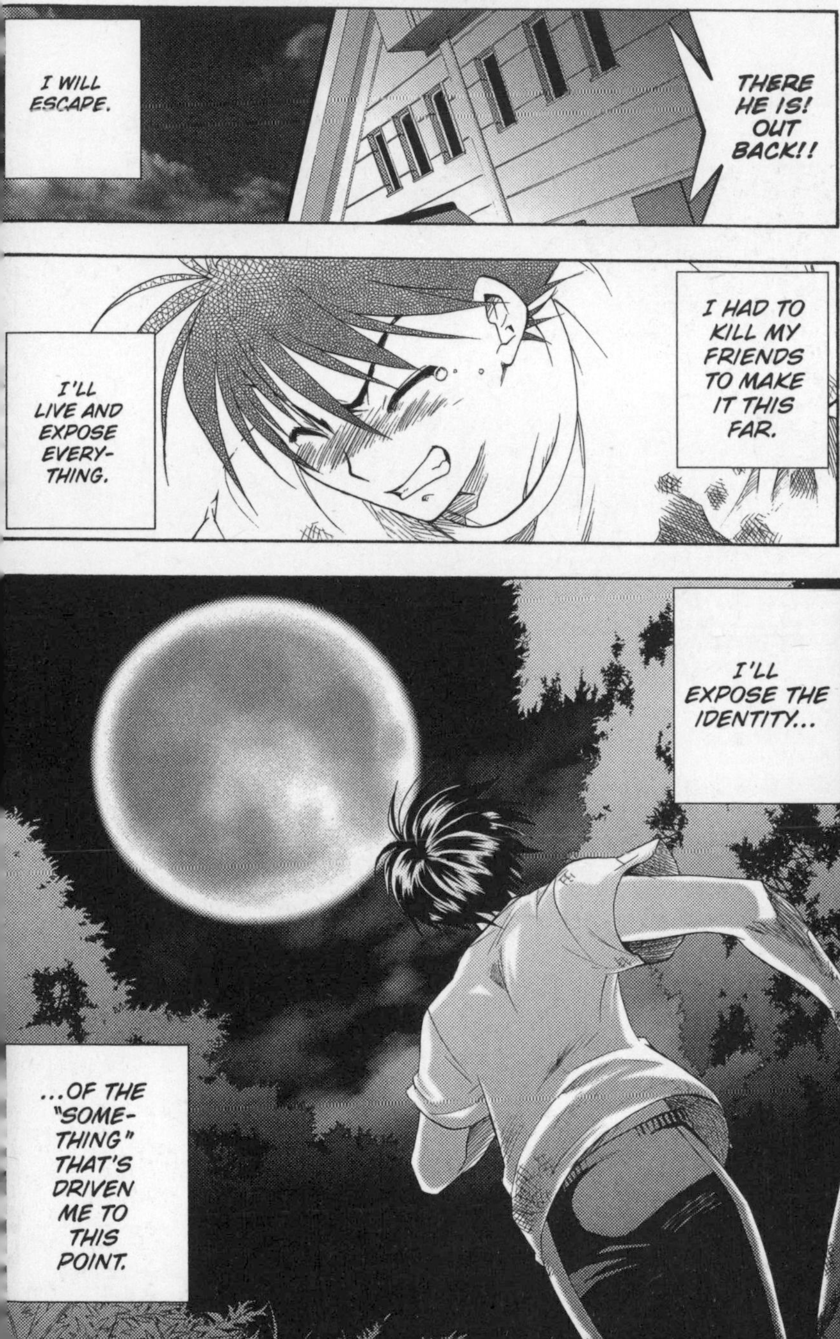
THERE HE IS! OUT BACK!!
I WILL ESCAPE.
I HAD TO KILL MY FRIENDS TO MAKE IT THIS FAR.
I'LL LIVE AND EXPOSE EVERY-THING.
I'LL EXPOSE THE IDENTITY...
...OF THE "SOME-THING" THAT'S DRIVEN ME TO THIS POINT.

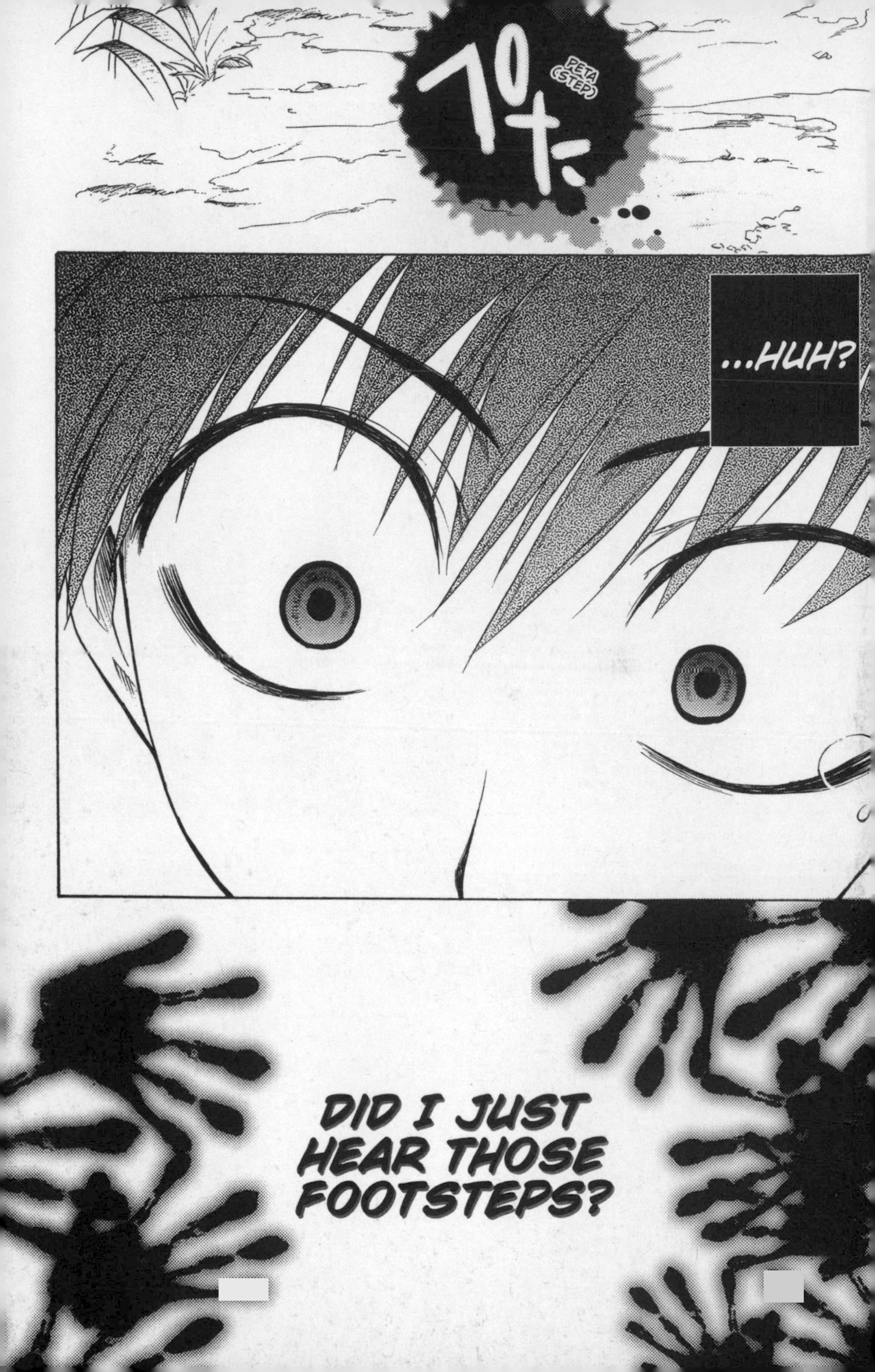
ぺた
PETA (STEP)
...HUH?
DID I JUST HEAR THOSE FOOTSTEPS?

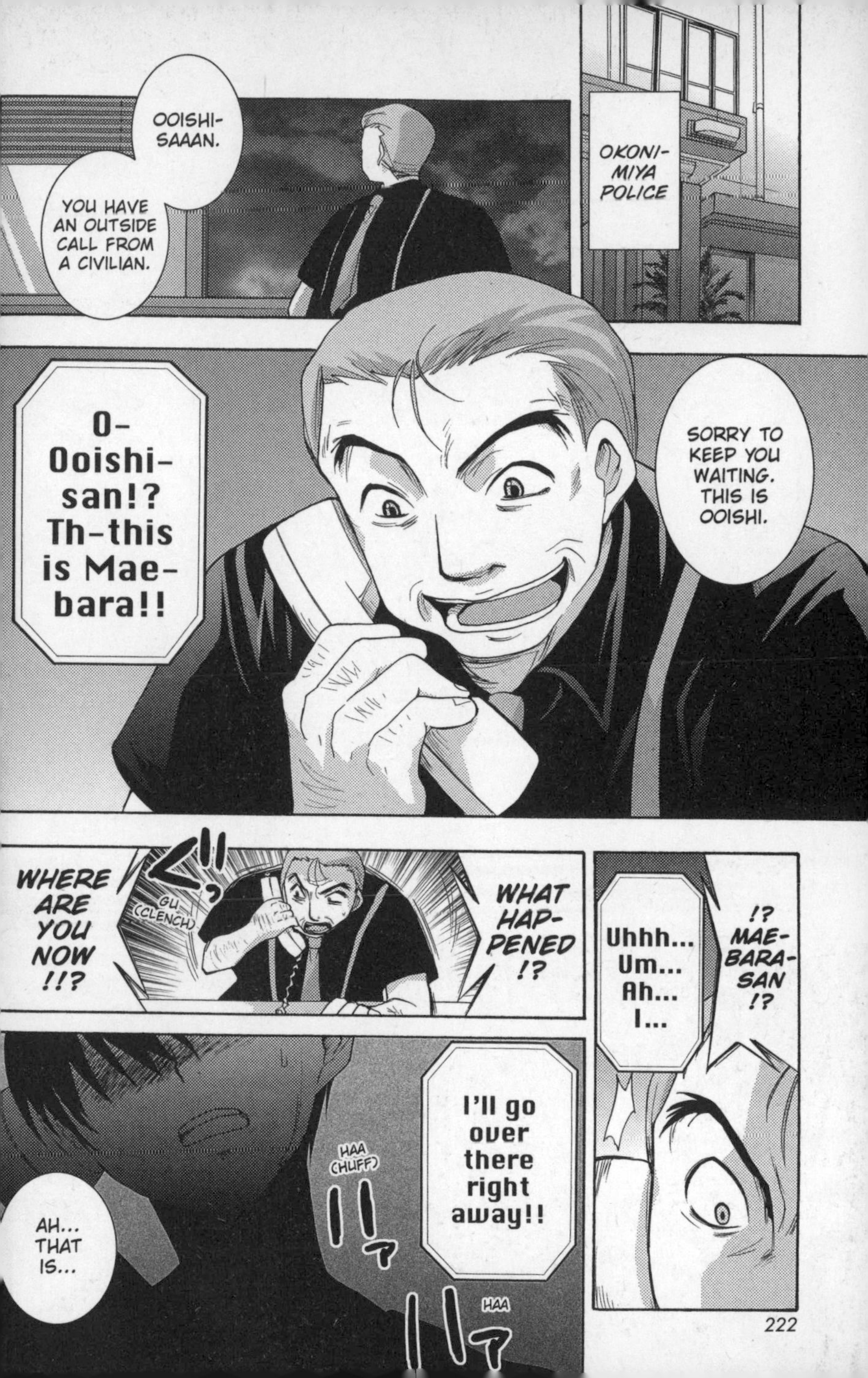

OKONIMIYA POLICE
OOISHI-SAAAN.
YOU HAVE AN OUTSIDE CALL FROM A CIVILIAN.
SORRY TO KEEP YOU WAITING. THIS IS OOISHI.
O-Ooishi-san!? Th-this is Maebara!!
!? MAEBARA-SAN!?
Uhhh... Um... Ah... I...
WHAT HAPPENED!?
GU (CLENCH)
WHERE ARE YOU NOW!!?
I'll go over there right away!!
HAA (HUFF)
HAA
AH... THAT IS...

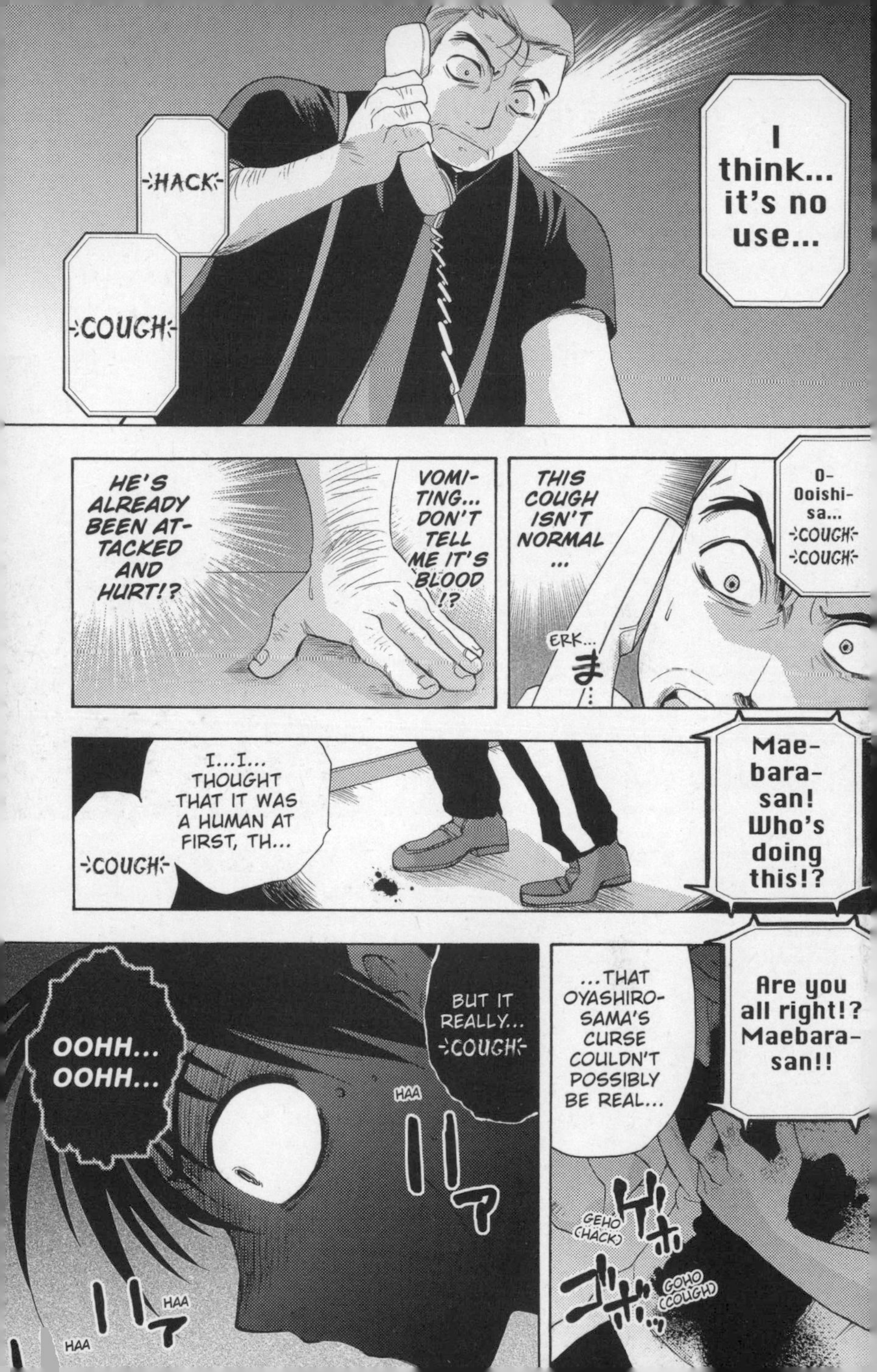
I think... it's no use...
HACK
COUGH
O-Ooishi-sa... COUGH COUGH
THIS COUGH ISN'T NORMAL...
ERK...
ま...
VOMITING... DON'T TELL ME IT'S BLOOD!?
HE'S ALREADY BEEN ATTACKED AND HURT!?
Maebara-san! Who's doing this!?
I...I... THOUGHT THAT IT WAS A HUMAN AT FIRST, TH...
COUGH
Are you all right!? Maebara-san!!
...THAT OYASHIRO-SAMA'S CURSE COULDN'T POSSIBLY BE REAL...
GEHO (HACK)
GOHO (COUGH)
BUT IT REALLY... COUGH
OOHH... OOHH...
HAA
HAA
HAA

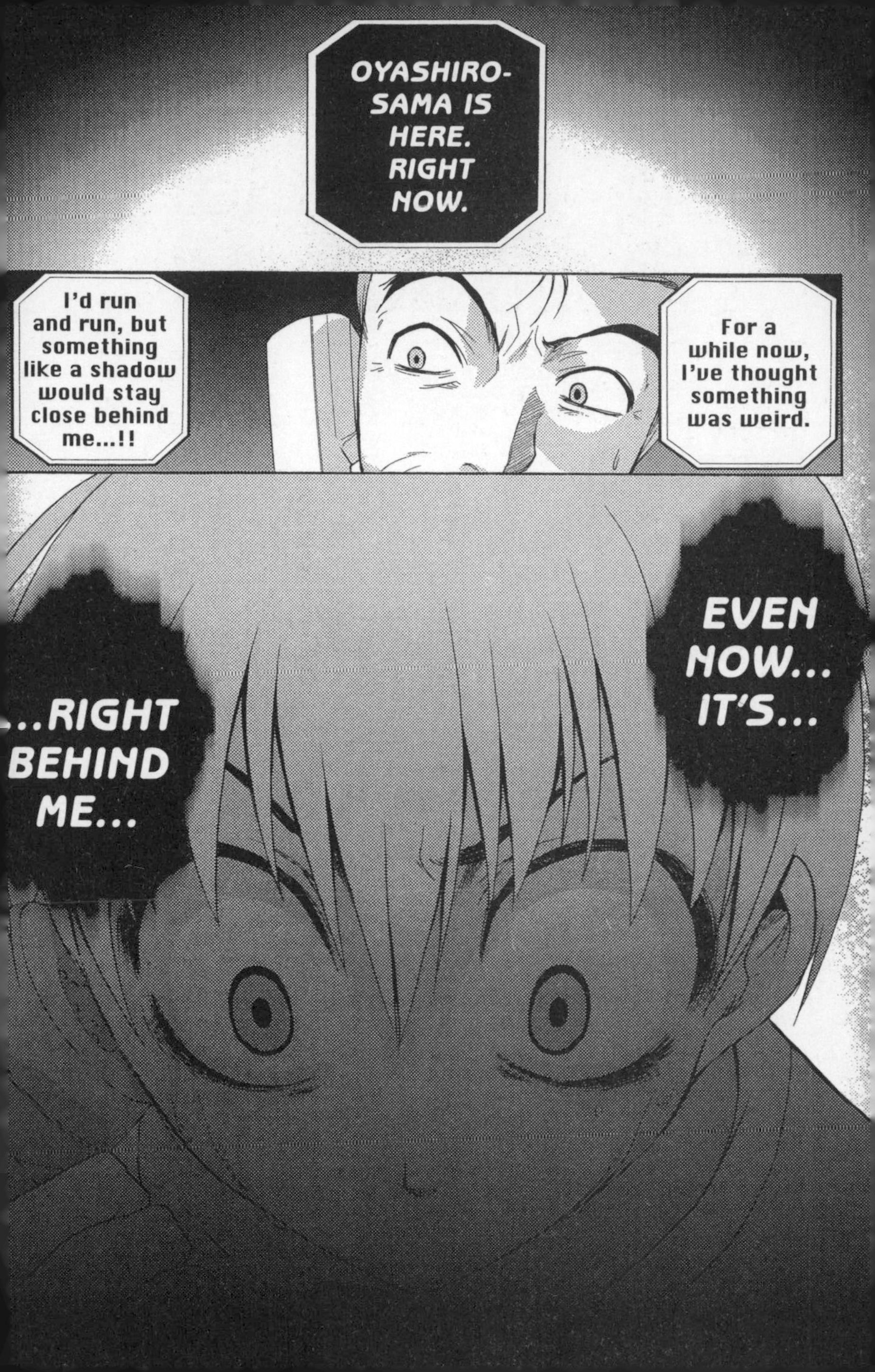
OYASHIRO-SAMA IS HERE. RIGHT NOW.
For a while now, I've thought something was weird.
I'd run and run, but something like a shadow would stay close behind me...!!
EVEN NOW... IT'S...
...RIGHT BEHIND ME...

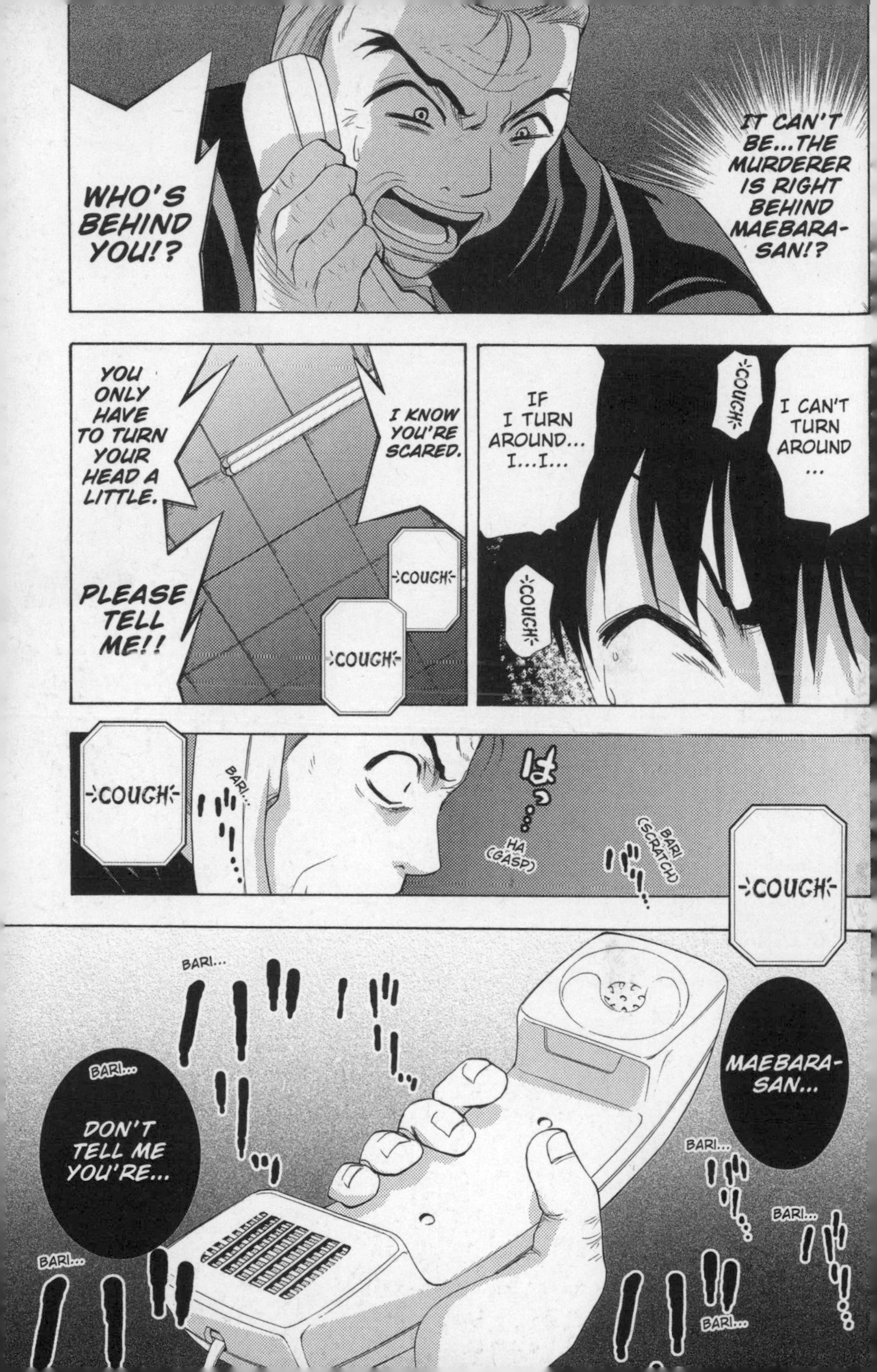
IT CAN'T BE...THE MURDERER IS RIGHT BEHIND MAEBARA-SAN!?
WHO'S BEHIND YOU!?
I CAN'T TURN AROUND...
COUGH
IF I TURN AROUND... I...I...
COUGH
I KNOW YOU'RE SCARED.
YOU ONLY HAVE TO TURN YOUR HEAD A LITTLE.
COUGH
PLEASE TELL ME!!
COUGH
COUGH
BARI (SCRATCH)
はっ…
HA (GASP)
BARI...
COUGH
MAEBARA-SAN...
BARI...
BARI...
BARI...
BARI...
DON'T TELL ME YOU'RE...
BARI...
BARI...

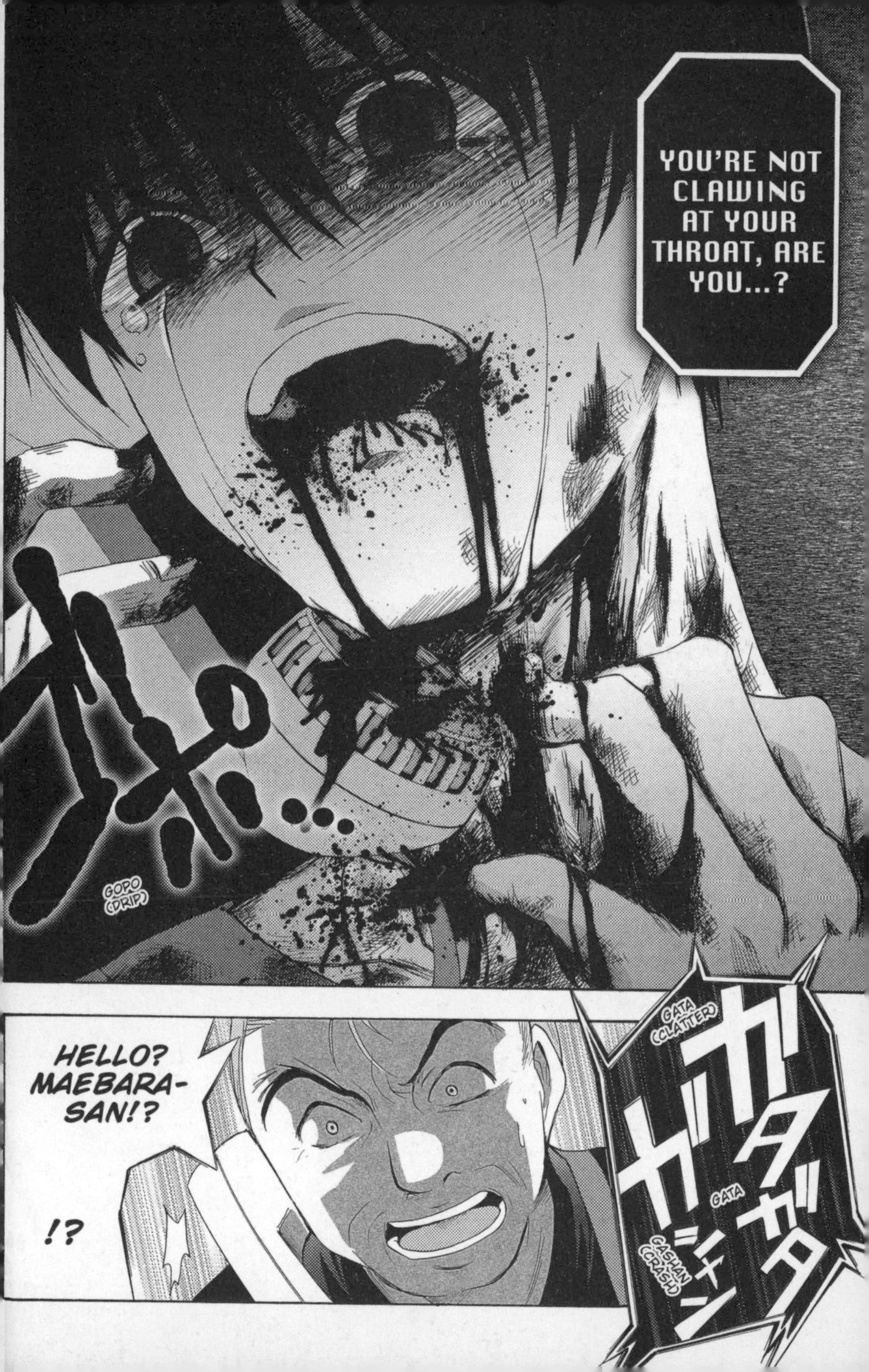
YOU'RE NOT CLAWING AT YOUR THROAT, ARE YOU...?
GOPO (DRIP)
GATA (CLATTER)
GATA
GASHAN (CRASH)
HELLO? MAEBARA-SAN!?
!?

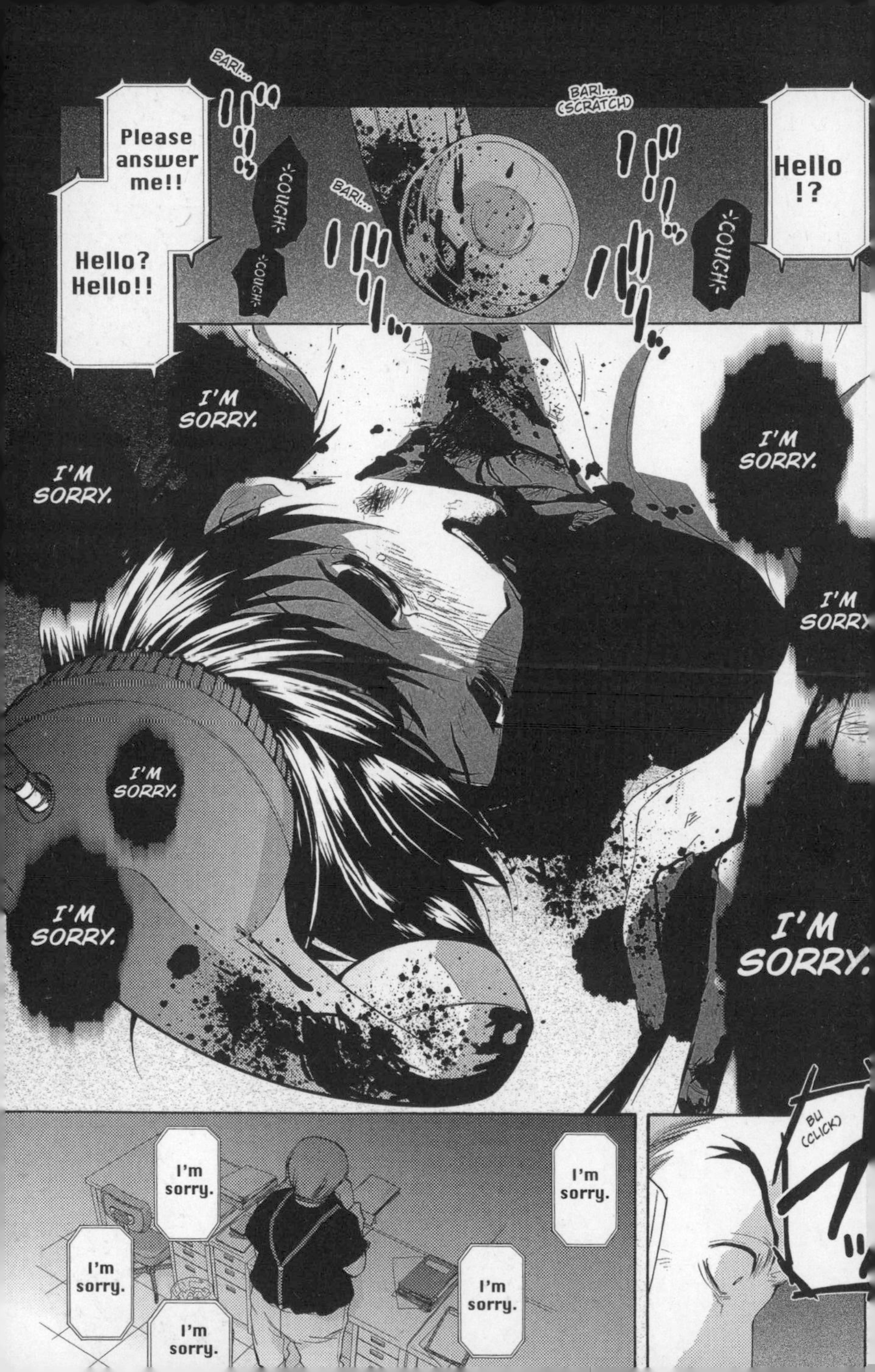
Hello !?
COUGH
BARI... (SCRATCH)
BARI...
BARI...
COUGH
COUGH
Please answer me!!
Hello? Hello!!
I'M SORRY.
I'M SORRY.
I'M SORRY.
I'M SORRY.
I'M SORRY.
I'M SORRY.
I'M SORRY.
BU (CLICK)
I'm sorry.
I'm sorry.
I'm sorry.
I'm sorry.
I'm sorry.

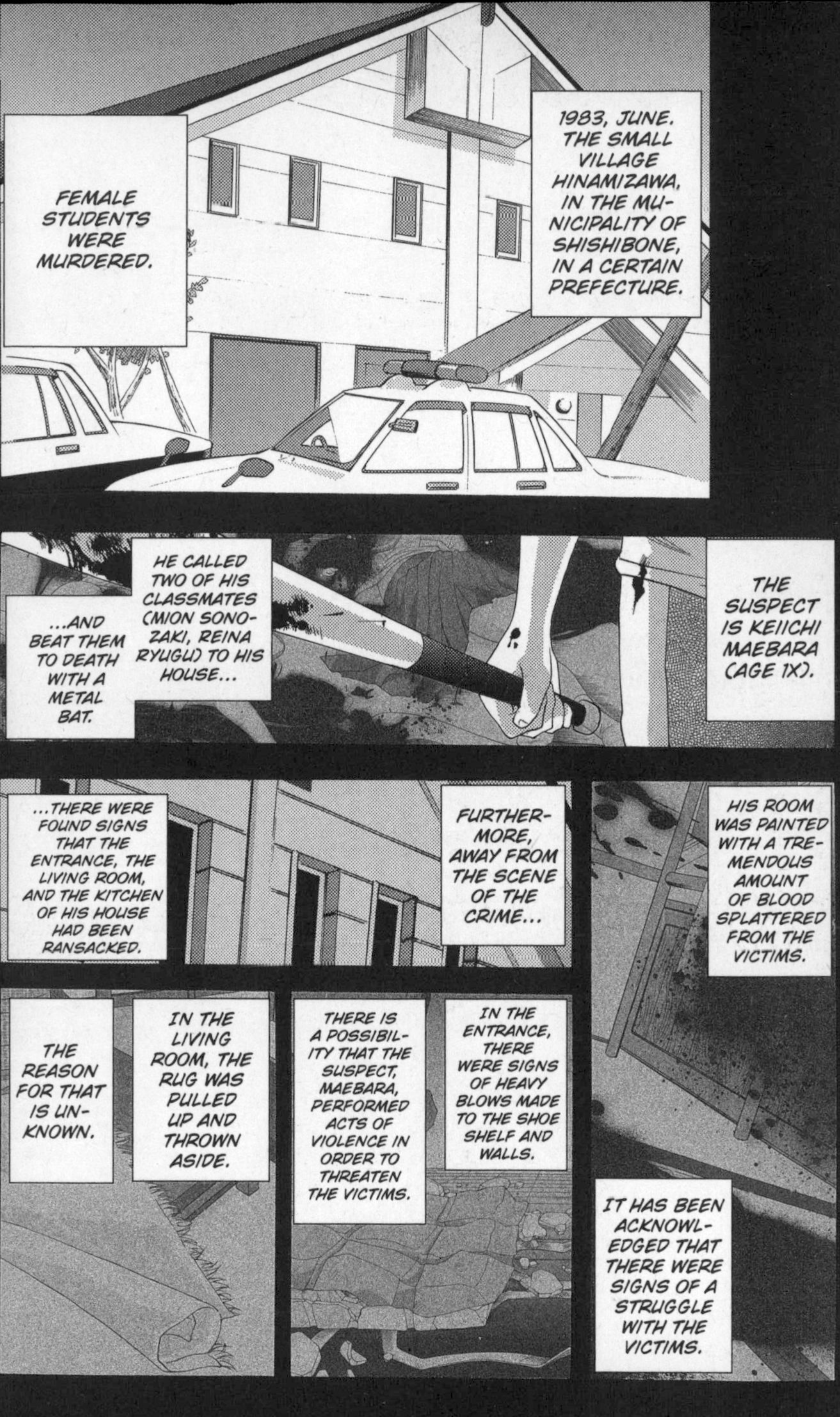
1983, JUNE. THE SMALL VILLAGE HINAMIZAWA, IN THE MU-NICIPALITY OF SHISHIBONE, IN A CERTAIN PREFECTURE.
FEMALE STUDENTS WERE MURDERED.
THE SUSPECT IS KEIICHI MAEBARA (AGE 1X).
HE CALLED TWO OF HIS CLASSMATES (MION SONO-ZAKI, REINA RYUGU) TO HIS HOUSE...
...AND BEAT THEM TO DEATH WITH A METAL BAT.
HIS ROOM WAS PAINTED WITH A TRE-MENDOUS AMOUNT OF BLOOD SPLATTERED FROM THE VICTIMS.
IT HAS BEEN ACKNOWL-EDGED THAT THERE WERE SIGNS OF A STRUGGLE WITH THE VICTIMS.
FURTHER-MORE, AWAY FROM THE SCENE OF THE CRIME...
...THERE WERE FOUND SIGNS THAT THE ENTRANCE, THE LIVING ROOM, AND THE KITCHEN OF HIS HOUSE HAD BEEN RANSACKED.
IN THE ENTRANCE, THERE WERE SIGNS OF HEAVY BLOWS MADE TO THE SHOE SHELF AND WALLS.
THERE IS A POSSIBIL-ITY THAT THE SUSPECT, MAEBARA, PERFORMED ACTS OF VIOLENCE IN ORDER TO THREATEN THE VICTIMS.
IN THE LIVING ROOM, THE RUG WAS PULLED UP AND THROWN ASIDE.
THE REASON FOR THAT IS UN-KNOWN.

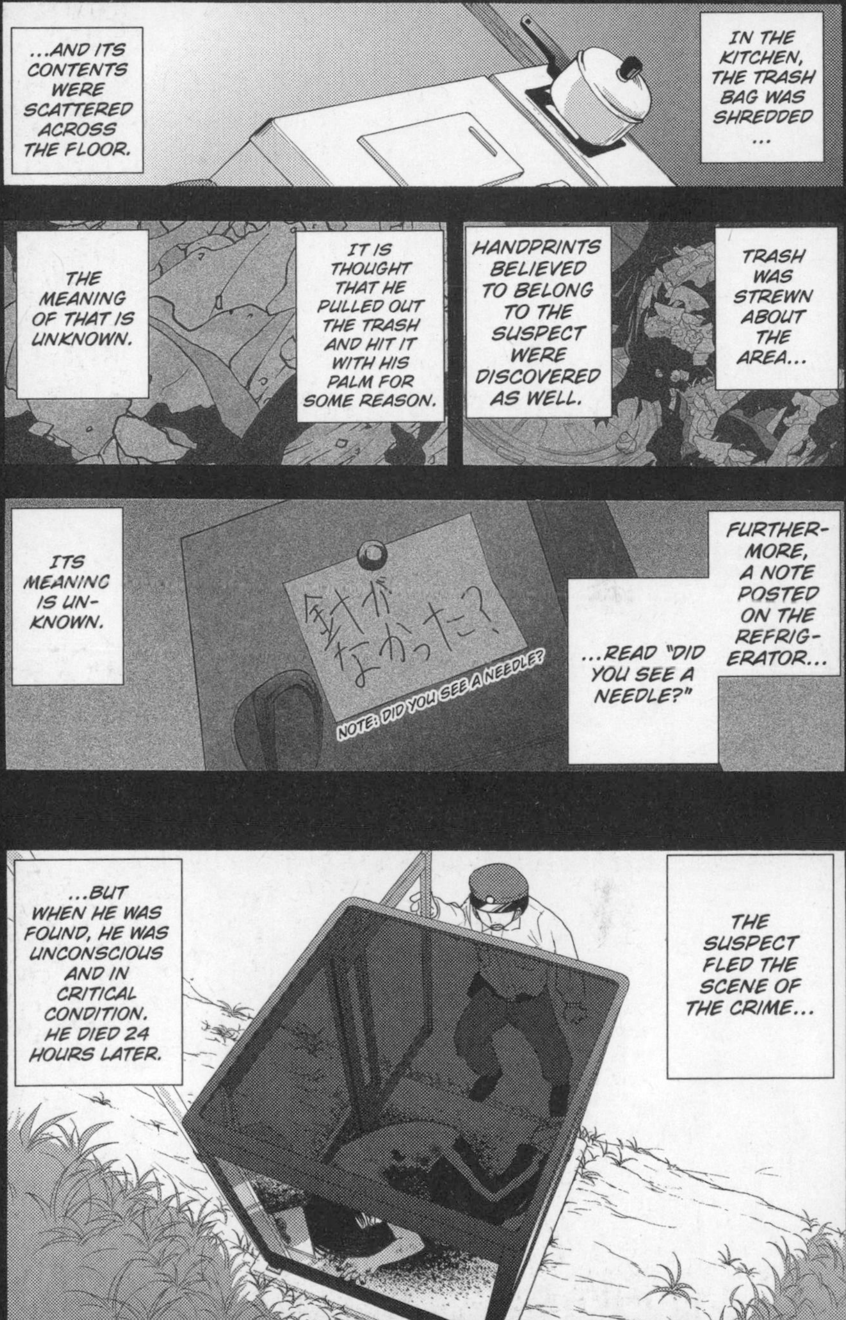
IN THE KITCHEN, THE TRASH BAG WAS SHREDDED ...
...AND ITS CONTENTS WERE SCATTERED ACROSS THE FLOOR.
TRASH WAS STREWN ABOUT THE AREA...
HANDPRINTS BELIEVED TO BELONG TO THE SUSPECT WERE DISCOVERED AS WELL.
IT IS THOUGHT THAT HE PULLED OUT THE TRASH AND HIT IT WITH HIS PALM FOR SOME REASON.
THE MEANING OF THAT IS UNKNOWN.
FURTHER-MORE, A NOTE POSTED ON THE REFRIG-ERATOR...
...READ "DID YOU SEE A NEEDLE?"
針がなかった?
DID YOU SEE A NEEDLE?
NOTE: DID YOU SEE A NEEDLE?
ITS MEANING IS UN-KNOWN.
THE SUSPECT FLED THE SCENE OF THE CRIME...
...BUT WHEN HE WAS FOUND, HE WAS UNCONSCIOUS AND IN CRITICAL CONDITION. HE DIED 24 HOURS LATER.

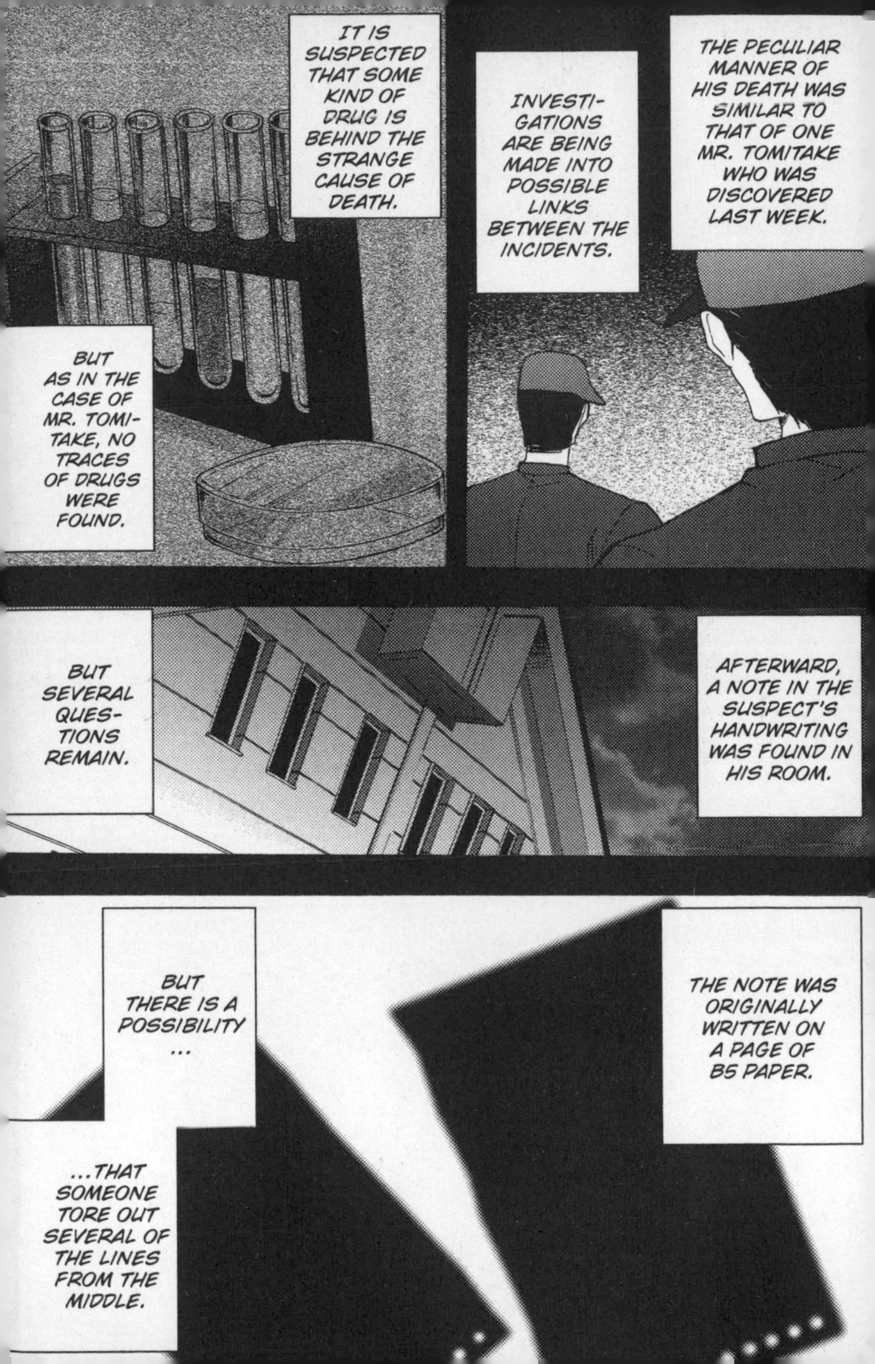
THE PECULIAR MANNER OF HIS DEATH WAS SIMILAR TO THAT OF ONE MR. TOMITAKE WHO WAS DISCOVERED LAST WEEK.
INVESTI-GATIONS ARE BEING MADE INTO POSSIBLE LINKS BETWEEN THE INCIDENTS.
IT IS SUSPECTED THAT SOME KIND OF DRUG IS BEHIND THE STRANGE CAUSE OF DEATH.
BUT AS IN THE CASE OF MR. TOMI-TAKE, NO TRACES OF DRUGS WERE FOUND.
AFTERWARD, A NOTE IN THE SUSPECT'S HANDWRITING WAS FOUND IN HIS ROOM.
BUT SEVERAL QUES-TIONS REMAIN.
THE NOTE WAS ORIGINALLY WRITTEN ON A PAGE OF B5 PAPER.
BUT THERE IS A POSSIBILITY ...
...THAT SOMEONE TORE OUT SEVERAL OF THE LINES FROM THE MIDDLE.

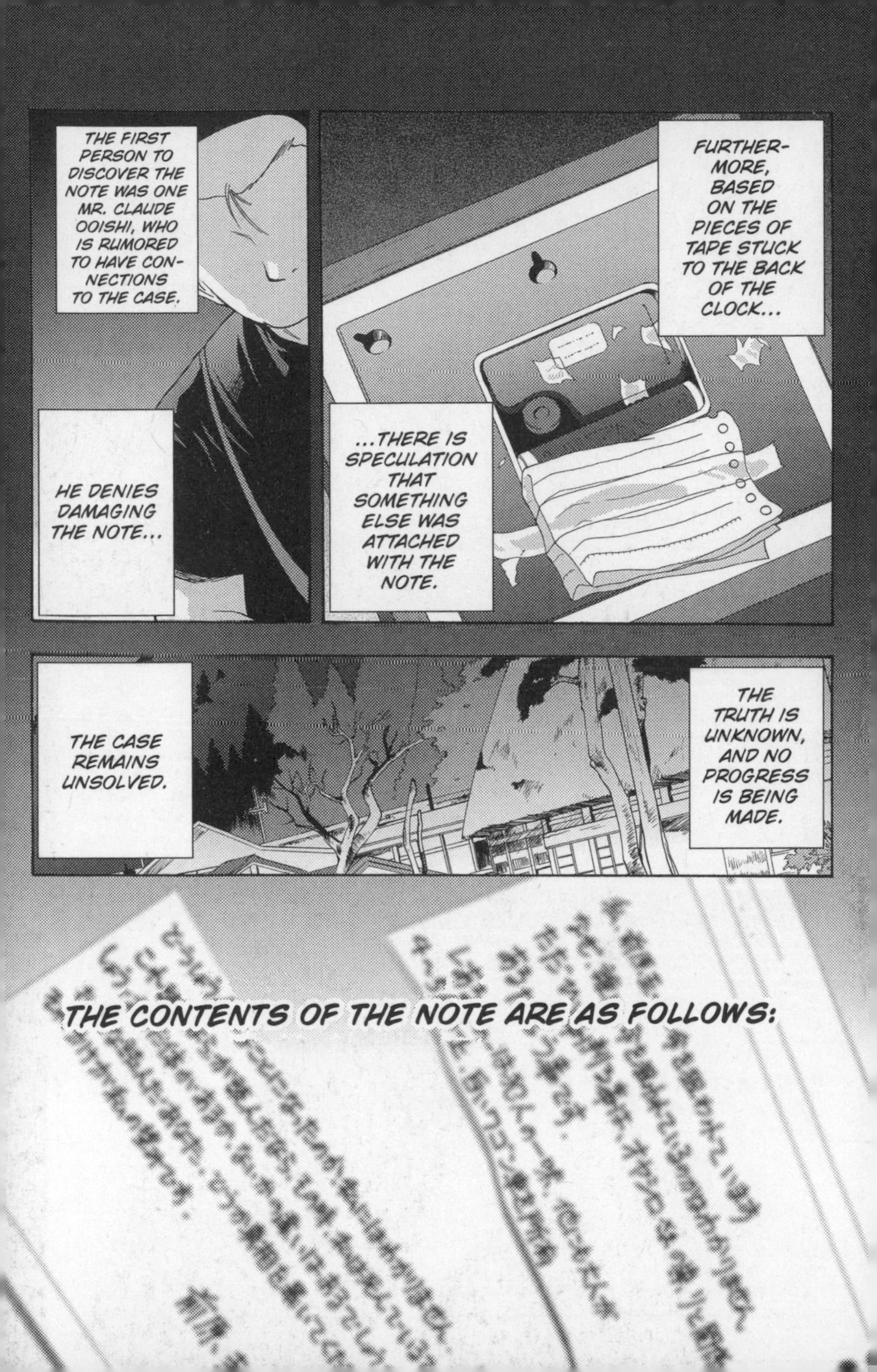
FURTHERMORE, BASED ON THE PIECES OF TAPE STUCK TO THE BACK OF THE CLOCK...
...THERE IS SPECULATION THAT SOMETHING ELSE WAS ATTACHED WITH THE NOTE.
THE FIRST PERSON TO DISCOVER THE NOTE WAS ONE MR. CLAUDE OOISHI, WHO IS RUMORED TO HAVE CONNECTIONS TO THE CASE.
HE DENIES DAMAGING THE NOTE...
THE TRUTH IS UNKNOWN, AND NO PROGRESS IS BEING MADE.
THE CASE REMAINS UNSOLVED.
THE CONTENTS OF THE NOTE ARE AS FOLLOWS:

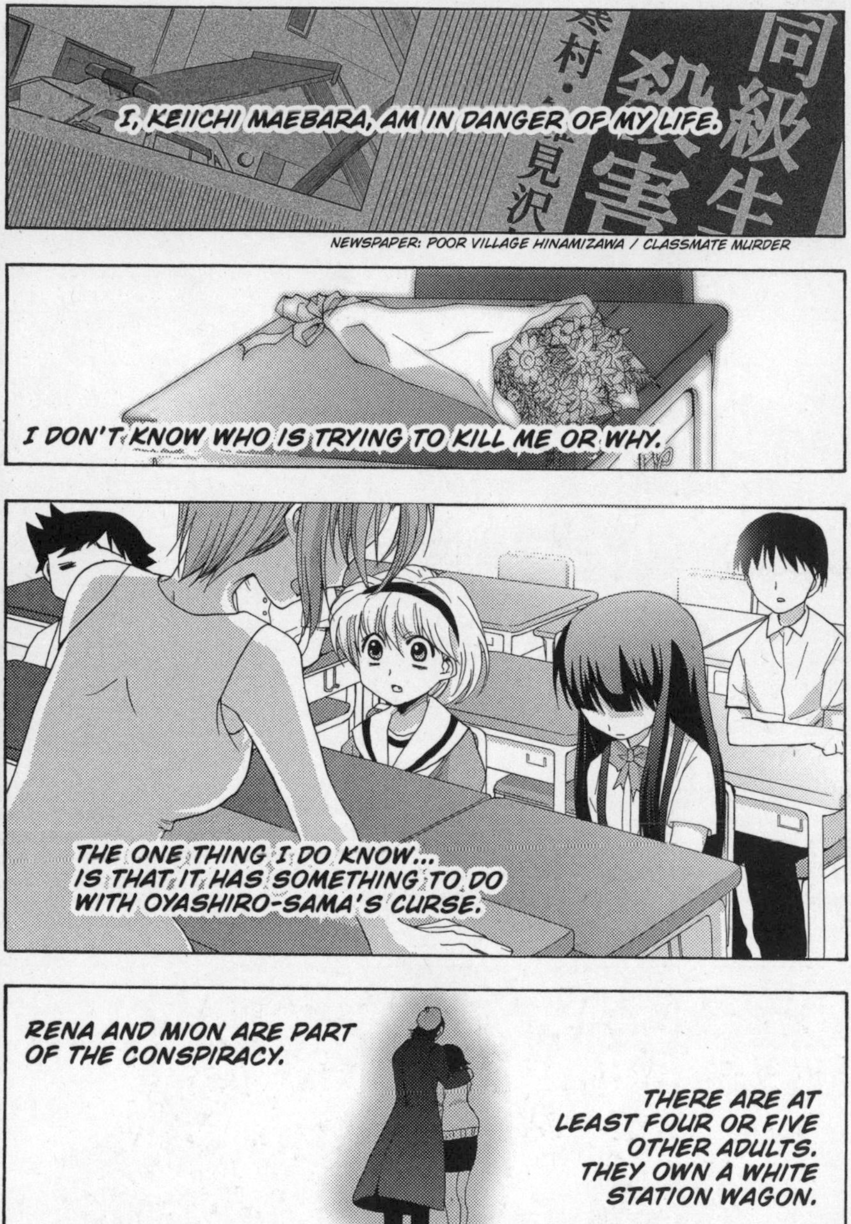
I, KEIICHI MAEBARA, AM IN DANGER OF MY LIFE.
NEWSPAPER: POOR VILLAGE HINAMIZAWA / CLASSMATE MURDER
I DON'T KNOW WHO IS TRYING TO KILL ME OR WHY.
THE ONE THING I DO KNOW... IS THAT IT HAS SOMETHING TO DO WITH OYASHIRO-SAMA'S CURSE.
RENA AND MION ARE PART OF THE CONSPIRACY.
THERE ARE AT LEAST FOUR OR FIVE OTHER ADULTS. THEY OWN A WHITE STATION WAGON.
(THE ABOVE IS FROM THE FIRST PAGE. THE NEXT PART WAS TORN OUT DIRECTLY HORIZONTALLY.)

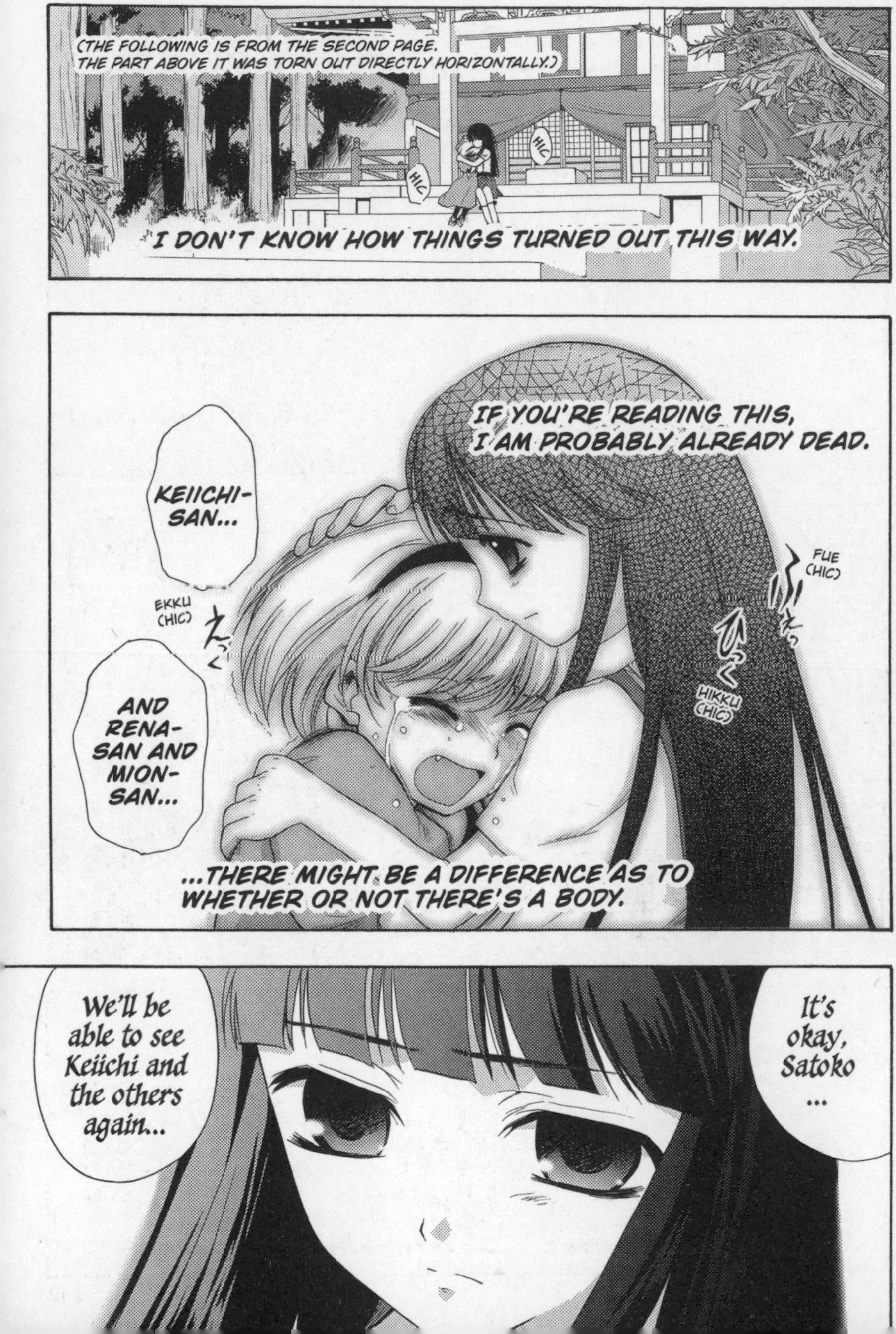
(THE FOLLOWING IS FROM THE SECOND PAGE. THE PART ABOVE IT WAS TORN OUT DIRECTLY HORIZONTALLY.)
HIC
HIC
I DON'T KNOW HOW THINGS TURNED OUT THIS WAY.
IF YOU'RE READING THIS, I AM PROBABLY ALREADY DEAD.
FUE (HIC)
HIKKU (HIC)
KEIICHI-SAN...
EKKU (HIC)
AND RENA-SAN AND MION-SAN...
...THERE MIGHT BE A DIFFERENCE AS TO WHETHER OR NOT THERE'S A BODY.
It's okay, Satoko...
We'll be able to see Keiichi and the others again...

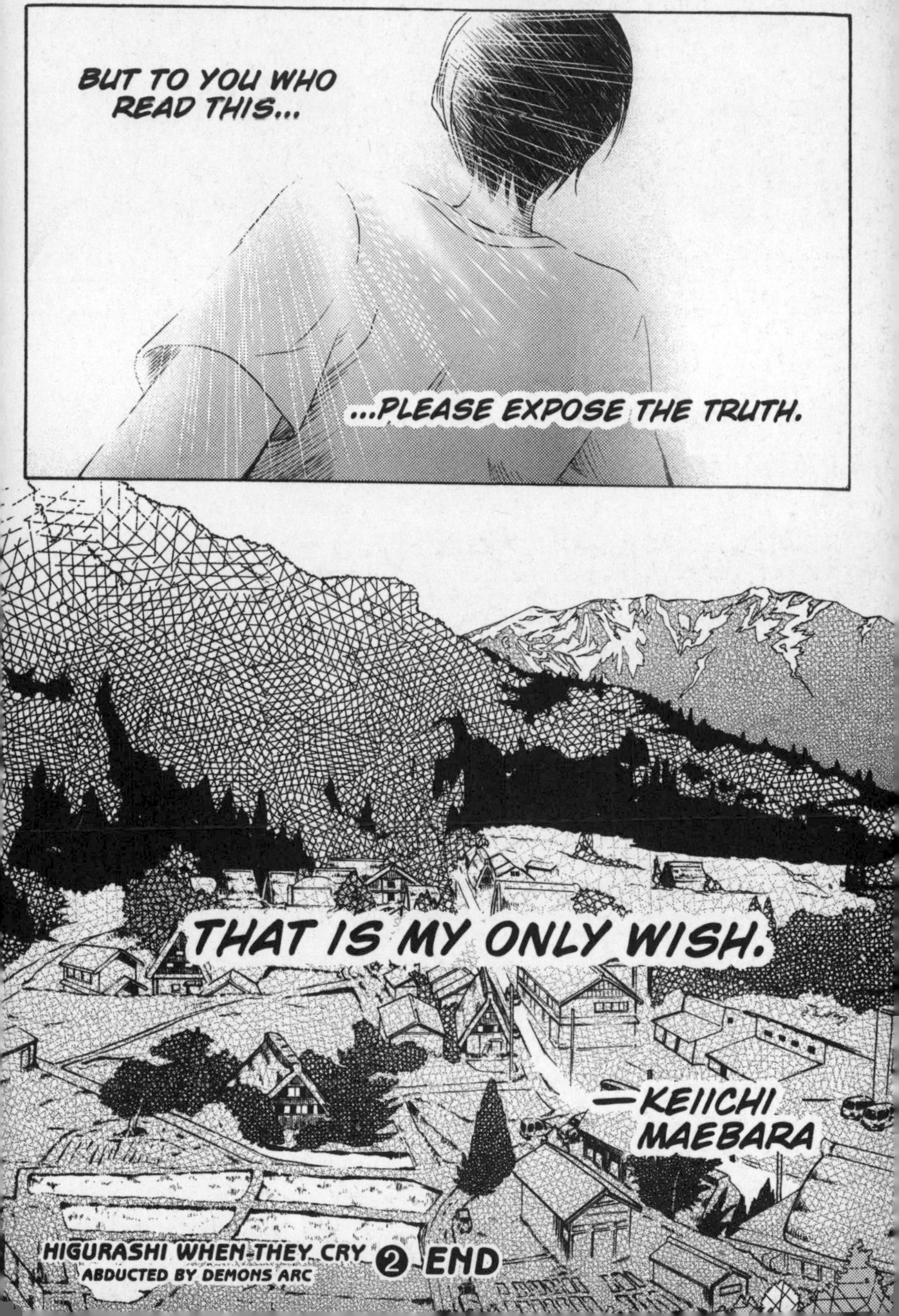
BUT TO YOU WHO READ THIS...
...PLEASE EXPOSE THE TRUTH.
THAT IS MY ONLY WISH.
—KEIICHI MAEBARA
HIGURASHI WHEN THEY CRY 2 END
ABDUCTED BY DEMONS ARC

TRANSLATION NOTES

Page 14
Onigafuchi
Literally means "pit of demons"; a fitting name for a village infested with them.

Page 28
Ohagi
Also known as *"botamochi"* or *"hagi no mochi," ohagi* is a Japanese treat made from sweet rice packed in a ball and coated with azuki red bean paste.

Page 85
Koushien
Koushien is a district in Hyogo Prefecture, known for holding the national high school baseball tournament.

Page 230
B5 paper
This is a Japanese category of paper size. B5 paper is a little bigger than seven by ten inches.

Higurashi
WHEN THEY CRY

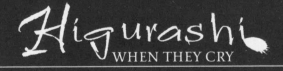

ABDUCTED BY DEMONS ARC

FIN

HIGURASHI WHEN THEY CRY

07th Expansion presents "Welcome to the series... WHEN THEY CRY."

ABOUT THE "ABDUCTED BY DEMONS ARC" THE ONE AND ONLY KEY

ORIGINAL STORY, SUPERVISOR: RYUKISHI 07

THE "ABDUCTED BY DEMONS ARC" IS THE FIRST STORY IN *HIGURASHI WHEN THEY CRY* AND DEPICTS THE THEMES I WANT TO DEPICT IN THE OVERALL STORY MOST SIMPLY. NOW, IF I WERE TO GO EVEN FURTHER, PERHAPS I COULD SAY THAT THIS "ABDUCTED BY DEMONS ARC" IS *HIGURASHI WHEN THEY CRY.*

TO GIVE A CRYPTIC EXPLANATION, THERE IS ONLY ONE KEY HIDDEN IN THE "ABDUCTED BY DEMONS ARC." THIS IS AN EXTREMELY IMPORTANT KEY, AND IF YOU CAN FIND IT, THEN THERE IS NO DOUBT THAT YOU WILL BE ABLE TO DELVE DEEP NOT ONLY INTO THE "ABDUCTED BY DEMONS ARC," BUT ALSO INTO THE "COTTON DRIFTING ARC" AND THE "CURSE KILLING ARC." BUT BECAUSE IT IS SUCH AN IMPORTANT KEY, IN ORDER TO HIDE IT, THERE ARE A LARGE NUMBER OF FAKE KEYS SCATTERED THROUGHOUT.

TO THOSE OF YOU WHO ARE TOUCHING ON THE WORLD OF *HIGURASHI* FOR THE FIRST TIME, I HOPE THAT YOU WILL ENJOY DROWNING IN THE SEA OF KEYS.

AND...TO THOSE OF YOU WHO ALREADY KNOW THE "KAI," THE "SOLUTION," TO THIS STORY, I HOPE YOU WILL WARMLY WATCH OVER THOSE WHO ARE ENJOYING DROWNING. BECAUSE, IN ANY EVENT, THE ONES ENJOYING THIS WORLD THE MOST ARE NONE OTHER THAN THE ONES STRUGGLING TO KEEP THEIR HEADS ABOVE WATER.

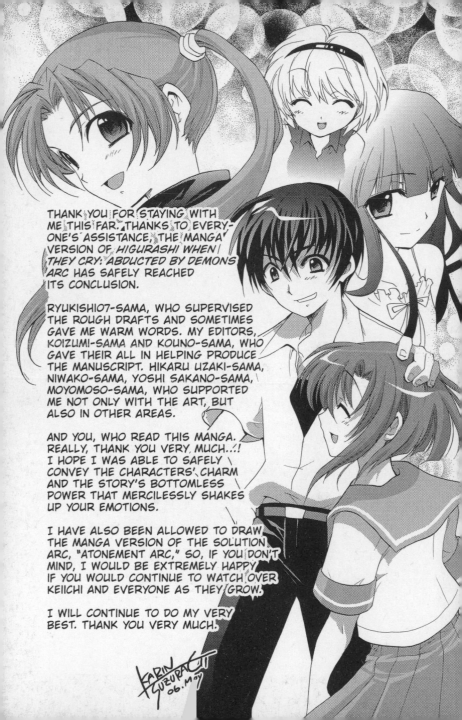

THANK YOU FOR STAYING WITH ME THIS FAR. THANKS TO EVERYONE'S ASSISTANCE, THE MANGA VERSION OF *HIGURASHI WHEN THEY CRY: ABDUCTED BY DEMONS ARC* HAS SAFELY REACHED ITS CONCLUSION.

RYUKISHI07-SAMA, WHO SUPERVISED THE ROUGH DRAFTS AND SOMETIMES GAVE ME WARM WORDS. MY EDITORS, KOIZUMI-SAMA AND KOUNO-SAMA, WHO GAVE THEIR ALL IN HELPING PRODUCE THE MANUSCRIPT. HIKARU UZAKI-SAMA, NIWAKO-SAMA, YOSHI SAKANO-SAMA, MOYOMOSO-SAMA, WHO SUPPORTED ME NOT ONLY WITH THE ART, BUT ALSO IN OTHER AREAS.

AND YOU, WHO READ THIS MANGA. REALLY, THANK YOU VERY MUCH..!! I HOPE I WAS ABLE TO SAFELY CONVEY THE CHARACTERS' CHARM AND THE STORY'S BOTTOMLESS POWER THAT MERCILESSLY SHAKES UP YOUR EMOTIONS.

I HAVE ALSO BEEN ALLOWED TO DRAW THE MANGA VERSION OF THE SOLUTION ARC, "ATONEMENT ARC," SO, IF YOU DON'T MIND, I WOULD BE EXTREMELY HAPPY IF YOU WOULD CONTINUE TO WATCH OVER KEIICHI AND EVERYONE AS THEY GROW.

I WILL CONTINUE TO DO MY VERY BEST. THANK YOU VERY MUCH.

KARIN SUZURAGI
06.May

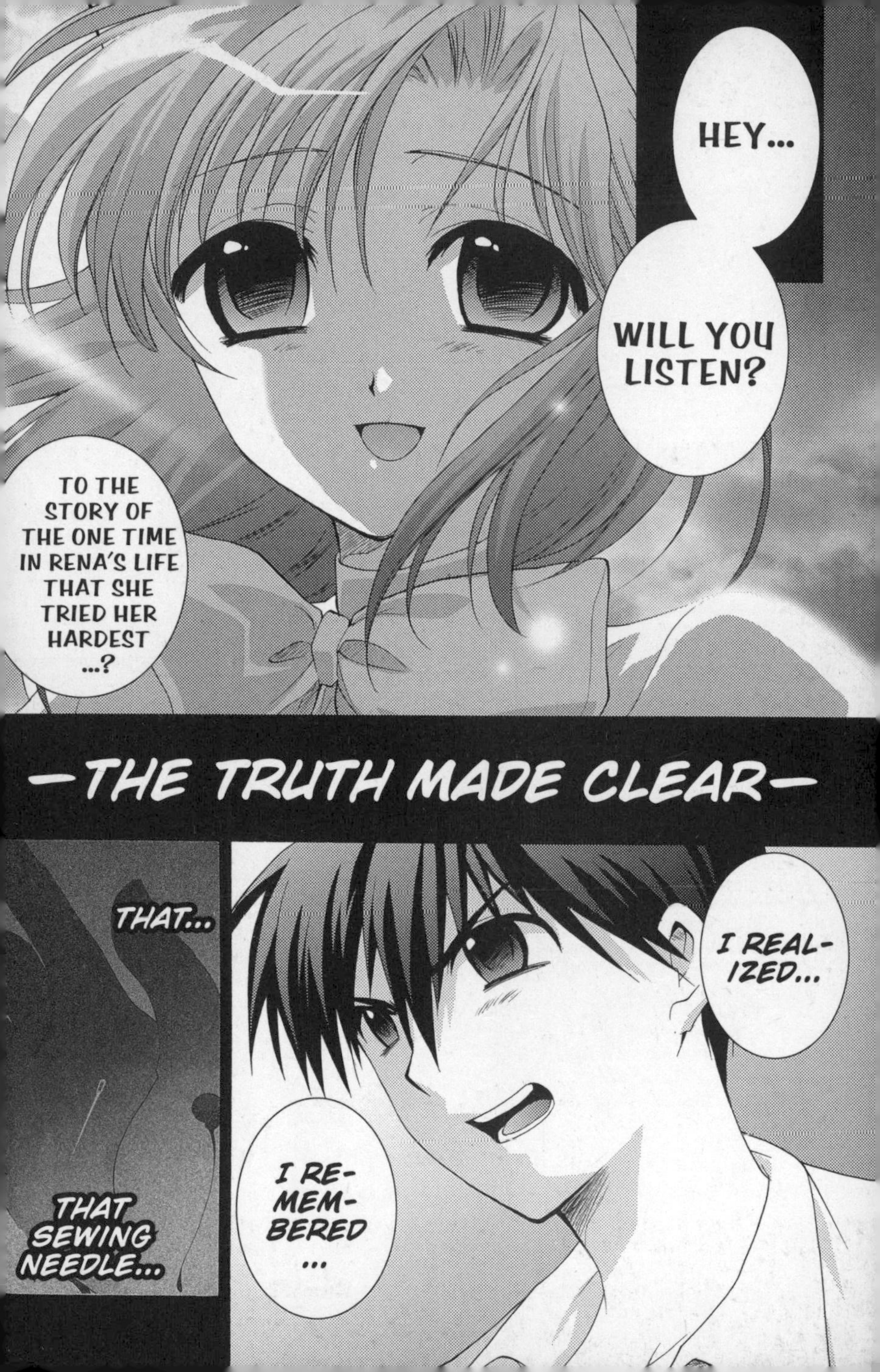
HEY...
WILL YOU LISTEN?
TO THE STORY OF THE ONE TIME IN RENA'S LIFE THAT SHE TRIED HER HARDEST ...?
—THE TRUTH MADE CLEAR—
I REAL-IZED...
I RE-MEM-BERED ...
THAT...
THAT SEWING NEEDLE...

—A NEW TRAGEDY—

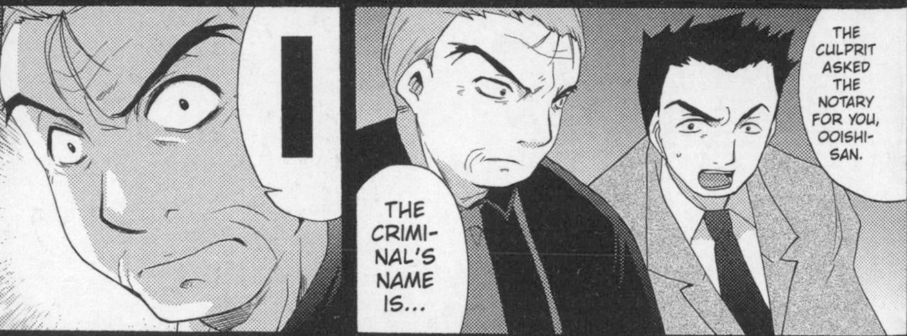
THE CULPRIT ASKED THE NOTARY FOR YOU, OOISHI-SAN.
THE CRIMINAL'S NAME IS...
!

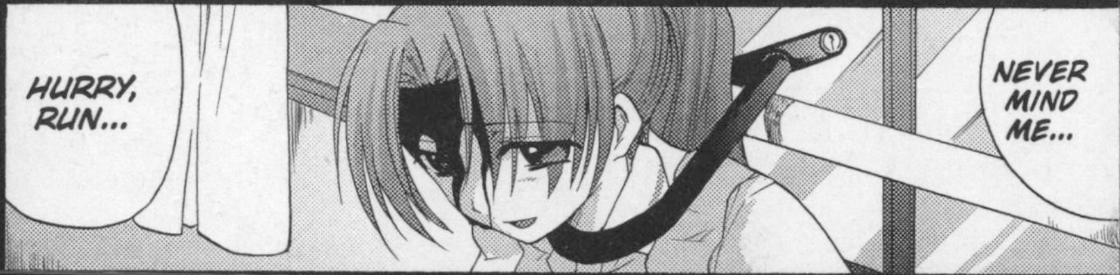
NEVER MIND ME...
HURRY, RUN...

—THE WORLD OF "HIGURASHI"—

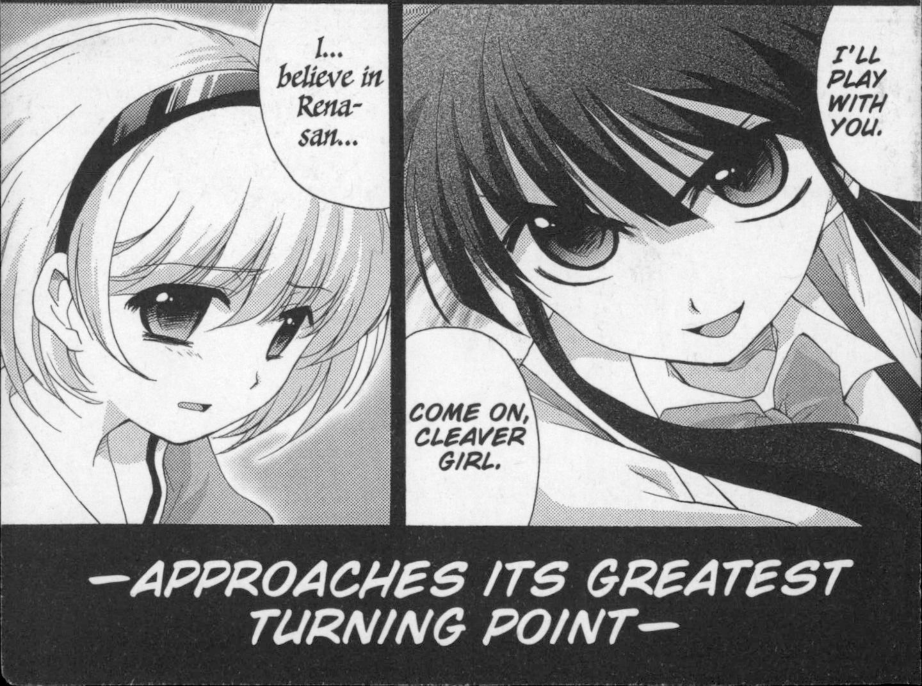
I'LL PLAY WITH YOU.
COME ON, CLEAVER GIRL.
I... believe in Rena-san...

—APPROACHES ITS GREATEST TURNING POINT—

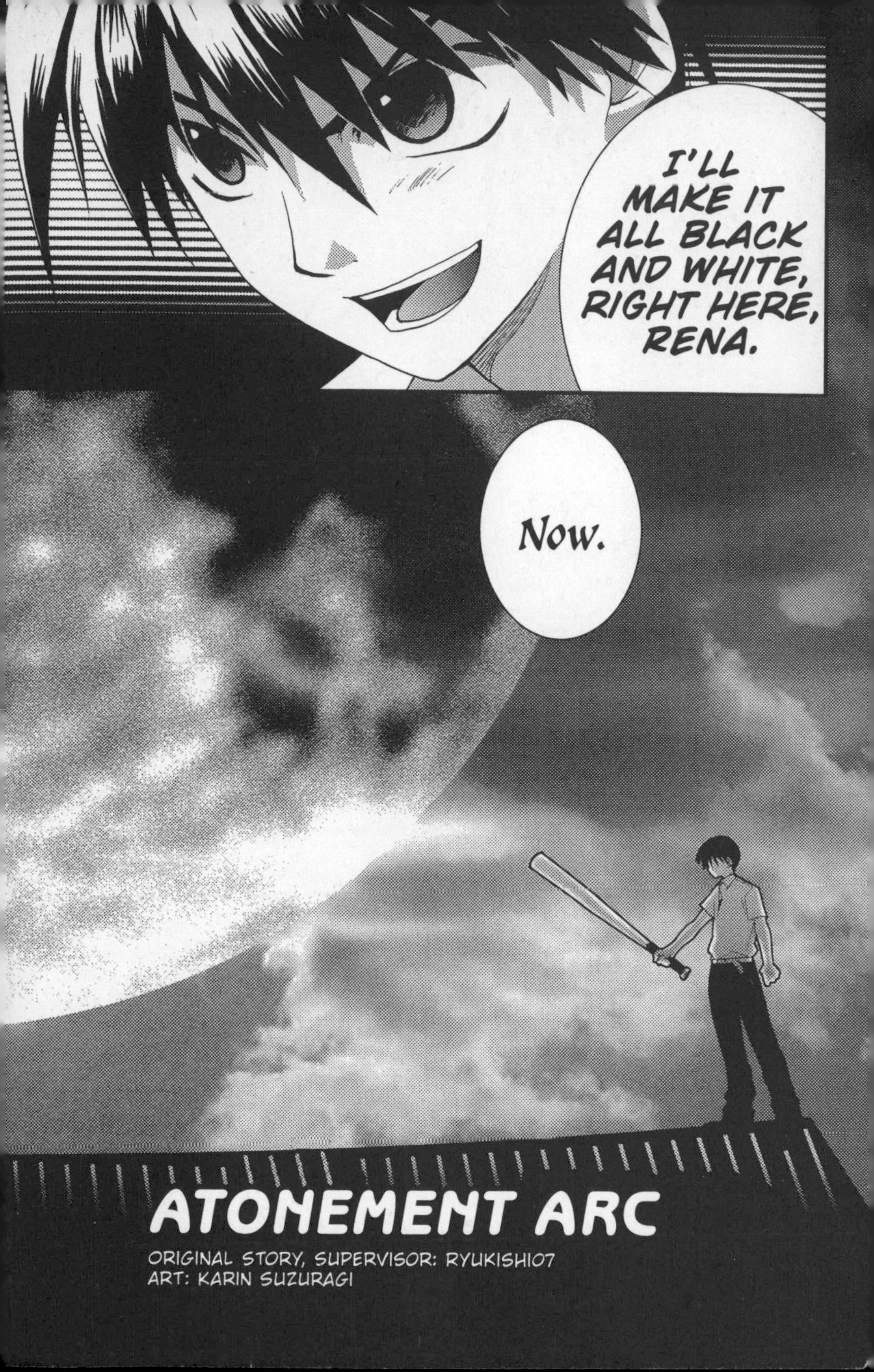
I'LL MAKE IT ALL BLACK AND WHITE, RIGHT HERE, RENA.
Now.
ATONEMENT ARC
ORIGINAL STORY, SUPERVISOR: RYUKISHI07
ART: KARIN SUZURAGI

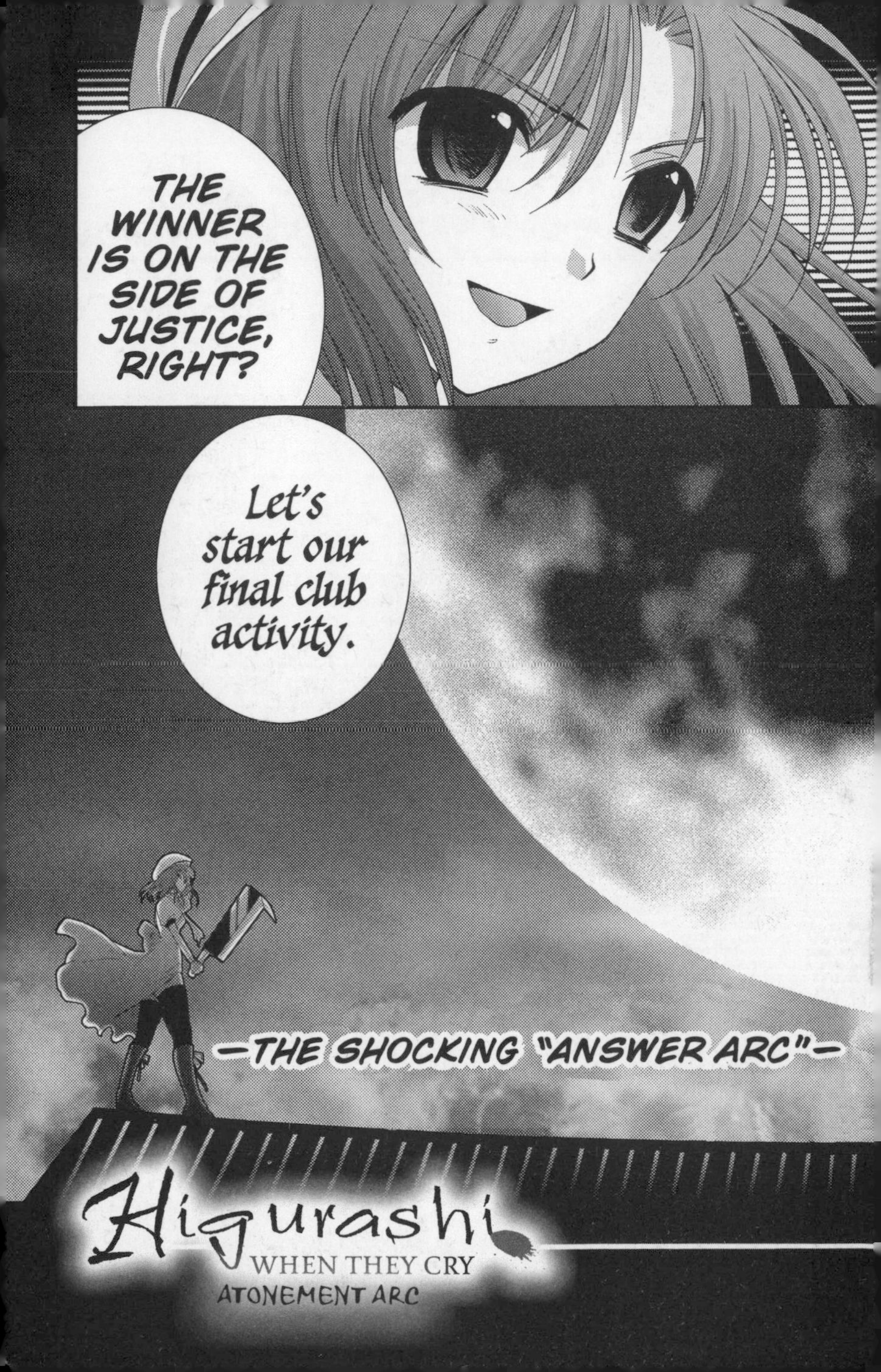
THE WINNER IS ON THE SIDE OF JUSTICE, RIGHT?
Let's start our final club activity.
—THE SHOCKING "ANSWER ARC"—
Higurashi
WHEN THEY CRY
ATONEMENT ARC

HIGURASHI
WHEN THEY CRY
ABDUCTED BY DEMONS ARC ②

RYUKISHI07
KARIN SUZURAGI

Translation: Alethea Nibley and Athena Nibley

Lettering: Shelby Peak

Higurashi WHEN THEY CRY Abducted by Demons Arc, Vol. 2 © RYUKISHI07 /
07th Expansion © Karin Suzuragi / SQUARE ENIX. All rights reserved. First
published in Japan in 2006 by SQUARE ENIX CO., LTD. English translation
rights arranged with SQUARE ENIX CO., LTD. and Hachette Book Group through
Tuttle-Mori Agency, Inc. Translation © 2009 by SQUARE ENIX CO., LTD.

Yen Press
Hachette Book Group
1290 Avenue of the Americas, New York, NY 10104

Visit our Web sites at www.HachetteBookGroup.com and www.YenPress.com.

Yen Press is an imprint of Hachette Book Group, Inc. The Yen Press name and
logo are trademarks of Hachette Book Group, Inc.

First Yen Press Edition: February 2009

ISBN-13: 978-0-7595-2984-7

20 19 18 17 16 15 14 13 12 11

BVG

Printed in the United States of America